MICHAEL ALBRIGHT

IT BEGINS

LitPrime Solutions
21250 Hawthorne Blvd
Suite 500, Torrance, CA 90503
www.litprime.com
Phone: 1-800-981-9893

Published by LitPrime Solutions   10/21/2022

ISBN: 979-8-88703-070-8(sc)
ISBN: 979-8-88703-071-5(hc)
ISBN: 979-8-88703-072-2(e)

CONTENTS

DEDICATION

To the center of my universe, my family, and to all those who run toward danger rather than away from danger.

PROLOGUE

No one witnessed it. No one even heard the noise. Scientific instruments on this world or any another did not record it. The effects were not felt by anyone. In fact, mankind as we know it would not even know of the event for millions and millions of years, and even then, it would become a matter of idle curiosity for most. For others, astronomers and astrophysicists, knowledge of the event would be a matter of great scientific curiosity and investigation. But in the overall scheme of things, it would not interrupt the busy daily lives of people as they raced to and from work, attended their children's sports programs, socialized with their friends, or perhaps read a bedtime story to an eager child lost in a make-believe world of dreams, wonderment, and possibilities. No, it wouldn't really matter to most, except for those who knew and understood.

Before the sands of time would record the passage of life, the universe was in its own evolutionary dance of existence. Millions of years ago, in the cold, lightless depths of space, at the outer limits of emptiness, where silence and the cover of darkness are companions, two massive bodies meandered on a fatal collision course. One, a cold and desolate orb of stone and minerals; the other, a hot volcanic planet engulfed in a gaseous cloud. Time was meaningless to these two massive bodies as they traveled through the emptiness of space. We know now that their journey lasted over one million years, a mere heartbeat in time, as they raced toward each other from opposite ends of the universe.

As the two heavenly bodies approached the intersection point of their travels, the gravitational field of each was felt and influenced by the other. Locked in a tug-of-war, each planet was drawn toward the other; closer and closer they raced, unable to escape the inevitable. As the gap between them closed, loose rock and magma from the fiery planet leaped through the void of emptiness separating the planets and slammed into the cold, desolate surface of the other. The desolate planet had five times the gravitational pull of the molten planet.

Volcanic activity increased as the planets drew closer. Magma spewed forth in immeasurable quantities as both planets danced their dance of death. Explosions began, more powerful than man could imagine, as the distance between the orbs rapidly decreased. When the collision occurred, each planet was rotating about its axis at over fifty thousand miles per hour, producing a force that can only be theorized and wondered about. We do, however, now know the result of that collision.

Millions of pieces of rock, and lava that cooled into rock, dispersed into space in every direction as a result of the explosion. Some were as large as the state of Rhode Island, and others as small as a grain of sand. In the eons that followed, some of these pieces crashed into other planets and became one with them; other pieces fell into orbit around larger masses, while still others began their own journeys through the galaxies of what we call space.

ONCE UPON A TIME...

T O SOME, LIFE IS A constant struggle. Nothing seems to go the way it is supposed to. It is as though life is a battle that must be fought each day in order to survive.

For others that are fortunate, life appears to be easy. But at times they, too, must struggle and claw their way. This struggle may appear easier than that of the less fortunate. However, this is not true. There is a difference. The fortunate ones never lose sight of their goals. They spend little time wandering down the twisted pathway of life. For them the path is clear and distinct.

Azizi was one of the fortunate ones, for he had come to experience the youthful dreams of life. His was not an easy road. He traveled a path of tradition mixed and at peace with the future. The odds of fulfilling his dreams were against him. But he persisted where others have faltered from the path. His goal was to help his family, his tribe, and his country by way of his dream.

As a child, Azizi, recognized that an airplane offered hope. It was an airplane that brought the doctors to care for the sick of his village. An airplane brought food in times of need and want. In good times, an airplane brought knowledge of self-sufficiency for the members of his village. Airplanes opened up a whole new world full of fascination, temptation, and most of all, hope.

It was from this association that a lifelong passion grew within Azizi. As a boy, he would run like the wind whenever he heard an airplane flying overhead. His destination was the small grass airstrip behind his village. As the plane landed, Azizi would run alongside the aircraft, pretending that he was the pilot in command of this fascinating machine. Most times the pilot of the aircraft was Tom Grissom, a volunteer pilot of the World Health Organization. Tom was used to children running alongside the aircraft whenever he visited a village. But Azizi was different. Perhaps it was the excitement in his eyes or the enthusiasm of his spirit. Whatever it was, Tom saw Azizi as different from the hundreds and hundreds of children he had come to know in the different villages throughout the plains of Africa.

Eventually, Tom was convinced that Azizi possessed the spirit and determination needed to be a pilot. On one visit to Azizi's village, Tom invited him to sit in the pilot's seat. He patiently explained the controls and the many gauges. Afterward, whenever Tom came to the village, he and Azizi would sit in the aircraft and talk about flying for hours on end. As a result of these talks, an inseparable bond matured between the two of them. From time to time, Tom would supplement their talks with gifts of books about airplanes and some airplane models for Azizi to build. Tom had become the teacher, and Azizi the more-than-willing student.

On the day of Azizi's fourteenth birthday, Tom made a special trip to the village.

As usual, Azizi ran alongside the airplane until it came to a stop. Once Tom opened the cockpit door, Azizi eagerly looked inside and asked where the cargo was. Tom stepped out of the airplane and explained that on this day there was no cargo. He withdrew an envelope from the inside of his shirt and handed it to Azizi. With great care, Azizi opened the envelope and read the birthday card. When he finished, Azizi looked up at Tom and thanked him. Tom explained that he didn't know what to give Azizi for his birthday and decided instead that it was time for him to get his first practical lesson in flying. At first, Azizi didn't know what Tom meant but quickly realized that he was actually going to fly. Not as a passenger, but as a pilot. Azizi smiled broadly as Tom simply said, "Let's go, kid!"

From that day forward, they were a team. Azizi and Tom would visit village after village, delivering food and medicine. During the next four years, Tom came to realize that the student had somehow become the instructor. Azizi was a natural. An airplane to him was an extension of himself; his feet were the rudder controls, and his arms and hands the wings.

When Azizi turned eighteen, he, like all other male children of his country, entered the military service. After basic training, he applied for the air service and was quickly accepted. For the next thirty-six months, Azizi progressed from flying propeller-driven aircraft as a cadet to becoming wing commander of a sleek, new jet fighter squadron. His love of flying never diminished but rather intensified within him. Azizi came to feel that the cockpit of an airplane was his cradle, and the sky his playground. But his life was at a crossroads.

The leadership of his homeland realized that the economic survival of the country depended upon a reliable transportation system. Toward that end, they expanded roads and developed a network of rail lines. The last piece of the puzzle was the establishment of a national airline to connect the various parts of the country to the world beyond its borders.

Naturally, the country turned toward its military to recruit qualified pilots. Azizi was one of them. Inwardly, Azizi had hoped that he would be offered a position in the management of the airline, but he realized that those positions went to those with political connections, and he had none. *Being offered the position of an airline captain in charge of a somewhat-new jetliner is no small accomplishment*, Azizi thought.

To Azizi, the path was clear. He would leave the military and take on this new role to help his country. As Tom had helped tie the country together, Azizi would help in a similar manner. There was simply no other course to follow.

Shortly after starting with the airline, Azizi met and married the woman of his dreams, Serwa. She, like him, came from the villages with hope for the future. Serwa stayed at home in their big house in the city and raised their daughter and twin boys. Azizi and Serwa were ever mindful of their backgrounds and made a special effort to see that the family visited their villages regularly. The visits were not so much to see the grandparents of the children but rather to teach the children tribal custom and its relationship to everyday life. After all, it is always good to remember where you came from.

Eventually, Azizi's hard work and dedication paid off. He was offered the position he had originally hoped for. However, becoming the director of operations for Transvaal National Airlines would not allow him to fly. Since flying was his passion, the decision was easy. Serwa wanted him to take the new job, but Azizi wanted to fly. He decided to continue to be an airline captain. This meant he would fly his regular route, going east to west across Zambia in four hops, and then back again each day. Azizi knew that his days were long and hard, but he was helping, in his own way, the people of his country.

Azizi felt satisfied with his life. He had a happy and fulfilling family life, he worked at a job he loved, and he had the opportunity to help his country grow. He also was successful at mixing traditional life with the pressures of modern-day city life. The only sadness that touched him during these times was the death of Tom.

What Azizi found difficult was the lack of closure for a life he had shared, if only for a whisper in time. Tom was flying government officials around one day when his plane simply disappeared. One minute it was on the radarscope, and the next second it was gone in a field of static that clouded the display. When the radar display cleared, Tom's plane was gone. There was a search, but the wreckage was never found.

Therefore, there was not a funeral or even a memorial service for Tom. Azizi felt as if the world forgot this kind and gentle man who gave of himself in the service of others.

Azizi knew that Tom's plane was somewhere in the jungle. But where, no one knew. Azizi recruited other pilots to always watch for a glimmer of reflective light coming from the floor of the jungle. But the aircraft eluded the searchers. After a while, Azizi stopped thinking of Tom as being a victim of an airplane crash; rather, Azizi thought of Tom as being his own personal guardian angel. Many times, especially when he was flying in inclement weather, Azizi would feel the gentle touch of Tom on the controls guiding him through to safety. In this, what some would call fantasy, while others call it reality, Azizi found comfort.

AIM HIGH

CAPTAIN DONALD RICHARDS WAS ONE of the less-fortunate ones. He meandered down a twisted pathway of life. As a youth, he couldn't understand the necessity of a high school education and quit, only to re-enter school and then quit again. He drifted from low-paying job to low-paying job, chasing the rainbow of an easy life that he never attained. That all changed one day when his nineteen-year-old car broke down for what seemed like the millionth time.

Standing alone on a highway baking in the midday sun, Donald could only curse his misfortune and pray for help. That help came in the person of Warren Davidson.

Warren was a meek and mild person on the outside but inside was a determined individual who knew what he wanted and was patient enough to wait for it. Those characteristics helped him in his current job. He was an accomplished salesman of sorts. But more properly, he was a recruiter for the South African Air Force.

When Warren stopped to help Donald, he saw in him the prospect of a recruit. His approach was as slick and determined, as if he were a cougar stalking his pray. Warren genuinely seemed concerned about Donald's car and knew enough about mechanics to realize that there was not a force on Earth that would make the automobile operate again.

After explaining the condition of the car to Donald, Warren offered to give him a lift to the next town.

During the one-hour-and-twenty-minute ride, Warren went to work. It was a very subtle, nonstop sales promotion. By the time they reached their destination, Donald was convinced that if he was to get direction in his life, the Air Force was the answer. During lunch, paid for by Warren, or, more properly, the citizens of South Africa, Donald signed his enlistment papers. Instead of heading home, Donald found himself on a bus to boot camp.

At boot camp, Donald was placed in a remedial platoon. While the main emphasis was on physical conditioning and introducing him to the Air Force way of life, equal emphasis was given to his education. In no time at all, Donald had finished his high school equivalency requirements. Twelve weeks later, he graduated and was off to aircraft mechanics school. By the time Donald graduated from school, he had acquired that certain sparkle in his eye that only pilots have. Donald knew what he wanted—he wanted to fly. But that would require a college education.

For the next seven years, Donald would go from duty station to duty station and attend college in his off time. He managed to graduate with a solid A average, much to the wonder of his classmates. Donald never appeared to study; instead, he took private pilot lessons and earned his license. In a short period, Donald was hired as a part-time instructor during his time off from the Air Force. It was as if he led three lives; he was in the Air Force, was a college student, and somehow managed to squeeze in his passion, flying.

When he finished college, Donald strode into the career office of the base he was assigned to. Proud of his academic accomplishment, he showed everyone in the office his diploma and announced that he wanted to take the examination for the position of Air Force pilot. The people in the office looked at Donald with skepticism in their eyes. However, they sat him in a room and administered the test to him. After an hour and a half, Donald left the testing room with his future in his hands. He walked up to the lieutenant in charge and handed him the test and his answer sheet.

Donald was directed to sit on one of those hardback slotted wooden chairs that are designed to be uncomfortable, and wait. He sat there nervously and watched as the lieutenant scored the test. He searched for any kind of facial expression on the lieutenant that would indicate how Donald did on the test. But the lieutenant sat there stone-faced. After what seemed like an eternity, the lieutenant gathered the papers together and walked over to Donald. Standing up erect, awaiting the verdict, Donald felt himself starting to sweat. The lieutenant extended his hand to Donald and, with a broad smile on his face, congratulated him. Donald had scored a perfect test. Not one question was wrong.

For the next eighteen months, Donald learned how to fly the Air Force way.

While his main interest was fighter jets, the Air Force thought otherwise. He was advanced to multijet aircraft and began flying the KC-10 tanker, an aircraft that refuels other jet aircraft in flight. While he was somewhat disappointed with his new assignment, Donald excelled in it. His talent for flying big jet aircraft was not lost on his superiors, and he was quickly promoted and given additional responsibilities. At first he was a squadron commander but was soon promoted to flight instructor. Donald liked flying with his squadron better, but he recognized the importance of teaching others how to fly the flying gas station.

It was during this assignment that Donald was selected to go to the United States and train as the command pilot of the South African Air Force's newest acquisition, the E-3 Sentry AWACS aircraft. The AWACS aircraft is an airborne warning-and-control system. In times of need, it serves as a control-and-command aircraft directing airborne and ground units in combat situations. Perhaps its greatest role is that of an early warning system. It is capable of tracking multiple targets at a distance of greater than two hundred miles, identifying those targets and making a determination as to whether a particular target is friend or foe.

DRIP, DRIP: OKAY, SO IT LEAKS

Today was like any other day to most of us, but to Azizi, no two days were alike.

He looked upon flying as a grand adventure. Each day was a new lesson to be learned. Sure, he would do the same thing over and over, but Azizi knew that no two flights were exactly alike.

At 2:50 p.m. this day, Azizi was walking around the aircraft doing an inspection check before the final leg of his homeward-bound trip. When he reached his number 3 engine, he looked first at the ground underneath. As usual, there were a few drops of turbine oil on the ground. For what must have been the millionth time, he pondered the source of the leak. Azizi had constantly referred the problem over to maintenance, with always the same result: no one could find the source of the leak.

Other pilots for Transvaal who knew Azizi would kid him about the leak. But Azizi, who loved this aircraft, would reply with a smile on his face, "Hey, I'm lucky. If it didn't leak, how would I know that it had oil in it?" Everyone knew that the aircraft was a labor of love for

Azizi, and in a way, they were jealous that they had not developed this same passion for their aircraft.

When Azizi finished his inspection, he boarded the aircraft and sat down in the cockpit. For the eighth time today, Azizi checked in with the airport meteorologist and received the latest weather update. Azizi found it hard to believe that there was a storm front developing in his flight path. The meteorologist made a vague reference to an area within the storm front that was very unsettled. To Azizi, this was double talk, and he thought that the weatherman must be some new kid. Azizi adjusted his flight plan to skirt around the disturbance, which would only add ten minutes to his estimated time of arrival. *Better to be safe than sorry,* Azizi thought to himself as he logged the new course into his flight computer.

Azizi then reviewed his flight manifest. On this trip he would be carrying light farm machinery, medical supplies for the new hospital, rice for the hungry, and some agricultural produce. Next, he turned his attention to the passenger list. Azizi always scanned the list to see if there were any children among the passengers. If there were, Azizi would make sure that they received a tour of the flight deck, in the hope of winning over a convert to the adventure of flying. Regrettably, there were no children on this flight. Azizi did, however, recognize the name of a repeat passenger, Jonathan Quinn.

Azizi was pleased to see that Mr. Quinn was crisscrossing the country again, for it could only mean one thing: jobs. Mr. Quinn was a lead representative of Spectrum Universal Computer Systems, a United States company that had recently invested millions in Zambia to build a manufacturing base for their African and Middle Eastern market. To Azizi, Mr. Quinn represented the future. Zambia would profit enormously from the investment, as thousands of people would be employed to manufacture computers. That was progress.

OFF THE COAST OF NATAL

A T 3:00 P.M., DONALD RICHARDS pushed the engine Start buttons on his aircraft, taxied to the end of the runway, and took off. The initial flight of the South African Air Force's newest acquisition, the AWACS, had begun. The flight plan called for Donald and his crew to fly up the coast and test all the aircraft search systems. At 3:10 p.m., Donald radioed to the flight controller that the aircraft was "feet wet"(out over the ocean).

Donald asked for a weather update, but the forecast was the same. A storm was building in the interior. After making a notation of the radio call, Donald checked in with the real star of the crew, Staff Sergeant Samuel Packman, or simply Sam to his friends. And Donald and Sam were friends. They had two things in common: surfing and an unending interest in the opposite sex. Together they enjoyed both, usually to excess.

Sam Packman came to the air force directly from high school. He didn't enlist out of a desire to serve his country, but rather, he did so to escape the ravages of poverty and its social consequences. When he underwent initial placement testing for the Air Force, Sam was found to have an uncanny ability with electronic equipment and computers, something he had never seen before. During training, it quickly became evident that Sam was outpacing his instructors. He could tweak the equipment to do what the designers thought impossible. The Air Force offered Sam the chance to go to college, but he refused. He liked surfing, and women too much. Anything beyond work would be too much of an interruption. Besides, Sam liked his current assignment of lead radar intercept operator on this new aircraft, which he regarded as his private playground.

Indeed, Donald had come to think of himself as Sam's chauffeur. After all, it is the techies who really run the world.

SHUT THAT THING OFF

A T 3:15 P.M., AZIZI TOOK off and headed home. After reaching their cruising altitude of thirty-five thousand feet, Azizi relaxed a bit and turned to his copilot and friend, Masud. They worked well together as a team. Each seemed to be an extension of the other. Today the cockpit chatter between the friends was about their monthly trip to Lake Victoria. Once again they would attempt to empty the lake of its fish. But the tales they would tell were often much better than the actual fishing.

Their conversation ended abruptly when a C note sounded throughout the cockpit.

Both men instinctively looked down at the weather radarscope, expecting to see danger, but the scope was clear. Azizi and Masud then looked out of the cockpit window and saw a clear sky. Masud checked the circuit breakers and found nothing amiss. Azizi made a note of the event in his log and made a decision to report the incident to maintenance when they landed. Reaching up to the overhead console, Masud turned off the alarm.

LOOK AT THOSE IDIOTS

Once airborne, Sam and his fellow technicians went to work. Within a few minutes, they had identified over two hundred aircraft within their surveillance zone.

Most of the flights were commercial aircraft, while others were military flights. Twenty-one, however, were unknown. These were either civilian private aircraft that were not broadcasting their identity or smugglers. They were able to determine that nineteen were legitimate single-engine private aircraft. The other two, however, could not be identified. Sam dispatched military aircraft to intercept these two unidentified aircraft.

As Sam was watching the intercept of the two unknowns, an alarm went off in the aircraft. Sam contacted the navigator, Lieutenant Gibson, to find out what was going on. Gibson was as confused as anyone and replied that a malfunction had occurred in the weather warning system.

Sam then went back to work tracking the aircraft, always looking for more. He surmised that in an aircraft with over a million parts and hundreds of electronic devices, something was bound to go wrong.

DON'T GO INTO THE LIGHT

AT FIRST, AZIZI THOUGHT HIS eyes were playing tricks on him. In front of his aircraft, white clouds were suddenly appearing and rapidly spreading across the sky. Azizi thought he could make out some sort of a vague dark shape in the clouds, but he wasn't sure. Turning toward Masud, Azizi tried to speak, but suddenly a thousand different things were bombarding his senses. An intense white light filled the cockpit. Azizi resisted the temptation to close his eyes and instead turned back around to look outside. In an instant the white light enveloped his aircraft and Azizi felt slight pain throughout his body. Fighting to control his thoughts and ignore the pain, which was growing in intensity, Azizi glanced at Masud. Azizi saw and heard his friend screaming as Masud covered his eyes.

Feeling intense pain now, Azizi somehow managed to hold on to the control column with his left hand and reach for the engine controls with his right. Thinking that it might be possible to outrun the light, Azizi pushed the throttle controls forward to increase the speed of the aircraft. After a few seconds at full power, Azizi knew that his efforts had failed, and he reduced the speed of the engines. He then tried to turn his aircraft to the left and gently dive in an effort to escape the light. Instead, his aircraft remained level, and it seemed as though all forward movement had come to a stop.

Azizi was now confused. The logical-thinking pilot left him. Panic and fear were beginning to enter his mind, but Azizi fought it back. Just when he thought he was in control again, Azizi felt as if the aircraft was rising straight up in the sky. Logic told him it was impossible, but the sensation of vertical lift told him otherwise. Azizi was sure of one thing—as the sensation of vertical flight increased, so did the pain.

Hearing the screams of the passengers and Masud, Azizi needed to do something to help. But the intensity of the pain he felt left him immobile. Azizi couldn't move. His hands fell off the control column as they contorted into fists while trying to manage the increasing intensity of the pain. The only thing Azizi could do was stare straight ahead as the light continued to grow in brightness. He stared into the light as long as he could, but his eyes were now pulsating, as if they were going to explode.

Through the pain, Azizi felt the taste of blood in his mouth and a warm, wet liquid running down his neck from his ears. He thought it strange that he could not hear the screams of the passengers or Masud anymore. Trying desperately to look over at Masud, Azizi felt defeat, as he could not move his head. All sensation seemed to be leaving him. Azizi wanted to scream out in pain but closed his stinging eyes instead. He focused his attention on a mental picture of his family, and for a second, the pain receded as a feeling of complete love washed over him. It was the last thought of Azizi's life.

OH, GET UP AND GO TO WORK

A SCREECHING GUITAR BLARED FORTH ITS unnerving sound. Simultaneously in the background, a drum beat incessantly as a clanking metal sound followed along in an offbeat tempo.

The hard-rock music that filled the room had accomplished its purpose. A hand emerged from under the covers and began a determined, snakelike dance for the Snooze button of the alarm clock. Finding its prey, a solitary finger pressed the magic button, which allowed another seven minutes of silence before the music would return. The hand slithered back under the covers, only to begin its haunting dance again and again as Dustin Grey wished the alarm clock away and intermittently fell back into the bottomless void of sleep.

When the alarm went off for the ninth time, Dustin, with great reluctance and hesitation, threw the covers off. In one quick motion, he lifted himself from the bed and stood erect in the darkness. Dustin carefully walked the few feet from his bed to the window, stumbling along the way over his shoes, which he had kicked off that morning before going to bed.

Groping in the dark for the bottom of the heavy-duty, light-blocking window shade, Dustin began to wake. He was excited at the prospect of going to work. Successfully finding the bottom of the shade, Dustin gave it a tug and then let go, sending the shade upward as it coiled around its spring-loaded cardboard cylinder. Gazing out upon a cloudless, starlit sky, Dustin concluded that his work would be relatively easy this night; it was a good night for astronomy. He glanced at the alarm clock and noted once again that he was late for work. He was supposed to arrive at work, or, rather, his love, by 11:00 p.m. But as usual, that meant he wouldn't leave for work until 11:00 p.m. To him time was an irrelevant concept. Dustin refused to live his life according the dictates of an earthly clock. He was attuned to the time and passage of the galaxies, the stars, and the planets. No, being on time for work to Dustin meant going to a place where he could gaze upon the wonders of the universe. Time itself did not dictate such things; conditions did.

Dustin reached up and turned the light switch on. He pulled down the window shade, blocking the view of the sky, which moments before had been his silent gateway to worlds and celestial events yet undiscovered. Crossing the bedroom, Dustin entered the adjoining bathroom and hurriedly shaved and showered. Donning a faded and somewhat-tattered T-shirt with a logo of a surfboard company, which was now too worn and faded to read, Dustin momentarily thought of learning how to surf but quickly dismissed the thought. There was not a force upon this Earth that could tear Dustin away from the powerful telescope permanently affixed upon the mountaintop. Dustin knew his sole purpose in life was to explore the heavens.

Dustin complemented his shirt with an equally faded pair of blue jeans torn at the knee. The jeans were not purposely cut to peruse a fashion trend but were worn from wear. To complete his roguish appearance, Dustin put on a dirty pair of sneakers, which were once gray but were now covered and stained with a mixture of dirt, oil, and grease. As an afterthought, he grabbed a baseball cap, which was once green but was now faded beyond recognition and torn at the peak of the brim.

When one saw Dustin, as he had a penchant for dressing this way, people would often think of him as a study in contradiction. People were always quick to draw conclusions about his lifestyle from his clothing, but when they saw his crew-cut hair, they didn't know what to think.

The haircut was actually a remnant from his days spent in the Marine Corps as a rifleman. While the discipline from the Corps didn't last, the haircut did. Most people thought Dustin to be what he was not. No one ever guessed that he was an astrophysicist, and not just any astrophysicist, but the one who discovered DG122.

Victoria Stockwell, known to her friends as Victoria, and to Dustin as simply Vicky, glanced out the window of her office to the darkened valley below. Off in the distance, Vicky spotted two headlights as they pierced the darkened landscape. She watched and followed the headlights as if transfixed by their light. At first, the lights went to the left and then to the right, and then back to the left again as they ascended the twisting, turning road up to the summit.

Vicky knew it was Dustin, late as usual, but she wouldn't say anything to him about his tardiness, hoping instead that he would someday correct this annoying behavior. After all, it was Dustin who had saved all their jobs amid an atmosphere of budget cuts and high inflation. Their facility, Midpoint Observatory, had fallen victim to a bean counter's pencil point and erasure. Hell, in today's world few people were interested in astronomy, much less understood it and its importance. Then, slightly more than one year ago, Dustin, the ever-present resident genius, detected an asteroid the size of Rhode Island emerging from deep space at an unprecedented rate of speed, hurtling toward Earth. Dustin had detected the asteroid when it first emerged. Therefore, the asteroid was named DG, for Dustin Grey, and designated *122* for the 122nd asteroid that would pass in close proximity to Earth.

Dustin's calculations laid bare the facts. The asteroid would pass near the Earth at an approximate distance of two hundred thousand miles. The general public would come to believe what the newspapers and the television stations had proclaimed: "A close call for planet Earth." Vicky knew that in astronomical terms it was a very, very close call. In fact, as Dustin often said, the asteroid would be a mere whisper away.

Dustin had almost lost control of his discovery as other rouge or would-be astronomers throughout the world issued press releases almost daily. Some cried doom, while others maintained that the moon or Earth would disappear in a spectacular collision with the asteroid.

Amid this panic and hysteria, Dustin's patient methodology proved its worth. Through careful calculation, Dustin had determined that the gravitational pull of the Earth and moon would have some influence on the asteroid but that it would pass peacefully by and continue on its journey. It was a hard time for truth when fear sells myths.

Eventually, though, truth won out and Dustin prevailed. However, it wasn't for a few months until the world community found out all that Dustin had discovered.

Another possibility Dustin considered was that DG122 would pass through a meteor belt as it approached Earth. Dustin, because of the mass of the asteroid, declared the meeting of these two heavenly events as a nonissue. As the meteors collided with the giant asteroid, they would not influence its course; instead, the mass of the meteors, as they slammed into DG122, would shatter, and their mass would then either be added to the asteroid or become forever locked in the tail of debris following behind. Dustin was really more worried about gravitational influence and focused his attention in that direction.

Dustin was convinced that the asteroid would pass safely by the Earth this time and continue on its cosmic journey. But that was the first of three possible scenarios that he had worked out. The second scenario, and one he feared, dealt with the unlikely possibility that the gravitational pull of the Earth and moon would influence the course of the asteroid as it passed by. If this happened, the asteroid could become locked in a new trajectory and become an ever-present danger in our galaxy, always to be watched and feared. The third scenario was an extension of the second and was the one Dustin dreaded most of all. If, and he felt it wouldn't, the gravitational pull of the Earth or moon was strong enough to influence the asteroid, then the asteroid could become again locked in a new trajectory that would send it on an elliptical course around the Earth, drawing in ever closer with each pass until the unthinkable happened, a collision with Earth.

At an international conference on astronomy, Dustin received the accolades of his peers regarding his discovery of DG122. He was also invited to present his findings for final judgment in the academic world. In a cold, impersonal, and determined manner, Dustin presented his scenarios. His peers, who also acted as his judges, were stunned by Dustin's conclusions. They could not, however, argue against what they had all come to realize through the sheer logic and fact of Dustin's presentation. That day, he won vindication over the detractors and foretellers of doom.

Once Dustin had received international favor for his discovery and conclusions, the United States government reversed the budget ax and funded the Midpoint Observatory for the next twenty years, with promises of continued funding after that. Midpoint was also made part of a small group of professionals throughout the world who search for and track asteroids that have the potential to collide with the Earth and affect the solar system. *Yes,* Victoria Stockwell, thought, *Dustin has saved the proverbial bacon.*

Vicky smiled to herself as she watched Dustin park his 1973 limited edition bright-yellow sports bug Volkswagen Beetle in the small parking lot. *How come it's always the brilliant ones that don't seem to care about material things?* Vicky wondered to herself. But she knew that Dustin was more than comfortable in his world and wouldn't think of driving any other car.

Dustin bounced up the steps to the observatory, reached into his pants pocket, and extracted his electronic identification card, which allowed the holder access to the facility. It took Dustin three attempts to get the little red light to change to green and unlock the door. Dustin couldn't imagine why he just wasn't able to open the door and walk in. After all, this was the middle of nowhere.

As Dustin walked into the hallway, he checked his mail slot and saw that, as usual, it was crammed full of magazines, personal mail, and a pile of memos. Dustin liked Vicky a lot in ways he probably shouldn't, but as an administrator, he regarded her as a destroyer of forests. Dustin, for lack of a better description, regarded Vicky as a micromanager. There were daily memos about everything. There were memos about shortages, how to use a computer disk, newspapers left in the lunchroom, reminders not to kick or punch the vending machines. His favorite, though, was a three-page memo about what one should do to prepare for vacation regarding his or her work. But Vicky had her good points too. She worked endlessly to see that everyone had everything they needed to do their jobs. Vicky was also constantly trying to improve the complex and the equipment. She was a tireless campaigner for outside grant money and endlessly argued with the government for more money. Her efforts always paid off in new equipment and other small improvements.

Dustin looked upon Vicky as more of a friend than a supervisor. Perhaps one day, if either of them were able to pierce their working relationship, they might become lovers.

"Hey, Dustin!" Vicky called out in her traditional greeting.

"Hey, Vicky!" Dustin answered while melting inside as he heard her sexy, deep, drawn-out Southern accent.

They both stared at each other for a moment, as they always did, until one of them broke the awkward silence. "What's the latest on our friend?" Dustin asked in a somewhat-nervous tone. Since its discovery, the position of the asteroid had been updated every half hour, with its location marked on a star map in the computer room of the observatory.

"Exactly on course, as you predicted, Dustin, and just fifty-eight days and seventeen minutes until event," Victoria answered with admiring eyes as she wondered exactly when Dustin was going to get up the nerve to ask her out. She decided then and there that once this damn asteroid thing was over, she would take the plunge and ask him out. *Why waste all this damn time?* she thought. Since the asteroid came into their lives, nothing was the same. There once was a time they would eat their midnight lunch together and talk endlessly about their favorite science-fiction shows and what was going on in their lives. They had even agreed to take motorcycle lessons together and vowed to buy bikes and travel the back roads. Vicky couldn't care less about motorcycles and was actually a little afraid of them, but if it meant getting closer to Dustin, she would overcome her fear. But since DG122 was discovered, the subject never came up again. She had once tried unsuccessfully to broach the subject, but she realized Dustin wasn't listening, as he was probably thinking about her nemesis.

"See you later, Vicky," Dustin replied as he began walking toward the computer room.

"Yeah, see you later. Hey, Dustin, your pants are on fire and your hair is falling out!" Victoria answered, knowing that he was already lost in his own world of DG122.

"Thanks, Vicky!" Dustin answered as he hurried on, having no idea what Victoria was saying.

Once in the computer room, Dustin did what he did every night. For what seemed like the millionth time, he confirmed the position of the asteroid and then meticulously recalculated its projected course. Each night the answer was the same. The asteroid was exactly where it was supposed to be according to his original calculations. In fifty-seven days, the asteroid would pass through the meteor belt and, one day later, would pass the Earth. There would be little opportunity for direct observation, as it would pass closest to Japan. That is, unless he could talk Victoria into spending some of the budget money for two tickets to the other side of the world. Dustin, of course, would suggest that Victoria accompany him. He secretly dreamed of himself and Victoria on vacation after the asteroid passed, but he would have to plot his scheme during his off hours. He was at work now, and nothing mattered but the asteroid. Dustin put his legs up on his desk and stared intently at the computer screen, watching his asteroid proceed across the cosmos. The rest of the night would pass, and Dustin would fend off conversation, forget to eat, and only go to the bathroom when his bladder screamed out in pain.

I DON'T HAVE A TICKET FOR THE ROLLER COASTER

A T THE SAME INSTANT THAT Azizi's aircraft was beginning its experience, a sonic wave slammed broadside into Donald Richards's brand-new AWACS plane. Immediately the aircraft was pushed violently to the right. The left wing dipped downward, placing the aircraft in danger of rolling over. Donald and his copilot, Arthur Kennedy, fought the controls to regain level flight. After what seemed like an eternity in hell, they edged the aircraft level. At the same time, the electrical systems, which powered the radar screens the technicians used, went blank. Then the aircraft began to lose speed, and it slowed dangerously close to the stall speed. Donald knew that once their speed slowed so much, the airplane could no longer fly. They would drop like a stone into the ocean.

Donald reasoned that he had to build up speed, and quickly. He decided to dive the aircraft, nose first, to build up speed, which would allow him to hopefully restart the engines that just stalled out. Both men knew that this was a dangerous maneuver with an airplane this size, but their options had run out. Donald glanced over at Arthur and saw his smiling face as if he were enjoying the position they were in. Arthur nodded to Donald. Donald winked back, and then together they pushed the control column forward, applied pressure to the flaps, causing the plane to dive downward toward the surface of the ocean.

The only thought that went through Donald's mind was a hope that the person who designed this aircraft knew what he or she was doing. Trusting his own life and those of his men to his skill as a pilot, Donald was determined that the aircraft would fly even if he had to get out and push it along.

In mere seconds, the aircraft fell fifteen thousand feet. Donald went thought the restart procedure, while Arthur kept his hands glued to the control column. At first, the engines coughed, and then, miracle of miracles, the engines started. Immediately grabbing for his control column, Donald screamed out, "Now, let's get this baby back up!" Together both men used every bit of strength they had. They pulled and pulled on the control column. Ever so slowly, the nose of the aircraft began to rise just as the surface of the ocean was getting uncomfortably close. At three thousand feet, the aircraft leveled off.

Slowly Donald and Arthur nudged the aircraft up to thirty thousand feet and leveled off. After he was satisfied that the aircraft was stable, Donald reported into the base and informed them what had happened. Being ordered to return immediately, Donald called the navigator and asked for a heading. After setting the new course, Donald directed Arthur to take over for a few minutes while he checked on the crew.

Donald left the cockpit and walked back into the crew area. First, he checked the electrical circuit breakers and tripped them back on. One of the circuits drew his attention as it was flickering when all the others were out. Even when he turned them back on, the same one continued to flicker. Deciding that he could pay attention to it later, Donald checked on the crew.

Everyone seemed all right, but a few of the men had minor bumps or bruises from hitting their consoles during the incident. Sam was okay and excited as ever. He motioned for Donald to come over to him and spoke in a hushed tone. "Donald, you won't believe this shit.

When the scope came back on, all the planes we were tracking were still there except one. A commercial airliner disappeared over Zambia."

Donald was use to this kind of mood in Sam, whether it was over girls or the surf. "Sam, are you sure the aircraft didn't simply land?" Donald asked, almost dismissing the aircraft.

"No, man. The thing disappeared. One second it is there, and the next it is gone!" Sam answered, as if he knew something Donald didn't.

"Maybe it was hit with the same thing that hit us and crashed," Donald speculated.

"Impossible! I reconstructed the event and the sonic wave, if that's what is was, began over one hundred miles from the aircraft, and came toward us away from the Transvaal flight," Sam replied, with a hint of superior knowledge in his voice.

"Okay, do me a favor and review the tapes—that is, if the digital recorder is working. Also, send out an inquiry to the Air Ministry in Zambia to see if one of their passenger planes is missing," Donald ordered, still not believing the aircraft disappeared.

Donald went back into the cockpit and helped Arthur prepare for landing, as they were now less than forty minutes from their air base. As a precaution, they dumped their excess fuel out over the ocean. Next, all nonessential electrical systems were shut down to decrease any risk of fire. When they were on final approach, Donald reminded the crew to tighten their seat belts and put away any loose items that could be a hazard if they had to crash-land.

Ever so gently, Donald eased the aircraft down. First, the wheels under the wings touched the runway, followed by the nose landing gear. Once the aircraft was stopped, an airport panel truck with a large sign on the back that read "Follow Me" pulled in front of the aircraft. Donald and Arthur looked at each other with puzzlement on their faces but did as they were instructed.

They were led to a secluded part of the aircraft parking area. Donald thought that this was being done for safety reasons, considering what they had been through. Once they were parked, Donald and Arthur shut down the engines and turned off all nonessential power running through the aircraft. Looking out of the window, Donald knew that he was wrong about the safety issue, as he watched his aircraft being surrounded by Air Security Police. Wondering just what was going on, Donald gathered his crew by the exit door. Not knowing what to expect, Donald instructed them that if questioned, not to answer any questions outside of the realm of a normal debriefing. Giving a nod to Staff Sergeant Josephs, Donald breathed deeply as the sergeant opened the door. Immediately, a stairway was rolled up to the aircraft so they could disembark.

Dispensing with normal protocol, Donald exited the aircraft first. When he stepped onto the stairway, he was immediately beckoned to come down the stairs by someone who looked like he was in charge. When Donald reached the bottom of the steps, two of the security policemen approached him. Each of the policemen grabbed one of his arms and led him to a waiting car. Rather roughly, he was shoved inside the back seat and the doors were locked. Donald strained to see through the darkened windows as he looked back toward the aircraft. He managed to see each member of his crew being treated the same way, except they were shoved into two passenger vans.

After a few minutes, the car Donald was in drove away, followed by the passenger vans. Fifteen minutes later, the motorcade pulled up in front of an old, weatherworn building that appeared to have been abandoned a long time ago.

Donald was taken out of the car by the same two security policemen and held as he was before by his arms. He was forced to watch as his men were shoved, pushed, and forced into the building. After his crew were all in the building, a burly-looking man dressed in a plain black flight suit approached him. He walked right up to Donald and pointed a handgun toward his chest. The security officer told Donald to get into the building and keep his mouth shut.

Donald tried to take a step toward the security officer, but he was still restrained by the other two security men that had almost dragged him out of the car. In frustration, Donald spoke those immortal words of confrontation: "Fuck you!"

"Fuck me? No, asshole, fuck you!" the security officer replied and then directed the other two security policemen, "Show this piece of shit into the building and put him in room number 4."

As Donald was dragged by his arms into the building, he turned his head around and hollered, "Who the fuck do you think you are? You're just a fat old man in a black suit trying to look like a tough guy!"

"Fuck you! I'll kill you now, asshole! You flyboys think that your shit don't stink. Well, guess what, asshole? You're just a turd to me, and your life ain't worth a shit!" the security officer shouted back as Donald was pushed into the building.

Donald was led, or rather shoved and pushed, down a darkened hallway and thrown into a room. Slamming against the far wall of the room, Donald immediately turned around and charged the door just as it was closing and locked from the outside. Donald tried pulling on the doorknob, to no avail. Taking his anger out on the door, Donald slammed his fists against the door and hollered out, "You assholes!" Striking the door with his fists once more, Donald settled down a little and took stock of his situation.

The room he was in was sparsely decorated. There were no windows. There was nothing on the wall but an old calendar four years old. The only furniture in the room was a wooden desk with a metal chair behind it, and another chair in front of it. At first, Donald paced around the room, which was no larger than six by six feet, and then sat down in the chair behind the desk. Donald opened every drawer of the desk and found them empty and dirty. Pushing himself and the chair backward a little, Donald put his feet up on the desk and waited, and waited.

Two and a half hours later, just as Donald was starting to fall asleep, the door suddenly opened and in walked Air Marshal Lester Kingman. Donald immediately stood at attention and saluted the air marshal. Lester Kingman returned the salute and ordered Donald to sit in the chair in front of the desk. Not one to be intimidated, Donald stood in front of the desk and bellowed, "Sir, I want to protest and file a complaint about the treatment my men and I received from your air security people!"

The air marshal, who was standing behind the desk, turned red in the face and exploded, "I don't give a shit about your protest or your fucking complaint! If I were you, I would sit down and shut the hell up. Otherwise, Lieutenant, you will be flying a latrine brush in some godforsaken outpost, where the sun don't shine!"

Donald wondered for a second where on Earth the sun doesn't shine and then, not to be outdone, replied, "Need I remind the air marshal that I am a captain?"

Donald didn't think it possible, but Lester Kingman's face turned even redder, and he exploded again, "Fuck you, sit down, and shut up! Otherwise, you will be a recruit by the time I finish with you!"

Understanding what the air marshal said, Donald sat down. He thought that the air marshal's last explosion was loud enough for everyone in the world to hear except the deaf and the dead. Donald sat rigidly in the chair, with both feet squarely planted on the floor and his hands on his legs. But Donald was not intimidated and stared straight into the air marshal's eyes, waiting for the next explosion.

Lester Kingman sat down behind the desk, took a digital recorder out of his pocket, turned it on, and placed it between himself and Donald. Staring at Donald with an unblinking intensity, which seemed to rivet him to the chair, Lester Kingman ordered him to describe the events of the flight.

As Donald described the flight, he noted that the demeanor of the air marshal changed. He seemed to have gotten over his anger, if in fact it was anger or some kind of act. In any case, Donald talked and the air marshal listened. When he had finished, Donald felt as if a great weight had been lifted off his shoulders. It was good to talk about what happened. Lester Kingman then turned off the recorder, sat back, and asked why Donald felt that the aircraft was hit by a sonic wave.

"Well, sir, when we experienced what felt like something slamming into our aircraft, I noticed a high, piercing sound that penetrated my headphones. It seemed to be all around us and coming from outside of my aircraft. The sound lasted only a few seconds, but it was enough to give me a slight feeling of disorientation. I recovered quickly, and well, you know the rest," Donald replied, purposely saying the words *my aircraft*.

"Captain, can you say with certainty that all the instrumentation went down and that no telemetry was being recorded when the event occurred?" Lester Kingman asked in a quiet tone.

Donald picked up on the word *captain* and wondered if he still had his job. Carefully Donald answered, "Sir, nothing about the flight could be said with exact certainty except the fact that we took off and then landed. After the event, I retripped the circuit breakers and all instrumentation came back online. Before landing, I shut them down again in the interest of safety." Donald left out the fact of the flickering light in the circuit breaker going to Sam's station. The flickering could only mean one thing; Sam had somehow rewired his station so that it always had direct power no matter what.

Donald was comforted by the fact that knowing Sam, no one would ever find a trace of the rewiring.

Lester Kingman stared at Donald for a moment, cleared his throat, and stated, "Captain!" *Still a captain!* thought Donald. "Each of your crew is being reminded that they have signed the National Security and Secrets Act. If anyone talks about this incident to each other or to anyone else without proper authority, I can guarantee that they will be dealt with to the full extent of punishment allowed. That includes hard time in a military prison for the rest of their lives. Is that clear?"

"Crystal clear, sir," Donald quickly replied.

Lester Kingman appeared to relax a little more. He unbuttoned his uniform jacket, put his arms on the table, and began, "Captain, I'll tell you what we know about this incident. But whatever I say, and I caution you again, is protected by the National Security and Secrets Act.

"Your aircraft was not hit by a sonic wave, but rather, it was subjected to an electromagnetic pulse. This magnetic pulse was so big that we could not even accurately measure its intensity. It originated in the upper atmosphere, but who in the hell shot it off is anybody's guess.

"The electrical systems of your aircraft tripped off and were not permanently damaged because, as you know, those systems are shielded from such an occurrence. Up to this incident, all the shielding was theory, or so we thought. You and your crew are very lucky individuals. There is, however, some fallout from the incident.

"Right now in our country and in our neighboring countries,

the situation is confusing. When the electromagnetic pulse occurred, anything within its immediate zone that did not have such shielding is not operating. Everything that depends on nonshielded computer chips is dead. That includes such things as a simple toaster to an automobile, and of course computers and computer-driven machinery. Regrettably, a commercial aircraft flying over Zambia apparently was not shielded and crashed, probably with a total loss of life.

"In short, Captain, other than the fact that we know there was an electromagnetic pulse, we have no idea what is going on. Nor do our neighbors. At first we thought that some fool started World War III, but the event is localized. Hell, the only ones with the technology are the Americans, and they are just as confused as we are."

"What do you mean, sir?" Donald interrupted.

"In the early 1980s, the Americans exploded an experimental low-grade electromagnetic pulse bomb in the atmosphere twenty-five miles off the coast of Georgia in the Atlantic Ocean. They wanted to monitor the event and measure the results, but all hell broke loose. Even at that low a grade of an explosion, the electrical power grid in the entire Southeast of the United States was knocked out. Automobiles that depended on early computer chips, computers, and everything else that depended on computer chips were fried. Power companies scrambled to restore power for two days. No one understood what happened. The American public took it all in stride, like they do any adversity, and continued on. That was the last time that they attempted an atmospheric blast, but they did refine their capability. Hell, today they can drop tiny bomblets from a fighter aircraft that can explode over an enemy's power station and knock out the power without damaging the generating equipment.

"The only real thing we know for certain is that no major power in the world caused this. We have asked the Americans for help in determining the cause of the explosion, and they have been most gracious." Lester Kingman concluded, took a breath, and added, "Captain, I'm grounding your aircraft for three days while we check it out and make sure that it is fit to fly. Tomorrow you and your crew will report to medical services for physicals. I want to make sure that everyone is okay."

Standing up, Lester Kingman continued, "For now, go home and get some rest. You and your crew need it. By the way, Captain, that was some bit of flying you did. Congratulations!"

Donald stood up and replied, "Thank you, sir." He then saluted the air marshal as he left the room.

THE DAY THE ANGELS CRIED

S TORM CLOUDS WERE GATHERING OVER the airport. Azizi's wife, Serwa, and her children were sitting in the waiting area of gate 5 in the Zambia International Airport. Serwa was waiting for her husband to return. She and the children enjoyed their daily pilgrimage to meet the center of their universe, Azizi, when he returned from a hard day's work. Every time Azizi walked up the passenger ramp, hugged her and gently kissed her on her lips, well, Serwa fell a little bit more in love. Azizi would then get down on his knees, hug, and give generous, loving kisses to each of his children. Hand in hand the proud young family would then leave the airport, only to return another day and do it all over again.

This day was different. Azizi was hardly ever late, and certainly not this late. Serwa saw the notification on the flight monitor that indicated that flight 143 was delayed. But somehow a feeling of dread was creeping into her. It was as if she knew something was terribly wrong, but she didn't know what. To dispel some of her nervousness, Serwa rose from her seat and walked over to the big window that overlooked the area where Azizi always parked his aircraft. As she stood there, the feeling of dread increased and she raised her left hand and placed it on the window. As she did so, a gentle rain began. For an instant she watched as the drops of rain ran down the outside surface of the window. Serwa then took her hand away from the window, turned around, and with a mother's smile on her face, walked back to her children. Together the young family sat and played a rhyming game as they waited.

For a few precious moments, the feeling of pending doom left Serwa as she played the game with the children. Together they laughed as only a family could. The feeling of doom, however, returned when she saw Etaba, the operations manager for Transvaal Airlines, walking toward her and the children. She and Azizi had known Etaba for the past five years, and Serwa could never recall him looking so glum as he did then.

Etaba slowly walked over to where Serwa and her children were sitting. Serwa instinctively stood up as Etaba approached them. They exchange silent looks for a moment, and then Serwa asked, "How serious is it?"

Etaba looked at the children and then back at Serwa and whispered so the children wouldn't hear, "His plane disappeared. There was a power outage, and when the radarscopes came back online, Azizi's plane was gone." Etaba coughed and tried desperately to hold back tears and then added, "The military has already launched a search-and-rescue operation. I'm…sorry… Serwa. Azizi is the best there is, and I'll bet he's on the ground somewhere caring for his passengers. Serwa, if there is anything…"

Etaba stopped speaking when Serwa shook her head and held up her hand to motion for him to stop.

Serwa turned toward her children and, with a tear in her eye, announced that they were going home. The children protested, saying that they wanted to wait for their daddy, but Serwa took their hands and walked away. Etaba watched as a proud family walked away from gate 5, and he felt the pain that Serwa was feeling.

I DIDN'T DO IT, AND YOU CAN'T PROVE THAT I DID

Donald was offered a ride back to his quarters but decided to walk the three miles so that he could get some exercise. He had been cooped up all day and needed to do something. As he walked, Donald thought about what the air marshal had said about the electromagnetic weapon. He reasoned that a weapon of such magnitude could cause instant havoc wherever it was used. Donald understood strategy, and he knew that if the Americans had such a weapon, then the Russians did also, and who knew what other countries had the weapon? *Surely, the Israelis do,* Donald concluded. Lessons in international strategy taught Donald that if each side knows the military capability of the other, then there is peace. It's when one side doesn't know what the other has that causes a conflict. Donald was lost in these thoughts, but he knew the answer to what really happened lay with Sam. He had to find out what Sam knew.

Twenty minutes later, Donald was outside of Sam's quarters. Since the lights were still on, he decided to knock on the door. Sam opened the door and physically pulled Donald into the living room and slammed the door closed behind him. "Sam, what the hell are you doing?" Donald hurriedly asked.

"Just being careful, Cap," Sam answered as he, at first, peered out of the living room curtains and then sat down across from his friend Donald, whom he affectionately called Cap out of respect for his rank.

Both men sat there for a moment, each waiting for the other to speak. Sam broke the ice and offered Donald a beer, which he declined. Donald observed that Sam had already consumed more than a few beers and was acting very nervous. Donald knew that this was out of character for his friend. *If Sam was drinking a lot, that would mean something was really wrong,* Donald thought to himself.

"Sam, through the years we have shared a lot of good times, a lot of beers, and maybe even a few women here and there," Donald began, which drew laughter from Sam and a comment.

Sam replied, "Yeah, Cap. Do you remember Janet? That surfer girl—"

But he was cut off by his friend.

"Sam, you know I'm not here to relive old times." The smile disappeared from Donald's face as he continued, "Sam, I know that your radarscopes were up and running after the circuit breakers tripped and shut down the rest of the electronics." At this, Sam nodded, with a slight smile on his face. "I didn't tell the air marshal about it because I knew that you would have covered your tracks. I just want to know what you saw and if you told anyone."

"No, Cap, I didn't tell anyone that my station was up and running. And yes, my tracks are covered nine ways till midnight. Look it, Cap, I reconfigured the electrical pathways during the retrofit a few weeks ago. Remember, I was in charge of it. My only problem was that I couldn't get rid of a little flicker in the monitoring bulb. I guess that's why you are here," Sam replied, letting it all out since the whole incident was driving him nuts and he just had to tell someone.

"You got that right, you crazy son of a bitch. Why did you do it?" Donald asked.

"Ah, I was just fooling around a bit, and I tweaked it a little," Sam answered proudly.

Donald turned real serious and tried to find out what he needed to know. "Look, Sam, something very odd is going on. I just want to know what you saw on the scope. I promise I will never reveal what you say to anyone."

Sam stared at him for a long second and asked, "No one else, agreed?"

"I promise, Sam. I won't tell a soul. And besides, if I did, I'm quite sure that the air marshal would have me shot," Donald promised.

Sam laughed slightly, turned real serious, and replied, "One of the aircraft I was tracking went vertical about the same instant the wave, or whatever it was, hit us. I don't mean it went vertical because it climbed into the sky under controlled flight. I mean the fucking thing went straight up like an elevator and disappeared when it reached forty-five thousand feet."

"Come on, Sam, aircraft don't go vertical, and they don't disappear!" Donald pleaded.

"I'm telling you, Cap. The damn thing went straight up and disappeared. Just like magic!" Sam swore.

Donald looked hard at his friend and instinctively knew that he was telling the truth. They then tried to reason through what would make a plane go vertical and, more incredibly, disappear. Finding no answers, Donald decided to call it a night. As he was leaving, Donald turned around and said, "Hey, Sam, that Janet girl, she really was something, wasn't she?"

"Fucking A, Cap," Sam replied as Donald closed the door and left.

Donald walked the rest of the way home more confused than ever. After he climbed into bed, he lay awake staring at the ceiling, wondering what could make a plane go vertical and disappear. He knew that there had to be a logical explanation, but he could not find one. As he lay awake, Donald said a prayer for the souls aboard that aircraft and hoped that whatever happened to them never happened again to anyone else. A restless sleep soon came to Donald, as tomorrow would be another day.

BUT THIS ISN'T WHAT THE RECRUITER PROMISED

REAR ADMIRAL CHESTER BRADDOCK FOLLOWED a very twisted path during the formative years of his life. As a child, he was raised in a strict Catholic family where there was always more mouths to feed than money available to feed them. He was the fourth child of eight born into a lower-middle-class family. Chester's life was one of hand-me-down clothing, toys, and wisdom from his older brothers. Luxuries were few and precious, but laughter and a sense of family were ever present. Chester was different, though. Most adults who knew him often said that he followed the beat of a different drummer as he matured. His mother was always being called to school and informed of his many misadventures. While other kids played after school let out for the day, Chester was usually in detention. Chester was simply being Chester. One thing Chester realized, though, was that it was up to him to make opportunity happen, rather than wait around for it to come knocking. Opportunity never knocked on Chester's front door, so he went to look for it.

Chester had seen the recruiting posters for the Navy. There was always a sailor in some foreign country. The catchphrase "See the World" ignited a fire in Chester. It wasn't a question of what he wanted to do but when he would do it. Deciding that he would leave after his birthday, Chester knew that he had to tell his parents. He wanted desperately to tell his mother, but he knew that she would never let him go. So instead he decided to tell his dad. That conversation did not go well, but once his father realized the depth of Chester's determination, he reluctantly agreed. There was, however, a price.

Chester had to promise to finish high school, write often, and if possible, go on to college. Agreeing to the conditions, Chester was now more determined than ever. The only regret he felt was not telling his family, especially his mother, but his father would take care of that.

On the day after his sixteenth birthday, Chester dressed for school as he normally did. But this day was different. Instead of rushing through breakfast, Chester lingered, taking mental pictures of his family. On his way out the door, he kissed his mother, as he always did, but the kiss was softer this time. When Chester went out the front door, his father was waiting for him. Chester ran into his open arms and hugged his dad. And then he did something he hadn't done since he was a child: Chester kissed his father goodbye. Breaking the embrace, Chester hurried to get away. If he lingered any longer, he knew that he wouldn't leave. As Chester rounded the corner of his block, he looked back and saw his father standing there with slumped shoulders, waving goodbye. Chester waved back with a smile but didn't see the tears cascading down the face of his father. Instead of getting on the school bus that day, Chester took a bus to the next town.

Walking proudly into the Navy recruitment office with a forged birth certificate that made him out to be nineteen, Chester declared that he wanted to join the Navy.

The recruiter smiled and asked for a birth certificate. Chester handed over the piece of paper and was relieved when it was given back to him. There were no questions about high school, as the recruiter simply checked off that Chester was indeed a graduate. In fact, the whole process went smoothly.

Chester passed the written test with a very high score. The physical was nothing—Chester was breathing, was walking, and could move his arms. Later that day, after calling his mother, who cried during the entire conversation, Chester found himself on a bus going to boot camp.

His fist assignment in the Navy was aboard a missile cruiser. Chester was assigned to the Combat Information Center of the ship, where all the elements of intelligence, radar data, and weapons melted into one cohesive plan of action. It was during this assignment that Chester found direction for his life. He decided that he wanted to be a naval officer in intelligence and not just any officer. He wanted to be an admiral.

Chester decided upon a plan and stuck to it. Secretly he obtained his high school equivalency diploma, and during the succeeding years, Chester attended college whenever he had the opportunity. Once out of college, he went on to earn two master's degrees; one was in electronic engineering, while the second one was in finance. *Might as well know how to get the money to do the engineering,* Chester thought.

Through the succeeding years, Chester had a brilliant career. Always rising in rank and responsibility in the intelligence field. Twenty years later, Chester had achieved the rank of rear admiral, and then one day his life changed forever. Chester went to work for Admiral Morrison, his friend and mentor, who was in overall charge of Space Command.

At Space Command, Chester was to be the second-in-command, which in Navy lingo meant he was the one in charge while Morrison took care of everything else. But Morrison left Chester alone. Morrison always seemed to be traveling all over the place, but mostly he was always going to Colorado. Chester didn't know the reasons for the many trips and really didn't care at the present time. When the time would come, Chester knew that Morrison would tell him when it was necessary.

In his position, Chester oversaw the operation of sixty-three military satellites.

While the main purpose of the satellites was to provide the military with instant communications throughout the world, the hidden purpose was using the satellites to spy on other countries. Chester's satellites could provide photographic and real-time video as well as electronic surveillance of anyplace in the world at any time. But there was one other thing Chester used the satellite net for: the tracking of UFOs.

BUT I DON'T HAVE A SILVER SPOON IN MY MOUTH

MICHAEL SCOTT WAS A UNIQUE individual. People, for some reason, were naturally drawn to him. Perhaps it was because he treated everyone as if they were important. And to Scotty, as his friends called him, everyone was important. It could be that he always told everyone the truth, even if it might emotionally hurt them. He didn't like to hurt people, but he figured that not to tell individuals the truth would be a sin of disrespect. Maybe it was because of his sense of humor or the great value he placed on friendship. Some might even say it was because Scotty was always there to give a helping hand. Whatever the reasons, Scotty was one of those people who are natural-born leaders. Others simply looked to him and willingly followed his lead.

Scotty did not come from a privileged background. Both his parents worked, and worked hard. His father, after whom he was named, was a construction worker in New York City. There were often long periods of unemployment for his dad, followed by eighteen-hour days when he did work. Catherine, Scotty's mother, worked equally as hard. She was a sales clerk in a large prestigious department store. After long days of standing on her feet, serving unappreciative customers, Catherine would go home, cook her family their supper, and then help Scotty with his homework.

Scotty was not one to ignore the hard work of his parents. When he was twelve, he went to work after school. He wanted to contribute in whatever way he could. At first, he took a job at a local grocery store, making deliveries to people who were too old to brave the streets of New York. The people he delivered groceries to also became a new source of income for him. When Scotty had the time, he would run errands for these same people to ease their lives and, at the same time, earn a little extra cash. From his jobs, Scotty earned his spending money and would purchase his clothing. This helped ease the expenses of the family and gave Scotty a sense of self-pride.

Scotty's formative years were spent in the public school system in New York City. Here he excelled academically beyond the expectations of both his parents and teachers. Some would call him a nerd, but he didn't fit the mold. Instead of being studious, Scotty was busy being Scotty. He was the center of attraction at parties, the hero of the football and baseball teams, and one of the biggest discipline problems in the history of public education. If he wasn't in detention, Scotty was always busy somewhere else. But one thing remained constant, his love of family.

In college it was the same story. Excellent grades, but always in trouble. Never studying, but always partying. Scotty was on a course to nowhere, until he had the opportunity to attend an air show on the beaches of Fort Lauderdale in Florida. Oh, Scotty didn't go there for the air show; he traveled from New York to Florida to attend a party the night before. Waking up on the beach the next morning with a pounding headache because of a hangover, Scotty found himself surrounded by people and loud noises overhead. He lay there and watched as almost every type of military aircraft flew overhead. In that brief span of time, Scotty fell in love.

From that moment on, Scotty knew that he wanted to fly. Returning to college, he settled down somewhat. Most of his time was now occupied with reading about airplanes. Just before graduation, Scotty visited a naval recruitment office and made an appointment to take the naval aviation test. For the first time in his life, Scotty was nervous about an exam. He traveled to the nearest naval air station for his two-day examination.

The first day, he aced the written exam. That night, he ate dinner in the officers' dining room surrounded by naval aviators. Scotty took in the atmosphere as the aviators joked with one another and recounted their most harrowing flights. Scotty wanted into this inner fraternity of pilots and pictured himself as one of them. After dinner, he walked back to his quarters but took a detour and went over to the runway. Sitting down, out of sight of the Shore Patrol (Military Police on a naval base), Scotty was mesmerized by the sight of fighter jets landing and taking off on night training exercises. He imagined himself as one of the pilots as he flew through the night sky.

After two hours of sitting by the runway, Scotty returned to his quarters and fell fast asleep. The next morning, Scotty ate a light breakfast and walked to the medical unit for his physical test. All day long he was poked, probed, and examined. They tested everything from his vision to his toes. At the end of the day, he was told that he passed, but the toughest part was yet to come—the review board, which would decide his fate.

Scotty sat on the hard wooden chairs outside of the conference room with his fellow candidates. Since they were being interviewed by alphabetical order, Scotty was dead last. He watched intently as each candidate left the room. Very few were smiling, as most had looks of total dejection on their faces. When it was Scotty's turn, he stood up and slowly walked into the room as if he were expecting the worst. Scotty sat down and glanced at the members of the board, who looked back at him with blank stares. One of the pilots asked Scotty why he wanted to be a naval aviator.

Scotty's fate was almost doomed within the first ten seconds of his answer. Scotty began by giving the standard answer every member of the examining board hated to hear: "I want to be the best of the best, and naval aviators are the best." But there was something different. When Scotty talked, his eyes sparkled, and his voice was enthusiastic.

For the next ten minutes, Scotty went on and on about flying and the challenges it presents. Finally, one of the members of the board told Scotty to stop talking. In muted silence, each member of the board looked at one another, and with a simple nod, Scotty was on his way to becoming the "best of the best."

After graduation from college, Scotty entered the Navy and was sent to flight training. As he progressed from propeller aircraft to jets, Scotty drew the attention of his instructors. It was almost as if Scotty were born to fly. But it was his love of flying and his inborn ability to handle an aircraft that set him apart. Due to his abilities, Scotty was given the opportunity to choose the type of aircraft he wanted to fly. Scotty chose the Navy's premier multipurpose fighter, the F-18.

For the next three years, Scotty's time was divided between sea duty and shore assignments. His skills as a pilot and a leader continued to improve. People just naturally looked to him for direction and guidance. Eventually, Scotty was chosen as squadron commander. His reputation spread throughout the Navy, and the brass (a slang term for the leadership of the Navy) expected great things from him. Admiral Morrison, who was an old family friend, reveled in Scotty's success. Privately, however, Admiral Morrison was waiting for the wild streak in Scotty to disappear under the pressures of command. That just never seemed to be the case.

Each naval aviator, upon being assigned to a squadron, is given a call sign (a word that describes the individual, which could be funny or serious). That individual is then known by that call sign. At first, Scotty was known as Harpo, after the famous entertainer who was well-known for his good humor and never-ending pranks. His call sign was later changed, however, due to one of his better-known pranks.

When Scotty was assigned to the USS *Eisenhower*, due to Scotty being Scotty, he was well-known to the crew. Everyone seemed to know him. Scotty had time for everybody. His aircraft crew regarded him as one of their own. When they were working on the aircraft, Scotty was always there, helping out any way he could. Scotty was the first naval aviator to ever ask them for their opinion. He made them feel that they were more important than he was. Scotty would say that he was just the driver of the aircraft and it was the crew that really ran the show.

But Scotty always went out of his way for every member of the crew. Once, when he found out that a crew member was going to be the father of triplets, Scotty went about organizing a party for the man to help give the family a good financial start. Scotty assessed each member of the crew three dollars, each officer under the rank of lieutenant ten dollars, each officer above the rank of lieutenant twenty-five dollars. The admiral Justin Brewer was assessed fifty dollars. But the party needed something more.

Scotty sought out his friend and computer whiz kid Seaman Wilton "Jonesy" Jones, and with them together a plan was hatched. Jonesy was able to hack into the supply computer system of Aviano Air Base in Italy. Together, the sense of humor of Scotty and the computer skills of Jonesy were a deadly combination. The world was not safe when they plied their antics.

Somehow they were able to "acquire" six hundred cases of nonalcoholic beer, six thousand hot dogs and buns, seven thousand hamburgers and rolls, and of course, all the accompanying condiments. Jonesy implanted flight orders into their computer system for a cargo plane to fly their "wares" to the naval air station in Saudi Arabia.

The next morning, three Sea King helicopters lifted off from the deck of the *Eisenhower*. They headed for Saudi Arabia to meet the cargo plane from Aviano. Aboard one of the helicopters were Scotty and Jonesy. Scotty was dressed in a "borrowed" captain's uniform, while Jonesy was masquerading as a lieutenant.

When they arrived at the naval air station, the cargo plane was waiting. One of the Air Force officers approached Scotty. Identifying himself as Captain Aldridge, Scotty signed the necessary papers to receive the cargo. For the next thirty minutes, Navy and Air Force men and women worked together to load the cargo aboard the Sea Kings. When everything was loaded, Scotty approached the Air Force officer in charge and thanked him for his help and cooperation. The Air Force officer replied, "My pleasure, Captain Aldridge!" and returned to his waiting aircraft.

Scotty boarded one of the helicopters and, while laughing, ordered, "Let's get the hell out of here before they catch on!" The three helicopters then departed and raced back to the *Eisenhower*.

Unknown to Scotty, Admiral Brewer, later that night, was awakened by a radio call from the commander of the Aviano Air Base. The commander demanded the arrest of a Captain Aldridge, who masterminded the theft of valuable morale material from the air base. Admiral Brewer replied in a very calm voice that there was no such person aboard the *Eisenhower*. The admiral then added that beer in any form was not allowed aboard naval vessels, unlike the Air Force, which allowed it on their bases and openly sold it to willing airmen. Admiral Brewer then hung up the telephone, rolled over in bed, and laughed, as he knew Scotty was at it again. But the admiral realized that he had to talk to Scotty. He just had to stop acquiring things from the Air Force. The last time the Air Force called, Scotty had spirited away two jet engines and assorted aircraft parts as well as couches and rugs for a compartment off the hangar deck where the crew could relax. As the admiral closed his eyes, he did so with a smile on his face because life sure was interesting with Scotty around.

The next afternoon, most of the aircraft were moved up to the flight deck in order to make way for the party. Scotty stood in the middle of the cavernous area, directing his shipmates on what to do. Cooks were laboring over charcoal grills, cooking the hamburgers and hot dogs. Other cooks were busy belowdecks, preparing salads. Other sailors were chilling the beer, while their shipmates were setting up tables. Two Marines were dispatched by Scotty to arrest the would-be father and held him in the ship's brig (a small jail aboard ship). After convincing one of his shipmates to dress up like King Neptune, Scotty was able to relax. After all, it isn't every day one gets to throw a party for about five thousand (the approximate number of people it takes to keep a ship like the *Eisenhower* at sea) of his closest friends.

At 1800 hours (6:00 p.m.), the festivities began. Those who were off duty converged on the hangar deck and waited as the father-to-be was hauled before King Neptune in leg irons and handcuffs. King Neptune read a royal decree declaring the wretched soul before him a man among men—a father. Ordering the shackles and cuffs to be removed, the king handed over a check for twenty-three thousand dollars so the expectant family could get off on a good start. All hands present began clapping as the young sailor, through weeping eyes, thanked his shipmates.

Once the party began, Scotty walked over to Admiral Brewer and handed him a bottle of beer. The admiral gratefully accepted it and then asked Scotty to thank Captain Aldridge for him. Scotty's jaw dropped a little as he tried to smile and slithered away.

Later that day, the aviators in Scotty's squadron changed his call sign to Pirate. The next time he climbed aboard his aircraft, Scotty hesitated a moment when he saw a skull and crossbones painted under his name.

I REALLY DIDN'T WANT TO HEAR THAT

CHESTER FOLLOWED HIS NORMAL ROUTINE this morning. He rose promptly at 4:00 a.m., donned his jogging clothes, and ran a few miles before most people even opened their eyes to greet the new day. After running, Chester allowed himself a few minutes' rest as he watched the early-morning news. Once satisfied that all was well with the world—at least there were not any wars going on—he showered and donned the uniform he loved so much and called his driver. Within minutes, Chester was on his way to work.

As they drove across the bridge from Alexandria to Washington, DC, the first few rays of sunlight were breaking through the light early-morning cloud cover. This was Chester's favorite time of the day. He loved to see the first light of the day wash over the Capitol building and the Washington Monument. To Chester, it was beauty in its own way. A few more blocks and Chester entered the underground parking garage of his office building.

After taking the elevator up to his floor, he stopped in the kitchenette and made a cup of freshly ground coffee. Chester didn't add milk or sugar; he preferred the full taste of the coffee undiluted. As he walked to his office, he held the coffee in one hand, withdrew his morning paper from under his arm, and glanced at the headlines.

Chester entered his office and sat down behind his large sweeping desk shaped like a boomerang. He preferred it this way, what with the clutter of paper and three computer screens occupying a large part of the top of the desk. Sitting down in his high-back desk chair, Chester glanced at the large stack of briefing papers and copies of overnight communications. Sitting back in his chair, he decided that work could wait a minute as he enjoyed his coffee. After a few more minutes of rest, Chester put his coffee down, picked up a stack of papers, and began reading.

After five minutes of reading the overnight briefing repots, he picked up another pile of papers, which was the overnight correspondence. Most of the material dealt with future requests to use the satellite net for spy missions. It was the piece of paper on the bottom of the pile that made Chester's heart skip a beat. It was a request from Air Marshal Lester Kingman of the South African Air Force. Reaching across his desk, Chester buzzed his secretary, Tina Marie, and asked her to locate Admiral Morrison while he re-read the document for the third time.

"Admiral, Admiral Morrison is on the line," Tina Maria announced over the intercom.

Chester pushed the Hands-Free button on the telephone and greeted the admiral. "Good morning, Arthur."

"Good morning to you, Chester. Now, why in the hell are you calling me so early?" Morrison asked, trying to clear the cobwebs from his mind.

"Arthur, I received a cable over the MILNET[1] from Air Marshal Lester Kingman of South Africa," Chester replied and then paused.

Morrison was still a little irritated that he was awakened from his sleep, and shot back before Chester could continue, "And…what does he want? Does he want you to go on a safari or something?"

Chester detected the note of sarcasm in Morrison's voice, but this was too important to put off till later. "I wish that were the case," Chester replied, hoping to cheer his friend up, and then continued, "He is asking if we detected the electromagnetic burst over Zambia yesterday."

"That's not so bad!" Morrison declared, then added, "We can send him the data we collected, but I think we should tone it down a bit. Do you agree?"

"Yeah, I think we should. But there is more. He is also asking for any information we may have relative to any aircraft in the targeted area of friendly, unfriendly, or unknown origin just before or after the event. And get this: he wants to know if such an aircraft was capable of spaceflight," Chester replied and waited for a response.

After a few seconds, Morrison spoke up. "Chester, I'm in Colorado. Clear your schedule. We have some talking to do. There's something you should know. I've been keeping a secret from you for a while. It was to protect you. But it's time you know.

"In the meantime, send a reply asking for clarification of the request. Send it through normal channels—regular dispatch—as if it's not important.

"I'll be there in about three hours. See you then. Oh, do me a favor. Send out for a tuna hoagie for me and one of those brownies. Thanks, Chester." Morrison quickly hung up the telephone, as he always did, leaving the other party with no one to talk to.

Chester did as he was instructed and forwarded a reply by regular routing. That would guarantee that it would arrive at least six to eight hours later. It was a simple reply, nothing that would alert anyone to what was really going on:

> *Please clarify request regarding aircraft. Feel that you must consider a piece of space junk.2 Will forward all data on electromagnetic burst.*

Reaching for the telephone, Chester dialed his head technician, Lieutenant Rodriguez, and directed him to gather the material on the Zambia incident and download the photographic logs from all satellites in the area at that time as soon as possible. In Navy lingo, that meant drop everything and get the job done.

Allowing himself to relax a bit, Chester pushed himself back in his chair and put his legs up on his desk. He recalled the details of the report regarding the electromagnetic burst. He knew it was off the scale, and the report did mention the possible presence of an alien spacecraft, but Chester would need more proof before he believed that. It was unfortunate about the passenger aircraft being in the wrong place at the wrong time, but Chester felt it was too much of a stretch to tie it to a UFO.

When Chester first took over the responsibilities of Space Command, if someone mentioned the word *UFO*, he would have thought the person crazy. But that had changed. Over the years, such words as *UFO, alien spacecraft, alien presence, alien abductions*, and *alien technology* had become somewhat commonplace in the reports that crossed his desk.

Chester, like a lot of the people who had worked in Space Command for a time, had become a true believer.

The alien presence bothered Chester. In fact, for the past few years, Chester had been bothering Morrison to push for the establishment of some sort of military response to fight the aliens and stop them from coming to Earth. But his pleas were falling on deaf ears. Morrison at least acknowledged the alien presence, but that was about it. Morrison would ask Chester how it would look if he went into the president and told him aliens existed and now they had to fight them. Chester's stock reply to Morrison was just "Tell the truth and show him what we know." Morrison would then always change the subject and close off any further discussion about aliens.

But Chester was worried. He recognized that trends in alien activity were beginning to appear. For one thing, the number of alien craft detected in Earth's atmosphere had risen dramatically. Secondly, there seemed to be at least three different types of spacecraft visiting Earth. There was the classic saucer-shape aircraft, then the long tubular-type spacecraft, and lastly, the sleek-looking spacecraft with the recurved wings, but those sightings were very rare. It was mostly the first two types of aircraft that were detected. Chester wondered if multiple alien civilizations were visiting Earth, or was it that the alien spacecraft were evolving, much like we had progressed from the Wright brothers biplane to the space shuttle? And then there were the disappearances.

At first, when Chester's techno spies started detecting landings of alien craft, the event was simply notated. As a matter of pure curiosity, Chester started scanning the local newspapers where landings had occurred. He was mainly interested in reading what the locals had to say about the event, if in fact it was reported in the papers at all. Most times it wasn't. At first, Chester didn't notice or glance over certain articles that appeared within two days of a confirmed UFO landing. Then one day, in a small newspaper from Western Canada, two lead stories occupied the top half of the front page.

The first story was about local residents reporting seeing unusual lights in the sky.

One resident went so far as to say that he had seen a flying saucer land in the woods. The second reported story disclosed the mysterious disappearance of a local resident, one Jacques Bernard. His family and friends were interviewed and basically said the same thing—Jacques was a family man who loved his children and simply would not leave home. Some people reported seeing him the afternoon of his disappearance as he was heading home. But he never arrived. It was as if he vanished into thin air.

The two stories running side by side hit Chester right between the eyes. What he had been seeing but not paying attention to suddenly became an ugly reality. When a UFO landed, people disappeared. Chester started to research the sightings that Space Command had confirmed as landings and re-read the local newspapers. In every instance, whether a UFO sighting was reported or not, there was a reported disappearance of at least one and sometimes two or three individuals. To say the least, Chester became alarmed but did not say anything until he had documented over six hundred cases.

Chester approached Morrison with his research, but once again, he was put off. Morrison offhandedly dismissed Chester's claim as mere coincidence. Disappointed, but not discouraged, Chester continued to record the disappearances—for what purpose, he didn't know. At one point, he thought of trying to investigate the cases on his own, but the responsibilities at work were too time-consuming. So Chester just continued to document case after case after case. Eventually, he had to give up his documentation as it was slowly becoming a full-time job. There were just too many disappearances.

-------- ✦✦✦✦✦ --------

[1] Military communication network between friendly nations.

[2] Worthless satellites and space stations that periodically re-enter Earth's atmosphere and don't entirely burn up during re-entry.

ANYTHING FOR TRICK OR TREAT

CHESTER GOT UP FROM HIS desk and walked over to the small kitchenette in his office, and as he thought about the air marshal's request, he stood there and made a fresh pot of Columbian coffee. Extrastrong—the way he liked it. He often thought that the lifeblood of the Navy was coffee. Throughout his career, no matter where he was, coffee was the one constant. It was always within easy reach, whether he was on board a ship or on land.

Coffee was always there. Chester liked to refer to the Navy as the Coffee Cup Navy.

Nothing would ever get done without this magic elixir.

Chester retreated to the comfort of his desk chair and sipped his steaming coffee. As he sat there, he wondered what Morrison was coming to see him about. Maybe he was finally going to see the president, after all. After thinking about it for a minute, Chester dismissed the thought. *That old war dog only does things his way,* Chester concluded.

His repose was interrupted by Tina Maria calling, "Admiral," over the intercom.

Chester put his cup of coffee down and answered the call. Lieutenant Rodriguez was in the outer office, anxious to see him. Chester had begun to get up and open the door when Lieutenant Rodriguez flung the door open and entered with piles of paper stacked across his chest and a slim plastic DVD case clenched between his teeth. Before Chester could say anything, Rodriguez walked over to the conference table and put down his papers and removed the plastic case from his mouth.

Whenever Chester saw Rodriguez, he wanted for the days of old. Gone were the days of spit and polish. This new breed of technological sailors was different. They were brilliant beyond description; however, they paid little attention to detail when it came to dressing. Oh, Rodriguez wore the uniform—otherwise, Chester would have him in the brig—but it seemed that instead of the man wearing the uniform, the uniform appeared to be wearing the body. Rodriguez always looked disheveled. His shirt was pressed, but it was always coming out of his pants, which seemed to anyone who looked at him were a size or two too big. Beyond Rodriguez's looking disheveled, however, Chester noticed that something else was wrong. Rodriguez, usually an easygoing person, almost to the point of being in a coma, looked worried. *No, it isn't worry,* Chester thought. *He looks downright scared.*

"What did you find, Lieutenant?" Chester asked.

"Well, sir, I... I... I found all the data on the electromagnetic discharge. And I have to tell you, we could not even measure the strength of the discharge. It's off the scale," Rodriguez answered and then paused to catch his breath.

Chester took advantage of the pause and tried to put the man at ease. "It's okay, Lieutenant. Just take your time and relax a second. I know that you have been working almost around the clock since we detected the discharge. And don't think for one minute that I don't appreciate what you have done for us." Chester smiled at the man and directed him to sit down at the conference table. Chester walked around to the other side of the table, sat down across from Rodriguez, and directed, "Now, Lieutenant, let's start again."

Rodriguez looked up and into the eyes of his commander, a man he had deeply come to respect. After clearing his throat, Rodriguez asked, "Admiral, can I speak off the record for a moment?"

"Of course, Lieutenant. I never want anyone in my command to think that they cannot speak bluntly to me about anything. I am always interested in what you think and what you have to say," Chester reassured him.

Rodriguez stared at Chester for a second and then began, "Sir, when you first asked me to start looking for and recording possible landing of UFOs, well, sir, I thought that I had landed in an insane asylum. And I thought that you were crazy. But that all changed when we were able to track the first one and actually record its landing, departure, and return to space.

"Right after that, I became a convert and started reading up on all the ufology material I could find. And I got to tell you that there is a hell of a lot of it. I read everything and watched every science-fiction movie that had anything to do with aliens.

"A lot of the stuff was pure bullshit created by some crackpot just out for the dollar. But at least half of the stuff was the real thing.

"This incident that we are looking into is the stuff of nightmares. The discharge, like I said, was off the scale. With all our present technology, we cannot even measure a burst as intense as this was. I was able to determine that the burst occurred at slightly over fifty thousand feet. It was directed over Zambia and targeted at the aircraft that the world thinks crashed. I was—"

Chester interrupted Rodriguez.

"You mean the plane didn't crash!" Chester declared more than ask a question.

In a very serious and somber tone, Rodriguez replied, "No, sir, it didn't crash."

"Then where the hell is it?" Chester hurriedly asked.

"It was taken inside the object, sir," Rodriguez answered and then quickly added, "Let me explain." He searched through his pile of papers and extracted a file buried halfway down the pile. Opening the file, he first looked at a photograph and then handed it to Chester. After allowing a few seconds for Chester to examine the photograph,

Rodriguez continued, "Sir, I took this photograph off the photo log of one of the satellites. It shows an alien spacecraft stationary over Zambia. As you can see, it's one of the tubular spacecraft. Now, sir, if you would look in the absolute lower right-hand corner, you will see a small aircraft below the object going out of the frame of film.

"I was able to determine that the aircraft was a small private airplane. Once I was able to determine its size, and allowing for altitude variables, I was able to roughly determine the size of the alien spacecraft. Sir, I know it's hard to believe, but it is roughly the same size as one of our aircraft carriers. But this one flies."

Chester looked a little ashen in the face as he spoke up. "Son, are you absolutely, positively sure that this is for real?"

"Yes, sir!" Rodriguez declared, then added, "Sir, when the object became stationary, a cloud began to form around it in order to mask it. It's kind of like steam coming out of a pipe. It's a vaporous matter, but it has the effect of clouding our vision. But we have the capability to see through the vapor. From the photograph, I ran a spectra analysis and found that the object had traces of Alpha Zuron radiation. As you know, sir, only objects that have been in space will emit Alpha Zuron radiation.

"I ran a further analysis on the cloud, and the results were a little surprising. I was able to determine that one of the components of the cloud is helium, and a few other chemicals that we cannot presently identify. On a hunch, I went a few steps further and found that as the cloud is formed, it is charged with electromagnetic properties. I'm guessing now, but once the cloud is formed, a very wide broadband radio transmission is then broadcast, which has the effect of fuzzing out conventional radars.

"This would account for the possibility that UFOs may be coming to Earth a lot more frequently than we think. Our satellites can track them, but if they slip in between our net, then they can come and go as they please, largely undetected. If people see a UFO, they mostly keep the sighting to themselves. If airline pilots, or, hell, even our own military pilots, see a UFO, they are not going to report it, for fear of losing their jobs and being branded insane. But there is a golden lining in all this."

"Excuse me, Lieutenant. You were able to tell all this from a photograph?" Chester spoke up.

Rodriguez smiled a slight smile and replied, "Not from the photograph alone. The photograph, combined with the monitoring instrumentation on two of our satellites, gave me what I needed. It was just a matter of thinking outside of the box and combining the facts that determined the answer."

Chester knowingly shook his head but really didn't understand what he was talking about, then changed the subject. "Son, you mentioned a golden lining."

"Yes, sir. Given the conclusion that I have reached, it would be possible to tweak our present radar system to see through the masking system the aliens use. Therefore, our military planes and civilian radar systems would be able to detect alien craft more readily," Rodriguez answered and then sat back in his chair. Then he added, "There is one more thing. The masking system they use appears to be environment friendly. While they use some unidentifiable chemicals in the system, I took the liberty of running a health check around the areas where we have detected alien landings. Assuming that they employed this system using chemicals, there is a possibility of increased cancer risks. But when I checked for cancer clusters around such landing sights, nothing remarkable appeared beyond normal statistical expectations."

Chester paused for a moment and commented, "Wow, you sure have said a mouthful."

"It's all there, sir. We can do it. There is one more thing, though," Rodriguez answered as he rose from his chair and removed the DVD from its case and put it into the player. He then continued, "The satellites in the area also recorded the event. As you know, each satellite takes digital photographs every ten seconds. I downloaded the photo logs from the two satellites in the area at that time, put them on this disc, and speeded up the time lapse so we could view the event mostly as it happened." Rodriguez then pushed the Play button and stepped back as the monitor screen came alive.

For the next minute and a half, Chester sat there with his mouth open and watched. The film began as the alien craft came into view and then slowed down until it was stationary in the sky. Next, the cloud Rodriguez was talking about began to form and spread across the sky. For a few seconds, nothing happened until the airliner came into view, and then a bright white light extended from the alien craft and washed over the airliner. For the next ten seconds, the Zambia airliner was pulled, tugged, or dragged into the alien craft. A few seconds later, the alien craft moved away amid the clouds it had created.

When the film was over, Chester let out the word *shit*! Recovering from his shock, Chester asked, "What about the people on the airliner? Where did the alien ship go?"

"Sir, we don't know what happened to the airliner or the people. The government of Zambia has launched an extensive search-and-rescue operation, but as of yet, they have not found anything.

As far as the spacecraft goes, fifteen minutes later, it was detected over the Atlantic Ocean, swooped down low, and sped away into outer space," Rodriguez answered as he removed the DVD and handed it to Chester.

"You have done an excellent job, Lieutenant. Admiral Morrison will be here later this morning, and I would like you to show him what you showed me," Chester ordered.

"My pleasure, sir," Rodriguez replied, saluted Chester, and left the office. Chester went into his kitchenette and poured himself another cup of coffee.

Returning to his desk, Chester sat down and wondered about the people aboard the airliner.

I'VE GOT A SECRET, NAH, NAH, AH, NAH, NAH

As Chester was sitting at his desk, Morrison walked through the door with a wide grin on his face. After the pleasantries between the two friends were completed, Chester told Morrison of the morning's activity. Morrison was eager to meet Rodriguez and hear for himself what the man had to say. He showed some interest in the video, but not too much. Chester thought that it was almost as if he had already seen it, but that was impossible.

Chester summoned Rodriguez into his office, and for the next hour, he made another presentation. Morrison questioned him extensively about how he reached his conclusions regarding the alien masking system. Rodriguez once again played the video, but again Morrison almost made an effort to show some interest. At that time, Chester knew that something was up. It was obvious that Morrison had seen the video before, but it couldn't have come from Chester's group.

When Rodriguez had finished the presentation and was gathering up his papers, Morrison asked the lieutenant if he wanted to change jobs. He offered him "the biggest challenge in his life to serve not only his country but also the world." Rodriguez at first declined, stating that he liked his present assignment and, in particular, he liked working for Admiral Braddock. But Morrison offered him an immediate promotion and access to a laboratory to pursue his work with unlimited resources. Rodriguez hesitated again, but Morrison was insistent and came close to ordering him to accept the offer. Reluctantly, Rodriguez accepted his new assignment without knowing where he was going and what he was actually going to do. But in a way, when Morrison ordered him not to speak to anyone about his reassignment, it intrigued him.

"Mind telling me what that was all about? I just lost one of my best men," Chester more demanded than asked Morrison after Rodriguez left the office.

"That's one brilliant kid!" Morrison declared, ducking the question for the minute.

"Every person that works in this facility has at least two master's degrees, and some have more than one doctorate degree. Hell, they are all brilliant in their own individual ways! Now, tell me why I just lost Rodriguez!" Chester replied and steered the conversation back to the central issue.

Morrison looked at Chester for a moment with a somber look upon his face.

Clearing his throat, Morrison began, "Chester, I'm afraid that for these past four years, I have been keeping something from you. It wasn't because I don't trust you. Hell, I trust you with my life. I did it to protect you. If I failed in my endeavor and it became public, it would have ruined my career in the Navy. I didn't want to drag you down with me. If I was successful—and I am—I knew when it would be the right time to bring you in on my little secret."

Chester was intrigued by what Morrison was saying but was a little disturbed that his friend hadn't confided in him. "I'll accept that. So what is the big secret all about?" Chester asked, anxious now to find out what was really going on.

Morrison picked up a hint of displeasure in Chester's voice, as he thought that he would. Looking at his friend, Morrison began, "Chester, since you have been in your present assignment, you have excelled beyond expectation. Your work and dedication are unmatched by anyone I know. I have come to rely on you not only as a friend but also as an extension of myself. That being said, here it is.

"You and I have been thinking along parallel lines for a long time. You were always trying to urge me to go to the president and alert him to the fact of the alien presence and the possible threat they pose. You also suggested that an independent force be formed in order to combat the growing alien presence and the abduction of our citizens by the aliens.

"Well, I have done what you suggested. With the—"

Morrison was interrupted.

"You mean that you saw the president? I knew it! What did he say?" Chester excitedly asked.

Morrison paused for a second and then continued, "I wouldn't exactly say that. I kind of didn't tell the president. In fact, he knows nothing about what I did. It just kind of evolved as a result of our conversations.

"Look it. The long and short of the matter is, I secretly built a base in Colorado specifically to combat the alien threat. This base has been operational since the past year. At present, we track alien activities, and like you, I realize the threat they pose not only to our nation but also to the world as a whole. We also do research on the alien capability and work around-the-clock trying to develop weapons to fight them effectively. In fact, we have developed a fighter aircraft that will revolutionize air travel as we know it. It is capable of taking off from a land base, travel, and fight in outer space. But that is only the beginning of the things that we have accomplished," he said. "Oh, we also have a few of the alien spacecraft, which we are trying to reverse engineer."

Chester interrupted. "What? How in the hell have you managed to keep all this a secret?"

"That is the easy part. Each member of the force is sworn under the National Secrets Act. But they are such a dedicated group of people that the unthinkable will never happen," Morrison answered and paused, waiting for Chester to ask another question.

When he didn't, Morrison continued, "Our fight is not alone, though. Over time I have forged alliances with my equals in other countries. We don't let politics stand in our way. Each one of us has recognized the danger that the aliens represent. At present, we are not united on a military basis. That will come later. I hope before it is too late. But for now we meet on a somewhat-regular schedule, discuss the problem, and formulate plans for a unified response.

"On the regular, though, we report to one another any alien contact or activity within our respective countries. We manage to do this through regular communications, and when the occasion presents itself, we meet in person. You know that conference on international terrorism that's coming up soon? Well, we will use that conference as a cover. All the principal members will attend the conference representing their countries. Sometime during that conference, we will schedule a meeting of the members. I would like you to attend that conference, if at all possible." Morrison concluded and felt pleased with himself.

Chester was stunned. Regaining his composure, he looked at his friend and superior officer. In a matter-of-fact manner, he stated, "I just have one thing to say." He then paused and continued in a heightened voice, "Arthur, you've been my friend for a very long time, and I love you like a brother, but when did you take leave of your senses? You built a secret base in Colorado, staffed it with a private Army, and decided on your own to wage war! And then forged allegiances with foreign countries because you want to fight aliens! This is crazy! Forget about your career—you have committed career suicide, and you just don't realize it! Get real, Arthur! The United States is not your private playground. You better tell the president!"

Morrison was taken aback quite a bit and then began a hard sell. For the next two hours, Morrison talked and talked. The only time he came up for air was when two tuna hoagie sandwiches and two brownies were delivered and promptly consumed. But even then, Morrison continued his sales pitch between bites. When he finished talking, Chester was sold. But he wasn't sure if he was sold on the idea out of loyalty to his friend and mentor or he simply didn't want to hear Morrison talk any more.

Once that was settled, Morrison reached into his briefcase and withdrew a DVD. Crossing over to the player, Morrison inserted the DVD and asked Chester to watch the movie. What Chester saw was a carefully orchestrated presentation. It depicted a busy underground facility with people in military uniforms—Navy, Air Force, and Marines—doing what they did best, their jobs. There was a large hangar deck with every type of aircraft carefully parked and looking ready for combat. Then there was the sleek-looking aircraft that Chester had never seen before parked off in the corner of the deck. Next came a virtual tour of the massive communications room and the regular facilities one expects to find on any military base, from sick bay to sleeping quarters. Lastly, the video depicted another view of the hangar deck, and at the end of the deck, two massive doors slowly opened. Chester was alarmed when he saw three classic round-shaped flying saucers just sitting there. At that point, the film ended.

Morrison quietly walked over to the DVD player and extracted the disc. After returning it to his briefcase, Morrison sat back down across from Chester and asked him what he thought.

Chester was still not completely sold on the idea that such a facility should remain a secret from the president, but he let it go. He was, however, intrigued that such a base could exist and somehow remain a secret. But he was completely sold on the idea that a military force should exist to combat the alien threat and presence. Speaking up, Chester declared, "I know that I have been bothering you about establishing a force to combat the aliens, but hell, I expected you to see the president and talk about it. I didn't expect you to go out on your own and do it!"

Morrison laughed slightly and spoke up. "But it was all your idea!"

"Yeah, but who the hell ever figured that you would carry it this far? Damn, Arthur, you're on a one-way train straight to Leavenworth. Forget about retirement—you'll be breaking big rocks into little ones for the rest of your life!" Chester replied, a bit emotional, but with a hint of admiration. Chester actually liked the idea of a secret base operating outside the limits of the military and the government. This was old-fashioned get-it-done-and-worry-about-it-later thinking.

"But what do you really think?" Morrison asked coyly.

Chester took a deep breath and, with a hint of laughter, answered, "I love it! May God forgive me, but I think that it's great! I'm with you. I guess we better reserve two rooms in Leavenworth. I hope we get rooms with a view, though."

OH, DON'T PULL OUT THE FAMILY PICTURE ALBUM

O NCE CHESTER HAD ACCEPTED THE inevitable and bought into the program, there was still one thing that bothered him. Morrison was a visible man. His rank required of him certain social functions and, of course, the endless parade of lunches, where the real business of government gets done. Already Chester had covered for him on countless occasions, and his repeated absences from Washington, DC, was beginning to be noticed. Chester was getting tired of giving the standard excuse that he was off on an inspection tour of some remote satellite-tracking outpost.

"There is one more thing I want to discuss with you before we break for dinner." Chester spoke up and then added, "I know that you are into this thing up to your eyeballs—or should I now say that we are?—but you have to appoint someone you can trust to run the operation for you. You are too visible of an individual to be constantly off somewhere. I have tried to cover for you as best as I could, but quite frankly, they want to see you and not your second in charge."

Morrison paused and knew that Chester was right, and so right that Morrison had been thinking the same thing for quite some time. As he stood up and walked over to the coffeepot and poured two cups of fresh coffee, Morrison replied, "I have been thinking about that for a long time. Like you said about me being visible and all, the same thing applies to you. Therefore, I have been looking elsewhere. I read personal file after personal file, and it always comes down to one person." Morrison put down one cup of coffee in front of Chester and held on to the other one as he sat down and asked, "You've heard me talk about Richard Scott and his family quite a bit. We were shipmates on the USS *Brooklyn* when she was first commissioned. After the war, Richard left the service. He got married late in life and had a wonderful son. His name is Michael Scott. Richard passed away a few years back, but I still keep in close contact with the family. Also, I was Michael's guardian angel when he was on active duty. I still keep close tabs on him, though. You may—"

Chester interrupted Morrison. "I know all about Michael Scott. Hell, I don't think there isn't anyone in the Navy above the rank of captain who hasn't been on the receiving end of one of his pranks. I'll give you this: there certainly isn't a more-colorful figure around. But isn't he still restricted from active service for a while yet? Last I heard, he's a weekend warrior[3] somewhere, still flying the F-18."

"Yeah, he is. But he is also a lot more. What isn't written up in his file jacket is the fact that two weekends a month he volunteers his time for the Angel Flight Program. He flies sick children and adults around the country so they can receive lifesaving treatments for their illnesses," Morrison sharply replied.

Chester felt a little embarrassed, but he didn't know that part of Michael Scott's life. Looking at his boss, Chester offered, "I didn't know about that. He sounds like a good man, but are you sure you want him to get involved in this? I mean, if he's the commander of the base, then wouldn't he be just as guilty of operating outside the military structure as we are? And do you want to expose your friend's son to what could possibly happen?"

Morrison has been wrestling with that very question and felt guilty that he would expose the son of a lifelong friend to such a danger, but he knew what he had to do. "I know Chester. That's what makes it so hard. But my first duty is to this country. I am duty bound, as we all are, to do what is right and best for this country. The best man for the job is Michael Scott," Morrison replied and then added, "Everybody calls him Scotty."

"You're right. I can see your point. He's a natural-born leader and one of the best aviators ever to come out of Pensacola. I know that he is also not afraid to speak his mind. Hell, he's the one who took on a UFO, right after his wingman was killed. It showed a lot of guts to do that." Chester laughed a little and then added, "It's kind of ironic that the man who will be in charge of a secret base has the call sign of Pirate. It's as if he stole the whole thing."

Morrison smiled slightly at Chester's point of irony while reaching into his briefcase again. This time he pulled out a CD and asked Chester to put it in the player. As Chester did as he was asked, Morrison told him that the very reason he built the secret base was Scotty. "I carry that CD around with me to remind me of the reason I built the base. It's a transcript of Scotty's encounter with the UFO. What happened was, Scotty and his wingman, Ice, were in the ready aircraft[4] on the deck of the *Eisenhower*. The air cap[5] was nearing the end of their patrol time and were low on fuel. A radar operator detected an unknown target heading toward the *Eisenhower*. A decision was made to launch the ready aircraft when the target came within one hundred miles of the carrier. Scotty and Ice were launched, with orders to intercept the target and destroy it if it came within fifteen miles of the carrier. Once they were launched, they both proceeded toward the target. Scotty, of course, was the flight leader.

"The recording on that CD depicts a determined man who will do anything to get a job done. That's the kind of determination this country needs. And that man is Scotty.

"You are right when you said that Scotty attacked a UFO, but he did that only after his wingman disobeyed orders and went too close to the target. Scotty initially was not going to attack the UFO but was going to observe it. Circumstances forced him to attack, as you will hear.

"Chester, if you would, please give me the remote so I can shut it off at times and fill in the details." Morrison took the remote and pushed the Play button. Within a few seconds, the recording began.

> *Eisenhower*: "Pirate, I am handing you off to looking glass[6] call sign Thunder. Nest[7] out."
>
> Pirate: "Thunder, this is Pirate. Two birds,[8] out."
>
> Thunder: "Pirate, acknowledged. Proceed at 2-3-2 degrees. Unknown on that vector, 7-5 NM[9] at 2-0 feet,[10] object is now stationary. Thunder, out."
>
> Pirate: "Acknowledged, 2-3-2 degrees, unknown 7-5 out at 2-0 feet, object in hover. Will proceed at 2-0 feet. Pirate, out."
>
> Pirate: "Ice. Sweep cold.[11] At 2-0 NM out, enable radars and go weapons hot."[12]

Morrison pressed the Pause button on the remote control and, looking at Chester, added, "During the debriefing of Scotty, he stated that as they approached the object, Thunder called out their distance to the object every ten miles. When they were twenty miles away, both Scotty and Ice enabled their radars and immediately had weapons lock.[13]

"Scotty first had a clear visual on the object when they were about one mile away.

"At first, the object appeared to be a gleaming orb stationary in the sky. As he and Ice approached closer, Scotty could make out its shape. He described it as about the size of a small jet, like one of those private executive jets. It had wings, but they were short and delta shaped. The tips of the wings were recurved back toward the main fuselage. It was long and sleek-looking, with an extended, pointed nose.

"Scotty planned to fly by the object to the right and then arc back and overfly it, but that was when things went wrong, as you will hear." Morrison concluded and pushed the Play button.

Ice: "Pirate, you ever seen anything like this?"

Pirate: "Negative, Ice. Stay at my seven."[14]

Ice: "Pirate, what is it? I've never seen anything like this. Look how it is just sitting there. I'm going in for a closer look."

Pirate: "Negative, Ice. Stay on my seven. Am breaking right."

Ice: "Pirate, look at it."

Pirate: "Stay on my seven. Acknowledge!"

Ice: "I'm going in for a closer look."

Pirate: "Negative, Ice! Follow me!"

Pirate: "Ice! Break off! Break off!"

"At this point," Morrison said, interrupting, as he pushed the Pause button again, "Scotty broke to the right and, when he didn't see Ice on his seven, came back around and flew toward the unknown. He watched as Ice made a close pass by the object and then quickly came around and headed right for the object. Telemetry from Thunder, the E-2C directing them, confirmed that Ice was headed right for the unknown, at six hundred miles per hour, on an interception course. When Ice closed to within a distance of one hundred yards, the unknown emitted what Scotty described as a blue light. When the light reached Ice's aircraft, the F-18 disintegrated.

"Scotty saw all of it happen. Instead of backing off and requesting help, Scotty was Scotty and attacked. But I am getting a little ahead of the story. Let me turn the transmissions back on." Morrison concluded as he pressed the Play button.

Pirate: "Nest! Nest! Unknown fired on Ice and splashed[15] him!"

Nest: "Pirate, this is Nest. Acknowledged. Ice splashed. Back off and observe. Await aid."

Pirate: "Negative, Nest. Am attacking."

Nest: "Pirate! You are ordered to break off and wait for help!"

Pirate: "Negative!"

Nest: "Back off, Pirate, and wait for aid! Acknowledge!"[16]

Nest: "Acknowledge, Pirate!"[17]

Nest: "Pirate! Acknowledge!"

Pirate: "Nest! Have engaged the unknown. All missiles were downed by a blue light. Send me some damn help!"

Nest: "Pirate, this is CAG.[18] You are ordered to break off."

Pirate: "Negative! Send me help, and now. Am going in for another attack."

Nest: "Pirate, this is CAG. You are ordered to break off now, goddamn it!"

"At this point, it became a little hairy," Morrison began after pausing the CD again. "When Scotty and Ice approached the unknown, a radio technician took it upon himself to broadcast the encounter throughout the ship. As a result of this, the *Eisenhower* began acting as one. Without orders or direction, the crew began preparations to launch additional aircraft. Aircraft were fueled and armed, pilots ran to their aircraft and made sure they were ready to be launched, the catapults were brought up to full launch capability, and in short, the whole ship was ready for a battle. When Ice was splashed, the admiral put the *Eisenhower*, as well as the escort ships, on full alert.

"Everyone was ready for battle except for CAG.

"Unfortunately for himself and Scotty, he went into a panic mode. CAG just lost it. Maybe it was the continued stress of his job, or maybe he just couldn't believe what he was hearing. In any case, he failed Scotty and his ship. The sailors and officers in the Combat Information Center[19] were pleading with him to give the order to launch aircraft in order to help Scotty. CAG seemed to focus on Scotty and replied to the pleas, something to the effect, 'Why doesn't Pirate listen and break off the attack?' Finally, Captain John Steward stormed into the CIC,[20] took the microphone from CAG, and ordered additional aircraft to be launched. But it was a little too late. Help was already on the way from the British carrier HMS *Illustrious*, which was on patrol in the area and had heard Scotty's pleas."

"Wasn't CAG, Captain Jeffrey Bittle, the same Jeffrey Bittle that earned the Silver Star for air combat during the Iraq War?" Chester asked.

"Yes, regrettably, it was. He was a very brave aviator, but for some reason, he just lost his edge. Hell, it can happen to any of us at any given time. Unfortunately, he lost it in a combat situation, and he could have gotten some people killed.

"I didn't want to see a man of his caliber lose his pension and be disgraced during a court-martial. But I'm getting a little bit ahead of the story. Let me turn the recording back on so you can hear what happened next," Morrison concluded as he pressed the Play button.

> Victor: "Pirate, HMS *Illustrious* here! Heard you need some help. Four birds[21] here, call sign Victor, closing on your 2-0[22] weapons hot, fires lit,[23] on your six.[24] Suggest break and reacquire[25] with aid. ETA, 4-5."[26]

Pirate: "Acknowledged. Am breaking right. Have you on my radar. Will join up ten miles from target and make our run. I'll lead and break left. Suggest your group, then break right after launch."[27]

Victor: "Sounds good. We are forming up on you now. We will lie back a few hundred yards and will launch after you break left."

Pirate: "Acknowledged. And, Victor, thank you."

Victor: "We aim to please. Now, let's splash this bastard! Victor, out."

Nest: "Pirate, this is Nest. All ready craft launched. Advise you wait for help."

Pirate: "A little late, aren't we, Nest? I have all the help I need. Beginning attack run…six missiles away."

Victor: "Pirate, break left now! Unknown is firing…all missiles destroyed. Pirate, hit the deck! Blue beam of light coming your way…flight[28] fire and break right!"

Pirate: "Victor…stick heavy.[29] I think that I'm hit! Trying to level off. Where is the bastard?"

Victor: "Shit!"

Pirate: "What?"

Victor: "We're coming around. That damn thing went vertical after it destroyed our missiles. No impacts. No impacts! We'll be on you in a few seconds. Sit tight."

Pirate: "Victor, I'm having trouble trying to turn. Do a visual on me."[30]

Victor: "Be there in two seconds."

Pirate: "Copy that."[31]

Victor: "Have a visual…will check for damage. The top half of your rudders were cut clean off. It looks like a laser made a clean cut to your rudders. Apparently, the unknown didn't mean to kill you. Will sweep underneath to see if there is any other damage… All clear. Only visible damage is to the rudders. Suggest you eject."

Nest: "Pirate, rescue craft launched and closing on you. Also suggest you eject."

Pirate: "Negative. Negative! Will try and make home. Victor, will you escort?"

Victor: "Affirmative. We need to turn on a heading of 3-2-5 degrees to get you home. Can you execute?"

Pirate: "Trying now…tail is sluggish…going to reduce power to port side and use the engines to turn…reducing by one quarter…coming around…just a little more, and there we are. Power matched on both engines."

Nest: "Pirate, we have you seventy-five miles out and on course. Anything we can do?"

Pirate: "Negative! Going to eject when I reach you. Bleeding off altitude. Down to twenty-two thousand. Will eject at one thousand."

Nest: "Copy that. Now have you fifty miles out at fifteen thousand."

Pirate: "Roger that."

Victor: "Pirate, this is Victor. We are pulling away to give you a clear sky for ejection. Will provide air cap[32] until rescue."

Pirate: "Thank you, Victor. Please thank your ship for me. Hope I can return the favor someday."

Nest: "Pirate, this is Nest. Have you fifteen miles out at four thousand. Rescue aircraft on station.[33] Do you need anything else?"

Pirate: "Nest, a big steak dinner would be nice!"

Victor: "Pirate, Victor, out."

Nest: "Dinner will be waiting. Have you at eight miles out at two thousand, speed at 3-0-0. Suggest you slow speed."

Pirate: "Slowing…feels very sluggish…like it's going to break apart…aircraft shuddering…"

Nest: "Pirate, eject."

Pirate: "Negative. Want to make sure this baby is going to hit the water and not the ship."

Nest: "Read you three miles out at one thousand. Time to eject."

Pirate: "Negative. Riding down to two hundred feet. Have some dry clothes ready."

Nest: "Copy that. How do you want your steak? Seared as usual?"

Pirate: "That would be great. Picking up a lot of vibration…don't think I'll make two hundred…what's my track?"

Nest: "One mile to port. Have you one and a half mile out at seven hundred and fifty feet. Time to go, Pirate!"

Pirate: "Affirmative!"

Scotty's training took over at this time. He drew his legs in toward the seat, reached upward, and with both hands, pulled a face curtain over his face and helmet. This set off a sequence of events. In less than a tenth of a second, the canopy of the aircraft was shattered by an explosive charge to clear the way for Scotty to eject.

Almost simultaneously, in less than one-quarter of a second, an explosive cartridge was ignited automatically, which began to propel Scotty's pilot seat upward. Rockets then ignited under the chair, which launched Scotty slightly over two hundred feet into the air in less than half a second, well clear of his disabled aircraft. Scotty fought off unconsciousness as the g-forces on his body increased. Finally, a small drogue parachute was then fired away from the chair, which deployed the main parachute, slowing him down. Another explosive charge then ignited, which separated Scotty from his pilot's chair. As the chair fell toward the ocean, Scotty's life raft inflated and dangled from his harness, ready for use when it hit the water. As Scotty drifted downward toward the ocean, he watched as his aircraft slammed into the water and quickly sank. His thoughts were not about himself and how lucky he was, but rather, they were mainly of Ice. But his thoughts were also of CAG. Anger was growing within Scotty toward CAG.

Why didn't he launch fighters to help me and Ice? Scotty asked himself over and over.

As Morrison pushed the Stop button on the remote, Chester spoke up. "That's some recording." And then he declared, "There's a lot of different scuttlebutt about what happened next. Some of the stories say Scotty damn near killed CAG when he got back to the *Eisenhower.* Some other stories have Scotty throwing him overboard. Just what the hell did happen?"

Morrison laughed a slight laugh, almost like a giggle, and then spoke up. "I guess it's the stuff that legends are made from. Scotty didn't beat him up or throw him overboard, but I imagine that he would have liked to.

"As soon as Scotty was in the water, the rescue helicopter was on top of him.

"Divers went into the water and helped hoist him into the helicopter. From the time Scotty went into the water until the helicopter carried him back to the *Eisenhower,* which was only a few minutes, almost the entire crew gathered onto the flight deck.

"When the rescue helicopter landed, the crew gathered around Scotty. Emotions were running high as they congratulated Scotty on his rescue and survival. CAG then appeared on the flight deck and stood by a hatchway to the conning tower. As if by magic, the crew felt his presence. They separated and cleared a pathway between Scotty and CAG.

"Scotty was all smiles as the crew were congratulating him. However, when he saw CAG standing there, his mood instantly changed. He threw his helmet down on the deck and started walking toward him with a look of grim determination on his face. As he passed through the crew, he ignored their pleas of 'Don't do it' or 'He's not worth it.' A few of the crew members even tried to restrain Scotty, but he quickly threw them off as he edged closer to CAG.

"When Scotty reached CAG, they stared at each other for the briefest of moments.

"Scotty then shouted out, 'You fucking coward!' as he drew his arm back and let CAG have it right on the jaw. CAG, of course, fell to the deck and struggled to get up. Scotty stood over him and shouted, 'What were you trying to do? Get me killed? You should have sent me help, you no-good piece of shit!'

"CAG eventually stood up and hollered at Scotty that he was under arrest. Scotty stared CAG down for a second and then pushed him aside as he entered the hatchway. CAG shouted after Scotty that he was under arrest and that his naval career was over, but he was shouting at a ghost. Scotty had gone directly to sick bay for a medical exam after his ordeal.

"CAG remained on deck for a few minutes and turned around to face the crew still gathered on the flight deck. CAG shouted at them, 'You are all witnesses. Pirate's career is down the drain! You all are going to have to testify at his court-martial.' CAG then repeated himself at least three more times over and over. One of the crew members then shouted out that nobody saw anything, and the crowd dispersed.

"Upon learning of the incident, Admiral Brewer proceeded to sick bay and had a talk with Scotty. In no uncertain terms, the admiral laid the law down to Scotty and confined him to his quarters once the doctors released him. He then turned his attention to CAG. Admiral Brewer knew, just as CAG inwardly knew, that CAG was finished as an effective leader. When it counted most, CAG froze. The problem was how to quell tempers and restore morale throughout the ship."

Chester cleared his throat and spoke up. "Well, that's a little different from most of the stories going around. CAG had it coming, that's for sure. I heard that CAG left the *Eisenhower* that night, never to be heard from again. But why did Scotty leave active service? It sounds to me like a court-martial board would have dismissed any charges."

Morrison thought for a moment and then replied, "Admiral Brewer contacted me right after the incident. He and I discussed the problem and decided that it would not do the Navy any good to have to go through two courts-martial. On the one hand, CAG would have been charged with 'cowardice under fire,' and Scotty would have been charged with 'striking a superior officer.' I agree with you that Scotty's charges would have been dismissed, but then there was the possibility that the existence of UFOs might have to be discussed in the courtroom. It was a no-win situation for the Navy and the officers involved.

"I had Admiral Brewer offer CAG a full retirement, provided he retired on the spot. Otherwise, he would be prosecuted, and if found guilty, which he would have been, he would have lost his retirement pay and would have wound up doing time in prison. To keep Scotty out of trouble, I directed that he be released from the regular Navy and be assigned to a reserve unit, which would allow him to keep on flying. My plan was to bring Scotty back after five years or so and move him into a command position. The Navy simply can't afford to lose men like him.

"You're right about one thing: CAG did leave that night. After he signed his retirement papers, he was flown off the ship. Since then he has been living a quiet life in one of those retirement communities in Naples, Florida.

"Scotty left the following day. When he went up to the flight deck, every member of the crew who were off duty said goodbye. I know someone slipped him a recording of his encounter with the unknown, and since that time, he has been conducting his own little investigation." Morrison concluded and took a sip of his cold coffee.

"Has it become an obsession of Scotty's?" Chester inquired.

"No, Scotty has always been grounded in reality. He does, however, spend some of his time delving into UFO groups and tries to stay current with the material. That's just an added plus for our purposes," Morrison replied as he stood up and poured himself another cup of coffee.

"How do you know that?" Chester asked, suspecting the answer.

"Oh, since I decided that Scotty was the right man to run our little endeavor, I've had some of our agents keep him under loose surveillance," Morrison replied as he sat back down.

"Loose? That doesn't sound like you," Chester pointed out.

"Okay, so not so loose. They keep an eye on his social life and monitor his business activities," Morrison replied as he winked at Chester and then smiled sheepishly.

"Business activities? What does Scotty do?" Chester asked.

After taking a sip of his coffee, Morrison cleared his throat and answered, "He is an international lawyer. His practice is basically limited to contracts."

"A lawyer! I would have never figured that Scotty would become part of the establishment. How the hell did that happen?" Chester asked, surprised at the answer he had received.

Morrison smiled and remembered that at first he was surprised when he heard that Scotty was going to law school. After sitting back in his chair and getting comfortable, Morrison answered, "His mother, Catherine, always dreamed that Scotty would one day become a lawyer. When Scotty first was accepted into flight school, she often remarked that if God intended that man should fly, he would have given him wings. She didn't like the idea of Scotty flying jets and made no secret about her feelings. After a while, though, Catherine gave up and accepted the inevitable.

"When Scotty was released from active service, he naturally returned home.

"Catherine, of course, renewed her campaign to make him a lawyer. Out of love for his mother, and mostly because he needed something to do, Scotty entered law school. He found that he liked it, and in particular, contracts. For the first time in his life, Scotty found something truly challenging. He buckled down and studied. His efforts were rewarded when he finished first in his class and went to work for one of his teachers, a Simon Pickney.

"Pickney was a highly sought-after international contracts attorney. In international negotiations, he is widely known as the 'guru of the deal.' Somehow he always worked his magic for the benefit of his clients. But he is a very fair man, and both sides of any deal he negotiated always felt as if they received the upper hand in a contract.

"When Scotty entered law school, Pickney had volunteered his time to teach. He immediately recognized the potential of Scotty. Over the next three years, he became Scotty's mentor and cultivated him. When Scotty graduated, he immediately went to work for Pickney. You see, Pickney wanted to retire, and since he was in a solo practice, he needed someone to carry on his firm. That someone was Scotty.

"Scotty took to it like a duck to water. In no time at all, Scotty was acting independently, negotiating multibillion-dollar deals all over the globe. Within a year, Pickney turned his entire practice over to Scotty, lock, stock, and barrel.

"Scotty moved his practice into an old firehouse up on West Forty-Fifth Street in New York City that had already been converted into a doctor's office. The doctor, a world-renowned surgeon, was moving his practice closer to the hospital. After restructuring the building into a law office and a home, Scotty moved in. You really have to see—"

"Wait a second." Chester interrupted as he shuffled through some papers on his desk. Retrieving a receipt, Chester asked, "What is the address on West Forty-Fifth?"

"Ah, 24 1/2," Morrison replied, knowing that he was trapped.

With a big smile on his face, Chester pressed on, "Let me guess. Scotty's secretary wouldn't be named Marlene Jackson, would she? The same Marlene Jackson that you have me send flowers and chocolates from the Charlestown Chocolate Company to monthly."

Having turned red in the face, Morrison sheepishly answered in a low voice, "Well...yeah."

"I knew it!" Chester declared with laughter in his voice and then, for effect, added, "So our 'For God and country,' the admiral has a girlfriend!"

"Hey, look, she is a very vibrant, beautiful woman. Any man would be proud and lucky to be with her!" Morrison shot back with irritation in his voice.

With a hint of laughter and admiration in his voice, Chester responded, "I think it's great, Arthur. It's about time you settled down. I'm happy for you."

"Well...thanks, but who said anything about settling down?" Morrison replied as Chester looked down at his desk with a smile on his face as he hummed "Here Comes the Bride" in a barely audible tone. "What's that?" Morrison quickly asked.

"Oh...nothing. I was just thinking out loud," Chester replied as he lifted his head and glanced at his friend. Managing to suppress his laughter and a smile, Chester searched for something to say. "You were talking about Scotty's office. What is it like?" he quickly asked.

Settling back down, Morrison answered while closely looking

at Chester for any hint of a smile, "It's a four-story building. On the first floor there is a receptionist's area, and then a secretarial area for his secretary, Marlene. The rest of the floor is Scotty's offices and a law library." Not detecting even a hint of a smile on Chester's face, Morrison continued, "The second floor is Scotty's living area. There is a living-roomdining-room combination, a large kitchen, and a home theater area. On the third floor, Scotty has his bedroom as well as three guest bedrooms. There is also a room he calls his private area, which is essentially a computer room that he uses for research. This is where he conducts his investigation into UFOs. The fourth floor is his game room and storage. You wouldn't believe the pool table he has up there. All hand-carved from a single piece of wood. Beyond the pool table there is a dartboard, which Scotty is always playing, and a few video arcade games. There is also a personal gym up there."

"Sounds like every man's dream," Chester observed. "Is there a woman in his life?" Chester inquired as an afterthought.

"Not as far as my agents can tell. At least not a steady one. He goes out on a lot of dates, but I guess that he is still searching," Morrison replied.

"That's a shame," Chester added.

"Not really. I have someone in mind for him," Morrison declared.

Not being able to resist, Chester spoke up. "A matchmaker too. Will wonders never cease?"

"Can it!" Morrison ordered.

Recovering quickly and knowing he had pushed his friend far enough, Chester changed the subject. "So how do we get Scotty to take command of the base in Colorado?"

"Well, that's the beauty of the whole thing," Morrison coyly answered and then drank some of his coffee. After readjusting himself in his chair, Morrison continued, "The secret to Scotty is to have him get interested in something and then spring, shall we say, the trap. The incident in Zambia is the perfect bait.

"We should investigate the disappearance of that airliner rather than just document it as we have already done. With Scotty's help, we will be able to get a team in there to perform a physical search. It would be nice to find that aircraft and see what happened."

"How is Scotty going to help us do that?" Chester interrupted.

"Scotty only has about ten clients from time to time. But they are the largest corporations throughout the world. One of those clients is Spectrum Computer Corporation. As you may know, they recently completed a multimillion-dollar deal in Zambia. And guess what? Scotty was the one who brokered the negotiations. During the process, he even established a friendship with the president of Zambia," Morrison proudly declared with just a tinge of regret that he would use friendship to accomplish his goal.

Chester was endlessly amazed at how his friend thought and the way he always seemed to work things out. "That's one neat little package, but how do you know that Scotty will go for it?" Chester inquired.

"I'm not 100 percent sure. But given the fact that a UFO is involved, and it happened in Zambia…well, it's a puzzle that Scotty won't be able to resist. It's just a matter of giving him enough facts and letting him loose," Morrison replied, and then he quickly added, "I'll have to step up surveillance on Scotty. Let me do that now, and then there is something else we have to talk about." Morrison then walked over to the desk, turned the telephone around to face him, and quickly dialed a number. In a few minutes, he ordered an increase in surveillance on Scotty to around-the-clock and assigned additional agents to watch him.

"Just one thing." Chester spoke up and then continued, "That UFO that Scotty encountered, its description is different from the standard saucer shape. Do we have any idea where it comes from?"

"No, it just seems to show up from time to time. At first, we thought that it was somehow connected to the saucer-shaped ones. Kind of like a command ship. But it doesn't appear regularly, and when it does, it just seems to be observing the other alien craft," Morrison replied and, as an afterthought, added, "It doesn't seem to be a threat like the saucers and the cigar-shaped craft do."

"But it killed Scotty's wingman," Chester pointed out.

"Yeah. But it also could have killed Scotty and that flight of British fighters. It didn't. Instead, it chose to leave. I believe the pilot of that craft was acting in self-defense. Ice probably came too close to the spacecraft and posed a threat. Remember, the alien craft downed the missiles that Scotty and the British fired at it. Just as easily, the alien craft could have taken out all the fighters.

"For some reason, this alien is different. I just wish that we could contact him somehow," Morrison concluded with a hint of regret in his voice.

[3] *Weekend warrior* is a name attached to someone who serves in a reserve unit of the military.

[4] Usually two fighter aircraft with their pilots sitting in the airplane, with the engines running on low idle, waiting to be launched into the air on a moment's notice if a threat presents itself.

[5] A squadron of fighter aircraft that are assigned to provide air cover for the carrier.

[6] A surveillance aircraft capable of tracking multiple targets at once and direct fighters to the targets. The aircraft designation is E-2C and can be described as an early warning radar system. Each naval carrier has as a regular compliment of such aircraft.

[7] The call sign of the USS *Eisenhower.*

[8] Two aircraft ready for attack run.

[9] Nautical miles.

[10] Twenty-thousand-foot altitude.

[11] Radar off.

[12] At a distance of twenty nautical miles from the object, Pirate instructed Ice to turn his radar on and activate his weapon system.

[13] Attack radars will establish the exact position of the object being attacked and transfer that information to the weapons computer, which in turn will activate the attack radar of the missile designated for the target.

[14] Positions are designated like the hands of a clock. For example, if someone said "On my six," that would mean behind the person. In this case, like the hands of a clock, Ice was to stay close to Scotty off to his left, slightly behind him.

[15] Shot him down.

[16] There is a pause of ten seconds in the record of the transmission.

[17] Another ten-second pause.

[18] Commander of the air combat squadrons aboard a carrier. His word is final in all matters related to the aviators and their aircraft.

[19] The central office on a naval ship, where aircraft and the battle readiness of the carrier are directed from.

[20] Combat Information Center.

[21] Fighter aircraft.

[22] Location.

[23] On afterburners.

[24] Coming up behind you.

[25] Break off the attack and then form up and attack together.

[26] Estimated time of arrival of Victor flight would be forty-five seconds.

[27] Once the antiaircraft missiles are launched.

[28] The British fighter aircraft.

[29] The control column is sluggish, and it is hard to control the aircraft.

[30] Scotty was asking another pilot to check his aircraft to see if any damage is visible.

[31] Scotty understood the transmission.

[32] When a pilot is downed, his fellow aviators will fly a protective cover over him. This is done to not only protect him from any possible enemy but to also pinpoint his location for the rescue helicopter.

[33] The rescue helicopters are airborne, ready to come in and pick him up.

BUT I REALLY WANT TO BE IN PHILADELPHIA

"Sir, I have a reply from the air marshal," Chester's secretary announced over the intercom.

"Okay, bring it in, please," Chester replied as he looked at Morrison with a look of surprise on his face. Taking the message from his secretary, Chester thanked her and waited till she left the room before opening the envelope.

"What does it say?" Morrison quickly asked.

As Chester unfolded the transmission, he couldn't understand how the air marshal responded so soon. Speaking up, Chester read the message:

> *Seek aid in investigation of the electromagnetic burst relative to the existence of an unidentified flying object in the area at that time.*

"Well, that was quick and to the point!" Morrison declared, then added, "I guess that we can't put him off any longer. It also gives us the opportunity to bring him into the fold, so to speak."

"How so?" Chester asked.

"Well, it's what I wanted to talk to you about. I want you to meet with the air marshal in Bermuda. Show him the video and bring him into the fold. We need a presence in that part of the world," Morrison ordered.

"What if he doesn't agree?" Chester asked, almost afraid of the answer.

"Let's just say that, should he disagree, his aircraft will meet with a tragic accident somewhere over the Atlantic," Morrison declared. Then he continued, "I'll contact him directly and arrange the meeting for two days from now. I'm going to tell him that in exchange for the information he desires, he is to give us full disclosure on all alien activity his government has monitored or encountered.

"If at any time during your meeting you feel that he is not being frank with you, end the meeting. Contact me immediately and say that the fishing was so bad you didn't catch a thing."

"A little dramatic, aren't we?" Chester asked. "What if everything is okay?"

"Okay, it's a little dramatic, but I love that kind of code-talk stuff," Morrison replied, laughing, and then continued, "If everything is okay, just say that you found that fish for my aquarium."

Chester looked at his friend with a smile on his face, masking his thought: *Oh boy, what have I gotten into?*

As Morrison reached for the telephone, he directed, "Chester, one more thing. Have your boys run a mineral and natural resource scan of Zambia. It will be a nice gift for Scotty to give the president and save his country millions in exploration costs. When that is done, run a scan for Alpha Zuron radiation over Zambia. If that plane was taken aboard a spacecraft and dumped somewhere in Zambia, it will have a radiation trace, as anything will that has been in space."

"Aye, sir," Chester replied as he stood up and left Morrison alone to call the air marshal. As Chester walked down the hallway toward the satellite surveillance room, he mumbled to himself, "This is just great, a secret base in Colorado, a private army, aliens up the wazoo, a plane full of people that disappeared, and the most incorrigible person in the world is going to be put in charge of it. What's next? Little green men from Mars setting up a coffee shop in the center of New York City?" A grin crossed Chester's face as he said to himself, "Ah, what the hell!" and laughed slightly as he shook his head back and forth.

DON'T FORGET THE SUNTAN OIL

CHESTER GAZED OUT OF THE small window of the executive jet as it came in for landing in Bermuda. Hearing the screech of the wheels as they made contact with the runway, Chester sat up and put the papers he had been studying back into his briefcase. If all went well, the air marshal would be landing shortly.

Chester's aircraft was directed to hold at the end of the runway for an escort.

Shortly, a small yellow truck appeared in front of his aircraft, with a "Follow Me" sign attached on the back. The pilot of the aircraft pushed the throttles slightly forward, followed the truck into a cavernous hangar, and stopped. After the engines were shut down, six naval investigative agents exited the aircraft. Once the agents were satisfied that the area was secure, Chester left the aircraft and was shown into an office against the outside wall of the hangar.

Two other agents then exited the aircraft, each carrying bulky soft-sided bags.

They went directly into the office area and began setting up an electronic umbrella over the area in order to defeat any attempts by anyone to eavesdrop on the meeting. Chester, in the meantime, stood by and watched as the agents worked. Everything in the office was removed, including the carpet. Two tables were then brought in and set up. One was placed in the center of the room with two high-back executive swivel chairs placed around the table. On the other table, a buffet lunch was set up with a variety of bottled water and soft drinks.

While Chester was waiting, one of the agents approached and informed him that the air marshal's aircraft would be delayed. Chester suspected that something might be wrong, but his fears were dismissed when he was told that the air marshal's aircraft was delayed due to the weather. In order to pass the time, Chester decided to take a walk. Leaving the hangar, he walked to the end of the complex and sat down on a bulkhead that overlooked the ocean. Here Chester could look out over the sea and be alone with his thoughts. He wasn't totally alone, though. An agent remained a respectable distance away, ready to protect Chester if a hidden danger arose.

Chester allowed himself to drift back through the pages of time. As always, Chester was thinking of his beloved Peggy. She had been dead now these past seven years, but to Chester she was still with and within him. It was on this very base that they first met. He was a young lieutenant, proud of his uniform and his rank, and she was the daughter of the base commander. When Chester first saw her from across the room of a summer cocktail party, he fell immediately in love. Cupid's arrow was buried deep within his heart. An arrow must have also struck Peggy, for she as well fell immediately in love. Within six months they were married in the base chapel and honeymooned in the town of Saint George.

During the succeeding years of their marriage, Chester and Peggy would return to the island each year for their vacation. Their favorite hotel was just outside the town proper of St. George. It stood atop a long hill. Each room overlooked the historic Fort Saint Catherine and the endless ocean beyond. To Chester and Peggy, there was not a lovelier place on the planet.

Their favorite place to socialize was not in the hustle and bustle of Hamilton, but rather, it was in a small out-of-the-way bar and restaurant that bordered the town square in, where else, but the town of St. George. It was a place where one immediately felt at home. There were no white linen cloths or a maître d' dressed in the phony finesse of refinement, but rather, it was a place where you were made to feel at home. Everyone accepted you as you were. Chester and Peggy would spend endless hours there lost in conversation and laughter. They came to regard the people they met there as their family, and indeed, Peggy and Chester were made parts of their families. It was in this place that they met their lifelong friends Tom and Laura Milby.

Both of Chester and Peggy's children were also conceived in Bermuda. Their daughter, Janet, over her father's objection, was a pilot of an E-2C aboard the USS *Eisenhower* in the Blue Tail Squadron. Their son, Joseph, broke with family tradition and joined the Marine Corps. His most recent assignment was to the Pentagon as a finance officer. While Chester would have preferred his children to have chosen nonmilitary careers and lead a normal life, if such a thing existed, he and Peggy had brought them up to be freethinkers. But if that was what they wanted to do with their lives, then so be it. Chester and Peggy were extremely proud of their children, and the primary importance of life was their happiness.

Bermuda, however, held very bittersweet memories for Chester. It was in Bermuda, on one of their vacations, that Chester became aware of Peggy's illness. On a beautiful, sunny day, Chester and Peggy were relaxing on the beach. Chester pleaded with Peggy to go swimming with him. Peggy tried to refuse, but Chester's pleas won out.

After almost an hour of frolicking in the water, the vacationers returned to the beach. Peggy lay on her beach towel to bask in the sun, while Chester sat down, picked up his book, and began reading. Suddenly, Peggy screamed out in pain and drew her body into the fetal position. Chester, attentive as always, drew close to his wife and tried to comfort her. He insisted on calling help, but Peggy was more insistent and passed it off as a stomach cramp from swimming.

During the next few days, Peggy continued to have pain but was able to hide her suffering from Chester. For his part, Chester tried to talk her into seeing their friend Tom Milby, who was a medical doctor, but Peggy continued to refuse. Chester was, however, able to secure a promise from his wife that she would see their family doctor when they returned home. Peggy reluctantly agreed to the promise, but fear was growing within her. She tried to convince herself that she was simply having stomach cramps.

On the last night of their stay on the island, Tom and Laura Milby threw a going-away party for Chester and Peggy. All their friends from the bar were invited, as well as a few neighbors. Soft jazz music gently echoed throughout the home and washed over the patio by the in-ground swimming pool. Most of the guests preferred to sit around the pool, sipping their tall tropical drinks. Chester, however, was in the living room, talking about fishing.

Chester stole a loving glance at Peggy as she was standing on the patio, talking to Laura. Suddenly, Peggy dropped her drink glass and fell to her knees in pain. Tom Milby rushed to her aid, picked her up, and sat Peggy in a chair. Chester ran up, knelt beside his wife, and asked what was wrong. Peggy ran her fingers through Chester's hair and told him that the pain had passed. Tom, however, knew better. He was used to seeing the expression of pain and asked, "Peggy, the truth, how long have you had this pain?"

Peggy gritted her teeth, looked up at Chester, and replied as she then faced Tom, "For the past two months." She then looked at Chester and declared, "I'm sorry, Chester."

Chester didn't know what to think or do. The trained naval officer able to see through a problem and reason through it was now lost in the abyss of indecision and emotion. He could only speak from the heart: "I love you, Peggy."

Tom looked at his friend and told her that he wanted to examine her at the hospital. Laura stayed by Peggy and Chester as she called for an ambulance. Peggy could only look at Chester with wondrous eyes. Chester saw his best friend and the center of his universe in pain. He prayed that Peggy would be all right, but mostly, he asked that Peggy's pain be transferred to himself.

Chester and Tom rode in the ambulance with Peggy. Remarkably, no one spoke, as they each seemed to be lost in the depths of their own thoughts. Peggy realized that she should have told Chester about her pain, but she feared the worst. She had wanted to wait until after their vacation was over. Peggy realized now that she had made a mistake.

Chester was experiencing doubts about his life. He knew that Navy life was difficult at best. It had meant long stretches away from home, but Peggy never complained. *Regrets always seem to be the child of adversity,* Chester thought to himself. Tom was looking at his good friends and seeing the love and compassion between them as only a friend could. He hoped that Peggy would be all right, but his experience told him otherwise. He truly liked Chester and Peggy. They were good, real people. Their friendship was true, and that was a precious gift that he and Laura treasured.

Once at the hospital, Peggy was wheeled away toward an examination room, while Tom was hurriedly issuing orders to the head nurse and, at the same time, placing telephone calls to various specialists, requesting their presence. Tom looked over at Chester, who was lost among the chaos of the emergency room. Seeing a hospital social worker in the room, Tom directed her to Chester after explaining the situation.

Kathy Denman had been a social worker for over the past eighteen years. She was used to seeing people in despair, but in all her years, she had never seen such a sad and fearful face than the one Chester was wearing at that moment. She approached Chester and directed him to a quiet part of a waiting room. Together they sat, drinking coffee. Chester talking about his life with Peggy, and Kathy listening. When Chester had finished relating his life story, Kathy tried to reassure him that Peggy was just in for testing and at present there were no results. Kathy then left Chester alone, after making sure that all his immediate needs had been met, and went to seek out Dr. Milby.

After Kathy left, Chester looked around the rather-large room and was surprised to see other people there. He momentarily wondered why he hadn't seen them when he arrived. He took special notice of a woman he guessed to be at least seventy years old sitting in the corner of the room. Her head was bowed, and she was weeping the silent cry of desperation. Chester smiled a sympathetic smile as he watched her children try to comfort her. Chester then realized that he was in either the room of broken dreams or the room of dreams yet to be realized.

Trying to pass the time, Chester thumbed through a stack of magazines, but nothing could hold his interest. All his thoughts were of Peggy and what she must be going through. Pacing offered no relief other than to release excess energy and some pent-up anger. He was not angry with Peggy, but rather, he was angry with himself for not having seen any sign that she was sick. Surely, if he had realized that she was sick, he would have immediately brought her to a doctor. The dark thoughts of Peggy's death came to Chester, but he was able to suppress them. Time passed ever so slowly for Chester. Each moment of thought was a lifetime of terror for him.

"Chester!" Tom called out as he entered the room.

Chester turned around and saw Tom walking toward him. Trying desperately not to look like he felt, Chester managed to put a slight smile on his face and greeted his friend. Tom directed Chester into a small private room off the main waiting room. Both men sat down in comfortable chairs, with a coffee table between them. Chester sat back in the chair while Tom sat forward, with his elbows on his knees and his hands folded together. Tom began by saying that Peggy was resting comfortably upstairs and had been given morphine to help ease her pain.

Chester immediately asked if he could see Peggy. Tom cut Chester off with a sense of urgency and told him that they had to talk first. Tom first explained about the various blood tests that were being run. Additionally, Peggy had been x-rayed and had received CAT scans of her entire body. Tom was hesitant to tell Chester of his fears, but Chester alleviated that problem.

"Tom, please get to the point. Just tell me what you feel, not what you know, which I guess is very little right now."

Tom looked at Chester and saw fear. The same fear he felt. Realizing that the only way to tell Chester was the direct way, Tom replied, "Chester, there is no easy way to say this. I think Peggy has advanced ovarian cancer. I'm hoping that it has not spread to other parts of her body. It depends on whether or not any cancer cells have violated or left the tumor. I took some biopsies, and the results are being rushed. In the morning we should have some of the results.

"On the positive side, if the tumor has not been violated, I feel that I can operate and remove the tumor. After some follow-up chemotherapy, Peggy will be fine."

"You really don't think that there is a chance, do you, Tom?" Chester shot back.

"Chester, you and Peggy are my dear friends. I wouldn't insult you by not telling you the way things are. Everything depends on whether or not the cancer cells have violated the tumor. Chester, we have to wait until at least the morning to know anything," Tom answered, seeing the fear growing within Chester.

Chester quickly asked, "If it has been violated, what then?"

Tom looked his friend squarely in the eye and replied in a tone of compassion, "It would depend on what organs the cancer has spread to. Chester, it's simply too early to tell. Why don't I take you to see Peggy? And then you can come home with me."

Once they reached Peggy's room, Chester's eyes filled with tears. Nothing on earth could have prepared him for what he saw. Here was Peggy, his vibrant, full-of-life, let's-go-do-this-and-then-that lover, best friend, wife, and mother to his children, lying horizontally in a hospital bed, sleeping. She was wired to monitors that beeped in somewhat of an erratic pattern. Both arms were connected to what seemed an endless array of plastic tubing connected to bags and bags of liquid being pumped into her body. Once Chester absorbed the shock of the scene, he crossed the room and kissed his Peggy ever so softly on the forehead. Chester then sat down in a chair next to Peggy's bed. With the greatest of care, Chester took her hand in his and held on to Peggy for dear life.

Tom tried his best to get Chester to leave, but he refused. After Tom left, promising to return early in the morning, Chester silently cried as he held on to Peggy. Throughout the night, Chester held Peggy's hand and listened intently to her shallow breathing. Chester was remembering the good times and the not-so-good ones, their hopes and dreams, and their plans yet to be fulfilled. But pure fear made the night seem like a thousand years for Chester, with the next day being but a dream away.

Chester awoke from a short nap when Tom and a small army of doctors and nurses entered the room in the morning. After pleasantries were exchanged and introductions made, Tom went over to Peggy and gently shook her shoulder in an effort to wake her up. Peggy slowly opened her eyes. She looked into Chester's eyes and smiled the passionate smile of love. Chester, while still holding on to her hand, rose up from his chair, bent over Peggy, and kissed her softly on the lips. Peggy wanted to hug Chester, but she could not raise her arms. Looking around the room, Peggy realized that they were not alone. Her face slightly flushed when she realized that the others had witnessed their kiss. Seeing that Peggy was now fully awake and alert, Tom again made the introductions and explained what each doctor and nurse did to care for her. Peggy thanked them all for their efforts and then looked back at Chester, smiling.

The doctors and nurses, except for Tom, politely left the room. Tom, Peggy, and Chester, for a moment, stared blankly at one another, afraid of what was to come. Tom tried to speak, but the words were not coming out. How could he tell this gentle person that she was close to death? Tom's eyes welled with tears as he unsuccessfully tried not to cry. Peggy looked at Tom with compassion and knew what was to come. Then looking over at Chester, she saw tears in the eyes of the man she loved. "My God, look at you two. You both are behaving like children that had their favorite toys taken away. Things have to be said and discussed, so let's get on with it and then some breakfast. I'm hungry!" Peggy declared, snapping Tom and Chester back to reality. Chester sat upright in his chair and wiped away his tears. Tom turned his head slightly away from Peggy to hide himself as he also wiped away his tears.

"Peggy, I'm so sorry... I...," Tom began, stumbling over his words.

"Tom, I love you and Laura, and I deeply cherish our friendship. But unless you tell me what you have to say, I'm going to get out of this bed, come over there, and kick your butt!" Peggy interjected.

"Okay, here it is," Tom began, then continued, "All the tests show advanced ovarian cancer. It has spread to the lymphatic system and has entered the lungs and liver. There are treatments that may halt its advance, but they may be of little use."

Peggy cut him off and asked, "Tom, how much time?"

Tom replied, "Five to six months at best. If we start treatments immediately, who knows—'"

But he was cut off again by Peggy.

"Tom, thank you. Please leave us alone for a while," Peggy sharply replied. She felt as if she had been hit by a freight train, but she realized that Chester was an emotional wreck. If things could ever be normal again, Peggy realized that she would have to make it so.

For the next two hours, Peggy and Chester talked and cried together. They held each other ever so gently, as if they were holding a newborn baby for the very first time. They talked about the children and how they were going to tell them. But mostly they talked about their life together and how wonderful it was and how wonderful it was yet to be. Peggy didn't want to undergo any treatments, but for the sake of Chester and the kids, she would go along with it. She knew from her mother's experience that the treatments didn't always work and might not extend life. But Peggy would subject herself to the treatments; after all, she was a fighter and was married to the best man in the world.

Three days later, Chester and Peggy returned to Tom and Laura's home for two more days of rest. The goodbyes were hard, as each believed that it might be for the last time. But Tom and Laura were to be constant visitors. After all, no matter what the adversity, true friends are always friends.

Once Peggy and Chester returned to their home in Virginia, life seemed almost to continue as normal—Peggy made sure of that. In fact, there were even days that Chester forgot the impending doom as he was occupied with Peggy's projects and varied interests. On the outside, life appeared normal, but the cloud of uncertainty and fear was always present somewhere.

Even Rusty, the family pet, a golden Lab, sensed the impending doom. When Peggy first returned home from Bermuda, Rusty seemed to have known that Peggy had been sick. Chester at first thought it was because they had left him behind when they went on vacation, but no, it was more than that. Rusty became attentive to Peggy as a human would have. If someone came to the house, Rusty would implant himself between the visitor and Peggy and stare at the individual. If Peggy sat in a chair, Rusty would sit beside her. He took to sleeping at the foot of her bed, something he never did before. As the days drifted by and Peggy's pain increased beyond the toleration of the pills, Rusty was there. At such times Rusty would place his head on her lap if Peggy was sitting down. If she lay down, Rusty would lie beside her with his head on her stomach, as if he could take away her pain. If Peggy was walking and fell to the floor in a pain spasm, Rusty would stand by her and take her weight as she tried to get up. Separation, even to go to the doctor's, became intolerable for Rusty. Eventually, Rusty would accompany Peggy wherever she went, even to the doctor's. To Chester, Rusty became Peggy's guardian angel.

After seven months of pain and suffering, on a cool, misty day that signaled the change of seasons, Peggy slipped into the stillness of death. It was not a lonely passing. Chester, the children, Tom and Laura, as well as Rusty were there.

Peggy was resting in bed, and of course, Rusty was lying beside her. Everyone in the room was talking in hushed tones when suddenly Rusty raised his head and let out a chilling howl. At the exact same moment, Peggy shouted out, "Chester!" Chester rushed over to his beloved wife, but it was too late—Peggy had breathed her last breath. Chester bent over, kissed Peggy on the lips, and whispered, "I love you," and ran from the room, weeping. Tom went over to Peggy and confirmed what the others already knew.

There was only one place in the world for Peggy to sleep her final sleep; it was in a cemetery one block from their home. A prettier place didn't exist. It was located on a gentle slope surrounded on all four sides by flowering dogwood trees in whites and pinks. A warm, gentle breeze always swept over the cemetery, bringing with it comfort and peace. Chester felt that Peggy would like it there, surrounded by beauty.

After Peggy passed way, the emptiness Chester felt was with him every waking moment. He took a leave from the Navy to try to work through his loss, but it was to no avail. Everywhere he went and everyone he saw reminded him of a gentler time. A time when there was always a smile on his face and happiness in his heart. But now there was a void there.

Rusty fared no better. Every day he would disappear. Chester always found him lying across Peggy's grave. He was still the ever-present guardian angel. Three weeks after Peggy died, Chester, as had become his routine, went to the cemetery toward evening to bring Rusty home. One day, Rusty didn't come as he always did when Chester called. As he walked up to Peggy's grave, fear grew within him—Rusty was not moving. When Chester reached him and knelt down to pat Rusty, his fear was confirmed. Rusty had died. Chester left the cemetery only to return with a shovel. In the blanket of darkness, Chester buried Rusty next to Peggy. It was just the right thing to do.

After another week of moping around the house, Chester knew that he had to return to work. He would never be able to fully deal with the loss of Peggy, but he had to refocus his attention for his own peace of mind. It was Morrison, his friend and mentor, who picked Chester up, shook him out, and gave him his job in Space Command. The challenges were demanding and pressure-filled, but it saved Chester. Since that day, Chester had devoted himself to his command and his friend.

"Admiral!" came a cry from behind Chester.

Chester slowly turned around and faced his security escort and replied, "Yes, son."

"Sir, I have just been notified that the air marshal's aircraft is on final and will be here in five minutes. I've directed a car to pick us up and bring us back. Is that all right, sir?" the agent answered.

"That's fine, Agent," Chester replied and then turned back toward the sea and looked out over the ocean. With his right index finger, he wiped a tear from his eye and then kissed the tip of his finger and blew the kiss toward the heavens and his love.

Chester turned back around and walked over to the car that had just arrived. As he was getting in, Chester felt gentle wisp of moisture on his cheek. He stopped and looked out over the ocean at the horizon and saw a rainbow. Chester smiled and winked toward the rainbow, for Peggy had just whispered, "I love you."

SO WHERE IS THE BEACH?

ONCE BACK IN THE HANGAR, Chester didn't have to wait long for the air marshal's aircraft to arrive. Within minutes, his aircraft pulled into the hangar and came to rest across from Chester's plane. Chester was glad to see that the air marshal chose an aircraft devoid of any markings. It wasn't much, but it didn't tell anyone who was watching anything.

Once the door to the aircraft was opened, Chester strode up to the stairway and warmly greeted the air marshal. An aide to the air marshal handed two very large briefcases to one of Chester's security forces as the air marshal spoke. "Admiral, in those two cases are our complete files and photographic evidence of the subject matter I discussed with Admiral Morrison. I hope they may be of some aid to you in your investigation."

"On behalf of Admiral Morrison, I thank you for your assistance. I am sure that the material will be most useful. Now, would you please follow me? I have arranged for some refreshments for us while we talk," Chester replied and directed the air marshal into the hangar office.

In the meantime, Chester's security force checked the contents of the briefcases and the briefcases themselves for any trace of explosives or electronic eavesdropping equipment. Once satisfied that they were clean, the security force gave the cases to Chester.

As the two men, from opposite sides of the world, tried to relax in each other's company, Chester's agents went to work. They closed up the hangar and completed the electronic umbrella over the hangar. Next, they searched the air marshal's aircraft, "for security reasons," and formed a defensive perimeter around the hangar.

Chester took a bottle of water off the refreshment table and walked over to the conference table. He asked the air marshal if he was hungry and invited him to eat. The air marshal poured himself a cup of black coffee and sat down across from Chester.

Since the day promised to be long, Chester went right to work. "Air Marshal, I would like to thank you for agreeing to this meeting and coming so quickly. I'm sure that this meeting will be of mutual benefit to us both. We have a common interest, and I believe that we both recognize the threat these visitors pose, not only to our respective countries, but also, in a larger sense, to the world," Chester opened, to see where it would go.

"I can't agree more, Admiral," the air marshal replied, then added, "But just one thing. Please call me Lester."

"Okay, but only if you call me Chester and not Admiral," Chester quickly replied.

"Good," the air marshal answered and then continued after taking a sip of coffee, "Chester, I know that you and the admiral are wondering about my request regarding the presence of a UFO on the day the airliner disappeared over Zambia. As requested, I brought all my government's files on the UFO problem. I am asking for help and direction to deal with this problem.

"I am quite sure that you have reviewed your country's intelligence report on me. I, as well, have reviewed my country's intelligence reports on both you and Admiral Morrison. I came to you because you have a reputation as being a person who speaks his mind and a straight shooter, no bullshit, just the truth. I am the same way. Therefore, I feel that we can forge a relationship to work together and hopefully repel these alien invaders.

"As proof of my intentions and honesty, I want to tell you what I have done. You see, I know what the hidden agenda of your agency is. That being the tracking of UFOs. I know this because I directed the penetration of your agency with a spy. Her job was to report back to us from time to time on the inner workings of your department and gather whatever intelligence data you may uncover relative to my government. The attempt failed when our spy quit and married her target, one Samuel Gibbs. I also tried on two other occasions to penetrate your command, but each attempt has been unsuccessful.

"I did this because I am a scared man. I am scared because of what we have been monitoring regarding the UFOs. My government and my people need help to combat this invasion. I have read your country's literature on the subject, and there are strong parallels in my country. From people claiming to having been abducted to people just disappearing.

"I tell you all this as an expression of friendship and so that you will know that you will hear nothing but the truth from me."

Chester was stunned by what he was hearing. On the one hand, the man was promising to work with him, and on the other, he just admitted that he tried to penetrate Space Command with a spy on more than one occasion. Chester knew immediately whom the air marshal was talking about. It was Carolyn Gibbs. Chester thought he knew her well. After all, it was Chester who had walked her down the aisle at her wedding and gave her away. He felt sorry for her because she had told him that her parents had been killed in a private airplane crash years ago. It was because she respected Chester so much he was honored to oblige her request. Chester regretted that she and her husband would have to be interrogated and polygraphed when he returned, but that was the price that had to be paid.

When the air marshal finished talking, there was a slight pause in the conversation. Chester just wanted to reach across the table and rip the man's lungs out. *How dare he send a spy against my command!* he thought and then realized that spying is just a chess game of nations. After all, when each side knows what the other has, it is that knowledge that actually keeps the peace between nations. Quickly, Chester dismissed his anger by saying, "Lester, I think that you are one brassy son of a bitch. Were we somewhere else on different business, I would do my absolute best to kick the ever-living shit out of you and then feed you to the sharks!" Chester then paused to let his comment sink in, then continued, "That being said, let's get down to it. Why don't you begin by telling me the status of UFOs in your country?"

The air marshal was taken aback a bit by Chester's comments but recovered quickly.

For the next two hours, the air marshal talked about what was going on in South Africa and the surrounding countries relative to UFOs. At first, Lester attributed such activity to atmospheric radar distortion, because whenever a UFO was detected, they would immediately launch fighter aircraft to the location. The fighters would always be met by empty skies. The mysterious radar blip would simply disappear off the scope.

That all changed one day when a close friend of the air marshal admitted that in responding to such an incident, he observed a round saucer-shaped object disappear at a high rate of speed. The pilot in question did not file a report, for fear of being listed as psychologically unfit for duty. Lester described his friend as being scared, but more importantly, he believed him. From that day forward, Lester became a believer.

Over the years, the sightings increased, and Lester began to formulate a plan of action. He picked the best of the pilots to receive advanced air-to-air combat training and pushed them to enhance their low-level attack techniques. For the time being, the pilots were still in different squadrons, but Lester would shortly bring them together into one unit. Lester further explained that the pilots would be formed into two battle squadrons. One would be placed in the northern part of the country, while the other would be in the south.

Lester then went on to cover the growing trend of UFOs actually landing within South Africa. At first, reports by civilians were dismissed by local authorities until a ufology subculture developed that cut across ethnic, social, and economic boundaries. Once the idea of UFOs took hold, the same local authorities that dismissed such reports were now constantly calling the Air Ministry for assistance. Later, the reports took a new turn. People began reporting being abducted, undergoing physical exams, and then being released. During the last two years, the reports took on a more-ominous tone. Some of the same people who had reported being abducted had disappeared without a trace.

"Chester, I'm scared, not only because of what I think is going on, but mostly because no one seems to care. I breached the subject very casually with my superiors, but to a man they laughed it off. As far as I know, there is no one officially looking or interested in the matter. Hell, the only people looking into the situation are a few people in the ufology community, and they are scoffed at, but tolerated.

"If I were to take a public stand on this matter, I would be labeled as unbalanced and sent off to some Happy Acre Retirement Home. I figure that it is better that I keep my mouth shut at present and quietly prepare. If I don't, then my country would be wide open for the aliens to do what they want.

"Chester, that was why I contacted your command. I need help. I have no one else to turn to, and I am desperate," Lester concluded, pleading.

Deciding that Lester was an honest man, Chester decided to share with him the information on Zambia. Chester knew that from this day forward, the life of the air marshal would change forever. True, he would owe allegiance to his country, but he would also dedicate himself to the association of military leaders throughout the world banded together to fight the aliens.

"What do you say we take a break for a short while and have some food?" Chester suggested.

"Sounds like a good idea to me," Lester agreed.

During the next hour, as they ate, Chester and Lester became friends. They swapped tales of their military service, their backgrounds, and their families. Chester was amazed that Lester's private life paralleled his own. They both each had a son and a daughter serving in the military service. Like Chester, Lester was a widower. His wife did not die from cancer, though. A nineteen-year-old drunk driver killed Mary, Lester's wife of twenty-seven years. Sure, the man paid his "debt" to society, but it was Lester and his family that paid the real debt, loneliness and despair every day of their lives.

Once Chester and Lester cleared away the plates from the table, it was time to return to the purpose of the meeting. Chester began by confirming that his command was indeed keeping track of incursions by UFOs into the United States and throughout the world. He went on to acknowledge that the tracking of UFOs was on the increase throughout the world, and so were the reported abductions and disappearances. In fact, the pattern was the same: first came an increase in reported sightings, then reported landings, then abductions, and finally disappearances.

Like in South Africa, the ufology community were the ones sounding the alarm, while the government sat back and did nothing. In a similar vein, Chester agreed that a response force should be formed to fight the aliens, but politics would prevent the establishment of such a force. After all, what government will publicly announce that they believe that little green men are visiting Earth and absconding with its citizens?

Chester just laid the hook to recruit Lester. *Now for the bait,* Chester thought to himself.

Chester began by summing up the original request of Lester. He then immediately launched into his own dissertation of the event. Chester confirmed that there was an electromagnetic burst, and its intensity. After discussing the disappearance of the airliner over Zambia, Chester thought it best to inform Lester of the capability of the satellites under his command. As he talked, Chester slowly reached into his own briefcase and withdrew two portable DVD players connected together.

When Chester finished talking about his satellites, he said in a monotone voice, "We were able to confirm that there was indeed a UFO in the area, and the electromagnetic burst came from the unknown. We were able to photograph the unknown, which we placed on a disc, to try to get a feeling of the event in a real-time sequence. After we watch the video, I'll show you the still photographs."

Chester then reached into the breast pocket of his jacket and removed a DVD. After putting it in the player, he quickly pushed the Play button. Instead of watching his own player, Chester took special note of the expression on Lester's face. At first, Lester looked interested, but then he looked very, very scared. When the movie finished, Lester pushed his chair back and stood up. Pacing around the room, he exclaimed, "What the fuck was that thing? Are we dead or what?"

Chester let him pace around for a minute or so in order to heighten the drama of the moment. Reaching down into his briefcase, Chester withdrew a large photograph of the UFO and placed it on the table. He watched as Lester looked at the table and zeroed in on the photograph. Lester walked over to the table, bent over, and then gazed at the photograph. He then looked at Chester, who was wearing his best poker face, and asked, "How in the name of God are we supposed to fight this thing? What the hell ever happened to 'Take me to your leader, I come in peace'? Don't these aliens watch your American science-fiction shows?"

Chester fought back the temptation to laugh at the movies comment and answered, "It's like walking through a nightmare, but we are awake. It is my belief that if we work together, we can overcome this threat."

"What do you mean work together? How are we going to do that?" Lester asked.

Chester replied, "I believe that the day will come when we can oppose these aliens and keep them from coming to our world at their will. We must appear as easy pickings to them. But if we present a united front, well, they lose and we win. But first, we must—"

And he was interrupted by the air marshal.

"How are we going to do that, Chester?" Lester asked. "Our governments can't agree on anything right now."

Fish nibbling at the bait, Chester thought to himself and then spoke. "For right now we can establish lines of communication outside of our government. At the same time, we move to establish an offensive force in our respective countries, much like you have done. I believe, like you, that such a force is necessary if we are to protect our citizens. Once our forces are in place, we will be better able to respond to the situation. Right now we can monitor and learn their moves. Sure, we can chase them off, but it is just not time to take the offensive unless it is absolutely necessary. Together we can win. Divided we will fail."

"But, Chester, how can two countries on opposite ends of the world fight this menace?" Lester asked.

"If you agree to work with us, you will find that we will not be alone. In fact—"

Chester was interrupted.

"You mean that there are others?" Lester quickly asked.

"As I was saying, we do have an association of military leaders from other countries. Men much like ourselves that recognize the problem and are willing to risk their lives and careers for the ultimate security of their countries. We cooperate in secrecy and are bound by a common goal, the sanctity of life on Earth.

"Each of us fully realizes that should our countries become angry at one another, all contact must cease, but the association must continue. Make no mistake about this, Lester: if you join our group, there is no turning back. Once committed, you are to remain in the group. Should you ever reveal the association to your government or any individual, you will be sanctioned. By that I mean killed, as well as those you tell. So it's put-up-or-shut-up time. Are you in or out?" Chester concluded.

Lester looked hard at Chester, saw an expressionless face staring back at him, and replied, "Yes, I'm in. It can only help my country."

Fish on the line and in the boat, Chester thought to himself and then replied to Lester, "Welcome aboard!" He then continued, "Next month you are scheduled to attend the international conference on terrorism. During the conference, the association will meet. It will give you the opportunity to meet the others. We use such conferences and NATO meetings as a cover so that we can get together."

For the next hour, Chester and Lester worked on putting a communication system and established code words they would use. When their meeting was over, both men relaxed a bit and talked about their plans for the future. They, like others, would walk a lonely path, but that path would be a bridge to the future. No matter how fragile that future was.

After their meeting was over, Chester escorted the air marshal to his aircraft. After they said their goodbyes, Lester asked, "Chester, what would have happened if I didn't agree to join the association?"

Chester looked at him straight in the eye and replied, "Your aircraft would have suffered structural failure over the ocean. Regrettably, all souls would have been lost. Have a safe flight home."

Lester looked at Chester for any indication that he was kidding. Finding none, he replied in a nervous voice, "Thank you for the straight answer to a question I shouldn't have asked. Hope to see you soon, Chester."

After the air marshal's aircraft left, Chester called Morrison on a secured line. "Hi, Admiral. I just wanted to let you know that I will be heading home now."

"How did the inspection of the weather station go?" Morrison asked.

"Just fine. Oh, I almost forgot. I found a new fish for your aquarium," Chester replied.

"That's great. I owe you dinner tonight. See you then. Have a safe flight," Morrison replied.

"Thanks, Admiral. I'll…" Chester stopped talking as he realized that Morrison had already hung up.

After Chester boarded his aircraft for the ride home, he settled into a seat midway in the cabin. He pushed the seat halfway back and stared out of the window. He watched as the airport faded away as they lifted up. Once airborne, Chester continued to watch as they flew over the lush green vegetation and the pastel colors of the homes. Within a few seconds, they were out over the crystal-blue sea and on the way home.

HEY, YOU WANTED TO BE AN AIR TRAFFIC CONTROLLER?

ANTHONY CHILDS CLIMBED THE STAIRS to what he came to think of as a blockhouse. Devoid of any windows, drab in appearance, and totally uninteresting to anyone. He realized that this must be the thousandth time he had made this trek. Climbing the stairs was the only exercise he could look forward to. The demands of his job all but eliminated any outside activity. His social life disappeared, except for an occasional date once in a while.

At first, he had liked his job and looked forward to being at work. Recently, however, he had begun to feel the pressures of the everyday life and death decisions he made. When he was in the Air Force, where he had learned his trade, he never handled the volume of aircraft he was currently responsible for. Working with antiquated equipment, ever-increasing flights, and the expectation that the future would mean more flights was an express train to a nervous breakdown. No one in the military ever told him that being a civilian air traffic controller was going to be like this. Hell, no one even hinted at it.

It is a lot of people like Tony that keep the system moving. They are the true guardians of the flying tin we call airplanes. But with Tony, the challenge was gone. He was slipping into the depths of despair and edging on the border of depression. Today, though, his supervisor promised him an easy day. He was to handle incoming flights from the islands. The work volume was less. The only problem was slipping the airplanes into the overall system, but most of that was handled by a few flight control centers around the country.

As Tony settled into his world of flat-screen computer monitors that glowed orange or green, the ever-present smell of grease pens, and little plastic strips that were constantly being shuffled to show the status of different flights, he was briefed by the person he was relieving. Once Tony scanned the status boards, he noticed that flight Charlie 3-4-8 had just lifted off from Bermuda, was climbing to twenty-five thousand feet, and was heading into Washington, DC.

SO MUCH FOR PARADISE

After Chester felt the aircraft level off, he allowed himself to relax. Flying, after all these years, still made him nervous. Whenever he saw a 747 come in for a landing, Chester would wonder how something so large could possibly stay in the air.

Sitting in his seat, Chester allowed himself to daydream. His thoughts, naturally, turned to Peggy, as they did constantly every waking hour. Chester was actually glad that he had returned to Bermuda. Sure, it brought back a lot of memories, but they were mostly good memories. He realized now that he had stayed away for really no reason at all.

Chester decided, as he looked out across the ocean, that his very next vacation would be spent in Bermuda. He resolved that one of the first things that he would do was visit one of their favorite restaurants in Hamilton. Chester decided that he would walk into the Hog's Penny at happy hour, take a seat at the crowded bar, and have a beer. Peggy would want Chester to live his life, and he would. Peggy once told him that she regarded each morning as a new dream, each day a new adventure, and each night a memory to be cherished. Yes, Chester resolved, he would go back to Bermuda.

"Admiral! Admiral!" the copilot called out.

Chester returned his chair to the upright position, stood up, and walked to the cockpit as he cursed the interruption.

WHO PUT THAT THERE?

Tony couldn't believe his eyes. Out of nowhere a blip appeared on the radar screen on an intercept course with Charlie 3-4-8. The unknown was at the same altitude and airspeed at a distance of twelve hundred nautical miles away. Reacting fast, Tony called Charlie 3-4-8 and notified them of the intercept. He then called his supervisor over and briefed him.

His supervisor confirmed that it was an unknown aircraft that was closing on Charlie 3-4-8. He frantically attempted to contact the unknown and left Tony to handle Charlie 3-4-8.

WHO IS THAT MYSTERY MAN?

ONCE CHESTER REACHED THE COCKPIT, he leaned on the bulkhead separating the pilot's area from the passenger side. The copilot informed Chester that they had just received a message from New York flight control that there was an unknown aircraft heading right at them twelve hundred miles out. Chester was then handed a pair of headphones, which he gladly took, and put them on. He could now listen to the transmissions between the pilots and the air traffic controllers. He didn't have to wait long.

"Charlie 3-4-8, unknown is still inbound. Instruct you climb to 3-2,[34] hold your heading. All attempts at ident[35] negative," Tony radioed.

"New York, this is Charlie 3-4-8, climbing to 3-2. Out," Chester's pilot radioed back.

"Affirmative, 3-4-8. See you at 2-7 feet and climbing," Tony radioed back and was now satisfied that a midair collision had been avoided. That is, until the radar made another sweep. "Shit!" Tony said out loud to no one in particular. The unknown had also climbed to thirty-two thousand feet and was still on an intercept course. The gap between the two aircraft had now diminished to nine hundred nautical miles. Pressing the button on the transmit wire to his headset, Tony immediately radioed, "Charlie, 3-4-8, UFO[36] has matched 3-2. Gap is now...8-5-0 inbound. Instruct a 9-0 degree turn to right and climb to 3-7. Do not acknowledge. Out."

Tony intently stared at his radar display and saw that Charlie 3-4-8 executed a ninety-degree turn and climbed to thirty-seven thousand feet. Seconds later, the unknown craft changed course and altitude to match Charlie 3-4-8. The distance between the two aircraft was closing rapidly. Tony keyed his microphone again and frantically called, "Charlie 3-4-8, UFO has matched change, closing on you. Instruct immediate evasive action. Will call all the markers. Do not acknowledge!"

When Chester heard this, he immediately held on tight to the bulkhead wall with both hands. Chester scanned the sky but could not see anything. Just then, an onboard anticollision alarm went off in the cabin.

The pilot looked down at the display and saw the blip, which represented the unknown coming right at him. A few quick mental calculations and the pilot estimated that the unknown was going to hit them on the port (left) side in less than a minute. "Shut that damn alarm off!" the pilot called out.

"4-5-0...4-0-0...3-2-5...2-7-5...," Tony radioed as he said a prayer for Charlie flight.

Chester bent down slightly, trying to find the damn thing that was going to kill him. All that he could see was a shiny object that looked like a classic saucer shape coming at them.

"2-0-0...1-2-5...7-5...echoes merged, echoes merged!" Tony cried out.

Charlie flight and the UFO became one blip on the radar screen.

When Chester's pilot heard "Echoes merged," he pulled up on the stick, pointed the nose almost vertical, and pushed the engine levers all the way to the maximum setting.

The engines screamed from the power as the aircraft began to lose lift and was close to stalling. The pilot then nosed the aircraft over to the left and dived at the last known position of the unknown. Chester's pilot recovered from the dive and leveled off. Just then, the unknown and Chester's aircraft passed within fifty feet of each other. And then the unthinkable happened.

"Charlie 3-4-5!" Tony called out over the radio.

Chester's aircraft lost power. The engines shut down, and the instruments went dead. "Hold on!" the pilot cried out as he eased the nose almost straight down. Chester, still standing in the doorway, fought back the effects of gravity and was able to keep his footing. He stared out of the cockpit windows and was slightly transfixed by the sight of the ocean coming closer and closer with each passing second. He was surprised that he did not feel any fear, but rather, he silently prayed. Somehow he managed to block the calm but excited dialogue between the pilot and his copilot. The only sound he heard was the high-pitched whistle of the air as it raced over the wings.

"Charlie 3-4-5!" Tony again called.

On their second try, the pilots managed to restart the engines. Within a few seconds, the instrumentation came back online. The pilots fought a gallant battle to bring the nose of the aircraft up. Ever so slowly the nose inched upward, and after a few more seconds, the aircraft leveled off.

"Charlie 3-4-5! Please respond!" Tony anxiously radioed. A few seconds later, his heart stopped racing when he heard, "New York, this is Charlie 3-4-5. What the hell was that?"

Tony began to answer, "No idea. It just—"

But his headset was taken off his head by the supervisor. "You are relieved. Report to my office and wait there," the supervisor ordered Tony.

Tony's supervisor then keyed the microphone and radioed, "Charlie 3-4-5, this is Supervisor Thornton of New York Control. Do you wish to report an encounter with an unidentified flying object?"

Chester's pilot turned around and looked at him. Thinking for a moment, Chester shook his head, indicting no. The pilot turned back around and radioed in a low, monotone voice, "Negative, sir."

Supervisor Thornton answered, "Understand negative. Will hand off to approach control for final. New York, out."

Chester left the cockpit area and returned to his seat. He suspected why the UFO was hard to see. The answer was something that had been bothering him for a while. The answer came to him one day, while watching a science-fiction show on television. The aliens were using some type of optical masking technology. His naturally suspicious mind then went down another road.

Why now? And why this aircraft? Chester tried to answer his own questions, but the answer was not clear. If the unknown was masking its appearance, then what made the illusion disappear when Chester caught a sight of it? The only conclusion Chester could reach was that the encounter was a deliberate act, as if the saucer were trying to scare them or, at worst, kill them. But there was another question left unanswered. If the saucer was trying to intercept his aircraft, then they must have known about the meeting Chester just held. If the aliens knew about the meeting, then who told them? These were questions that Chester would bring up to Morrison at dinner that night that must somehow be resolved.

Once Chester's aircraft landed back at Dulles, the crew and the security team were ordered not to talk about the incident to anyone. Everyone was to report to Space Command for debriefing the next morning.

· ·◆◆◆· ·

[34] Thirty-two thousand feet.

[35] The identity of the unknown aircraft.

[36] Tony used the term *UFO* because it took less time to say than *unknown*. In this situation, milliseconds are often the difference between disaster and a near miss.

I THOUGHT I SAW A FLYING SAUCER

Tony sat in his supervisor's office for over an hour. He didn't know what to expect but feared that his career was over. Sure, a change in employment could somehow be a good thing, but he would never find a job at the amount of money he was making.

Supervisor Thornton walked through his door with a slight smile on his face. Walking over to his desk and sitting in his chair, he faced Tony. "Why look so glum, Tony?" he asked.

"It's just been a tough shift. Why did you relieve me?" Tony asked, perking up and having decided that he would fight for his job.

"Standard procedure dictates that when an anomaly occurs, the controller is to be relieved and debriefed," Thornton replied.

"Oh. Am I going to be debriefed?" Tony asked.

"Only if you want to be. Look it, Tony, I reviewed the tapes. The unknown appeared suddenly on your scope. Your actions were classic textbook, and you remained calm. That was very good work. You are to be commended," Thornton answered.

"What about the UFO?" Tony asked with a hint of hesitation in his voice.

"What UFO?" Thornton asked with a smile on his face.

"Sir, it was there. You know that," Tony replied.

"Tony, what good would it do anyone if you filed a report? That report would mean the end to your career. Why do that? You're a good person, Tony. Don't blow your job over a UFO that no one cares about," Thornton replied.

"Why is it that everyone is afraid of UFOs? Hell, you know as well as I do that every controller here has seen a UFO painted[37] on his or her radar screen. I even remember you telling me that you experienced the same thing when you were a working controller," Tony answered with a little anger in his voice.

"That's all true. Everyone here has, at one time or another, seen UFOs. But everyone knows that if they were to report it, they would be classified as psychologically unfit for duty," Thornton replied, hoping Tony would listen. "Go home, Tony. Take your motorcycle out for a ride and relax. It just isn't worth it. Maybe one day the world will change, but not now."

Tony looked long, hard at his supervisor, then rolled his eyes in desperation and replied as he rose from the chair, "You're right. See you later, boss. Thank you." Tony then shook Thornton's hand and went home.

---

[37] Seen.

WHAT DO YOU MEAN YOU DON'T HAVE ANY KETCHUP?

That night, Chester was in heaven. Morrison treated him to dinner at Hogates Restaurant along the river in Washington, DC. Chester had his favorite personal-reward dinner, filet mignon cooked well, topped with caramelized onions, garlic mashed potatoes, and fresh-baked biscuits. Chester wasn't interested in talking; he was there to eat. And eat he did. When his meal was finished, Chester ordered a big slice of chocolate blackout cake topped with a scoop of vanilla ice cream smothered in hot fudge. When he was finally finished, he then ordered a large cup of black coffee and was ready to talk.

Chester quietly related the day's events to Morrison, who listened intently. He agreed with Chester that the UFO was no mere coincidence; it had to be a purposeful act.

The only conclusion they could reach was that the aliens were somehow monitoring their activities.

The conversation eventually drifted to Scotty. The increased surveillance that Morrison had ordered was in place. "So far, there is no indication that Scotty knows that he is being followed. I will probably call there tomorrow and tell them that I am coming for a visit," Morrison told Chester.

"Won't Scotty's antenna be up if you call out of the blue and tell them that you will be just dropping in?" Chester asked, a little unsure of Morrison's plan.

"No. They are used to me just dropping in," Morrison reassured Chester.

With a devilish smile on his face, Chester added, "Ah, you probably just want to go and see Marlene, anyway!"

A little flushed in the face, Morrison replied, a little annoyed, "Well, I can see that it has been a hard day on you. I guess it's time that we old warhorses retreat home. Let's go."

SOMETIMES IT'S GOOD TO BE THE BOSS

Admiral Morrison arrived at his main office in the Pentagon at his usual time, shortly before 6:00 a.m. He liked this time of the day because, even though the Pentagon was actually open twenty-four hours per day, there was still relatively quiet in the building. The large mass of people who worked here during the day would not start arriving for at least another two hours.

As he entered his office, one of his aides, Lieutenant Doreen Stark, was just placing the morning briefing papers on his desk. This daily ritual was necessary in order to keep current with developments. In less than an hour, Morrison would be able to read a summary of world and military developments, with particular attention being paid to the Navy.

"Good morning, Lieutenant," Morrison called out with the usual grin on his face as he strode over to his desk.

Lieutenant Stark turned around and replied in a cherry voice, "Good morning, Admiral. Can I get you a cup of coffee and something to eat?"

"No, thank you, Lieutenant. Oh, don't forget that we leave for New

York City at 0800.[38] Did you pack everything that you need for a few days?" Morrison inquired.

"Yes, sir. I'm all ready. I have also reviewed Mr. Scott's jacket[39] again. I must say that I find him to be a very interesting individual. Do you think that he will go along with our plan?" Doreen asked.

"Knowing Scotty the way that I do, he won't be able to resist a puzzle. Lieutenant, please let me know when it is seven thirty. And please, no interruptions," Morrison ordered.

As Doreen was leaving the admiral's office, she stopped by the door and turned around. She wanted to know one more thing. To get Morrison's attention, she cleared her throat and spoke up. "Admiral, I couldn't find anything in Mr. Scott's jacket that indicated whether or not he has recently married since he left active duty. I know that the reserves are sometimes slow to update files. I wouldn't want there to be a mistake," Doreen stated.

Morrison looked up at her with a smile on his face and answered, "No, Lieutenant, Mr. Scott is not married and, as far as I know, is not seeing anyone at the present time."

"Thank you, sir. I'll note that in the file," Doreen replied as she smiled to herself and left the office, quietly closing the door.

Morrison laughed a little to himself as he crossed his office to the credenza. After pouring himself a cup of coffee, Morrison picked up the first of three corn muffins he would consume for his breakfast. Doreen arranged this snack every morning for him. He always enjoyed her thoughtfulness but never let her know it.

Returning to his desk, Morrison sat down in his high-back leather executive chair.

He moved his chair off to the side and pushed back into the chair to a semireclining position. He then put his feet up on the desk. While staring at the ceiling, Morrison did not think about work; his thoughts were mainly about Scotty and Doreen.

Morrison thought about Doreen and how their relationship had grown since that time. It truly was a father-daughter relationship. He counted himself lucky that he had found her. When Morrison was looking to hire a new aide, he had interviewed more than forty-three candidates, and none of them seemed right. It was a friend that recommended Doreen to him.

When Morrison first read her file jacket, to say that he was impressed would be an understatement. She was a graduate of the naval academy and ranked number 5 in her class. After graduation, she was posted to naval intelligence. During her off hours, Doreen somehow managed to earn advanced degrees in astrophysics and aeronautical engineering. All her fitness reports (a yearly evaluation report completed by her current commanding officer) were excellent. Her responsibilities continually increased, and she met every challenge with success beyond her superior officer's expectations.

What interested Morrison the most was the fact that Doreen was the daughter of a fourth-generation Marine Corps general. She had two brothers, one a Harrier pilot in the Marines, and the other an officer in Marine Recon. Morrison wondered what made her break with family tradition. To be sure, it was a gutsy move on her part. He could only imagine the havoc and arguments her decision must have caused in the family. A family of jarheads (slang word for a *Marine*) with a squid (slang word for anyone in the Navy) among them. But Doreen stuck to her plans to join the Navy, and Morrison respected that.

When Doreen first appeared in his office for an interview, she was the picture-perfect representative of a naval officer. She stood ramrod straight in a perfectly tailored uniform with not a crease in her clothing or a thing out of place. When Morrison directed her to a chair, her posture, even sitting down, was perfect. Her diction was exact and to the point.

Within the first five minutes of the interview, Morrison knew that he had found his new aide. However, the interview continued for the next two and a half hours.

They discussed her education and present assignment in great detail. They then covered naval affairs, ranging from weapons to naval deployments. Her answers, of course, were right on the mark. Having read her file jacket, Morrison had one area left to cover.

He asked her if, in her lifetime, she had ever observed anything that she could not explain. Without the slightest hint of hesitation,

Doreen answered. She explained that one night, while she was at the academy, she was walking guard duty. Her area was the dock. While on duty, she observed a bright light in the sky over the bay. At first, the light seemed to hover and then sped off at an incredible rate of speed. Doreen had reported the sighting to her superior officer and entered the incident into her duty report. Morrison was surprised at her candor in making that report, but he would expect nothing less from someone he worked with.

It was when the interview concluded that Morrison noted just how beautiful Doreen was. In low military-style heels, she stood approximately five feet, four or five inches. Her body was very well sculptured, without a hint of extra weight. Her dark-auburn hair was cut short, her skin was a natural light-olive color, and she possessed beautiful but piercing brown eyes and a thin Roman nose. This was topped off with a smile that melted men's hearts.

Morrison had thought that Doreen must turn heads no matter where she went. He envisioned that men must lose their concentration when she walked by. It was then that Morrison thought that she and Scotty would make the perfect couple, but in the future.

During the years that followed, Morrison would plant little seeds about Scotty into their conversations. And it seemed to work. Every time he brought up Scotty or related a story about him, Doreen would pay full attention to every detail and would question some of the finer points. Morrison knew that Doreen had a reputation of ending many a suitor's plans with an icy stare or a response that she simply wasn't interested. Morrison inwardly hoped that Scotty would be treated differently. They just seemed to be a perfect match, if ever that would happen.

For Doreen, the intervening years had been challenging ones. Each day she described as a new adventure. Most importantly, she developed a fierce loyalty toward Morrison. Her responsibilities were always increased, especially in the area of sensitive matters. Just how much Morrison trusted her was evident one day when he called her into his office. Morrison had four out-of-focus photographs laid out on his conference table. He asked her what she thought they were. Doreen studied each photograph and then replied, "Admiral, these appear to be photographs of what are commonly referred to as UFOs. The one on the right closely resembles the light I saw while I was at the academy."

Her simple but honest statement sealed her fate forever. Morrison brought her into the fold, so to speak. He warned her of the risks involved. But that didn't matter. The challenge and her loyalty to Morrison dictated her course of action. She was instrumental in the establishment of the Colorado Project and other support projects. Her crowning achievement, however, was being given the task of developing and being in charge of the design of the X-44 aircraft. Within a short period, Doreen brought the project from a design stage to production of a brand-new airplane. It was mainly a fighter, but a giant leap ahead of its time. The X-44 was an offshoot of the next generation of space shuttles. Like the new space shuttles, it was designed to take off from land like an airplane, but it was also designed to fight the aliens in outer space. Yes, Morrison thought, he had picked the right assistant.

After reminiscing for a while, Morrison relaxed in his comfortable position and reviewed what he had to accomplish that day. First and foremost, Morrison had to somehow convince Scotty to call the president of Zambia and convince him to allow a team to come in and search for the missing airliner. Secondly, if the president of Zambia allowed a search, then he had to further convince Scotty to head up that search. Thirdly, if Scotty agreed to go, then he had to convince him that Doreen was a necessary part off the search. Morrison needed a pair of eyes on the ground to assess the overall situation. Fourthly, he wanted to begin working on Scotty to bring him back into active service and convince him to head up the Colorado Project. His last goal was to finally bring Doreen and Scotty together and see what happens. At that last thought, he smiled to himself, sat up in his chair, and began reading the morning briefing reports.

✦✦✦✦✦

[38] 8:00 a.m.

[39] Military jargon for a personnel file.

I REALLY NEED A NEW PAIR OF SNEAKERS

SCOTTY AWOKE AT HIS USUAL time, 5:00 a.m., without the need of an alarm clock. After getting out of bed, he crossed the hallway to the bathroom and began his morning ritual.

Scotty donned an old T-shirt, a pair of running shorts, sweat socks, and old, ragged sneakers, which were in desperate need of replacement. *But they sure are comfortable,* Scotty would often think to himself. As he did every morning, Scotty ran down the stairs into the office area and snatched his keys from the counter. Once he stepped outside, Scotty hesitated a moment and breathed in the fresh air of the early morning. He then walked the block and a half to Central Park. Once he entered the park, he began his stretching exercises. It was then that he felt that presence again.

For the past few days, Scotty felt that he was being followed. It wasn't until late yesterday afternoon that he saw a man following him. He recognized him from his days in the Navy. He knew that the man was a naval intelligence agent. Scotty tried to confront the man, but when he approached him, he vanished into the afternoon crowd along

Fifth Avenue. What Scotty couldn't figure out was why he was being followed.

Perhaps, Scotty thought, it had something to do with his research on the internet into UFOs. But he never made a secret out of that. In fact, Scotty openly talked about UFOs to whoever would listen. Sometimes he would even go to fairs or lectures on the presence of UFOs. He wasn't yet, however, a full-fledged member of the ufology community.

Scotty felt that the people that were following him were real close this morning. He wanted them to know that he knew that they were there. He began his morning run by jogging real slow and then suddenly broke into a sprint. Somehow, he had to draw them out from the multitude of other joggers in the park at this hour.

After what Scotty estimated to be a half mile, he took a switchback trail. This allowed him to look and see if anyone was behind him. As he turned, Scotty noticed a young man and woman that seemed to be scanning the runners. They were dressed in dark-bluet shirts and gray shorts with a yellow stripe imprinted with *USN*. But he had to make sure.

Scotty decided to remain on the trail that he was on. A mile farther up, the trail entered a series of tight turns up a small slope. In order to give his followers a run for their money, Scotty began another sprint up the slope. He felt that the run would make them sweat. At the top of the hill, Scotty would confront his shadows.

When Scotty reached the top of the hill, he darted over to a park bench that was partially hidden from view by a boulder. About thirty seconds later, the man and woman reached the top of the slope and stopped. They were both breathing hard and were bent over, with their hands on their kneecaps.

"Where the hell is he?" the woman asked, barely able to speak.

The man stood upright and looked around as he answered, "Beats the hell out of me."

Seeing that her partner was standing up straight, she thought that he was getting ready to run again. She stood up and pleaded, "I can't do this anymore. Just give me a minute."

Scotty had seen what he had wanted to. When they were bent over, their sweaty shirts clung to their bodies. Hidden underneath their shirts,

Scotty was able to detect the silhouettes of Glock 9mm pistols and a small two-way radio. In order to get their attention, Scotty coughed slightly and began walking toward them. When he drew near to the agents and was about to walk by them, Scotty uttered, "Tell the admiral I said hello."

"Yes, sir. It will be my pleasure," came a quick reply from the male agent as Scotty passed them.

Scotty turned around and smiled at the agents, turned back around, and began walking away. As he walked, he heard the female agent, in a sarcastic voice, say, "Yes, sir. It will be my pleasure. Why didn't you just tell him who we are? You dummy, the admiral is going to fry our collective asses now!"

THE MOUSE CAN
SMELL THE CHEESE

P RECISELY AT SEVEN THIRTY, DOREEN buzzed the admiral and reminded him of the time.

Morrison reached for his telephone and pressed the Speed Dial button and then the number 9. The telephone rang three times before he heard the friendly voice of Scotty. "Good morning, Scotty," Morrison began and then added, almost as an afterthought, "How are you doing?"

"I'm fine, Admiral. How are you?" Scotty answered, knowing that Morrison wanted something else.

Morrison acknowledged the pleasantry but, as usual, went right to the point. "Scotty, I'll be in New York City around 11:00 a.m. Would it be all right if I stop by?"

"Of course, Admiral. I'm looking forward to seeing you. Say, would you like to go to dinner tonight, if your schedule isn't too tight?" Scotty asked, knowing the answer would be no.

"I'd love to, but is it all right if we play it by ear? I might have to leave late in the afternoon," Morrison replied.

"Okay, Admiral. I look forward to seeing you. Say, Admiral, is everything okay?" Scotty inquired.

"Yes, Scotty, everything is fine. I'll see you later," Morrison answered and immediately hung up the telephone.

"Goodbye, Admiral," Scotty answered, knowing Morrison had probably hung up already. Scotty wondered for a moment about the tone in the admiral's voice. It usually meant that he wanted something but didn't want to ask. *Oh well, I'll find out soon enough,* Scotty thought and shifted his attention to the arrival of his secretary, Marlene.

Marlene Jackson was somewhat of an enigma to Scotty. They first met when Scotty went to work for Murdoch. From the first day, Marlene doted on him. Every need he had, Marlene fulfilled. Marlene was the most efficient person Scotty ever met, and she was the best secretary anyone could ever hope for. When Murdoch retired and Scotty decided to move into his own office, he didn't have a chance to ask Marlene if she wanted to go with him.

Instead, when Scotty first talked about the move, Marlene declared that she couldn't wait to be in the new office. When the time for the move came, Marlene came along with the furniture and the files.

Scotty truly loved this woman, who was another mother figure in his life. Last year, when Marlene turned sixty-five, Scotty made the mistake of asking if she was thinking about retirement. That miscalculation resulted in a one-hour lecture on how work gives life meaning. Scotty really didn't want to see her leave, but he didn't want to see her waste her life working. Scotty reasoned that she should be out enjoying the rest of her life. He didn't realize that she was enjoying her life. To Marlene, Scotty was the son she never had, and work provided a type of family environment for her.

Even though Marlene didn't want to retire, Scotty made sure that she had enough money for the rest of her life. Scotty had realized that Marlene was a big reason for the success of his business. He did all the talking, but Marlene was the one who kept them up and running. One day, Scotty called Marlene into his office and announced that they were partners. They were to split the profits evenly. Marlene didn't like the idea and said so. But Scotty insisted and dismissed her objections. Today,

Marlene had investments worth slightly over four million dollars. It perplexed Scotty why she never spent any of the money on herself. The only thing she would spend it on were a few charities. Scotty wanted her to go out and live her own life, but Marlene was Marlene, and nothing he could do would change that.

I DON'T KISS AND TELL

SCOTTY GLANCED OVER AT THE clock and saw that it was just fifteen minutes until interrogation time. Over the past few years, Marlene and his mother, Catherine, had decided that it was their sacred duty to find him a wife, and try they did. He was constantly amazed at the number of introductions they had arranged. Of course, Scotty had to fulfill the script Marlene and Catherine had written and take every one of their choices out on a date. Scotty often wondered just where in the hell they were getting these women from. At times, when he would inquire, Marlene would reply that the prospective Mrs. Scott was a niece of so-and-so and qualify that with a complicated lineage of personal association. Quickly Scotty resolved that it just wasn't worth asking about.

Going down to his office, Scotty busied himself until he heard Marlene coming through the front door. Precisely at 8:00 a.m., as usual. She called out "Good morning" to Scotty, who tried to answer her greeting. But as was also her habit, Marlene then announced that she would be in with the tea in a few minutes. Marlene then shouted out that she wanted to hear all about his date. Scotty ran his fingers through his hair in frustration but knew that he was trapped.

In less than five minutes, Marlene burst into his office carrying her silver tea tray. She put it down in the corner of his desk and then poured them each a warm cup of morning tea. Marlene then opened the tin containing the daily supply of shortbread cookies. She only allowed Scotty three cookies each day. If he dared to ask for another, experience taught him that he would be in for a lecture on weight control. Once satisfied that they were ready, Marlene sat down in a high-back leather chair across from Scotty.

Scotty tried to start off the conversation by telling Marlene that Admiral Morrison would be visiting that day. But with a dismissive wave of her hand, Marlene indicated that she didn't want to discuss that. Leaning forward in her chair while balancing her teacup on its saucer, Marlene launched into her usual list of questions: "How did it go last night?" "Where did you go for dinner?" "What did you have?" "What did she have?" "Did you drink?" "Did she drink?" "How many drinks did she have?" "What was for dessert?" "What did you wear?" "What did she wear?" "How did she wear her hair?" "How tall is she?" "Is she pretty?" "Was she nice?" "Was she easy to talk to?" "Did you both get along?" "Has she ever been married?" "Does she have children?" "Are you going to see her again?" And then there was Scotty's most favorite question of all: "Did you kiss her good-night, or was there more?" It was only after each question was answered to her satisfaction that Marlene would sit back in the chair and ask, "Okay, boss, what's up for today?"

Scotty informed Marlene that Admiral Morrison would be visiting later in the morning. He then asked her to order a deli spread, soft drinks, and bottled water for approximately ten people. That way, Scotty was assured of having leftovers for tonight and he wouldn't have to face the prospect of cooking. Somebody once complained that he could actually burn water.

Since Scotty and Marlene had recently finished up a contract, they really had nothing to do today. While Marlene was busy ordering lunch, Scotty retreated upstairs and donned a blue business suit. After dressing, he returned to his office and played darts to pass the time.

BUT I WANT TO SIT BY THE WINDOW SEAT

Anxious to leave, Doreen pushed the admiral out of the office by 8:00 a.m. After a quick ride to Edwards Air Force Base, they boarded an unmarked executive jet. Morrison, without hesitation, walked through the cabin to the cockpit. He always made it a habit to meet his pilots and question them briefly about their qualifications. Today's pilots seemed to be kids just out of school, and Morrison wanted to make sure that they knew what they were doing. Once satisfied, but nervous, Morrison walked back through the cabin and sat down in an executive chair. Doreen then sat down across from the admiral and buckled in.

Once Doreen and the admiral were settled, a steward welcomed them aboard and offered them a light snack and something to drink. Morrison, offhandedly, instructed him to return to his station and not disturb them. The steward didn't act offended but simply retreated to the rear of the aircraft. Doreen raised an eyebrow at the admiral, with a frown on her face. Morrison took the chastising well and replied, "Okay, so I don't like flying." Doreen smiled slightly and sat back in her seat.

Once airborne, Morrison reached into his briefcase and withdrew his file on Zambia. Doreen knew better than to interrupt the admiral when he behaved like this. She sat in her seat and watched him closely for a hint of what he was thinking. But he didn't reveal a clue. For the next forty minutes, Doreen gazed out of the window while the admiral read his file. After reading the entire file, and satisfied that he knew the file by heart, Morrison returned it to his briefcase. Stretching his arm, he pushed the overhead panel to summon the steward.

"Admiral, I was directed to give you this package when you were free," the steward announced and handed Morrison the package.

Morrison put his hand in the bag and took out a box of chocolates from the Charleston Chocolate Company. Morrison laughed to himself and returned the candy to the bag. Silently he thought, *Thanks, Chester, you old romantic.* Morrison looked up at the steward and uncharacteristically said, "Son, I apologize for my behavior earlier. Could I please have a bottle of water?"

"No problem, sir. I could tell that you seemed preoccupied. I'll get the water." Turning toward Doreen, he then asked, "Lieutenant, would you like something?"

Morrison spoke up for her. "She will have coffee, black. Thank you."

Doreen was used to the admiral ordering for her. What she really wanted, though, was a cola. But she appreciated the thoughtfulness of the admiral and vowed to break him of this habit one day.

Once their drinks were served, Doreen leaned forward and asked, "How are you going to play it?"

After taking a sip of water, Morrison thoughtfully replied, "There is only one way to do it. With Scotty, you have to tell him the straight story. If he thinks for even one minute that you are deceiving him, it turns him right off. He won't say that he suspects that you are deceiving him, but he will never deal with you again. He's kind of the silent type, and most people consider an individual like Scotty as being a bit dangerous.

"Should he seem uninterested, I will gently remind him of Ice and explain that this is an opportunity to seek the truth about the aliens firsthand. I should also say that, if he takes the assignment, he might discover something about the way the aliens operate. But I don't think that I will have to apply that pressure. I think Scotty will be intrigued enough by the facts and the photographs and will be more than willing to help."

"Are you going to mention the Colorado Project?" Doreen asked.

"Not yet. I'm going to wait until your trip to Zambia is over. Perhaps, by then, Scotty might be interested enough to take command of the facility. If I flat out ask him now, he will turn me down. I would like to try to ease into it."

"I hope you are right, Admiral. It's going to be an interesting day," Doreen replied.

"Oh, it will be more interesting in more ways than one," Morrison replied with a slight grin on his face. He was more interested at this point to see how Scotty and Doreen would react to each other. "There is one more thing, Lieutenant. I hope that you like deli food and all the side salads," Morrison added.

"I love deli food!" Doreen answered. "Why do you ask?"

"Whenever I visit Scotty in the daytime, he always caters a deli lunch. He knows I love the stuff, but he and his secretary, Marlene, refuse to tell me where he buys the food. After we finish eating, he will tell me that I should be watching my triglycerides," Morrison replied.

"He's right, you know," Doreen curtly replied.

"Yeah, yeah. Now, hush up and leave me alone. I want to think for a while," Morrison replied and pushed his chair into the reclining position and closed his eyes.

Doreen also relaxed. For the remainder of the flight, she looked out of the window and watched as the landscape slipped by below them. She was somewhat surprised at herself.

Doreen was feeling a bit nervous about meeting Scotty. There was also a growing pain in her stomach. *All this from photographs,* she thought to herself. Every day she would look at the two photographs of Scotty that the admiral had in his office. One of them was of Scotty in his naval uniform, with an American flag in the background. The other photograph showed Scotty in his flight suit, looking like he just returned from a mission. After the admiral began telling her stories about Scotty, Doreen found herself saying "Good morning" to the photographs when she was alone in the admiral's office. Her thoughts gradually returned to the reason for their visit, but Scotty was always in the back of her mind. Those thoughts, however, did not include the mission.

AH, AH, PLEASED TO MEET YOU

SCOTTY WAS STILL THROWING DARTS, playing a game of 301 against an imaginary challenger, when he heard the front doorbell ring. As he looked out of his office, Scotty saw Marlene glance up at the security camera display, which showed who was at the front door. Scotty also looked at the security monitor as he left his office to retrieve his suit jacket from the law library. He noticed that it was the admiral, accompanied by a woman officer. Marlene hollered out, "Showtime!" as she pressed the button to automatically unlock the front door.

As Scotty entered the reception area of the office, Morrison was hugging Marlene and softly kissed her on the cheek. "Now, where has this beautiful creature been hiding all this time? I bet the boys go crazy over you!" Scotty heard Morrison utter and thought to himself, *Laying it on a bit thick today, aren't we?* Scotty then called out, "Admiral, it sure is nice to see you!" and walked over, waited for him to release Marlene, and then shook his hand.

As they were shaking hands, Scotty's attention was diverted to

Doreen, who suddenly appeared next to the admiral. Scotty let go of the admiral's hand and turned to face Doreen. He was thunderstruck. Here right in front of him was the most beautiful woman he had ever seen. The moment was not lost on Doreen. She was standing with her hands clasped in front of her, holding her small briefcase. Her head was bent slightly downward, being somewhat embarrassed by Scotty's stare. Doreen could feel her pulse quicken and her face slightly flush.

The moment was also not lost on the admiral. Hesitating for the moment, in order to heighten the excitement, Morrison smiled to himself. He then took Scotty's forearm and guided him closer to Doreen as he said, "Scotty, I would like you to finally meet my assistant, Lieutenant Doreen Stark." When Scotty and Doreen were less than two feet away from each other, Morrison released Scotty's arm and continued, "Lieutenant Stark, I would like you to meet Commander Michael Scott, call sign Pirate."

Scotty extended his hand and said, "It's a…a…pleasure, Lieutenant."

Doreen took his hand and shook it and replied in a nervous tone, "The…a…a…pleasure is all mine, Commander."

Scotty looked deeply into her eyes, which were a beautiful shade of brown in the center and slightly darker on the edges, and managed to say, "Please call me…ah, Scotty."

"I'll tell you what? I like the name Michael. I think I'll call you Michael. If that's okay with you? And you can call me Doreen," Doreen answered with a slight air of authority, with an edge of anxiety in her voice.

"That's great!" Scotty quickly replied and then added, "I…er… mean that will be okay, Doreen."

"Good!" Doreen confirmed.

Morrison noted that through the pleasantries, Doreen and Scotty were still holding hands. Neither one seemed willing to let go. Here was Scotty, a hardened naval aviator and a brilliant attorney, and Doreen, a highly educated, razor-sharp naval officer, both of whom were acting like teenagers about to go off on their first date. Morrison couldn't have been more pleased with himself and was trying desperately to hold back his laughter. He couldn't take it anymore and turned away and let out a slight laugh, which he masked by coughing.

Scotty let go of Doreen's hand and turned toward the admiral and asked, "Admiral, did you say something?"

"No, I was just clearing my throat. I think I have a cold coming on," Morrison replied with a slight grin on his face.

"Oh! I have just the cure for that. Plenty of bed rest and some tender loving care!" Marlene declared and then reached up and kissed him lightly on the cheek.

The tables had suddenly turned. Morrison was now nervous and cleared his throat while mumbling, "I'm sure that I just need some vitamin C." He paused and then added, "Could we…ah…sit down? There's something I want to ask you, Scotty."

"Of course," Scotty replied.

"But first, I must meet your assistant." Marlene spoke up as she walked over to Doreen. After Marlene introduced herself and the pleasantries were over, she turned toward Scotty and said, "Mr. Scott"— she always called him Mr. Scott when someone was in the office, much to his objections; otherwise, it was Scotty or Michael—"why don't we get you all settled before lunch arrives?"

"Yeah, that's a good idea. Why don't we do that?" Scotty quickly replied.

"Oh, I almost forgot," Morrison declared as he reached in his briefcase and withdrew the box of chocolates and handed them to Marlene.

"Arthur, you remembered. That's so sweet of you," Marlene answered and then reached up again and kissed him on the cheek. "Wow, three kisses in one day—people will be talking!" Marlene stated and then continued as she grabbed the bottom of his tie and led him toward the conference room, "Come on, you big teddy bear, let's get you comfortable!"

"Marlene!" Morrison protested, to no avail.

Doreen was amazed. She turned toward Scotty and commented, "Are they always like this? I've never seen this side of him."

"Every time! Maybe one day they will actually go out on a date,"

Scotty answered as he stepped aside and let Doreen go in front of him. As Scotty walked behind Doreen, he watched her every movement, especially the gentle sway of her hips.

Marlene directed Morrison to his usual place at the head of the table and placed Doreen on his left, and Scotty across from Doreen. Bending over to whisper in Scotty's ear, Marlene stated so no one could hear, "Looks like your mom and I have been looking in all the wrong places," and left the room after asking if anyone needed anything. Racing to her desk, Marlene dialed Catherine and gave her the intelligence report on Doreen's and Scotty's reactions to her.

Once Morrison was comfortably seated, he surveyed the room as he usually did on every visit. This was his favorite room in Scotty's home. In the center of the wall on the left, there was a functioning fireplace. On each side of the fireplace were floor-to-ceiling bookcases running the length of the wall. These housed the tools of Scotty's trade, lawbooks, which Morrison couldn't care less about. On the far wall was a collection of wall clocks set to the times of different major cities around the world. Each clock had a brass plaque underneath it with the city whose time the clock represented. In the center of this collection hung the admiral's favorite clock. This clock was square and depicted the time in each major time zone and showed which sections of the Earth were in darkness and which sections were in daylight at the present time.

The wall on the right was occupied with glass display cabinets. These housed Scotty's model collection. There was a vast array of wooden ship models from the eighteenth century. And one large display model of the USS *Eisenhower*. Alongside the *Eisenhower* model were two aircraft models. One was of an F-18 that Scotty had flown and still flew then in the reserves. The other one was of an elegant and sexy aircraft that Morrison recognized as being modeled after the alien craft that shot down Ice. Morrison reasoned that if Scotty could display a model of the alien craft, he must be fully recovered from Ice's death and must really be into investigating the aliens. That would be a big plus for Scotty if he was going to take over Space Command in Colorado.

Along the wall behind where the admiral was sitting, there was a long credenza. In the center of the credenza was a large vase of fresh-cut flowers, which were replaced every day. On each side of the vase was a model of horse-drawn fire engines.

The admiral then took a hard look at the conference table he was sitting at. He always commented that he wanted Scotty to sell him the table because of its beauty. It was made out of California burled wood. It was a wood mostly unique to itself. Highly polished as it was, it brought out the subtle colors of the wood, rich blacks, browns, a hint of purple, and a few other colors. Around the table were gathered eight high-back leather chairs. Morrison appreciated the extra room these chairs provide. In front of each chair was a leather blotter and a banker's lamp. Each workspace also had a multiple-line telephone, the wires skillfully hidden in the wood. In the center of the conference table was a conference call device, which gave everyone in the room an opportunity to talk and likewise hear what the person on the other side of the line would say.

As the admiral relaxed in his chair, he reclined it slightly. He put his hands behind his head, interlocked his fingers, and extended his elbows outward. He glanced over at the display models and centered on the one of the USS *Alfred*, the Navy's first flagship authorized by the Continental Congress for its fledgling naval service. Morrison allowed himself to momentarily daydream about what it must have been like to sail on her (sailors always refer to their ships as women because they fall in love with their ship). He imagined himself as an officer on watch (naval term for *working*), manning the poop deck (the command deck in the stern, where the ship is steered from), gazing out at the ocean as the sun was setting. Just before the gentle kiss of darkness, the sun gives off its full radiancy in a color spectrum of greens, violets, pinks, blues, in a stunning rainbow of color.

Scotty and Doreen looked at the admiral lost to his thoughts and then looked at each other in puzzlement, wondering what he was thinking. The awkwardness of the moment was resolved when Marlene walked into the conference room and announced that lunch was served. Hearing the word *lunch*, Morrison snapped out of his daydream, sat upright in his chair, and announced that he was hungry. He then ordered, more than asked, Doreen and Scotty to join him and Marlene for lunch.

THIS USE TO BE CALLED A DAGWOOD—PLEASE PASS THE MUSTARD

MARLENE POSITIONED HERSELF NEXT TO the admiral as they sat down at the kitchen table. This ensured that Scotty would sit next to Doreen. In the center of the table was a deli lover's feast. There were more-than-generous piles of roast beef, smoked turkey, pastrami, salami, pepperoni, three different kinds of ham, Swiss and Italian cheeses, New York-style coleslaw, macaroni and potato salads, three different kinds of breads, and of course, a selection of pickles and pickled tomatoes. For liquid refreshment, there was a selection of flavored seltzers, colas, root bear, and cream sodas. Of course, the ever-present coffeepot was brewing up its magic elixir.

Not one to stand on ceremony, Morrison dug right in. Between two slices of rye bread, he managed to squeeze every type of meat. On top of that he placed a mount of coleslaw topped by a few slices of cheese. Add some Thousand Island dressing and his sandwich was completed. But he wasn't finished yet. Reaching for the largest pickled green tomato, he quickly cut it up in slices and laid it beside his monstrous sandwich. Of course he needed something to drink. He took the top off a cream soda and placed it strategically in front of his sandwich. As Morrison picked up his delight, which was bigger than his mouth, he noticed three pairs of eyes on him. "What?" he uttered as his taste buds were watering, and ordered, "Dig in, everyone!"

Doreen, Marlene, and Scotty looked at one another in silence and followed the admiral's example. Their sandwiches, however, were less than a third of Morrison's. Rather than have soda, they all chose a bottle of seltzer, followed by a cup of coffee.

The conversation around the lunch table was dominated by the admiral and his favorite subject, New York City during the Victorian era. He could recount, from his readings, what he knew of the era and spice it up with his vivid imagination. Morrison created colorful images of what the city looked like during the late 1800s. From his descriptions one could imagine horse-drawn carriages conveying their Victorian-dressed passengers to afternoon socials or teas. The streets would have also been crowded with delivery wagons carrying a wide variety of goods. Of course, street vendors would be selling their varied wares to the crowds. The sidewalks would be crowded with people hurrying to their destinations. Or perhaps, couples would be strolling casually down the avenues.

Children would be running in every direction, playing games. Some of the children would be playing a serious game of jacks or sticks.

When darkness fell upon the city, the admiral was able to describe down to the smallest detail the dress fashions of the gentlemen and ladies as they attended the theater or sporting events. With a sparkle in his eye, Morrison recounted the favorite entertainment of the rich and not-so-rich of that time, the beer gardens. For the price of a nickel to two bits (a term taken from a colonial piece of eight coin, which would have equaled a dollar and could be broken into eight pieces; two bits would have equaled a quarter in today's coinage), one could dine, drink beer, and watch an elaborate floor show.

Everyone had been drawn into the admiral's conversation and had been able to imagine what life might have been like back then. Scotty received approval for his comment about women's fashions back then. He imagined that, while the style of dress covered all parts of a woman's body, it left everything to the imagination while maintaining an air of mystery. But Scotty, like Doreen and Marlene, concluded that he would rather live in modern times. They reasoned that, while the problems of the past are basically the same as the present, today more tools are available to surmount any obstacles.

The admiral ended the conversation about Victorian New York when he asked Marlene if that chocolate cake on the counter was for eating or decoration. Marlene laughed as she cut a rather-large piece for him. The others also had a piece of cake for dessert, but not half as large as the admiral's.

Scotty was thankful for one thing: the lively banter at lunch had helped ease the tension between himself and Doreen. They were now laughing together and felt comfortable in each other's company. Most importantly, they were stealing looks at each other and smiling when they were caught by each other. Like his comment about women's fashion in the Victorian era, Scotty found her name not only beautiful but alluringly mysterious as well.

After dessert was finished, Morrison asked Marlene if it was okay if he made another sandwich for a snack in the afternoon. Marlene just looked at him and stated that she thought he had eaten quite enough. Scotty couldn't help himself and reminded the admiral that he should watch his triglycerides and back off the deli meats.

Morrison laughed a slight laugh and glanced over at Doreen. She was trying to hold back a laugh but was unsuccessful and let it out. Upon hearing Doreen laugh, Scotty turned toward her and asked, "What? What did I say?"

Doreen looked at Scotty, reached out with her hand, placed it on Scotty's, and replied, "It's nothing, Michael. I say the same thing to him each time he has a deli sandwich. But he never listens." Turning back toward the admiral, but leaving her hand on top of Scotty's, she replied, "May I suggest a nice Caesar chicken salad for dinner tonight, Admiral?"

"Careful, Lieutenant. That smacks of treason!" Morrison replied with a smile on his face.

Scotty felt the soft, warm touch of Doreen's hand upon his and decided that he liked it. He wondered where the admiral had been hiding her. But that no longer mattered; she was here now, and that was all that mattered. True, he found her beautiful and a vision of Venus, but what he liked most about her was the fact that she was equal to all and second to none.

Marlene saw Doreen's hand on top of Scotty's and smiled but realized that they had just met and thought it improper. Deciding to break up this momentary repose, she announced, "Now, if you would all get back to your business—not that you will ever tell me what it is about—I'll clean up this mess and get back to my own work."

Doreen released her hand and offered to help as she rose from her chair, but Marlene wouldn't think of it. "No, thank you, Doreen. You're a guest in this house today. Perhaps next time. Now, all of you get out of here!" Marlene replied and then winked at Morrison and added in a soft voice, "Arthur, I'll have a sandwich and some cake ready for you to take."

"Thank you, darling. I'm surprised that some handsome man hasn't snatched you up," Morrison declared, trying to smooth her over.

Marlene busied herself gathering up the dishes as she mumbled to herself, "Not that you would notice, you big oaf. I've been waiting all these years for you to take me to dinner."

Morrison thought that he heard Marlene say something as he was leaving the kitchen. He turned around and asked, "Excuse me, Marlene, what did you say?"

Marlene looked at him and replied, "No...nothing... I was just thinking of the weather out loud."

"Oh. I thought I heard you say something to me," Morrison replied and then continued, "I'm sorry, I neglected to thank you for lunch." As he walked out of the room, he added with a smile on his face, "An oaf like me sure does like that food!"

Marlene couldn't believe that he had heard her. In frustration, she threw the sponge that she had been wiping the table with into the sink and silently swore to herself, *Someday, I'm going to get him!*

THE MOUSE TAKES THE CHEESE

Aﬀter resettling into the library, Scotty noticed a change in the admiral's demeanor. Gone was the good-hearted joking and the fooling around. Suddenly, the admiral was deadly serious. Scotty watched as the admiral set up a notebook computer in front of himself and then placed a portable DVD player in front of Scotty. Looking at the player, Scotty wondered what it was he was going to watch. He glanced over at Doreen, hoping for a hint of what was about to come, but she just smiled at him and then looked at Morrison as if she were waiting for a cue. Whatever it was the admiral wanted, Scotty had a feeling that it wasn't going to be good. He didn't have to wait much longer.

Morrison looked up at Scotty, glanced at Doreen, and then looked back at his computer.

After putting a DVD into his computer drive, the admiral sat back in his chair, cleared his throat, took a sip of cream soda, and began as he looked at Scotty, "I want you to take what I am about to say as no small measure of the faith I have in you and your abilities. If I didn't know your capabilities, I wouldn't be here.

"Scotty, I don't mean to sound dramatic, but I have a problem, or rather, I should say that the world has a problem. I need your input and assistance partially because of your current position. I am not going to ask you to violate any confidences or infringe upon your friendship. I believe—"

"Admiral!" Scotty interrupted and continued, "Why don't you just get to the point? Otherwise, I'll have to go upstairs and put on a pair of boots to wade through the bull." Scotty was getting a little impatient.

Morrison laughed a nervous laugh and glanced over at Doreen as if to say, "I told you so." After taking another sip of his soda, Morrison tried the straight approach. "I know that since the death of Ice you have been seriously investigating the UFO phenomena. From the short talks that we have had on the subject, I know that you are still trying to understand a few things about them. First, both you and I want to know where they come from. Secondly, we have no idea as to why they are here and just what in the hell they are up to.

"Prior thinking about alien visitation in our world was ridiculed and dismissed by the government. We both know that was not the case. The government took the matter very seriously, but they apparently did nothing to halt the visitations. In essence, they allowed the aliens to come and go as they pleased, and today the matter is officially scoffed at. And yet the alien incursion into our country and countries throughout the world continues. Lately, things have changed. Not with our government or other governments, but rather, the behavior of the aliens has taken on a new twist.

"As you know, there have always been stories of abductions whenever an alien presence has been reported. Largely, they were just that, stories. I'm not saying that all the reported abductions were mere fantasy. There were a few that were genuine in so far as there was no evidence to repudiate those claims. But recently, within the past five years, there has been an increase in reported abductions. A large portion of these people has been given lie detector tests. And guess what? They have been passing them. Not only that, but when they are examined by doctors, their claims of physical examination appear to be provable. But I'm not telling you anything that you don't already know." Morrison paused as he looked at Scotty and knew that he had his full attention.

After taking another sip of his cream soda, which was beginning to get warm, Morrison closed in for the kill. "This change in alien tactics reached a new height five days ago. An Antonov An-12, belonging to the national airline of Zambia, with passengers and crew aboard, was on its last trip of an uneventful day when it simply disappeared from its assigned altitude and flight path.

"At the same time, the military of South Africa had an AWACS aircraft up patrolling its eastern coastline. The AWACS was running a track on the Zambian airliner as a training exercise when it was hit with an electromagnetic burst. When the EMB[40] hit the AWACS, all its instrumentation and radars went out. At the exact same time, all radar in Zambia went out. When both of these events happened, the Antonov, according to the South African Air Force and the government of Zambia, disappeared.

"Chester received an inquiry from the air marshal of South Africa requesting any information related to the EMB. He ran a satellite check and downloaded the photographic log from some of the birds."[41] Morrison paused for the sake of drama and then pressed a button on his laptop computer and continued, "Scotty, if you would please watch the DVD player in front of you." As the film was being played, Morrison added, "We took the stills from the satellites and animated them as best as we could so that we can watch the event as close to real time as possible."

Scotty watched the short film and was horrified by what he saw. He immediately thought of Ice, but this was far worse. He couldn't imagine what might have happened to the people. He felt for the pilots of the aircraft and wondered what they were thinking when this happened. But he recognized the alien craft. Scotty tried not to show any emotion, but a lump formed in his throat. He knew what the admiral, that crafty old dog, wanted. But Scotty decided to let the admiral ask the question.

When the film ended, Morrison leaned forward in his chair and removed the DVD from his computer and returned it to his briefcase. Scotty folded the portable DVD player closed and waited for the admiral to shut off his computer. Glancing over at Doreen, Scotty received a sweet smile that told him that she really didn't want to be a part of the con job that was coming.

As Morrison finished putting his computer away, Scotty began asking questions about the fate of the airliner. When he was told that not a trace of the airliner was ever found, it confirmed what Morrison wanted. The admiral wanted him to go and search for the airliner. But first, Scotty thought, *I'll play it out.*

"Admiral, I'm sure that you are familiar with the alien craft in the film. But what you may not know is that the first modern published report of such a craft was actually in the early 1890s. Two of these aircraft were observed, in broad daylight, flying over mining camps somewhere out west. I believe that it was in Colorado, or it could have been in Wyoming. The report in the newspaper was accompanied by sketches and numerous eyewitness accounts. But if I recall correctly, these craft were first seen over fifteen thousand years ago. We know this because images of the spacecraft were painted on walls of caves occupied in prehistoric times in France. My question is, Why are you showing me this?" Scotty asked, hoping to see him squirm a little more for the fun of it.

Morrison paused before answering. He knew that he had to choose his words very carefully; otherwise, Scotty, even though he was a friend, would refuse him. After looking over at Doreen, who was looking at Scotty, Morrison stated, "One of the passengers aboard the Zambia airliner was a Jonathon Quinn of Spectrum Computers. His family, through Spectrum, has requested the Department of State to look into his disappearance.

"The State Department, in turn, contacted the Joint Chiefs and the CIA to see if they could be of any help. What State would like is for us to commit a satellite to overfly Zambia and search for any trace of the aircraft. I'm more than willing to do that, but at the same time, I would like to do a bit more. I should mention that the chief executive officer of Spectrum is an old college buddy of the president who contributed pretty heavily toward his campaign. The president, of course, would like to help out his friend. And that, Scotty, is where you come in.

"I know that in your negotiations with Zambia, on behalf of Spectrum, you became good friends with the president of that country. What I would like you to do is contact your friend and offer him the assistance of our government in searching for the aircraft. Further, I would like you to be the overall director of the search. I would also like Lieutenant Stark to accompany you and serve as your assistant. I—"

The admiral was interrupted by Scotty.

"Admiral, I know you. You couldn't give a damn about politics, and much less our revered president. I know that, given the film you just showed me, you don't really believe that the airliner will ever be found. I think that for the first time in your life, you are scared of something. You're not here asking me to just search for a missing plane. There's something going on in the background. So what do you really want?" Scotty asked in a cool, monotone voice.

Morrison considered what Scotty just asked and thought, *What the hell! I might as well tell him everything. It's the only way he will go. And who knows, things might just work out.* Looking Scotty directly in the eye, Morrison answered, "Okay, what I am about to tell you is absolutely secret, never to be revealed. I will not insult your integrity by asking you to sign the National Secrets Act, but be advised that you are bound by it.

"For the past few years, I have been forming a loose association with my peers in other countries. The purpose of this association right now is to openly exchange information about the aliens and the threat they pose to our world. Each of us has done this without the knowledge of our respective governments because we recognize a growing problem that one day will have to be dealt with," Morrison replied without hinting at what he was really after.

"That being said, you're right, I am afraid. I'm afraid that if that airliner is not found and the people are not safe, it will mean that an alien spacecraft entered our atmosphere, snatched a commercial airliner out of the sky, and did who knows what with the people aboard her. I want that airliner found in one piece, with the passengers sitting under the wing, sipping tropical drinks, waiting to be rescued. Otherwise, it's a whole new ball game. And guess what? We're losing big-time."

Morrison finished and waited for Scotty to speak.

Scotty looked down at the conference table, then across at Doreen, who avoided his glance, and then at Morrison. Without blinking, Scotty replied, "Okay, Admiral, I'll do it. But first, I have some questions, and I want some specialized equipment."

"Go ahead," Morrison quickly answered.

"Is there any question that the airliner was taken by the alien spacecraft?"

"Yes and no. Yes, we can't say 100 percent that it happened that way. No, only because we think that's what happened. That is why it is imperative that we search for the aircraft," Morrison almost pleaded.

"Were you able to track the alien craft? Did it leave our atmosphere?" Scotty asked.

"It flew out over the Atlantic and then disappeared. We believe that it then left our atmosphere," Morrison answered quickly.

"Any idea of its flight or armament capability?"

The admiral cleared his throat again and answered, "No to both parts."

"What is Zambia doing to search for the aircraft?" Scotty asked, imagining that they could do very little, knowing their resources.

"They are following regular procedure, conducting a ground and air search. They are starting on the known course of the airliner just before it disappeared. The search pattern is then widening out just past the maximum distance the airliner could have traveled on its known fuel reserves. So far, not even a trace of the aircraft has been found," Morrison replied, resigned to what he feared.

Without losing a beat, Scotty switched gears. "Okay, Admiral. Now to my conditions, which are not up for negotiation.

"First, I know that NASA has been experimenting with what's called synthetic aperture radar and has four aircraft so equipped. From what I have read, this new radar can find trace elements of metals that conventional radar cannot. I want two of those planes, with technicians flown to the Canary Islands immediately. The crew must be civilian, without any hint of military affiliation. The aircraft are to be devoid of any identification, except lettered on the outside as geological survey craft," Scotty started off.

"Done. Next?" Morrison answered as he was making some notes.

"Secondly, I want Chester to do a global sweep for me to try to locate sources of Alpha Zuron radiation on a mass equal to or slightly above the mass of the missing aircraft."

"Done," Morrison replied, hoping there wasn't another condition.

"Thirdly, I want a funeral urn prepared containing ashes to be presented to Mrs. Quinn, should we not find her husband. I know it sounds cruel, but I am thinking of the family. It will allow them to have closure."

Raising an eyebrow, Morrison replied, "If you insist. Is there anything else?"

"Just one more thing. I want a friend of mine to accompany the NASA aircraft crew and oversee the operation. His name is Vinson Howard, an ex-naval investigative agent. He had Cosmic Alpha security clearance before he left the service," Scotty asked more than demanded.

"Okay, if you guarantee he is okay," Morrison concluded, feeling a little unsure about this man. "I have a couple of demands as well." Morrison spoke up, paused, and then continued, "I want Lieutenant Stark to accompany you as your assistant. She's not there to spy on you, but to help in any way she can. Secondly—"

Morrison was interrupted by Scotty.

"That would be my pleasure, Admiral," Scotty blurted out, trying not to sound too enthusiastic.

"Now, if I could finish, Scotty?" Morrison replied with a hint of laughter in his voice.

Looking over at Doreen, he saw her blushing slightly, and turning back to face Scotty, he continued, "I want each of you to carry a satellite phone. I have two of them that are encrypted and equipped with burst transmitters."

"Agreed," Scotty answered and then continued as he looked at the clocks on the far wall, "Let's see…it's almost 7:00 p.m. in Zambia. I'll go upstairs and make the call in a few minutes. And then I'll call

Vinson. If this goes off, and it should, I want to leave first thing in the morning and meet the aircraft in the Canaries.

"I want the both of you to stay here tonight. There is plenty of room. That way, we can finish making plans. Okay?"

"Sounds good," Morrison replied as Scotty got up and left the room.

✦✦✦✦✦✦✦

[40] Electromagnetic burst.

[41] The military love to call satellites *birds*.

YOU HAVE THE WRONG TELEPHONE NUMBER

Once Scotty was upstairs, he crossed his living room and settled into his favorite chair, an oversize green leather recliner. Once seated, he pushed on the back of the chair with his body and changed it to the reclining position, clasped his hands behind his head, and stared up at the ceiling. It was time to think and plan. In the back of his mind, he wondered if he would be able to convince his friend to allow him to join in the search. Experience taught Scotty that while the admiral was calm on the exterior, there was an element of fear within him. For Morrison's sake, Scotty had to convince the president to let them into the country.

There is something else, though, Scotty thought. He had a feeling that there was a hidden agenda going on in the background. Morrison wasn't talking, and neither was Doreen. Scotty couldn't figure out what it was, but he knew that it was really the overriding reason for their visit. That, combined with the fact that he was being shadowed, told him enough. It had something to do with himself.

Scotty's thoughts then turned to Doreen. *My God,* Scotty thought.

She sure is beautiful. And what a sweet personality! His thoughts centered on Doreen for the next few minutes, and yes, for a few moments, he fantasized about her. But those thoughts were interrupted by the sound of the admiral's footsteps on the stairway.

Scotty returned his chair to the upright position and asked if anything was wrong. The admiral replied that there wasn't and informed Scotty that the aircraft that he requested had been obtained complete with the civilian crew running the experiments on the new radar.

Additionally, the aircraft would be leaving California around midnight for the Canary Islands.

With some hesitation in his voice, Morrison told Scotty that he had asked Admiral Braddock to perform a mineral and natural resource sweep of Zambia and that the results were on their way. The admiral suggested that the maps could be used as a bargaining chip to get the search teams into Zambia. Scotty took some offense to this and countered, "Admiral, the president is my friend. He may be a distant friend, but nonetheless, he is my friend. I will not lower myself or injure his self-esteem by bargaining. What passes between us is done through friendship. If he agrees to allow us to search, then so be it.

"Should we be able to search, then I will present the maps as a gift of our government. If he doesn't, my price for asking is the maps, and I will then forward them to him as a gift from our government. Are we clear on that?"

Morrison agreed and retreated back downstairs to help Doreen finish making the plans and securing equipment. As he walked downstairs, Morrison thought to himself, *Goddamn, he's good,* and smiled.

Once the admiral beat a hasty retreat down the stairs, Scotty reached for his Rolodex, found the president's number, and telephoned his private residence. A security agent speaking perfect English, the official language of Zambia, recognized Scotty's voice immediately. After they caught up on old times, the security agent excused himself while he notified the president of his call. A few minutes later, Scotty was greeted by a friendly voice. "Scotty, my friend, is it all well with you?" the president asked

"I'm fine, Mr. President. How is your lovely wife and those two adorable children?" Scotty replied.

"They are all fine, Scotty. I'm sure that they want to say hello. Just hold on a minute and let me go get them," the president replied and put the telephone down.

For the next twenty minutes, Scotty and the president's family caught up on old times. Scotty deflected questions about his private life and just when some lucky girl was going to tie him down. Relief came when he spoke to the children. He delighted in hearing about their latest triumphs and adventures in exact detail. While the president's children, a boy aged seven and a daughter aged nine, were young, they spoke as if they were much older. When Scotty told them that he might be coming for a visit, they made him promise to stay with them and have a picnic. Scotty laughed with happiness as he recalled his last visit, when they spent the day at Lake Victoria. In the background, Scotty could hear the president trying to get the children off the telephone. Suddenly, both children said goodbye and hung up the telephone. Sitting in his chair, Scotty looked at the dead telephone, laughed, and then called back.

This time the president answered, and before Scotty could get past the word *hello*, the president apologized and stated, "I heard the children talking that you may be coming for a visit. That's great. Of course you will be my guest!"

"Well, sir, that would depend on what I am about to ask you," Scotty declared, then continued, "I'm afraid that this is regrettably a business call and not entirely social."

"That's okay, Scotty. As long as we get to see you," the president answered. Then he asked, "How can I be of service to you?"

For the next half hour, Scotty and the president discussed the missing airliner. The president explained in great detail the efforts to locate the plane, and those of his neighboring countries. But their efforts went unrewarded. The aircraft simply could not be found. The president summed it up best when he said, "It's as if the heavens opened up and snatched it away." This simple statement sent a chill through

Scotty as he feared that it was quite prophetic. It did, however, offer Scotty an opening for his proposal.

Scotty explained that the family of Mr. Quinn, an employee of Spectrum Universal Computers, had approached the United States government for assistance in aiding in the search. He then explained about the experimental new radar and how successful it was. When Scotty offered the availability of this new radar to conduct a search, the president didn't hesitate.

While his country could use the additional help in the search, the offer impressed the president. But what impressed him even more was the fact that Spectrum had made such a request. Spectrum had recently made a decision to eventually invest billions in Zambia. They were in the process of building multiple factories to build computers for distribution throughout Europe and Asia. Spectrum had found an educated workforce in Zambia with a president that cared more for the welfare of his people than anything else. Zambia welcomed the investment because it would allow the country to diversify its economy from being almost entirely dependent on mining and copper production to manufacturing.

The president was delighted by the fact that Spectrum showed, by its request, the value it placed on its employees. "Of course, I would welcome the assistance. However, there is a price," the president responded.

"What would that be?" Scotty asked, a bit surprised by the demand.

"That you come along as well and be my family's houseguest. The kids keep asking when Uncle Scotty was coming back," the president replied.

Laughing, Scotty answered, "It would be my honor, Mr. President!"

Scotty then offered to have his assistant contact the minister of the interior to work out the details, which was agreeable. When the president heard that Scotty had an assistant, he found it very curious that it was a female. A barrage of question ensued that led to Scotty admitting that, yes, he would like to date her. The president didn't need to hear any more and immediately directed that the mysterious Doreen would also be a guest in his home.

Scotty next called his good friend Vinson. It took them all of two minutes to catch up on old news since they had lunch together a couple of days ago. The hard part came when Scotty explained that their old employer had need of their services. Vinson wanted to know the details, but Scotty told him that, since they were talking over an unsecured telephone, it couldn't be discussed. Vinson protested, reminding Scotty that military service was behind him. When Scotty explained that it would only be for approximately four days and that he needed his keen eyes and investigative talent, his objections disappeared. There was a strong bond between these two men that matured through a long friendship and mutual trust. Either one of them would do what the other asked, no matter what the risk.

When Vinson heard that two naval investigative agents would be at his home in a few hours to pick him up, take him to the airport, and give him a briefing about the mission, his curiosity was really piqued. The only response he could get out of Scotty was to dress for warm weather.

After talking to Vinson, Scotty sat back in his chair for a moment and thought about what gifts he should bring along for the president's family. He knew that they would not have time to shop, since they were leaving in the morning, so he reached for the telephone number of Everett's Department Store. Everett's had been a family department store since the early 1800s. It survived a couple of depressions, numerous recessions, and numerous inflationary periods for the simple reason that they gave excellent service to the customers.

Scotty had been using the "executive gift service" of Everett's since he started practicing law. At the conclusion of every international contract, it is the custom to exchange gifts between the parties. Everett's maintained a gift registry for its customers. They would not only select, wrap, and deliver, but they also keep a detailed record of the gifts given, their value, and the date of the gift.

For the president, Scotty selected a slim black leather briefcase engraved with his initials. For the president's wife, the beautiful Edenausegboye, he chose a porcelain sculptor of a pride of lions in honor of her dedicated work to protect the wildlife of Zambia. For the baby of the family, Mawuli, Scotty chose a pair of remote-controlled cars, hoping he would get to play with one of the cars. For Mawuli's older sister, Titilayo, Scotty chose a selection of computer games and software.

Once the gifts were chosen, the clerk from Everett's asked how the gift cards were to be inscribed. Scotty pondered the question for a minute and then instructed the clerk to sign them "With Love, Doreen and Scotty." Scotty realized that this might have been a bit presumptuous on his part but reasoned that if Doreen was going to be staying at the president's home, then her name should also be on the gift cards. After being assured that the gifts would be delivered to his home within a few hours, Scotty reclined his chair again and thought that he would relax for a few minutes.

After daydreaming for an hour, mostly about Doreen, Scotty went back downstairs. As he was descending the stairs, he heard the sound of laughter. When he reached the library, Scotty wondered what was so funny. Doreen spoke up. "Forgive us, but Marlene was just telling us some stories about you. And I have to tell you, this photograph album is absolutely precious! You really were a cute baby. The picture of you in the first grade with the curly hair…well, you must have been a lady-killer even back then!"

Scotty frowned and glanced down at the photo album as he declared, "Yeah, well, let's get back to business. The president has agreed to let us help in the search, and Vinson is a go." Scotty then handed Doreen a slip of paper and directed that she call the minister of the interior to make the final arrangements.

As the admiral beamed from ear to ear and thanked Scotty, Marlene discreetly rose from her chair. She picked up the photograph album and returned it to the cabinet. Before she left the room, Marlene informed Scotty that she would make dinner arrangements and suggested that they all stay overnight. Scotty realized that he messed up and told Marlene that he had already told them to stay over as they were leaving early in the morning. "Oh…good," Marlene almost whispered and left the room. Scotty rightly so detected a note of being hurt in her voice and chastised himself for not telling her of their overnight stay.

Doreen went to the end of the table and placed her call while Scotty and the admiral talked. The admiral congratulated Scotty on securing permission for the search. He then went on to explain that Vinson would be flown to the Canaries, where he will meet the search aircraft. Doreen and Scotty would leave early in the morning and also meet the search teams in the Canaries. When Doreen finished her telephone call, she informed them that all was arranged and that they should be on the ground tomorrow night in Zambia. She then looked at Scotty and remarked, "You, sneak, you. How come you didn't tell me that we are staying with the president and his family? I have to go shopping. I don't have a thing to wear."

"That kind of just came up. Besides, you would look beautiful in whatever you wear!" Scotty replied, being a bit surprised at himself for his candor. Then he added, "There's one other thing you should know. I had the gifts signed 'Doreen and Scotty.' I hope you don't mind, but since we will both be staying with the president's family, I thought it only appropriate." Scotty searched Doreen's face for a hint of disapproval. Instead, he received a wink and a big smile from Doreen as she said, "You, little devil, you."

Marlene then re-entered the library and told Scotty that she had made early dinner reservations for him and Doreen at his favorite Italian restaurant, Antonio's. As she looked at the admiral, she added that both she and the admiral would enjoy a quiet, catered dinner also from Antonio's at home. At the mention of this revelation, the admiral began acting like a teenager about to go out on his first date. Marlene then turned back toward Scotty and instructed him to be back no later than eight o'clock as Everett's, in addition to delivering gifts that someone forgot to tell her about, would also be bringing over a selection of clothing for Doreen to try on, from which she would pick out what she wanted. Doreen looked at Marlene with a look of shock on her face and was about to speak when Marlene cut her off. "I told them a size 4. Is that about right?"

Doreen replied, "Why, yes, that's exactly right, but—"

And she was cut off by Marlene, again.

"Oh, don't thank me, dear. When I overheard you say that you didn't have a thing to wear, I decided to call Everett's for you. It was the least I could do. And don't worry about the cost. I told them to charge it to Mr. Scott's account. That weasel of a person he calls an accountant will figure out a way to make it tax-deductible. Now, off, you two, and get ready for dinner!" Marlene ordered.

Doreen looked at Scotty with her mouth open, as if she were searching for something to say. Seeing her dilemma, Scotty said, "Don't even try. It's a losing battle. Once her mind is made up, it's easier to just go along with the program."

"I'm not going to allow you to pay for some clothes for me. It's not the way I was brought up!" Doreen declared.

"Don't worry about it. Marlene is right, you know. My accountant will probably figure out a way to make sure that they are tax-deductible," Scotty replied and, seeing that she wasn't satisfied, then added, "If it makes you feel uncomfortable, you can donate the cost of the clothes to charity. Okay? Now, let's go and eat. I am starving, and you are just going to love Antonio's cooking."

TABLE FOR TWO

OVER A CANDLELIT DINNER IN a quiet back corner of the restaurant, with soft jazz playing in the background, the nervousness between Scotty and Doreen melted into the background. They truly enjoyed each other's company. She talked about her childhood and growing up in a house full of Marines. She also talked about her plans for the future, which included marriage and a family. Scotty also talked about his childhood and his life in the Navy. Doreen asked him why he decided to practice law. It was a question that he could not really answer, but he told her that he was getting real bored with it. Scotty was getting really tired of hearing his clients constantly complain about their bottom line, but in reality, they were making a fortune. Most importantly, their conversation was punctuated by the pre-relationship jitters. They both lightly touched each other on the arm or hand as they talked, as if they were seeking each other's approval or reassurance that the other was actually there and not part of a dream.

Meanwhile, the admiral was spending a very nervous evening trying to fend off Marlene. As they sat around Scotty's dining room table, Marlene seemed to be inching closer and closer. He could smell the sweet aroma of her perfume and admitted to himself that he found it quite intoxicating. But all those years of bachelorhood had taught him certain survival skills. He was about to execute one of his survival tricks when, to his delight, his cell phone rang.

Morrison was so nervous that he dropped his cell phone when he withdrew it from his belt. Quickly, before it stopped ringing, he answered. He was happy to hear Chester's voice on the other end. Chester just wanted to know if the survey maps had arrived yet as they should have or would momentarily. But Morrison kept him on the phone with stupid questions. Chester tried to hang up, but his boss just went on and on.

Marlene, not to be daunted by this ploy, moved even closer and reached out and put her hand on top of his. In a very soft, warm voice, she demanded, "Arthur, hang up the phone. Tell him that you will call him back!" Just when all hope of escape seemed lost to him, the doorbell rang. Marlene withdrew her hand, uttered "Damn," stood up, looked at the admiral, and went to answer the door.

To her amazement, the people from Everett's were there with two clothing racks full of clothes. As she was showing them in, a naval officer arrived with a package for the admiral. With a sharp tone of resignation, Marlene admitted everyone. She put the people from Everett's into the library and sent the naval officer up to see the admiral.

Marlene sat on a chair at the back of the room as the people from Everett's droned on and on about the attributes of each particular piece of clothing. Automatically, she would answer yes to repeated questions if the recipient of the clothing would like something. Her thoughts were of an opportunity lost, but not lost forever, she vowed. Just then, she eyed the admiral as he stood in the doorway as a mute witness to the chaos. He smiled softly to Marlene and motioned that he was going upstairs. Marlene smiled back, but quickly the smile faded into a frown.

I'LL JUST TAKE A PEEK

ONCE UPSTAIRS, MORRISON WALKED OVER to the pool table. He racked the balls and began playing a game of eight ball against himself. He was losing to himself four to three when he decided to sneak a look into Scotty's computer room. Carefully he crept along, stopping to check and see if he could hear Marlene coming up the stairs. When he felt safe, Morrison slowly opened the door.

Almost creeping in, Morrison felt like he was betraying a friend, but the room interested him. The computer room was only five by ten feet, with one continuous desk running the length of three walls. On the vast desk were three computers. Two of them were made by Spectrum—little surprise there—but the third one was the one that interested Morrison the most. It was devoid of any manufacture decals. At first, the admiral thought it odd that it was not connected to a cable. But he reasoned that it was the one computer Scotty was using to tabulate information. The stack of papers lying next to this computer confirmed his suspicion. Leafing through them, Morrison realized that Scotty was plotting the trajectories of the aliens when they entered the atmosphere and cross-correlating that information with reported sightings.

Morrison was about to jump out of his shoes when suddenly one of the printers came to life. He picked up the two pages and read a report on multiple sightings of mysterious lights in the sky off the coast of Brazil. The report went on to detail that the same lights were seen up and down the entire seacoast almost at the same time. When all the reports were taken together, one was able to see that the source of the lights traveled in a south-to-north direction. Not knowing what to make of it, Morrison replaced the papers exactly how he had found them. Backing carefully out of the room so as not to disturb anything, the admiral went back to his game of pool.

Morrison was still losing to himself when he heard a commotion downstairs and realized that Scotty and Doreen had returned home. After clearing off the pool table and returning the cues to the rack, the admiral decided that he should go downstairs and see what all the noise was about.

As Morrison entered the library, he laughed to himself about the scene in front of him.

The people from Everett's were crowding around Doreen, showing her piece after piece of clothing. While making her selections, Doreen consulted Scotty on each piece. Morrison didn't know what could have happened between Doreen and Scotty at dinner, but their initial nervousness was over. The admiral smiled at that thought and was happy with himself.

Turning back around, Morrison retreated back upstairs to watch some television while he waited for the chaos downstairs to end.

After what seemed like an eternity to the admiral, Doreen, Marlene, and Scotty came upstairs and joined him. When Morrison asked Doreen if she was happy with her clothing choices, she replied that she couldn't have done it without Scotty's help. Morrison smiled to himself and thought that she was laying it on a bit thick since they had just met earlier today. But Morrison acknowledged that this day seemed like a week. If things continued the way they were going, Morrison knew that he would shortly be looking for a new assistant. His thoughts were interrupted when Marlene, always the host, asked if anyone would like something to drink.

With his bachelor survival in fine tune, Morrison cleared his throat and suggested that they all go to bed now as they would be waking up at 4:00 a.m. Everyone followed his lead and wished one another a good night's sleep. Marlene offered to show Doreen to her room, but before they started up the stairs, Doreen crossed the living room to where Scotty was standing and kissed him on the cheek. Softly she whispered, "Thank you for a lovely day." She then turned and followed Marlene up the stairs, but not before looking back at Scotty with a sweet smile on her face. Scotty was left standing there with his mouth slightly opened.

As Doreen ascended the stairs, Scotty called out, "Ah…good night."

Morrison watched the flirting between Doreen and Scotty with a big smile on his face.

When Doreen disappeared up the stairs, he threw his uniform jacket over his shoulder, walked over to Scotty while laughing, slightly slapped him on his arm, and said "Good night." As he walked up the stairs, he whistled "Here Comes the Bride" just loud enough for Scotty to hear. As Morrison walked to his bedroom, he thought, *I hope they at least invite me to the wedding!*

SOMETHING SMELLS REALLY GOOD

S COTTY ROSE A FULL FORTY-FIVE minutes earlier than when he was supposed to. He thought he would be the first to get up, which would allow him some quiet time before they were supposed to leave, but he heard the stirring sounds of his houseguests. Quickly he shaved, showered, and dressed. When he left his bedroom, the smells of cooking had drifted upstairs.

He could smell bacon frying and what he hoped would be French toast. As he was about to go down the stairs to investigate breakfast, he heard the door to Doreen's room open.

Scotty hesitated at the top of the stairs and waited for her. When Doreen came within view, Scotty was surprised to see that they were wearing the same clothes. They both wore pale-blue linen shirts, white linen pants, brown belts, and brown loafers. The likeness of their clothing was not lost on Doreen. She greeted him with a big smile and a happy-sounding "Good morning." She then complimented Scotty on his fine taste in clothing. Scotty stumbled over his words trying to make a joke. He really just wanted to reach out and kiss Doreen but decided that such a bold move would have to wait. The same idea crossed Doreen's mind, and she surely would have welcomed such boldness, but she decided to let nature take its course, although prodded along occasionally. Together they descended the stairs and walked into the kitchen; however, neither Scotty nor Doreen was prepared for the sight that welcomed them.

Standing over the stove was the admiral, dressed in his finest uniform. His uniform jacket was replaced with a full-length flower-patterned apron. He was fully involved in cooking bacon and French toast. Marlene was busy setting the table and making coffee. After Doreen and Scotty greeted the would-be chefs, Morrison turned toward them and, while shaking a spatula in their direction, said, "Don't say one word, Scotty. Not one word!" Morrison then looked Doreen in the eye and ordered, "Lieutenant, you either. And so help me if you breathe just one word of this, you will be posted to an atoll in the South Pacific, taking weather readings for the rest of your career. And don't dare laugh! That's an order, Lieutenant!"

Scotty stood there taking in the scene, while Doreen put a hand over her mouth and ran into the hallway. As Scotty was about to speak, everyone in the kitchen heard Doreen laughing. With the hint of a laugh in his voice, Scotty commented, "Why, Admiral, I think it is very practical and looks very becoming on you. What do you think, Marlene?"

Marlene walked over to the admiral and patted his back as she replied, "Why, I think that he just looks adorable!" She then kissed him on his cheek and added, "Don't you agree, Mr. Scott?"

"Yes, Marlene, he just looks a-d-o-r-a-b-l-e! I'm just wondering if this will become a fashion statement around the Pentagon. I would, however, suggest that the color of the flowers be a bit brighter. That way, they wouldn't clash so much with the admiral's red face," Scotty replied, knowing he was walking on thin ice.

Once Doreen came back into the kitchen, they sat down and enjoyed the admiral's cooking. When they were finished, Doreen and Scotty carried their luggage down to the office area, while Marlene and the admiral cleaned up.

Once the admiral came downstairs, he went outside and summoned two agents into the office area. He directed them to put the luggage in the car and wait outside. Marlene then came down with a picnic basket in one hand and a small box in the other. She handed Doreen the basket as she said, "I fixed you both a snack from the leftovers of yesterday's lunch. I hope you enjoy it." Before Doreen could thank her, Marlene turned toward the admiral and handed him the box as she said, "I also prepared a lunch for you, your usual selection of deli meats and salads."

"Why, thank you, Marlene! What would I ever do without you!" Morrison replied as his taste buds could hardly wait to experience the treasures within.

Marlene, in almost a whisper so no one would hear, replied, "I'd like to know what you would do with me."

"What was that?" Morrison asked, not letting on that he had heard her. "You're welcome, Admiral," Marlene replied in a disappointed tone.

"You know, Admiral, you should really watch it. You had a lot of deli meat yesterday," Scotty declared.

"He's right, Admiral!" Doreen added with a tone of concern.

"Lieutenant, you're out of line!" Morrison spoke up but was very touched by her concern. Turning toward Scotty, he continued, "Mr. Scott, mind your own business. This lovely woman fixed me a nice lunch, and not to eat it, well, that would be downright rude. It would not be the honorable behavior expected of a naval officer. Now, let's get to the airport."

Marlene kissed Scotty goodbye and instructed him to take care of Doreen. Doreen then kissed Marlene goodbye and thanked her for everything she had done for her. Marlene then told Doreen to watch out for Scotty and related that she had a feeling that she would be seeing a lot of her in the future. Marlene then turned her attention toward the admiral. She planted a big kiss on his lips and instructed, "Now you hurry back, darling."

Morrison ignored the remark and, without skipping a beat (his bachelor survival skills in fine tune), explained to Marlene that he had assigned two agents to be posted to her and Scotty's residence. Scotty was a little surprised but agreed with the admiral and directed her to make herself at home upstairs until they returned. Marlene couldn't see why she had to stay there, but she was up against two very strong-willed individuals. There was only one thing she could do, and that was do as she was directed.

After another round of goodbye kisses and hugs, Doreen, Scotty, and the admiral entered the awaiting car and drove off while Marlene stood in the doorway, waving goodbye with one hand and wiping tears from her eyes with her other hand.

YOU LOOK A LITTLE YOUNG TO BE A PILOT, SON, YOU SURE THAT YOU KNOW HOW TO FLY THIS THING?

ARRIVING AT THE AIRPORT, SCOTTY was glad to see that the aircraft that they would be using was devoid of any markings except for the international registration number and small lettering that identified the plane as a "geological survey" aircraft. After walking around the aircraft, doing his own safety check, Scotty, with Doreen, followed the admiral on board. They sat down into two oversize and stuffed leather chairs as the admiral headed directly for the cockpit.

Scotty and Doreen listened with smiles on their faces as the admiral conducted his inquisition. They could hear him asking whether or not the pilots ever flew an aircraft over the ocean before, just where they received their pilot training, if they were sure that they had enough fuel, if they knew how to land on water in an emergency, and a hundred other questions. Once satisfied that the pilots met his minimal standards, the admiral wished them a safe flight and turned his attention to Doreen and Scotty.

Morrison stood in the middle of the aisle with a somewhat-troubled look on his face. He spoke in a firm but soft voice. "I want you both to know how much I appreciate what you are doing. My two favorite people in the world are leaving. I just wish that I could go and watch over you."

"Ah! Come on, Admiral. I thought that Marlene was your most favorite person in the world!" Scotty spoke up as he glanced at Doreen and saw her smile and look back at him.

The admiral's face turned a slight shade of red as he first cleared his throat and continued, "Mr. Scott, let me continue without the editorial commentary. Thank you!" After a few seconds' pause, the admiral continued, "In the luggage compartment is a gray cylinder. It contains the survey maps that Chester ran. Scotty, please give them to the president with our compliments.

"Also, I have taken the precaution of placing a few M16s, four .45-caliber handguns, some stun grenades, and more than an adequate supply of ammo behind the bulkhead panel in the kitchen. I know that you don't want the weapons, but I feel much better that you both can defend yourselves should something happen. I want each of you to watch out for the other, and I don't want either of you to take any unnecessary risks. Just be safe. Remember, if any situation smells bad, it is. Just get out of there quick. And that's an order."

"But, Admiral, we are going to one of the most beautiful places on Earth. The people are absolutely fabulous. It's the kind of place where if you are there for a while, you feel that you've lived there all your life," Scotty interrupted.

"I know, Scotty, I know. It's just that you are both going so far away. Please, both of you, just be safe," Morrison said, wanting to get his point across.

Doreen, overcome with emotion, released her seat belt, stood up, and hugged and kissed the admiral on his cheek. As she sat back down, she coyly added, "Why, Admiral, I'm becoming jealous of Marlene."

Morrison was once again flushed red in the face and was a little nervous over Doreen's sudden show of emotion. He bellowed out, "Lieutenant, remember that you are a naval officer!" With that declaration, Morrison exited the aircraft mumbling, "May you have smooth sailing and following seas." Once the engines started, Morrison stuck his head back into the aircraft and hollered out, "Be safe, you two. That's an order!" He then closed and locked the door to the aircraft, much to the dismay of the ground attendant. When the aircraft began to move, Morrison backed out of the way, but not before gently touching the wing and whispering to himself, "Be safe, my children."

With a rare show of true emotion, Morrison stood there and watched as Doreen and Scotty's aircraft taxied out on the runway and took off. Reaching up to his eye, Morrison wiped away a tear. He then walked over to his waiting aircraft and returned to Washington, DC, full of anxiety over the unknown.

SOUTH OF THE BORDER, IN OLE BRAZIL

Each day is different, but for Enrique, each day began the same way. He rose before dawn, ate a hearty breakfast of a mixture of oat and cornmeal, drank several cups of strong Brazilian coffee, kissed his sleeping children goodbye, gathered up his meager necessities, kissed his wife goodbye accompanied by a slap on her posterior, and walked the short distance down to the beach and his fishing boat. Nothing changed. It was the same each morning.

Once checking that everything was as it should be, Enrique started the engine and headed directly out to sea. When the sun began to rise, Enrique steered directly toward the bright-orange orb. It was as if he wished that the sun would bless his modest craft, and perhaps he secretly desired it to do so. Truly, he was naked each day of his life against the elements of nature. But through the long years that he had spent at sea, Enrique had come to regard the sea and the sun together as his mother, the giver of life. Enrique did not think of himself as one against nature, but rather, he viewed himself as working in concert with the sea and, to a larger extent, the life that it contains. For the bounty of the sea provided his family with the lifeblood of their existence. But that existence was becoming harder to obtain.

In the last few years, Enrique's, as well as the other fishermen's, very survival had been threatened. The threat didn't come from nature. Nor did it come from Enrique or his fellow fishermen. It came from greed and a disrespect for nature. Without warning, large fishing ships of foreign nations became regular visitors to the waters Enrique's family had fished for centuries. These big ships took without regard for the creatures themselves or for the future of the ocean life.

Enrique cursed these big ships, but he was powerless to stop them. Men from his government, in their store-bought suits and ties, would come to his small village and tell the fishermen that they were the backbone of the nation, carrying on a proud and vital tradition. Then these visitors would tell them of the government's efforts to stop the big ships from coming. But like always, their briefcases contained nothing but empty promises. After a while, the men of the village stopped listening. A quiet resolve overcame them. If they were to survive, they would have to work longer and much harder than they knew. Enrique would often think back to the time he first went to sea, not as a youngster who was proud to accompany his father, but when his childhood ended and work became its own definition.

Enrique was born into a small family; he had no brothers and only one younger sister.

His mother, he could remember being a very beautiful woman ever watchful of his needs and desires. His father, well, his father was his hero and the one he most wanted to be like. Enrique loved and was devoted to his family, but especially to his sister.

Enrique was six years old when his sister was born. He remembered it as being a cold, windswept, rainy night. Since his family couldn't afford a doctor, a midwife came to his home, a shack by most people's standards, but a castle to him, that night to help in the birth. He could remember his father nervously pacing back and forth across the small kitchen in anticipation of his sister's birth. Enrique paced also, carefully following in his father's shadow.

For hours, Enrique anxiously awaited the arrival of his sister. He could hear his mother screaming occasionally, and he wanted to run to her. But his father always restrained him with just a smile or a wink of his eye. Enrique found reassurance in his father. He was, after all, the strongest and wisest man he knew.

When his sister was finally born, he could remember, the midwife came out from behind the curtain that divided the kitchen form his mother's bedroom. She was tenderly carrying a bundle in her arms wrapped in a blue blanket. Enrique ran over to her and strained to see.

Pulling the blanket back, Enrique saw his sister for the first time. She moved ever so slightly and cried the cry of new life. But something was terribly wrong. The midwife was weeping and offering prayers up to the heavens. Enrique turned toward his father and saw the look of sadness on his face. His father walked over to the kitchen table and slowly sat down. His hands covered his face, and he began crying. For the first time in Enrique's young life, he saw his father cry. It would have been natural for Enrique to run to his father, but instead, he ran into his mother's room.

Crying out, "Mama, Mama!" Enrique stood by her side and saw that she was not moving as she lay in her bed. Tears began to well in his eyes as he stood over his mother, begging her to wake up. At first, he tried pushing her shoulder to wake her up. Then he slightly lifted his mother's head up and cradled her with his small hands. He kissed his mom softly on the cheek as he begged and begged her to wake up.

When he felt his father's strong hand on his shoulder, Enrique gently put his mother's head down. He turned around and looked up at his dad. Picking Enrique up in his strong arms, his father held him, and together they looked down at his mom. It was through teary eyes and a strained voice that his father told him that his mother had died. It was as if someone reached in and took a large part of Enrique's heart that night. For surely a part of him died as well.

As the succeeding years passed, Enrique became his sister's protector. Each day he would run home from school, not so he could go and play with his friends, but to pick his sister up from the babysitter. When she was old enough to attend school, they would walk to and from school together. She had become his best friend, and he her parent. Together they dreamed of the day that they would leave their village and visit the wondrous places their teachers talked endlessly about. Their father was included in their dreams, as he would have to come along and show them the way.

At nighttime, their father would have them read aloud from their schoolbooks.

Afterward, they would discuss what they read, guided by their father's gentle persuasion. When the subject of the world outside their village was raised, their father would tell them that before they ventured out into the world, they would first have to understand it. And the key to understanding lay in education. Together they were a happy family united by a deep love and respect they had for one another. Enrique was in his last year of high school when that love was to be tested.

One morning, his father had set out to sea before the first rays of sunlight had warmed the Earth. Alone, his father set his nets and began trolling for fish. After a few hours, his nets seemed full and he began hoisting them aboard. He was standing in the back of the boat, guiding his catch aboard, when a small rogue wave slammed broadside against his boat. Immediately, his father lost his balance, and somehow he became entangled in the steel wire guide ropes. He fought frantically to free himself, but the more he tried, the more he became entangled. The wire tightened around him and dragged him toward the winch. At the last second, his father was able to grab a gaff hook. Extending it in front of him, Enrique's father jammed the hook into the teeth of the motor, which stopped it. But the damage had been done. He was bleeding badly, and the wire had cut his leg down to the bone.

For the next hour, in between periods of unconsciousness, his father managed to free himself. Taking off his belt, he applied a tourniquet above where the wire had cut into his leg. Crawling along the deck on his stomach, he was able to reach the pilothouse (the area of a boat where one steers the boat). Pulling himself up, Enrique's father was able to start the engine and steer toward his village. He fought off searing pain, doing his best to remain conscious. But from time to time, darkness would cloud his vision from the outer edges of his eyes until it completely covered them and he would pass out. After a few minutes, he would wake up and readjust his course homeward.

Enrique and his sister were waiting for his father when he arrived at the village well after dark. With an experienced hand, Enrique's father beached his boat on the soft sands. Sensing that something was terribly wrong, Enrique and his sister ran over to the boat and quickly climbed aboard. They were not prepared for what they saw: their father was lying down on the deck in a pool of blood. Enrique and his sister knelt down by their father and gently held his cold hands. When they realized that he was dead, they cried the cry of death. That night, Enrique closed his schoolbooks forever and repressed his childhood dreams of the world outside of his village.

Enrique liked to remember, for it helped pass the endless hours away. It also brought back the many lessons his father had taught him. One came to mind. It was an old mariner's saying: "Red skies in the evening, sailors delight; red skies in the morning, sailors take warning." Since Enrique saw tinges of red skies bordering the horizon, his instinct told him to turn his boat in close to shore and fish the shallow water. He wasn't disheartened by the weather, but rather, he felt happy. Today he would be able to beach his boat and enjoy his lunch in his private place, a small horseshoe cove his father had shown him.

It really wasn't much. The cove was only about sixty feet long and surrounded on all sides by high hills of earth and rock. It really wasn't that wide either, maybe fifty feet if that. But it was Enrique's private place. He would enjoy his lunch on its pristine beach and linger as long as he could, surrounded by its simple beauty. Enrique was sure that others had seen this beach, but he liked to think that he was the only one who had actually set foot upon its welcoming sand.

WHOSE TURN TO WASH THE DIRTY LAUNDRY

S INCE CHESTER RETURNED FROM BERMUDA, he had ordered round-the-clock surveillance placed upon Samuel and Carolyn Gibbs. He couldn't believe that security had somehow let a spy slip through their net without even a hint of a problem. After reading and re-reading the background report prepared on Carolyn by the director of internal security for military affairs, Chester could only conclude that someone really screwed up. The director had personally handled the original request to investigate her background. It seemed now that all he did was retell what Carolyn had told friends and prospective employers. She claimed that she had wanted a change of scenery after the death of her parents. So she left South Africa in search of her fortune and a new life.

Chester knew that Director Eric Hyman was typical of a lot of senior supervisors in government service—out of touch with reality and always depending on people who were just out to feather their own nest. Somewhere along the way, the mission and goals of their office were lost to them. Instead, they were there to ride out the wave until retirement. If Chester were to have his way, and he would, Director

Hyman would be removed from government service, but not before being demoted.

What Chester had to focus on was Carolyn and just how much damage had been done. He took a moment to reflect and feel sorry for Samuel Gibbs. This was going to cause a lot of havoc in not only his personal life but in also his career. *Or maybe not,* Chester thought.

As part of the ongoing surveillance, a new background investigation was conducted.

So far, it showed nothing remarkable. Samuel Gibbs was a naval officer, and Carolyn Gibbs was employed as a travel agent. The only other steady job she had was at the Internal Revenue Service for a short period. Samuel and Carolyn paid most of their bills on time, drove subcompact leased vehicles, and were not affiliated with any clubs or associations. Their only exercise was riding bicycles on the various bike paths around Washington. Together or individually, they never traveled outside of the United States, and neither of them had a passport. Everything seemed normal, except for two telephone calls made to South Africa within the last year. One call was around Christmas, and the other was last July. The telephone number in South Africa was registered to a female named Sophia Judd, a retired civil servant of the South African Air Ministry.

To check out the telephone calls, Chester contacted a friend in the National Security Agency (NSA). Since the NSA monitors millions of telephone calls each day, Chester knew that its computers search for certain key words in monitored conversations. If a word is mentioned, that call is then forwarded to an agent to determine if it requires further investigation. Chester wanted them to check their computer records for the key words *space command*, *UFO*, *aliens*, and *unknowns*.

The words *space command* were a frequent match, but only on military and intergovernmental telephones. There was not a record of those words being used in communications between South Africa and the United States. The words *UFO*, *unknowns*, and *aliens* were another matter entirely. There were literally millions of calls containing those words. Most between private homes or to police departments. But again, nothing going to South Africa. And the Gibbses' telephone number did not show up as a call mentioning any of those words. Cell phones, text messaging, and the internet likewise did not show a connection to the Gibbses.

Chester then turned to the Central Intelligence Agency. He provided them with all the information he had on Carolyn and what he suspected about her. Within a day, Chester received the information he was seeking. Carolyn Gibbs was once Carolyn Judd, born to Sophia and William Judd, of Johannesburg. They were able to track her through the public school system and on to university records. She was an A+ student all throughout college and two graduate schools. Carolyn had advanced degrees in theoretical computing and theoretical physics.

The title of her graduate-degree thesis in computing was "The Application of Offensive Computer Invasion During National Emergencies." In reality, her thesis was a handbook on how to hack into the computer systems of other governments. It came as no surprise to Chester when he read the last entry detailing her education. She was a scholarship student sponsored by the Air Ministry of South Africa.

When Chester finished reading the CIA report, he picked up the telephone and ordered the immediate arrest of Carolyn. She was to be treated as a threat to the United States, and as such, if she resisted, Chester gave the order to suppress with prejudice any resistance. She was then to be brought to Space Command and kept in seclusion.

IS THERE A MOVIE ON THIS FLIGHT?

ONCE THEY WERE AIRBORNE, SCOTTY and Doreen settled back in their oversize leather chairs and relaxed. Scotty thought about the mission and the pleasure of seeing his friend and his friend's family again. But his silent repose was interrupted by Doreen when she launched into a barrage of questions. She wanted to know everything there was to know about the president and his family, about the trip itself, and about Zambia. With the patience of a man who was falling in love, Scotty answered each question in detail so as not to curb her enthusiasm. He realized that Doreen was on an adventure and was excited about the sudden turn of events in her life. But the mission had to come first. Changing the subject of the conversation, Scotty prompted Doreen to review with him what they hoped to accomplish and how they were going to do it. It was then Scotty realized that the trip couldn't have been organized so quickly if it weren't for her. Surely, she deserved to be a part of every facet of the search, but Scotty knew what she had planned for herself just wasn't going to happen.

Scotty knew he had to tell her without dampening her spirit. So he began by briefly explaining the social customs of Zambia and their importance in everyday life. He knew that Doreen would be invited by the president's wife to go on a tour of the national parks. Scotty explained that to decline such an offer would cause Edenausegboye to lose face in front of her family. Such an insult would not only jeopardize the mission but would also affect Scotty's relationship with the president. As Scotty talked, he looked for a telltale sign of disappointment on Doreen's face. Instead, he saw expressions of excitement. It appeared that Doreen was delighted at the prospect of seeing the country rather than being cooped up in a search aircraft for the next few days. Relieved, Scotty suggested that they try to get some sleep. After pushing their chairs into a reclining position, they both fell into a restful sleep.

I CANNOT TELL A LIE: I CUT DOWN THE CHERRY TREE

At 11:35 a.m., Carolyn was arrested at her place of employment, much to the horror of her coworkers. The entire contents of her desk were seized, as well as her computer. The entire operation took less than five minutes. Carolyn was handcuffed and roughly thrown into the back of a panel van and quickly driven away. Ten minutes later, she was at Space Command. Instead of taking the elevator, the agents physically pushed her up six flights of stairs. She was ushered into Chester's office, and each of her hands was then handcuffed to the arms of the chair she was sitting in. Chester sat at his desk and watched the drama unfold in front of him. He didn't smile or wince at the treatment she received. When the agents finished, they left the office, except for one who stood behind her with his gun drawn and pointed at her head. Carolyn wanted to scream, but she knew the day she dreaded had arrived. Her nightmare became reality.

Chester sat in silence for a moment. He wanted Carolyn to squirm. But instead, she just sat there staring back at him. With a smile on his face, Chester opened, "Carolyn, so nice to see you again." Getting up from behind his desk, Chester walked around it and sat on the front, across from Carolyn. He stared at her a moment and began, "As I see it, you have a choice to make. And you only have one chance to make that choice. You can cooperate with me and tell me everything, or you can refuse to talk. Should you choose silence, then I will find the deepest hole in the ugliest prison there is and throw you in it. When all is said and done, no one will ever hear from you again. The only company you will have are the cockroaches and an occasional rat that passes by. We could, of course, shoot you, but that is really messy, and besides, the carpet in here is new. We could take you down to the basement, though, and shoot you there. Yeah, that's a good idea. So what's it going to be? Cooperation, death, or being gnawed to death by rats in a dark cell? It's your call."

Carolyn lifted her head up and looked at Chester through teary eyes. In a very low voice, she spoke. "I'll cooperate."

"Okay, now, here is the way it is going to happen. I will ask you questions, you will answer them. After which you will take a polygraph test. If you lie to me or on the polygraph, you will immediately be taken from this place, never to be seen or heard from again. No one will ever come to your rescue because no one—and I mean *no one*—will ever know where you are," Chester threatened in a strong and somewhat-loud voice. He was really just playacting, as he was just as anxious as anyone to get the entire mess over with.

Carolyn nodded, indicating agreement to his terms. She sat erect in her chair but could not look Chester in the eye. She tried, however, to look out of the corner of her eye for the agent, but she couldn't see him. She guessed correctly that he was standing behind her with his weapon still out, ready to shoot her. "What is your name?" Chester began.

"My birth name is Carolyn Judd, and my married name is Gibbs," Carolyn answered in a nervous voice.

"Are you an agent of the South African government?" Chester got right to the point.

"I *was* an agent for the South African government, but I quit," Carolyn replied, trying desperately to maintain her composure.

"When did you first start working for them, and in what capacity?" Chester asked, calming down a little.

Carolyn momentarily gathered her thoughts and spoke with a slight trace of conviction in her voice. "I began working for the Air Ministry right out of school, after I received my physics degree. That was roughly a little over five years ago.

"Since I already had an advanced degree in computers, I was first assigned to the computer programing section. I wrote software for offensive weapons systems. After that—"

She was interrupted.

"What kind of weapons systems did you work on?" Chester hurriedly asked.

"South Africa has a small fleet of medium-range missiles. I rewrote the software programs to make them more accurate. I did this by tying the onboard computer system into the international global positioning satellites. This gave the weapons an accuracy to within ten feet from the center of the target. All these weapons were functioning when I was reassigned," Carolyn concluded.

"Before I interrupted you, what were you going to say?" Chester asked.

Carolyn was a bit more relaxed now. She was on familiar territory and began to speak with ease. "I was then assigned to a research program entitled Dragon Fire." Carolyn paused and knew that she had to tell all. "Dragon Fire was an attempt to launch standard artillery shells into the upper atmosphere and have them fall back to Earth directly over their targets. Instead of being able to fire a standard artillery shell accurately only twenty-five miles, South Africa would now be able to fire that same shell a little over three thousand miles."

"How?" Chester asked.

"The principle is based upon the long gun Saddam Hussein was trying to build before the Iraqi War in the tail end of the twentieth century. He was trying to build a gun—I believe it was called the ball gun—that would have been capable of hitting the United States. You know, it is like the long gun that your country has in Puerto Rico that you use to launch low-altitude satellites." Carolyn paused for a second, looking for some type of acknowledgment from Chester, but she received none. She could only continue, "Our approach was a little different. Instead of shooting a standard military round up a long barrel, we took that same standard shell and altered the explosive charge and added a small rocket motor. Essentially, the explosive charge in the shell fires off and launches the shell. When it reaches the apex or the projected highest point of its travel, the directional fins deploy and then a rocket motor fires. The shell enters space and comes back down over the target."

"Was it successful?" Chester asked.

"I was only with the program for eleven months, but yes, the initial tests were successful. But as far as I know, the project was canceled," Carolyn answered, paused, and then continued to tell all. "After that, I was assigned to head up an offensive computer warfare group called Octopus. Our job was to attack a target country on two fronts. We were to attack the economy of a country as well as the military computer systems of that country.

"For example, the economic attack would be directed at the governmental financial structure. In essence, we would empty their banks through electronic transfers. We would then attack the communication system of a country, followed by an attack on their energy grid. This would then be followed by an attack on their transportation system. Basically, we would scramble every computer system we could locate. The objective was to cause complete and total havoc.

"The same goals applied to the military attack. We would first target the communications network of the command structure. At the same time, another unit would begin to issue false orders to the targeted country's military and confuse their response capability.

"Admiral, I don't mean to imply that South Africa was thinking of utilizing this type of warfare. Just the opposite was true. My original directive was to defend against a computer-borne attack. I realized that in order to defend against such an attack, I would have to first know how to do it offensively. So with permission, I designed the best offensive system I could and then tore it apart to build a defensive system."

"Did South Africa ever use the system to attack a country?" Chester asked.

"No, but I was ordered to apply the system against Space Command," Carolyn stated, wishing this were a bad dream. She then continued, "I was ordered to hack into your computer system in order to see what you are really up to. I tried three times, but each time I was unsuccessful. In fact, when we launched the third attack, your security system must have recognized our footprint and immediately sent a worm into our system and caused over ten million dollars in damages. The air marshal then abandoned the idea of a computer attack.

"I was then directed by the air marshal to come to the United States. My assignment was to secure employment within your department and get the information that way. For some reason, the air marshal has a real obsession with your department. I know he's into UFOs and all, but what that has to do with spy satellites, I don't know."

"What happened then?" Chester asked, guessing the rest.

"When I arrived in Washington, I rented an apartment in a middle-income neighborhood and made all appearances as if I were a hardworking girl trying to take on the big city. I figured that the best way to snoop around in your department was to do it from the inside. So I applied for a job here and actually had two interviews, but that eventually failed. In the meantime, I was able to get a job at the Internal Revenue Service in the computer department. I did pretty good there and was promoted to programmer within two months. But I still had my assignment.

"For the next few months, I was able to kind of put your building under surveillance. I watched your employees to see where they ate lunch and followed some of them to Clancey's Bar, where they hung out after hours. Naturally, I started hanging out there, and then one day I signed up for a bus trip to Baltimore to go to a baseball game.

"It was on that trip that I met Sam. I felt immediately that my mission was over. I know that this may be hard to believe, but I fell in love with him that day. One thing led to another, and as you know, since you gave me away, we were married. I quit the IRS and took a job in a travel agency.

"After I had met Sam, I sent a report back to the air marshal and told him what he wanted to hear. That your department was looking into UFOs and conducting research into alien technology. And that was it," Carolyn concluded. She was actually relieved that the truth was all coming out. It felt as if a great weight was lifted off her shoulder.

"Did Sam ever discuss his work with you or, in any way, indicate what he does here?" Chester asked, looking for the slightest hint of a lie.

"No, Admiral. Sam never discusses his work. I asked him once what he does for you, and he told me that he has a boring job doing computer entry work and sometimes monitors the disposition of satellites. I never asked again, and Sam has never told me anything else.

"You have to understand something. The only thing that matters to me is that Sam and I are together. I couldn't care less what he does," Carolyn answered in a firm voice.

"Did the air marshal or any other representative of the South African government ever contact you again?" Chester asked, ready to conclude the questioning.

"Yes. They threatened me with death, imprisonment, exposure, and worst of all, they threatened to make life very difficult for my mother. I was able to fend them off, though. As you can see—"

Carolyn was interrupted by Chester.

"What do you have over them?" Chester anxiously asked.

Carolyn smiled slightly as she tried to readjust her sitting position, but the handcuffs restricted her movement. She then answered, "Before I left South Africa, I microdotted the entire files on Operation Fire Dragon, all the software I worked on for the weapons systems, and all the data relative to the computer warfare program. I did this because I knew that there was no way in hell that I would ever return to South Africa.

"When I worked at IRS, I managed to create an untraceable file on their computer system. The file contains copies of all the material I just mentioned. It is set up so that if I don't reprogram a clock in the file every sixty days, the information will be forwarded to every free government in the world and all the major newspapers throughout the world.

"When their threats didn't work, they sent an agent to see me. I gave him a copy of all the material and told him, unless they leave my mother, Sam, and myself alone, the material would be sent out. I haven't heard from them since."

"Okay, like I said, you are going to take a polygraph now, and if it's truthful, we'll talk. Before the test, I want you to give the agent all the details on how to recover the data on the IRS computer," Chester replied, quite impressed with the woman before him. "Agent, uncuff her and escort her to the examination room," Chester ordered and waited for them to leave.

Once Chester was alone, he realized that Carolyn was actually a gift from above. He would get his hands on an offensive-and-defensive computer system and a project that could shoot an artillery shell into space. He figured that one day both things might just be handy to have around. Most importantly, he had the air marshal between a rock and a hard place. Sure, he would call the air marshal and thank him for giving up his spy, but Chester would also tell him that the computer bomb Carolyn planted could not be found. The air marshal would get the message, cooperate, or suffer the consequences. His thoughts were interrupted when his intercom buzzed and he was informed that Lieutenant Gibbs was waiting in the outer office.

"Tell him to get comfortable," Chester ordered and then relaxed in his chair and began to think about Peggy.

WHO HAS MY SUNGLASSES?

A HALF HOUR BEFORE THEY WERE due to land, the flight attendant gently nudged Scotty and Doreen on their shoulders to wake them up and inform them that they were going to be landing in the Canary Islands shortly. Scotty stood up, stretched, and walked up to the cockpit to check on the pilots. Doreen remained in her seat and sipped on a cup of freshly brewed coffee as she checked on the weather data for Zambia for the next few days. She was relieved to learn that the weather was going to be clear and favorable for flying. Doreen was glad that something was going in their favor and hoped that it was a favorable omen for the trip.

Once Scotty was satisfied that all was well with the flight crew, he returned to his seat and idly looked out the window. In less than twenty minutes, they landed. Their aircraft was directed to the back side of the airfield, coming to rest in a large hangar. Arrangements had been made to service Scotty's aircraft as well as the two search planes, which were already there.

As Scotty stepped off the aircraft, he was immediately greeted by the big smiling grin of his longtime friend and confidant, Vinson. "Scotty, you son of a bitch, I can't believe that we are doing this!" Vinson stated in a cheerful voice. He then stepped back when he saw Doreen and declared, "You must be Doreen. Scotty told me that you were beautiful, but he didn't say that you are a goddess! Pleased to meet you."

Doreen blushed at Vinson's remark, turned her head ever so slightly downward, then raised it again, extended her hand, and shook Vinson's as she replied, "Pleased to meet you as well. Michael said that you were a charmer, but aren't you laying it on a bit thick so early in the day?"

"Ouch!" Vinson replied as he turned around and then introduced William Patterson, the chief of operations and his assistant, Bill Finningham, for the search aircraft, to Scotty and Doreen. After a brief exchange of pleasantries, they all decided to go to the terminal and get something to eat. Vinson, noting that Scotty was looking in the direction of the two 737 search aircraft, explained that the aircraft were being serviced under the watchful eyes of some men Admiral Morrison had sent to meet them when they landed. How they managed to arrive before the aircraft, Vinson could only guess, but he was impressed by the efficiency of the admiral. Scotty commented to Patterson that he was glad to see the "geological survey" markings on the aircraft. Patterson replied, "We aim to please. Your admiral is one persuasive son of a bitch, or one damn powerful person to get us here so quickly. I'm not complaining. My men and I are actually excited at being here. We are getting a chance to actually look for something rather than flying test patterns all the time."

"Yeah, the admiral is a son of a bitch, but a good son of a bitch. On top of that, he is one powerful person. He lives by the words *can do*, and anything less is unacceptable. The government of Zambia hasn't had any luck so far finding the aircraft. That's why you, your men, and your aircraft are so essential," Scotty explained.

Patterson began, "Mr. Scott—"

But he was interrupted by Scotty. "Please call me Scotty. Everybody does," Scotty pleaded.

"Okay, Scotty, but call me Bill," Patterson replied, then continued, "If that aircraft is there, we will find it for you."

"Good. Now, let's get something to eat!" Scotty ordered, then asked, "Bill, have your men been fed?"

"You won't believe it, but there is a Burger King in the airport. They are all over there, eating," Patterson replied.

"Who would believe it, a Burger King in the middle of the ocean!" Vinson interjected.

"Could we eat now?" Scotty ordered more than asked.

Vinson motioned to someone by one of the search aircraft, and a long black limousine pulled up next to them.

"I'm not even asking where you scrounged this from," Scotty commented.

As Vinson opened the back door to the car and motioned for them to get in, he stated, "My lady and my lords, your carriage awaits."

HOW MANY DID YOU SAY?

CHESTER WAS STILL SITTING IN his comfortable desk chair, daydreaming about Peggy, when from the back of his mind he remembered that he had to check on Scotty's request. Instead of just doing a satellite scan for Alpha Zuron radiation in Zambia, Chester decided to do a worldwide scan. He was curious to see just how many hits they would get at the one millirems (small unit of radiation measurement) reading. Then they would determine if other scans were necessary. Picking himself up out of his chair, Chester walked down six flights of stairs and entered the underground brain center of Space Command.

Chester walked over to the work area of Lieutenant Richard Cunningham. When Lieutenant Cunningham saw Chester approaching, he stood up and held a salute until Chester was in front of him and returned his salute. Chester was tired of reminding Cunningham not to salute every time he saw him, and so he just went along with the ritual.

When Chester asked Cunningham about the sweep, he was told that the results of the first sweep were being analyzed by the computer and should be printing shortly. Cunningham invited Chester to accompany him to the grid map printer, which could print a document sixty inches wide and whatever length the operator desired. As they both stood there waiting for something to happen, Cunningham filled the void with meaningless chatter about last night's football game. Chester would occasionally grunt in agreement to what Cunningham was saying, but he didn't have the slightest idea or interest in what the young lieutenant was saying. His mind was still on Carolyn and what would happen if she failed the polygraph. As if on cue, the printer whined to life and saved Chester the torture of being entertained while waiting.

Both men stood there watching as a map of the world was being printed. There was, however, an unexpected problem. There were thousands of red dots all over the map, which indicated a trace of Alpha Zuron radiation. Chester was surprised and spoke out loud. "You have to be kidding! There's that many trace elements of material that landed on Earth."

Lieutenant Cunningham was equally surprised at the amount of hits they obtained.

After looking at the map briefly, Cunningham replied, "Sir, at the level you ordered the trace, we picked up everything from small meteorites to who knows what. With this type of scan, we cannot differentiate one item from another."

Chester pondered the problem for minute and then asked, "Lieutenant, can we run scans based upon mass and not necessarily the degree of radiation emissions?"

"That's not a problem. I can use the radiation tag as a baseline and then reconfigure the computers to run a mass analysis. All the basic programming is done. All that I have to do is assign the mass value of the object. Where would you like me to start?" Cunningham replied in a curious tone.

"I want you to run an initial scan on a mass of at least ten tons. If that's successful, I want future runs with an increase of ten tons until you get no more hits. Then start running scans starting at nine tons all the way down to one ton," Chester ordered.

"Wow…that's some big meteorites, Admiral! Or are we looking for something else from space?" Cunningham asked but was met by a cold, hard stare from Chester. Cunningham realized that he had crossed the line. Almost stumbling over his words, he added, "I'll start immediately, sir." Cunningham then saluted the admiral and went back to his workstation.

Chester was left standing by the printer. He saw the look of resignation on the young lieutenant's face and realized that the kid was anxious to please and he had cut him off.

Chester walked over to Cunningham's workstation and thanked him for the excellent work he had done. He then told him that the other runs were a matter of national security and were urgently needed. To inspire him further, he instructed Cunningham not to discuss the matter with anyone. Chester's little pep talk had the desired effect— Cunningham attacked his work with a new zeal.

Chester returned to his office, taking the stairs again, in an attempt to stay in shape. That is, after he took two rest periods in his pursuit of physical perfection. Once back at his desk, Chester called Morrison to bring him up-to-date on the day's events.

Their conversation first covered the satellite runs that Cunningham was performing. Morrison was particularly interested and wondered what the runs would top out at. When it came time to discuss the Gibbs matter, Chester quite bluntly told Morrison that Carolyn Gibbs would be a valuable asset to the Colorado Project. He then detailed what she had told him. Morrison was a bit more reserved about his enthusiasm and suggested that the results of the polygraph would speak for itself.

Morrison then asked Chester what he was going to do about her husband. Chester explained that Lieutenant Gibbs was waiting in the outer office and that he would talk to him shortly. Chester had already decided that Samuel Gibbs would also have to take a polygraph, and if he passed, he could stay. Chester's real test would be if he tendered his resignation. If he did so, then Lieutenant Gibbs was an honorable man worthy of saving. Morrison agreed, but he was most interested in Carolyn despite the fact that he passed her off while Chester was trying to promote her to him. Morrison instructed Chester to call him when both of the polygraphs were over. He quickly hung up the telephone before Chester could say goodbye. *A man on a mission,* Chester thought to himself and then hung up the telephone.

I GUESS THAT HE HAD A BAD DAY

As Scotty, Doreen, Vinson, and Bill Patterson were walking through the terminal building in search of something to eat, Scotty eyed the Burger King. Scotty had hoped to share a meal with the search crew before the work started. He thought it would be a good way to break the ice so that they all could work more cohesively together. When they reached the Burger King, Scotty was disappointed when he saw that everyone had finished eating.

Everyone was just sitting around, talking.

Scotty told Bill that he wanted to introduce himself to the crew and thank them for being there. Bill stood in the entranceway to the Burger King and called the men to order. He asked for their attention for the next few minutes as he wanted to introduce the people who would be signing their paychecks. Bill first introduced Scotty as the overall director of the operation. He then turned his attention to Vinson. Saving the best for last, he then introduced Doreen. After a few drawn-out seconds of complimentary whistles and hubba-hubbas, Bill settled them down again.

Scotty began in a light laughing tone, "Well, I'm glad that you all approve of Ms. Stark's presence. I think that you will find her a most capable individual possessive of advanced academic degrees that are too numerous to mention. Besides, I can't even pronounce half of them." Receiving light laughter in return, Scotty continued, "But seriously, we have a very important job to accomplish over the next couple of days. I want you to know how much I appreciate your presence here. I am assured that your employer will likewise not forget your dedication and personal sacrifice. I am sorry that I had to pull you away from your homes and family on such short notice, but time may be running out for the passengers of the downed aircraft. As Vinson has told you, all attempts so far to locate the aircraft have been unsuccessful. The job has therefore fallen to us. I wish you all good luck, and let's find that aircraft!"

As Scotty concluded his remarks, an agitated voice shouted above the din of the good cheer, "Excuse me, but why in the hell are we on the other side of the world, giving help to people we don't even know? I had plans for this weekend, and instead, I'm sitting in a restaurant on an island I couldn't care less about."

Scotty's face tightened a bit as he fought back the anger that was rising within him. He knew that he had to rise to this challenge and win; otherwise, he would lose the respect of the men and women on the search teams. Carefully he responded, "Sir, we are here to assist the government of Zambia in locating any surviving passengers of a downed airliner. Just maybe someone is alive and praying that someone is coming to rescue them. That, sir, is the reason that we are here. If you were that survivor, you would be hoping that a group of people, as is assembled here, would come to your aid. I can think of no better sacrifice one can make for his fellow man than to—"

Scotty was interrupted by the angry voice again.

"Well, I'm not waiting to be rescued. I know where I am. I'm right here on this fucking island!"

Scotty was doing his very best to maintain his patience but felt like he was about to lose his cool. In a deliberate, controlled voice, Scotty stated, "Sir—and I use the term lightly—I learned a long time ago that a person such as yourself, a selfish son of a bitch, is a danger to fly with. Not only to yourself, but to the dedicated crew that must fly with you. You—and I hesitate to call you *sir*—are relieved. You will not be going with us."

Vinson, who had been standing alongside of Scotty, made a quick call to the agent in charge of security for the aircraft. He requested that two agents come to the restaurant immediately. Vinson knew from experience that Scotty was about to walk over to the man, grab him by the neck, and throw him out. It would be better if the agents were to do it rather than Scotty, Vinson thought.

"You can't fire me, you bastard! Who the hell do you think you are?" the angry voice shouted out.

Scotty took a step toward the man, but Vinson grabbed his forearm. That halted Scotty, and he looked at Vinson for a moment as if to thank him then turned back toward the man. While trying even harder to control himself, Scotty answered, "I'll tell you who I am. I'm the wrong person to piss off."

Just as Scotty finished talking, the two agents arrived. They rushed over to the angry man, each grabbing him by one arm, and escorted him toward the exit to the restaurant. The man, not to be outdone, shouted out, "You fucking asshole! I'll kill you when I get a chance! Who the fuck do you think you are?"

Scotty walked over to the man, stared at him straight in the eyes, and said in full earshot of everyone, "Agents, present this excuse of a human being to El Captain Perez. Tell him that Michael Scott requests that he be locked up. Then ask Captain Perez if he would do me the honor of dining with me at the cafeteria. You will find his office one level down." Just to rile up the man a little more, Scotty added, "You know, they still break large rocks into small ones in prison here. You're going to be breaking enough rocks to build a new road. Oh, and by the way, don't drop the soap in the prison shower. You never know what might happen." Scotty then turned away and faced the rest of the aircrew. Before he could say anything, the entire restaurant erupted in applause.

It appeared that the altercation had a positive effect on the search crews. Each member of the search crew walked up to Doreen, Scotty, and Vinson and introduced themselves. Some thanked Scotty for getting rid of the man. Once the crew were on their way back to their aircraft, Scotty asked Bill Patterson what had just happened. Patterson explained that the man was a real pain in the butt, always complaining about everything and second-guessing every order and directive. While Patterson had tried on several occasions to fire the man, he seemed to have a guardian angel who protected him. Scotty then asked what the man's job was and was told that he was an equipment technician. Patterson went on to explain that his absence would mean an added workload for some members of the crew but they would willingly handle the extra work now that the bad apple was gone.

As they then walked to the cafeteria, Scotty explained that Captain Perez was an old friend of his. Scotty had wanted to stop in and visit with Captain Perez before they departed but guessed that he would be busy now since he had sent him some business. Scotty said that he would stop in on him after lunch.

When they arrived at the cafeteria thirty minutes later, after allowing Doreen to window-shop in the airport stores, Scotty put a wide grin on his face when he eyed old Hector Perez standing at the entrance. Mentally, Scotty noted that Hector was still short and still robust, but he sure looked impressive as hell in his uniform. While Hector's uniform was meant to impress and immediately establish his authority, he had more brass on him than an Army general.

Hector spotted Scotty and, with a big smile on his face, walked up to him. They exchanged a hug and kiss on each other's cheek, the traditional European greeting that American men find uncomfortable. "Scotty, you old devil, why didn't you tell me that you were on the island?" Hector asked.

"Hector, it's great to see you. I just wish that I could stay a while. Unfortunately, we are on our way to Zambia to search for a missing aircraft, and time is of the essence. I'm sorry that instead I brought you some trouble," Scotty greeted his friend.

"No trouble at all. That man is a most unhappy person. Your agents told me that he threatened your life—a very unpleasant business. Rest assured that he will receive free accommodations for a very long time on our island paradise," Hector replied while slightly shaking his head back and forth.

"I would appreciate it if you could hold him overnight, and I'll have those two agents escort him home," Scotty asked.

"If you insist, but I think that he should be prosecuted. We do not take such behavior lightly here. But if you insist, I'll release him in the morning," Hector replied and then looked over at Doreen. "Now, who is this Venus standing next to you?" Hector asked.

"I'm sorry. Hector, I'd like you to meet Ms. Doreen Stark. And this is Vinson, who is assisting in the search. And this is Bill Patterson, the overall director of the search aircraft," Scotty introduced everyone.

Hector shook hands with Vinson and Bill but turned his attention toward Doreen. After kissing her on the cheek and hugging her, he interlocked his arm in hers and, while leading her toward the cafeteria, said, "Now, before you marry this old Pirate friend of mine, let me tell you some stories about his misspent youth."

As Hector and Doreen entered the restaurant, Scotty, Vinson, and Bill were left behind momentarily, staring after them. Quickly they caught up to them as Hector began one of his stories. All during lunch, Hector kept them entertained, at Scotty's expense, with stories of their many adventures, most of which ended in disaster.

After an hour of laughter and some excellent wine, it was time to leave. Hector drove them back to the aircraft and said his goodbyes. He did manage to extract a promise from Scotty. Scotty promised that he would return with Doreen for an extended vacation sometime in the near future. As Scotty and Doreen were about to board their aircraft, Hector hugged

Scotty and Doreen wished him well. Turning to Doreen, Hector hugged her as well and kissed her on the cheek and then said loud enough for Scotty to hear, "Now, don't go marrying this scalawag and forget to invite me to the wedding."

"Hector, we are not even—"

Doreen had tried to reply but was interrupted by Hector. "Don't tell that to an ole Latin lover like myself. I have eyes, you know. I see the way you look at each other!" Hector answered, sure of himself.

"Thanks, Hector!" Scotty called out as he stepped aside to allow Doreen to enter the aircraft.

"Catch you on the return trip!" Hector called out above the noise of the aircraft engines.

While Vinson and Bill walked over to their aircraft, Scotty went aboard his aircraft and sat down. As the plane began to taxi for takeoff, Doreen turned to Scotty and asked, "Why does he think that we are getting married?"

"I don't know. It must be the climate and the romantic surroundings. Besides, Hector is an old romantic," Scotty replied as he looked out of the window and saw the two search aircraft following his plane. After takeoff, Scotty relaxed and took a short nap, while Doreen tried to imagine what was going to happen next.

I THINK YOU DIALED THE WRONG NUMBER

After finishing his conversation with Morrison, Chester wanted to make one more telephone call. It was time to call the air marshal. Fumbling through the papers on his desk, Chester found the number and, with a sly grin on his face, dialed the telephone. When the air marshal answered, Chester began by inquiring about his family and then quickly got to the point. "I wanted to let you know that I have cleared up the matter you told me about regarding that intruder. She was picked up and interrogated. Boy, what a story she had to tell! The most interesting part was when she gave me a little package detailing her computer expertise while she was in your service. Why, Air Marshall, your shop has been up to some very interesting things."

"What…what would that be, Admiral?" the air marshal asked with dread in his voice.

Almost laughing, Chester replied, "Oh, the games people play over the internet!"

"I assure you, Admiral, we play for defensive reasons only. Basically, it is only for training purposes," the air marshal quickly replied while silently cursing to himself.

Chester decided to get this over with fast. He had to let the venerated air marshal know, in no uncertain terms, just who was in charge. "Air Marshal, this is the way it is and how it is going to be. Our copy of your computer game will remain secured, unless you try to engage my command in a computer game again. If that should happen, your material and plans will be released throughout the world. You'll be a very famous man because you will be in every major newspaper in every country.

"There is a downside, though. Carolyn's plans are still out in cyberspace somewhere, waiting to go off as well. You could say that it is sort of like a backup plan.

"There is one more thing. Sometime in the future, Carolyn may become our liaison to your department. This will allow her to visit her mother on occasion. One other point of information. Should anything—I mean *anything*—happen to Carolyn or her mother, you will be front-page news. At that point, your country will be very alone in the world. Is there any part of this you don't understand?"

"I understand completely, Admiral. I will comply with your wishes. I feel like I just made a deal with the devil, though," the air marshal replied with resignation in his voice.

"You mean *devils*." Chester paused and then added, "You know, I almost forgot. I wanted to ask you how Fire Dragon was coming. I'm quite sure that we can incorporate it into the negotiations for the aircraft we spoke about. What do you think?"

Sheepishly the air marshal replied, "Speaking for my country, we will be more than glad to supply that material to you free of cost."

"You take care of yourself, Air Marshal. I'm sure that we will have a very beneficial relationship in the future. Goodbye, Air Marshal," Chester declared and then quickly hung up the telephone—a trick he learned from Morrison.

"Goodbye, Admiral," the air marshal stated as he hung up the telephone visibly shaken.

ARE YOU REALLY THE PRESIDENT?

As their aircraft prepared to land in Lusaka, Doreen, being concerned about meeting the president of a country and, more importantly, friends of Scotty, excused herself. Grabbing her makeup bag, Doreen headed for the bathroom. Although most people who saw Doreen were readily impressed with her natural beauty and skin tone, she wanted to make last-minute adjustments to her mascara and lipstick. When Doreen emerged and sat back down, Scotty could only think to himself, *My God, she is beautiful and intelligent to boot. What a killer combination!*

Once their aircraft touched down, it was directed to the far side of the field and parked next to a large empty hangar. Almost immediately, a long black limousine pulled up close to the aircraft. The president and his family emerged and stood in the heat of the day, waiting for Scotty.

Unable to curb his enthusiasm any longer, Scotty bent down, looked out of the window of the aircraft, and upon seeing his friends, began waving. The president and his wife likewise waved when they spotted him. The children, however, seemed a bit confused and turned to their mother for help. Edenausegboye bent down and pointed at Scotty. The children then immediately began to wave and were about to dart to the aircraft when their mother grabbed them by their arms and restrained them. Scotty then called Doreen over to the window. Once she looked out, Doreen recognized the president and his family from the photograph of them Scotty displayed in his living room. Not to be left out, Doreen then also began waving. When Mawuli first saw Doreen, a questioned look appeared on his face. He then pointed at the plane and looked at his mother. He was obviously asking who Doreen was. Edenausegboye then bent over and answered his question. Mawuli then turned back toward the aircraft and began waving again, but not as enthusiastically.

Once the engines of the aircraft shut down, the flight attendant opened the doorway and invited Scotty and Doreen to deplane. As Scotty approached the doorway, he stood aside for Doreen to leave first. "No, Michael, you go first," Doreen pleaded.

"Why, ma'am, I'm just trying to be the perfect gentleman," Scotty declared in a lighthearted tone and then asked, "Doreen, why are you so nervous? Are you okay?"

"Yes…it's just that I've never met the president of a country before, and I so want to make a good impression on your friends," Doreen replied.

Scotty, with a kind and concerned look on his face, replied, "Doreen, just be yourself. They are just like you and me. I'm quite sure that they will find you as charming as I have. Besides, you sure did charm the pants off Vinson and Hector."

"Well, I don't know. They are not the president of a country," Doreen added.

"Doreen, just be yourself. You'll do great," Scotty replied as he winked.

"Okay, Michael, but just don't leave me alone. Do I curtsy or anything?" Doreen hastily inquired.

"No, just shake hands. And relax!" Scotty replied.

Doreen then ducked her head out of the doorway and stepped down the three short steps to the runway. Scotty was close behind. Once Scotty was out of the aircraft, Titilayo and Mawuli ran to him, shouting, "Uncle Scotty!" Scotty knelt down on one knee and outstretched his arms; the children excitedly ran into them. After an exchange of numerous kisses, Scotty stood up with the children in his arms. He then turned toward Doreen and introduced his precious bundles to her. The children each replied with a cautious hello while they tightened their grip around Scotty's neck. After looking Doreen over from head to toe, Titilayo asked, "Are you going to marry my Uncle Scotty?"

Doreen was surprised by the question but recovered quickly and replied, "Now, what is a beautiful young girl like you asking a question like that for? Besides, we are just friends, and I work for your Uncle Scotty." Then she reached out and tickled her young inquisitor.

Sensing no danger to her world, Titilayo reached out for Doreen to hold her.

Doreen immediately took advantage of the situation and took her from Scotty. Doreen was immediately rewarded with a kiss on her cheek from her passenger.

"Oh my god!" Scotty exclaimed, pretending that he had forgotten something. "I forgot. We have to go back on the plane and get the presents."

"Presents!" Mawuli shouted.

"Yes, presents. Will you help me, Mawuli?" Scotty expressed.

"You betcha, Uncle Scotty!" Mawuli cried out as he struggled to free himself from Scotty's hold.

Scotty and Mawuli climbed into the aircraft, and together they opened a closet door. As Scotty reached in and took out the first orange flight bag, Mawuli took it from his hands and ran out of the airplane. "Presents!" he shouted as he left the aircraft. Scotty then grabbed the second bag and likewise left the aircraft. Scotty also shouted when he emerged, but it had nothing to do with presents. "Slow down, Mawuli!" Scotty pleaded.

While Scotty was in the aircraft, the president and Edenausegboye had already introduced themselves to Doreen. The nervous Doreen, who a few minutes ago didn't want to be left alone with strangers, seemed perfectly relaxed. She was telling her willing audience about the trip and the beauty of Zambia as she saw it from the air. The president politely excused himself, walked over to Scotty, and hugged him while saying, "Scotty, I am so glad to see you. It has been too long, my friend."

"Yes, it has been too long, Mr. President. I have missed you and your lovely family," Scotty replied.

"Will you quit addressing me by Mr. President? Call me by my given name, Asukile," the president pleaded.

"Yes, Mr. President," Scotty answered while laughing.

"Oh, shut up, you two. Now, give me a big hug and kiss, Scotty!" Edenausegboye commanded.

As everyone was exchanging greetings and talking, the two search aircraft arrived.

They were directed to park in the large hangar, which would serve as their search headquarters. Asukile then introduced Kamau to Doreen. Doreen recognized his name as the individual she had made all the arrangements with before they had left New York. Within earshot of the president, Doreen praised Kamau for his kindness and valued assistance.

Doreen then asked if she could introduce Kamau to the flight crews and to Vinson, the coordinator of the search teams. Asukile gratefully gave her permission and added that Kamau would see to the needs of the people who had come to help his country.

When Doreen returned, she, Scotty, and the president's family entered the limousine and proceeded to the presidential home. Along the way, Mawuli could not take his eyes off the orange bags. To his repeated questions as to when the presents could be opened, the president would patiently reply, "When it's time, Mawuli, when it's time."

BOY, I WISH TODAY WERE A HOLIDAY!

As days go, this was not what Chester would characterize as a great one.

Although it did have one highlight: he sure enjoyed that call to the air marshal. The downside of the day was the plain and simple fact that he really liked Carolyn as a person. He had been deeply honored when she had asked him to give her away at the altar when she and Samuel Gibbs were married. Chester wasn't proud of the fact that he had threatened her life, but he realized that it was just the job and service to his country.

Chester longed for the simpler days when he executed the orders of his superiors.

But now he was giving the orders that had an indirect impact on the personal lives of those under his command. After allowing himself a few more minutes of moral self-examination, Chester decided that the day must go on no matter what might happen.

Reaching across his desk, Chester called his secretary and directed her to show Lieutenant Gibbs in.

Lieutenant Gibbs stood erect before Chester and saluted. Chester stood up and returned his salute and directed him to sit down. Chester paused and then began, "Lieutenant, as you know, from time to time, all personnel are subject to passing a polygraph exam. This is done in order to determine if the individual has in some way violated the National Secrets Act. I know that this is the second time that you will be taking the test, and as I told you before, the secret is to just relax.

"Before you take the exam, I am giving you the opportunity to state here and now any indiscretion you may have made regarding your assignment in Space Command. So I ask you, Do you have anything to report?"

"No, sir," Lieutenant Gibbs answered with conviction in his voice.

"Nothing, Lieutenant? Have you ever told your wife what your real assignment is here? Or anyone else, for that matter?" Chester asked.

"No, sir. I just told my wife that I monitor satellites," Gibbs answered.

"Okay, Lieutenant, return to my outer office and wait until you are called," Chester ordered.

After Gibbs left, Chester called Lieutenant Cunningham to check on the satellite runs. Cunningham informed him that the ten-ton run was completed, and showed 367 hits. Chester was a little amazed at that number but realized that the run would have picked up spacecraft that had returned to Earth and probably some very old meteor residue that struck the Earth hundreds, if not thousands, of years ago. But the number seemed awfully large. Before hanging up, Chester asked him to call when the runs zeroed out at no returns.

For the next hour, Chester busied himself with the day-to-day business of running his command. This was the stuff that Chester disliked. Approving leave requests, reviewing purchase orders, or reviewing attendance reports were not exactly the "adventure" Chester was promised when he joined the Navy. But it is the little things that make the bigger things work. His journey into the routine was interrupted, much to his relief, by the naval agent who administered the polygraph to Carolyn.

Chester was delighted to learn that Carolyn passed the polygraph. Now, Chester knew that she could be saved. But there was still the test that her husband would have to pass. Chester ordered that Carolyn be detained in an empty office, be given something to eat, and remain in the office under the watchful eye of an agent while her husband was tested. With a smile on his face, Chester dismissed the agent and then put his feet up on his desk and relaxed. He withdrew a cigar from the inside pocket of his jacket and tumbled it around in his fingers. Chester wanted to have a celebration smoke, but the words *smoke-free environment* echoed in his mind. Frustrated, he returned the cigar to his pocket.

BUT I DON'T HAVE A THING TO WEAR

Once at the presidential home, Scotty and Doreen were given adjoining bedrooms on the second floor. The decor was simple, but functional. Their rooms each had a queen-size bed with a hand-carved bed board decorated in the native fauna of the country. Next to the beds were simple nightstands with lamps made out of wood and what appeared to be shades made of bark from a limewood tree. Against the far wall of the bedroom was an armoire made of highly polished tigerwood. To complete the room, two chairs were placed around a small circular table. The table was placed in front of French doors, which led to a private balcony. The balconies overlooked the extensive tropical gardens in the back of the house. As an added conveyance, each room also had a private bathroom and shower. The walls were decorated with numerous photographs of the wildlife of Zambia.

When Scotty and Doreen were alone in their rooms, their thoughts were of each other. They both dreamed about what it would be like to be with the other. But those dreams were not for now. They were there to accomplish a mission, and that had to come first.

After showering, Doreen had a dilemma. The president had told them that dinner was to be informal. To Doreen, there was informal/formal, casual-dress clothing, and then there was really informal, jeans and a T-shirt. Wanting to make just the right impression, Doreen left her room in a short camisole and a pair of purple thong underwear. She marched the twenty or so feet to Scotty's door and knocked.

Within seconds, Scotty opened the door. Before Scotty could speak, Doreen said, "Scotty, I—"

But she stopped speaking almost immediately as her audience of one had a strange look on his face.

When Scotty opened the door, he was not expecting the sight he beheld. His mouth dropped open and his eyes widened. After gazing upon Doreen's face, Scotty's eyes looked down upon her body. He first saw the nipples of her breasts erect and hard against the sheerness of her camisole. Pressing onward, his eyes followed the curves of her body downward past her thin muscular legs, right down to her toes.

Doreen, unaccustomed to this look on Scotty's face, looked down at herself. Upon realizing what she was wearing, Doreen let out a scream and ran back to her room, closing the door firmly behind her. She leaned against the closed door for a moment. With the open palm of her hand, Doreen slapped herself on the forehead and hollered out, "Stupid, stupid, stupid!" A moment later, Doreen suddenly smiled at herself as she was quite pleased with her little indiscretion. Doreen was still smiling as she crossed the room and slipped on a long light-blue linen dress. When she looked at herself in the full-length mirror, Doreen was disappointed that the panty line of her thong showed. Bending over slightly, she removed her underwear. Hearing a knocking on the door, Doreen threw her thong on the bed and answered the door.

Doreen was pleased to see Scotty standing there with a smile on his face. As they walked together down the hallway, Scotty complimented her on her dress. Doreen coyly asked if he really liked her dress. Scotty answered, "Yes, of course, you look absolutely beautiful." But being unable to resist the temptation, he added, "But I have to say that I had no objection to your first choice. It might have raised some eyebrows, but what the hell." Doreen laughed slightly and then, as they started down the stairs, slapped Scotty across the stomach. Scotty lost his balance momentarily, but he just had to say, "It sure was casual!" Not to be outdone, Doreen replied, "Best thing you have ever seen!" as she winked at him. Scotty stopped walking and was left speechless for a second. Together they walked into the kitchen arm in arm, smiling and laughing with each other.

WHO, WHAT, WHERE, HOW BIG—YOU HAVE TO BE KIDDING!

CHESTER WAS STILL THINKING ABOUT that cigar when his telephone rang. He had been thinking of going outside to smoke, but somehow the thought of an admiral standing around in the front of the building, smoking, didn't sound right. Slowly Chester reached for the telephone. The disappointment in his voice changed to excitement when he heard Lieutenant Cunningham's voice on the other end. Chester anxiously asked where the satellite runs had zeroed in.

He was surprised when Lieutenant Cunningham told him that after a run at 320,000 tons, the next run was zero. With his heart beating a little faster now, Chester asked just how many returns there were at that level. He didn't know what to expect, but one thing he didn't expect was the answer he received. Chester thought that perhaps millions of years ago, a meteorite that large could have hit the Earth, and if it contained metal or iron, it would account for the reading. When Cunningham said that there were four returns at that level, Chester swallowed hard and asked where they were. Cunningham read with deliberate slowness: "One is in Siberia, one in Chile, one in the North Pole, and one off the coast of Hawaii." "Just how big are these things?" Chester asked but was disappointed when Cunningham related that it would be hard to estimate but they would appear to be at least a few hundred feet long.

Chester realized that these were crashed UFOs. What worried him was the realization that one was in Russia. He visualized that the Russians were probably taking one apart right this minute. But then he knew that if they had one and were working on one, it would be impossible to keep such a secret. Getting back to the present, Chester asked if any of the runs showed anything in or around Zambia. He thought that since the UFO brought the aircraft into itself, there would be radiation traces on the aircraft, assuming, of course, that the aliens had later put the aircraft down somewhere.

Chester held on, as he could hear Cunningham sorting through some papers. After a few minutes, Cunningham came back on the line and announced that he had one reading of thirty tons that didn't show up on the forty-ton run. There was also a faint return, but the reading was too weak to accurately determine its size and location. Cunningham went on to explain that the thirty-ton-plus return was located off the coast of Angola on a direct line from coastal town called Tombua. Cunningham quickly added that the object was in international waters and its exact location had been plotted. Realizing that it was probably the missing airliner, Chester directed Cunningham to plot all the returns onto topographical and ocean maps in categories of tonnage. Chester added that it was a matter of utmost urgency vital to the interests of the nation. Once again, he gave Cunningham a sense of inspiration. Cunningham answered with a strong "Yes, sir!" and went back to work kind of wondering what was really going on.

After hanging up, Chester went on the internet and was able to determine that an Antonov-12 weighs approximately 30.8 tons, with a maximum weight of 38.6 tons. It seemed to Chester that the object in the ocean off Angola might indeed be the missing aircraft. In order to confirm this, they would have to somehow get a look at it.

Feeling confident that Cunningham had found the missing airliner,

Chester thought that he should call Morrison and tell him the news. But it was too late to recall Scotty, so he decided to let it go until later. He was beginning to think about that cigar again when his telephone rang again. Chester was told by the polygrapher that Lieutenant Gibbs also passed his exam. Chester directed him to bring Gibbs into his office.

When Gibbs arrived, Chester invited him to sit down. Chester remained standing while he started talking. "Lieutenant, I am pleased to inform you that you passed your polygraph examination. However, there is an additional matter that we must discuss. It seems that a few years ago you crossed paths with an espionage agent of a foreign government. That agent is in this building, and I am going to give you the opportunity to confront this individual. I want you to accompany a naval investigative agent and see this individual. You are to determine if, in fact, there was a breach of security. After that, I want you back here and report any security violation that may have occurred. I want to be able to conclude this matter immediately."

Gibbs began, "Sir, I would never, under any circumstances, compromise the Navy or your command. I—"

But he was interrupted by Chester.

"I know, Lieutenant. Your polygraph bears that out, but I need you to see this person and determine if, in fact, there might have been a breach. You are dismissed," Chester answered and waited as Gibbs left his office.

PLEASE PASS THE SALT

DINNER THAT NIGHT WAS A welcomed relief for all. For Scotty and Doreen, it was the best part of a very long day. For the president and his family, it was relief that their friend had returned. Doreen took immediate notice that Scotty was regarded much more than as a friend. It was as if he were an immediate member of the family. She also fell under the charm of the family. The time passed in a cloud of laughter and joy. When Scotty saw that Doreen was relaxed and joining in the fun, he was happy. Happy to see her as she really was and not the officious naval officer she would have most believe that she was. He felt close to her and hoped that the feeling might, in some way, be returned. But time itself would be the judge of that, he resolved.

Doreen was enjoying herself. She had come halfway around the world to visit with people that made her feel as if she, too, belonged here. Doreen realized, for the first time in her life, that friendship is not something that has a price, but rather, it is a love of sorts that is unconditional, in that no one seeks or demands something from the other.

During the course of dinner, Doreen would constantly steal glances at Scotty. She saw the genuineness of his character. She wondered why feelings for him were growing within her. Although they had only known each other for almost two days, it seemed to Doreen as if they had shared a lifetime together. A few times she had caught Scotty looking at her, and Doreen felt arousal. She tried to fight these feelings, but Doreen was beginning to realize that it was a losing battle. Of one thing she was sure: Scotty would belong to her. But she had to find out if he felt the same way. Doreen thought that he might, and she more than desired it so.

As dinner was nearing the end, Mawuli began his endless assault on the pivotal question regarding the presents. His mother reminded him that dessert was yet to be served, and after that, perhaps if he was good, they would open the presents. Titilayo excused herself from the table once the adults finished eating. Scotty asked if she was all right, and Edenausegboye told him that she had worked all day baking him a chocolate mousse cake. Shortly, Titilayo re-entered the dining room carefully carrying the cake. She placed it down in front of Scotty, who commented over and over how good it looked. He then picked her up, sat her on his knee, and gave her a big kiss on the cheek. Scotty then cut the cake while Titilayo distributed the pieces and then returned to Scotty's lap.

Together they enjoyed the delicacy she had prepared. Not to be left out, Mawuli picked up his cake, carefully carried it around the table, and also sat on his Uncle Scotty's lap.

During dessert, Asukile asked Scotty what his plans were for the next day. Scotty explained that he intended to fly with the search aircraft during the first sweep of the country. Edenausegboye interrupted him and stated that on the second day, he had a most important engagement at Victoria Falls. As Scotty looked at her with a puzzled look on his face, Edenausegboye simply stated, "Family picnic!" At the sound of those two words, the children let out a loud "Yeah!" with Doreen joining in.

With a slight laugh in his voice, Scotty continued, "On the second day, I have plans of going on a picnic to Victoria Falls." This led to a second loud cheer from the children, but this time the cheer was led by Doreen.

Edenausegboye then turned her attention toward Doreen. She informed Doreen that she had made plans to show her the country.

"While Scotty is off doing his flying thing." Pretending to offer slight protest, Doreen explained that she was there to assist Michael, but enthusiastically, with a broad grin on her face, she answered that she would love to see the country. With the plans concluded, everyone finished their dessert, while Mawuli continued to eye the gift bags in the corner of the room.

When the dessert dishes were cleared away, Mawuli ran over to the gift bags and dragged them to Scotty. Reaching into one bag, Scotty withdrew a very large box. After pretending that he didn't know whom it was for, Scotty placed it in the outstretched arms of Mawuli. As Mawuli tore at the wrapping paper, Scotty and Doreen passed out the rest of the presents. Mawuli let out a big cheer and held up the two remote-controlled cars for all to see as the others opened their gifts. Titilayo was equally excited by her gift and ran to Scotty and gave him a kiss and a hug. She then did likewise to Doreen, who was surprised at the gesture but recognized that a simple kiss marked her acceptance into the extended circle of the family.

Titilayo then looked at her mother and asked her if it was time now. Receiving a nod, Titilayo disappeared again and returned with two presents, which she presented to Scotty and Doreen.

Doreen, caught up in the emotion of the moment, tore at her present as eagerly as Mawuli had. When Doreen opened the velvet box, she looked upon the most beautiful emerald she had ever seen. Carefully she removed the emerald, which was on a golden chain, from the box as tears welled in her eyes. She offered a very large thank-you and politely protested that she couldn't accept such a gift, but Edenausegboye cut her off. "Nonsense! You are a guest of my country, and this is just an expression of thanks from us. Besides, Scotty chooses his friends carefully. If you are here with Scotty, then you are special to him, and therefore special to us."

Doreen stood up with teary eyes and walked over to Edenausegboye and, while giving her a hug, said, "Thank you! You and your family are special to me too." Turning around, Doreen sought out the assistance of Titilayo to put the necklace on. Scotty then opened his gift and was surprised to receive a pilot's chronometer watch. On the back of the watch was a simple engraving: "To Scotty, our brother, with love." Followed by all the family members' names. Mawuli, of course, removed Scotty's other watch and placed the new one on his wrist.

Asukile, Mawuli, and Scotty disappeared into the hallway to play with the cars, as Edenausegboye, Titilayo, and Doreen went to the computer room and loaded the new software. After an hour of play, the adults chased the children off to bed. But not before an ample supply of hugs and kisses was exchanged between Titilayo, Mawuli, and the four adults.

Once the children were safe and snug in their beds, the adults shared a sherry and some light talk about the day. Scotty began to feel very tired and expressed that it was time for him to get some sleep. The rest of the adults agreed and decided to call it a night.

As Scotty and Doreen climbed the stairs back up to the second floor, Doreen commented that she just loved his friends. Scotty expressed that he loved them dearly and they apparently felt the same way toward her. Arriving at her door, Scotty gently kissed Doreen on the lips. Doreen anxiously returned this slight show of emotion, and then they said good night as they entered their individual rooms. Scotty went over to his bed to lie down for a moment but fell fast asleep. Doreen climbed into bed thinking about Scotty and the exciting day she had had. Thoughts of the mission were the furthest things from her mind as she fell asleep.

ANYBODY SEE A SPY AROUND?

Lieutenant Gibbs followed the naval agent to a small office at the end of the hall.

After the agent unlocked the door, he stood back and let the lieutenant enter. As he entered the office, Gibbs stopped dead in his tracks when he saw Carolyn sitting in a chair, crying. He slowly walked over to Carolyn, knelt down beside her, kissed her on the forehead, and asked her what she was doing there. After Gibbs asked the question, the answer came to him in a millisecond. Emotionally it hit him as if he had been run over by a truck.

Gibbs stood up, turned his back on his wife, and saw the agent standing in the corner of the room. He turned back toward Carolyn and asked if their marriage was a sham or part of some kind of plan on her part. Carolyn stood up, walked over to her husband, took his hands in hers, and directed him to sit down. Carolyn then began to explain what she never had the courage to tell him but had wanted to so often.

Chester, of course, was watching and listening to the whole scene over a closed-circuit video connection. He watched as they cried together, then hugged and eventually kissed. After almost an hour, Gibbs asked the agent if they could see the admiral. Chester sat up erect, turned off the monitor, and prepared for their arrival.

Once in Chester's office, Lieutenant Gibbs asked for permission to speak. Chester nodded his approval, and Gibbs began, "Admiral, I would like, on behalf of my wife and mine, to apologize for the dishonor and embarrassment we have brought to your command. It was never my intention to hurt you in any way. You have been like a father to me, and there is no one in the world I respect more than you.

"I have dishonored myself, my country, and my fellow servicemen. I do not deserve to be here. I hereby submit my resignation from the United States Navy.

"I am very sorry, sir. I just wish to leave. I realize that, to say the least, the future is shaky, but I love my wife and will stand by her no matter what the outcome. You, sir, are too good a man to pay the price for my stupidity. I—"

Gibbs was interrupted by Chester.

"Lieutenant, sit down and shut up! No one will be leaving the service today. What is done is done, and Carolyn will have to live with that. Let's try to rebuild from the ashes. Toward that end, Lieutenant, you are relieved from your duties here." Chester noted the look of despair on Gibbs's face and continued, "You are immediately promoted, which would have happened in another month, anyway, and I am reassigning you to a more challenging position. Carolyn will be debriefed for the next couple of weeks and then will join you. She will be put to work in our theoretical science department, where her skill will be of great aid to our efforts." Turning toward Carolyn, Chester asked, "Do you agree, Carolyn?"

"God, yes, Admiral. I'll do anything for you!" Carolyn quickly answered.

Chester nodded, then continued, "Neither of you will be able to return to your home. Carolyn, you will stay here and be debriefed. You, Lieutenant, will receive immediate transport to your new assignment. Your possessions will be packed up and shipped to you, your bills will be paid off, and your leased automobiles will be turned in and paid off. The cost of all this will be subtracted from your future pay. Any questions?"

Gibbs and Carolyn wanted to ask a thousand questions but thought quite the better of it. Seeing that neither of them was going to ask any questions, Chester dismissed them and called for an agent to escort them out of his office and see to it that the lieutenant receive immediate transport.

Lieutenant Gibbs saluted Chester and thanked him over and over. He then walked over to his wife and gave her a long, passionate kiss. Chester spoke up. "Lieutenant, there is a time and a place for that!"

Lieutenant Gibbs and Carolyn broke their embrace and left the office, but not before thanking him again. Chester felt the presence of Peggy again and knew that she, too, was smiling. He was sure that he felt someone ever so softly kiss him on the cheek but concluded that it just itched there. After all, could Peggy reach through the shadow of death and kiss him? No, Chester concluded, but he sure wished otherwise.

HEY, THIS IS MY BEACH

Enrique was hungry as he approached his private place. He looked forward to sitting on the warm beach and having a late lunch. As he came closer, Enrique could just barely make out what appeared to be shapes in the sand on the narrow beach. He wondered if something had washed up on the beach from the depths of the ocean. *No,* he thought, *the shapes seemed to be evenly separated and arranged in neat rows.* "My god, don't tell me that someone is going to destroy my beach!" he murmured to himself. But something was even more strange. The sun was reflecting off the shapes as if they were glass or made of a shiny metal.

Cautiously, Enrique approached the beach. He slowed the speed of his boat down as he neared the cove. For an instant, Enrique wondered if he should pass by and come back another day. *No, this is my beach, and if someone has come here, I want to know what is going on,* he thought to himself.

As Enrique edged closer to the beach, he could definitely see that most of the shapes were about five to six feet long, about two feet wide, and approximately one foot in height. The smaller shapes were about half as long but otherwise were the same dimensions. To Enrique, the shapes almost looked like sleeping bags that people use on camping trips. He had never been to camping himself, but he remembered seeing them in an adventure magazine a few years ago. *Yes, that must be it. There were campers on my beach!* Enrique thought. He just hoped that they were neat and would take their garbage away with them when they left. *But where were the people?* Enrique didn't see anyone walking about. *Why would they leave their sleeping bags there and walk away?* Enrique couldn't reason through the questions that were clouding his mind. Enrique sped up a little now and came closer and closer to the shore. Then he saw what was on the beach.

Delicately, Enrique edged his boat onto the sand. As an added precaution, he threw his anchor into the sand. He knew that in about an hour the tide would come in and lift his boat off the sand. Once he left the boat, Enrique approached one of the shapes and knew immediately what lay before him. He could easily see that a man was lying there, covered over by the silvery material, as the material clung to the man's body shape.

Slowly Enrique reached down and touched the material. He expected it to be sharp, since Enrique had concluded that it was made from very small pieces of metal or glass. But it was the softest material Enrique had ever felt. Not finding a zipper or buttons to open the material, Enrique pinched the material between his thumb and forefinger to examine it. As if by magic, the material split apart in a straight line from where he pinched it to the end of the top of the material. Inside the material was a body of a man.

Immediately, Enrique dropped the material from his hand and stepped back in horror. At his feet lay the body of a man, his chest split open down the center, revealing a nearly empty chest cavity, as most of the organs had been removed. The cloth, as if guided by invisible hands, closed over the body and sealed itself once again.

Unable to move, Enrique felt his heart begin to race. He felt as if his heart were about to leap out of his chest. Enrique could not imagine how a man could possibly do that to another human being. Fear now began to overcome him, but Enrique was able to see past the fear. He knew that he had to see what was under the other covers. Enrique wondered if all the shapes contained bodies, and if so, were they all desecrated, or could someone possibly be alive? He simply had to look.

While constantly looking around for the person who might have done this, Enrique approached another shape, which he guessed to be a woman. Slowly he pulled the material back and was sickened by the sight. He was right; it was a woman, or what was once a woman. She, like the other person, had been opened from the chest downward. Again, the internal organs had been removed. Letting go of the material, Enrique approached a small shape as he called out, "No, no." He knelt down next to the small shape and feared what was under the material. Tenderly, Enrique knelt down and pulled the material back. The sight he beheld sickened him even more. The child had also been cut open, and his organs removed, but where his eyes should have been, the eye sockets were empty. Enrique dropped the cloth covering the child. He put his hands in the sand, and while kneeling on all fours, Enrique vomited and cried, "God, why?" Enrique kept repeating this as he knelt there. When his stomach was empty, Enrique stood up and looked across the beach and knew that more bodies were under the other covers.

Fear told Enrique to run, just get in his boat, and leave. But inwardly, Enrique knew that he had to make sure that there was no one alive. He prayed that someone was left alive. As if in a coma, Enrique went from one body to another, looking for a survivor. Survived what, he couldn't imagine. Enrique felt the bile rise within him, as each sight he saw was more horrible than the last. While most had their organs removed, a few others, who appeared to be elderly, were untouched. But they were dead just the same.

With each passing moment, his fear, which Enrique had been fighting back, began to grow as he hurried in his ghastly mission. When he reached the end of the beach, Enrique came upon another small shape. He looked toward the heavens and shouted out, "Please, God!" Enrique hesitated after he knelt down. He didn't want to look but knew that he had to. With utmost care, Enrique pulled the covering back. He saw the body of a small girl, but she was not desecrated. Knowing that she was also dead, Enrique let go of the material. As the material closed over the girl, Enrique heard the girl coughing. She then sat up and threw off the covering. As Enrique let out a cry of joy, he took off his shirt and covered the girl's nude body.

Enrique gently picked her up in his arms and began to run toward his boat.

Stumbling through the surf, Enrique fell among the waves and dropped his precious cargo. Gingerly he picked her up, holding her even closer as he raced toward his boat. Enrique looked over his shoulder to make sure that the unseen demon who perpetrated this ghastly work was not pursuing him and his precious bundle. Fear continued to grow within him, but determination to reach safety drove Enrique onward.

Once Enrique reached his boat, he was able to place the girl on the deck as he stood in the rising surf. Satisfied that she was safe, Enrique scampered aboard. He picked the girl up and placed her on a seat by the wheelhouse. Quickly he ran to the bow, and instead of pulling the anchor aboard, Enrique cut the rope. Running back into the wheelhouse, Enrique tried to start the motor, but his hands were shaking uncontrollably.

He stood there for a minute, trying to calm down as he reached within himself for that last bit of inner strength. Trying again, Enrique turned the key to the On position and pushed the Start button. The engine coughed to life and then ran smoothly. Trying to get away from the horror on the beach, Enrique guided his small craft straight out to sea. When he was approximately three hundred yards from shore, Enrique throttled back his engines to a dead-slow speed. He then tied a rope to the wheel, which would guide the boat in a wide continuous circle.

Once Enrique was satisfied that the boat was going in a circle, he knelt down in front of the little girl. He reached for his canteen and gently washed the girl's face. He was hoping for some kind of a reaction, but he received none. Putting the canteen to her lips, Enrique forced water into her mouth. The small girl coughed and spit out the water, but then she drank eagerly. Slowly her eyes opened, but it appeared that she could not or did not see Enrique. He tried talking to her over and over, but she didn't answer. He correctly thought that she was in shock. After wrapping a blanket around her, he fastened a rope around her so that she would not fall out of her seat. Enrique bent over and gently kissed her on the forehead. At that moment, she reached out to him and grabbed his hand.

Enrique stood there holding her hand as he reached for the boat's radio with his other hand. While looking at the girl, Enrique pressed the Talk button on the microphone and called for help.

His pleas were answered by the Maritime Police. Enrique tried to sound calm, but even he detected the fear and nervousness in his voice. To the unending questions of the person on the other end of the radio, Enrique repeatedly described what he had found. "Blood? No, there wasn't any blood!" he shouted back and thought about that for a second. *How could there not be any blood? There should have been blood all over the place!* Enrique thought. Frustrated, he again gave the radio operator his position and screamed for him to send help. Enrique then threw the microphone down. Opening the door to a small compartment, Enrique fumbled with the contents until he found his handgun. He checked to make sure that the gun was loaded and then put it in his waistband.

Bending over, Enrique untied the child and lifted her into his arms. As he stood there, holding her, he tried to center his mind on a small bit of reality. But this was a nightmare come true: Enrique remembered all the strange things he had seen over the years. He would also listen to the stories of other fishermen about things they saw while at sea. But nothing could compare to this. All the stories and his experiences had to do with lights in the sky at nighttime. He remembered wondering what they were the first time he saw them. They would zoom back and forth and then disappear out to sea. Over the years, they had become common to Enrique, and he soon disregarded them. Once, he had even seen a circle of light pass beneath his boat and move off into the distance. Even that he had accepted.

The only time he had been scared of the lights was on a dark, moonless night. He was five miles out to sea, heading homeward, when a light from above approached his boat. When the light engulfed his boat, Enrique looked up into the light. Immediately he felt intense pain. Quickly closing his eyes, Enrique fell to the deck, screaming in pain. Within a few minutes, the light moved off into the distance and

Enrique recovered. He told his story to fellow fishermen more than a few times. He was surprised to learn that they, too, had had similar experiences. But that was in the past. Enrique scanned the skies now for the lights, thinking that the lights might offer help. But there were none to be seen.

Determined not to let his mind wander, Enrique began to pray for help and protection for himself and the girl in his arms. Remaining vigilant, Enrique waited for some sound or sight that help was on the way. He stood there alone against not only the elements but also the unspeakable horror that befell those people on the beach. Enrique cradled the girl against his chest with one hand as his other hand stroked her hair. He softly sang her lullabies against the backdrop of the unknown and a darkening sky.

DON'T HANG UP ON ME

CHESTER WAS HAPPY WITH HIMSELF. The Gibbses were on their way to a new life, and hopefully a closer relationship. *At least that's the way it seems,* Chester thought.

Getting back to business, Chester picked up the telephone and dialed Morrison. Once his friend was on the telephone, Chester told him about the Gibbses and what he had decided. Morrison welcomed the addition of Carolyn, but he wasn't quite sure what to do with her husband.

The really big news of the day, Chester saved for last. Once he told Morrison of the work of Lieutenant Cunningham, the tone of the conversation changed—Morrison was no longer relaxed, but rather, he was excited. When asked, Chester repeated the coordinates of the Alpha Zuron radiation trace found off the coast of Angola. When Chester added that the mass of the return should match that of the missing airliner, Morrison couldn't contain himself any longer. He asked what seemed like a hundred questions and concluded that the return must, in fact, be the missing airliner. Morrison then told Chester that he would check on ship dispositions and see if he could find a research vessel in the area to investigate it.

Morrison was about to hang up when he suddenly recalled a

conversation he had had earlier in the day with an associate member from Brazil, General Salas, about the forthcoming conference on international terrorism. When the association would meet, using the conference as a cover, Salas was interested in making a presentation about the apparent increase in UFO activity within his country. Morrison went on to explain that lately there had been a rash of sightings up and down the coast of Brazil. But nothing of any worth had been reported. It was basically the same story: once fighters were scrambled into the area, the UFOs sped off.

As an afterthought, Morrison added that a regional jet aircraft belonging to Air Brazil with forty eight souls (in the airline industry, passengers and crew are referred to as souls) aboard apparently crashed on a return flight from Brasilia to Rio de Janeiro. Just to be on the safe side, Morrison asked Chester to have his resident genius, Lieutenant Cunningham, check the runs for the Brazilian airliner. Chester asked if he suspected that they had another Zambia incident on their hands, but Morrison replied that he thought they should check for the hell of it.

Morrison then reminded Chester that they were to meet for dinner promptly at 6:00 p.m., one hour from then. Chester tried to convince his friend that they should go to a restaurant, but Morrison insisted that they go to one of his favorite delis. Chester was about to protest again when the line went dead. As usual, Chester was sitting there, talking into a dead telephone.

WHAT DO YOU MEAN MOTION SICKNESS?

CAPTAIN GEORGE MONTGOMERY WAS A happy man contented in his life's work and avocation. He was the captain of a naval research ship plying the oceans of the world for the good of mankind. The mission of the USS *Salisbury* was to study the migratory patterns of various species of fish. In addition to this, different ways were explored to increase the fish population as a whole, thereby ensuring a stable food supply for the ever-increasing population of mankind. George laughingly thought of himself as the taxi driver for the scientists on board, but deep down he knew that it was his skill as a sailor that allowed the scientists to carry on their work.

The scientists on board thought the world of George and recognized him for the professional that he was. There were many times that they sailed through storms thinking that their lives were over. But there would be George, calm as a cucumber, issuing orders to the bridge crew, while the seas towered above their small ship. Whenever anyone would pass a comment about a storm that they had just been through, George would always retort that they must be pissing off King Neptune with all the gear they dragged through the water for their studies. Everyone felt safe aboard the *Salisbury*, because George was the constant. He would always be there to either save their lives or simply to help them along.

There were parameters with George, though. Safety was his main concern, and to ensure that, he ran a tight ship. Every man and woman on board, whether civilian or enlisted, knew their responsibilities and the proper way to accomplish them. If anyone slacked up, there would be George, giving what some referred to as an instructional lecture to the violator. One thing was sure: George never had to give the same lecture twice. That is not to say that life aboard the USS *Salisbury* was not enjoyable. Actually, people fought hard to get aboard George's ship. Some educational institutions even went so far as to petition their congressman, seeking help to get their researchers on his ship. While George was uncompromising about safety, he did his best to have a happy ship. He made sure that the enlisted crew blended well with the civilians. Together everyone worked toward a collective goal and helped one another out. It was not uncommon, at the end of a voyage, that a scientist would have experience in the engineering department of a ship, and an enlisted sailor would know how to read the enzyme levels in a fish. It was a belief of George's that diversification is the key to mutual understanding and respect, and lo' behold the individual, whether scientist or sailor, who didn't follow it.

The message he had received from Admiral Morrison caused George much concern. He knew that Morrison was a man that didn't do things lightly; he must have a damn good reason to interrupt their work, George concluded. If Morrison wanted his ship at a set of coordinates within twenty-four hours, George would do his best to be there in twelve. He owed Morrison an incalculable debt. Hell, George owed him his very life and happiness, and he would do anything for him.

It was approximately four years ago when George went to see his old boss, Admiral Morrison. George had a problem that he thought for sure would chain him to a desk somewhere in the hinterland, approving the purchase of toilet paper, while waiting for retirement. George had previously been the captain of a guided missile cruiser and was on track for promotion when the next opening became available. The problem was that George had begun to question himself and his decisions. He made the right decisions, but his mind was becoming clouded and confused by technological overload. He knew that he was a good and capable captain, and indeed, George felt at ease with his job. But the mask was beginning to crack.

When George graduated college in the late sixties, the word *computer* was spoken of in theoretical terms. Upon entering the Navy, he first became acquainted with rudimentary computers. He had thought of them as merely aids to getting things done. By the time the nineties rolled around, it was a computer Navy. The modern Navy depended on the damn things for everything from hot water to the most sophisticated weapons systems. During these years, George, and those around him, adapted to this new age. But for George it was a struggle.

George realized that it was not his responsibility to know everything about computers, but only to evaluate the information he was given from them. The problem was that the information was overwhelming. George knew how to command his ship, but the computers offered so may alternatives for every little decision. George felt that his decision-making process was slowing down due to information overload. Simple decisions were now complex. The bridge of his ship, as well as most compartments, had come to look like a spacecraft. Everywhere there were sailors huddled over computer screens, monitoring this or that and not paying attention to the world around them. They knew their one job and little else.

George knew that he was a dying breed. He realized full well that those who could not readily adapt to a computerized world were doomed to the abyss of low-paying jobs in a noncomputerized surrounding. This became crystal clear one day when he attended a conference entitled the "Workforce of Tomorrow." George came away from the conference with the realization that companies were presently interested in hiring college graduates who had graduated in the late 1990s. The overall belief was that these individuals possessed the necessary computer skills to survive in today's economy. George knew that people like himself would be constantly trying to catch up while always slipping behind.

There was not one event that pushed George into this decision; it was a growing feeling within himself that concluded his career aboard the missile cruiser. The technology was constantly changing, and just when George learned that system, it would be replaced by a new system with a whole new set of operating procedures. George was convinced that he could never keep up. He loved his job, and it was out of this love that he made his decision.

While on leave, George made an appointment with Morrison. It was not easy to tell his boss that he felt himself incompetent to handle his command because of his inability to readily adapt to change. But once the words were out, George felt as if a great weight was lifted off his shoulders. Morrison tried to talk to him about it, but George remained steadfast. He requested to be relieved before he endangered the ship and crew he had come to regard as family.

Reluctantly agreeing to his request, Morrison thanked him for his honesty and told him that he was not going to get off that easily. The *Salisbury* needed a captain, and George fit the requirements. Two weeks later, George found himself in the middle of the Atlantic Ocean, the proud captain of the USS *Salisbury*. Yes, there were computer systems aboard, but not the overly complicated ones you find on a ship of war. George had been reborn, and the ole sailor within him flourished.

Overseeing the operation of the *Salisbury* from the bridge, George picked up the transcript of Morrison's transmission and wondered about the last part of it:

> *Maintain radio silence until arrival STOP use only burst satellite uplink STOP all preparations for search STOP all haste STOP Godspeed STOP*

What could have happened that was so bad that they must maintain radio silence? Somebody must have lost something really important for all the cloak-and-dagger stuff, George thought. In all his years aboard the *Salisbury*, they never had to use encrypted burst transmission through a satellite net. The other part was easy. All the equipment aboard the *Salisbury* was always maintained in an operational ready mode. Just in case, George ordered an equipment check from the thrusters, which would allow George to position his ship directly over the coordinates and maintain that position down to the cameras on the underwater vehicles. As an added preparation, he ordered a cutting torch and a mechanical arm added to one of the vehicles. Why, George didn't know. It just seemed like a good idea. He also ordered a preflight check of the onboard helicopter in case they had to utilize it during the search. The only thing George was certain about was the fact that Morrison sure wasn't interested in fish.

HEY, WHERE'S MY PICKLE?

W HEN CHESTER ARRIVED AT SAL'S Deli, Morrison was already there, sitting at a table in the back of the dining area. As he walked past the deli counter, Chester received a big hello from Hector. Chester couldn't understand why the owner of Sal's was named Hector. He attributed the name to a business decision, but he couldn't reason through it.

When Chester reached the table and sat down, Morrison was eagerly cutting a pickled green tomato into slices. "Have some?" Morrison offered. But Chester declined the offer and picked up the menu. Chester really didn't need it since he always ordered the same thing—brisket on a hard roll, an order of onion rings with ranch dipping sauce, and two bottles of celery soda. After placing his order, Chester smiled as Morrison ordered pastrami, turkey, coleslaw, and Russian dressing on a long roll, one large order of fries accompanied by a large order of onion rings, a side order of coleslaw, red-skinned potato salad, and lastly, a very large cola. He was just amazed that Morrison could eat so much.

But eat he did.

During dinner, Chester and Morrison talked about the events of the day. They were both delighted that things turned out the way they did for Carolyn. Morrison expected her to be a big help in the theoretical science department. As far as her husband went, Morrison would find something for him to do, as he said earlier. When Chester explained what Lieutenant Cunningham had accomplished, Morrison was impressed with his work and hinted that he might be a good addition to the Colorado Project as well. Chester feigned off the remark and wondered if he would have anyone left to do the job they were originally hired for.

Morrison explained to Chester that he had located a research ship one day's sail away from the location off Angola. He went on to describe that the ship was equipped with underwater cameras and should be of great aid in locating the airliner. Chester asked who the captain was and was pleased that it was George Montgomery. While he didn't know him personally, only heard of him, he knew that he was one of the best sailors around. Chester knew that he was a friend of Morrison's and he had a lot of faith in him. So that was good enough for him. After explaining that the *Salisbury* was on her way to begin the search, Chester expressed that he hoped Scotty would find the airliner and the people alive.

Morrison agreed but inwardly felt that Captain Montgomery would find the plane.

Chester then asked if Morrison had heard from Scotty. Morrison stated that he didn't expect to hear from Scotty or Doreen for at least two or three days, when they were on their way home. While he didn't like the idea that they would be out of contact for so long, Morrison felt it necessary to let them operate on their own.

Morrison then asked if Chester's wonder boy, Lieutenant Cunningham, had found the missing Brazilian airliner. When Chester told him that it didn't turn up on the scans, Morrison was relieved. At least it wouldn't be another Zambia case. He guessed that the airliner just crashed, and was thankful for that, but at the same time he felt for the people aboard her.

When they had finished talking about work, the conversation drifted over to sports. It was then Morrison realized something. "Hey, I didn't get a pickle. Where is that waiter? Whoever heard of a deli not serving pickles with a sandwich?" Morrison stood up and walked to the front of the deli to claim his long-lost, but not forgotten, pickle. Chester just laughed.

BUT I DON'T WANT TO GET OUT OF BED

A T 5:00 A.M., SCOTTY AROSE out of a nice, comfortable bed. He quickly showered, put on a flight suit, and went downstairs very quietly, lest he wake the household. As he neared the kitchen, Scotty could hear voices and the sound of laughter. He was surprised to see Doreen standing at the stove, cooking eggs and ham while keeping a keen eye on her homemade biscuits as they baked. Edenausegboye was setting the table for four.

Doreen explained that she had heard Scotty showering and decided to surprise him with breakfast. Scotty went over to Doreen and kissed her softly on the cheek. Edenausegboye simply smiled and told Scotty to sit down as she poured him a cup of coffee. As Scotty was drinking his coffee, Asukile arrived and, after greeting everyone, sat down at the table.

After the last egg was cooked and the last biscuit was buttered, everyone sat down to breakfast together. Scotty ate hardily for the long day ahead. When it was time to leave, Scotty stood up, walked over to where Doreen was sitting, bent over, and after kissing her on the cheek, thanked her for the breakfast. Doreen stood up, faced Scotty, and then hugged him tightly. "Be safe!" she whispered before releasing him. As Scotty was about to leave, Asukile stood up and called in a security guard named Chike. After introducing Chike to Scotty, Asukile explained that Chike was assigned to him as both a bodyguard and driver. Scotty didn't particularly like this situation but accepted it. After saying goodbye and wishing the others well for their day, Scotty left with his protector in tow.

BUT I JUST WENT TO BED

Captain George Montgomery spent a restless night in his cabin. Retiring early the night before, George had hoped to get a full night's sleep. He wanted to be fully prepared for the work ahead. But it was not to be so. His body was tired, having felt not only the nervousness and physical exertion of preparing the ship for whatever mission they had to accomplish but also the effects of the anxiety of wanting to perform perfectly. While his body lay prone in his bunk, desperately trying to relax, George's brain was in high gear, constantly checking and rechecking the day's preparation. He wanted to be sure that no stone was left unturned and that everything was as it should be.

At 0530 hours (5:30 a.m.), the telephone rang in George's cabin. Slowly he reached up over his head and picked up the receiver from its cradle on the bulkhead. In an exhausted voice, George stated, "Captain here."

"Sir, we have reached the coordinates, and thrusters have been engaged. Are there any further orders?" came the reply from a very young voice that sounded wide awake.

"No, Lieutenant, I'm on my way," George replied, thinking that these damn young kids today seemed to have endless energy.

After replacing the telephone back into its cradle, George lay on his side, pulled the covers up to his neck, and lay there wishing that he had slept through the night. But duty calls. Slowly George threw the covers off and sat up, placing his feet on the cold steel deck. While sitting on his bunk, George rubbed his face with his hands, trying to shake the cobwebs of sleeplessness away. After convincing himself that he had to get moving, George stood up and walked into his private head (bathroom on a naval ship), shaved, and took a colder-than-normal shower. As he dressed in a fresh uniform, George again reviewed the preparations for the mission he had accomplished. Convinced that all was ready, he left his cabin and proceeded to the bridge, ready to take on the world and whatever it was Morrison was searching for.

Once on the bridge, George was handed the first of what would be an endless stream of hot coffee for the remainder of the day. Crossing over to the computer that controlled the ship's thrusters, George studied the display screen and was satisfied that all was operating as it should. The ship's position was being maintained at the exact coordinates that Morrison had given him. Turning away from the computer, George walked over to his captain's chair. Stepping up approximately a foot and a half to the footrest, he then shifted his body and sat down. From this vantage point, George had an unobstructed view of the ocean ahead of him.

As George sat there and gazed over the calm seas, he wondered just what he was doing there. Checking the time and doing the mental calculations to determine the current time in Washington, DC, George determined that Morrison was either in bed or just going to bed. He really didn't want to wake him up, but orders are orders. George reached over to his telephone, called the radio room, and instructed the radio operator to call Admiral Morrison over a burst satellite link. When the operator asked him for the setting code, George reached into his pocket and extracted a carefully folded piece of paper.

Unfolding the paper, he read the operator the frequency code. George remained on the line while the connection was being made. He carefully refolded the paper and was placing it back in his pocket when George heard the admiral's phone ring.

Morrison was actually wide awake. During his free time, besides reading about Victorian New York, the admiral liked to collect and paint toy soldiers. At this moment, he was in his study, surrounded by his toy Armies and Navies that were carefully placed in glass-enclosed bookcases. For the past six weeks, he had been painstakingly painting a vignette of the American Revolution. The scene depicted the period right after the battle of Princeton, New Jersey. It consisted of three pieces, a father, a mother, and a small child. The father was a member of the New Jersey militia who had been wounded in the leg during the battle. The soldier had his arm around his wife's shoulder for support as he limped away from the battle. His young son was proudly walking in front of his parents, cradling his father's musket in his small arms. Morrison found that as he painted, he relaxed and the worries of the nation were lifted from his shoulder, if only for a short period. When one of the telephones on his desk rang, Morrison reluctantly placed his delicate paintbrush into an open bottle of cleaning solution as he picked up the receiver. Stealing a glance at his handiwork, Morrison answered, "Yes!" with a trace of anger in his voice.

George began, "Admiral—"

But he was interrupted immediately.

"Yes, George, what do you have to report?" Morrison immediately asked.

"Sir, we have reached the coordinates and are on station," George replied, noting the trace of anger in the admiral's voice.

"You sure did get there fast," Morrison replied, the anger in his voice gone now, and continued, "When will you begin operations?"

"Sir, the sun will be up in approximately forty-five minutes, and I prefer to wait until then. It's a safety issue. During underwater operations, the deck is crowded with technicians and cable. We can commence operations immediately under deck lights, but it's much safer when the sun is up," George replied.

"That's fine, George. But I don't want you to begin operations until you hear from Admiral Braddock's office. I want to set up a live satellite feed," Morrison ordered. "By the way, George, you did real good." And then he added, "Goodbye, George."

"Goodbye…," George began to answer but heard dial tone as the admiral had already hung up.

After Morrison returned the telephone to its cradle, he removed his paintbrush from the cleaning solution. After wiping it off with an old rag, he placed it in a drying tray. He looked at his artwork again, then covered the vignette with a piece of wax paper.

Having returned his paints to their container, he glanced once more at his silent armies and then reached for the telephone.

Chester, likewise, wasn't sleeping; he was sitting in the family room of the house he and Peggy had shared. He wasn't occupied in a hobby or reading a book or watching television, but rather, he was sitting in a darkened room, illuminated only by the soft glow of a single light in the adjoining kitchen. Staring into the darkness of the room, Chester was remembering. He was thinking of the good life he had been fortunate to share with Peggy, and of the plans they had made for their future together. Plans that would remain unfulfilled but could be dreamed about. The sound of the ringing telephone snapped him back into reality. Sitting up, he reached over and picked up the receiver. It took Chester a second to recognize the admiral's excited voice.

Their conversation was brief and to the point. Chester felt that this was going to be another sleepless night spent at the office. But he didn't mind. Inwardly, Chester knew that he had one of the most interesting jobs in the world. After Morrison hung up, while leaving Chester on the line, he called his office and issued the orders necessary to establish an encrypted video and audio satellite link to the *Salisbury*. He then informed the duty officer that he and Admiral Morrison would arrive shortly, and to make sure that there was a very large pot of coffee and some sweet buns available. As an afterthought, Chester ordered that Lieutenant Cunningham be present to see the fruits of his labor.

IS THIS THE COMMUTER FLIGHT?

When Scotty arrived at the airport, he was glad to see that the crew were readying the aircraft for the day's work. After looking at the aircraft, Scotty caught up to Vinson and Bill Finningham. They informed Scotty that the aircraft had been fueled and serviced.

Additionally, all adjustments to the radar had been made, and the search grid maps had been prepared and distributed. Finningham noted that the crew were in good spirits and were anxious to get started. He attributed this in no small way to the royal treatment everyone was receiving from their hosts.

Vinson then briefed Scotty about a meeting he and Bill had with the representative of the Zambia Air Force, who had overseen the search so far. Of great benefit, they received a map that plotted all the radar returns of their search. These returns or "hits" had then been checked out by ground units. Unfortunately, all the hits were negative for the airliner. Finningham then had that information overlaid onto their computer search maps so that they wouldn't waste time chasing returns the Zambians had already checked out.

As final preparations were underway, Scotty took Vinson aside and asked him to spend the morning with the government representative. The idea was to have Vinson shown around the airport and hopefully be introduced to the everyday workers of Transvaal airlines. Scotty felt that, this way, Vinson might be able to get a feeling about the flight crew of the missing aircraft and their capabilities. Scotty also wanted Vinson to talk to the maintenance people to find out what the mechanical status of the aircraft was.

Vinson gladly received Scotty's orders, as he was not anxious to get back aboard an aircraft after the long flight to Zambia.

At precisely 7:00 a.m., both the search aircraft rolled out of the hangar and taxied to the runway. They didn't have to wait long for clearance to take off. Within minutes, both aircraft were in the air and proceeding to their search areas. Scotty decided that he would stay in the cabin area of the aircraft and not the cockpit. He wanted to observe how the search was being done.

The cabin area was different from what he was used to. All outside light was blocked from entering the cabin so that the sun would not cause reflections on the screens of the electronic equipment. While the cabin was bathed in electronic light of reds, greens, blues, and oranges, the eerie glow was reduced by soft overhead lighting. Here, Scotty was able to observe firsthand the mechanics of the search. As the technicians paid close attention to their monitors, Scotty went from station to station in an effort to understand what each person's function was. Two technicians operated the experimental radar, while three other men operated additional search radars. In another part of the aircraft, one technician monitored an instrument that measured any magnetic deviation from the known magnetic field of the ground below. A magnetic deviation would therefore indicate the presence of some type of errant metal. As an added plus, the aircraft was equipped with infrared imaging scanners that would detect any survivors in the area.

For the next ninety minutes, Scotty remained where he was, watching with increased interest as one search grid was completed and another began. They had started to confirm the contacts the Zambian Air Force had examined, but no new contacts had been revealed.

Scotty's concentration was interrupted by the pilot of the aircraft when he requested his presence in the cockpit.

Once in the cockpit, the copilot motioned for Scotty to put on a set of headphones.

Reaching up and taking a pair from the bulkhead, Scotty put them on. The pilot asked Scotty if he would sit in the jump seat for a while. Reaching behind the copilot, Scotty took the jump seat out of its holder and unfolded it. After locking it into the floor of the cockpit between the pilot and copilot, Scotty sat down and put on his seat belt. Scotty began by asking if there was a problem. The copilot first checked the transmission select switch to make sure that only those in the cockpit would hear what they were going to discuss.

Sensing that something was amiss, Scotty quickly scanned the instruments and noted that the flight computer was flying the aircraft. There was, however, one oddity: the pilot had his hands very close to the steering column but was not touching the wheel.

Scotty thought that it was as if the pilot expected the computer to go down at any second and he was preparing to manually fly the aircraft. Scotty then glanced over at the copilot, who was now turning to his side to face him.

"Sir, about twenty minutes ago, a single bright light appeared on our port wing about one mile out. Right after that, we noticed another one on our starboard side in the same relative position. We thought that they were escort aircraft from the Zambia Air Force and the light was just a reflection off the canopy glass. When we executed a turn a minute ago, the light on our port side fell into our shadow. And guess what? It's no aircraft I've ever seen. When it was in our shadow, it remained a bright circular light," the copilot stated and waited for an answer, as Scotty was now looking at the lights and confirming their presence.

"Do they register on radar?" Scotty asked as he was looking out the window to the left and watching the light.

"Negative!" came a quick reply.

"Have they come in close and threatened our aircraft in any way?" Scotty asked.

"No, sir. Since we noticed them, they have maintained the same relative position. They even hold that position when we turn. When we slow down, they slow down. If we increase altitude, so do they. They are just always there in the same position," the copilot replied.

Scotty detected an edge in the man's otherwise-calm voice. In order to take the edge off the pilots, Scotty knew that he had to come up with something. The last thing he needed were edgy pilots who didn't want to fly. "Have you heard from Tango 2?" Scotty asked.

"No, sir!" came another quick reply.

Scotty reached within the recesses of his mind and pulled out an explanation. "Gentlemen, what we have here is Foo Fighters—"

"Foo Fighters! What the fuck are Foo Fighters?" the copilot interrupted and then apologized for his language.

"Shit, I know what you are talking about. I remember hearing about them, but what the hell are they?" the pilot asked, speaking up for the first time. "Sorry, sir," he added.

Scotty was glad to hear the pilot speak up for the first time. He then watched as the pilot then relaxed and turned toward Scotty as he continued, "Foo Fighters were first reported during World War II by both Allied and Axis fighter and bomber pilots. The lights would appear out of nowhere, mostly in daylight and rarely at night. Some pilots reported that they pursued the lights, but no matter how fast they flew, the lights always outpaced them. There are also reports of pilots seeing them during the Korean and Vietnam Wars. Today, commercial airline pilots see them, but they are afraid to report them officially, lest they be labeled crazy, or worst, they could be singled out as having seen a UFO. And we all know that is nothing but a quick trip into oblivion and retirement.

"What's odd is the fact that the lights disappear just as quickly as they appear. Some pilots think that the lights are angels watching over them, while others truly believe that they are UFOs."

"Has anyone ever figured out what they are?" the pilot asked, clearly interested in the conversation and noticeably much more relaxed.

"No, but all authorities agree that it is a natural phenomenon," Scotty began, trying to sound logical as he was in the process of making something up to relax these men. He then continued, hoping they would buy into what he was about to say, "It seems that when an aircraft flies through an atmospheric disturbance of some sort, the electrostatic charge that we emit, combined with our magnetic field, further disturbs the air and supercharges it. Those circumstances combined produce the lights that we see. Sometimes the light or, like in our case, lights stay like they are, but they have also been known to circle an aircraft as it proceeds along its flight path.

"When we leave the area of atmospheric disturbance, the lights disappear. For example, the warm thermals coming off the ground clash with the cool air of our altitude and will cause such a disturbance. We know that the weather forecast for the next several days calls for intermittent showers, so we know that the air is definitely in a disturbed state."

"Yeah, you're right. I remember reading that now," the pilot responded, completely relaxed.

"Hey, the lights are gone!" The copilot spoke up as he glanced out of the window. "Well, I'll be—Foo Fighters! Who would figure it?" he continued.

Scotty was relieved to see the operation of the cockpit return to normal. Both of the men went back to the business of flying the aircraft. It was hard for Scotty to believe that they believed his explanation, since he made most of it up. Privately, Scotty had come to believe that the mysterious lights were for real, and hidden in the light was something much more ominous than a static charge.

As Scotty was preparing to leave the cockpit, he heard Tango 2 call in and report the same mysterious lights. There were two of the lights off their starboard side.

Scotty then sat back down and watched and listened as his pilot responded, "Tango 2, you are flying a perpendicular course to us. Be advised that we just left that area and encountered disturbed atmospherics. What you are seeing is natural light and nothing to be worried about. Richard, I can't believe that you have been flying all this time and have never seen Foo Fighters!"

"Foo-What?" came a quick reply.

"Foo Fighters! Richard, it's just an electrostatic charge in the atmosphere and no threat to the aircraft," Scotty's pilot responded.

"Oh yeah, Foo Fighters, I've heard of them. Good hunting, Tango 1. Tango 2, out," Richard replied.

Scotty and the two pilots shared a good laugh over the conversation, but Scotty's laugh had a nervous edge to it. Praying to himself, Scotty hoped that Chester had a satellite overhead, watching the whole thing. He realized that Chester was powerless to come to his aid, but if something went wrong, at least someone would know what happened. After refolding his jump seat, Scotty excused himself and re-entered the cabin area.

Once back in the cabin, Scotty settled in behind the operator of the experimental radar. The man was busily at work, making constant adjustments to the instrumentation. Scotty figured that shortly they would reach the end of their search pattern for the morning. After that, they would return to the airport, service the aircraft, and give the crew a lunch break. Thirty minutes of boredom resulted in a second of excitement as the operator Scotty had been watching called out a hit.

Scotty quickly perked up and paid full attention to what the operator was doing. As the technician busied himself with more dials and switches, he informed Scotty that it was a low-level hit, not near the size of the airplane they were searching for. His mind racing, trying to think of alternatives, Scotty asked what size it was. He was disappointed when the technician told him that it was bigger than a car but smaller than a tractor trailer truck. Realizing that it could be a piece of the aircraft they were searching for, Scotty ordered the technician to mark its location. The technician turned toward Scotty and told him that he would do better than that and launch a marker buoy.

As Scotty was talking to the technician, the flight supervisor came over and explained that when they get a hit during a search, it is normal procedure to launch a marker that they can fly right to the object. Scotty was a little uncertain what the supervisor was talking about and envisioned a rocket of some sort being launched from the aircraft toward the target. The flight supervisor saw the hint of puzzlement on Scotty's face and elaborated. He informed Scotty that the aircraft would now come back around over the object. At that time, another technician would then launch an unpowered marker buoy out of the tail of the aircraft. As the buoy fell to the earth, it trailed out a carbon filament wire impregnated with metal dust that was attached to the launch tube. That, in turn, was connected to a flight computer. Once launched, the buoy was flown by the computer through manipulation of directional fins on the buoy, usually to within a few feet of the target. Once the buoy came in contact with the ground, the sharp nosecone went into the soil, and from the shock a homing signal was activated. The signal would last usually for five days or until the battery died.

Scotty asked if the wire was long enough to actually reach the ground, since the aircraft was constantly moving. He was surprised to learn that the wire was fifty miles long and as thin as human hair. Becoming more interested in the process, Scotty asked how the signal was sent down the wire if the wire did not have a metal core or optical fiber to carry it. He was quite impressed to learn that the metal powder within the carbon wire was magnetized and the directional signals were carried down the magnetic field surrounding the carbon strand. Intrigued now, Scotty asked if it was reliable. The supervisor told him that while it was still in the experimental stage, the process had been 98 percent accurate.

While they were talking, the marker buoy had been launched. The technician confirmed that the buoy had hit the ground and that the transmission signal was strong. Scotty was anxious now to land and check out the buoy to see what was there. But they still had another forty-five minutes of flight time left to finish their search pattern. For the remainder of the flight, Scotty went back up into the cockpit, sat in the jump seat, and looked out for Foo Fighters. Thankfully, there were none.

MAKE ME LOSE A NIGHT'S SLEEP, WE'LL SEE ABOUT THAT

Captain Hector Perez spent a restless night after Scotty left. As he tossed and turned in bed all night with only intermittent naps, the anger was growing within him. The man locked up in his jail really bothered Hector. How dare this individual come onto his island and threaten the life of a friend? While Hector had promised Scotty to put the man on an airplane today and forget the whole matter, he decided to make some inquiries before he released him. As he prepared for work, Hector concentrated on the man. Hector knew that something in the man's appearance was odd, but he just couldn't put his finger on it.

Over breakfast, his wife was chatting away, but Hector was consumed by thoughts of the man. When his wife would ask a question or require a comment on her thoughts, the best Hector could muster was an occasional grunt of agreement or an "Oh yeah" on cue. His morning kiss goodbye with his wife was more an act of automation rather than an expression of love and compassion. The man had gotten to him.

Getting into his car and driving through paradise didn't help much. Hector remembered the first time Scotty came to his home and remarked how beautiful the island was and how lucky a person he was to not only live in paradise but also see its beauty every day. Since that day, Hector looked at his surroundings in a different light. He had grown up here and never really appreciated what to him was normal. But today Hector didn't notice the warm, friendly people or the beauty of the land set against a backdrop of a pale-blue sky.

Arriving at the airport, Hector went immediately to his office and opened the file the arresting officer had prepared. Looking at the photograph of the man, Hector realized what had been bothering him. The man had big eyes, and it was as if his eye sockets were too small to contain them. Dismissing that thought, Hector read the scant information sheet:

> name: Stanley Thomas Merrick
> dob: April 26, 1956
> place of birth: Los Angeles, California
> residence: 9634 Fimble Tree Lane, Los Angeles, California
> telephone number: 469-2265
> marital status: Widower
> next of kin: None
> height: Six feet, one inch
> weight: 196 pounds
> scars: None
> distinguishing marks or characteristics: None
> hair color: Black
> eye color: Black, and a small notation indicating that the eyes were larger than normal.
> employment: Electronics engineer, Braswell Engineering Group, Los Angeles, California

Hector didn't get much from the file except the officer's notation that Merrick had large eyes. *Well, I guess that is not so unusual, but I have never seen a person with black eyes,* Hector thought to himself. Next, he scanned the property slip and didn't find anything unusual. There was the normal—wallet, keys, credit cards, change, and money.

Additionally, there was a duffel bag, which had been removed from the aircraft prior to its departure. Hector reached over and called the police property room and asked to have Merrick's personal property brought to him.

Together, Hector and one of his officers went through the duffel bag. They found what one would suspect they would find: shirts, pants, underwear, socks, an extra pair of sneakers, some reading material dealing with astronomy, and a shaving kit. Upon opening the shaving kit, Hector was surprised to find a beeper. Picking up the beeper, Hector wondered why Merrick would not wear the beeper. As he ran his fingers over the back of the beeper, Hector felt a screw sticking out a little.

With his fingernail, Hector patiently unscrewed the back cover of the beeper.

When he removed the cover, Hector was elated. The electronic part of the beeper had been removed, and in its place were two small vials of tiny orange pills. *No one would go through the trouble to hide something legal. Therefore, these must be illegal drugs of some sort. Now I got you, you bastard!* Hector thought.

Hector was going to honor Scotty's wish and release the man, but not right then. The drug charge would carry more time, due to the strict drug laws, than the threat to kill.

Hector was more than satisfied that Merrick would become a longtime resident of the Canaries, but he wouldn't be a tourist. Wasting no time, Hector handed the orange pills to the officer, along with the shell of the pager, and instructed him to have the pills tested.

Putting Merrick's belongings back into the duffel bag, Hector was smiling. *To think I lost a night's sleep over this creep. The resolution to the problem was there all along!* Hector thought to himself as he ordered Merrick brought to the interrogation room.

Patrolman Fernando Banderas, a recent graduate of the police academy, went to Merrick's cell and called him forward to the cell door. After opening the door, Fernando ordered Merrick to turn around to be handcuffed. In a very quick motion, as Merrick began to turn around, he reached out with his left hand and seized the nine-millimeter handgun that was not secured in Fernando's holster.

Merrick forced Fernando to turn around, then quickly put his right arm around his neck and pulled Fernando's body against his. With his left hand Merrick held the gun to Fernando's head. Together they walked out of the cell, into the main corridor, and toward the elevator at the end of the hallway. Fernando was pleading for his life as they walked. Merrick didn't see it, but Fernando managed to hit a red panic button on the wall as they passed it. Immediately an alarm sounded throughout the complex.

Two policemen on duty in the cell area drew their guns and ran to the jail cells.

As they turned the corner, the two policemen saw Fernando being held by the prisoner. As they approached Merrick, they ordered him to drop the weapon. Merrick pulled Fernando even closer to him as he shouted to the policemen to drop their weapons. But they didn't. The two policemen kept approaching Merrick with their guns aimed at his head. Merrick shouted out again for them to drop their weapons. Again, they just kept walking toward him. Merrick panicked and fired his weapon four times. Both policemen fell to the concrete floor, slumped over and unconscious.

COME OUT, COME OUT, WHEREVER YOU ARE

CHESTER AND MORRISON ARRIVED AT Space Command almost simultaneously. Their drivers parked alongside each other on the first level of the underground garage. Both men greeted each other warmly, but there was an undercurrent of anxiety lurking within them. They were each afraid of what might be found on the floor of the ocean. As they walked toward the elevator together, they busied themselves with idle talk about sports and the weather. Their conversation was interrupted by a Lieutenant Sanders, who informed Chester that all preparations for the satellite link had been completed. After thanking Lieutenant Sanders, Chester and Morrison continued to walk toward the elevator.

Lieutenant Sanders raced ahead of them and pushed the button for the elevator. As Chester and Morrison arrived at the elevator, the doors opened. Lieutenant Sanders stood at attention as the two admirals entered. Once they were on the elevator, Morrison turned toward Chester and asked, "Were we ever like that?"

"Yeah, I guess we were. And we sure must have been a sweet pain in somebody's ass," Chester answered as the elevator came to a stop on the floor his office was located on.

Morrison admired the framed prints of naval warships that adorned the walls of the corridor that led to Chester's office. His concentration was interrupted when Chester said in a soft voice, "I don't believe it."

When Morrison looked down the corridor, he saw Lieutenant Sanders standing at attention in front of the door to Chester's office. Morrison noted that Sanders was panting hard, and his face was a deep shade of red. As Morrison and Chester came closer to the office, Sanders opened the door and stood aside. Morrison walked in while Chester hesitated by the lieutenant. With the barest hint of a smile on his face, Chester stated, "Mr. Sanders, you shouldn't be panting like that after running up only six flights of stairs. You should really start working out. I don't want you getting sick on me. You have to stay in shape. Think of how it would look if one of my young lieutenants dropped dead of a heart attack. Hell, I'd be answering congressional inquiries forever! Shape up, mister!"

Smiling broadly now, Chester entered his office and quickly closed the door.

Once the door was closed, Morrison erupted in laughter and repeated Chester's pearls of wisdom: "You have to stay in shape. Shape up, mister!"

Chester, laughing now, also replied, "Yeah, well, on second thought, we were never that bad. He's a good officer, just a little eager to do well."

After the laughter died down in a few seconds, Chester crossed to his desk and telephoned the officer in charge at this time of the night. He ordered him to patch through the satellite link. Once Chester learned that Lieutenant Cunningham had already arrived, he directed him to his office. Chester then pressed a button concealed under his desk.

Immediately a picture of a seascape on the far wall rose up, revealing three forty-inch monitors. Crossing over to the monitors, Chester turned them on.

Two of the monitors had static lines running across them and told Morrison that when the underwater sleds began transmitting, their pictures would fill the blank screens. The third monitor showed two men. One of them was sitting down in front of some controls and a bank of small monitors. The other man was looking over the seated man's shoulder at the monitors, which were showing status readouts of the underwater sleds.

Morrison rose from the couch he was relaxing in and stood in the center of the room. "Good morning, George," he began.

The naval officer turned from glancing over the man's shoulder, faced the camera, and replied, "Good morning, Admiral. I'm sorry to have disturbed your sleep."

"That's okay, George. If it weren't urgent, we all wouldn't be here. George, I am here with Rear Admiral Braddock, and shortly, a Lieutenant Cunningham will join us. The lieutenant is the one responsible for all of us being here. Now, if you would, George, please explain to us what is going on," Morrison ordered.

George replied, "Yes, Admiral. And good morning to you, Admiral Braddock. As you know, we have two deep remote vehicles aboard, which we just launched and which are on their way to the targeted area. The reason that—"

But he was interrupted by Morrison.

"George, can you hold for a second, please? I believe Lieutenant Cunningham has arrived." Morrison interrupted when he heard knocking on the door.

Chester walked across the office and opened the door. Along with Lieutenant Cunningham, a steward arrived with a cart of hot coffee, sandwiches, and soft drinks. After directing the steward into the office and waiting for him to set up the refreshment cart and then leave, Chester thanked Lieutenant Cunningham for coming. He then introduced Lieutenant Cunningham to Morrison.

Morrison, likewise, thanked him for coming and offered him some refreshment.

Taking a bottle of water, Cunningham remained standing, waiting to be invited to sit down.

Morrison then began speaking. "Lieutenant, and this goes for you and your men as well, George, what we hope to see shortly is never—I repeat, *never*—to be discussed with anyone except those present, and then only on my order or Admiral Braddock's authorization. Is that understood?"

After receiving two quick replies of "Yes, sir," Morrison continued, "I don't know what, if anything, we may find, but it is absolutely essential that it remains among those present. George, I'm sorry for the interruption. Please continue."

"Yes, Admiral. Now, as I was saying, we have two deep remote vehicles on their way down to the target location. The reason you are not receiving video is that in order to conserve battery power, we don't switch the lights on until we are fifty feet from the bottom. Presently, we are just crossing the four-hundred-foot mark. So we should reach four hundred and fifty feet in a few seconds, and then the lights will come on.

"Both our vehicles are equipped with digital video and still cameras. Each still camera has extended memory, so we should be able to get more than enough usable stills. Also, each vehicle is equipped with various devices that will allow us to recover small items, should that be necessary. Ah! As you can see, the lights just came on. We should be able to see what's there shortly," George answered and then fell silent watching the ship's monitors.

Morrison, Chester, and Cunningham stood in mute silence as they watched the monitors. They were constantly going from one monitor to the other, looking for a hint of an object. Cunningham, as he watched, was mentally reviewing his satellite scans and his calculations. Silently, Cunningham was praying that something was there, because if there wasn't, he caused a lot of fuss for nothing.

Seconds seemed to pass like hours. Morrison stood in the center of the room, intently looking at the monitors. All he saw was silt being stirred up by the electric motors of the sleds. Then slowly an image began to take shape, but just what it was, he couldn't imagine.

JUNGLE? NO ONE SAID ANYTHING ABOUT GOING INTO THE JUNGLE

After the search aircraft landed, the crew were treated to an elaborate buffet lunch by their gracious hosts. Scotty ate with the pilots and enjoyed the kidding about the Foo Fighters. He was somewhat disappointed to learn that Tango 2 did not have any hits from their search. But Scotty felt that the aircraft was not going to be found—at least not here.

After lunch, Scotty met up with Vinson, who had spent the major part of the morning talking to people from the airline. Vinson told him that the general feeling was that the plane flew into something like a time door to another time dimension. The airline people were afraid that it might happen again. When Scotty asked about the crew, Vinson told him that the crew was considered the best there was and in fact there was no more-experienced flight crew around. Foul play was ruled out because the pilots were friends and their families always vacationed together. Vinson added that the captain was a nut about safety and would personally oversee repairs. He would even come into the maintenance hangar on his days off. Delivering his final assessment, Vinson concluded that foul play was ruled out, mechanical failure was a remote possibility, and any terrorism or any other purposeful crashing of the aircraft was highly unlikely.

Scotty thanked Vinson for his assessment, knowing that he never left any stone unturned. After informing Vinson about the radar hit this morning, Scotty asked him to arrange for some helicopters to take them out there to examine the object. When asked if he wanted to go along for the ride, Vinson hesitantly agreed, stating that the concrete jungle of New York, which he loved dearly, was as much jungle as he cared to visit. Scotty laughed as Vinson walked away to make the arrangements while mumbling to himself.

Shortly after the two search aircraft departed for their afternoon runs, two Zambian Army Black Hawk helicopters set down in front of the hangar being utilized by Scotty and his team. Major Ehioze was the first to leave the helicopters, followed by six heavily armed and professional-looking soldiers from each helicopter. The soldiers formed a line and stood at attention until Major Ehioze allowed them to stand at ease. The major then walked over and introduced himself to Scotty and Vinson.

After brief but warm and friendly introductions had been made, Scotty, Vinson, and the major walked over to a map that was attached to the wall of the hangar. Major Ehioze pointed to the area that they would be going to. He explained that, due to the thickness of the jungle, they would have to rappel from the helicopters. Scotty smiled at this revelation and took notice of the worried look on Vinson's face. Sensing that something was wrong, Scotty turned toward his friend and asked, "What's wrong?"

"I thought I was going to stay here and…you know…coordinate. You didn't tell me, back in New York, that we would be going into a jungle! And to me, the word *jungle* equals *snakes*. Well…and…snakes are not a good thing. It can't get any worse than this," Vinson replied with a very worried look on his face.

Scotty and Major Ehioze had a good laugh. Winking at Scotty, the major added, "There is one more thing. Poachers frequent the area to which we will be going. That is why my men are so heavily armed." The major then motioned to one of his men, who came forward carrying two large duffel bags and weapons. "I have brought some things for the both of you to wear and play with," the major added.

Major Ehioze opened one of the bags and handed the items to Vinson one at a time. Shortly, Vinson was dressed in a flak jacket, hands-free-communication headset, a Kevlar battle helmet, and a utility belt with two canteens, a machete, and rappelling gear. As if to add insult to injury, the major then handed Vinson a sawed-off shotgun and a bandoleer of shells.

Scotty then began to get similarly dressed and enjoyed a good laugh with the major as they listened to Vinson mumbling to himself about all the gear and the idea of going into the jungle. He was also complaining about the possibility of running into snakes, jumping out of a helicopter, and lastly, poachers who were trying to kill him.

Once Scotty was ready, the conversation turned serious. The major explained that they were receiving a good, strong signal from the marker that was dropped on the object. He then explained that it would take them about thirty minutes' flying time to reach the object. Major Ehioze then asked Scotty if he thought the airplane was there.

"No, I don't think the aircraft is there. If the aircraft had crashed there, it would have made a real mess of the jungle. That is, it would have created a wide path, knocking down trees as it crashed to the ground. Your search parties would have easily seen such devastation. I think what we might find is a piece of the aircraft. From that we may be able to find out just what happened," Scotty replied.

"From what I have been told, the probe should just about be on top of the object. So it shouldn't be that hard to find. I have a heavy-lift helicopter on standby to take the wreckage out and bring it back here. So if we are ready, gentlemen, we can get going. Oh, one more thing, we are going to have to hike out approximately five miles to an open field so that we can be picked up. So go easy on the water. Are we ready?" the major asked.

"Oh, great. Now we have to go for a hike through a jungle loaded with snakes while poachers will be shooting at us. You owe me big-time for this, Scotty," Vinson added as they walked to the waiting helicopters. Major Ehioze directed Scotty to the second helicopter and told him that he would take Vinson with him to keep an eye on him. Scotty thanked him and joined the soldiers by his designated helicopter as they were boarding.

Once seated in the helicopter, Scotty looked down at the lush countryside while the helicopter took off and headed out over the jungle. His thoughts turned to Doreen, and he realized just how much he missed her company and sense of humor. He was wondering what she was doing right then when the pilot of the helicopter announced over the intercom that they were two minutes from their destination. A yellow light started flashing, indicating that it was time to prepare to rappel out of the helicopter. Scotty then felt the helicopter slow down as the nose flared slightly upward, and then it leveled off, stationary, one hundred feet over the jungle.

SO YOU WANT TO BE A TOUGH GUY?

Hector was on his way to the interrogation room when he heard the alarm going off. Fearing that it involved the prisoner Merrick, Hector pushed open the door to the stairway and began a quick descent to the lower level. As he was about to open the door to the cell area, Hector heard the loud blasts from a weapon echoing back and forth against the bare concrete walls. For the first time in his career, Hector drew his weapon and took the safety off.

Opening the door very slowly, Hector lay on the floor and inched his way toward the hallway. Peeking around the corner, Hector saw Merrick against the far wall, about sixty feet from him, holding Fernando around the neck in front of him. Two policemen were about twenty feet from Hector and were lying very still on their backs. Merrick, seeing Hector, leveled his weapon and shot off a round toward the doorway. Hector withdrew his head just in time and saw a small piece of concrete blast away from the doorframe due to the impact of the bullet.

Hector picked himself off the floor and crouched against the wall, inside the doorway, with his weapon held firmly in his hands. He then called out to Merrick, ordering him to drop his weapon. This was met by another bullet landing against the doorframe.

Changing tactics, Hector then asked Merrick what he wanted. This time Hector received a reply: "I want to get off this fucking island, you asshole! Get me a fucking plane. Now!"

"Okay!" Hector shouted out without ever having the intention to get this creep an airplane, but he knew it was good to let Merrick think that he was in charge. "But the airplane is going to take some time. Let me come in and take the two officers before they die!" Hector pleaded as more police arrived on the stairway.

"Fuck you! Let the bastards die!" Merrick shouted back.

"If you let those two men die, you aren't going anywhere. I'll kill you myself. So let me come in and get them!" Hector replied as he gave the other policemen on the stairway hand signals to evacuate the building.

"You stupid ass, I still have one of your men! If you come in here, I'll kill him!" Merrick shouted out as he tightened his grip on Fernando.

"If you kill him, there is nothing in the world that will stop me from killing you. You're dead either way. So why don't we end this bullshit? Let me remove my two men and we'll get working on the airplane?" Hector shouted back.

After a few seconds, Merrick agreed and instructed Hector to throw his weapon into the hallway and to remove his shirt and pants. Hector held his gun in front of himself, removed the magazine clip and one bullet from the chamber of his automatic handgun. After tossing it into the hallway, Hector began undressing and threw his shirt and pants also into the hallway. In times like this, odd thoughts come into a person's head. In Hector's case, he thanked God that he wore boxer shorts today and not those damn tight short underwear his wife liked so much. The saving grace in all this was, Hector realized that at least he wouldn't look stupid. Raising his hands in the air, Hector shouted out, "Okay, I'm ready! I'm coming out!"

"Okay, no sudden moves!" Merrick shouted back.

Cautiously, Hector stepped into the hallway with his hands in the air. He saw his officers lying on the floor, and an anger rose within him, but Hector suppressed it as best as he could. *Now is not the time to get angry and lose control,* he thought to himself. When he reached the first officer, Hector knelt down next to him. He immediately realized that the man was simply unconscious due to the close-range impact of the bullet against the Kevlar vest the officer was wearing. Looking over at the other officer, Hector realized that the same was the case with him as well.

Pretending to examine the officer he was kneeling next to, Hector put his finger on the man's neck, checking for a pulse. He then looked up at Merrick with a slight smile on his face and announced that the man was still alive. He was somewhat transfixed when his eyes met Merrick. Hector found himself staring into two large black pools totally devoid of emotion. Breaking his stare, Hector acted as if he were trying to stop the man from bleeding. He put one hand on the man's chest and pressed down. With his other hand, Hector gently patted the man's torso, looking for the telltale bulge of another weapon. He found what he had been searching for just under the lower edge of the vest. Slowly Hector slid his hand under the vest and unsnapped the weapon. Satisfied with his actions, Hector withdrew his hand and squatted next to the downed officer while announcing that he was ready to move the man.

"You try anything and you're dead!" Merrick shouted with a nervous edge in his voice.

As Hector squatted there momentarily, he put his right finger on his chest and stroked it downward. He made eye contact with Fernando, who winked at him, indicating that he understood the signal. Hector then glanced at Merrick, who was waving his gun back and forth in the direction of the doorway.

Hector then bent over the officer, placed his left arm under the officer's neck, and slowly began to lift the man's torso into a sitting position. With his right hand, now totally out of view of Merrick, Hector slipped his hand under the vest and withdrew the weapon, a .357 Magnum short-barrel handgun, and released the safety. As he exhaled deeply, trying to calm his nerves, Hector shouted, "Now!"

Fernando shoved his elbow into Merrick's abdomen, which caused him to lose his balance momentarily. As Fernando fell to the floor, Hector raised the weapon, and after releasing his grasp on the officer, he put both of his hands around the weapon and steadied it. Hector then experienced those few seconds of sheer terror a policeman may experience once in his career, or the lucky ones never experience.

Merrick realized now what was going on and began to aim his weapon at Hector. Hector didn't hesitate as his training took over. In rapid succession, Hector fired three shots into Merrick's chest. As the shots landed, Merrick dropped the weapon, his body plummeting against the wall. A few seconds later, Merrick's lifeless body slid down the wall. He came to rest in a grotesque sitting position. His legs were twisted under him, his back rested against the wall, and his head was slumped against his chest.

Hector stood up and walked over to Merrick. He stood over Merrick for a minute.

Unable to control his anger, Hector raised his weapon, shouted, "You fucking bastard!" and shot Merrick twice more in the chest.

Dropping his gun as he turned around, Hector noticed that other policemen were in the hallway, attending to Fernando and the two unconscious officers. Hector began to walk toward the doorway to the cheers and adulation of his fellow officers. When he reached the doorway, a cold chill went through Hector as he realized that something was very wrong.

Turning around, Hector began to quickly walk back to Merrick. Some of the policemen slapped him on the back and congratulated him, but Hector didn't hear them. After taking a second to look at Merrick and the bloodstained wall, Hector turned around with panic in his voice and shouted for everyone to leave. As the policemen cleared the hallway and scrambled up the stairs, Hector closed the door to the hallway and posted a guard. No one but no one was to enter the hallway. As Hector ran to his office, his mind was racing in the panic mode. Something was very, very wrong.

I'LL JUST WAIT FOR THE TOUR BUS

A FTER EVERYONE RAPPELLED FROM THE helicopters and was safely on the ground, Major Ehioze directed four of his soldiers to establish a secure perimeter. He then directed two more of his soldiers to stand guard while the rest of the little expedition went to work.

Everyone removed their backpacks but kept their flak vests on and their weapons nearby, except for Vinson, who kept his weapon slung over his shoulder. Major Ehioze then directed his men to begin clearing the jungle growth. Within a few minutes, one of the soldiers found the buoy. Everyone then realized that their quest should be very close by, and attacked the jungle growth with a new vigor.

As Scotty was working, he noticed Vinson constantly scanning the ground in front of himself. Scotty walked over to his friend and asked him what he was looking for. In a matter-of-fact attitude, Vinson told Scotty that he was looking for snakes. Scotty laughed a little but let the comment pass. The major, however, upon overhearing the conversation, winked at one of his men and stated, "What about the snakes that climb the trees around here? Is anybody keeping an eye out for them?"

Vinson's eyes immediately were drawn skyward as he said out loud to himself, "Ah, shit, nobody said anything about snakes in trees. You got to be kidding me!"

"Everyone knows that snakes can climb trees around here!" the major replied, followed by a round of soft laughter from the soldiers and Scotty.

When the short comic interlude was over, the work continued. The growth was so thick in some places that they couldn't see a foot in front of them. Together everyone chopped endlessly with their machetes, clearing the growth to the ground and advancing mere inches each quarter-hour. Breaks were frequent in the unbearably hot, dry heat. Each time a break was called, the major would caution the men to go easy on the water as they still had to hike out of there.

After one such break, Vinson stood up and returned to work. Scotty noticed a soldier sneaking up behind Vinson as he held his machete in his outstretched hand. At the end of the machete, a large brown snake was coiled around the tip. The soldier saw Scotty and placed his index finger over his lips for Scotty to be quiet. All the men silently turned their attention to the drama unfolding in front of them. When the soldier was about three feet from Vinson's back, he flung the snake over Vinson's head. The snake landed in the branches of a tree right in front of Vinson. Upon hearing the sound of the snake falling in the branches, Vinson looked up and saw fangs right in front of his face.

At the top of his lungs, Vinson yelled out, "Snake!" as he fell backward and reached for his shotgun. While lying on his back on the floor of the jungle, Vinson aimed his shotgun at the offending snake and tried to fire. But he had forgotten to release the safety. At first, Vinson did not pay attention to the laughter around him, or perhaps he just didn't hear it. As he was trying repeatedly to fire his shotgun, the laughter finally penetrated his consciousness and he realized that he was the butt of what he considered a very cruel joke. Vinson then lay there for a minute as he laughed a little to show the men that he could take their kidding, but inwardly he was worried if there were any more snakes around.

The major restored order and directed everyone back to work. For the next half hour, the only sound to be heard was the endless chopping of machete-wielding men. Suddenly, the soldier alongside Scotty swung his machete and was rewarded with the unmistakable sound of metal hitting metal: *Clunk!*

Everyone immediately stopped working and went over to where Scotty was now standing. Even though they were standing right in front of the object, they couldn't clearly see it. For the next hour, the men worked feverishly, and their efforts were rewarded when it was completely uncovered. When the men were finished, they all stood together about ten feet from the object. Everyone's reaction was the same: "What the hell is it?"

Before them was a cylindrical object about four feet in diameter and approximately thirty feet long.

Scotty wiped his sweating forehead with a towel as he considered the object that they had worked so hard to uncover. What it reminded him of was a car that had been crushed into a small cube like the ones he had seen in junkyards back home. But what was this cylinder-shaped object in front of him? To his aeronautical eye, he began to distinguish small parts of an airplane, but it was so thoroughly mashed together that he couldn't be sure. He did know one thing: it was not the airplane or even a part of the airplane they were looking for. This object had been here for a while.

Major Ehioze asked Scotty what he thought it was. Scotty told him that in all likelihood, it was a small aircraft, like a Cessna or a Piper. Scotty then asked the major if any other aircraft had been reported missing within the last five years or so. The major thought for a minute, and then his face lit up as he remembered that a small airplane had disappeared about four years ago. The pilot was a volunteer from the World Health Organization who was flying some government people around when it disappeared from radar. The major recalled that an extensive search was conducted but nothing was ever found.

"Well, Major, I think we may have found it," Scotty replied, thinking more out loud than actually talking.

"How do you know that this is even an airplane?" the major inquired as the men now stood around Scotty, interested in his every word.

Scotty looked around for Vinson, who, true to form, was scanning the ground and trees for snakes, his gun now at the ready. Scotty then looked at the major and the men as he walked over to the object and pointed out, "The skin of an aircraft, such as this, is held together by screws and rivets. These are both steel and stainless steel. Stainless steel is weaker than regular steel, and therefore, stainless steel is used in nonstructural members of the aircraft. Steel fasteners are utilized in joints and other applications where structural integrity is important. The trouble with steel is that it corrodes, while stainless steel will not corrode under most circumstances."

Pointing to parts of the cylinder, Scotty pointed out, "If you would look here, you will notice corrosion points equally distanced apart, on what appears to be the skin of an aircraft, where it is joined to the frame members. While over here"—Scotty walked up to the front of the cylinder—"you can see stainless steel fasteners in almost-new condition. If you look hard enough, you can identify some parts of this object." Scotty walked around the object, followed by his interested entourage. "Over here we have part of a wing flap, while in this area is what looks like part of a wheel assembly, the kind found on a small light aircraft."

All the soldiers readily agreed with Scotty's assessment of the object and pointed out other parts that they could recognize, such as the tail as it wrapped around the cylinder. Scotty then directed Vinson to start photographing the object from all different angles. Scotty, meanwhile, stood there pondering the object.

"What's wrong?" Major Ehioze asked.

Letting out a breath of warm air, Scotty replied, "I sure would like to get a small piece of the airplane for analysis. We could nail down what kind of airplane this was."

"Aren't we going to bring it back?" the major asked.

"No. There is not much sense in that. I'm afraid that it would just be a lot of hard work for nothing. We have the photographs, and from what we know, we should be able to identify the aircraft. But it sure would be nice to have a sample of the metal for analysis," Scotty replied and was amazed when one of the soldiers placed a pair of heavy-duty bolt cutters in his hand. He thanked the soldier and then turned toward the major and asked, "I don't suppose that you have a swimming pool handy also?"

The major laughed and replied, "No, but if you give us a few minutes, we could build one for you."

Together, the major and Scotty laughed as they worked the bolt cutters against the metal. After ten minutes of bending and cutting the metal, their efforts were rewarded with a four-by-four-inch piece of the object. After putting the piece of the object in a plastic bag, Scotty announced that they were finished. The major instructed everyone to take a fifteen-minute break and eat something before they left. As an added precaution, Major Ehioze handed each man a salt tablet and stood by as each person took the pill.

After the rest period was over, the major called in the perimeter security detail.

Once everyone was assembled, he ordered two men on point to proceed directly to the pickup spot. The main body of men would follow, walking ten yards apart at all times, in order to make themselves harder targets for the poachers. Three of the soldiers were to follow the main body five hundred yards behind them. Major Ehioze explained that, should the main body be attacked by poachers, the rear guard would be in position to outflank the ambushers and attack them from behind. A nasty surprise for the poachers, but an effective tactic in the jungle.

Once their group began their trek, each person took a turn at hacking away at the jungle growth in order to clear a path. After an hour of this backbreaking work, their efforts were rewarded when they reached a forest. Vinson seemed much more relaxed now as they moved quickly through the tall trees. After another two hours of walking, they reached the pickup point. The major then radioed to the helicopters for a ride back to the airport.

As they were landing at the airport, Scotty was glad to see that the search aircraft had already returned. Once the helicopters touched down, Scotty made sure to thank each one of the soldiers individually for helping in the search. Scotty stood by as the helicopters lifted off, and waved to the soldiers as they headed back to their base.

Bill Finningham greeted Scotty and Vinson as they entered the hangar. Bill inquired about their trip, and Scotty told him that the trip probably cleared up an old mystery but did nothing for the present one. When asked by Scotty how his day went, Finningham explained that they had now overflown the entire country and no positive contacts had been found beyond the ones the Zambia Air Force had identified. Anxious to take a shower, Scotty requested Finningham to assemble the search maps and telemetry from the aircraft for review. Scotty and Vinson then headed for a long-awaited shower.

Donning fresh clothes after their showers, Scotty and Vinson were treated to some refreshments, courtesy of Finningham. As the three of them sat down at a table in the hangar, Scotty asked if anything unusual occurred during the afternoon search. Finningham was slow to answer but admitted with great hesitance that the Foo Fighters were with both of the aircraft throughout the afternoon search. Scotty didn't like this bit of news but was secure in the fact that the crew for both had returned safely.

After they finished eating, the threesome began reviewing the search results of the day. After approximately three hours of reviewing the search process, Scotty concluded that they had done an excellent job and had covered every possibility. Scotty then instructed Finningham and Vinson to stand down the search crew tomorrow, as it would serve no real purpose to overfly the search pattern again. Turning toward Vinson, Scotty asked him to arrange a photographic safari for the flight crew tomorrow. He thought they might as well enjoy some part of the country while they were here. Wishing them good night, Scotty walked over to his waiting car and relaxed in the back seat.

As he was leaving the airport, Scotty remembered that he wanted to ask Finningham something. After instructing the driver to return to the hangar, Scotty sat back and wondered about the man he had fired in the Canaries. As he reached the hangar, Scotty caught sight of Finningham and Vinson as they were about to enter the office area inside the hangar. Scotty called out to Finningham, who turned around and walked toward him.

"Bill, I'm sorry. There is one more thing I wanted to ask you," Scotty started out.

"Yes, Scotty, what is it?" Finningham asked.

"That guy I dismissed in the Canaries, has the crews said anything more about him?" Scotty asked.

"Not really. Everyone thinks he is a real son of a bitch that complained about everything and was condescending as all hell. But one thing in his favor, he sure did know electronics. I just hope my boss doesn't put him back on our project," Finningham answered.

Still not satisfied, Scotty pressed on, "Does anyone know anything about him beyond the job?"

"Not much. He always kept to himself. He sure didn't think much of his fellow employees. He used to call us a bunch of cavemen trying to act intelligent. There is one thing. The man said that he had a family and all, but no one ever saw them and he never talked about them. He just never socialized with any of us. I always thought that the man was a nut. Other than that, no one knows anything about him," Finningham answered, searching his memory for something else.

"Did he have any odd habits at all?" Scotty asked, trying to think of the right questions to ask.

"No, he is just a real mean person—wait, there is one thing. Well, actually two. He takes pills continuously, little ones. Says that they are for his asthma. Never saw him use an inhaler, though. My son has asthma, and he uses an inhaler and takes pills, but nowhere near the amount he does.

"The other thing that is odd—and don't think me crude—is the size of his eyes. They are large, the largest I've ever seen, and boy, are they dark! You would think that you are looking into a black pool when you look at his eyes. That's why he always wears sunglasses. One day one of the guys asked him about his eyes. He told him something about a genetic disorder and walked away. No one ever said anything about it ever again.

"Does that help you out?" Finningham concluded while admitting to himself that he knew very little about the mysterious Mr. Merrick.

"Yeah, thanks, Bill. Listen, you and your men did an excellent job. I don't know how to thank you and your men enough," Scotty added.

"It's been our pleasure, Scotty. Glad we could help, although we didn't find the aircraft. But we were able to prove that all our work for the past few years has been successful," Finningham answered.

"Okay, but thanks again. Enjoy your day tomorrow," Scotty answered and concluded the conversation.

Scotty then relaxed in the back seat of the car again as he headed back to the presidential home. Before the car left the airport, Scotty was fast asleep.

Once at the presidential home, Scotty awoke and entered the house. He was surprised to see Titilayo and Mawuli still awake as they charged their uncle. After a warm exchange of hello kisses and hugs, Scotty chased them upstairs into their bedrooms. After tucking them in bed, Scotty returned downstairs and found Doreen, Edenausegboye, and the president sitting at the kitchen table, enjoying a cup of tea.

When asked about his day by Doreen, Scotty told her the details of the search, from the Foo Fighters to his excursion into the jungle. Scotty was struggling to stay awake as he talked, but it was hopeless. His words faded as Scotty's head sank against his chest and he fell into a deep sleep.

The president helped Doreen and Edenausegboye carry Scotty upstairs to his bedroom and place him in bed. Excusing himself, the president left as Doreen and Edenausegboye started to undress Scotty. Together they removed his flight boots and began to take off his flight suit. As they were doing this, Edenausegboye asked Doreen what her interest was in Scotty. Doreen was taken aback a bit by the directness of the question and replied that she really liked him but wasn't sure if the feeling was returned. Edenausegboye laughed slightly and declared, "Anyone can see that you are both in love with each other!"

Doreen's face turned red as she replied, "Well, maybe."

"I don't mean to be forward. It's just that Scotty is very special to my family and to me. Scotty is a man who doesn't give his friendship easily, and the lucky few he extends it to are very grateful for its gift. My children absolutely love him, and Asukile trusts his advice and treasures his friendship.

"You're a lucky woman, Doreen. Never let your shyness stand in your way. If you know what you want, go after it before you lose what you seek," Edenausegboye added.

"Thank you, Edenausegboye. I appreciate your advice," Doreen answered as she looked at Scotty and smiled.

Once they took off his flight suit and tucked Scotty under the covers, Doreen gently kissed him on the forehead and whispered, "Sleep well, my…my…love."

As Edenausegboye and Doreen left Scotty's room and said good night, Doreen was surprised at herself for what she said when she kissed Scotty good night. Her true feelings were beginning to emerge. That night, she slept peacefully, aware now of those feelings.

JUST SEND HELP

Once in his office, Hector fumbled through his Rolodex and managed, somehow, to locate the telephone number of the coroner. While he waited for Juan Garcia to come to the telephone, Hector tried to calm himself. Thinking that he was back in control of his emotions when Juan said hello, Hector began shouting into the telephone for him to come immediately and to bring biological containment suits.

Juan couldn't make any sense of what his friend was talking about and thought that it was another one of his practical jokes. Just last month, Hector had called him and asked Juan to come over to the airport and pick up two stiffs. When Juan arrived at the airport, there were two stiffs, all right, two stiff drunks.

Trying desperately to calm Hector down, Juan could only understand that someone had been shot, and instead of bleeding red, the man's blood's color was pink. Now convinced that this was another joke, Juan asked Hector if the man was a blue blood. Hector disregarded the comment and pleaded with Juan to come, and come quickly. The panic in Hector's voice convinced Juan that this was for real. After promising to be right there, Juan made the necessary preparations.

When Juan and his team entered the hallway of the jail cells, they were dressed in individual biological containment suits. As they approached

Merrick, it was easy for Juan to see why Hector was so panicked. The body of Merrick was indeed bleeding a pinkish-color blood that seemed to froth upon contact with the air. After a short discussion among themselves, Juan and his team decided to wrap the body in heavy-duty plastic and seal every opening with a heavy-duty tape. The body was then going to be transported and immediately cremated since they did not have the facilities to conduct an autopsy in a safe environment. Juan left his crew as they set about their grisly work. First, they wrapped the body and then washed down the entire area with pure bleach.

Upon reaching Hector's office, Juan instructed him to get undressed as his clothing as well as those of anyone else who came in contact with the prisoner would have to be burned.

Hector was then escorted to a decontamination shower, where he and the rest of his men were hopefully cleaned of any remaining effects of their contact with Merrick.

After Juan and his team departed and things calmed down, Hector returned to his office and tried to think logically through the events of the day and what he would do next. All physical evidence of the existence of Merrick had been taken by Juan's team, including his clothing, wallet, and everything he had touched, from the mattress he had slept on down to the bed frame and the roll of toilet paper in his cell. Just then, Hector thought about the pills he had found in Merrick's beeper. He placed a call to Juan and informed him about the pills and that they had been sent to the narcotics lab for testing. Juan told him that he would make the necessary arrangement to get them. Hector pleaded with Juan to at least preserve one of the pills, and preserve it in such a way so as not to present a biological hazard. Juan reluctantly agreed to his friend's request, but only if it was feasible.

Hector felt that there must be something that he was missing. He re-read over the file on Merrick, and again nothing unusual stood out. Taking the fingerprint card of Merrick, Hector scanned it into his computer and performed a search of Interpol's database. After a few seconds, Hector found himself staring at the computer screen as it blinked, "No Matches Found."

Hector sat at his desk, thinking for a moment. What he needed was general information. If Interpol didn't have a fingerprint record, then no one else in the world would either. What he needed was a general search. He then tied into the FBI's database in the United States. Not expecting much, Hector was surprised to find a match for the name and the address of record. When the computer asked him if he wanted a hard copy of the file, Hector immediately clicked his computer mouse onto the Yes box.

After a few minutes, Hector was rewarded with three pages of data that told him that his Stanley Merrick was not the Stanley Merrick who had been a Los Angeles police officer that had died in the line of duty on September 20 in 1996. The essential details matched, such as date of birth, place of birth, address, and a general description of height and weight. But nothing else matched. The real Merrick had a degree in history and had never even taken an electronics course.

Hector stayed late in his office and waited until it was an appropriate hour in Los Angeles. He contacted the personnel department of Braswell Engineering under the guise of confirming his employment since Mr. Merrick had caused a disturbance in the airport. The personnel director, Mrs. Evans, found the whole affair humorous and pleaded with Hector to keep him locked up. Mrs. Evans did not pull any punches. She considered Merrick as the biggest bastard that she had ever met. Hector thanked her and hung up knowing that Mrs. Evans's feelings matched his own for the recently departed.

Before he left for home, Hector decided that he should try to reach Scotty to tell him what had happened. Once he placed the call to Scotty's home, Hector realized that he had a better chance of breaking into Fort Knox than he had with trying to get information out of Marlene. Out of desperation, Hector settled for a promise from Marlene that she would try to contact Scotty as soon as possible and request him to call. Satisfied that this was the absolute best that he could do, Hector decided to go home and leave the mysterious Mr. Merrick for another day.

As he walked to his car, Hector thanked God for this day and for the lives of his men. From now on he would live by Scotty's words and truly enjoy this paradise, which he knew he had taken for granted for far too long.

WHAT THE HELL WAS THAT THING?

A s the shape on the bottom of the ocean floor grew in size on the monitors, Morrison could clearly see that whatever it could possibly be was round in shape. He could not conceive of the fact that the object could be an entire airplane, but his mind imagined that it could be the jet engine of an aircraft they were looking at. Morrison was straining to see the object and make out any possible features when suddenly a bright light filled one of the monitors as a luminescent fish swam in front of the camera.

After a few seconds, the contrast of the picture returned to normal as each remote vehicle traveled the length of the object. A few minutes later, the vehicles reached the end of the object. As the vehicles turned around, their lights centered on the end of the cylinder-shaped object. Morrison and Chester knowingly looked toward each other as they recognized what surely must be the tail section of an airplane crushed into the end of the cylinder. Morrison cleared his throat and spoke up. "George, I want you to send each vehicle down a side of the object, photographing it every couple of seconds. Also, would it be possible to determine its size?"

"Yes, Admiral, we can pretty accurately estimate its size based upon our measurements, but we could be off by as much as a few inches. I'm beginning the run now," George replied as he gave the order for the remote vehicles to proceed down the sides of the object.

The impact of what Morrison and Chester saw was not lost on Lieutenant Cunningham. When he first began the task of identifying traces of Alpha Zuron radiation, he assumed that he was either looking for meteorites so that some scientist could extract its exotic metals or for some errant satellite that fell back to Earth. But this was different. Cunningham had seen and been a passenger on enough airplanes so that even he could clearly recognize the tail section of an airplane embedded in the end of the object. The thought that was occupying his mind now was just how the tail section of an airplane ended up in this hunk of metal on the floor of the ocean.

As the remote vehicles began their run down the sides of the object, Morrison could now see other telltale parts or pieces of an aircraft. Chester was likewise closely watching the video monitors and wondered about the people. He was concerned that they might be crushed somewhere in the object, and if they weren't, just where were they? It was as if the aircraft simply folded in on itself into a nice cylinder shape.

Cunningham inched forward from the back of the room, concentrating on the monitors, unaware of his movement, until he was abreast of the two admirals. Like them, he stood there with his mouth open in awe of the sight.

The threesome called out to one another parts of the aircraft as the remote vehicles swept over and by them. What looked like a jet engine crushed into the cylinder was picked out by Cunningham, Chester was able to identify a landing strut, and Morrison saw a section of the outer skin of an aircraft with holes in it where the windows once were. The area above where the windows should be, the three of them could see faint traces of the letters S-V-A-A-L. That revelation had an impact on Morrison and Chester immediately. Chester was the first to speak up. "See those letters, S-V-A-A-L? That can only mean Transvaal National Airlines. The rest of the letters are hidden as the metal folds into the cylinder…my god, what the hell happened to this aircraft and the people aboard her?"

"I don't think that you are going to find them here!" Cunningham spoke out loud, forgetting that he was there simply as an observer. After he had spoken those words, the full impact and implication of what Chester had said hit him hard. *He thinks that there were people aboard that aircraft. And if there were people aboard that aircraft, that could only mean that the plane had to be flying at that time. My god, what is going on here?* Cunningham wondered. Before he could finish thinking through the problem, Morrison interrupted his thoughts.

"What do you mean?" Morrison asked as he turned and faced the young lieutenant.

"Well, sir, this aircraft looks like scrap metal, much like cars are crushed and then sent for recycling. I must admit that I have never seen scrap metal in a cylinder shape before. What gets me, though, is, Why does it have traces of Alpha Zuron radiation? If the admiral thinks that there were people aboard the aircraft, then it would follow that the aircraft was in flight when an incident occurred. There can be no other explanation. If the aircraft has traces of Alpha Zuron radiation, then the object was either taken aboard an object that had been in space or crushed by an object that has been in space. Since the sheer size of such an object does not exist on Earth, then the object that did this is of alien origin. That would explain the radiation.

"Now, if an alien craft took the aircraft aboard, it did so for a reason. It sure wasn't to copy our technology. Therefore, the conclusion is obvious. The aliens are or were interested in the human beings aboard the aircraft. Otherwise, why go through this charade of hiding the aircraft on the bottom of the ocean?" Cunningham concluded and nervously awaited an answer, wondering if he had just uncovered the greatest deception of all time.

Chester turned toward Cunningham with a smile on his face and simply stated, "Bingo, Mr. Cunningham. Welcome aboard the express train to oblivion."

Morrison quickly added, "This is why your work is so important. You have given us the ability to locate any trace of alien visitation or incursion. I know this may be a little bizarre right now, but all will be explained shortly. Just remember, never talk to anyone about this. The results of any indiscretion are quite unpleasant. Now let's get back to business."

Captain Montgomery and his technician had heard the exchange between the admirals and Lieutenant Cunningham. As they worked, George and his technician would occasionally look at each other with looks of shock and surprise, but continued working, half afraid to speak. Their work was interrupted when Morrison spoke up.

"George!"

"Yes, sir," George answered, turning around toward the video camera.

"Okay, now you and your technician know what we are looking for. Somehow, this aircraft was crushed in space and returned to Earth or was crushed inside a vehicle that had been in space. That would account for the presence of Alpha Zuron radiation. The rules of secrecy apply to both you and your technician. Do I have your word that you will never speak about this incident?" Morrison asked, knowing the answer.

"Yes, sir," George immediately answered.

"Yes, Admiral," the technician answered as she also turned around and faced the camera.

For the first time since the satellite link was established, the technician had turned toward the camera. Morrison was surprised to see that underneath the baseball cap and baggy uniform was a beautiful woman about forty years old. "What is your name, Sailor?" he asked.

"Chief Petty Officer Janoski, sir," she replied.

"I'm sorry to get you both into this, but there is no other way," Morrison claimed.

"No problem, sir. If there is one thing that I learned in life, it is how to keep my mouth shut," Chief Janoski replied.

"Thank you, Chief," Morrison answered and then turned his attention toward George. "Now, George, can you give me the dimensions of the object?"

"Admiral, according to our data—but keep in mind that there is a margin for error—the object is approximately twenty feet in diameter and one hundred and thirteen feet in length.

"One of the remotes is equipped with a cutting torch. I'm going to try to cut into the object and see if we can get a sample of the metal. I figured that if we could get a sample, then someone might be able to test the sample against a known material. Then the object could be identified," George replied. Then he continued, "Admiral, I'm going to have the remote cut into the object now, so if you want to watch the monitor, you will be able to see what's happening."

"Good idea, George. We will be standing by," Morrison answered.

Morrison, Chester, and Cunningham remained standing in the middle of the office and watched the remote vehicle. As if on cue, the torch lit up in a bright-blue flame. Slowly the remote vehicle edged closer to the object. When it was within reach, a mechanical arm extended from the vehicle and the torch began cutting into the object. Suddenly, the sound from the monitors was filled with an alarm going off. Their attention was then drawn to the monitor they had talked to George over. But Chief Janoski was alone at her station. George was gone.

"Chief!" Morrison called out.

Chief Janoski turned around, facing the camera, and, in a calm voice, answered, "Admiral, our radar picked up a low-flying aircraft coming toward us at over six hundred miles per hour. The computers could not get a match on the aircraft. Captain Montgomery went up on deck to get a visual."

"Okay, Chief, please keep us advised and turn off that damn alarm!" Morrison ordered, but before he had finished talking, Chief Janoski had turned back around and gone back to work.

"Admiral, they stopped the cutting operation." Cunningham spoke up as he scanned the monitors.

"Wonder what is going on," Chester said as George came back into view on one of the monitors.

"Admiral!" George called out.

"Yes, George, what the hell is going on?" Morrison demanded.

"It appears that as soon as we lit the torch, our radar picked up an aircraft speeding toward us," George answered, breathing hard. Trying to catch his breath, George continued, "Admiral, it was a flying saucer. The thing was perfectly round, with a flat top about seventy feet across. It sped off to the east and out of sight."

"Okay, George, calm down. What are you going to do now?" Morrison asked.

"I've ordered the remotes back on board. We are making preparations to get underway…" George paused. "Admiral, just what the fuck is going on? Is my ship in danger?" he demanded, knowing that his ship had absolutely no defensive weapons with which to fight.

"George, you did the right thing. Secure all operations and get your ship underway." A brief pause. "Hold on a second, George," Morrison ordered as he turned toward Chester and held a hushed conversation. Cunningham took a respectful few steps backward, away from the whispering admirals. When they finished their private interlude, Morrison faced the monitors and spoke up. "George, I want you to listen to me very carefully. Here's what I want you to do. First, get all the memory cards from the digital cameras and any monitoring tapes as well as the telemetry tapes and lock them in your safe. Next, do your best to calm down your crew. Tell them it was one of our experimental aircraft or something. Just try to calm down the situation. Right now I want you to steer to the naval base in Puerto Rico. Do you have enough supplies and fuel on board?"

"I have a two-week supply of food. As far as fuel goes, I have a ten-day supply. We have more than enough to make Puerto Rico," George answered.

"Okay, good, George. We'll talk later. Right now, see to your ship. Admiral Braddock will contact you shortly. Smooth sailing, George. I'm breaking the connection," Morrison concluded.

"Goodbye, Admiral," George was able to answer before the satellite connection went dead.

THAT'S IMPOSSIBLE— IT CAN'T BE MORNING ALREADY!

Awaking to the sound of tropical birds greeting the new day outside of his window, Scotty propped himself up on his elbows and looked around his room, making sure of where he was. Peeking under the covers, he wondered what had happened to his flight suit. The last thing Scotty remembered was being at the kitchen table and talking to Asukile.

What he was talking about, Scotty couldn't recall. As he was thinking through this paradox, Scotty heard the sound of small footsteps running down the hallway. The footsteps stopped outside of his door, and the doorknob was beginning to turn very slowly. Quickly Scotty laid his head back down on his soft oversize pillow and pretended to be asleep.

When the bedroom door creaked open, Scotty peeked at the doorway and saw Mawuli and Titilayo enter the room and walk toward his bed on their tiptoes. They were trying to be quiet, but the giggles overcame their childhood scheme. Still pretending to be asleep, Scotty bit down hard on his lower lip in a successful attempt to control his own laughter. Once the children were on each side of the bed, Mawuli cried out, "Time to get up, Uncle Scotty!" Wanting to play this game a little longer, Scotty lay perfectly still, pretending to snore.

Being determined to wake his uncle, Mawuli gently placed his thumb and forefinger on Scotty's eye and pried open his eyelid. Scotty let out a howling roar, like a lion in the jungle, reached over, picked up Mawuli, and threw him on the bed. Letting out another roar, Scotty reached over, picked up Titilayo as well, and threw her on the bed beside her brother. Scotty then knelt over them, let out another roar, and to their absolute delight, began to tickle them. Their laughter carried his joyful message out of the room and down the hallway.

Doreen, upon hearing the laughter, threw her covers off and ran into Scotty's room. When she saw what was going on, Doreen just had to get in on the fun. She ran over to the bed, threw her arms around Scotty's torso from behind, and shouted out, "Let's get him!" Scotty fell to his side and was pushed onto his back by Doreen. She then held down his arms as the children vigorously tickled him. Resistance was futile, as laughter overcame Scotty to the point that his strength was sapped.

Edenausegboye then came into the room and, with a slight hint of laughter in her voice, called out, "Children, children!" Receiving no response, Edenausegboye said to herself, "Ah, what the hell!" as she ran over to the bed and joined in the fun. Asukile then appeared in the room and started laughing. In order to make his presence known, Asukile, in a laughing voice, hollered out, "Can't the president of the country get some sleep around here?"

Titilayo struggled through the laughter and cried out, "Get Daddy!"

Edenausegboye, Titilayo, and Mawuli then attacked Asukile, knocking him to the floor as they tickled him. Scotty and Doreen sat on the edge of the bed next to each other and watched a family that loved one another play.

After a few minutes of unending laughter, Asukile managed to escape the grip of his captors and proclaimed, "Breakfast and then a picnic!" The children let out a cheerful "Yeah!" and disappeared down the stairs. Edenausegboye and Asukile put an arm around each other's waist and began to walk out of the room but stopped to kiss each other.

Edenausegboye was a little embarrassed by this sudden show of emotion and slapped her husband on the behind to break his grip. Turning toward Scotty and Doreen, Edenausegboye said, "Time to go, you two," as she and Asukile left the room, their arms still around each other's waist.

Scotty answered, "I'll be right down. I just want to take a shower first."

As Doreen stood up and walked toward the door, Scotty couldn't help but notice that she was dressed in short silk pajamas. Unable to resist the temptation, Scotty asked, "Going casual again, are we?"

Doreen stopped for a moment as a broad smile crept across her face, and she knew that he was referring to her little indiscretion of the other night. She then looked over her shoulder at him and countered, "Be nice now. Who do you think took your clothes off and put you in bed last night? Just remember one thing: I saw you naked, and I have pictures." Doreen then ran out of the room as Scotty rose from the bed and walked toward her.

She had left Scotty for the second time standing at his doorway with his mouth open. Had she looked back, Doreen would have seen desire in his eyes and puzzlement across his face. If this were a game of chess, Scotty had just been checkmated.

Breakfast was a nosy affair. The children talked endlessly about the forthcoming day and the promise it beheld. Everyone was in the spirit of the day, except for Scotty, who was playing it a little cagy. He wasn't quite sure if Doreen was playing a joke on him or if she really had taken a couple of photographs of him. When the children finished their breakfast and scampered off to get ready, Asukile asked Scotty if something was wrong. Scotty looked up and asked, "Okay, just how did I get to bed last night?"

Edenausegboye spoke up. "After you fell asleep, we carried you up to your room. Doreen and I undressed you and put you under the covers."

Nervously, Scotty asked, "Did—"

Doreen cut him off and replied, "No, but the pictures will be ready by eleven. We ordered the panoramic ones." Her comment was met by laughter from everyone except Scotty, whose face turned red as he put his head down and continued to eat.

"Oh, Scotty, smile. It's not like we are going to sell the pictures to anyone," Edenausegboye added and then continued, "At least not anyone you know."

Realizing that there was only one way out of his predicament, Scotty chimed in, "I hope you got my good side at least."

Doreen, having some fun with Scotty at his expense, countered, "We got your good side, all right. But I can't promise you that it was your face!"

Scotty looked at Doreen and made a comical face as he stuck his tongue out at her. Quick to recover, Scotty replied, "Well, as long as you spell my name right and my mother doesn't see them, it's okay."

Doreen was about to answer when Mawuli came into the kitchen and pleaded with everyone to hurry up. Not wanting to disappoint a child, everyone cleaned up and left the house. Edenausegboye had saved one of the prettiest sights in the world for the location of the picnic, Victoria Falls.

MURPHY'S LAW? WHO THE HELL IS MURPHY?

AFTER FINISHING THEIR CONVERSATION WITH Captain Montgomery, Morrison, Chester, and Cunningham sat around discussing what was found on the floor of the ocean. Together they tried to imagine what possibly could have happened to the passengers of the airliner. They couldn't really come up with anything other than hope that somehow they were alive and well. Their conversation was interrupted when the telephone on Chester's desk rang. Answering it, Chester was informed that a flash message for Admiral Morrison had just been received from General Salas of Brazil. He was requesting to speak with Morrison on an encrypted satellite uplink. Chester instructed his secretary to put it through as soon as it was ready.

After hanging up the telephone, Chester told Morrison that the call would be coming through shortly. "It must be something to do with that crashed airliner in Brazil," Morrison declared and then spoke what he was thinking: "God, I hope we don't have another situation like the one in Zambia."

Lieutenant Cunningham spoke up, directing his question toward Chester. "Admiral, should I leave the room?"

"No, Lieutenant, you're in the club now, so you might as well hear what the man has to say," Morrison replied before Chester could answer.

Just then, the telephone rang. Morrison crossed the room and picked up the telephone. After confirming that it was General Salas, Morrison told him that he was putting it on conference speaker. When the change was made, Morrison replaced the handset to the telephone and stated, "General, I am here with Rear Admiral Braddock and a Lieutenant Cunningham, who is a new member of our group. Please speak freely."

"Okay, Admiral. Chester, how are you?" General Salas began.

"I'm fine, Carlos. How is that lovely family of yours?" Chester replied.

"They're fine…for now, but I…" There was a momentary silence as Carlos searched for the right words. When he started speaking again, his voice was cracking. "I don't know if…if anyone is safe anymore."

"Carlos, take your time. Just tell us what is wrong," Morrison pleaded.

"Thank you, Arthur," General Salas began and then, after swallowing hard, continued, "Admirals, Lieutenant, I'm standing in a field outside of a temporary morgue we set up a few hours ago. It's just outside of a small coastal fishing village. You know that plane I told you about? Well, we never found it, but we found the passengers and crew. That is, if you can still call them people after what has been done to them. Hell, some of them don't even resemble a person anymore, just pieces of flesh." One was able to imagine the tears falling from General Salas's eyes as his voice continued to crack, and his breathing was shallow and rapid.

"Carlos, please take a moment," Morrison implored, feeling compassion for the general.

"I'm okay. It's just so horrible," General Salas replied.

"It's okay. Just take your time," Morrison answered as he looked at Chester's face and saw a hint of confusion on it.

After a pause of approximately fifteen seconds, General Salas continued, "A local fisherman stumbled upon forty-eight bodies, or rather parts of bodies. They were neatly arranged in rows covered by a material no one is familiar with.

"Two seamen from our Coastal Patrol were the first on the scene. They, in turn, contacted my headquarters, and we responded. No one could have been prepared, in their worst nightmares, for what we found. Each body has been dissected. I don't just mean cut apart. Remember high school biology class when we had to dissect worms and small animals and remove the major organs? Well, it's like that, but my god, these are, or rather *were*, human beings.

"In each case the body had most of, if not all, the internal organs removed. In others the limbs were removed as well. In some cases, the brains were even removed. My morgue officer told me that the incisions were not made with a knife, but rather with a new type of surgical laser much more precise and clean-cutting than he has ever seen. The odd thing is that there is no blood anywhere. It's as if the bodies were sucked dry before the monster began cutting the people.

"The desecration had to have been done elsewhere, and then the bodies were dumped on the beach. The young girl that survived, may God have mercy on her, was—"

Morrison interrupted General Salas. "What, you have a survivor?"

"Yes! I'm sorry, I thought that I had mentioned her. The fisherman found her wrapped in the same cloth as the bodies. The poor girl is in a deep state of shock and can't talk or communicate. It's like she is in a coma, but awake. She just stares as if she doesn't see you. We believe her parents were passengers on the aircraft, so we can only imagine what she must have seen. I have her under the care of my staff psychiatrists, but so far, they cannot get a response out of her.

"My medical doctors conducted a detailed physical examination of her. They found that her vagina had been violated. Internal scarring indicates that some small samples of her tissue have been removed. The doctors also found that a very thin needle entered her neck. When they x-rayed the area, they were able to determine that the needle tracked up into her brain. They concluded that another tissue sample was taken.

"Oh, there's one more thing. Another probe was sent up into her nasal cavity and deposited what can best be described as a BB. The object has been removed by our doctors and is currently undergoing testing. We have tried to x-ray it, but the film comes out foggy. We've even tried to cut it open with a laser, but no luck there either. Somehow we'll figure out what it is and what it's purpose is.

"Arthur, I don't know what is going on. I need your help. This alien thing has taken on a whole new twist. I'd like you to come down here and see this for yourself," General Ramos concluded.

"Are you sure that this is alien activity?" Morrison asked, knowing the answer. "There is not a force on Earth that could have done this. You know that, Admiral. I have all the military forces of my country on alert status only because I don't know what else to do," Carlos quickly replied.

"I know, Carlos. I was just hoping that there was a possible alternative to what we have feared for so long. I'll be down there late today. Also, I am going to bring a Lieutenant Cunningham with me. He's the newest addition to our organization. That is, if that's okay with you?" Morrison commanded more than asked. Then he added, "I'll have Lieutenant Cunningham contact your base and coordinate our arrival."

"That's fine with me. Arthur, just get here as soon as you can," Carlos pleaded. "We'll be leaving around 1400[42] hours. Oh, there is one other thing. I have a team in Zambia looking for a downed airliner. The leader of the search is the man we talked about to head up the association. They should be finished today, and I would like to have their input on your situation. I could have them there probably tomorrow. Would that be all right?" Morrison asked, this time knowing that Carlos would agree.

"Anything, Arthur. Just get here, will you?" Carlos pleaded again.

"We'll be there today, Carlos. I promise," Morrison quickly answered, a little worried about the edge in his friend's voice.

When they said their goodbyes and hung up, Morrison, Chester, and Cunningham momentarily stared at one another as they thought about the victims Carlos had described. Cunningham was a little confused about everything. In the short span of a few hours, he lost one job and found another, aliens had suddenly become a threat, and it seemed as if he was joining a secret club to fight aliens. *Why in God's name did I answer the telephone?* Cunningham thought to himself.

Chester's intercom broke the awkward silence. "Admiral!" a voice pleaded through the speaker. Instinctively, Chester pressed the button and answered the frantic voice. "Sir, the operations room called. Since you were on a call to Brazil, they thought that you might be interested. One of the satellites has detected an unknown aircraft crossing the Atlantic Ocean at well over Mach 3, heading straight for Brazil."

"Okay, patch the feed through to my monitors immediately," Chester ordered as Morrison walked over to the telephone on the conference table and tried calling Carlos directly on his satellite phone. "Are you sure that it is not an errant missile?" Chester asked, somewhat hoping it was.

"Admiral, it is a confirmed UFO and not a missile," the frantic voice answered.

As Chester broke the connection, his monitors came alive. "Carlos!" Morrison shouted into the telephone once the general had answered. "We are tracking an unknown heading toward your twenty.[43] Coming low and fast from the east. Suggest you go to red alert status. Please instruct your pilots to observe and not engage!" Morrison cried out.

Carlos replied, "Ordering red alert now. But how—"

But he was interrupted by Morrison.

"I'll explain later. Please just observe and do not engage," Morrison pleaded.

"Will do!" Carlos replied and then hung up as his attention shifted to preparing for the arrival of the UFO.

As Chester stood in the center of his office, staring at the computer monitors, Morrison made another telephone call, this time to Colorado. His order was simple: put the base on red alert. If Carlos was right and indeed the game had changed, then it was anybody's guess as to what would come next.

After hanging up the telephone, Morrison joined Chester and Cunningham, who was now standing alongside his superior officer, and waited for the drama to unfold. They didn't have to wait long. Within a few minutes, the UFO slowed its speed and came to a complete stop approximately twenty-five miles from the coast of Brazil and just hovered there. From the satellite picture, the threesome could clearly see that the UFO was the classic saucer shape. Very faintly they could see what looked like a green light coming from the underside of the UFO, shining down on the ocean. It was as if the UFO was looking for something on the surface of the ocean.

Cunningham, who was scanning all the monitors, noticed four radar blips suddenly appear on a monitor that displayed a radar image of the area. "Admirals, something is happening. It looks like fighters are moving toward the UFO," Cunningham stated out loud, and as he finished, a box appeared under the four blips, which identified the aircraft as four F-15 fighter jets. All eyes then became transfixed on the live satellite video feed. They watched as the F-15s flew by the stationary UFO and then turned back around and headed directly at it. The UFO started moving away toward the north, but not at an accelerated rate of speed. It was as if the UFO was toying with the fighters. Correcting their course, the fighter jets followed the UFO northward. When the jets closed to within ten miles of the UFO, missiles suddenly left the wings of the fighters headed for the UFO.

Silently, Morrison, Chester, and Cunningham cheered on the pilots, even though they were disobeying orders. They each wanted to see the UFO shot down, but their hopes were soon dashed. A red light came out of the saucer and instantly blew up the pursuing missiles. When this happened, the fighter jets turned toward the east and flew away from the saucer. Not letting the fighters escape quite so easily, the UFO reversed course and now was following the fleeing pilots. Morrison had an inner feeling of what was going to happen next as he silently hoped that the UFO would turn away.

As they stood and watched, the distance between the UFO and the fighters narrowed rapidly. When it looked like the UFO was about to fly past the fighter jets, a red beam of light came out of the saucer and hit each one of the fighter jets. In an instant, the four F-15s exploded in a spectacular explosion that lit up the night sky. The UFO flew through the explosions and sped away to the south, gaining altitude as it disappeared off the display.

Morrison was the first to speak. "Goddamnit, why didn't those pilots just follow orders and just observe? I admire their courage but curse their stupidity. I'll tell you one thing: Carlos is right, the game has changed. I just hope that we are not too late to survive."

"Arthur, they seem to follow a shoot-if-shot-upon approach. Like Scotty's wingman and these poor devils. If we can keep our cool until we are ready, then we should be okay," Chester answered.

Turning toward Chester, Morrison pointed out, "But what about the two airliners? Are we supposed to sit by and let these bastards attack the human race anytime they want? We have to stop them somehow and keep them away."

"I know, Arthur. And no, we can't sit by and let them do what they did in Zambia and Brazil. But I don't think it will happen again, at least not right away," Chester answered, trying to calm his friend down.

"Why not, sir?" Cunningham asked before Morrison could find the words.

"Well, let's try to look at it objectively. Zambia is the first recorded incident of the aliens snatching an aircraft while it was in flight. Why haven't they done it before? To answer that, we have to ask ourselves, Why now? I believe that the answer is, they simply didn't have the capability until now.

"Look it. They have been visiting the Earth for hundreds of thousands of years. To be sure, they must have interfered with the human race and continue to do so. What they did in Zambia is something entirely new to them. They didn't do it in the United States or any other country in the world that is capable of fighting them. No, they chose a developing country that doesn't possess a fully modern military machine. Zambia was an experiment and nothing more. They proved that they could do it, and that was what they were after. The trouble is, they got caught. We saw them on the satellite net, which means they don't know the capabilities of our satellites and they didn't count on South Africa having their surveillance aircraft up and monitoring the skies.

"They did it again in Brazil, because we caught them at their game. They wanted to demonstrate to us that they can do it at their will. I think that both incidents were thoroughly preplanned. But I am quite sure that they are aware of one other factor. That is, if they do it again, we will fight them, and that they don't want. I believe that like us, they simply are not yet ready to take on the human race in an outright war.

"The aliens need time to prepare, and so do we. I hate to sound like doom-and-gloom, but I don't think that they are her to explore or say that they come in peace or even ask permission to live here. No, I think that there is a much more sinister plan going on, and it is not to benefit mankind. In the meantime, though, they will continue their game and maybe become a little bolder, but not again on the scale that they showed us they could act.

"We, at the same time, must prepare and do it quickly. Our day is coming, and we must be ready. We have to be able to recognize any change in their tactics, figure out how to take advantage of it, and then continually probe for weaknesses. The hunted must become the hunter. Otherwise, we are doomed," Chester answered, now knowing what must be done.

Morrison had listened to every word his friend had said. He knew that Chester was right. Turning toward Cunningham, Morrison ordered, "Lieutenant, go home and get some sleep, if you can. Pack a bag for a few days and be ready to leave at 1000 hours.[44] I'll have someone pick you up at your home."

"Aye, aye, sir," Cunningham answered as he saluted and left the room.

After Cunningham left, Morrison and Chester sat around talking about the incident in Brazil and Zambia. Their conclusions were the same: Mankind was in for the fight of its life. They both agreed that Scotty was the one needed to run the Colorado Project, and they needed him now. He was the one man who could put the pieces together and form what they both hoped would be an effective offensive force against the aliens.

Morrison reached into his shirt pocket and withdrew Doreen's telephone number; it was time to get her and Scotty on their way to Brazil. "Don't you think it might be too risky to send Scotty and Doreen to Brazil?" Chester asked.

As Morrison began to dial, he looked at Chester and replied, "It may be risky, but if it's as horrible as Carlos said it was, it might just be the thing we need to push Scotty into taking command of the project."

Chester looked at his friend with raised eyebrows and uttered, "Oh," as Morrison continued to dial.

[42] 2:00 p.m.
[43] Location.
[44] 10:00 a.m.

OKAY, WHO BROUGHT THE ANTS?

THE BEAUTY OF NATURE SURROUNDS our very existence every day of our short visit upon this planet that we call Earth. From the budding of a flower to the gentle rolling hills of the countryside, from the crashing of the surf upon the shore to the soft, gentle kiss of a snowflake upon our face, from the first cries of life to the gentleness of parenthood, and from the beauty of a sunset to the vibrance of life anew held within the promise of a sunrise, Mother Nature reveals her bounty. We are truly fortunate creatures to walk this gentle Earth and gaze upon its wonders. Our mission—nay, our duty—is not simply to enjoy what nature has given us, but rather, we are to act as custodians of this natural gift, for the future. That is, if the survival of mankind is our ultimate goal.

Mother Nature has created areas of this Earth to remind us of her gift, her beauty, her mystery, and mostly her majesty. In some areas of this planet, she has evidently worked overtime to drive this lesson home. One such place is Victoria Falls. Here man has lived in harmony with nature for the past two and a half million years.

When one approaches the great falls from the vantage point of an airplane, one is immediately struck with the thought that the Earth is belching forth great clouds of angry steam from its inner depths. But upon closer examination, you realize that the steam is not steam at all; rather, it is the mist of Victoria Falls rising in the air, only to fall back to Earth and provide the foundation of life to the surrounding rain forests.

Looking even closer, one will forever be struck with awe of the power and majesty of the sight in front of them. Millions upon millions of gallons of water plummet down a cliff face 420 feet high and approximately one mile wide, being fed by the wondrous Zambezi River. It was against this backdrop of natural beauty and wonder that Edenausegboye wanted to share her family with Scotty and her new friend, Doreen.

When the presidential party arrived at Victoria Falls, they and their guests were immediately surrounded by well-wishers. Asukile and Edenausegboye took the time and patience to greet each person individually with a smile, a few words, and a traditional handshake. While this was going on, Scotty, Doreen, Mawuli, and Titilayo, under the scrutiny of a few presidential security agents, managed to sneak away to the Mukuni Craft Village to await the presidential party. In the village, vendors sold every type of native craft. The variety of crafts included carvings in stone, wood, and precious gems to jewelry and, to the delight of Mawuli, toys. Scotty and Mawuli stole off to a vendor selling hand-carved animated animals, while Doreen and Titilayo visited a booth containing native dolls.

Mawuli immediately saw what he wanted, a hand-carved elephant with legs that moved in a walking gait, which in turn animated the elephant's ears to flop back and forth, and the trunk to rise up and then fall back down. Scotty looked at the elephant with wonder and couldn't imagine the delicate work and the patience it took to make such a toy.

As Scotty was examining the toy, an old man shuffled out from the back of the stall and approached him. Speaking in a chipper voice, the old man asked Scotty if he needed some help. Scotty admired the work so much that he heaped praises upon the old man for his work. The old man, with a prideful smile on his face, went on to explain to

Scotty just how the elephant was made and the simple mechanics it took to animate the elephant. Mawuli, of course, was jumping up and down, eager to get his hands on his new toy, and waited impatiently as the two grown-ups discussed his treasure.

After five more minutes of discussion, Scotty decided to purchase another one for himself and asked the old man how much they were. Unblinking, the old man looked Scotty in the eye and told him forty dollars. Taking out his wallet, Scotty immediately withdrew forty dollars and held out the money in his hand for the man to take. The old man first looked down at the money in Scotty's hand and then looked him in the eye. The smile was now gone from the old man's face, and it was replaced with a hurtful look.

Looking down at the money again, the old man snatched it from Scotty's hand, turned his back, and shuffled toward the back of the stall with his head hung low. Scotty called out, "Thank you," but the old man did not acknowledge him. Mawuli was already playing with his elephant as Scotty picked his up, and together they went to look for Doreen and Titilayo.

Walking a few stalls down, Scotty found Doreen engaged in a lively discussion with the owner. Scotty could not believe what he was hearing: Doreen was telling the owner of the stall that the dolls—there were two of them, one for Titilayo and one for herself—were not worth the money she was asking. After what seemed like an eternity, Doreen and the woman settled upon a price. When Doreen paid for the dolls, the woman warmly thanked her and declared that it was a good bargain. Once outside the shop, Scotty asked Doreen why she haggled with the woman about the price. Doreen explained that bargaining is part of the culture. If you don't haggle the price, the merchant will not only lose face but it is also like telling the seller that you have no respect for whatever it is the person is selling. Scotty realized his mistake and felt sorry for the old man. He loved the elephant and respected the workmanship, but it was too late and the damage was done. Scotty decided that Doreen would handle any more purchases they made, which she did with skill and compassion.

After approximately an hour, Asukile and Edenausegboye caught up with the shoppers and admired their purchases, which by now included some native drums, a few hand-carved masks, and some clothing for the children and Doreen. Asukile informed them that their picnic was being readied and that it was time to leave. Scotty and Mawuli protested slightly, as there were a few unexplored toy stalls left, but by then their hunger was winning the battle and the thought of eating overcame their enthusiasm.

Walking down a winding path through a part of the rain forest, Edenausegboye kept Scotty and Doreen mesmerized as she pointed out what seemed like endless varieties of plants and trees along the way. She not only explained their function to the overall ecosystem but also related the efforts underway to preserve the forest for future generations. Victoria Falls, like most natural attractions throughout the world, is being inundated with visitors. While efforts are underway to preserve and protect this gentle forest, much more is needed. Scotty knew that Zambia was indeed a fortunate country to have people like Edenausegboye crusading for preservation and ensuring that what they saw today would be here tomorrow.

As they came to the end of the trail through the rain forest, they emerged onto a bluff overlooking the Zambezi River. Mawuli and Titilayo ran to the edge of the bluff and called for Scotty and Doreen to come quickly. Ignoring the thunderous noise of the nearby falls, Scotty and Doreen ran to the children, thinking that something was wrong. Mawuli, holding his elephant in one hand, was pointing off to his left with his other hand. Scotty and Doreen looked in the direction Mawuli was pointing and saw a sight that took their breadth away. Before them was Victoria Falls, in all her majesty and power. Water thundered down the monstrous face of the fall at a tremendous rate. Scotty and Doreen stood there silently, each to their own thoughts, as they gazed upon this natural wonder.

Mawuli broke the silence by taking Scotty's hand and led him toward the picnic area, lamenting that he was hungry. Titilayo took Doreen's hand and, likewise, led her away.

OKAY, WHO FORGOT THE MUSTARD?

DOREEN THOUGHT THAT THE PRESIDENTIAL chef and his staff had truly outdone themselves. As the head chef and his serving stewards stood behind the serving table, ready to assist the hungry picnic-goers, Doreen paused and took in the sight. Before her was a table covered in white linen decorated with wild orchids accenting the feast. The food included a variety of both hot and cold meats, various varieties of cheeses, a few types of breads, numerous cold and hot vegetables, and plenty of fresh fruits. For dessert there was a selection of puddings and chocolate cake to die for. Doreen took a plate and wanted a little bit of everything.

Once everyone had filled their plates and sat down on the soft grass, Asukile invited the staff, including the security detail, to eat with them. At first, they offered polite protest, thinking that it was not their place to sit and eat with the president, but Asukile would not hear of it. Once they were all sitting together, all lines of rank and position disappeared as they all shared a meal and, most importantly, enjoyed one another's company as friends should.

After the meal was finished, the adults seemed to languish, as they relaxed after the feast. Titilayo ended their repose when she threw a soccer ball into the center of the group. Mawuli decided who should be on each team and directed each person to his or her assigned position. At first, everyone took the game a little seriously, but that quickly disappeared as the players careened into one another and laughter took the place of competition. After a half hour of play, Asukile excused himself and prepared cold liquid refreshments for the group. As the group rested, Doreen and Scotty walked to the edge of the bluff and out of sight of the group.

Together they stood in seclusion, looking at the waterfall. At first they didn't speak, just shared the sight together. Breaking the awkward silence, Doreen turned toward Scotty and said, "Michael, I want you to know how much the past few days have meant to me. I feel as if I am on an adventure and have known you forever. Your friends are the nicest people I have ever met. And Titilayo and Mawuli, well, if I ever have children, I hope they are just like them."

Scotty was standing close to Doreen, staring into her eyes. He looked at her with compassion as desire rose within him. Trying to focus on her statement, Scotty struggled, "They like you too, and you're right, they are wonderful people. I only wish…"

But he fell silent as he reached up and pushed an errant strand of hair off Doreen's forehead.

Instantly they embraced in a long, soft, passionate kiss. As her body pressed against his, Scotty could feel the warmness and firmness of her breasts against his chest. As their bodies melted into one, Doreen could feel the passion and excitement arise within Scotty, as it was within her. Scotty then broke the kiss and, pulling his head back, offered, "Doreen, I'm sorry. I shouldn't have—"

"Oh, yes, you should have!" Doreen declared, interrupting Scotty, and then drew him in even closer as their lips and tongues melted into one.

Just then, Scotty heard a telephone ringing. Doreen heard it also but chose to ignore it. Scotty broke their kiss and, with his forehead resting against Doreen's but still holding their embrace, said, "You're ringing."

In a voice of resignation, Doreen replied, "Yeah, I know it," as she broke their embrace and withdrew the cell telephone Morrison had given her. Opening the telephone, Doreen pressed the green Answer button and put the telephone up to her ear. "This better not be a wrong number!" Doreen spoke in an angry voice.

Admiral Morrison was taken aback a bit by the angry tone of her voice and asked, "Lieutenant?"

"Yeah. Who the hell wants to know?" Doreen countered and then recognized the admiral's voice. Doreen offered, "Admiral, I'm sorry. I wasn't expecting you to call, and I thought it was a wrong number."

"Understandable, Lieutenant," Morrison answered but knew he must have interrupted something really important, and continued, "I know that Scotty is out with the search teams, but is there any way that I can contact him? There has been a similar incident, and I have to reach him as soon as possible."

"He's right here, Admiral," Doreen replied as she withdrew the telephone and handed it to Scotty, saying, "It's the admiral. Something about another incident."

Doreen turned away, looked down at the ground, kicked at the grass, and saw Titilayo standing about fifty feet away, staring at her. Bending down on one knee, Doreen outstretched her arms. Titilayo ran into her beckoning arms and, while hugging Doreen, asked, "You are going to marry my Uncle Scotty, aren't you?"

Doreen looked at her through teary eyes and replied, "I don't know, but if I do, I promise that we will get married on this very spot and you will be my bridesmaid. Is that okay?"

"What's a *bridesmaid*?" came a quick reply.

"A bridesmaid is the very best friend of the bride. She is the one that the bride trusts the most," Doreen replied and, seeing the questioning look on Titilayo's face, added, "It's a very important job."

The questioning look on her face turned into a broad smile as Titilayo stated, "Okay, I'm going to go tell Mawuli!" broke the embrace, and raced off.

"Wait!" Doreen cried out, to no avail. Standing up, Doreen looked at Scotty. He was facing away from her, talking on the telephone. She wanted to run over to him, throw the damn telephone into the river, and do a lot more than just kiss him, but that was a dream and not the present reality. Frustrated, Doreen decided to walk back to the picnic.

"Admiral, what's this about another incident?" Scotty began.

"First, tell me what's going on there," Morrison ordered.

Frustrated himself, Scotty answered, "We covered the entire country, and the aircraft simply isn't here. Not even a trace of it."

Anxiously, Morrison replied, "I think we may have located it on the bottom of the ocean. We can't be sure, though. From what we can tell, there is no trace of the occupants."

"Let me guess, the aircraft you found is a hunk of scrap metal in the shape of a cylinder. Right?" Scotty inquired, anxiously waiting for the answer.

"That's it exactly. How did you know?" Morrison quickly asked.

Having the upper hand for once, Scotty slowly replied, "We found what I believe to be a small Cessna. It disappeared with some government officials aboard her about six years ago without a trace, up until now, that is. The pilot was a very experienced and respected bush pilot for the World Health Organization. At that time, there was no evidence of foul play. The plane simply disappeared off the radar screens. Just like the aircraft we are looking for.

"If both cases are similar, then it's a fair assumption that our visitors have been doing this for some time. But not on the scale that they have just done." Scotty paused for a second, thinking about what he had just said, and asked, "Now, what about this new incident, Admiral?"

"It appears that a similar disappearance occurred in Brazil. An airliner disappeared. While it hasn't been located yet, there are bodies," Morrison began, but his voice began to quiver. "The...bodies...were desecrated beyond description. Major organs have been removed, as well as some limbs. Scotty, it's...terrible." His voice then perked up as he continued, "But guess what? There is a survivor. She is a very young girl. Right now she is in shock, the poor thing, and can't talk. But that could change at any moment.

"I promised my counterpart that I would come down there for a look-see. Scotty, I would like you and Lieutenant Stark to meet me there.

I need your opinion. So can I count on you being there?" Morrison nervously asked.

Without thinking, Scotty answered, "Yes, of course. I want to see for myself what these bastards did. But I also want Vinson along."

"Agreed. Now, let me talk to Lieutenant Stark and she can make the arrangements," Morrison ordered.

Looking around and not seeing Doreen, Scotty answered, "Admiral, she's not here right now. Can you call her back later? We'll leave as soon as possible, Admiral. Goodbye." Scotty concluded the conversation and hit the Hang Up button on the telephone in an effort to let Morrison know what it felt like to be talking to dead air at the end of a conversation with him.

Titilayo had run back to the picnic area and announced to the group that Doreen and Uncle Scotty were getting married and that she was going to be a maid to the bride. "A very important job!" she announced. Doreen arrived back at the picnic about a minute after Titilayo had made the announcement and was warmly congratulated by Edenausegboye. Realizing the misunderstanding, Doreen set the record straight. She began by saying that Titilayo must have seen Scotty and her kissing, and any talk of marriage was of the future. Doreen concluded this rather-embarrassing moment by adding, "If I should ever be lucky enough to meet the right man, and I think that I have in Michael, I want to get married right here. It would be my honor to have Titilayo as my bridesmaid and Mawuli as my ring bearer. You all have made me feel like a part of your family. And your country is truly an Eden, and the people make it so. I love you all and will miss you very much when we leave." Her eyes were now watering.

Mawuli, who had sneaked up and hidden behind his mother, peeked around her legs and asked, "Why don't you and Uncle Scotty stay?"

"I would love to, but..." Doreen's words stopped as she began to cry, not a cry of sorrow, but a cry of someone who has come home. Edenausegboye hugged Doreen and understood what was not said.

Asukile thought that something was wrong. Scotty should have come back with Doreen, but he was nowhere to be seen. Getting up, he walked over to where he thought Scotty was. Mawuli tried to follow, but his father asked him to remain behind and suggested that he have a piece of chocolate cake. Mawuli's eyes lit up at that suggestion, and he raced back to the desserts.

Scotty thought about what the admiral had said. If the bodies were desecrated, just what in the hell was the purpose behind that? he wondered. *Maybe it's a warning not to interfere with them, or maybe our bodies possess something they really need,* Scotty silently half-concluded. Suddenly he realized that all the crew were out on a safari, including his pilots. *God, I hope they all haven't been drinking alcohol,* Scotty wished as he dialed Vinson's cell number.

Scotty was somewhat relieved when Vinson answered on the second ring. Getting right to the point, he asked if either of his pilots had any alcohol to drink. He was disappointed to learn that everyone had some mixed drinks with lunch. To the casual observer, this question would seem harmless, but to a pilot it meant delay. Scotty would have to wait at least twelve hours until it was safe for his pilots to fly. Vinson sounded okay, but Scotty thought it odd that he didn't hear any background noise coming through the telephone, and asked his friend where he was.

"We are all out on that damn safari you asked me to arrange," Vinson declared.

"How come I don't hear anyone in the background?" Scotty asked out of curiosity.

"Oh, they're out walking through a field to get a better view of some kind of animal. I decided to stay behind with the trucks. The head guide wanted us to walk through some tall grass up to my waist. If that guy thought that I would walk through that grass knowing that snakes love tall grass, he's nuts!" Vinson replied with conviction.

"Vinson, listen, when my pilots get back, I want you and them to return to the airport and prepare the aircraft for departure. I want the plane ready to leave first thing in the morning. Also, the search teams are free to return home, so make sure that they get ready as well.

"I'd like to leave sooner, but since you guys had some drinks, we have to wait at least twelve hours. Oh, Vinson, we have one more stop to make before we return to New York. We have to go to Brazil first," Scotty instructed and waited for the inevitable protest from Vinson.

"Brazil? I don't want to go to Brazil! I want to go home," Vinson protested.

"It's important, Vinson. One more stop and then we go home. I promise," Scotty ordered.

"Okay, one more stop and then home. But you have to promise me that there will be no more jumping out of helicopters, and no more jungles," Vinson pleaded.

"I promise, Vinson," Scotty swore. Then he asked, "Say, Vinson, where exactly are you?"

"I'm sitting under a big tree, waiting for the nature lovers to come back. It's so damn hot here," Vinson replied.

Deciding to have some fun with his friend, Scotty asked, "Say, Vinson, are there any holes in the ground where you are sitting?"

"Yeah, there are lots of small holes. Why?" came Vinson's expected reply.

"Well, I can only think of two things that live in holes in the ground. Really big bees and—"

Scotty was interrupted when Vinson shouted, "Shit!" into the telephone. Scotty called to Vinson, but all he could hear was the panting noise of someone running, followed by a clunk and the sound of someone walking on metal. The next words Scotty heard were of Vinson shouting, "You were going to say *snakes*, weren't you?"

"Well, no. I was going to say mice, but come to think of it, snakes do live in holes in the ground," Scotty replied, trying desperately to hold back his laughter.

"Get me out of here, Scotty! I want my air conditioner. I want to sit in my living room and watch TV. If I want to see nature, I can see it on TV. I don't have to go chasing after it through the jungle. I want to go home, Scotty!" Vinson pleaded.

"We'll get there, Vinson. Calm down. Where are you now?" Scotty asked.

"I'm standing on top of a Land Rover, and I'm going to stay here until they come back. Goddamnit!" Vinson shouted and then added in a nervous voice, "There's an elephant walking this way, and he looks pissed off!"

"Vinson, get down off the truck and get in it. He's probably just passing through," Scotty instructed and offered comfort.

"How do you know? Are you some kind of freaking expert on elephants now?" Vinson pleaded more than asked questions.

"No, just get in the truck," Scotty ordered.

"Okay, I'm in the truck. He's turned away and is walking in the direction he came from," Vinson reported and then pleaded, "Scotty, get me out of here!"

"We are, Vinson. Just remember what I told you," Scotty replied.

"Yeah, yeah, I know. Get the planes ready to take off," Vinson answered.

"See you later, Vinson. Goodbye." Scotty concluded the conversation and hung up the telephone.

When Scotty put the telephone in his pocket, he noticed Asukile walking toward him. Scotty called out to him and tried to turn his friend's attention to the falls by remarking on its beauty. But Asukile was not to be fooled. He looked at Scotty and, for the first time, saw a footprint of fear on his friend's face. Asukile decided that the best approach was the most direct one and asked, "Scotty, tell me what is really going on here. It's my impression that your visit here, which I more than welcome, is about much more than a missing aircraft."

"You're right, Asukile. But if you believe one thing that I am about to tell you, it's that no one wanted to find the aircraft and, most importantly, the crew and passengers more than me," Scotty began as he looked his friend in the eye and wondered if Asukile would still be his friend when their talk ended.

Asukile knew that Scotty was dead serious, by not only the tone in his voice but also the fact that this was one of the first times he had called him by his given name. A hint of fear spread over Asukile as he replied, trying to put his friend at ease, "I believe you, Scotty, as I always have. There has never been deception between us from the start. Truth was the building block of our friendship and will always remain so. Come, let's walk as we talk. I find it most relaxing."

"Okay, but know this well: from this moment on, your life will change and you will begin to question some of your values and beliefs.

There is one other thing. I was going to tell all this before I left. I just didn't know how to bring it up. I am breaking an oath to my country, which I hold most dear, but, my friend, you have a right to know. I only ask that you not repeat or act on this information until the proper time, whenever that is. Do you agree?" Scotty replied.

"Yes, of course. As long as it does not harm my countrymen and our beloved land. I cannot promise inaction if it hurts my people," Asukile replied while the fear within him continued to grow.

Scotty was relieved that Asukile had asked him what the real purpose of the trip was. After all, one could not casually say that he believed that an alien spacecraft snatched an aircraft weighing more than thirty tons out of the air as it flew along. And who knew what happened to the people? It was odd, Scotty thought, but he was beginning to feel as if a great weight was being lifted from his shoulders as he began to talk.

As the two friends walked along, Scotty began his tale with his first encounter with an unknown craft when he was flying for the Navy. He told Asukile of Ice and his death when he approached the spacecraft, of his own reckless attack, and of the years he spent investigating what everyone referred to as UFOs. Scotty told Asukile of Admiral Morrison and described in detail the pictures the satellite net had taken of the unknown craft, of his failed efforts to find the aircraft on land, and of the admiral's discovery of the missing plane on the bottom of the ocean. Sadly, Scotty talked of the missing people and of their probable fate. He thought it best to include what the admiral told him of the similar event in Brazil, and the fact that there was a survivor among the carnage. Scotty concluded that he, Doreen, and the rest of the search teams would have to depart in the morning.

Asukile listened intently as Scotty talked, and tried to comprehend every fact down to the smallest detail. But what he was hearing was incredible. Sure, he had read about UFOs, but that was science-fiction stuff and was not for real. It was something one saw in the movies, and the people of Earth always defeated the aliens. If he was hearing this from anyone other than Scotty, he would have called the person a liar and looked into having the person examined for mental illness. But Asukile knew that it was true. He felt it, but he didn't want to accept it. His thoughts naturally turned toward his family and how he could possibly protect them.

When Scotty finished talking, both men remained silent for a few minutes.

Asukile spoke up first. "Can we fight them, Scotty?"

"Yes, we can fight them, but I don't know if we can beat them," Scotty replied in a voice of resignation.

"Shouldn't the world know about this and unite together and fight this threat?" Asukile anxiously asked his friend.

"In a perfect world, yes. But our world is far from being perfect. It would be all of two minutes before any unification would break down and national interests prevailed over the common good. Never mind the possibility that one country would try to strike a deal with the aliens and sell the rest of us down the river.

"Eventually, you're right, the world has to know, but not just yet. Before that can happen, we have to somehow gain the upper hand. Otherwise, we become the proverbial sheep being led to slaughter. I know that it may sound crazy, but for right now we have to sit back and watch what they do as we somehow prepare for the day that we can effectively strike back.

"When I attacked that alien craft, my weapons were useless against it. We need better weapons and delivery systems that come close to their own capability. Then and only then should we fight back aggressively," Scotty replied, beginning to see through the problem for the first time.

"You're probably right, but how many people are going to disappear in the meantime? How many lives have to be sacrificed before we can fight back? Most importantly, why in the hell are people being taken away?" Asukile asked in frustration.

"I don't know, my friend. I just don't know," Scotty replied, also frustrated, and then added, "But I do know that right now is not the time to fight back. We have to prepare, and during that time, we have to learn everything we can about the aliens. We have to know where they are vulnerable, and we have to go into the fight with a chance of success. Otherwise, the human race will pass into extinction. You know what gets me? Right here and right now, we couldn't even prove that aliens are for real."

"What do you mean? We have the aircraft you found in the jungle and the other one in the ocean. And don't forget, we are still missing those people. Additionally, I'm quite sure that proof exists in, say, your country, and what about those photographs you talked about of the spaceship that captured the airliner? There's proof out there, we just have to find it," Asukile replied with conviction.

Scotty looked at his friend with compassion and understanding and knew that he was right, but there were some basic truths that must be told. "Asukile, you're an honorable man who relies on the honesty of others. Right now I can't think of one government that is ready to admit what they know. I'm damn sure that there is plenty of evidence in existence, but how in the hell can you or I get access to it? Governments, by their very nature, lie and mislead. The photographs that I told you about would be in the shredder the minute their existence was revealed. Yes, we do have the wreckage of one of the aircraft, and Admiral Morrison believes that he may have found the wreckage of the airliner, but what are they and what, by themselves, do they prove? They are two large hunks of scrap metal, and that is all. People would say that you are trying to hide something and that's why you had the aircraft scrapped. No, Asukile, we have precious little of anything at all," Scotty replied.

"What about the people?" Asukile asked, trying to find something to hold on to. "The mere fact that they are missing should count for something."

"And what about the people? They are just missing. The world will think that the airliner crashed in a secluded part of the jungle and just hasn't been found," Scotty replied in frustration.

"I guess that you are right, Scotty. I just feel that we must do something and not sit around pretending that all is well while people are disappearing or being murdered by these alien creatures. We have to do something!" Asukile answered with determination in his voice.

Trying to calm his friend down, Scotty answered, "There is something you can do. You can enhance the training of your military pilots. I'll help you petition the United States to further train your pilots in advanced air combat. In the meantime, have your pilots up and flying as much as possible until the sky becomes as commonplace to them as their home. Keep their skills sharp and their morale high. Have your Army train and retrain, and when they are so tired they can't stand up, start training them over again. Try to compress your airline flight schedules to the times and areas that your Air Force is up training or on patrol. In essence, prepare for the day that we can fight back.

"Promise me one thing, though. Try to keep your flying at a minimum. Don't go out alone. Always have a security force around you and your family."

"I appreciate the thought, Scotty, but my duty to my country and my people comes first," Asukile replied, knowing that Scotty was speaking from his heart.

"I know, Asukile, but I care deeply for you and your family. I don't want to see any of you threatened or harmed in any way," Scotty pleaded.

Asukile looked at Scotty and saw the concern on his face as he replied, "Thanks, Scotty. We will all be safe." He paused. "I think we should be getting back now. Everyone is probably wondering what happened to us, and I don't want to upset those security guys. They can be a real pain in the butt."

Scotty and Asukile laughed slightly as they turned around and began to walk back to the picnic. They each walked in silence, left to their own thoughts. Both men became closer that day. They were now truly brothers united in the basic task of survival. When they reached the picnic, Doreen walked up to Scotty and kissed him on the cheek. Scotty took her hand and never let go of it for the rest of the day. She had become his reality in an insane situation, and he held on to this gentle woman who had become the fire of his life.

DON'T YOU EVER ANSWER YOUR TELEPHONE MESSAGES?

As DAYLIGHT BEGAN ITS ENDLESS journey into night, Asukile proudly announced the evening plans that both he and his wife had arranged for the group. First, there would be an evening dinner, not that anyone was really interested in eating again after the picnic, aboard the Victoria Falls Safari Express Train, followed by a relaxing night in the Zambia Tree Lodge Hotel.

To remove the puzzled look on Doreen's face, Asukile explained that the rooms of the hotel were actually built in large trees along the Zambezi River. Each huge ebony tree had a platform built on it, upon which was constructed a hotel room, which offered the visitor a rather-unique perspective of the river at night. Doreen seemed to understand but was struggling to imagine a hotel in the trees. She looked to Scotty for interpretive words, but he simply shrugged and offered her a comforting wink. Asukile then mentioned to Scotty that he would have preferred to head home after their talk but thought it best to follow through on the plans that had been made. Asukile had learned early on in his presidency that each canceled presidential visit or trip produced nothing but controversy.

As they were preparing to leave, Doreen's telephone rang again. This time, Scotty answered and was annoyed that it was Morrison again interrupting their day. Scotty and Doreen had forgotten all about him the rest of the afternoon, but as usual, he always popped up. This time Morrison talked to Doreen about their schedule and expected arrival time in Brazil. Morrison had made all the arrangement himself, except for their departure from Zambia. Doreen took care of that detail as soon as the admiral hung up. Doreen was disappointed that they would have to leave directly from the hotel and go to the airport, but she was secure in the thought that she and Scotty would shortly return for an extended restful visit.

As an afterthought, Scotty decided to call Hector before they left for the train. He wanted to see if Hector would be available for lunch since they would be landing in the Canary Islands to refuel just after noontime. After being put through to his office, Scotty was surprised to hear Hector answer in an excited voice, almost on the verge of hollering. This was not normal behavior for his friend, whom he often regarded as a natural Zen Buddhist. Scotty immediately became concerned and asked Hector if he was all right.

"Scotty, thank God that you are okay! I've been going nuts waiting for you to call. Didn't you get my message? Is that lovely creature Doreen okay?" Hector excitedly asked.

"I never got your message, and yes, Doreen is fine. She is right here with me now. Catch your breath and tell me what is wrong," Scotty demanded.

Hector replied, "You know that guy you had trouble with and kicked off the search team? Well, he wasn't what you and I would call normal. He tried to kill a few of my men, but I killed him. But that isn't the really weird part, though. He didn't bleed like you and me. He…he…he…bled pink blood that bubbled. And another thing, he had these really big eyes. I mean *really* big eyes. The largest I've ever seen. And dark. It was like you were looking into a coal mine or something. Scotty, I don't—"

Scotty interrupted him. "Hector, you been hitting that Madeira again, ole buddy?" he asked for the benefit of anyone listening in on Hector's unsecured cell call.

"He may have looked like you and me and may have talked like you and me, but he sure as hell didn't bleed like you and me. Scotty, I don't know what kind of shit you are into right now, but grab Doreen and run away from it before it gets you. You both can live here with me. Get the hell out of it, Scotty, and now!" Hector pleaded.

"You know that I can't do that. I have to see it through," Scotty replied, trying to calm his friend.

"Okay, but be on your guard. I know that you hate handguns, but make damn sure you carry one." Hector again found himself pleading.

"We're okay. We are surrounded by security guards. I'll see you tomorrow, and we can talk then," Scotty replied again, trying to calm his friend.

"Okay, but I am going to have some jet fighters escort your aircraft in. They will meet up with you as soon as you cross into international waters," Hector answered, now giving the orders.

"I wish you wouldn't do that. I don't want to attract attention. Let's just have lunch tomorrow, okay?' Scotty pleaded.

"Sure thing. But please watch your back," Hector demanded while not agreeing to anything.

After Scotty hung up, he told Doreen what Hector had to say. Scotty then told her why they were going to Brazil, since the admiral apparently had not. Doreen took the news well, but Scotty could see the look of concern on her face. He also knew that he had to tell her one more thing, but he was hesitant to do so. But Scotty realized that if he and Doreen were to be more than, shall we say, friends, then that relationship must be built on mutual trust. Scotty knew that this was something he never did before. He swallowed hard and began, "Doreen, there is one more thing I have to tell you. You can tell Morrison if you want to, and I know it is your duty to do so, but I told Asukile everything. He had a right to know. He's my friend, and I care for him and his family as if they were my own. I know that it was wrong, but that is just the way it is."

Doreen looked Scotty in the eyes and, with a slight smile on her face, answered, "The admiral doesn't have to know a damn thing about it. If you didn't do it, I was going to. This trip has changed everything for me. For the first time in my life, I can see what is really important. It's not about chasing aliens around the world, although they do have to be stopped. What it's about is love and friendship!" Doreen replied as tears began to well up in her eyes, and continued, "I also have some things that I want to tell you, but not here and now."

Scotty reached out and drew Doreen close against his body, not caring who was watching, and kissed her again. This time it was to the cheers and whistles of the group.

Their kiss was interrupted when Titilayo began tugging on Doreen's shorts. Breaking their embrace, Doreen knelt down and asked her what she wanted. Titilayo asked if it was time to be the maid of the bride. With slight laughter in her voice, Doreen replied, "Not yet, but I'll let you know when."

Scotty, upon hearing the question, knelt down also and asked Titilayo who was getting married. Titilayo answered that it was a secret. Scotty then asked if he could be a maid of the bride also. Titilayo thought hard about the question for a moment and then replied, "Yes, but I think you have to be a girl. Mawuli is going to be a ring man, and maybe you can help him. Can Uncle Scotty help Mawuli, Doreen?" Titilayo asked as she looked up at Doreen.

"We'll see. It looks like it is time to leave, Titilayo!" Doreen declared, trying to avoid any more questions and hoping for an end to the conversation. Relief came when Titilayo then ran over to the table and picked up her doll.

As Scotty and Doreen were standing up, he asked, "What was that all about?"

Doreen gave Scotty a short kiss on his cheek and replied, "Oh, nothing, just girl talk," as she turned away and walked away toward the others. Doreen glanced back once as she was walking away. She saw Scotty standing there, staring at her, with his mouth slightly open and a puzzled look on his face. *It's good to keep him a little confused!* Doreen thought to herself.

ALL ABOARD!

A RRIVING AT THE TRAIN STATION just before sunset, the presidential party was greeted warmly and was shown to their private coach. Asukile made sure that the entire party was seated before he would sit down. The security personnel protested that they should ride outside of the coach, but Asukile would not hear of it. The entire group was here to enjoy themselves, and that was it. Scotty and Mawuli, however, stole away from the coach, since they wouldn't be leaving for at least twenty minutes, and went to look at the steam engine that would be pulling their train. Mawuli asked endless questions about how the engine worked, but Scotty was way out of his league. The train's engineer heard Mawuli's questions and came to Scotty's rescue. He explained the inner workings of the engine in simple terms and invited the eager travelers into the cab of the engine. Mawuli sat in the engineer's seat and was delighted when he was allowed to reach above him and pull the cord that blew the whistle. When the train was ready to leave, Scotty and Mawuli raced back to their car and climbed aboard.

Doreen was in awe of her surroundings. She was sitting in a passenger car right out of the 1920s, perfectly restored to the glory of its day. There was no detail left undone, from the hand-rubbed wood adorning the car down to the handmade rugs on the floor.

There were lace curtains on the windows and linen tablecloths on the dining table. The attendants were even dressed in period clothing. Doreen closed her eyes and tried to imagine what it must have been like in the late Victorian era as passengers relaxed in the car and casually watched the vistas of Africa pass by as the train chugged along. She wondered if the travelers of that day came to love and appreciate Africa as she had in a few short days. The enchantment of the people and the country had won her over. Doreen was shaken from her thoughts when the train began to move.

Slowly the engine huffed and puffed as it chugged away from the station, pulling the cars filled with people seeking a unique view of the countryside and an enjoyable evening. As the train moved out of the station, it quickly came to a stop. An errant elephant chose that time to cross the tracks ahead of the train. When the elephant passed over the tracks and was safely in the jungle, the train continued its journey. After a short while, the train came to rest in the center of the Victoria Falls Bridge. The passengers were rewarded with a magnificent view of the falls as the sun set. Doreen sat transfixed as the last embers of daylight danced across the water and faded into darkness.

Once darkness fell, the train once again began its journey. The group was served a sumptuous buffet of native meats and vegetables accompanied by a wide variety of dinner wines. This was followed by a light dessert of fruits and sweet cakes of every description. The conversation over dinner was light and enjoyable, as it had been this afternoon.

Doreen was surprised that she was accepted into the group as if she were a long-lost family member. She felt warm surrounded by these people, and in particular by Scotty. She wanted to tell him of her involvement in the Colorado Project and grow that much closer to him, but this was not the time and surely not the place. After two hours, the train was back in the station and the presidential party was whisked away to the hotel.

BUT I NEVER LEARNED
TO CLIMB A TREE

Arriving at the hotel, Scotty and Doreen stood for a moment to take in the sight.

There was a square building that served as the lobby of the hotel, and an adjoining Olympic-size pool softly illuminated by pastel-colored lights. Surrounding the lobby was a massive stand of tall ebony trees. In each tree was, as Doreen later described it, a small house perched delicately about fifty feet above the ground. Each tree had a connecting wooden bridge suspended by ropes from the others. Some trees also had a wooden staircase leading up to the individual platforms. This truly was different from anything she had ever seen, but then the past two days had been filled with sights and sounds that were totally new to her.

After checking in, the party was led to their individual rooms by a host of stewards who carried battery-operated lanterns to illuminate the way. To say that Doreen was impressed with her room would be a vast understatement. What she had described as a small house when she was standing on the ground was not adequate. Her room was approximately twenty feet long and more than half as wide. Inside there was hand-woven carpeting on the floor. The walls were made of tightly interwoven reed with a screened window on each wall, except the one that the four-poster double bed rested against. Next to the bed were two small nightstands that held small table lamps and an alarm clock.

Across from the bed, on the far wall, was a small table and two chairs. On top of the table was a large fruit basket decorated with the same orchids Doreen had seen at lunchtime.

Against the far wall was a small bureau, which had a bowl and water pitcher placed upon it. Doreen guessed correctly that it was for washing. As Doreen was looking up at the thatched roof, Titilayo came running through the door and announced that she was going to sleep with her Aunt Doreen. Having achieved "aunt" status, Doreen could not have refused. Her plans of inviting Michael over for a good-night "piece of fruit" were dashed.

Scotty had likewise been thinking of inviting Doreen over to his tree house, but when he saw Titilayo enter Doreen's room, he knew that his fantasy was over. He could only look longingly at her tree house and dream of what could have been. That night, Doreen and Scotty slept a restful sleep surrounded by the sounds of the jungle and wrapped in a blanket of peace that only Mother Nature could provide.

Asukile roused Scotty from his sleep just as the rays of the sun were penetrating the thick cover of the trees. It was obvious that his friend had spent most of the night awake. Probably thinking about their talk, no doubt, Scotty thought to himself. He was right, as Asukile wanted to go over every detail of what Scotty had told him. For an hour they talked, and it was a good talk, as it helped each of them gather their thoughts and see through the situation. Scotty tried to reassure his friend that the aliens would probably not come back, as they apparently had moved on to South America. But Asukile was not at ease. Their conversation ended when Doreen and Titilayo arrived and announced that breakfast was now being served.

Knowing full well that this was probably the last time that they would share a meal together for a long time, Scotty and Asukile pushed their earlier conversation aside and filled the occasion with light banter. There was talk of the visit to Victoria Falls and promises of times yet to come. Scotty could see that Doreen was saddened by the fact that they had to leave, and would probably stay if given the opportunity. Scotty knew that he would like to stay as well, but he had made a promise to Morrison and promises have to be kept. His thoughts were interrupted when he saw an aide whisper in Asukile's ear.

Asukile then announced that it was time to leave for the airport.

Once at the airport, Doreen knew that it was time to say goodbye. Her eyes filled with tears as she exited the limousine. Doreen saw that their aircraft was ready to take off. She turned to Edenausegboye and hugged her. Together both women wept the cry of friendship and separation. Bending down, Doreen hugged both of the children. Titilayo begged her to stay. Doreen explained, as best as she could, that she had to leave, but promised to return very soon.

It was equally hard for Scotty to say goodbye. He loved these people and had come to think of them as his brothers and sisters. He hugged and kissed the children goodbye, and then, as he kissed Edenausegboye on her cheek, she whispered, "Scotty, now, don't you let that gentle creature get away. You marry her or you are a fool!"

"Someday, if she will have me," Scotty whispered back.

"Oh, she will!" Edenausegboye quickly added.

The goodbyes were interrupted by the flight attendant of Scotty's aircraft. He approached Scotty carrying a large black leather cylinder. Inside were the satellite maps Chester had prepared. Taking the case and turning toward Asukile, Scotty said, "This is a gift from my admiral. Inside you will find satellite maps of your country detailing your country's natural resources, and an agricultural assessment of your land. He wanted me to give you this as an expression of friendship between our two countries."

Asukile looked down at the cylinder and replied, "Would you kindly thank your admiral for me? I am quite sure that our interior department will find them most useful and save us a lot of work." Looking Scotty in the eyes, Asukile pleaded, "Scotty, please come back real soon!"

"I will. I promise," Scotty replied as he heard the engines of his aircraft slightly increase in pitch, indicating that it was clearly time to leave.

After another round of hugs and kisses, Doreen and Scotty boarded the aircraft. Doreen took a seat so that she could see her new friends and wave goodbye. Scotty said hello to Vinson, who was sitting in a seat close to the cockpit, facing Doreen. Scotty bent over Doreen to peer out the window and also waved goodbye as the aircraft began to taxi toward the runway.

Within a few minutes, they were airborne. Scotty sat down next to Doreen, and seeing that tears were rolling down her cheeks, he put his hand on her arm to comfort her. Doreen flexed her arm, casting his hand away as she said, "Oh, shut up!"

Scotty, perplexed by her response, looked at Vinson, who raised his eyebrows and made a face as if to say, "I don't know." Vinson then left his seat, walked to the back of the aircraft, and returned with a handful of tissues. Carefully he placed them on Doreen's lap, but she did not acknowledge his gesture as she continued to stare out of the window. Vinson made another face at Scotty and then retreated to the back of the aircraft.

Scotty tried to put his arm around Doreen, but she rebuffed the gesture. Staying next to Doreen, Scotty then put his chair in the reclining position and fell asleep. He didn't hear Vinson announce that fighter aircraft were flying alongside both sides of the aircraft. When Scotty was asleep Doreen looked over at him and smiled. Softly she kissed him on the cheek and then snuggled her head against his protective shoulders. She didn't see the slight smile cross his face. Scotty lay awake for a few minutes and breathed in the sweet smell of her hair, and then he fell back to sleep until they arrived at Grand Canary Island.

WEREN'T WE JUST HERE?

As their aircraft was on final approach into the Canary Islands, Doreen reached over and gently shook Scotty awake. Scotty looked around and saw Doreen smiling at him, obviously somewhat recovered from the separation blues. He felt a little guilty for having caused her some pain. After all, it was unfair to thrust her into a new land with new friends and suddenly to have taken it all away with one telephone call. Scotty knew that Doreen had enjoyed herself in Zambia, and he vowed one day to take her back there. But this time it would be for much longer, and definitely not on the admiral's business. He also longed for Zambia because, for some reason, the country made him truly relaxed and really brought home to him just what life was really about.

Reaching over to take Doreen's hand and kiss her, Scotty had momentarily forgotten about Vinson, who interrupted his intentions when he cried out, "Hey, Scotty, glad to see you finally woke up. Now, what about the promise of going home? When exactly are we going to get there?"

Scotty released Doreen's hand and turned around to face Vinson. After letting out a sigh of frustration, Scotty replied, "Vinson, I promise that as soon as we leave Brazil, we will head right back to New York."

"Okay, but you promised, and a promise is a promise. Besides, remember, we have tickets to a basketball game in three days," Vinson countered, driving his point home.

Scotty turned back around and took Doreen's hand in his and smiled warmly at her. Doreen smiled back and then kissed him softly on the lips. They both then smiled at each other and sat back in their seats, contented. In a few minutes, the landing gear lowered and their aircraft touched down on the runway. They were directed to the back of the airfield, where small charter and private aircraft were sent for servicing. Once their aircraft was parked and the doorway was opened, Hector came aboard and welcomed them back. After welcoming handshakes and a kiss for Doreen, Hector explained that they would be having lunch in his office, as it would provide more privacy than a restaurant. Hector then led them off the aircraft and into the warm, moist air of the tropics.

After a short car ride to the terminal building, they settled into a conference room adjacent to Hector's office. Everyone was glad to see the lunch buffet Hector provided, as they were all hungry after their light breakfast. Unable to contain their hunger any longer, they helped themselves to sandwiches and platters of fresh fish. As everyone sat around the conference table, eating, Hector wanted to know everything about their trip into the Wilds of Africa, as he called it.

Doreen was eager to talk about everything she saw and did. In particular, she dwelled on their visit to Victoria Falls. When it was Vinson's turn, he managed to mumble something about trekking through the jungle, which he didn't fail to note was full of snakes and was hotter than hell. Scotty, told Hector of the search they conducted and its dismal results. While Scotty was talking, he saw that Hector was preoccupied about something. Knowing that it was about the mysterious Mr. Merrick, Scotty decided that the most direct approach was the best. "Hector, when we talked yesterday, you mentioned the man we left in your jail had threatened to kill some of your officers and that you had shot him. Could you tell us what happened?" Scotty asked, eager to find out about the incident.

Hector went into great detail how he had found the small orange pills and how, thinking that they were illegal drugs, he decided to press charges against the man. He then detailed the events leading up to the shooting, the subsequent death of Merrick, and his eventual cremation along with all his possessions. He also explained his efforts to find out something about the man and his discovery that Merrick was actually an impostor, who had taken the identity of a deceased policeman. Nervously, Hector added, "Scotty, the really weird thing was the man's blood."

"Yeah. You mentioned that it was pink and not red. What exactly do you mean by that?" Scotty asked, trying to help his friend along with his story.

"After I shot the guy and he was dead, I started walking away, but I realized that something was very wrong. As I said, I walked back to him and looked at his wounds. He was bleeding, all right, but his blood was pinkish and foaming as it left his body. It was as if, when his blood was exposed to air, it caused it to foam, much like shaving cream does when it leaves the can. It was for that reason that the incident was treated as a biological contamination problem. Everything the man came into contact was also burned. Hell, our people even cremated his ashes after his initial cremation," Hector explained.

"Did anyone keep any samples of his blood for later study?" Doreen asked, hoping someone had saved a sample.

Turning toward Doreen, Hector replied, "No, the coroner thought it best to immediately dispose of everything. Hell, he even burned my underwear and socks along with my clothes, and the same thing with all my personnel who were present at that time.

"You see, we don't have any real state-of-the-art biological containment facilities on the island. That was the reason for the quick action."

"It was probably for the best, Hector. But you mentioned the orange pills. I don't suppose that some of them are still around?" Scotty inquired.

Hector stood up from the table without saying anything. He went into his office and returned a few minutes later. As he placed a small round stainless container on the table, Hector stated, "I was able to save one of the pills for you. Our people insisted putting it in this container." Hector sat back down and continued, "You can take it with you and have it tested. Our people ran some tests on two of the pills, and the results were a little weird. In fact, our lab people couldn't identify some of the ingredients. Perhaps your people will have some better luck.

"I'm sorry that I could only get one pill for you, but at least it's something. All the other pills were burned along with the other stuff."

"Do they have any idea what kind of pill it is?" Vinson asked, becoming interested now.

"Well, that's another puzzle. As best as the lab people could determine, the pill is some kind of oxygen enhancer. What that means is that when someone takes the pill, the pill will cause more oxygen to enter the blood and, at the same time, enhance the action of the lungs.

"It was as if Merrick, or whatever his name really is, could not breathe adequately. He needed more oxygen, and the pills, based upon what little we know, helped him. Either he suffered from some weird affliction or, I'd have to guess, he was one of your aliens from outer space," Hector concluded as he looked around the room for some kind of confirmation on the faces of his guests. Receiving blank stares in return, Hector added for more effect, "And those eyes…whoever had seen someone with large deep black eyes?"

Scotty coughed a nervous cough and didn't know what to say. He looked around the room and saw that both Doreen and Vinson were looking downward, as if they themselves were trying to figure out something to say. Hector sensed their uneasiness and relieved the stress of the moment by saying, "Scotty, what I told you over the telephone, I sincerely meant. I get the feeling that you are involved in something that may be too damn big to handle, not that you couldn't. You are more than welcome to stay here, as well as Doreen. And you, too, Vinson.

"Scotty, don't go down this road. If this guy, or whatever he was, is any indication of the people you will be dealing with, then, partner, you all are in some deep shit. It's time to get out, Scotty. This thing isn't normal, and this guy Merrick sure wasn't from around here, was he?" Hector asked, hoping his friend would give up whatever he knew.

Scotty looked at Hector and wanted to tell him everything but knew that he couldn't. It was the second time in two days that he wanted to violate his oath and knew that he would. Hesitating a moment longer,

Scotty began, "Hector, I, like Doreen and Vinson, took an oath to our country that we simply can't break. You deserve a straightforward answer, and—"

Scotty ended midsentence as he was cut off by Doreen.

"Michael!" Doreen spoke up and then continued as she looked at Vinson, "Vinson, can I trust you not to reveal what I am about to say?"

"Hell yeah! The man deserves to know. Besides, when the trip to Brazil is over, it's back to good old New York City for me and you can keep this alien business to yourself," Vinson replied with conviction and determination to get home in his voice.

Hector picked up on the word *alien* and looked over at Scotty with a confused look on his face. Scotty saw his friend look at him and nodded in agreement. Doreen spoke up, getting his attention. "Hector, as you know, we went to Zambia to search for an airliner that disappeared while in flight. What you don't know is that at the time of the disappearance, our satellite net managed to photograph an alien spaceship that was shaped like a long cylinder in the same area. In essence, the spaceship snatched the airliner out of the air," Doreen continued, and together she and Scotty told him everything they knew, including the fact that they were on their way to Brazil to investigate a similar disappearance.

Hector didn't really want to believe what he was hearing. Inwardly, he did, as he never knew Scotty to lie to him. After another twenty minutes of discussion, Hector was a convert. "Are they a threat to my island?" Hector asked, feeling the fear in his voice.

"They would appear to be a threat to the entire world," Scotty answered in a somber voice.

"Is there any way that we can fight them, or is there a way I can prevent them from coming here?" Hector asked, trying to figure out a way to protect his island.

"I don't know. At this point we don't know a hell of a lot," Scotty answered. "There is something you can do." Doreen spoke up and hesitated for a moment for effect. "You can be our eyes and ears here. My boss belongs to an international association that has been monitoring, as best as they can, the frequency and locations of the aliens visits. The idea is to try to get a picture as to why they are here.

"If you should spot anyone like our Mr. Merrick going through your airport, try to find out where they came from and where they are going. That information would be most helpful in trying to develop an overall picture. But please don't detain them, unless they break some kind of law. Let's just try to find out what they are up to.

"I'll be your contact, and we can arrange a system of communication. If that's all right with you."

"God, yes! But you have to promise me that if anything changes, you will tell me," Hector replied, knowing that his life had just changed.

"Agreed!" Scotty replied, then added, "I'm sorry for all this, Hector."

"Nothing to be sorry about, ole buddy. It is just part of life. I just wish that Merrick never came here. Nothing has been the same since, and it sure doesn't look like it ever will be again," Hector answered.

As Scotty, Doreen, and Hector continued to talk, Vinson stared out of the window. He couldn't help but think of events over the past few days. His peaceful, safe world had been invaded. He was there, trying to help a friend, and he knew that Scotty would likewise have come to his aid no matter what the circumstances. But dealing with aliens—who would have ever thought? His views were changing, though. While Vinson continued to complain about wanting to go home, there was a feeling growing within him that he would become a visitor to his home rather than a resident of his home again. Vinson could see the problem of aliens unfolding in front of him, and he wanted to do something about it. Just what he could do, he didn't know. Vinson had seen the worried look on Scotty's face over the past few days, and he knew that life would never be the same for him as well. Yes, Vinson concluded, Scotty would somehow see this thing through no matter what road it led him down. Vinson also reached another conclusion, or rather a reality: if Scotty was to become committed to fighting the aliens, then he would stand by his side, no matter what the consequences. Vinson's thoughts were interrupted when he heard Doreen call out his name.

When Vinson turned around, he was surprised that Scotty and Doreen were preparing to leave. It seemed that Vinson had been thinking for quite a while. Doreen reminded him that they had to hurry back to the airplane if they were to make their scheduled takeoff time. Vinson would have liked to visit the island for a few days, as he was not especially in a hurry to get to Brazil. He was somewhat afraid of just what they might find.

Once back at the airplane, Scotty waited patiently as Hector shook Vinson's hand and wished him well. Next, Hector gave Doreen a big hug and a kiss on the cheek and told her to keep an eye on Scotty as he tended to get into trouble easily. Doreen vowed to keep both of her eyes on Scotty to keep him out of trouble.

As Doreen and Vinson entered the aircraft, Scotty hugged Hector goodbye and simply said, "I'll see you later," as he stepped back.

"Scotty, you ole pirate, you take care of that girl and watch yourself. I got a feeling that from now on you and Doreen are going to be in constant danger. And Vinson, well, he is kind of hard to figure out. On the one hand, he says that he wants to go home, but his eyes tell a different story," Hector cautioned.

"Yeah, I think the lives of all four of us changed with this trip," Scotty replied, and hesitating for moment, he added, "Hey, Hector, I'm real sorry that you got involved in this business."

"I wouldn't have it any other way. You know that," Hector replied, trying to relieve the anguish his friend was feeling.

"I know. Hector, from what you told me, Merrick got what he deserved. It was a good shooting. Let it go. It's over," Scotty replied.

"It just never goes away, Scotty," Hector replied with regret in his voice and then perked up when he said, "Listen, have a safe trip, and may God smile warmly on you all."

As Scotty turned toward the aircraft, he winked at Hector and added, "And may God hold you safely in his hand. Goodbye, Hector."

Hector stood where he was and watched as their aircraft taxied out onto the runway and took off. He waved goodbye at the aircraft, knowing full well that his friends couldn't see him. As Hector re-entered his automobile, a thought came to him. *Hey, they never told me what to do with an alien if another one winds up in my jail!*

COULD YOU SHOW ME
THE WAY TO RIO?

FIVE HOURS LATER, UNDER THE growing cover of darkness, Scotty, Doreen, and Vinson were wide awake. They were full of anticipation as their aircraft touched down at a Brazilian Air Force base close to the shore of the Atlantic Ocean. When their aircraft came to a rest inside of a hangar, Scotty opened the door and pushed the button on the bulkhead that lowered the small stairway. Scotty was the first to emerge and didn't know what to expect as he walked down the stairs. When he reached the bottom and looked around, he was surprised to see Admiral Morrison waiting for them. He had thought they would see him tomorrow once they were transported to the scene of the discovery.

The admiral approached Scotty and eagerly welcomed him. Shortly, Doreen and Vinson emerged, and Morrison greeted them warmly as well, as if they were long-lost family members. He explained to them that before going to the scene, they would visit the survivor, who was in the base hospital. Afterward, they would spend the night on the base and be transported in the morning to the site. Reluctantly agreeing, Scotty asked the admiral if they could get going because he wanted to take a nice, long shower before dinner, adding that a change of clothing would be nice since they left most of their clothes in Zambia due to their quick departure. Morrison chuckled at Scotty's predicament and promised to find him something. He could not, however, resist the temptation and added, "Boy, you really are lost without Marlene to constantly look after you. Wait until I tell her that you lost your clothes."

Doreen then spoke up in what she thought would be Scotty's defense. "Admiral, I don't have any clothes either. We simply didn't have time to pack. The president surprised us with an overnight trip."

"What, Lieutenant? You mean to tell me that he lost your clothes also?" Morrison added as he shook his head from side to side and laughed as he turned toward Scotty. He continued, "Just wait till I tell Marlene that you lost this poor girl's clothes as well. Marlene is going to kick your butt clear across Central Park, Scotty." Now, turning his attention to Vinson, Morrison asked, "And I suppose that you lost your clothes as well, Agent?"

"Agent? I'm no longer an agent. I'm a civilian. That's C-I-V-I-L-I-A-N. I live in New York City and I'm a passenger on my way home. And no, I have my clothes. Thank you," Vinson proudly replied.

"Whatever you say, Agent!" Morrison replied as he laughed to himself and walked to a waiting Humvee. Opening the door, Morrison glanced at Doreen, Vinson, and Scotty and, as he was getting in, shouted out, "Let's get in the car, children."

"Where are we going, Admiral?" Scotty asked as he climbed in.

"First to the hospital, to see the child, then you can have your shower and something to eat. Then early to bed. We'll be leaving early in the morning," Morrison answered.

On the way to the base hospital, Morrison somberly explained that he had been at the scene of the grisly discovery earlier in the day and that a Lieutenant Cunningham was presently there, working with the Brazilian military documenting the remains of the passengers and crew. Morrison described in detail what he saw, not because he wanted to be hard on them, but rather to prepare them for tomorrow. He thought that if they were prepared for the horror of what they would see, then they just might be able to remain objective in their conclusions. The admiral knew that it would be difficult for them, but he needed their insight, especially from Scotty and Doreen. Vinson, he didn't know that much about, but if Scotty trusted him, Morrison felt that it was good enough for him.

As they pulled up in front of the hospital, Morrison explained that the young survivor was still in a deep state of emotional shock, unable to respond to any type of stimulation. Speaking somberly again, Morrison began to choke on his words as he related, "They can't even identify her yet. They are trying to gather all the dental charts they can, but the process is too damn slow. The poor girl just sits in bed with her eyes wide open, staring straight ahead. I'd give anything to get my hands on whoever did this!"

Doreen was taken aback by this seldom-seen show of emotion on the part of the man she worked for, but she had an idea and decided to pursue it. "Admiral, have they tried aroma stimulation?"

"What do you mean?" Morrison asked.

"Well, sir, you mentioned that the bodies appear to have been operated on by the use of some type of new surgical laser and that there is a total absence of blood. Further, that major organs, and, in some cases, whole limbs, were removed. Let's take it one step at a time.

"First, the blood had to go somewhere, and as you know, there is a very distinctive smell to blood. If they could hold a vial of blood under her nose, it just might shock her mind alert and bring her out of it. I know that it may sound cruel, but it just might work.

"Secondly, if the limbs and organs were removed for some purpose— let's say to study them—then they had to be put into a suspension liquid to preserve them. I'm not saying that they use our solutions, but the smell might just be similar enough to do the trick.

"Lastly—now, this is where it really gets sickening—I read somewhere that when a laser cuts flesh, it gives off a distinctive smell unlike all others. If they could get a piece of steak and cut it with a laser in front of her, it might work.

"Oh yeah, there is also sound stimulation. They should be exploring a wide range of different sounds from a synthesizer. You never know, there could be a matching sound," Doreen explained.

"You're scaring me, Lieutenant. But that's real clear thinking. I'll suggest your idea, and you're right, it just may snap her out of it. I'm impressed!" Morrison responded. "Now, let's go inside."

Once they were inside the hospital, Major Pilar Roman, the resident head psychiatrist, greeted them. As Major Roman led them down the hallway toward the girl's room, she explained the treatment the girl was receiving and updated her condition. They listened intently as Major Roman explained that the girl was in perfect physical condition and, at present, was being fed intravenously and being forced liquids. She went on to explain that the girl's urine was being collected from a catheter and was analyzed. The analysis thus far from blood and urine indicated that she was given some type of strong sedative. As Major Roman stepped in front of the door and opened it, she added that since the girl was given a sedative, she was probably asleep during the ordeal.

As they entered the small room, the nurse, who had been sitting in the corner of the room, reading a magazine, stood up and walked over to the foot of the bed. The girl was lying down with her upper torso raised at a forty-five-degree angle. She had a blank expression on her face as she stared at a small television mounted on the opposite wall. The television was blaring out the sound effects and words of some cartoon character that Doreen didn't recognize. The admiral, Scotty, and Vinson stood at the end of the bed near the nurse, while Major Roman went over to the left side of the bed. Maternal instinct overtook Doreen, and she went over to the right side of the bed and sat down facing the girl. She took the girl's hand in hers and interlocked their fingers. Scotty could see that tears were welling up in Doreen's eyes. He slowly walked up behind Doreen and gently placed his hands on her shoulders, offering some comfort and support.

As tears began to fall from Doreen's eyes and slowly roll down her cheeks, Major Roman explained that the girl would not respond to physical stimulation. To illustrate her point, the major took out what looked like a dental probe with a curved sharp hook at the end. As the major placed the probe on the girl's forearm, Doreen spoke up in a sharp tone. "Don't you dare! You leave her alone. She's not some test animal for you to play with!"

Major Roman, from the expression on her face, was obviously not used to being talked to in such a manner. She glanced over at Morrison, who knew that he had to defuse the moment, even though he agreed with Doreen. "Lieutenant!" Morrison quietly called out.

Doreen, while still holding the girl's hand, protested, "But, Admiral, she was going to stick her with that thing!"

"I was going to rub her arm with it to show you what I am talking about. See!" Major Roman countered as she took the probe and very roughly rubbed it up and down the girls arm while looking directly at Doreen.

Scotty could feel Doreen begin to get up as Major Roman illustrated her point.

Not wanting to see a war erupt in the room, Scotty gently, but firmly, held Doreen's shoulders down. Doreen turned her head toward Scotty and whispered, "Okay."

It was then that Doreen felt the girl's fingers tighten around her hand. Doreen quickly looked around the room, and her attention settled on the television. A cartoon character was running away from some weird-looking animals, and as the character did so, there was a swishing noise. As Doreen looked back at the girl, she heard the noise again, and sure enough, the girl's grip tightened again. Unable to contain herself, Doreen let go of the girl's hand and, while wiping the tears away from her eyes, blurted out, "She is reacting to the noise on the television, the swishing noise!"

"I'm sure that she did, honey, but don't bother yourself about it. We have tried everything and have never gotten a reaction. It's probably just a muscular contraction," Major Roman answered in a condescending tone.

Doreen began to reply, "But I tell you—"

But she was interrupted by Major Roman. "Admiral, I think it is time to leave now. The patient needs her rest!" Major Roman loudly ordered more than suggested.

"Yes, Major," Morrison replied as he opened the door and waited for everyone to leave the room.

Once outside the hospital, Doreen turned toward the admiral and, in a very loud voice, swore, "That bitch! She doesn't give a goddamn about that girl. I'm telling you, Admiral, she reacted to that noise, and that bitch isn't going to do anything to help that poor girl! I'm going to tell that bitch Dr. Know-It-All just what I think of her!"

As Doreen turned toward the front entrance of the hospital and took a step in that direction, Morrison reached out and grabbed her arm. Speaking firmly, more as a father than a superior officer, he ordered, "Lieutenant, now is not the time, nor is it the place, to do anything. I saw how Major Roman treated the girl, and I am as appalled as you are. I promise you that I will do something, but it can't be now. We're here on an important mission, and we have to accomplish it first. Then we will do something for the girl."

Doreen seemed to relax a bit and turned toward Scotty and cried out in a low voice, "Michael?"

"I want to see her butt get kicked also, Doreen, but the admiral is right. Now is not the time," Scotty answered as he put his arm around her. Doreen sank her head in his shoulder as they walked back to the waiting vehicle.

On their way to the bachelor quarters, Morrison emphasized that they were invited there and were guests of the military. While he appreciated and sympathized with the plight of the girl, Morrison explained that such matters were best handled in a diplomatic manner. He then begged everyone not to reveal their true feelings should a similar incident occur. He stressed that it would be best to observe the situation and then talk about what they saw among themselves. Morrison again vowed that he would see to the situation the girl was in and promised that he would try to get her a new doctor. Through his own diplomatic way, Morrison managed to have Scotty, Doreen, and Vinson promise that they would hold their tongues if they saw something wrong.

Arriving at the bachelor quarters, they were each shown to their individual rooms. Scotty was pleased to find two fresh flight suits, GI underwear, and socks neatly folded on the bed, and a new pair of flight boots on the floor. Doreen and Vinson found similar clothing waiting for them. Deciding to take his long-awaited shower, Scotty entered the adjoining shower and found a toiletry kit for his use. After shaving, Scotty stood under the relaxing, warm water of his shower for nearly an hour. After dressing, Scotty left his room and walked down to the lobby. Waiting for him were the others, all dressed in a similar fashion. "Either we are quintuplets and our mother dressed us alike or we are going to some party for lost pilots," Scotty blurted out, hoping for some kind of comic reaction.

"Very funny, Mr. Scott. Now, let's go and eat, shall we? We have been waiting for over half an hour for you," Morrison ordered while, at the same time, chastising Scotty.

No one really ate their dinner, except for the admiral, who attacked his steak with the vigor and hunger of a man that hasn't eaten for a few days. The admiral, in between bites, saw that his companions were just picking at their food and looking somewhat somber. *Probably a result of the visit to the hospital,* Morrison thought. Knowing that it was up to him to lift their spirits, he launched into a detailed story of one of his favorite subjects, Victorian New York. To the dismay of his audience, tonight's lecture was on the theater district. As the admiral droned on and on, Scotty, Doreen, and Vinson exchanged smiling glances at one another, knowing full well that they were there until Morrison decided that he was finished. The lecture concluded when the bill was placed on the table. The admiral reached into his pocket and placed money on the table as he informed everyone that it was time that they went to bed.

Scotty and Doreen decided to walk the mile or so back to their quarters. They said good night to the admiral and Vinson once they were outside of the restaurant. Holding each other's hands as they walked, Scotty and Doreen talked about their trip to Zambia and Victoria Falls. They vowed to one day return there on a long vacation, free from their responsibilities. Doreen then directed the conversation toward the young survivor. Doreen wanted to bring her back with them to the United States. She felt that the girl would be able to receive proper care back home in Washington, DC. Scotty was quick to point out that eventually the local authorities would identify her and reunite her with some relatives. Doreen knew that Scotty was right and that the girl would be better off with her family, but she wanted to do something for her.

In what seemed like two minutes but had to be much longer, Scotty and Doreen found themselves in front of the bachelor quarters. Still holding Doreen's hands, Scotty turned toward her and looked into her eyes. He wanted to say something but stumbled over his words. Finally, he let go of her hand and put his arms around her and kissed her with all the passion within himself. Doreen welcomed this gesture of affection and pressed her body against his. Their kiss was interrupted by, yeah, you guessed it, the admiral clearing his throat. "There's a time and place for that, and in front of the bachelor quarters isn't it, children!" Morrison bellowed and then ordered, "Now, let's get to bed. And I don't mean you two together. The sun gets up here pretty early, I'm told."

Breaking their embrace, Doreen walked over to the admiral, kissed him on the cheek, and said, "You, old romantic, you. Good night." She then walked up the front stairs of the building, turned around, and said, "Good night, Michael. See you in the morning." She then blew him a kiss and went inside.

The admiral and Scotty watched Doreen as she entered the building. Once she was out of sight, Morrison said, "That's some woman, eh, Scotty?"

"Yes, sir," Scotty softly replied.

"Make some lucky man a good wife someday. Don't you think so?" Morrison asked as he turned to face Scotty.

"She sure will, Admiral," Scotty answered as if in a trance.

"Mr. Scott!" Morrison called out, trying to bring Scotty out of his own fantasyland.

"Yes, sir," Scotty answered as he turned toward the admiral.

"Let's get some sleep. We have a hard day tomorrow," Morrison directed as he grabbed Scotty by the arm and led him up the small stairway to their quarters.

Once he was lying in bed, Scotty could only think of Doreen. Nothing else mattered to him right then. He would love to go to her room, but he knew that the admiral was in the next room. If Scotty left his room, Morrison was sure to know and would follow him. Jet lag eventually overcame Scotty as he was thinking of Doreen and what it would be like to get away from all this.

DON'T ANSWER THAT TELEPHONE

CAPTAIN GEORGE MONTGOMERY WAS ON the bridge of his ship when a call was received over the secure net from Rear Admiral Chester Braddock. George directed the radioman to put the call through to his cabin in a minute. Rising out of his chair, George scrambled to get to his cabin so as not to keep Chester waiting.

Entering his cabin, George went over to his desk, sat down in his old-fashioned wooden armchair, and waited for the telephone to buzz. A few seconds later, the call was put through. As George let out a big sigh, he picked up the receiver and said, "Hello, Admiral. It's good to hear from you."

"Hello, Captain Montgomery. I hope all is well aboard your ship," Chester replied.

"Everything is shipshape, Admiral. Although everyone is still talking about our recent visitor," George answered, hoping for a conversation in which Chester would explain about the UFO.

"About that, how is the overall mood?" Chester inquired, not taking the obvious bait.

"Well, sir, the crew and civilians seem to argue among themselves as to whether or not they actually saw a flying saucer. Some are absolutely convinced that they saw one, while the rest say that there is no such thing. The crew followed my direction that it was some sort of experimental craft. Hell, some of the crew and civilians now swear that they saw an American flag painted on the craft.

"No two people see the same thing. If ten people witness something and later are asked to describe what they saw, you would get ten different answers. It's all a matter of personal interpretation.

"I checked, and no one had a camera with them at the time the craft flew over. So there are not any photographs that could pop up in the newspapers.

"I know that I may be out of line, but, Admiral, just what was that thing? Was it a real flying saucer?" George explained and asked the big question.

"Officially, it was an experimental aircraft, George, and nothing else for now," Chester answered tersely.

"Yes, sir," George quickly replied.

"George, I wanted to talk to you for a moment about your orders. When you arrive at the San Juan Naval Base, your ship will be met by some NIS[45] agents. They will debrief the civilian researchers aboard your ship and request—well, more like demand, if they value their freedom—that they do not discuss with anyone the Navy experimental aircraft that overflew your ship. Since the aircraft represents a leap in aviation technology, it is important that it remains top secret for the present.

"Afterward, they will be free to head home or wherever they want to go. We will, of course, provide them with transportation.

"What I want you to do is prepare them for their debriefing. You can tell them, let's say, that some NIS agents want to talk to them about the experimental aircraft that they saw, or something to that effect. Do you see any problem with this?" Chester asked more out of courtesy.

"No, Admiral. As I said, half of them believe that they saw an American flag on the aircraft as it flew over. If anything, it will just confirm what they already believe," George answered, quite sure of himself.

"That's good, George. Now, when you dock in San Juan, I will be coming down to see you. I am afraid that your crew cannot receive liberty[46] beyond the naval base. If they go ashore, the entire crew must be back on board no later that 1800 hours.[47] Is that clear?" Chester ordered.

"Crystal clear. Sir, if I may, will the crew also be debriefed?" George asked, now concerned because it sounded like something was coming and it didn't sound good.

"Not at this time. You are to caution them, before you release them on liberty, not to speak to anyone about what they saw or may have thought they saw," Chester replied and, as an afterthought, added, "Remember, George, it was a naval experimental aircraft."

"Got it, sir," George quickly replied.

"Good. Now, when will you arrive in San Juan?" Chester asked.

"Sir, I should be there within two days. We shouldn't run into bad weather. The forecast is for clear skies and smooth seas." George mentally went over his estimated time of arrival as he spoke.

"That will be great. George, I know that we are asking a lot from you and your crew, but believe me, it is important, not only to your country, but, in a larger sense, to the world as well," Chester replied, trying to lift his spirits.

"I have a good crew, Admiral. There is not a complainer among them. They know their duty and perform it without question. You will not find a better crew anywhere," George proudly answered.

"They have a good leader. You will be receiving a teletype with official orders directing you to San Juan. I'll see you when you dock, George. Have a safe sail and following seas," Chester replied, concluding the conversation.

"Thank you, sir. See you then," George replied and hung up the telephone, wondering what might lie ahead.

George then left his cabin and went back to the bridge, where a teletype was indeed waiting for him. After reading his orders, George went over to the navigator and checked on their progress. When he realized that his ship was on course and on time, he decided to add a few more revolutions to the propellers, which would cut a few hours off their trip.

Being satisfied that all was well with his ship, George walked to the fantail (back of a ship), leaned on the chain that served as a guardrail, and stared at the ocean. Here, in solitude, George was able to think clearly. He found that he couldn't even guess what he and his crew had gotten into. He wished he had been on deck when the UFO flew over the ship, so he could have seen it for himself. At least then he would feel a little bit better about spreading disinformation. Dismissing his mental wanderings, George refocused on his world. He had a ship to safely sail across the Atlantic, and for right now, that was all that mattered. Letting go of the chain, George walked back up to the bridge and settled into the routine of running his ship. This was his world. He could touch it. He could feel it. He could even smell it. And by God, he loved it.

— ◆◆◆◆◆ —

[45] Naval Investigative Service.
[46] Being able to leave the ship.
[47] 6:00 p.m.

OH MY GOD

T HE ADMIRAL, TRUE TO HIS word, rousted everyone out of bed at 5:00 a.m. and ordered them to assemble in the lobby in a half hour or less. Scotty took the admiral's order in stride, as he knew that today was the closing act of the trip, and tomorrow, or even late tonight, he would be home. Scotty planned to try to convince Doreen to come and visit for a few days, but he decided to push that idea aside until after the day's work was done. Getting out of bed, he hurried into the bathroom and took a cool shower as he could feel the heat of the day beginning to build. Dressed in a fresh flight suit, Scotty left his room to wait for the others in the lobby.

When Scotty arrived in the lobby, he was surprised to find the admiral sitting with Doreen and Vinson, drinking coffee and munching on doughnuts. Upon seeing Scotty, the admiral stood up and handed him a large container of Brazilian black coffee and invited him to take some doughnuts. Scotty eagerly took the coffee but at first declined the offer of the doughnuts, hoping for some fried eggs and bacon. His hopes were quickly dashed when the admiral told him it was the doughnuts or nothing.

Reluctantly, Scotty reached into the box and took four of the circular delights. After Scotty finished breakfast, the admiral announced that it was time to leave. Spirits were high as the foursome left the building joking with one another about the heat and humidity and placing bets as to who would pass out first from the heat.

Once at the airfield, they were directed to a waiting helicopter. After donning flight helmets and connecting the intercoms, they settled back into their seats for the thirty-five-minute ride to the scene of the discovery and the adjoining location where the bodies were being examined. A few minutes into the flight, Scotty noticed Vinson staring out of the open doorway of the helicopter at the jungle below. As they flew over a river, Vinson spoke up. "Admiral, we don't have to cross a river, do we?"

"No, Agent. Why do you ask?" Morrison inquired.

"There's piranha fish in the rivers down here. I hear that they can eat a man in seconds," Vinson answered with concern in his voice.

"We'll be landing next to the emergency camp, Agent. And no, we will not be walking across or boating across any rivers," Morrison answered.

"Okay, I'm just checking. I'm not crossing any rivers or walking in any jungles," Vinson answered, adding his conditions.

Scotty nudged Doreen as they listened to the exchange between Vinson and the admiral, and they shared a laugh. Midway through the flight, Morrison explained that they would be met by General Salas, who would brief them first on their findings. After that, they would be shown the remains of the passengers and crew of the aircraft. Morrison pointed out that if anyone didn't feel up to it, they should speak up and he would understand. When he didn't receive a response, Morrison thanked them and suggested that if they should feel queasy while they were in the morgue tent, they should leave right away and get some fresh air. Assured that they would follow his instructions, the admiral fell silent and looked at the jungle pass by below him as he contemplated the sight he saw yesterday, grimacing at each passing thought.

When they landed at the camp, Lieutenant Cunningham and General Salas were waiting for them. After introductions were made among the group, Morrison pulled Cunningham aside and asked him if he had completed his work photographing the bodies and getting all the documentation he could. Cunningham replied that he had completed all he could and hoped that the admiral would tell him to leave, as he had had enough and couldn't take another moment inside of the tent. Morrison then excused himself and talked briefly with General Salas. When he was finished, Morrison walked toward Cunningham again. *My God, he is going to order me back into the tent,* Cunningham thought to himself. To his relief, mostly to the relief of his stomach, Morrison ordered him to get on the helicopter for the return trip to the air base. He was then to take the admiral's aircraft back to Washington, DC, and report to Rear Admiral Braddock.

Thanking the admiral, Cunningham at first extended his hand but quickly realized his mistake and saluted. Once the admiral returned his salute, Cunningham ran to the helicopter before Morrison could change his mind.

General Salas then led the foursome into a field tent, where they could talk in relative privacy. He began by explaining that Brazil, for the past few years, had witnessed a large increase in the number of UFO sightings. These sightings, he explained, were not concentrated in any one particular area but rather were witnessed from the far reaches of the interior to the coastline. Last year, there were over two thousand sighting reports given to local authorities. The general emphasized that he suspected that the majority of these reports could be explained away if he had the resources to conduct investigations.

Explaining that sighting reports in the past had been treated as idle curiosity by his government, the overall mood had recently changed. Citizens and government officials alike were starting to take notice of the events and were asking just what was going on.

Anticipating that once the gravity of the current situation was fully explained to the president of Brazil, the general believed, the entire country would be put on a heightened state of military preparedness, General Salas drove his point home by recounting how four of his fighter pilots were just killed by a UFO. Shocked by this revelation, Scotty spoke up as he turned and looked at Morrison. "Admiral, why didn't you tell us about this?"

General Salas spoke up. "I asked him not to. I wanted you to learn about it from me. Admiral Morrison tells me that the three of you are the best people that he has, and if anyone can figure this mess out, it is the three of you. I thought it best that you learn everything about this incident at once, rather than in parts. It may have been a bit unfair, but that was my wish."

Scotty, Doreen, and Vinson looked at the admiral as they heard this praise and didn't know whether to hit him for keeping some facts from them or thank him for the adulation.

"General, were all the fighter aircraft flying at the same altitude, or were they stacked in attack formation?" Scotty asked.

"Let me explain what happened. When we received a call from the admiral that we could expect a UFO heading toward our coast, I dispatched the four aircraft with orders to observe only, not to engage. Once the fighters were on station and were vectored in on the UFO by ground radar, all hell broke loose.

"The flight leader called in a description of the unknown, a round metal object approximately fifty feet wide and about thirty feet high, and was instructed again to observe only. For some reason, he ordered all aircraft to fly abreast of one another and then chase the UFO. What we suspect is, as they were chasing the UFO, each aircraft managed to get missile lock on it. When that happened, the UFO turned back toward them to counter the threat. The pilots then launched their air-to-air missiles, which were intercepted and destroyed before they could land on the UFO. Seconds later, all four fighter aircraft disappeared off the radarscope.

"I was informed by Admiral Morrison that the incident was caught on satellite, in an infrared mode, and that all four jets disappeared in a large explosion simultaneously.

"We, of course, searched the area and have only found small fragments of wreckage," General Salas explained.

"I am sorry for your loss, General," Scotty replied, feeling remorse for the lost pilots.

"Thank you, Mr. Scott. I understand that you lost your wingman to a UFO a few years ago. I sympathize with your loss as well," General Salas replied and instantly forged a bond between himself and Scotty.

"Thank you, sir," Scotty replied as he once again mentally relived the death of Ice.

Changing the mood, General Salas announced, "Okay, now, for the reason we are all here. As you know, the remains of the victims were located a short distance from here on a secluded beach. The fisherman who found them visited the beach regularly and has never noticed anything unusual in the past. It may be a stretch, but we could assume that the aliens never came to this beach before. Then why this spot? Again, I can only hypothesize, but I think they chose this particular beach because it is so secluded.

"The seclusion of the location would allow, as it has, for limited public exposure. It would therefore follow that we were meant to find the bodies, but exactly why we were supposed to find them, I can only guess at. I can only come up with one real reason. I believe that this incident is a warning to back off and leave them alone. That, I will never do. I and my country will fight them to the end. Who the hell do they think they are that they can kill so many innocent people and get away with it?

"That problem aside, let me briefly tell you what is going on now. All the remains have been removed from the beach. We are presently conducting autopsies, as much as we can, given the condition of the remains, to determine just how they all died. As you know, there is almost no blood left in the bodies. When we find traces of blood, it is collected for analysis later, as we do not have full laboratory equipment on-site. We are also photographing each body and taking measurements and weights as best as we can. I'm sure that the admiral has briefed you on the condition of the remains, so I won't dwell on that. I just don't understand why so many organs, and, in some cases, limbs, were removed from these poor souls. What's really odd is that in a few cases, the brains were also removed.

"Now, there's nothing that I can say to fully prepare you for what you are about to see. Our doctors have requested that everyone who enters the morgue tent wear a level-2 biocontainment suit with a self-enclosed breathing device. The reason we are doing this is that we have not yet been able to determine if there is indeed a biological hazard.

Please, if you should feel sick, go immediately to the wash-down station, where your suit will be decontaminated, and leave the tent. Are there any questions?"

Scotty spoke up and asked, "General, you mentioned that in a few of the cases, the brains had been removed. Did this removal also include the brain stem and connective tissue?"

"I'm not sure, Mr. Scott, but I will find out before you leave," the general replied.

Scotty spoke up again. "One more thing. Was the spinal fluid removed from the victims?"

"Yes. One of the first things our doctors sought out was a sample of spinal fluid. However, in each of the victims, the fluid had been removed. Why do you ask?"

"I don't know yet. This whole thing doesn't make any sense," Scotty answered, then asked, "Were there any foreign objects found in the bodies examined so far?"

"Yes. I was going to show them to you later. In two of the bodies, what could be described as BBs were found in the nasal cavity. They were extracted, and I will give the admiral one of them to take back with you, as well as a few of the cloths that the bodies were wrapped in."

"Any idea why the BBs were there?" Vinson asked.

"No. I'm hoping that our people and yours can work together on that problem, and maybe collectively we can solve the puzzle," General Salas responded, then asked, "Any more questions or comments before we go into the tent?"

"Just one, General." Doreen spoke up and asked, "Have you identified the victims yet?"

"We know who the they were from the flight manifest. At present, we are only able to make identifications through the use of dental charts. Our police are making great efforts throughout the country to obtain these charts and interview the neighbors of the victims in order to locate relatives of some of the deceased who have not come forward yet.

"We are excited about the fact that early this morning, our survivor was identified. There were only three children on the flight, and two of them were males. Therefore, we determined her identity. Unfortunately, both of her parents are listed on the flight manifest and are more than likely among the victims. From what we have learned about the family so far, there doesn't seem to be any living relatives of the girl. It's tragic, but—"

General Salas was interrupted by Doreen.

"What will happen to her?" she quickly asked.

"The best doctors we have will treat her, and then I guess she will be put up for adoption, provided that she recovers. I understand that you are very concerned about her, Lieutenant, but let me personally assure you that she will receive the best care available," the general answered. "Now, if you will follow me, we can get this unpleasant business over with."

Scotty could see that Doreen was pondering the general's answer as they walked over to the dressing area to don their containment suits. Two technicians helped each of them into the rather-thin yellow protective suit, which was attached to bulky, thick-soled boots. Once they were dressed, one of the technicians explained the use of the helmet. Each helmet was constructed of high-impact blue plastic with a wide visor and a self-contained breathing apparatus that filtered out noxious gases and odors. An internal wireless communication system, which allowed them to communicate with everyone else in the tent, was also built into the helmet. Once they put on the helmets and felt comfortable walking in the suits, they entered the autopsy tent, one by one.

After entering the tent, Scotty quickly scanned the interior. He guessed that the autopsy tent was at least 150 feet long and half as wide. Scotty estimated that there were approximately forty of the impersonal stainless steel autopsy tables neatly arranged in six rows, running the length of the tent. Huddled around most of the tables were a small army of doctors and medical technicians working on the remains of what once resembled human beings. The doctors were involved in the task of trying to perform autopsies on the poor, unfortunate souls, while the technicians were carefully gathering human tissue samples and carefully cataloging the horrible deaths. Against the far wall of the tent, Scotty could see stacks of military-standard aluminum coffins, or what they liked to call body trays. As the general led the small group to a nearby table, Scotty could hear the endless drone of air conditioners trying to keep the interior of the tent cold against the onslaught of the heat outside.

Once they had gathered around one of the autopsy tables, General Salas told them that the body before them, which was covered over by a thick black plastic sheet, was that of a man who was yet to be identified. The only thing that was known about him was that his age was estimated to be approximately fifty years old. The general, in order to prepare them for what they were about to see, went on to explain that all the man's internal organs, including the heart, kidneys, urinary track, lungs, and liver, had been removed, as well as the man's eyes and sinus cavity. Stepping back from the table, General Salas introduced Dr. Miguel Santoro, who was now standing next to Scotty, as the head medical pathologist. After introductions were made around the table, General Salas asked the doctor to explain the condition of the body they were about to see.

As Dr. Santoro began to speak about the general condition of the remains and what organs had been removed from the body, General Salas went to the other side of the table and began to peel back the plastic sheet covering the body.

As the general removed the covering, Scotty gasped at the desecration before him.

The man looked to Scotty to be in his late forties or early fifties. His jet-black hair was just beginning to turn gray in a few areas. His facial skin was deeply wrinkled, as if the man had spent his short years toiling in the sunlight or as if he had spent his life at sea. Where the eyes should be, there were two empty holes turned black around the edges. Scotty could detect two small slits under and over the eyes where surely they had removed some of the sinus cavities. Through his helmet, Scotty could hear the doctor talking, but he could no longer listen as he continued with his own physical examination.

Scotty's attention was then drawn to the man's torso. It appeared that the man was literally cut down the center of his chest. The ribs had been peeled back to remove the heart and lungs, leaving an empty cavity of raw red flesh. Below the rib cage, the entire lower torso had been removed down to the spinal cord, which Scotty could see sticking through the small amount of remaining flesh. Scotty noted that the general had failed to mention that the man's genitalia had also been removed. When he looked down at the man's legs, it appeared that they had also been operated on. There was a surgical cut that ran the length of the legs, from the top to almost the ankle. Trying to think clearly, Scotty remembered that someone told him that doctors sometimes will take a vein from a person's leg and use it to repair other veins in a person's body.

Taking a step backward from the table, Scotty could feel the bile beginning to rise within him. He desperately fought the sensation, trying to hold on to his composure.

Suddenly, he heard Doreen call out, "Michael!" and as he turned toward her, she buried her head in his chest. Instinctively, Scotty put his arms around her, as if to protect her from the sight of the carnage. As he began to gently rub her back, Scotty decided to take Doreen away from this and told her, "Come on, let me take you out of here."

"I'll be okay, Michael. Just give me a minute," Doreen replied, as she also was fighting back the urge to vomit.

"No! We are leaving," Scotty ordered.

Vinson eagerly volunteered, "Scotty, I'll take Doreen outside. You stay here and finish up."

"I'm with you, Agent!" Morrison quickly added and took ahold of Doreen by the arm and led her and Vinson to the decontamination wash-down area by the exit.

Scotty watched as his friends left the tent. He then turned his attention back to the remains before him. Speaking up, Scotty asked, "Doctor, from what you are able to tell, would you say that this man was in good health before this incident?"

"I'm sorry, but right now that is impossible to say. When we run cultures from his tissues, perhaps we will be able to tell something. I just don't know for sure. But based upon the muscular tone of his legs and arms, he appears to have been a fit individual," the doctor replied.

"What about the victims that you have been able to identify? Would you say that they were in good physical condition prior to the incident?" Scotty asked, pressing his inquiry on.

"We are presently lacking medical histories on the individuals that we have identified so far, with the exception of three of our soldiers who were victims. A review of their medical histories indicates that they were each in prime physical condition.

"It was in one of these soldiers that I found what you would call a BB in the individual's sinus cavity. I couldn't tell you just how it got there, but it couldn't have been by accident," the doctor replied and then looked at the general when he mentioned the BB.

"Yes, Doctor. General Salas mentioned the BBs to us," Scotty replied, then asked, "Beyond the presence of the BB, was there anything else odd about it? What I mean is, was it just lying there, or was it attached to something? In other words, did it have any possible function that you could see?"

"It must have had some function, because when I removed it, the BB was actually attached to some nerve endings. Other than that, there is nothing else I know about it other than the fact that the BB was implanted in the man.

"Now, if you will follow me, I'd like to show you the condition of the other victims, which, as you know, varies from the poor fellow before us to others who only have a limb missing," Dr. Santoro replied and directed Scotty's attention to the remaining victims.

As they walked down the aisle, the doctor would remove the plastic sheet covering the victim and explain the condition of the individual and detail what organs were removed. At each table the horror was the same. What had been a living, breathing person was mutilated beyond belief. Scotty was managing somehow to fight off the urge to vomit, but his stomach was beginning to win the battle.

When they came to the last table in the aisle, Scotty noticed that the body under the plastic appeared to be somewhat smaller than the others. As the doctor pulled back the plastic sheet, Scotty instantly became ill. Before him lay the lifeless body of a young boy. Like most of the others, the child's chest had been cut down the center and peeled back.

And all the poor child's major organs had been removed.

Scotty momentarily stared at the empty cavity of the child's chest and saw part of his backbone sticking through the remaining flesh. Scotty then looked at the child's face and saw that his skin was removed on the left side of his cheek.

Scotty couldn't take it any longer; he quickly began walking toward the exit, with the general chasing after him. He didn't hear General Salas calling out his name, or, for that matter, anything else. Scotty knew one thing, and that was that he had to get out of the tent. As he neared the exit, Scotty reached behind his head and began tugging at the helmet, trying desperately to get it off. As he entered the decontamination area, Scotty was successful and pulled the helmet off. After throwing the helmet on the floor, he began pulling the containment suit apart. The technicians started to wash Scotty down and pleaded with him to keep the suit on, but he blindly lashed at the suit with his hands and was finally successful in ripping it off his body, as well as the boots. Once the suit was off, he ran toward the exit doors.

Doreen, Vinson, and Morrison were sitting on a wooden bench outside the exit doors, drinking ginger ale, to calm their stomachs, when they heard a commotion on the other side of the exit. Standing up to see what was wrong, Morrison approached the exit doors just as Scotty came crashing through them. Morrison was knocked to the ground by Scotty's charge, with Scotty lying across him. Scotty quickly picked himself up and ran over to a topless fifty-five-gallon drum that was serving as a garbage can. Placing his arms on the rim of the can, Scotty bent his head over the drum and began to vomit.

Doreen walked over to Scotty and gently began to rub his back in an attempt to comfort him. The admiral stood up just as the general came through the exit doors of the tent, and together they walked over to Scotty. Vinson, in the meantime, reached into a cooler that someone had thoughtfully placed by the exit doors and took out a ginger ale for his friend. When Morrison reached Scotty's side, he asked the question that all obviously sick people are, for some reason, asked, "Are you okay?"

As Scotty hung over the barrel, he managed to reply in a very low voice, "Organ harvesting."

Morrison looked first at General Salas and then back at Scotty as he asked, "What?"

Scotty vomited again and then said, in a much louder voice this time, as he spit the remains from his mouth, "Organ harvesting! The bastards are here to steal our organs!" Scotty vomited again and then added, "Look, it's like this. The world is their laboratory, and guess what? We're the fuckin' rats in the maze! They are not here to help us. They want us. You, me, and everyone else, that's what they want! We are what's valuable to them."

Feeling a little better, Scotty stood up and took the can of soda from Vinson's outstretched hand. Scotty opened the can, took a long, hard drink, and then continued, "They must have figured out a way to transplant our organs into their bodies. If the guy that we had trouble with in the Canary Islands is an example of their physiology, then they would appear to be a pretty close match to us, with the exception of their eyes and lungs.

"I think that they extract our eyes to implant into their bodies so that they would fit in better and not draw attention to themselves. The guy in the Canaries had really large eyes. It's obvious that he didn't have implants. But there was one other thing: that same alien took a pill, which we know to be an oxygen enhancer. Therefore, they immediately need human eyes to fit in with us, and lungs to breathe easier in our atmosphere. The whole thing is nothing but a horror movie that suddenly became real.

"Those BBs the doctor found could have two purposes. First, the BBs could be a device to monitor a person's health and bodily functions, and secondly, the BBs could also be a tracking device so the aliens could quickly locate a person when his organs are needed."

"Are you saying that the BBs led the aliens to the airliner?" General Salas asked.

"If the BB acts as a tracking device, and I am betting that it is part of their function, then yes, it may have led the aliens to the airliner to get the people they were implanted in. The other passengers were an added bonus for the aliens," Scotty replied. Then he warned, "I would suggest that those BBs be crushed as soon as possible, or placed in a lead container. For added safety, broadcast a wide-spectrum static jamming radio signal around the container."

"I'll do that. But tell me, why is all this happening now?" General Salas followed up.

"This…this wasn't originally meant to be. Look, let's assume that they have been doing this for a long while. We have all heard the stories of people being abducted from their homes at night or from some secluded spot away from any witnesses. Sure, some of the stories are so wild that they couldn't be true, but I'm now betting that a large portion of the stories are actually true.

"The presence of the BBs has been documented for a long time. They are usually discovered by accident. Typically, a person will go to his or her doctor complaining of recurrent sinus problems. Their physicians, as a prelude to treatment, will often order a series of sinus x-rays. At this point, the presence of the BBs is detected and removed. The cases have been well documented in everything, from prestigious medical journals to sci-fi magazines.

"The story is always the same. The victims of the implants don't have any idea of just how the BB got there. They are as surprised as their doctors. I think that these people were either used as guinea pigs in a study or possibly were intended transplant victims monitored throughout their lives as to their physical condition until it was to be their time.

"To answer your next question, no one has ever monitored these people to determine if they are reimplanted with another BB. I would think that the aliens would give up on them, as it may be too risky to reacquire them," Scotty replied.

"But then why all this?" General Salas asked as he extended his arm and pointed at the autopsy tent.

"This is a guess, but I think this is a warning. It's a warning done out of fear. I believe that they know about your association to monitor their activities, and they are afraid that the countries of the Earth will one day unite and fight them.

"What they are telling us is this: Let them come and go at their will to do what they must, and they will let life continue on as it has, at least for the immediate future. Expose them and they will conquer us now, even though it would hurt or retard their overall aim of taking our planet for themselves.

"You have a war on your hands, gentlemen. A war like you have never seriously even contemplated. Your choice is simple: roll over and ignore them or fight them!" Scotty drove his point home, and then, as he turned and faced Morrison, he declared, "Me? I'm for fighting them. I don't want these bastards ever to do this to another human being again. Give me the tools and I will fight your war!"

"Count me in!" Vinson spoke up.

"That goes for me too, sir," Doreen added, forgetting for the moment that she was already doing her part to fight the aliens.

"Okay, we'll talk about this later," Morrison replied, knowing that at last his desire to have Scotty head up Space Command was now assured. "Are you feeling okay, Scotty?" he then asked.

"I'm okay, sir. But is there a place where I can lie down for a while?" Scotty asked, feeling a bit weak.

General Salas called over a soldier and directed him to show Scotty to a tent where he could rest.

While Scotty rested, the rest of the group engaged themselves in a lively conversation regarding the aliens and the conclusions that Scotty had talked about. After an hour of discussion, each one of them reached the same conclusion: fight the bastards. While Morrison, Vinson, and General Salas continued the conversation, Doreen excused herself and went to check on Scotty. She found him awake and very glad to see her. As they held each other, they knew that their lives had changed this day. The tenderness that they felt suddenly became even more precious, and something that they would always cherish.

As Scotty and Doreen hugged each other, they didn't speak. Their communication was silent. In that silence, all emotion was spoken as if it were shouted so all could hear. Yet it was private, as it always is between lovers. Their peace was interrupted when Vinson burst through the flaps of the tent and announced that they were ready to leave.

As their helicopter lifted off, Scotty looked down at the autopsy tent and felt sadness for the victims and their families. He silently vowed to avenge their deaths and prayed for God's help in his mission.

When they landed back at the military base, Morrison suggested that they go and wash up as they would be leaving in half an hour. Scotty walked to the bathroom and didn't see Doreen and Vinson drive away in a Humvee. Scotty washed his hands and splashed water over his face and neck, seeking relief. As Scotty was about to leave, he noticed a clean flight suit neatly folded and lying on top of a small counter in the corner of the room. Scotty looked around and, seeing no one, changed into it. Although the flight suit was a couple sizes too big, he felt better.

Leaving the bathroom, Scotty looked around and didn't see Doreen, Vinson, or the admiral. Thinking that they were off somewhere, getting some food, Scotty walked over to their waiting aircraft, went aboard, sat down, and fell into a deep sleep.

HOME, I AIN'T EVER GOING TO GET HOME

FEELING SOMEONE SHAKING HIS SHOULDER, Scotty slowly opened his eyes and looked up. Vinson was standing over him and saying something about the admiral wanting to see him. Scotty told Vinson to leave him alone so that he could get some sleep. Vinson shook Scotty's shoulder again until he was awake. Getting up from his seat, Scotty momentarily forgot where he was. Looking around, he found himself on an airplane and asked Vinson if they were home yet. Vinson laughed a hearty laugh and informed him that the plane had become his home away from home. Both men then left the aircraft and met the admiral as he was pacing back and forth by the small stairway used to get into the airplane.

"What's wrong?" Scotty asked when he saw the concerned look on Morrison's face.

"Scotty, Vinson, I have to know one thing. What each of you said back at the autopsy tent about wanting to fight the aliens, were you serious about it, or was it just a response because of what we saw?" Morrison asked, looking each of them squarely in the face.

At first, Vinson and Scotty looked at each other and nodded in acknowledgment. Scotty spoke up first. "Admiral, I meant what I said. You give me the capability to fight the aliens and I'll do it. A lot has changed in a few short days. I couldn't turn my back and walk away as if nothing has happened." Scotty paused and then added, "I simply couldn't live with myself if I didn't do anything."

"Okay, what about you, Agent?" Morrison asked as he acknowledged Scotty's answer and then turned and faced Vinson.

"I feel the same way, Admiral. After what the aliens did to those poor people, well, sir, it just isn't right. No one deserves that. And you know, it could have just as easily been my mother or father aboard that aircraft. Fight them? Hell, I'd like to kick their collective ass back to where they came from!

"Besides, where Scotty goes, I go. Someone has to look out for his ugly face and keep him out of trouble!" Vinson replied with a slight laugh at the end of his vow.

"It means that you will not be living in New York City regularly anymore, Agent," Morrison pointed out.

"That's okay. It is getting too crowded anyway," Vinson declared.

"Good! Glad to hear it, Agent," Morrison responded and then, while looking toward the front of the hangar, added, "Let's get back aboard. We will be leaving as soon as my pilots and Lieutenant Stark get back."

"Sir, Doreen is aboard the aircraft, waiting for us," Vinson pointed out.

"I didn't see her, Vinson," Scotty stated with a puzzled look on his face.

"She was in the bathroom when I got you up," Vinson coyly answered.

"Good. Then we should be about ready to shove off," Morrison declared as he turned around. Then he proclaimed, "Ah, here come our pilots now!" As the two pilots joined them, Morrison introduced them, "Scotty, Vinson, may I introduce you to my pilots, Captain Megan Carroll and Lieutenant Warren Pierce. Two of the best damn pilots I have ever met." Morrison then realized that he just made a major mistake, so he added, "With the obvious exception of yourself, Scotty!"

After the introductions and hand-shaking were completed, Megan Carroll boarded the aircraft and began her preflight check, while Lieutenant Pierce did the walk-around inspection of the aircraft, checking the tires, landing gear, looking to see if any liquids were leaking, and the overall general condition of the flight surfaces. A few seconds later, the twin jet engines of the aircraft started and the admiral, Vinson, and Scotty began to enter the aircraft. As Scotty was walking up the stairs, his attention was drawn to a Humvee that was rapidly approaching their aircraft with its siren blaring. Scotty stepped off the aircraft and stood next to the admiral, waiting for the Humvee to stop. Once it came to rest, General Salas jumped out of the vehicle and ran over to Morrison and Scotty.

"Admiral! The girl is gone!" General Salas shouted above the whine of the jet engines.

"Gone? What do you mean *gone*?" the admiral shouted back.

"The doctor went to check on her and the nurse was passed out, the window to the room was open, and the girl was gone. I've locked down the base, and I'm having a complete search done. You don't think the aliens have returned for her, do you?" General Salas asked, afraid of the answer.

Pondering the question for a moment, Morrison answered, "Not in broad daylight. They would have had to land a ship near here. It's too risky." Thinking for another moment, Morrison then pointed out, "If the aliens look like the man Scotty had trouble with, then yes, they may be on the base right now disguised as one of your soldiers. You better match everyone—and I mean *everyone*—against their personnel records and fingerprints." As an afterthought, he asked, "Any idea when she disappeared?"

"It was in the past hour or so when the doctor went to check in on her," General Salas answered.

"Is there anything that we can do to help?" Morrison asked.

"No. For your safety, it's best that you leave right now. I am going to follow your advice and treat everyone as a suspect. I just hope that we have not been infiltrated.

"Oh, one more thing. I've ordered a fighter escort for you as far as Panama. I would suggest that you radio ahead for your fighters to meet you there," General Salas suggested.

"I'll do that, General. Good luck with your search. Be sure to let me know what happens next. See you at the conference. Goodbye for now. Just remember, together we can fight and beat these devils!" Morrison offered.

"I hope so. Be safe, Admiral. And you too, Scotty. Have a safe flight," the general answered.

After Scotty and the admiral entered their aircraft, Morrison proceeded up to the cockpit and informed the pilots of the fighter escort that they would be receiving and ordered an escort to meet them close to Panama. Returning to the cabin, Morrison sat down across from Vinson. He noticed that Doreen was sitting across from Scotty, facing him, but she didn't appear to be her usual self. Doreen had her head uncharacteristically buried in a magazine, which she didn't appear to be reading. Wondering what was wrong, Morrison asked, "Lieutenant, are you feeling okay?"

"Yes, Admiral, I'm fine," Doreen answered as she momentarily moved the magazine away from her face and then returned to it immediately.

Morrison looked to Scotty for support, but all Scotty could do was shrug his shoulders, as he couldn't even guess what was bothering Doreen.

Once they were airborne, and seeing that the fighter aircraft escort was flying alongside their aircraft, Morrison ordered the flight attendant to serve lunch. Vinson and the admiral eagerly attacked their roast beef sandwiches, while Scotty nibbled at his, but Doreen didn't even look at her lunch, preferring to remain quiet and look at her magazine. When Morrison finished his lunch and had drunk the last sip of soda, he excused himself and declared that he had to go to the head (Navy lingo for the *bathroom*). Vinson sat up erect as the admiral stood up and asked, "Admiral, did I ever tell you that my great-grandfather was a fireman in New York City in the 1800s?"

Sitting back down, Morrison instantly became interested in what Vinson had to say. Vinson went on to detail what little he knew of his great-grandfather's life in the fire department. He knew that the fire engine was steam powered to pump the water and that the engine itself was pulled by horses. Beyond that, Vinson didn't know much else but relied on his own imagination to fill in the gaps. For the next half hour, he did a superb job of entertaining the admiral.

Vinson was interrupted when Captain Megan Carroll announced over the intercom, "Lieutenant Stark, we have crossed into international airspace."

All eyes, except Vinson's, turned toward Doreen, seeking an explanation. Vinson simply let out a sigh of relief, having kept the admiral, and everybody else, for that matter, away from the bathroom. Doreen threw her magazine down and raced to the bathroom in the back of the aircraft. Vinson stood up and followed her lead.

The admiral turned around in his seat and looked toward the back of the aircraft just as Doreen entered the bathroom and Vinson bent down outside of the doorway to the bathroom. What the admiral saw next, he couldn't believe. Vinson stood up with a child in his arms and gently placed her into one of the executive seats in the back. Reaching over to the window, Vinson pulled down the shade just in case the escorting fighter pilots could see in the window. He then reclined the seat a little to make the girl more comfortable. Doreen emerged from the bathroom and went over to the girl and covered her with a blanket. Taking a bottle of water from Vinson, Doreen put the bottle to the girl's lips, and she miraculously took a few sips.

"Lieutenant!" Morrison bellowed as he rose from his seat and walked to the back of the aircraft. "Don't tell me that's the girl from the hospital?" the admiral shouted as he looked down at the girl and immediately recognized her. "My god, it is!"

"I couldn't just leave her there! You saw how they were treating her!" Doreen pleaded.

Putting his hands on his rather-large hips, Morrison again raised his voice and stated, "Lieutenant, you kidnapped a foreign national from her own country and put her aboard a United States-government jet. Do you realize just how much trouble you are in?" Turning toward Vinson, he continued, "And you, Agent, you should know better! How does the rest of your life in a federal penitentiary sound?"

"Hey, I'm no agent. I'm a civilian, you know," Vinson replied, setting the record straight.

"Civilian or not, you're in it up to your neck!" the admiral challenged in an impatient, loud voice.

"Admiral!" Scotty spoke up as he walked toward the back of the aircraft. "What's done is done. We can't change that, and hollering only makes it worse.

"Doreen is right, the girl was not being treated right. There is not one among us, including yourself, that didn't want to wring that doctor's neck. I am quite sure that they have very capable doctors there, but she was not one of them. If things progressed the way that they did, then the girl might not have ever recovered. You saw the way she dug into the girl's arm with that probe. How many times do you think she might have done the same thing just to prove a point? That doctor's behavior went beyond normal. She was just a disaster.

"Admiral, we just can't bring the girl back and say we found her on our aircraft or, worse yet, say, 'Sorry, General, but we thought your psychiatrist was a nut, so we kidnapped the girl.' If we did that, do you honestly think that he would ever trust us again? Admiral, we need him, and he needs us, if your association is going to work. Right now he thinks aliens entered his base and took her. Let him keep thinking that. To do otherwise would destroy what you have worked so hard for.

"Look it, we can get her the proper treatment she deserves at home. You yourself were upset at the way she was being treated. Doreen and Vinson saw a wrong and did something to correct it. Granted, their behavior may have slightly crossed the line—well, maybe they were *way* over the line—but nonetheless they rescued the girl.

"Let it be, Admiral. There is nothing to be gained by going back. Let's just go on from here. I'm only upset that they didn't let me in on their plan," Scotty concluded after pleading their case.

Admiral Morrison looked long and hard at Scotty. He knew that everything Scotty said made perfect sense. To go back and return the girl would be a disaster. At home, she would receive the proper care. Morrison then looked down at Doreen and the girl. A big smile came over his face as he asked, "Okay, how can I be of help?"

Doreen stood up and kissed Morrison on the cheek and then high-fived Vinson.

Squeezing past the admiral and Vinson, Doreen walked up to Scotty, whispered, "Thanks," put her arms around his neck, and gave him a big kiss on the lips. When Doreen turned around, the admiral was sitting next to the girl as if he were her protective father.

He was holding a bottle of water up to her lips and coaxing her to drink. To everyone's surprise, the girl's lips parted and she willingly drank the water as the admiral held the bottle up.

"Why, Admiral, you're a natural!" Vinson offered.

Morrison looked up at Vinson for a moment and ordered, "Agent, tell my pilots to radio home base when we are in US airspace and inform them that we have a medical emergency on board." Just to throw salt on the wound, Morrison added, "Oh, Agent, you are not a civilian, as you may think. Actually, you are in the Navy again. You really should have read the National Secrets Act a little more closely before you left New York." Morrison enjoyed the look of shock on Vinson's face.

"What?" Vinson replied in surprise, then asked, "Scotty, did you know about this? I suppose that you are going to call me *Agent* for the rest of my life, huh, Admiral?"

Looking up at Vinson, Morrison announced, "No, I think *Commander* is much more appropriate." Turning his attention to Doreen, Morrison continued, "Lieutenant Stark, I will be calling you *Captain* from now on. Congratulations!" Then looking at Scotty, Morrison smiled even more and declared, "Scotty, I anticipated that you would join us sooner or later, and I have had your promotion approved to rear admiral. Congratulations, Admiral! It has been long overdue."

A big smile crossed Scotty's face as Doreen offered her congratulations in the form of a long, passionate kiss. Vinson seemed a little puzzled and asked, "But, Admiral, how can I be a commander? I wasn't even in the reserves!"

"Yours was the easiest. I brought you in under the management program. We are allowed to bring people into the military, provided that they possess special skills, at an officer's rank. Scotty needs your skills, and that is good enough for me, Commander," Morrison replied.

"Thank you, Admiral," Vinson replied, grinning from ear to ear. Turning toward Scotty and Doreen, Vinson congratulated them.

After the congratulations were exchanged, everyone's attention was refocused on the girl. Everyone tried as best as they could to make her comfortable and discussed the horrid sights she might have seen. Scotty was becoming antsy and asked the admiral if he could fly the aircraft for a while. Morrison knew that pilots hate to be passengers and instructed him to go and have some fun.

As Scotty entered the cockpit, Captain Carroll asked him if he wanted to take the controls for a while. Of course Scotty eagerly agreed, and Lieutenant Pierce climbed out of the copilot seat on the right. After Scotty settled into the seat, Captain Carroll gave him a quick tour of the instruments and briefed him on the relative course they were following, as well as their position. Within a few minutes, the Brazilian fighter escort turned and went home as a flight of Navy F-18s took over the escort duty. Scotty suggested to Captain Carroll that she direct the fighters to fly in a staggered position to starboard (to the right) at different altitudes separated by at least five hundred feet.

Once Captain Carroll directed the fighters to their new positions, Zebra Flight, the call sign of the fighters, separated and two aircraft flew above them while the other two flew below them. Once they were in position, the flight leader of Zebra Flight called Lima, Scotty's aircraft designation, and informed Captain Carroll of their position.

Captain Carroll then ordered that the fighters turn off their search radars to reduce their electronic signal. Turning toward Scotty, she offered, "Just an added precaution. Never can be too careful, you know, given what you guys are dealing with. Ground radar should pick up any traffic headed our way and warn us."

"It's a good idea, Captain. We should be able to sneak right into the base now," Scotty reassured her but really not knowing what to expect. Trying to change the subject, Scotty asked, "We are approaching the Gulf of Mexico. Okay if I contact NAS[48] Pensacola and check in?"

After receiving the captain's permission, Scotty keyed the radio. "NAS Pensacola, this is Lima 2-4-6. Do you copy?"

"Lima 2-4-6, this is NAS Pensacola. Read you five by five.[49] Make you over the Yucatan Channel at 3-2-0[50] proceeding north-northwest. Over."

Scotty listened to the voice from NAS Pensacola and thought that he recognized it from his days aboard ship. Taking a chance and disregarding procedure, Scotty called out, "This is Lima 2-4-6. Red, is that you?"

"Pirate, you old sea dog, I thought that was you. What happened to the civilian life?" Red asked.

"It was okay, but really boring," Scotty answered.

"Glad to see you back, old buddy. It hasn't been the same without you," Red offered.

"Hey, Red, I thought you vowed to stay at sea after the last divorce?" Scotty reminded him.

"Yeah, but my new girlfriend wants me to keep my feet dry,"[51] Red answered.

"I don't blame her. Okay, Red, I'll get in touch. I better close before we get a reprimand. Be safe, Red, and kiss her for me. Lima 2-4-6, out."

"Lima 2-4-6, road is clear. Fly safe. Out," Red concluded.

"Okay, Admiral, you are going to have to explain that. And who the hell is Red?" Captain Carroll asked Scotty.

Scotty related that Red was, without a doubt, the best ATC (air traffic controller) in the entire Navy. He explained that Red was once an aviator but had a severe crash and could no longer fly. Wanting to stay in the Navy, Red went into air traffic control as an alternative and had saved the lives of many a nervous aviator trying to land his aircraft in bad weather and especially at night. Red would patiently talk an aviator down until they landed safely on the carrier.

Scotty pointed out that Red's weakness were women. Red had taken the saying "A girl in every port" to mean "A wife in every port." As a consequence, Red had been divorced five times, but now with a new girlfriend, he would probably remarry. Concluding Red's story, Scotty stated that every naval aviator owes a debt to people like Red who guide pilots safely through the night and bad weather. Captain Carroll offered her agreement to that simple truth.

For the next ten minutes, Scotty enjoyed himself. He had taken the aircraft off automatic pilot and he did what he liked best, flying a plane. His excitement was short-lived, however, when he heard Red calling in an excited voice. "Lima 2-4-6, have two unknown aircraft at your altitude coming at you fast and true, estimated speed 9-0-0 on intercept at your seven o'clock[52] position. Do you copy?"

"Copy!" Scotty radioed as his small cockpit became alive with activity. Captain Carroll radioed Zebra flight and ordered them to turn on their search radars and weapons. She then ordered two of the aircraft to intercept the unknowns. Immediately, two F-18s broke formation and headed toward the unknowns. They radioed in that they had acquired the targets on radar but could not get a visual as they closed to within one mile of their radar contacts. In a few seconds, the F-181s overflew where the unknown craft should have been. Turning their aircraft around, the pilots again acquired the unknowns on their radar but could not see them.

"Lima 2-4-6, unknown aircraft are two miles from your seven," Red reported in a much calmer voice.

At that moment, Morrison entered the cockpit and instructed Scotty to dive the aircraft and then turn in on the unknowns' position. Scotty pushed the stick over as Captain Carroll placed her hands on the control column, ready to help out if necessary.

Scotty dived the aircraft two thousand feet. He then banked the small executive jet to the left. The remaining two fighters followed Scotty's lead and armed their missiles, ready to fire at the unknown craft.

"Pirate, they are matching your dive," Red reported.

The admiral remained in the cockpit and steadied himself on the back of Captain Carroll's chair. He was scanning the sky above them when he exclaimed, "Son of a bitch! There they are. I knew they couldn't stay invisible in a dive!"

"If that isn't a fuckin' UFO, I don't know what is!" one of the pilots of Zebra flight radioed.

"Admiral, this is bullshit. Let's work our way out of here!" Scotty called out and then radioed the fighter aircraft and instructed them to obtain missile lock on the UFOs, but under no circumstances, unless they were fired upon first, were they to fire on the UFOs. Scotty then pulled the aircraft up to thirty-three thousand feet and to the right, away from the UFOs. As he performed this maneuver, his heart almost stopped. In front of him, to the left, was an aircraft that looked exactly like the one that had shot Ice down. The sleek craft with recurved wings raced by him toward the location of the UFOs.

Scotty heard over the radio what happened next.

"Shit, there is a third one—only it looks like an airplane without real wings!" one of the fighter pilots radioed.

"The two saucers took off and are speeding away. The third one, the one that looks like an airplane, is chasing after them!" another fighter pilot called out.

Captain Carroll directed Zebra flight to reform on her aircraft and end the radio chatter. Scotty looked up at the admiral, who said, "I'll explain later. Right now let's get to Colorado. Send the fighters home when we go feet dry."[53] After pausing for a few seconds, he then added, "I think I will hire those guys. They showed guts and didn't lose their cool." The admiral then turned around and went to the back of the aircraft to check on their precious cargo.

Captain Carroll and Scotty looked at each other, thankful to be alive. Once their flight quieted down, Scotty radioed Red and thanked him for his help. Red asked what it was all about. Scotty told him that some admiral was running a drill on them and that, thanks to him (Red), they passed the exercise. After Scotty thanked Red again, his flight was handed over to Colorado Flight Control. Within a few minutes, they crossed over land and Zebra flight broke off and returned to their base.

Scotty decided to stay in the copilot's seat for the rest of the flight. As they continued, Captain Carroll and Scotty remained in a heightened state of readiness, in case the aliens decided to come back. Scotty, as he flew on, allowed himself to think about the aircraft with the recurved wings. It appeared that this mysterious UFO had come to their rescue by chasing off the aliens in the saucer-shaped craft. *Or did the saucers leave because the fighters were able to acquire missile lock on them and the UFO with the recurved wings merely observed what was going on?* He pondered this question but couldn't come up with a reasonable answer.

Scotty did, however, reach once conclusion: this incident was no chance encounter; the aliens were after the admiral and knew exactly where to find him. Saying a silent prayer to himself, Scotty thanked God that they were alive, and wondered if they could really fight these bastards.

When they were close to their destination, Captain Carroll told Scotty that she would fly the approach. As they began their descent, Scotty listened in on the radio, and when he heard that they were ten miles away, he looked out of the window. He was puzzled that he couldn't see any landing lights marking where the runway was. All he could see were snowcapped mountains in the distance, with lush green fields in the valleys below. Scotty became alarmed as the aircraft continued its descent, and felt the landing gear being lowered and locked in the open position. He scanned the ground before them and still didn't see the airport. Unable to contain himself any longer, Scotty demanded, "Captain, just where in the hell are we going to land?"

"I'm sorry, Admiral," Captain Carroll responded as she reached into a recess in the panel above her and withdrew a pair of glasses just like the pair she was wearing. Handing them to Scotty, she directed, "Here, put these on."

Once Scotty put the glasses on, he could clearly see the blinking lights that outlined the runway. Choosing to concentrate on the landing, Scotty pushed his obvious questions aside for the moment. Once they landed, Captain Carroll taxied to the end of the runway and stopped in the center of a very large red circle painted on it.

After turning the engines off, she informed Scotty that they had to wait for a few minutes. Scotty turned toward Captain Carroll and asked her to explain why he could see the runway lights with the glasses and only saw green without them.

With a knowing grin on her face, Captain Carroll explained that the green field he had seen over the runway was a holographic image. The light emitted from the runway lights was projected at a different wavelength from regular light. This way, the runway lights were invisible to the naked eye and to a camera lens. The special glasses allowed the wearer to see through the holographic image and revealed the runway lights. She went on to explain that the holographic image was then around them and over them, and asked Scotty to remove the glasses and look outside. When he did, Scotty could only see green outside the aircraft's window. When he looked up, he could only see green. Putting the glasses back on and looking out the cockpit window, Scotty could clearly see the runway and the sky above. Removing the glasses once again, he then sat back in the seat and asked what was next.

As if on cue, Scotty felt the runway shake and the sensation that the aircraft was descending. Seeing the puzzled look on his face, Captain Carroll explained that they were on a large elevator, just like an aircraft carrier had, and like on a carrier, they were descending to the hangar deck of the base.

Scotty stared out of the cockpit window and was amazed at what he saw as they descended. They were being lowered into a large concrete area that seemed to run on endlessly. Along each wall was every type of military fighter aircraft, helicopters, and a few small executive jets, like the one he was on. Additionally, he spotted a group of sleek-looking black jet aircraft that he had never seen before or even heard of. These were much sleeker-looking than the famed stealth fighters. These mysterious aircraft looked mean and fast. Instinctively, Scotty wanted to rush out and see them, but his thoughts were interrupted by the admiral when he entered the cockpit and announced, "Welcome to my toy shop, Scotty," as their aircraft came to rest on the floor of the immense hangar.

Scotty began, "Admiral—"

But he was cut off by Morrison.

"I know. Scotty, I will explain everything to you and the commander after you have had a chance to rest. Right now we have to get our young visitor to sick bay," Morrison ordered as an aircraft tow truck latched onto their aircraft and towed them to a parking space. Once parked, the admiral opened the door to their aircraft and admitted a medical team to take care of the young girl. As the medical team was leaving the aircraft, carrying the girl on a stretcher, Doreen told Scotty that she would see him later. She wanted to make sure that the girl was going to be well cared for and made comfortable.

Once they left the aircraft, the admiral directed Scotty and Vinson to take a seat on a golf cart. Vinson sat in the back, while Scotty sat in the front seat, next to the admiral. As soon as Scotty sat down, the admiral pushed the accelerator to the floor and the cart took off at a high rate of speed toward the end of the area, a good mile or so away, Scotty noted to himself. As they passed the aircraft lined up on each side of the cavernous area, Scotty mentally recalled the specialty of each aircraft. He knew that each type of aircraft parked here was mainly for air-to-air combat, with a few fighter-bombers thrown in. When they passed the mysterious black aircraft, Scotty drooled over them and couldn't wait for the chance to fly one of them. At the end of the aircraft area, the admiral brought the cart to a screeching stop and skidded it almost completely around in a full circle.

"God, I love to drive that thing!" Morrison declared as he left the cart, then directed Scotty and Vinson to follow him.

The admiral led them down a long corridor, past what Scotty estimated to be at least fifty offices. At the end of the corridor they entered an elevator and descended five levels. Once again the admiral took the lead and led them on another small hike. This time they ended up in the housing office of the complex.

There Scotty and Vinson were introduced to the housing officer and were led on another hike, this time without the admiral. After fifteen minutes of walking at a quick pace in one direction and then another, making left and right turns every few minutes, they arrived at what the housing officer described as their quarters. Scotty was glad that their rooms were across from each other—at least they wouldn't get lost trying to find each other. The housing officer then handed each of them a small pamphlet, suggesting that they read it over and pay special attention to the base maps that it contained.

Once satisfied that Scotty and Vinson could find the elevators and the mess hall, the housing officer left them on their own, but not before telling them that the admiral had ordered him to inform them to get some sleep as the admiral would wake them up early in the morning.

Scotty and Vinson were left alone in the hallway, looking at each other with puzzled looks on their faces. Then Vinson broke the silence. "Well, ole buddy, what did you get me into?"

"Beats me," Scotty replied and then, with a smile on his face, added, "Good night, Commander! See you in the a.m."

"Good night, my admiral!" Vinson replied with slight laughter in his voice.

Scotty turned toward his friend and directed, "Very funny. Let's get some sleep, Vinson. It's been a trying day." Turning back around toward the door to his quarters, Scotty turned the key in the lock and opened the door.

When Scotty entered his quarters, he stood a few steps into the room momentarily and wondered if he was in the wrong room. He found himself in a room at least thirty feet long and almost as much wide. The floor was carpeted from wall to wall in a thick, plush neutral color. In the center of the room were two large leather couches facing each other, with a coffee table between them. Off to the right side were two matching recliners in front of bookcases that ran from the floor to the ceiling, crammed full of books ranging from light fiction to technical manuals on every conceivable subject having to do with aircraft and spaceflight. Against the left wall was an entertainment center containing a large-screen television and a stereo unit. At the back of the room was a desk, which Scotty estimated to be over twenty feet long.

As Scotty walked over to the desk, his attention was drawn to a brass nameplate displayed in the center of the desk in front of the accompanying chair. Picking it up, Scotty stared at it for a minute and read the inscription, "Rear Admiral Michael Scott." Putting it back down, he then walked to the back of the desk and sat down in the high-back executive leather chair. Scotty examined the desk and rubbed the highly polished walnut wood that the desk was made of. He then examined what the desk contained.

There were a few large drawers down each side of the desk, with combination locks on each of the top drawers. On the top of the desk, in the center, three computer monitors were embedded below the writing surface of the desk, covered over by glass, angled upward so Scotty could see them from his chair. A keyboard slid out on a try from the center of the underside of the desk. On his immediate right were four telephones, each a different color. There was a red one, a blue one, a green one, and a black one. To his left six television monitors were mounted on a wall, which showed changing screens of different levels and parts of the complex. To his left a series of clocks was mounted on the wall depicting the local time in different capitals of the world. Beneath them, Scotty was glad to see a clock like the one in his study in New York. It showed not only the time in each major time zone of the world but also where it was daytime and nighttime.

Getting up from his desk, Scotty crossed over the room to his left and opened a door in the center of the wall. This led into a small hallway with a half bath on one side and a somewhat-large kitchen and dining area on the other side. Opening the refrigerator, Scotty was pleased to find an ample supply of his favorite soft drinks and junk food.

Pulling on the freezer door, he was more than pleased to find a few containers of chocolate raspberry ice cream waiting for him. Satisfied by what he found, Scotty went back into the living area of his quarters and crossed over to another door on the opposite wall.

Opening that door, Scotty found himself in his bedroom, which was almost the same size as his living room. Against the far wall was a four-poster king-size bed with end tables flanking the sides. Opposite the bed was another entertainment center containing the same equipment as the one in his living room. Adjoining the bedroom was a full bathroom and a dressing area, as well as a very large walk-in closet. Peeking into the closet, Scotty saw a series of uniforms hanging there next to some flight suits. The uniforms had the rank of rear admiral sewn on them. Taking one of the uniforms off the rack, Scotty was amused when he saw his name and rank engraved on a small nameplate mounted on the breast area. *The admiral really does think of everything,* Scotty thought to himself as he returned the uniform to the rack.

Scotty then left his quarters and knocked on Vinson's door. Opening his door, Vinson stood in the doorway with his desk nameplate in his hand. Before he could speak, Scotty spoke up. "I see that you got one of those too. Uniforms also, I suppose, as well as a full wardrobe that fits."

"Yeah, it seems like we were set up, Scotty," Vinson replied, then added, "The admiral somehow knew the answer before we could even think of the question."

"It kind of seems that way, doesn't it? Well, just think of those poor people in Brazil and Zambia. That's why we are here. And it looks like we are in it up to our eyeballs. Good night, Vinson," Scotty replied and then turned around and walked across the hall to his quarters.

"You're right, Scotty. Good night," Vinson answered with resignation in his voice as he remembered the sights he had seen in the last few days.

Scotty was exhausted as he entered his bedroom and lay down on his bed. He wondered where Doreen was and realized that she was probably still in sick bay, looking after the little girl. Scotty wanted to get up and go see her, but he couldn't move.

Exhaustion overcame him and he fell fast asleep. He didn't hear Doreen knocking on his door a few minutes later.

◆◆◆◆◆◆

[48] Naval air station.
[49] In this case, *five by five* means "crystal clear."
[50] Thirty-two thousand feet.
[51] Stay on land.
[52] Position in this case is stated like the hands of a clock; seven would equal the little hand of a clock on the number 7.
[53] Over land.

ANYBODY SEEN THE TOUR BUS AROUND?

A T PRECISELY 5:00 A.M., SCOTTY rose out of bed and showered. When finished, he entered his walk-in closet, chose his underwear and socks—standard military issue, of course—and couldn't decide whether or not to wear a uniform. While the admiral told him of his promotion, Scotty hadn't seen anything official beyond his new uniforms hanging in the closet. It was indeed tempting to put on an admiral's uniform, but it just didn't feel right to him. So he chose to put on his old standby dress, a flight suit. As he looked at himself in the mirror to brush his hair, Scotty noticed his name badge on the flight suit: Rear Admiral Michael "Pirate" Scott. Oh, Scotty was proud enough of himself and his new rank, but he decided to remove the Velcro-mounted leather patch and put it in the breast pocket of his flight suit.

Walking into the living room of his new quarters, Scotty smiled slightly to himself, thinking that this might all be some part of a dream and not real at all. He wanted to pinch himself to see if he was asleep, but he then thought of the people, or what was left of them, in Brazil and knew that it was for real. Trying to shake the thought from his mind, Scotty left his quarters and walked over to Vinson's new home away from home.

As Scotty was about to knock, Vinson opened his door and, with a surprised look on his face, said, "Scotty, I was just going to get you. I'm starved! What do you say we get something to eat?"

"Yeah, me too! If I remember correctly, the housing officer told us that the main mess hall is about half a mile that way," Scotty replied, motioning to his left.

Vinson and Scotty walked down a long maze of twisting and turning hallways, trying to find their way. Occasionally they would come across a "You Are Here" map posted on the wall. They seemed to be heading in the right direction, but both men felt that they were lost, though they wouldn't admit it to each other. "Hey, Vinson, how come you didn't put on a uniform?" Scotty asked, trying to pass the time as they walked.

"I don't know. It just didn't feel right. I think that we should be sworn in or something first. Besides, I kind of like these clothes you flyboys favor so much," Vinson replied.

"Yeah, I kind of feel the same way," Scotty answered and then, in an excited tone, declared, "Hey, look. There's the mess hall!"

"Thank God! If we had to walk any farther, I would have died of malnutrition!" Vinson added.

As they entered the mess hall, Scotty noted that the vast open room was almost filled to capacity. Everyone was eating and talking as they prepared for the day's work. Just what work all these people did, Scotty couldn't imagine. As he and Vinson entered the main area of the mess hall, it suddenly became quiet. There was not a sound anywhere as a few thousand eyes stared at them. Leaning over, Vinson whispered, "Do you have this effect on people wherever you go?"

Scotty turned toward Vinson with a big smile on his face and then, turning toward the crowd, shouted, "Good morning, all! How's the chow?"

To Scotty and Vinson's surprise, the room erupted in "Good morning, sir," and then everyone started clapping. A young naval officer called the room to attention, and everyone stood erect, faced

Vinson and Scotty, and saluted. Scotty took one step forward and proudly returned the salute. The same young officer then shouted out, "Welcome aboard, sir."

Scotty wasn't quite sure what to say but felt that he had to say something. He decided to shout back, "Thank you. But how's the chow?"

In time-honored tradition, everyone shouted back, "It stinks, sir!"

"Glad to hear it! May we join you, ladies and gentlemen, for breakfast?" Scotty asked.

"Yes, sir!" came another eruption, followed by more clapping as the crowd sat back down.

Scotty waved to them and motioned for them to settle down and continue their breakfast.

Vinson and Scotty then walked over to the end of the food line, picked up a tray, and took their place at the end of the line. Vinson asked Scotty what was going on, but Scotty could only look at his friend and shrug his shoulders. As Scotty turned back around to look down the food line, two Marines in front of him stepped back and came to attention. Scotty returned their salute and asked why they stepped back. The sergeant spoke up. "Sir, the new base commander may step ahead."

"Sergeant, I thank you for your courtesy, but no one is special here, and if I see the new commander, I will tell him. Please take your place in line, Marines," Scotty replied.

The sergeant then shook Scotty's and Vinson's hands and welcomed them aboard.

Everyone else in line likewise welcomed the two strangers. Scotty asked the sergeant just what all the fuss was about. He didn't like the answer. The sergeant told Scotty that the previous base commander never ate with the men. He then took the liberty of pointing out that it was good for the morale of the base to see the new commander sharing a meal with everyone. Vinson nudged Scotty and again asked what was going on. Scotty almost whispered his reply, "I think you are right: Morrison set us up. We agreed to fight the aliens, but these people think that I am the new base commander, and I have no idea who they think you are."

"What should we do?" Vinson asked with concern in his voice.

"Let's just play it out and see where it all leads," Scotty offered as his tray was heaped with scrambled eggs, bacon, and some French toast. As an afterthought, Scotty also took a few fresh blueberry muffins. Vinson likewise took a more-than-generous amount of food.

When Scotty and Vinson exited the food line, they decided to follow the Marines that they had met in line to a table. Over breakfast they were engaged in conversation by all the people they were eating with at the long table. After introductions were finished, everyone offered their own bits of advice on how to find their way around the facility and the many shortcuts they would have to learn should they ever have to get somewhere fast.

After finishing breakfast and wishing everyone well, Scotty and Vinson walked the half mile or so back to their quarters. Scotty had wanted to get there before the admiral, but when they turned the last corner, there was the admiral pacing back and forth in front of Scotty's door. "Good morning, Admiral!" Scotty called out.

Morrison looked at them and then answered, "Good morning, Admiral, Commander. Been out exploring, I see." Pausing for a moment to catch his breath, Morrison stated with a devilish grin on his face, "I've ordered breakfast in your quarters, Scotty. So let's go in." Almost as an afterthought but really for effect, he added, "Oh, I've asked Commander Stark to join us. I hope you don't mind."

"No, sir!" Scotty enthusiastically replied as he opened the door to his new home away from home. Morrison strode in as if he owned the place, which he really did, and invited Scotty and Vinson to sit down around the coffee table. The admiral asked, more out of courtesy than concern, how they liked their quarters. Vinson didn't shy away from the obvious and asked Morrison why he referred to the room he slept in as "his quarters." The admiral could only offer a nervous cough in response and then announced that Rear Admiral Chester Braddock would be arriving later this afternoon. He was about to go on talking when there was a sharp knock on the door.

Scotty answered the door and admitted a steward, who was pushing a rather-overflowing cart full of food. As he was about to close the door, Scotty saw the love of his life coming down the hallway. Half-closing the door behind him, Scotty at first stood in the hallway, waiting for Doreen, but then rushed to her. Looking up and down the hallway, and not seeing anyone, Scotty and Doreen shared a short good-morning kiss. While Scotty thought he was out of sight of everyone, he was not out of sight of the steward.

When they broke their brief embrace, the steward excused himself and began to walk away but then turned around and approached Scotty and Doreen. "Admiral, I'd like to welcome you and your command aboard. It will be a pleasure serving under you," the steward began. But then he warned, "But, sir, there is one thing you ought to be aware of. If you will look up at the overhead,[54] you will notice security cameras, which are constantly on." He then pointed at the camera mounted on the ceiling.

Scotty looked up to where he was pointing and noticed the tiny camera, no bigger than a dime, embedded in the ceiling. Not being able to control himself, Scotty smiled and waved at the camera. Turning back toward the steward, Scotty introduced himself and found out that his assigned steward was Seaman First Class William Jacobs. Scotty then thanked him for his welcome and for pointing out the camera. *Great!* Scotty thought. *I haven't been here for more than twenty-four hours and now everyone knows about Doreen and me.* As an afterthought, Scotty concluded, *Ah, what the hell!*

Once Doreen and Scotty entered his quarters, the admiral ushered everyone into the dining area and invited them to eat. When Scotty and Vinson politely refused and took only coffee, the admiral insisted that they eat a hearty breakfast since they had a long day ahead of them. While still offering resistance, they lost the battle when the admiral prepared plates for them of generous helpings of scrambled eggs (real eggs and not the military powdered eggs), bacon, and quite a few sweet rolls. Neither Scotty nor Vinson would dare admit at this point that they had already eaten, so with great reluctance they put their forks and knives to work and pretended to enjoy the meal that the admiral had so thoughtfully dished out.

Before Scotty would let the admiral monopolize the breakfast conversation, he asked Doreen how their little visitor was doing. Doreen explained, in great detail, that she was resting comfortably in sick bay. She further explained that the doctors seemed hopeful that after some proper rest and nutrition, they would be able to start trying to bring her out of her present condition. Proudly, Doreen announced that the doctors took her suggestion of sensory stimulation seriously and invited her to partake in the process. Vinson, Scotty, and the admiral expressed happiness about the girl. The admiral concluded the conversation by admitting that it was probably a lot better for the girl to be there with them than to be left to the witch doctor in Brazil. To Doreen this meant that the admiral now fully approved of her actions.

In the course of breakfast, the admiral explained that the base was originally designed as part of the MX Missile System, an ill-conceived plan to frequently shuttle offensive nuclear missiles on mobile launchers underground to new launching sites. When the MX plan was deemed a failure, the complex was turned over to the Office of Emergency Planning. That office expanded the facilities to provide underground living facilities for six thousand people in the event of a nuclear war. When the relative threat of nuclear war was all but eliminated, the facility was handed over to the Navy, simply because no one else wanted it.

At first, the Navy didn't know what to do with such a facility so far from the oceans of the world. However, it gradually came into use when the Navy began deploying its own satellite net. The site offered the Navy a unique opportunity to carry on its space interests away from the prying eyes of foreign governments and competing national interests. The Navy continued to make an investment in the facility and continually updated the base for satellite reconnaissance with replicated systems in Washington, where the central command was located.

When the alien threat was realized as a serious one beyond idle curiosity, Morrison explained that reconstruction and updating of the complex accelerated. Quickly the landing strip was added, as well as the construction of the hangar deck. The surrounding mountains were ringed with an offensive missile system, as well as a laser offensive system, and a plasma cannon, a byproduct of the Star Wars Program.

The admiral further explained that the facility occupied a land area of roughly forty-three thousand acres, of which the base occupied a little over one thousand acres. The rest of the property was open land ringed with sensors to detect the presence of unwanted visitors. To deceive an intruder, most of the security force was dressed in Park Ranger uniforms. They explained to trespassers that the area was a fragile environmental zone and therefore off-limits to the casual guest. If a trespasser persisted in crossing the land, he was arrested and prosecuted under Federal Environmental Law. The area was also a no-fly zone to commercial, military, and private aircraft.

Continuing on, Morrison explained that the complex was a collection of six separate and independent underground structures. Each structure was protected against nuclear, neutron, and electromagnetic bomb blasts as well as biological attack. All the buildings were interconnected through the use of an electric train, a walkway, and moving sidewalks as well as elevators. The admiral explained that last night they entered the complex through the hangar deck, which was a separate building but connected by the elevator they rode down on to the section they were now in. The other structures consisted of a fuel depot for the aircraft and vehicles, a weapons depot connected to the hangar deck and capable of moving weapons on a moment's notice to awaiting aircraft, research facilities, generator plant, and of course, the building that they were now in served as the main housing unit for the base personnel.

Scotty listened intently as the admiral talked, while picking at his second breakfast.

Finally, he pushed his plate away and let the others know that if he ate another morsel he would burst. Morrison reminded him that they would be doing a lot of walking and suggested that he should reconsider eating his breakfast. Reluctantly, Scotty ate another forkful of eggs and a piece of bacon. He followed this last morsel of food with a large gulp of coffee and asked if they could get on with the tour. Looking around the table, Morrison noted that everyone seemed to be finished, and as he was about to get up, the admiral noticed that there was a lonely piece of bacon on his plate. The admiral picked up the bacon with one hand and simultaneously picked up a biscuit with his other hand. In one lightning-fast motion, he broke the biscuit in half, made a bacon sandwich, and in two quick bites, ate the last of his breakfast. Washing it down with a sip of coffee, Morrison declared breakfast to be over and that it was time to leave.

Once in the hallway outside of Scotty's quarters, they began walking down the seemingly endless corridors of what was to become their new home. Scotty and Vinson walked alongside the admiral, while Doreen, who obviously was quite familiar with the layout, led the way.

The admiral lectured that on the level they were on was the main housing area, where each person, unlike traditional military style, was assigned a private room, including their own bathroom. This was done to help ease the strain and demands of living underground, shut off from the rest of the world. Every possible accommodation was afforded the staff of the complex to make them feel at ease. Each room had cable television, radio, and high-speed internet access. In addition, the cable service served as a local base news network as well as an electronic message board and email system. While everyone was given total access to the internet, all outgoing and incoming emails were filtered through decrypting programs to determine if anything was being sent or received in code.

As they walked down hallway after hallway, Scotty listened intently to the admiral's droning on and on while they passed by two Olympic-size swimming pools; a bowling alley; handball, racquetball, squash, basketball, and tennis courts; exercise rooms; a tanning salon, beauty salon, and hobby workshops; a three-hundred-seat movie theater and auditorium; and meeting rooms for every possible interest. Scotty was very impressed when they arrived at a very large department store that simply sold everything. Concluding the tour of the main living area, while having skipped the main mess hall, Morrison led them up to the next level.

Exiting the elevator, they were all immediately confronted by three Marine security personnel. Scotty recognized the sergeant as the man he had met in line in the mess hall.

Everyone, including the admiral, was asked for identification as their presence was logged into a computer that kept track of visitors and employees while they were on the floor.

Morrison explained that each individual was tracked by computer so that at any given moment each person could be located and a determination made as to what they were doing. Doreen added that the security measures were necessary because this level was the heart of the complex and only accessible to those who worked on said level.

As Doreen led the way again, Morrison pointed out that the computer center and the main research laboratories were located on this level. Scotty easily reasoned the function of the computer lab, but he was curious why the complex had so many research laboratories. Morrison explained that each lab had a specific function, from designing state-of-the-art aircraft, engines, theoretical physics, metallurgy, to almost any subject dealing with the threat from UFOs.

As they reached the end of the laboratories, Scotty and Vinson were surprised to emerge into an atrium three stories high filled with trees and walkways, through an elaborate multilevel garden. With a big smile on her face, Doreen told them that this was her favorite place to come and think and relax. She also would spend endless hours here just sitting on a bench, reading a book.

On the other side of the atrium, they entered the main computer area, which seemed to stretch on forever. Behind its glass walls, people sat at consoles, immersed in their own little worlds. Scotty was impressed when, as they walked through the area, he counted nineteen supercomputers and what must be hundreds of smaller computer banks. The admiral explained that the computer area was beyond state-of-the-art in the civilian or military world. Such computer capability, the admiral pointed out, was necessary in order to carry on one of the main functions of the complex, the interpretation of incoming data from the satellite net.

Proudly, Morrison explained that Chester had recently assigned one Carolyn Gibbs, who was a whiz at theoretical computing and other related research, to the complex. Morrison detailed that Ms. Gibbs and her team, in less than a day, had just made a breakthrough in tracking UFOs. She had developed a computer program in which raw data was fed in regarding a UFO approaching Earth's atmosphere, and based upon numerous observations, the program was able to reliably predict the probable destination of the UFO within seconds. That information was then fed into Space Command on the next level. It was then displayed, in real time, on the computer screens. It was hoped, Morrison enthusiastically mentioned, that the program might be able to reverse-track a UFO in order to determine just where they were coming from. In a lower tone, Morrison added, "But that is a little ways away yet."

Needless to say, Scotty was impressed and, while glancing, first, at Vinson, and then at Morrison, spoke up. "If this is true, that means that we now have the capability to anticipate where a UFO is going. If we are able to do that, then we can dispatch forces to meet them, and just maybe we can break up their plans. But time will tell." Scotty thought for a moment and somewhat somberly added, "But I guess we would need one hell of a fast fighter aircraft, though."

With coyness in her voice, Doreen added to the comments, "Ah, we just might have that capability. But that's for later." And then turned around and walked down the hallway. Vinson and Scotty just looked at each other and then followed her lead.

Ascending to the next level, Morrison hurried them along to Space Command. He was anxious to show off his baby, and rightfully so. As they passed through another security checkpoint, the group entered the cavernous area through a massive vaulted doorway. Scotty walked up a slight incline and, upon reaching the top, was transfixed by what he saw. The room was at least two stories high, approximately three hundred feet long, and one hundred and fifty feet wide. On the far wall were numerous computer screens, each six feet high and twice their height wide. Scotty counted forty-five such monitors neatly arranged in three rows. He noted that there was adequate space for at least another fifteen monitors, and indeed it appeared that they were in the process of preparing the space for such an addition. Below the monitors, occupying the floor space were a little over one hundred computer operators busily at work in their computer stations.

As Scotty stood there studying the massive monitors, he noted that each of them showed a section of the world as seen from a satellite. He watched with great interest as one of the screens began to zoom in on a targeted area. The satellite rapidly zoomed in on a foreign warship passing through the Panama Canal. When the satellite continued to zoom in, Scotty was impressed as he could now plainly see the crew members of the warship on the deck of the ship. As the satellite continued to zoom in still, Scotty was able to read the newsprint of a paper one sailor on the warship was holding up as he was reading it.

Then, turning his attention to the other screens, Scotty noted that two had apparently gone blank, as if someone had turned them off. Turning to Vinson, who was standing beside him, and equally impressed, Scotty commented more than asked, "I wonder if they get MTV on this setup."

Vinson laughed as he continued to look around the room. He then turned toward Scotty and replied, "Man, if they can't, they sure got gypped!"

Morrison, who was standing behind Scotty and Vinson, was taken aback a bit by their humor. To regain their attention, he cleared his throat, and as if on cue, Scotty and Vinson turned around to face him.

"Well, what do you think? Pretty impressive, huh?" Morrison asked but did not wait for an answer. Instead, he began a long lecture as to what the multiple screens showed and what the small army of computer operators was doing. The admiral pointed out that each screen was a visual depiction of what a satellite was seeing in real time. Morrison went on to explain that Space Command received frequent request from other agencies for use of the satellite net.

While his office complied with each reasonable request, Morrison admitted that the demand for satellite time was ever increasing and was reaching the point that they would have to start turning down requests regularly.

"Admiral, what kind of requests do you get?" Vinson asked.

Morrison was not surprised by the question and eagerly answered, "The requests run the full gamut. We handle everything from military intelligence work to agricultural studies to surveillance work. During the first war with Iraq—you may remember it was called Desert Storm—and the second war with Iraq, the Washington office was filled with Army and Marine brass that simply wanted to watch the war as it happened. Sometimes we also track the migratory habits of whales, for the preservation groups.

"So you see, the requests are quite varied."

"But isn't the primary function of the satellite net communications?" Scotty asked.

"Yes, you're right, Scotty. Our chief concern is communications, and we carry a vast array of audio communications for the military, but the optical use of the satellites is ever on the increase. Right now we can point a satellite at an individual anywhere on Earth, and we are moving toward the day when we will be able to clearly hear what he is saying. In the meantime, we have to settle for eavesdropping on electronic conversations," Morrison proudly answered.

"Admiral, as far as Space Command is concerned, do you use the satellite net for all your communications?" Scotty followed up on his question.

"Yes, we do. But all our communications are sent out encrypted and in a burst transmission," Morrison answered and then asked, "Why do you ask, Scotty?"

"Oh, nothing," Scotty answered in a thoughtful tone.

Admiral Morrison knew better than to press Scotty for an answer; he had seen Scotty like this before. Morrison knew that Scotty had to first think through a problem, and then eventually he would tell him his thoughts in a clear and concise manner. Deciding to leave Scotty to his thoughts, Morrison continued to explain the various functions of Space Command. He would look at Scotty as he talked and was glad to see that he appeared to be paying attention. When Morrison mentioned that, at present, they were capable of positioning a satellite over any spot on Earth within three minutes of a request, both Scotty and Vinson seemed to be adequately impressed.

Vinson then took notice of two of the monitor screens that, at first glance, appeared to be blank, as if they were showing a picture of nighttime. As Vinson stared at the monitors, he detected faint specks of white light and, occasionally, colored light moving across the screens. While he continued to look at the monitors, he asked, "Admiral, those two monitors that are darkened, what do they represent?"

Morrison explained that the monitors were showing, in real time, the depths of space. Currently they were depicting the stars that made up the constellation of Orion. Like the proud father of a child, Morrison detailed for Vinson the evolution of this capability. The same Lieutenant Cunningham he had met in Brazil and a computer research team had worked together to reconfigure a satellite to probe the depths of space while it remained in Earth's orbit. To accomplish this feat, they had also pirated the radio telescope in Puerto Rico, since it had fallen into disuse. Lieutenant Cunningham and his team had written a software program to combine the information from the radio telescope and the telemetry from a satellite to produce the rendering that they were now seeing. Morrison added that this new tool might just give them an added plus in trying to track the UFOs. Once he concluded his comments, Morrison asked Doreen to show Scotty and Vinson sick bay, as he had to do something, and promised to catch up with them later.

As Doreen, Scotty, and Vinson left Space Command, they passed what Scotty correctly took to be a flight ready room. Doreen explained that the combat pilots were housed on this level in order to be close to the hangar deck in case of an emergency. Also, given the fact that four pilots were always kept ready to fly on a moment's notice, it made sense to have them close to their aircraft.

When Doreen finished her explanation, Scotty changed the subject. Scotty wanted to ask her a question out of earshot of the admiral. "Doreen, what is going on? Everyone seems to think that I am the new base commander, and Vinson has some role to play also."

Doreen stopped and waited for two Marine security personnel to pass by. She then turned toward Scotty and Vinson and told them a little secret. "Remember back in Brazil when you said that you wanted to fight the aliens? Well, you know the admiral." Doreen reached out and took Scotty's hand in hers and continued, "Michael, you are the new base commander, and, Vinson, you are going to be one of the executive officers of the base. You will both be sworn in today at 5:00 p.m. on the hangar deck, in front of all the base personnel."

"Wow!" Vinson exclaimed. "I guess it works for me!"

Doreen momentarily looked at Vinson when he spoke and then

turned back to Scotty and said, "Congratulations, Michael, or should I say Rear Admiral Michael Scott?" as she drew closer to Scotty and embraced him in a long, soft, passionate kiss.

Vinson looked up and down the hallway as Doreen and Scotty kissed. He then began to whistle as he continued to look up and down the hallway, hoping that no one would walk by.

After what seemed like a minute to Vinson, he coughed and said, "Er…the new executive officer of this fine base orders a cessation of the present fraternization between naval personnel."

Doreen broke the kiss for a moment, kept her arms around Scotty, and uttered, "It's not five o'clock yet. Sorry, Vinson, no power just yet." She then gave Scotty a quick kiss and broke the embrace, but not before Scotty gave her a pat on her behind.

As Doreen led Scotty and Vinson toward sick bay, they came to the main security office.

Scotty decided to enter and introduce himself. Major Jonathon Whitney, a career Marine, greeted him. The major explained that the purpose of his unit was to maintain absolute security over the base and to provide a rapid deployment force should that ever be necessary. Scotty, Doreen, and Vinson were then shown the housing for the Marines, which, in fine corps tradition, was neat as a pin and absolutely spotless.

As Major Whitney, or JW as his superiors called him, walked them through the housing unit, he explained that there were two hundred and fifty combat-ready Marines on the base all cross-trained in security, medical emergencies, as well as fire response. Scotty could immediately tell that the major was a proud individual and proud of his Marines. As they departed, Scotty told him that they should work well together.

Major Whitney snapped to attention and saluted. When Scotty returned the salute, the major said, "Thank you, sir. I would like to welcome you and your exec aboard. If there is anything—and I mean *anything*—you should ever need, just give me a holler." Before they left, everyone shook hands and wished one another well.

When they reached sick bay, Vinson asked if it would be possible to visit the girl he had helped spirit away from the hellish doctor in Brazil. Doreen, of course, replied that they would go to her room first. When the threesome entered sick bay, they were immediately surrounded by the staff. As they were introduced to each individual, Scotty realized that he didn't have a chance in hell of remembering their names. Patiently he met each individual and exchanged a few words with them, mostly about their work. When the introductions were over, Scotty asked about their visitor. One of the doctors, Commander Jerome Hewitt, the doctor in charge of emergency services, stepped forward and informed Scotty that she was sleeping comfortably and should not be disturbed.

It might have been the arrogant tone in the man's voice, or maybe it was just the way he looked, but it was enough to trigger something in Scotty to make him slightly angry when the doctor spoke. Scotty looked Dr. Hewitt in the eye and, in a controlled voice, spoke. "I'm sorry, Commander, but I must insist on seeing her right away!"

"Very well, sir. After all, you're in charge," Dr. Hewitt replied with a hint of resignation in his voice, but even with that he still said it in an arrogant tone.

Scotty stood his ground, and in an elevated, strong voice so that there would be no mistake ever about it, he countered, "That's correct, Mr. Hewitt, and you would do well not to forget it! Now, Doctor, let's see the girl."

"Yes, sir," came a quick reply from Commander Hewitt, and he immediately showed them to the girl's room.

Once they entered the girl's room, Scotty was very surprised to find that it was darkened except for a little light coming out of the bathroom. He noticed that the television had been removed and that the walls were devoid of any pictures. The poor girl lay in bed with her eyes opened, staring up at the ceiling. Trying to control his anger, Scotty turned to the doctor and opened up with, "Doctor, I thought that you told me that she was sleeping."

"She must have just woken up," Hewitt quickly replied.

Scotty continued, "Listen to me very carefully, Commander. You misinformed me, and I don't like that one bit. When I ask a question, I expect the answer to be exact and not a guess.

"Now, I am not even going to ask why there is not a nurse in here. You will order round-the-clock nurses in here immediately. You will also see to it personally that pictures—and I mean nice, pretty ones—are put on the walls today. I also want this room to be brightened, and the television returned immediately. I want fresh flowers in here every day, and I don't care if you have to grow them yourself. Further, you will personally deliver to me every day, at 1600 hours, a report on her progress—and there damn well better be progress—as well as a copy of any nurse's notes and any entries you or any other doctor makes in the medical log.

"If anything happens to this little girl, even if she so much as catches a cold, I will hold you personally responsible. Is that clear, mister?"

"Yes, sir!" Hewitt quickly replied.

"See to it now, Doctor!" Scotty ordered and watched as the doctor scurried from the room and ran down the hallway, shouting orders to the orderlies and nurses.

"I'd say you burned his tail feathers a bit, Scotty," Vinson stated as Doreen walked over to the girl and gave her a kiss on the forehead, for which she was rewarded with a very, very slight smile from the girl.

"Did you see that?" Doreen excitedly asked.

"My god, yes! That's great! Looks like she has a chance, after all. You were right on the money, Doreen!" Scotty exclaimed as he looked down at the girl and then at Vinson, who was standing beside him with a wide grin on his face. "Doreen, why don't you stay here for a while? Vinson and I will track down the admiral. You can join us later," Scotty then added.

"Thanks, Michael, and I do mean thank you. With us around she has a chance to come out of this. I'll meet you on the hangar deck after the nurse comes on duty," Doreen replied.

"See you later! Take care of our kidnap victim, Doreen," Vinson added as he and Scotty left the room and headed back down the hallway.

"Vinson, do me a favor and call Major Whitney. Have him post round-the-clock security outside of her door. I want two Marines with sidearms at all times. If someone enters the girl's room, I want one of the Marines to go in with the person and record what they do," Scotty ordered.

"Expecting trouble?" Vinson asked.

"No. It's just that the doctor really pisses me off. I want him to get a message loud and clear," Scotty replied and thought out loud as the admiral approached. "There's just something about him that doesn't add up. Just what it is, I have no idea."

"Will do, Scotty," Vinson replied as he walked over to a telephone on the wall and dialed 0, hoping that the base had a telephone operator.

"Trouble, Scotty?" Morrison called out as he approached.

"Nothing, really. Just another stubborn doctor that thinks he is some kind of god. I made a few changes. Hope you don't mind," Scotty answered.

Morrison had a grin on his face and was laughing slightly as he replied, "Shot him down in flames is more like it. I already heard about it. It's good to see that you are taking command already, Admiral."

"Admiral! Not yet. It's not five o'clock yet," Scotty replied, now grinning himself.

"Oh, you know about that?" Morrison asked, the tables having now turned.

"Yes, sir. Admiral, if I may, how come you didn't tell me about all this? And base commander? Where did that come from?" Scotty inquired. "I expected to go back to combat flying and hunting down those bastards!"

"I know, Scotty. I am not going to insult you and heap you with praises, but you are simply the best man for the job. I don't know anyone else who possesses your skills and abilities. If anyone can run this place the way it should be run, it is you.

"I tried to run both this operation and the one in Washington, but I can't. This base needs a steady hand that is cool under pressure. If things go the way they seem to be going, you will be under a lot of pressure. I'm not doing you any favors. The work is going to be hard, and there will be a lot of sleepless nights. If I didn't think that you could do it, you wouldn't be standing here now. Rather, you would be back in New York, playing lawyer.

"So which is it, lawyer or the commander of a force that will eventually fight the aliens and push them back across the universe?"

Scotty looked the admiral in the eye and was half-tempted to punch him in the face for all the deception, but that was not to be. Thinking to himself, Scotty knew that he wanted to fight the aliens for what they did in Zambia and Brazil. If the only way he could do that was to run the show, then so be it.

A grin crept across his face as Scotty answered, "Okay, I'm in. But do me a favor: just tell me the truth from the get-go."

Morrison smiled broadly and shook Scotty's hand as he said, "You got it! Congratulations, Admiral."

Vinson then walked over to Scotty and Morrison and informed them that the security detail would be in place within a few minutes. Morrison smiled at Vinson and then added, "I must say, Scotty, your friend Vinson here was an added plus I didn't count on. You should both be proud of yourselves. You are about to embark on an adventure very few people will ever know about, but one that I am sure everyone would love to be involved with.

"Besides, I wanted to save the rah-rah stuff for later. I want to show you both first something that you will find irresistible. So let's get going. I don't want you to miss your swearing-in."

After they had ascended to the next level, as they walked on and on, the admiral explained that where they were was the next best thing to an airplane factory. Here they were able to fabricate almost any aircraft part and maintain the sensitive electronics in the airplanes. There were also state-of-the-art research labs working on new aircraft composition materials. Doing his best to hurry Scotty and Vinson along, Morrison walked and talked as fast as he could, all while taking deep breaths and giving only the barest of explanations for the things they saw.

When they ascended to the hangar deck, Scotty was glad to see Doreen waiting for them with an electric golf cart. Morrison motioned for Doreen to move over, but after stating that she would drive so that they would stay alive, Morrison coughed and sat in the front passenger seat. After Scotty and Vinson sat down in the back, Doreen took off at an acceptable speed of fifteen miles per hour.

As they drove down the hangar past the aircraft, Scotty was amazed by the array of aircraft he saw. He noted that since his arrival yesterday, there were now some additional aircraft there. Scotty counted six Black

Hawk attack helicopters; sixteen F-18 fighters, more advanced than the one he flew; eight A-6s, an out-of-date aircraft but one hell of a close-in bomber; eight Dragonfly airplanes, again a way-out-of-date aircraft but the best close-in ground support fighter-bomber ever built; a few business jets; six Osprey aircraft, capable of getting into an area quickly and either hovering or landing vertically; six Harrier fighters, capable of vertical takeoff and landings; three C-130 cargo planes, capable of short takeoffs and landings; eight stealth fighters; and lastly, sixty of the mysterious black jets.

Doreen stopped the cart in front of one of the black jets and invited Scotty to take a look. He was amazed as she, at first, stood in front of one of the jets. Before him was an aircraft no larger than his old F-18, yet it had less than a third of the wing area. In fact, this aircraft had almost no wing area at all. What wing it did have was swept back along the fuselage, with the wingtips recurved in a circle. In place of a conventional tail, there were three very short stubby vertical surfaces with just the barest hint of a rudder to steer the aircraft. The glass of the cockpit was a transparent gold color.

His attention was drawn to two opened forward gunport doors. Scotty examined the openings and was impressed to see a small Gatling gun in each of the openings. Doreen and Morrison watched with admiration as Scotty then walked around the aircraft while touching its surface. Excited as a child, Scotty crawled underneath the aircraft and looked up at the rotating missile launcher hidden in the belly of the craft. He then climbed up on a wing and squeezed his way into the cockpit, examining every switch and control. When he finished his tour of the cockpit, Scotty stood up and shouted out, "When can I fly her?"

"In due time, Scotty," Morrison answered while laughing.

"Where the hell did you get these beauties?" Scotty anxiously asked.

"I'll let Doreen answer that, since she's in charge of the project. Come on down. We have to get going!" Morrison hollered back.

After climbing down from the aircraft, Scotty walked up to Doreen and asked, "Come on, Doreen, where did you get the aircraft?"

With a broad smile on her face, Doreen replied, "Calm down, Michael." Becoming a little more serious, she then continued, "As you know, NASA has been designing a new type of space shuttle capable of taking off like a conventional airplane from a runway, climbing into space on its own onboard power, achieving orbit, and then landing at any airport in the world. Their concept is great and will work one day, but they are still in their initial design-and-testing phase.

"We needed something similarly capable if we were to react quickly and fight the aliens either in the atmosphere or in space. We simply took their plans, gave them to our designers, and voilà, what you see is the result of their work. We call it the X-45 because of the number of designs we went through until the finished product was completed. But the aircraft is still evolving. Future enhancements will include laser and plasma weapons on board."

After pausing for a moment to let what she said sink in, Doreen then continued, "The X-45 has the capability to take off and land on runways slightly under three thousand feet. The complex wing design allows for that as well as tremendous speed capability. I—"

"Excuse me, Doreen," Scotty interrupted and then asked, "That wing design is the same as the one on the UFO that shot down my wingman, and was on the UFO that apparently came to our rescue yesterday. Is that right?"

Doreen looked away from Scotty for a moment to gather her thoughts and then, turning back around, answered, "Yes, Scotty, you are right on all three counts. The original design for the recurved wing came from your accounts of the encounter you had in which Ice was killed. Since that time, ships of the same design have been seen around the world.

"We decided to try it, and after a lot of trial and error, it not just worked but worked way beyond our expectations. Speed capability in the atmosphere is roughly Mach 6, and it is more than capable of going much faster, but that is as far as we tested it. It seems that its only speed limitation is restricted by the skill and physical fitness of the pilot. In other words, our bodies limit the speed we can push it to. In space we have tested it at a speed of one hundred and eighty thousand miles per hour. But again, it is capable of much faster speeds.

"For fuel, we presently use standard jet fuel, but tweaked up a bit, to take off and fly it in Earth's atmosphere. When the aircraft enters space, another engine takes over that is plasma based. One day we should be able to use the plasma full time, but just not yet.

"Basically, what we are looking at is fighter that is capable of completing its mission in Earth's atmosphere as well as in space. In the future we feel that this aircraft, with some further refinements, is more than capable of travel at the speed of light.

"It's major shortcoming is the fact that the aircraft is impossible to fly without the aid of computers. The aircraft has six computers aboard her. Two of them are needed to fly the aircraft. The other four are kept in the active standby mode.

"Let me explain that a bit more. The human pilot applies force to the controls and, in that way, tells the aircraft what he wants it to do. The computers then interpret those actions and make it happen. The aircraft is simply too difficult for a human to fly alone. The computers recycle the controls every one thousandth of a second.

"Oh, by the way, the six computers I spoke about are separate from the tactical and navigational computers. In total there are over eleven computers on board."

Doreen again paused and waited for Scotty or Vinson to ask a question. When neither of them spoke up, she continued, "For defensive and offensive capabilities, each aircraft has two forward- and one rearward-enhanced Gatling gun-designed rapid-fire cannons, which are controlled by separate targeting computers. Each gun is capable of delivering ten thousand hardened uranium rounds per minute over an effective distance of roughly three miles.

"As you noticed, Michael, the missiles are a totally new design as well. They are a penetrating weapon that will explode on contact, and then another charge goes through the outer and inner hull of a UFO and will then explode, sending shrapnel out in a mushroom pattern.

"The missile is a shoot-and-forget weapon in that once the target is acquired and weapons lock is established, the missile is shot and will continue to track its target at hyperspeed of roughly Mach 12. Each aircraft carries eight missiles in a rotating launcher inside its belly.

I should mention that all eight missiles can be shot off in less than fifteen seconds.

"I should also mention that we are in the process of adding laser- and plasma-based weapons to the aircraft. But let me continue.

"The aircraft is also capable of converting into the light-bomber mode. The missile launcher is removed and a bomb rack is submitted. The bombload is twenty smart bombs per aircraft. These, like the missiles, are penetrators but also have the capability of burrowing into the ground thirty feet, and then they explode the outer casing. Once the outer casing is blown away, a small penetrating missile is activated that will pierce almost any structure." Doreen concluded her mini lecture and smiled to herself as she could clearly see the look of surprise on Scotty and Vinson. For effect, she then asked, "Any questions?"

"Wow!" Scotty exclaimed, then asked, "I have a thousand questions. But first, you said that the missiles are capable of penetrating the hull of a UFO. How do you know that?"

Doreen began to answer, "Because we have—"

But she was interrupted by the admiral. "Let's save that surprise for later, Captain," Morrison ordered.

"Okay, then what is the aircraft made out of?" Scotty asked. "It sure doesn't feel like aluminum."

"You're right. There is no metal in the structure of the aircraft, not even for the internal framing. The aircraft are constructed out of mostly composites and ceramics. The combination of materials makes the aircraft stronger, faster, and much lighter than any other aircraft on Earth. The ceramics, again mixed with the composite material, allow the aircraft to re-enter Earth's atmosphere without incident. In fact, the outer skin after re-entry will actually be cool to the touch.

"In short, gentlemen, you're looking at an aircraft that defies aeronautics as we know it. It's revolutionary in design and capability. And I don't think we will know its full potential until years of testing are done. But for now we have the weapon to carry the fight to the aliens," Doreen answered.

"How in the hell did you develop all this ceramic and composite material stuff?" Vinson asked, wondering just what really was going on.

"Actually, we didn't develop it all. Our team reverse engineered the composite material and added enhancements to its molecular structure. The stuff is really remarkable. If it weren't for the crashed—"

The admiral again interrupted Doreen.

"Captain, you are going to ruin the surprise!" Morrison bellowed.

Looking over at Morrison and back at Doreen, and trying to rescue her, Scotty asked, "What is its radar signature?"

Doreen smiled and answered, "Virtually none, Michael. In the tests we have run, radar doesn't even know that it is there. While the stealth fighters leave a small radar signature, this aircraft is invisible to radar. Even when an operator knows what to look for, he can only find it less than 1 percent of the time," Doreen replied.

"How many of these aircraft do you have?" Vinson asked.

"Right now we have seventy-two, each fully tested in space and operational. There are fifty-two more ready for delivery shortly, and another two hundred on order. We have been talking about boosting production and will probably do so shortly.

"As I said before, future enhancements will include a laser and plasma cannon in the nose of the aircraft," Doreen concluded.

"Where are they all?" Scotty asked.

"They are secreted at military bases around the United States, and a few in Canada," Doreen replied.

"Okay, that's enough, children!" Morrison interrupted again and then ordered, "Back in the cart, ladies and gentlemen. I have a surprise for you."

Once they were all back in the golf cart, Doreen drove to the end of the hangar deck. She stopped in front of two large steel garage-type doors. As they stood in front of the doors, Morrison shouted, "Okay, open them up!"

As the doors opened, Scotty and Vinson looked at each other and then back at the sight in front of them. Neither Vinson nor Scotty could believe what they saw. Inside the huge space were four conventional-looking flying saucers. They were just sitting there on platforms. Each saucer had a ramp going into it, which technicians were using to gain entry. Off to the right side of the room was another saucer that had obviously crashed and had either broken apart or was taken apart by technicians. On the other side of the room was a triangle-shaped black craft in mint condition, just parked there.

Scotty asked, "Admiral, how on Earth did—"

But he was cut off by Morrison.

"Not how on Earth but where on Earth is the question," the admiral responded. "One of them we found off the coast of New Jersey, lying on the ocean floor in four hundred feet of water. We raised it and brought it back here. After a year we were able to determine that its propulsion system had failed. They had either landed it there and couldn't get it off the bottom or it crashed there. In any case, the crew was dead.

"Two of the others, we forced down with aircraft and surrounded them after they landed not far from here. We had wanted to make contact, but for some reason, they were dead when we opened the hatch. Our doctors later determined that they all had committed suicide.

"The last saucer flew over our base a few months ago. We launched a squadron of the X-45 aircraft, and one of the aircraft fired a two-second burst into the saucer. It crashed, and we recovered it. Three of the crew were dead, but two were just barely alive. We tried to save them, but they died as well.

"That craft over there on the right is the infamous Roswell spacecraft. I should point out that it didn't crash in Roswell but rather about three hundred miles to the southwest. Again, the flight crew were dead." Morrison concluded and, upon seeing that he had a captive audience, revealed his last little surprise. "That last craft over there, the one shaped like a triangle, is our invention, or, rather, I should say our adaptation of a flying saucer. Hopefully, it is going to be the next generation of the X-45 aircraft. It is powered solely by a plasma engine and is faster than a lightning bolt. We have flown it all over the world, and it has even been reported to local authorities as a UFO."

"Wow! This is quite a collection." Vinson spoke up as his mind raced to catch up with reality, and then asked, "Admiral, what about the dead aliens? What were they like?"

Morrison looked at Vinson with a slight smile on his face and then answered, "Well, they are two basic body types. Apparently, they live in some type of harmony together, but I suspect that it is more like an alliance type of relationship.

"First, there is the classic 'Gray' being, which I suspect is the true worker civilization. They are between four and four and a half feet in height, a somewhat-pale-gray skin, four fingered and toed, very large eyes, and a very slight build. The other type looks much like you and me. They are between five and six feet tall, with scalp hair, five fingered and toed, medium build. But the one thing that sets them apart is their eyes—they are very large. From what I know about your Mr. Merrick in the Canary Islands, he definitely was an alien. God only knows just what he was doing on the search teams." Morrison concluded, looked downward, and then looked back at Scotty and Vinson. "It's odd, but I use to feel pity on the aliens. They seemed to be very fragile creatures. Of course, I'm talking about the Grays. That is, up until the events in Zambia and Brazil."

"What did you do with the bodies?" Scotty asked, wondering if they were still around.

With a slight laugh in his voice, Morrison answered, "We don't keep them in giant test tubes like they do in science-fiction movies, if that's what you are thinking." He paused, then continued, "After they were autopsied and studied, we buried them with military honors." Morrison then felt that he had to add, "I know that it may sound a bit silly, but they…or rather, I used to think that the aliens were explorers on a mission of peace for their civilizations."

Scotty and Vinson were silent, pondering what the admiral had said. Morrison was a bit somber also and then perked up. "Look, it's almost lunchtime. Why don't you and Vinson look around for a while? And then I'll meet you in my, or rather *your*, office, Scotty, in Space Command in, say, one hour? Chester should be arriving any minute as he managed to get away a bit early, and I want to meet his plane."

"Okay, Admiral. One hour from now," Scotty answered.

Doreen then took over as tour guide again. She showed Scotty and Vinson around and in the UFOs. At first, Scotty had difficulty understanding the flight instruments of the saucers, but after Doreen explained the function of each lever and switch, he couldn't wait to take a saucer out for a spin around the world. Taken as a whole, Scotty was amazed at the pure simplicity of the craft, but in that simplicity there lurked a threat. As Doreen lectured about the spacecraft, Scotty became more and more aware of the alien threat and their capabilities.

❖❖❖❖❖

[54] Navy jargon for *ceiling*.

FOOD FOR THOUGHT

When Doreen and Vinson arrived at Scotty's new office in Space Command, Rear Admiral Chester Braddock and Lieutenant Cunningham had already arrived and were sitting around the conference table, talking. Morrison was paying close attention to the deli meat platter he had ordered for their buffet lunch. With great diligence and patience, he was creating another masterpiece of culinary delight. Having finished, Morrison sat down at the table and stared at his creation and a plate heaped with potato and macaroni salads, as well as a few pickles. As he picked up his sandwich with both hands and maneuvered it toward his mouth, Morrison managed to ask where Scotty was.

Doreen explained that Scotty wanted to walk for a while on the hangar deck and think about something. Morrison looked over at Chester and realized that they both had the same thought. They were afraid that Scotty was in the process of changing his mind about taking over command of the base. Such thoughts, though, would not deter him from his food.

Morrison took a big bite out of his treat and moaned ever so slightly. Doreen, upon hearing the familiar moan, looked over at the admiral and knew that he was unconsciously expressing his delight. But she wanted him to feel a little discomfort as he ate and reminded him that he should watch his triglyceride intake. Morrison looked up at Doreen and managed a little smirk, accompanied by a grunting noise, and then turned his attention back to his hobby, eating.

As Morrison continued to enjoy his snack, Scotty walked into the room and greeted everyone. Before Scotty could sit down, Morrison ordered him and the others to eat. After making himself a small sandwich, Scotty sat down in the chair next to the one Doreen had been sitting in. Needless to say, Scotty was relieved when Doreen sat down next to him with her food. Under the table, Scotty and Doreen angled their legs so that they would be touching, out of sight of the others.

Chester watched the two lovebirds and knew what they were doing. He could see the admiring looks that they had for each other, but he was concerned with what he also saw on Scotty's face. He detected an ever-so-slight frown of concern on his face. Trying to lighten the moment as everyone ate, Chester began relating some of his funnier stories from his years of service. And he was relieved when Scotty added a couple of stories of his own to the conversation.

After everyone was finished eating and the table was cleared, Morrison wanted to get down to business. But first, he continued to play the host and asked if anyone wanted a cup of coffee before they began. Everyone, with the exception of Scotty, poured a cup. Scotty chose a bottle of water instead. Once they were all settled around the table, Morrison cleared his throat, looked Scotty in the eyes, and asked him what he thought of the complex.

Scotty hesitated, gathering his thoughts, and carefully answered, "Admiral, what can I say? I think the base is absolutely fantastic. I'm floored! I can't imagine how you managed to keep this place a secret. And those aircraft, the X-45, my god, they are going to revolutionize flying! Behind the Wright brothers, this is a giant leap in aviation." Hesitating for another moment, Scotty continued, "But I'm not sure I am capable of the job you have given me. This is all so new. It will take me a long time to play catch-up and get up to speed on everything."

Morrison spoke up in a sharp tone of authority. "Let me stop you right there. As I told you before, if you weren't fit for the job, you wouldn't be sitting here. It is because of your capabilities that you are here. So let's cut the crap. Are you in or out?"

Without any trace of hesitation, Scotty returned Morrison's stare and replied, "I'm in, Admiral!"

Without any expression on his face, Morrison turned toward Vinson and simply asked, "Commander?"

Vinson looked back at Morrison and answered, "Like I said, where Scotty goes, I go. I'm in for the duration."

This time, Morrison showed a hint of a smile and turned back toward Scotty to ask, "Why the long face? I thought that you would be smiling from ear to ear by now."

Scotty looked down at the conference table and folded his hands. *How can I tell the admiral that the security of the base has been compromised?* Scotty thought to himself. At the present time, he couldn't prove anything, but the feeling that he was right was crying out within him. Looking up at Morrison, Scotty began, "With all due respect, Admiral, I think that there is a spy, and perhaps more than one, in the complex. I don't mean a spy for a foreign country, but rather an alien spy." *There, I said it,* Scotty thought as he looked around the table and noticed the look of displeasure and shock on Morrison's and Chester's faces.

With a hint of slight agitation in his voice, Chester asked, "How did you arrive at that conclusion? Do you know that Arthur and I have taken extraordinary steps to protect the security of this base?"

Scotty looked directly into Chester's eyes and knew that this would be a defining moment if he was to succeed as commander of the base. Scotty chose his words very carefully as he spoke. "Anyone can plainly see that the security measures that you and the admiral have taken are way beyond ordinary. Otherwise, the existence of this base would have been common knowledge. You are both to be congratulated for what you have accomplished.

"But the fact remains that I believe an alien spy or spies are operating inside of the base.

"Please indulge me for a few minutes and let me explain how I reached that conclusion.

"The admiral told me of your encounter with a UFO on your way back from Bermuda. Granted, that alien craft have been known to operate inside of the Bermuda Triangle, but to approach your aircraft on your way back from a meeting about the alien threat, and in broad daylight, well, that's too much of a coincidence.

"When we were returning from Brazil, we ran into the same situation, except there were more than one. Luckily, we apparently received some help from another UFO that was similar to the one that shot down my wingman, Ice. But that's another area of inquiry entirely.

"Now, take the facts of the two encounters and combine them with the fact that Space Command knows where both of you are at all times and you'll realize the encounters are far from a chance happening. Also, Space Command was aware of the mission of the USS *Salisbury*, and what shows up the minute they located the wreckage of the aircraft from Zambia? A flying saucer. Also, how the hell did our mysterious Mr. Merrick wind up on the search teams?

"And what about the flying saucers that you have? Two of them were found nearby. What are the odds of that happening? And why would the crew commit suicide?

"To me, all this indicates that there is a spy on the base. The spy is to blend in with the people on this base and report on your whereabouts and the capability of this base.

"The real question is how to ferret out the spies. Merrick was easy to identify because of his eyes, and since no one has mentioned anything about someone with larger-than-normal eyes, we have to assume that they have transplanted human eyes and adopted them to their bodies. Remember Brazil. Some of the victims had their eyes removed."

Morrison and Chester listened intently as Scotty talked, and they began to see the logic of his argument. Together they reluctantly agreed with his conclusions and realized that somewhere along the line they must have overlooked something.

Morrison was the first to speak up. "Scotty, I'm afraid that I have to agree with you. There is a possibility that there may be spies on the base. But how do we identify them? And how could they possibly be getting their information out? This base is always in a lockdown mode, and we take every conceivable security precaution."

"Unfortunately, I don't know how to identify the spy just yet," Scotty responded. "But there are a few things we can do to shut the base down a little tighter. We can install biometric identification and security system that will rely on a combination of retina identification and fingerprint scans as well as personal identification. I know that it is like trying to close the barn door after the horse has run away, but it's a start. Further, there must be a way to find out if someone has had a transplant. But we can work on that.

"As to how they get the information out, it must be electronically and it has to have something to do with the satellite net. Why do you think the aliens haven't taken out the satellite net yet? Surely, not because they are benevolent creatures who want to see that we use our satellites for our benefit. After Brazil and Zambia, it's clearly evident that there's nothing benevolent about these bastards. No, it's because they have their own use for the satellite net. They use it as a source for their own intelligence. Hell, they probably know more about this base than we do."

Scotty had made his argument.

"Do you want me to send you some naval investigative agents right away?" Morrison asked.

"No, Admiral. Any investigation has to be done very slowly and quietly. We could turn this base upsides down and not identify the spies, but our hand would be tipped. This has to be done with great care, and very gently. For now I'll work with the head of security, Major Whitney. But if you could lend me Lieutenant Cunningham for the time being, I have other plans for him and Vinson to begin their own quiet investigation," Scotty said.

"Done!" Morrison replied as he turned toward Cunningham and stated more than asked, "Hope you don't mind, Lieutenant?"

"No, sir. It sounds very interesting," Cunningham quickly replied.

"Is there anything else you would like, Scotty?" Morrison asked, a little shaken now.

Quick to answer, Scotty replied, "There are a couple of things. First, while I want to know yours and Chester's location twenty-four hours a day, the satellite net should not be used to convey that information.

I want to stick to land-based, hard-line communications, encrypted, and sent in burst transmission format. The code, however, should be changed every day. Secondly, fewer people should handle all sensitive information. The circle has to be kept small. Also, I noticed that the shredders in each office we visited were the standard strip kind. Crosscut shredders should be installed immediately. The shredded paper should be collected every day and either be burned or chemically washed. Thirdly, I don't know what your current training flight schedule is, but I would like each pilot up and flying every day. Also, I want each pilot to rotate through Top Gun school each year. Those pilots from Zebra squadron that escorted us in are the type of aviators I want. They were cool and relaxed under pressure. They didn't mind taking on the UFOs. They simply did their job and didn't hesitate."

Scotty was on a roll, but Morrison cut in.

"You're right about the first two points, but we have to talk about the flight schedule. We try to get each pilot up as much as possible, but you have to remember that we are trying to keep this place a secret. If we put each pilot up every day, well, it won't be long before somebody takes notice, and there goes the neighborhood," Morrison pointed out.

"You're right, Admiral. So we should then rotate the pilots every other month to a nearby base, where they could keep their skills sharp. On the base, however, they should at least be flying every third day." Scotty conceded to a good point and tried to strike a deal.

"That's reasonable, as long as most flying is done at nighttime," Morrison countered.

"Agreed!" Scotty quickly replied.

"Anything else you need right away?" Morrison asked.

"Yes. I want to bring in two more people immediately," Scotty demanded more than requested.

"Oh, and who would that be?" Morrison asked, wondering what was coming.

"There was a fellow on the *Eisenhower* with me named Wilton Jones. The man is an absolute whiz with computers. Also, I would like a friend of mine, Art Giovanni. He's an ex-Marine. He was in Force Recon and cross-trained in intelligence. Right now he is living in Mt.

Pleasant, South Carolina. It's a small town outside of Charleston. Both men would be a valuable asset to the base," Scotty replied as he looked at the admiral and wondered what he was thinking.

With a sheepish grin on his face, Morrison asked, "Let me see. I think I recall the name Seaman Wilton Jones. Didn't he, at one time, serve under the infamous Captain Aldridge? He was in supply, wasn't he, Scotty?"

Scotty began to laugh slightly as he spoke. "Yes, Admiral, he was in supply, and damn good at it."

For the benefit of the others, Morrison, who was now laughing, recounted how a Seaman Jones and a mysterious Captain Aldridge hijacked a shipment of beer for a party aboard the *Eisenhower*. The admiral concluded the story by relating that the Navy looked high and low for Captain Aldridge but just couldn't seem to find him. Scotty just sat in his chair, staring down at the table, a little red in the face.

Morrison stopped laughing and then stated, "I'll have Jones located and transferred here immediately, provided that he is still in the Navy. As to Giovanni, give me the particulars, and if he passes a background, you can have him as well."

"Sounds fair, Admiral. Thanks!" Scotty happily concluded.

Much more serious now, the admiral spoke up. "Scotty, there is one thing that I have to show you. After your aircraft crashed following your encounter with the UFO, I had a search conducted to locate your aircraft. I wanted to have the metal from your aircraft analyzed to determine the type of weapon that was used against you. We were somewhat successful in that our scientists were able to determine that the weapon was a type of laser, but one we haven't even conceived of yet.

"There was a bonus in this effort. We were able to also recover the gun camera from your aircraft. The disc was slightly deteriorated, but there was enough for the technicians to work with."

As Doreen stood up, turned the lights down, and inserted a DVD into the player, Scotty became a little nervous. He didn't want to relive the incident, but it looked like he really didn't have a choice. A panel of the wall Scotty was facing moved aside, revealing a bank of monitors.

Two of the monitors, one at least thirty-two inches wide and the other a smaller one, came alive.

There right in front of Scotty was the scene he relived in his mind a thousand times over. Sitting in the sky was the UFO with the recurved wings as Scotty approached it. Scotty shifted his weight in his chair to mimic the maneuvers he performed that day as he approached the UFO. Unconsciously, Scotty placed his hand on an imaginary flight control handle and pressed an imaginary Fire button as the film showed a missile leave on its way toward the UFO. The scene then shifted as Scotty had pulled away from the UFO after he had fired a missile. For the next few minutes, Scotty relived the attack and saw the unknown again and again as he maneuvered into a firing position. But there was something different in the movie that Scotty didn't recall about that day.

Doreen stopped the playback on cue from the admiral as he spoke. "Did any of you notice something about the UFO?"

Receiving no reply to his question, Morrison instructed Doreen to continue the film. He explained to the others that what they were going to see was just the UFO and, in particular, the front end of the pointed nose of the craft.

Scotty sat transfixed as he saw the picture of the UFO grow in size in front of him. The picture zoomed in on the nose of the aircraft, and Scotty could clearly see the cockpit area and a shadow of a figure behind the silvery-colored glass. His attention, though, was drawn to a flashing light just below and in front of the cockpit. The UFO was emitting a flashing light that didn't seem to flash in an automatic sequence, but rather, it was as if the craft was trying to communicate. When the film ended, Scotty looked directly at the admiral and pleaded, "Admiral, don't tell me that the UFO was trying to signal me and Ice that day?"

Morrison looked at Scotty with compassion in his eyes and explained, "Yes, Scotty, it was. At first, we thought the flashing light was some sort of a coded transmission. In reality, it was just plain old Morse code. The message the pilot of that craft was sending was, 'Danger, stand clear.' We suppose that when Ice approached the UFO and didn't turn away, the pilot had no choice but to fire. Scotty, when you began your attack, the pilot flashed that message, and when you started firing at him, he did what anyone of us would do: he fired in self-defense.

"That alien could have killed you, but he didn't. He simply disabled your aircraft so that you couldn't press on the attack. With the arrival of that British fighter group, the UFO departed the area as quickly as he could."

"Admiral, what you are telling me is that Ice's death was a mistake," Scotty declared.

"Scotty, as you know, a fighter pilot's life is spent in endless hours of training preparing for the few seconds of sheer terror he will spend in combat. For Ice, that terror occurred in a different form when you sighted the UFO. Ice became spellbound by the sighting, and instead of listening to you, he pressed onward.

"Scotty, that day you did all that you could have possibly done. There is no reason to blame yourself for what happened. When you get down to it, it was a simple mistake that you didn't cause." Morrison was trying to make Scotty feel better.

"He was my wingman, Admiral, and I will always feel responsible," Scotty replied in a somber tone.

"I know you do, Scotty. No matter what any of us can say, you will always feel the same. But when you think of Ice, think of the good times and not his death. Also, think of the positives. Ice was a good man who contributed a great deal to naval aviation and its future. Remember, it was Ice that made the recommendations regarding the ejection seat in the F-18, which made the seat much safer to use.

"Ice was a credit to naval aviation, Scotty, and we are the better for having had him in our midst. He would not want you to be sitting around and kicking yourself in the ass over his mistake," Morrison replied, trying to console Scotty.

"Yes, sir. You're right, of course," Scotty replied with a slight smile on his face and understanding in his tone. But he had to ask the obvious question. "One thing, sir. Why didn't he just radio us instead of using that damn light?"

Morrison didn't really have an answer but offered, "The only thing that we can reason is that his communication gear is incompatible with ours. If that pilot's society can build a craft like that, then the communication capability must also be quite advanced. The pilot probably just didn't have the time to reconfigure his gear to warn you away. He chose to communicate in the universal language of Morse code. I might add that the letters he was flashing were perfectly clear in English."

Vinson wanted to shift the conversation away from Scotty talking about Ice and get his friend back on track. Speaking up, he asked, "Admiral, have there been a lot of sightings of this new type of alien craft?"

"We knew that we had a new player on the field, but we didn't know what that meant. Approximately one year after Scotty's encounter, a shuttle crew observed one escaping Earth's atmosphere and speeding off into space. Since that time, there have been sporadic sightings. One dramatic sighting took place off the coast of New Jersey. A KC-135 tanker crew was flying at thirty-five thousand feet, waiting to refuel some fighter aircraft. While they were waiting, the entire crew watched as the spacecraft continued to lose altitude and slip into the ocean. An immediate underwater search was launched, but nothing turned up. We have to assume, from this encounter, that these craft are capable of underwater movement as well," Morrison responded. "I'd love to get my hands on one of these babies to see just what it is capable of. Also, I would like to thank the pilot that came to our aid when we were returning from Brazil."

"So then we appear to be dealing with three basic types of alien spacecraft. Is that right, sir?" Cunningham asked.

"That's right, Lieutenant. There is the basic saucer shape, which we have designated as Z-1; the cigar-shaped or tube-shaped craft, which we call Z-2; and now the sleek-looking craft that we will call Z-3.

"But that brings up another point. When you ran the mass runs a few days ago back in Washington, you detected a larger-than-normal mass in the ocean off the coast of Hawaii and, I believe, one similar mass in northern Russia near the Arctic Circle. Both of these areas would appear to be worthwhile looking into.

"At the present time, the USS *Salisbury* is proceeding to Puerto

Rico and then will be sent to Hawaii to investigate that site. The one in Russia, we will keep secret for the time being. What this possibly means is that there may be a Z-4 class that we haven't seen or discovered yet," Morrison replied.

"How long have these flying saucers been around?" Cunningham asked as a follow-up question.

"Doreen could best answer that question. Doreen?" Morrison deferred the question, not wanting to monopolize the free flow of the conversation.

Doreen had sat back down next to Scotty after the film and held his hand under the table, out of sight of the rest. Releasing his hand, Doreen stood up and walked over to a section of the wall where the monitors were and pressed a button. A 3D holographic image of the Earth then appeared floating over the conference table. The image rotated as the Earth, in like manner, rotates on its axis. She then picked up what looked like a small remote control with a keypad on it and began, "As best as we are able to determine, the first representation or report of a UFO sighting was approximately fifteen thousand years ago." Doreen then hesitated as she looked around the room and saw the look of surprise on Vinson's and Cunningham's faces.

Smiling at Scotty, Doreen continued, "Archeologists looking for early traces of man in France happened upon a cave that had, at some time, been occupied by early man. On the walls of the cave were pictographs of animals, a few representations of people, a rudimentary representation of the stars that they must have seen, and three drawings of classic flying saucers. The representations differed slightly from the ones we are seeing today in only the upper structure of the craft. Otherwise, the shape is basically the same.

"At first, the archeologists were convinced that the depiction of the flying saucers was the work of some jokesters that had been in the cave prior to their discovery. So they carefully removed some paint chips from the saucer paintings and from some of the other pictures.

"But when they had them analyzed, the results were the same: all samples carbon-dated back a little over fifteen thousand years ago. The painting medium—that is, the composition of the paints—was the same as well. A closer examination of the paintings revealed that the technique used to create the paintings was also the same. First, an outline of the picture was created using the quill point of a feather dipped in an earthen-tone paint. The feather itself then was used as a brush to color in the picture.

"Once the archeologists realized the relative importance of their find, they immediately published their results, not only including the traces of early man but also talking about the paintings of the UFOs. Regrettably, they were immediately scoffed at and ridiculed. Their valuable archeological work was likewise disregarded, and all funding for their research was cut off.

"Today the cave is part of an archeological museum. A small building has been erected near the sight, which contains artifacts of rudimentary tools from the cave. Visitors are allowed to enter the cave, under supervision, to view the pictographs. However, the area of the cave containing the pictures of the UFOs is walled off from the public area. Let me just add that no mention of the discovery is anywhere in the museum. If a visitor should have heard about the paintings of the UFOs and inquires about them, they are told that it was just a cruel joke of a deranged man seeking fame and fortune."

After taking a sip of water, Doreen pushed a button on her remote. A red dot appeared on the 3D image of the Earth where the cave in France was located. She then pushed another button, and another red dot appeared, but this time in China. Doreen then took another sip of water and continued as she looked around the table, "The Chinese language, as you all know, is a pictographic-based language in the written form. Around the time that our ancestors were writing, or rather drawing, on the cave in France, Chinese early man used a similar method of leaving his footprints behind. While there are also cave drawings in China, as far as we know, no flying saucer paintings have been found. But what have been found are some later inscriptions on some bones the Chinese used to write on.

"The early Chinese would frequently draw what they saw or whatever message they were trying to convey. They would inscribe these drawings on the bones of animals that had been ground down flat and were of a uniform size. Chinese scribes would tie these pieces of bone together and simply transport what we would refer to as a notebook of sorts. It was in such a 'notebook' that a reference to flying saucers was discovered. What is interesting is that this particular notebook was part of a traveling display on loan from the Chinese government.

"The overall theme of the display was an archeological record of ancient Chinese man and his culture. When the display reached New York, a young child visiting the museum with his father stood in front of the display case. The museum's head curator happened to be on the floor at the same time. He wanted to get a feeling for the public's reaction to the exhibit. The small child was looking at the notebook at eye level when he exclaimed in front of the curator, 'Look, Daddy, there's a flying saucer on that thing!' The child's father bent down, obviously annoyed, to see what his son was talking about. When he did so, the curator heard him tell his son, after looking at the notebook for a minute, 'You're right, son, that does look like a flying saucer.' The curator went over to the display after the man and his son had moved on, bent down, and saw the same thing.

"The curator anxiously waited for the museum to close that night. When it did, he, along with an expert in ancient Chinese languages, worked till dawn examining the bones and translating the text. What they found were three distinct references to flying saucers always accompanied with the pictograph of water. Wanting to share his discovery, the curator contacted the minister of culture in China and informed him of his discovery. Regrettably, the Chinese government canceled the exhibit the next day and all the material was crated up and sent back to China. The curator did, however, photograph the notebook before it was returned.

"In Africa, archeological evidence also points to the early visitation of flying saucers. While, as in the case of China, cave pictographic evidence is lacking, the find here is in pottery. Shards of ancient pottery that, when reassembled, resembles a flying saucer have been found. It seems that these pieces have no other function than to depict what people saw. Also, as one would expect, other pieces of pottery have been found depicting animals of the day. This early pottery is not inscribed with any form of writing but is decorated with abstract designs.

"In the area bordering the Mediterranean Sea, in almost every country, there is some sort of pictographic representation of alien visitation. These aliens must have appeared as some sort of god to the people. There is one interesting cave painting by the Dead Sea that shows a flying saucer in the sky with representations of people between the saucer and the land. No one has been able to determine if the painter was showing people falling from the craft or if the people were being levitated into the spacecraft.

"Information about these caves, as well as on many of the discoveries that I have talked about, are not available to the general public. The governments themselves don't even acknowledge their existence. Word of these discoveries seems only to spread through the scientific community," Doreen concluded and relaxed a bit as she entered more red dots on the globe in the area surrounding the Mediterranean Sea and Africa.

After putting the remote control down on the table, Doreen reached for her water bottle and took another sip of water. As she looked around, she could see that her audience was mesmerized. She didn't expect to be giving a brief history lesson, but she was trapped as much as her listeners were interested in what she was talking about. Continuing, Doreen reached even further back in time to make a point. "Let's put aside for a moment what we just talked about and step further back in time. When the great shifting of the continental plates took place and the Americas and other parts of the world broke away from the great landmass, the world was truly divided geographically. Archeologists may argue that due to the separation of civilizations, each respective culture would develop independently of its neighbors across the great oceans of the world. True, a land bridge did exist between North America and the far reaches of present-day Russia, and civilizations migrated that way, but let's look for one second at the early development of culture.

"What is it that all cultures throughout the world have in common? The answer is easy: they have a creation story. It may be varied in its form, but it comes down to the bare facts of creation and the establishment and credence of their society. Many civilizations, once established, retell their story and many other stories of how they came into being at the same time. It is in these other stories where our interest lies.

"Some civilizations talk of gods descending on fiery chariots to the Earth, while in some societies early stone carvings are found. One may interpret some of these carvings to depict men dressed in modern-day space suits walking the Earth. In one civilization, there are stories of two men who went from village to village instructing people on how to care for themselves, how to plant crops, and introduced a moral code on how to live. The same or similar thread can be found in many cultures. The names are different, but the results are the same. At some point in time, there was a visitation from an outside source, and these visitors were the wise and noble ones who taught the people. They didn't advance the civilization but rather gave its people a way or an avenue, if you will, of survival. I'm not saying that the aliens aided in the construction of the pyramids or anything like that. What I am saying is that at critical times in a culture, there exists evidence, intangible as it is, that alien visitation helped put a culture back on course. Some civilizations, for reasons of their own, either didn't accept this help or received none."

"Did the aliens act in a benevolent manner back then, Captain?" Cunningham thoughtfully asked.

"Based upon what we have recently seen, Lieutenant, I don't think that there is a benevolent bone in their bodies. They were obviously always acting in their own interest. Any help that they might have given to mankind had a purpose behind it, and it sure wasn't kindness," Doreen replied with conviction in her voice.

"What about when modern history began? Is there any reference to flying saucers then?" Cunningham eagerly asked.

Doreen took another sip from her water bottle as she considered the question. It was hard to summarize a few thousand years of history in a general discussion about aliens. But try she must. "There's not much. There are references here and there in official city or town records, or one can see flying saucers in some paintings of the time, always in the background, but there is nothing really tangible. Soldiers at that time also give mention of possible alien presence in their letters home and in some diaries. They would record that strange lights or shiny disks would appear over battlefields. There is also mention of the same thing during periods of great want on Earth, such as during the Black Death in Europe. While an alien presence was observed, there is no known record of interaction on the part of the aliens. There were, however, two curious incidents during the 1500s.

"The first of these took place in Basel, Switzerland, in the mid-1500s. Apparently, an air battle erupted between flying saucers in the skies over Basel. It is recorded that the round objects were firing colored lights, which we now know to be lasers, at one another. Some of the saucers exploded in the air, and a few were supposed to have crashed in the surrounding countryside. The event is well documented, but there is no follow-up documentation, such as reports on the crashed saucers, as far as I am able to determine.

"The other event is far less spectacular, but much more important. Recently, in a dusty storage room in Constantinople, a museum curator found an old map that belonged to an admiral in the Turkish Navy. We know the admiral as Piri Reis, and we know that he commissioned the map in 1500.

"Now, we must keep in mind that mapmaking back then was accomplished through exploration. Exploration then would provide the mapmakers of the day a new basis upon which they would draw their maps and charts. They tended to combine the best of the source maps, which they knew to be accurate, into a new map. The mapmaker to Piri Reis likewise drew upon source maps in order to make his map. Piri Reis apparently had requested a map of the then known world.

"What Piri Reis had received in 1500 is perhaps the most accurate map of the world as it is today. Keep in mind that Columbus discovered America in 1492. A mere eight years later, Piri Reis had a map that accurately depicted the east and west coastline of America, as well as all the major rivers.

"In essence, it would have been impossible to draw such a map in 1500. But that is only one example of the map. The map also showed the coastline of Antarctica at the South Pole. Now, never mind the fact that at the time of the Piri Reis map, the North and South Pole were well iced over. Therefore, it would have been impossible for anyone to have drawn a rendition of the coastline, yet the coastline is well defined on the map. In order to check the accuracy of the map, it would be necessary to see through the polar ice. Such technology did not become available until the early 1990s.

"The Piri Reis map was put to the test by the Air Force, and guess what? The map was found to be accurate down to the smallest detail. The question remains, How did the mapmaker know of such detail? No one has been able to answer that question. Some scientists say that the map could only have been made with a view from outer space and it would have to have been made well before 1500, unless the maker of the map had the technology to see through the ice. The only other alternative is that the map was made using alien technology. I leave it to you."

Doreen paused and reached for her water bottle again.

Wondering about the map and its maker, Cunningham asked, "Is there any information on where the maker of the map could have possibly obtained his source material?"

"At present, I am not aware of any of the original source maps being available. I am not even sure if any researcher is out there even looking for those maps," Doreen replied.

"Doreen, you said before that there is not a lot of material detailing or recording the aliens during this period. Why do you suppose that is?" Vinson asked.

"To understand that, we must keep in mind the period as a whole. Being able to read and write was the exception rather than the rule. Very few people received or could afford a formal education. In whole villages, there may not even have been one person among the population that could read or write.

"The great history writers of the time were mostly the monastic communities. Some of these communities kept detailed social histories of their area. In some of these histories, one can find vague references to flying saucers and visitors from another world. But they are talked about in very general terms and are often referred to as spiritual beings. You see, the monastic communities were mainly concerned with the spreading of their religion. Their problem, if they wrote such things down, was trying to reconcile the existence of aliens or superior beings within the beliefs of their religion. Somehow they had to transform alien beings that had form and physical appearance into the spiritual beings they preached about.

"Perhaps, at this time in history, the most powerful person was not the king or the people in charge, but rather, it was the storyteller. The storyteller would make his living by traveling from hamlet to hamlet, carrying the news of the day. Communities would hire him to talk about what was going on in the kingdom and relate any gossip about their neighbors in the next hamlet. Unfortunately, this type of oral history is lost to historical record. Such a person may have, in fact, told stories about lights in the sky or of mysterious people walking the Earth, but we will never know.

"Of course, the last possibility is that the aliens did not visit Earth as often as they do today. Society as a whole was leaving its infancy stage and was growing and advancing in maturity. The aliens might have plied their trade, like we witnessed in Brazil, back then, but their chances of getting caught were minimal at best. This was due to the ruralness of human existence back then. While there were great cities at that time, those cities had to be supported. The people who lived in the countryside grew the crops, raised the animals, wove the cloth, and mostly made the limited amount of consumer goods. These were the people at greater risk from the aliens," Doreen concluded and quickly took another sip of water before someone asked another question.

As Doreen was sipping her water, her attention was drawn to Cunningham as he asked another question. "Well, then when did the alien presence really become a threat?"

As Doreen screwed the top back on her water bottle, she replied, "Personally, I think that they have always been a threat, from the earliest known report of their appearance right up to the present."

Cunningham sat forward in his chair and pressed on with his questions. "I agree with you. But when did their presence really become a concern?"

"To the rest of the world who are not aware of what we and others know, there is really not a concern, but rather idle curiosity. You can buy toys of alien spaceships, pick up books about alien invasions, watch movies about aliens, buy alien magnets for your refrigerator, or even alien dolls. But what does this all mean? That there is a curiosity but not a solid belief that aliens are for real and are here on good old Mother Earth.

"On the other hand, if we define *concern* as curiosity, then I would have to say that the very first mention of the word *alien* was the turning point from ignorance to knowledge," Doreen replied in a flat but even tone of voice.

Vinson now had taken over where Cunningham left off. "Then when were flying saucers first openly talked about?"

"That's really hard to answer, Vinson. From what I know, the term *flying saucer* was first spoken in the late 1800s in this country. A farmer was the first one to report such a sighting to authorities in the Midwest. Then, also in the late 1800s, as a matter of fact, in Colorado, not far from here, a newspaper reported on two sightings of a class Z-2 spaceship over a mining community in broad daylight.

"When World War I started, there were the usual sightings over the battlefields in Europe. Then when the war was over, the number of reported sightings decreased. That is, until World War II. Again, the same pattern emerged of sightings over battlefields, but this time they were also seen during sea and air battles. To answer your question, though, UFOs became open conversation during the mid-1940s. That trend has continued up until the present.

"What is interesting is the fact that the alien presence seems to have dramatically increased with the dawn of the nuclear age. Apparently, at this point man became a threat. Once the first atomic bomb was exploded, suddenly there were reports of UFOs all over the globe. At every nuclear, and later hydrogen, bomb test site, UFOs were reported in the same area a few days later. When the first atomic power plants went online, the aliens would constantly overfly the plants, and they still do today. At first—"

Morrison cleared his throat, interrupting Doreen.

Once Doreen stopped talking and looked at him, Morrison took over. "Excuse me, Doreen. I don't mean to interrupt, but I want to point something out," he said. "Up until our trip to Brazil, our main goal in monitoring the alien presence was to track the UFOs that overfly our military bases and atomic power plants. They seem to have an interest in military bases not only in this country but also in places around the world where nuclear weapons are stored. Sometimes they also overfly nuclear missile silos and naval fleets around the world that are carrying nuclear weapons.

"You see, the UFOs usually enter our atmosphere in pairs and then split up. We tend to disregard the ones that are not headed over our military bases, fleets, and nuclear power plants."

Morrison paused for a second as he turned toward Scotty, then added, "Scotty, we can't disregard any UFO now, in light of our recent experience. We have to step up our surveillance and determine where each one of these bastards goes."

"Admiral, on average, how many UFOs do you track a week over the United States?" Scotty asked.

"Sometimes only one or two during an entire week. Other times we may detect six or more in a single night. There simply is no average, and there is no detectable pattern to their visits," Morrison explained.

"I know that we are constantly improving our ability to track where they come from, but does anyone have any solid guess where their home is?" Vinson asked.

With a look of frustration on his face, Morrison answered, "We simply don't know, Commander. We only know that they are capable of travel at the speed of light."

"I guess that's why we will always be on the defensive," Vinson mumbled out loud, not meaning to be heard.

"What's that, Commander?" Chester asked.

"I was just thinking that we will always be on the defensive and not be capable of taking the fight to the alien home world one day." Vinson spoke up.

"Why is that?" Cunningham asked for the benefit of all.

"Years ago, I read an article on the twin paradox. The article presented a simple explanation of travel at the speed of light. If I remember correctly, the idea was based on two young twin brothers. It was a hot summer day, and one brother sat on the curb in front of his house, not wanting to move. His twin wanted to go for a short bicycle ride, but the lazy one told his brother that he would wait for him. The twin on the bicycle drove at the speed of light and returned to his brother," Vinson explained, and everyone could tell from his voice that he was excited. "Now this is where it gets real interesting.

"When the child who drove his bicycle at the speed of light returned, he was the same age as he had left plus the few seconds it took him to go around the block. His twin brother, who was stationary during his ride at the speed of light had likewise aged but was now in his late nineties.

"So you see, when we become capable of travel at the speed of light and launch an attack, everyone the attacking force knew or loved would be dead when they returned. Also, the world might have forgotten just why they left in the first place."

"Unless they travel through a time door." Scotty spoke up, and all eyes turned on him.

"That, you are going to have to explain," Morrison ordered as he sat up erect.

"We know from physics that what Vinson said is correct about the universe as we know it now. But our understanding may be in the infant stage. We know that we have not uncovered all of its secrets. The aliens, on the other hand, may have somehow figured out a way to bend time and travel the galaxies through a sort of tunnel. For example, let's say we enter a tunnel in New York and travel for a few seconds and come out in China. We would be able to travel vast distances in an instant.

"Let's assume, for the sake of argument, that the alien home world is at the end of the universe. If they relied on travel at the speed of light, they would have the same problem we do. When they returned to their world from Earth, no one would be around that sent them on their trip. Therefore, there has to be an easier way to get here from there and back again."

Scotty was then interrupted by Vinson, who asked, "What about black holes or wormholes, like on TV?"

Scotty first looked at Vinson, and then around the table, and began, "Scientists have theorized for years about travel through wormholes and black holes. The problem with black holes is that they are so dense that they would collapse or crush matter and probably would not be an avenue through time and space. Wormholes, though, are a possibility, but it is not known if they likewise collapse matter or offer a passage through time and the vast distances of space. There is still the problem of stability that has to be answered before travel through a wormhole would be possible. Added to that is another problem. That is, the predictability of travel. If I enter at A, will I necessarily come out where I intended, at location B? These are questions that have to be explored and answered. But I don't think the answer lies in either black holes or wormholes. It lies somewhere else entirely.

"I know that what I am about to say is a little far-fetched. While there is no physical evidence to back it up, and based upon what I have already said, such a thing as a time door may not exist, I feel that we must explore the possibility that they do exist. I'll get to some examples in a second that may point to the fact that time doors may exist, but first, let me say that a time door would offer predictability not only of time but also of location.

"That having been said, I would like to tell you about three instances when aircraft simply disappeared without a trace, and one example when an aircraft disappeared and one year later returned.

"As I said, the first example has to do with the disappearance of three aircraft. Two of these were jetliners that disappeared within a year of each other in the exact same location at almost the exact same time of day. On Christmas Eve—I forget the year—a commercial jetliner with one hundred and twenty people aboard was on final approach to Miami International Airport at 10:34 p.m. The aircraft was over the Atlantic Ocean and was three miles from the runway. The pilot radioed that he had the airport runway lights in sight and had just lowered his landing gear. The air traffic controller later testified that he had the aircraft on radar one second and, in the blink of an eye, the aircraft disappeared off the radarscope. The air traffic controller tried to contact the aircraft but was unable to. At no time while the air traffic controller was in contact with the aircraft did the pilot indicate that there was trouble with the aircraft. As you might expect, there was a massive search launched for the airliner, but the results were entirely negative. There was nothing to be found of that aircraft, not even a piece of paper or an oil slick on the water.

"Now, just for a minute, think of all the paper products an airliner carries, from napkins to paper cups. Then there are the plastic products, from plastic structural items to a simple credit card. And what about the clothing that the people were wearing and whatever was in their suitcases? They didn't find a thing. It was as if the airliner never existed. After authorities have spent five days of searching, the flight was listed as 'lost to conditions unknown…presumption that all souls were lost.' Not a great comfort to the families."

Scotty paused and looked at everyone and saw immediately that they were listening to his every word. Looking around the table, he then continued, "As I said before, exactly one year to the day, location, and almost the same exact time, the same thing happened again.

"The aircraft was there one second and gone the next. At the investigative hearing, the air traffic controller testified that during the last radio contact, he could hear Christmas carols being sung by the passengers. This time the controller was in radio contact at the time the aircraft disappeared. As the pilot was reporting in, with the Christmas carols in the background, the controller heard the pilot say, 'Look at that, it's like the sky is moving right in front of us.' Again, nothing appeared abnormal about the flight up to the moment of its disappearance. The search, once again, couldn't even find a scrap of paper from the airliner or a hint that it even existed at all.

"The third incident was witnessed by most of the passengers on a luxury liner. This case involved the HMS *Queen Mary* as she was making a passage from England to the United States. On the second day of her voyage, the *Queen Mary* was approximately one hundred and twenty miles off the coast of Ireland. The weather was clear, with only sporadic high clouds, and the ocean was calm. An Irish private pilot was flying his aircraft, a single-engine sport plane, out over the Atlantic when he came across the *Queen Mary*. The pilot lowered his altitude to approximately four hundred feet and, for reasons of his own, began flying in a circle around the ship. As he did so, the passengers and crew who were on deck began waving at him. The pilot, in turn, waved back at the growing spectators. As he was making his third circle around the ship, and being broadside to the ship, in full sight of the spectators, the pilot and his aircraft simply vanished.

"At the same time the plane disappeared, an electromagnetic charge hit the *Queen Mary*, which disrupted her instruments for a few seconds. The captain of the *Queen Mary* ordered the ship stopped, and boats lowered to search for the missing pilot because, as he later stated, 'he didn't know what else to do.' He saw the plane disappear and knew that a search wouldn't turn up anything, but felt that he had to do something. For the remainder of the day, the *Queen Mary* continued her search until she was relieved by British warships that continued the search. But nothing was ever found.

"British intelligence agents boarded the *Queen Mary* and interviewed all the witnesses. The crew and the passengers told the same story: the aircraft didn't explode or disintegrate, just vanished.

"The last case is something even more odd. It involved a training flight out of Willow Grove Naval Air Station in Willow Grove, Pennsylvania."

Scotty paused as he was interrupted by Doreen.

"Excuse me, Michael. I don't mean to interrupt, but I thought you should know that we have a detachment of the X-aircraft stationed at the Willow Grove air station," Doreen informed Scotty and the group.

Scotty looked at Doreen for a moment and hoped that the same thing that he was about to talk about wouldn't happen to one of his pilots. "I'm sure that they will be fine there. That's a really good choice. Willow Grove is a nice air station," Scotty began, then continued, "For the benefit of those of you that are not familiar with Willow Grove, I should tell you that it is a shared facility with flight elements of the Navy, Marines, Army, and some of the Air Force. It's located just north of Philadelphia, in a really nice suburban area.

"On the naval side, the base is mainly a P-3 Orion naval reserve station for subhunting. Occasionally, though, a naval reserve fighter wing trains out of there. They conduct their exercises out over the Atlantic Ocean off the coast of New Jersey. On one such day, a flight of F-14s left Willow Grove and headed out to their practice area over the Atlantic Ocean. At 11:34 a.m., they arrived at their practice area in clear weather and unlimited visibility. As they were flying in a V formation and were executing a slow banking turn to the right, the lead aircraft disappeared in front of the other three.

"Like with the *Queen Mary* incident, the aircraft didn't explode or disintegrate, just disappeared. Also, like with the *Queen Mary* incident, the remaining aircraft had experienced an electromagnetic burst for a few seconds at the time the F-14 disappeared.

"The pilots stayed in the area, searching as long as they could. When they ran low on fuel, they returned to Willow Grove. A naval search of the area revealed nothing. A board of inquiry was hastily put together and investigated the matter, with no results. The three pilots from the flight were subsequently assigned to other units and were ordered not to speak about the incident. It was felt that the matter was put to rest, and the incident listed as a training accident with the loss of life of the pilot. That is, until a year to the day the F-14 disappeared.

"A P-3 Orion had taxied to the end of the runway at Willow Grove and was waiting for takeoff clearance when, all of a sudden, its instruments began to go crazy and the engines shut down. At the same time, the radar in the tower shut down. The air controllers in the top of the tower that monitor ground traffic on the runways, again at the same instant, saw a greenish glow at the end of the runway about four hundred feet up. Out of the glow, an F-14 emerged and landed. It screeched to a stop at the end of the runway and remained there. Airport Rescue raced to the aircraft and found the missing pilot, Commander John Parks, in the cockpit, unconscious.

"Commander Parks was admitted to the base hospital and then later transferred to a hospital in Philadelphia. Once the commander came out of his coma, he was transferred to Bethesda Naval Hospital for psychiatric care and evaluation. I should point out that his physical condition was excellent. In fact, according to his medical record before his disappearance, he actually came back physically better than when he left.

"While under psychiatric care, Commander Parks told a fantastic story of being on another world that was far more advanced than our own. The trouble, though, was he couldn't recall just how he traveled to this other world, and he had no idea just how he came back to Earth. He couldn't offer any details of his stay on this other world except to describe the inhabitants as being a lot like us, but with wider foreheads.

"Eventually, Commander Parks was allowed to return to flying, but it didn't go too well. He was subjected to constant criticism and kidding by not only his fellow pilots, commanding officers, but also by the enlisted personnel. He was given the call sign Spaceman, and they would often play cruel jokes on him. If anything, he was driven from the service by some very narrow-minded people who were probably, if truth be known, scared of him, because people always fear the unknown. Tragically, less than a year later, Commander Parks was killed in an auto accident.

"There are those that believe Commander Parks actually committed suicide, due to the circumstances of his death. He was driving on a major highway at that time and had just passed a tractor trailer when suddenly he pulled in front of the truck and was killed. Whatever the case, Commander Parks was an honorable man and a dedicated father. The real tragedy was that he left behind a wife and two small children. The Navy made sure, for his children's sake, that his accident was officially listed as an accidental death due to mechanical failure of his automobile. A representative from the Navy was assigned to the family and made sure that the family was well cared for and ensured that the children received an education. Today both of his children are in the Navy, and both are aviators."

"That's a real shame about Commander Parks. It's too bad no one was ever able to find out where he went and what he saw," Lieutenant Cunningham added, then asked, "Admiral Scott, what you said about time doors makes sense, but is there any hard evidence that they do exist?"

Scotty was still thinking about Commander Parks when Lieutenant Cunningham spoke up.

After a few seconds, Scotty's brain caught up with what he heard, and he answered, "No, everything is really in the theory process, whether it is time doors, black holes, or wormholes. But I'll tell you this: we have to start seriously, considering all possibilities of space travel, if we are to figure out where the aliens are coming from. I still believe that one day we will carry the fight to their home. If we can do that, then we might have an even chance of defeating them." When Scotty concluded, the room fell silent and everyone contemplated what he had said and wondered what was ahead of them.

Trying to change the subject and inject a little attempted humor into the moment, Vinson spoke up. "You know, a few days ago, I was at home in New York, watching a little TV, chasing women around, going to a ball game now and then, and having a good time, not knowing what was going on. I guess ignorance is truly bliss. But now I feel like I am in the middle of a science-fiction book and the bad guys are looking pretty bad."

There were slight laughs and chuckles around the table until Chester spoke up. "Yeah, I felt that way for a long time also. But, Commander, you will find that truth, especially in this business, is a lot stranger than fiction."

After Chester spoke, there was a slight silence in the room, but then Scotty looked at Morrison and asked, "Speaking about science fiction, have we found out anything about those BB objects that were removed from those victims in Brazil?"

Clearing his throat, more to get the full attention of those in the room rather than of need, Morrison answered, "We have found out some information, but...well...let me start at the beginning.

"When we arrived yesterday, I gave them to our scientific research department to look at. I remember what you said to General Salas, Scotty, and you were right on the money. We have seen these objects before, and yes, they come to us from civilian doctors who find them in patients who were complaining of sinus conditions.

"Our conclusion is the same as yours. We believe that they are some sort of monitoring-and-tracking device. When we receive a BB through normal channels, it is usually well after they have been removed. The ones we received in Brazil were only two days old—that is, since they were removed from the bodies. When we examined them yesterday, they were emitting a very low gain signal. Therefore, they have to at least be a location-tracking device. But I think, like you, they are also a monitoring device of some sort. Oh, we deactivated the device by crushing it. A metallurgical examination of the BB shows that it is made up of magnesium, platinum, a little aluminum, and some unknown metal that, according to our scientists, is stronger than our strongest steel.

"What is really interesting is the core of the BBs. They contain a silvery liquid much like mercury in its consistency. But Chester can best comment about that," Morrison concluded as he then looked over at Chester.

Chester returned the glance and then began, "As the admiral was saying, we believe that the objects are location beacons and a monitoring device of some sort. Each one that we have seen has been examined and found to be identical to the rest. We have started to collect background data on the people that had these devices implanted in them. It's a long, tedious process, but one day it may show that they all have something in common beyond the devices. Recently, there seems to have been a change in the objects and the location of their placement in the human body." Chester paused and reached into his shirt pocket to withdraw a small plastic bag with a kidney-shaped bright silver piece of metal inside. After taking the object out of the plastic bag, Chester passed it to Cunningham and told him to look at it and pass it around.

Reaching over and taking a sip of his now-cold coffee, Chester began, "The object that is being passed around appears to be a new generation of the BB implant. They are no longer being implanted in the sinus cavity, but rather, they have been found in the large toe of some patients, in the wrist area, or in the upper thigh of others.

"They first came to our attention a few years ago, when a doctor in the Southwest sent the object to his local medical university for identification. The university, in turn, sent it to the Office of Scientific Research. From there it found its way to us. I sent an agent to interview the doctor under the guise of interviewing him for a medical journal. During the interview, the agent turned the conversation around to the implant.

"The doctor told him that a patient had come to him complaining about a constant irritation in the wrist. He x-rayed the man's wrist and found what he thought to be some type of an old surgical staple. His patient, however, maintained that he had never been operated on in his life and had never even broken his wrist.

"The man asked the doctor to operate on him and remove the object as it seemed to be the source of his irritation. When the doctor opened up the man's wrist, he found that the object was tied into the man's nerve endings and embedded in the muscular tissues. What was going to be a thirty-minute operation turned into a six-hour ordeal. The doctor stated to our investigator that he knew of no surgical procedure available today that can so intricately rewire nerve endings. Postoperative checkup revealed that the man's irritation had disappeared.

"After this initial find, we sent out a medical alert under the guise of the National Health and Safety Foundation. We cautioned doctors to remove the object should they come across it in their patients. Our cover story was that it is an early design of an advanced type of surgical staple that could, over time, cause a toxic reaction in the body. Since we sent out the alert, we have received slightly over two hundred of these objects from all over the country.

"We built up dossiers on the people, including complete medical histories, and as much social background as we could reasonably put together. Dr. Hewitt was then assigned the task to look for something these people may medically have in common with one another. Dr. Hewitt could not find anything that they had in common except that which was statistically probable with a large group. For example, a certain number had the same blood type, some had the same medical problems, like the onset of diabetes and so forth. In other words, there was nothing remarkable about this group of people."

"Admiral, are the new objects made out of the same material as the BBs?" Vinson asked.

"Yes, Commander. The metallurgic composition is the same, but the volume of the mercury like liquid has vastly increased," Chester answered.

"Sir, how is the thing powered? If it broadcasts a signal, then it has to be powered by something," Vinson pressed on.

"Right now we think the body's own electrical field provides the power, especially since the objects are now tied into the nerve endings," Chester replied.

"Excuse me, Admiral, but you were going to talk about the liquid center of the objects," Cunningham pointed out.

"Oh, yeah. The liquid in the center of the objects is of the same consistency as the liquid in the BBs, although the relative volume of the liquid is about twenty times more than the BBs'. Like Admiral Morrison mentioned before, the liquid is like mercury, but it is definitely not mercury. From what we have been able to determine, the liquid is an exotic mix of elements—some of them known to us, but most of them we have never seen before—that when combined together form another mineral entirely.

"Then the real question is, What is the function of the liquid? At present, we can only guess, but we are making progress. We know the device transmits a radio wave. But what causes that? Our best guess is that the device itself is like a computer. The liquid, we believe, is similar to a central processing unit.

"Our scientists are currently designing an experiment to test that belief now. Their goal is to electronically feed data into the liquid and hopefully retrieve it. If we are successful at it, then maybe one day we will be able to feed erroneous information into the device and have it broadcast to the aliens. It would be interesting to see what would happen, but that is a long way off."

"Admiral, let's assume that you are right about the devices. What kind of information do you think the devices send to the aliens?" Vinson asked as he sat forward in his seat.

"We know the devices are probably monitoring the body functions and health of the individuals they are implanted in, but they are more than likely capable of much more. For example, using the individuals' body as kind of a laboratory, the devices could be capable of monitoring our atmosphere. Also, the devices should be able to record sound, not only of the host, but also all that he hears. It's really a scary situation.

The possibilities are really endless, until we can decode one of the devices and determine just what is really going on," Chester replied in a somber tone.

"Admiral, has everyone in Space Command been checked for one of these devices?" Scotty asked.

With a tone of confidence in his voice, Morrison answered, "There's no worry there, Scotty. Everyone receives a full-body scan each time they enter the base. You didn't know it, but each of you passed through one when the plane we were on came down on the elevator to the hangar deck. Also, once a year each member of this base receives a full-body x-ray and CAT scan as part of their annual checkup."

"Who is in charge of the process?" Scotty asked, wondering.

Unable to control a smile, Morrison replied, "The same doctor you reamed out earlier, Dr. Hewitt. He is really a big asset to this base, Scotty, but he sure can be a sweet pain in the ass at times."

Vinson, who had been listening very carefully to every word said, perked up and asked, "Admiral, these implants that you think may be tracking devices, do they have any relationship to the so-called men in black? That is, if the men in black are for real."

"Oh, they are for real, but we don't know who they are. We do know that they are not connected with the federal government. Although they claim to be National Security Association agents at times. They also like to pass themselves off as FBI agents.

"Basically, they seem to appear after a confirmed sighting of a UFO happens. They go to the witnesses of the event, usually the people that report it, and use intimidation and threats to get the people to recant their stories or to remain silent. Their tactics usually work." He paused. "Oh, one more thing: they really dress bad!" Morrison concluded with a chuckle in his voice.

Before Morrison stopped laughing, Vinson quickly asked a follow-up question. "I've heard that these men in black often threaten people. Do you know anything about that?"

"I was going to get to that next," Morrison replied, paused for a second, and then continued, "They have been known to threaten the witnesses with death or the deaths of their children for refusing to do as they say. Some of the witnesses leave their homes in the middle of the night and move away. They probably then establish new identities somewhere else. Other witnesses elect to stand their ground, and they successfully pass off the threats. In a few rare cases, the witnesses have been killed.

"In trying to deal with this, there is one main problem. That is, the lack of information. The people who succumb to the threats are not about to tell anyone. So the only ones we know about, at first, are the brave souls that risk everything and speak out. By the time we get word of the incident, it's usually too late and the men in black have moved on.

"What's interesting is that on the rare occasions that our investigators are able to get a physical description from a witness, it appears to match your Mr. Merrick. Each witness says the same thing—their eyes seem to be really large. That is, when they take their sunglasses off, which is quite rare. There are some witnesses that have stated that the men in black will even wear sunglasses at night. Overall, the main problem is that we are always chasing them and never seem to catch up.

"There is a certain irony here, though. The men in black, quite unintentionally, are actually carrying out the aims of our government by trying to suppress talk of UFOs and aliens. They are like those detractors that show up at UFO events. One side presents their views as to the existence of aliens, while the detractors attempt to explain why UFOs don't exist. The detractors are equally as passionate in their beliefs, but in reality, they have nothing to say. I guess, like most people, they chase their fifteen minutes of fame in the sun to later realize that they are in total darkness.

"In any case, the men in black are for real and are probably scattered throughout the world. They are an added threat to mankind. At some point, we will have to deal with them, but first, we have to figure out how to catch them."

"Admiral, is it possible that the men in black are also responsible for the cattle mutilations that we hear so much about?" Cunningham asked.

Morrison looked at Cunningham, and then at the people around the table, and began to explain. "I would have to say no, Lieutenant. I don't know for sure that, at some time, they didn't have anything to do with the cattle mutilations. But all the evidence we have uncovered points responsibility for the mutilations in another direction entirely.

"This may be hard to believe, but what we have uncovered in our investigation is that our government, or rather an organ of our government, is responsible for the mutilations. It is a combined effort of the Atomic Energy Association, the Department of Health, and the Office of Scientific Research reorganized under the Office of Departmental Interaction. Quite a name, isn't it? It means absolutely nothing.

"What they are doing is studying the long-term effects of nuclear radiation as a result of the atomic testing done during the 1950s and 1960s. You see, virtually all the mutilations take place around the original testing areas. Usually downwind from the testing areas, in what were considered safe areas at that time, and around the country where the winds may have carried the deadly material. It was clearly a period of insanity and arrogance for man to think that atomic testing could be carried out in a safe manner, but that's another matter entirely.

"You see, most of the mutilations center on the removal of the liver and soft-tissue areas of the cattle. The liver is the great filtering agent for the body, not only in cows, but in all animals and mankind as well. What better way to test the long-range effects of radiation poisoning then by dissecting the liver and soft-tissue areas? What is really scary is that they wouldn't still be carrying on these covert operations if they weren't still finding the effects of the radiation from the testing era present today.

"They are also probably testing for the effects of radiation in other parts of the country as well. For example, I remember reading about cattle mutilations taking place outside of Huntsville, Alabama, about twenty years ago. I backtracked through newspapers of the area, and what do you think I found?" Morrison looked around at the puzzled looks on everyone's faces and continued, "Approximately five years before the mutilations took place, there was a leak from an atomic reactor in the area. Put two and two together and what do you have? Medical research."

"Wouldn't it be easier just to buy the cattle you want to test?" Cunningham asked.

"Yes, it would. But how would it look for a government representative to buy one cow from farmers all over the place? Eventually, it would lead to too many questions. No, it's easier for them to do it the way they have been done. Besides, the public looks upon it as further evidence of alien activity and shrug their shoulders. What better cover could you possibly have than little green men from Mars who have a taste for cow liver? None!" Morrison concluded.

"What about human testing for the effects of radiation?" Cunningham continued his line of questioning.

"There are readily available health statistics that they collect in their targeted areas. What they mainly look for is an abnormality in the cancer rate or mutations of cancers and birth defects. It's truly sad that future generations have to suffer for the ignorance of a few a long time ago. Just look at the havoc that was caused when they thought that uranium was some great cure-all a little over a hundred years ago right here in Colorado.

"Since the thinking at that time was that uranium could cure people or prevent disease, water coolers, bathtubs, and even some houses and commercial buildings were constructed of stone that contained high levels of uranium. It was believed that by drinking water out of such a cooler, a person would be protected from illness. Street vendors would actually sell glasses of this new miracle drink to eager customers. In a similar vein, people bathed in the uranium bathtubs and worked surrounded by the deadly mineral. For those who couldn't afford such coolers or bathtubs, uranium cones were sold all over the country. People would place these cones in their bathtubs or in the center of the dinner table so that the whole family could reap the benefits of uranium. There are even stories of people placing the miracle cones under their pillows while they slept. Unfortunately, these people did nothing but hasten their own deaths," Morrison replied with a tone of sadness in his voice.

"You know, one thing that we haven't talked about is crop circles. They seem to be turning up all over the world. Does anyone know anything about them?" Vinson asked.

"Scotty, you were looking into them at one point, weren't you?" Morrison asked.

"Yeah, but it was largely a waste of time. Some weird people who want to cause a stir fake most of them. There are a few, however, that have proved to be of unknown origin.

"In those rare cases, a full scientific study has been completed with very few factual conclusions. What they know but really can't explain is that the ground has been compacted with tremendous pressure, as if the Empire State Building had been placed on the ground and left there for a few years. The ground also has been found to contain a low level of radiation residue. In one such case, I went to a crop circle soon after it was found. I was able to detect a trace of Alpha Zuron radiation, which confirmed that something that had been in outer space had been on the ground. What's interesting is the fact that crops that grew after the event experienced approximately a 25 percent increase in yield for two years, and then the yield returned to normal. Scientists have not been able to sufficiently explain the increase in yield of such land, the soil compression, or the traces of radiation.

"The designs that have been left in authentic crop circles, some believe to be a message or a warning of some kind. Others believe that the symbols are some basis of a language, but if the makers of the designs are trying to communicate, I believe that they would have done so through binary numbers. For myself, I think that the symbols are an address of sorts, or a map, if you will. My other thought is that the genuine symbols could be a massive jigsaw puzzle and each crop circle is another part of the puzzle. The main problem is that no one that I know of has even a hint of how to interpret the symbols. It would be ironic if the symbols were some sort of alien graffiti.

"In any case, the more interesting question is, Who made them? I doubt the race of aliens who did the damage in Brazil and Zambia would even bother to make such symbols. They could be made by the aliens in the Z-3 craft, or even by another race altogether," Scotty concluded, ending his mini lecture.

"You know, it seems to me, based upon what we have been talking about, that the general public has access to quite a bit of evidence regarding the existence of UFOs. I wonder if the government will ever admit to their existence," Vinson stated, directing his statement to no one in particular.

"As you know, Commander, the government, at the dawn of the modern UFO era, did take a more active role in trying to determine what so many people were reporting to their local officials. One of the first such studies was the infamous Project Bluebook, which was successful in explaining away approximately 90 percent of the sightings. It was the other 10 percent that caused concern. In subsequent years, other studies were commissioned, and the results were basically the same. But this time maturity took over where the emotion of fear left off. Many of my peers recognized the potential of the threat of alien visitation and undertook their own investigation. The result of my inquiry is the base that you are now in, and the hardware being developed to fend off this threat.

"The political end of the government—that is, the president along with the Senate and Congress—is fearful of what the results would be if the general public knew the truth of alien visitation. You see, our venerated leaders think that the public is not smart or mature enough to know the truth. I, however, happen to believe that the citizens of this country are a lot smarter than anyone gives them credit for. But my view is in the minority. As weird as it may sound, our government feels that there are economic, social, and now, get this, religious reasons not to reveal the truth."

Morrison paused. "Let me take a moment to explain," he then added. "It is the view of our elected leaders that if the presence of aliens were to be accepted as fact, our social structure would break down. For example, the government envisions people becoming lawless out of fear of an alien invasion. Our economic system would go to hell as people refuse to pay their bills, since if an alien invasion is to occur, their property would be gone anyway. After all, isn't that what happens in the movies?

"If an alien presence is accepted as fact, church leaders see their beliefs threatened. They see a redefinition of their beliefs and wonder how to reconcile their religion to fit the alien presence. The whole reasoning is flawed, but those in power traditionally hold that belief. That is, until President James recognized the maturity of the populace.

"His order was simple: prepare an exhibit to travel around the country detailing what is known about UFOs. President James also instructed that the exhibit include alien artifacts. The exhibit was prepared and included the Roswell craft, which you saw on the hangar deck, as well as other items that were found near other crashes. There was even an introductory film that portrayed the aliens as being part of the great cosmic community. The overall theme was one of peaceful coexistence. Just when the exhibits were about to be announced, President James pulled the plug. The exhibit was taken apart and everyone was ordered to never speak about it under the penalty of imprisonment.

"It's really a shame. The world might truly be united right now to fend off the aliens if only everyone knew the truth," Morrison concluded.

"But, sir, with all the sightings today caught on videotape, won't the truth have to come out sometime?" Vinson asked.

"You're right, Commander," Morrison began. "But there is a major problem within the UFO community. While it's true that practically everyone owns some type of video camera and more and more sightings are being filmed, there is a relative increase in the number of faked sightings. A lot of people are quite capable of faking a sighting with the aid of sophisticated computer programming. When faked film is passed off as a genuine article and testing reveals it to be fake, what do you think happens? More attention is given to the fake than the real sighting. Because of the people that fake sightings, abductions, and alien contact, the public movement for truth about UFOs suffers a very large creditably gap."

"What you say makes a lot of sense. It's a shame that the honest people are the ones who suffer, while the dishonest snakes that they are slither back into their holes to probably emerge another day." Vinson spoke his thoughts out loud.

Scotty took advantage of the slight lull between Vinson and the admiral to ask, "Admiral, Vinson told me that while we were under attack from the saucers yesterday, you said something about knowing that they couldn't stay invisible during a dive. Could you please tell me what you were talking about?"

"Okay, but first, let me refresh my coffee," Morrison pleaded, then left his seat and poured another cup of the hot elixir. Not one to pass up an opportunity, he also made himself another ham sandwich. The others then followed the admiral's lead and likewise poured themselves fresh coffee. Scotty, however, took another bottle of water and a nice brownie to sustain his hunger.

After everyone sat back down, the admiral, with the precision of a surgeon, wiped away the crumbs from his mouth and began, "The basic concept of invisibility is really as old as time itself. The main stumbling block is the application of the idea to reality. Science-fiction and horror movies have made great use of the concept to produce some stunning effects. As the world goes, science fiction oftentimes becomes the reality of tomorrow.

"You may find it interesting, as an aside, to know that during World War II, the British employed magicians to fool the enemy. One such magician was given the task of making the city of Alexandria in Egypt invisible to German bomber pilots. Since the Germans carried out their bombing at nighttime, the magician made the city invisible. He did this by creating, in the desert, a nighttime silhouette of the city by simply casting light into the sky to replicate what Alexandria looked like at night from the air. The city of Alexandria itself was then blacked out at night. Each and every time, the German bomber pilots bombed the illusion, even though their instruments told them that they were in the wrong place. So the problem is really one of being able to create an illusion. This example shows that a person can be tricked into believing one thing because he sees it, even though his logic, in this case, a pilot's reliance on his navigational instrumentation, tells him that it is not where it should be.

"If we take this case and reverse it, the objective becomes to place something where another person's senses tell him that the object is not there because he simply can't see it. Our military and the science community had fooled around with the idea since they realized its potential. What grew out of it was the art of camouflage. The Navy, with the aid of civilian science, took the idea to the extreme in conducting the Philadelphia Experiment.

"As you may know, the object of the experiment was to render a naval vessel, the USS *Eldridge*, invisible not only to the human eye but also to radar. The basic experiment was a success in that the ship did disappear from sight for a time and was invisible to radar. But the consequences were disastrous. There are stories of men being fused into the decking and bulkheads of the ship, and a host of other weird things. Since this experiment, military efforts in this area have been very low-keyed and minimal at best.

"Getting back to the present, though, about three years ago, we experienced a wave of unidentified radar returns overflying the United States in the daytime. When aircraft were dispatched to investigate, most of the time the pilots would not see anything even though ground and their own radar told them something was there. These incidents were written off as atmospheric anomalies even though different radars detected the same thing from different locations.

"A few rare times a pilot would report that he saw a UFO either diving or accelerating upward. Over time, we came to realize that the UFOs were employing some sort of masking device. To the naked eye, the UFOs were invisible as long as they maintained straight, level flight. They were not, however, invisible to radar. Our problem then was to reinforce our pilot training to have them believe in their instruments even though they can't see the UFO. Added to this—"

Morrison was interrupted.

"Excuse me, sir. Do we have that capability?" Cunningham excitedly asked.

Morrison looked over at Cunningham, a little displeased with the interruption. He then looked back at the group and continued, "I'm not going to say that we have that capability, but we are getting there. We have been working on the problem and have made a lot of progress, but we still have some work to do. Our approach was a little different. First, let me back up a little and start at the beginning.

"In order not to repeat the mistakes of the past, we tried to learn as much as possible about the Philadelphia Experiment. Our research kept running into brick walls from total deniability to vague references in obscure scientific publications. We were only able to get a taste of the science that had been used. Shifting direction, we decided that the problem had to have fresh thinking and a solution to meet our specific needs. Therefore, we established a set of goals that we had to accomplish. But that's where my part of the story ends. While directing the development of the X-aircraft, Captain Stark also directed the efforts on optical invisibility."

Morrison then directed, "Captain Stark, would you please continue?"

When Morrison mentioned Doreen, Scotty pushed his chair back slightly and smiled as he looked at her. *My god, when she said that she had a few things to tell me in Zambia, she sure wasn't kidding!* Scotty thought to himself. As an afterthought, he wondered if Doreen knew what the lottery numbers were going to be in the next drawing.

Doreen felt Scotty looking at her, so she stole a look at him and returned his warm smile. Turning back around, Doreen then pulled her chair slightly toward the conference table. Placing her folded hands on the table, Doreen looked around at the expectant faces and began, "As Admiral Morrison said, we first decided on what goals were to be accomplished. We had two main, somewhat-impossible objectives. First, we wanted the aircraft invisible to radar. Secondly, we wanted the aircraft to be invisible to the naked eye.

"During the development of the X-aircraft, we used the stealth fighter as a modern model of what we wanted. But the demands of our requirements called for a radical rethinking. As the aircraft developed, we would play with the shape until we had it just right. The end result, as you know, was complete invisibility to the most sophisticated radar in use today.

"Next, we wanted to somehow render our aircraft invisible to the naked eye. To experiment, we chose an F-18. Since we know the radar signature of the F-18, we could easily follow it on radar and hopefully make it invisible to the observer. We also knew that whatever we came up had to be affixed to the aircraft. It follows, then, that whatever material we affixed to the aircraft would have to be strong enough to withstand the pressures and velocities of flight. The last problem was that any such material would have to fully engulf the aircraft.

"Once we settled on the F-18, the research team studied its outline to determine the eventual shape that any covering material would have to conform to. At the same time, we took a real basic approach by painting the aircraft in different-shaped color schemes to break up the appearance of the aircraft to the naked eye. This was somewhat successful, but the illusion was totally lost when the aircraft was observed from another airplane.

"Along with this approach, we researched aircraft paint, which led us down some interesting paths. For example, we started fooling around with radar-absorption paint. For starters, we were then able to reduce the radar return of an F-18 by 72 percent. We were also very successful in developing very lightweight aviation paint. As an aside, we were successful in licensing off that technology to paint companies that service the commercial airline field. On an average airliner, the new paint means a weight savings of approximately six hundred pounds. To the airline industry, that is money in the bank. But let me—"

When Scotty heard the words *licensing off that technology*, he sat erect in his chair and, with a wide grin on his face, said, "Excuse me, Doreen. I apologize for the interruption." Then glancing toward Morrison, Scotty declared, "I knew you guys couldn't have possibly paid for all this from black project funds!"

Laughing to himself, Morrison replied, "I was waiting for you to ask that question."

"Come on, I know that I am right. How are you paying for all this?" Scotty asked. "Hell, one of those X-aircraft must cost at least two hundred million!"

"Actually, they cost two hundred and forty million each, but with production in full swing, the cost has been reduced down to one hundred and forty million each," Morrison said. "Let's let Captain Stark finish, and then we can talk about it," he ordered while still slightly laughing.

"Yes, sir," Scotty answered in a confident voice and then looked at Doreen and apologized, "I'm sorry for interrupting, Doreen. Please continue."

"That's okay, Scotty." Doreen accepted his apology and then glanced around the room and continued, "Once we ran through all possibilities of a covering material from paint to other polymers, we explored the use of electronic projection technology. But the weight factor was overly burdensome, and therefore we scrapped that idea. Next, we decided to look outside of our research labs to get better in touch with what is out there in the industry.

"We sent people to every imaginable trade show in the United States, Canada, Europe, and the Far East. And guess what? Our inspiration was found in a futuristic home show not one hundred miles from where we are sitting.

"What our research technician saw, and later the rest of us, was a window display. We were surprised when, at the touch of a button, the window went from being clear to what looked like its having a silver film over it. The window, as a result of the silver film, could not be looked through. As you can imagine, we deluged the window representative with questions until we found out the basic operating principle. Its simplicity was its genius.

"The manufacturer had fused a thin transparent film to the window. The film contained intersecting packets, or layers, if you will, of liquid crystal. When electricity was applied to the film, the atoms of the liquid crystal became excited and formed a silver sheet. This, in turn, rendered the window impossible to look through. The amount of light that was reflected by the silver sheet was slightly over 60 percent. This was great for the homeowner, but disastrous for us.

"Our goal was not to reflect light but rather to bend the light around the aircraft. This would make the aircraft invisible to the naked eye. By bending light around an object, you are simply distorting what a person sees. For example, if we are trying to hide an aircraft in the sky, we first have to absorb the surrounding light, slightly change its wavelength, and then reproject that light, but in a muted tone. The result is that someone looking directly at the aircraft sees nothing but empty sky. However, there may be a slight distortion of the light as the aircraft moves across the sky, but the overall effect is achieved.

"Briefly, what we have done is this: we took the original concept and produced a multilayered transparent film. The gas we utilize is inert so that it doesn't present any safety concerns. When we want the aircraft to become invisible, we excite the atoms of the gas with electricity from an auxiliary power unit on board the aircraft. And voilà, the aircraft becomes invisible. It's really quite impressive to see.

"Since the film medium we use is very flexible, it is no problem mounting it on the aircraft. I don't think that we are totally there yet, to have a fully functioning system, but we are advancing on the right track. The drawback of the system is that we cannot mount it on the X-aircraft if they go into space. The system would not last through the transition into spaceflight. But rest assured that we are working on the problem and will solve it."

"Wow!" Vinson thought out loud, then added, "Any more tricks up your sleeve?"

Doreen laughed slightly and then answered, "That all depends on what you ask for. We have a fine, dedicated, and brilliant research staff here. Given enough notice, they can solve almost any problem."

"I believe it," Vinson quickly answered.

"Thank you, Vinson." Doreen acknowledged his remark and then looked at Scotty and suggested, "Michael, you know that when you take command later, it's tradition for the new commander to give a sort of welcoming speech. Also, at the same time, it's expected that you will outline the goals and objectives of your command."

"Doreen is right, you know." Morrison put his two cents in.

"It is a good idea. Thank you, Doreen." Scotty smiled at her as he thanked her, and then he addressed the group. "I would also like to give a presentation on the incidents in Zambia and Brazil. We should be able to put together a short film of what we saw. I'd like to do that tomorrow, if at all possible. What do you think, Lieutenant? Can you get a film together and do a commentary?"

"I can get a film together tonight on Brazil, and I'll do an introduction on Zambia. Is there anything special you would want edited out?" Cunningham asked.

"I haven't seen the film you took in Brazil, but I trust your judgment. I don't want to soft-shoe the presentation. It should be shown just the way we saw it. It will give everyone a chilling reminder of just why we are here and the importance of the work everyone, from dishwasher to scientist, is involved in," Scotty directed. Then he asked, "What do you think, Admiral?"

"It's a damn good idea!" Morrison replied. "The people here have every right to know exactly what they are working so hard for. Besides, it will also have the psychological effect of establishing a new dedication to our goals with a new leader at the helm. It will symbolize the closure of my command and offer a renewed dedication under yours."

"Good. Doreen, would you please coordinate with Mr. Cunningham?" Scotty asked.

"Of course, Michael," Doreen replied with a smile on her face.

Smiling back at her, Scotty asked, "Doreen, just so I am clear on this, Do you mean to tell me that your group has managed to render an F-18 invisible to the naked eye and, at the same time, reduced its radar signature?"

"Yes, that's exactly it!" Doreen proudly replied.

"This I just have to see," Scotty demanded.

"I'll set up a demonstration for you tomorrow," Doreen replied.

"Thank you. I can't wait to see it!" Scotty thanked her and turned toward Morrison with a Cheshire cat smile on his face and asked, "Admiral, about the secret project money?"

"Okay, Scotty. But Chester will have to explain it since it's been his project as of late." Morrison answered Scotty's plea with an equally sly grin on his face, followed by a soft laugh. Turning toward Chester, Morrison called out, "Chester."

Also with a smile on his face, Chester pulled his chair in a little closer to the table. He then took a long sip of his coffee as a stalling tactic to gather his thoughts. Then putting his coffee cup down, Chester began in a soft voice, "I don't have to remind everyone here that whatever we talk about remains here within the group. All things that we have discussed and will discuss are to remain top secret." Chester paused and looked toward Scotty before continuing, "What I am getting at, I guess, is a little fatherly advice. Scotty, a few hours from now, you will receive command of a base that, as far as we know it, is unique in all the world. You will decide the direction your command is to move in. Not every decision you make will be the right one, but that is what human nature is all about.

"What I am trying to say, Scotty, is, understand a problem before you make a decision. Sometimes you will not have the luxury of time to react. In those cases, make your decisions with courage and conviction. What you must remember, though, is that you should not be afraid to alter your decision should the situation suddenly change.

"There is one more thing. If what you suspect about a spy on the base is true, then keep your circle of trust close. You should also compartmentalize the trust that you give others. For the time being, tell people what they individually have to know in order to perform their jobs.

"That being said, let me tell you a tale of government capitalism!"

Chester had a smile on his face when he concluded and then began his tale. "You're right, Scotty, all this couldn't have been paid for with secret project money. Each of the saucers that you have seen is an absolute treasure trove of technology. We realized early on that the technology that literally fell into our laps could be reverse engineered and adapted for civilian, industrial, and military use. In order to do this, a corporation was formed. It is known as the Unicom Research and Development Corporation. Unicom started out as a small office. Its main purpose is to license off to any national company whatever technology deemed to be safe for civilian use. Of course, whatever technology that we license cannot have an impact on national security. As more and more items were released, Unicom grew and grew. Today it is a real research laboratory employing over three hundred people. You see, we feed them the ideas and some basic designs. They will then refine the product and license it to the companies who will produce the items.

"The people at Unicom have no idea who their actual employer really is. As far as they know, they work for a private employer with the usual health and other benefits people have come to expect. The CEO of Unicom, however, is a naval officer masquerading as a civilian scientist. He, in turn, reports to me."

Chester paused as he quickly reached into his back pocket and withdrew a tissue. Just in time, he held the tissue under his nose as he sneezed.

Returning the tissue to his pocket, Chester added, "I should mention that after all expenses are met, our daily profit from this venture is currently a little over seven million dollars, and that is per day."

"What kind of products have you licensed out to the private sector?" Vinson asked.

Laughing slightly, Chester answered, "I'd like to say that the silicon chip was ours, but it wasn't. Our objective is to give gentle nudges or enhancements to existing technology. In other cases, we bring out giant leaps in technology when it is advantageous to our needs. There is, however, one exception. In the field of medical technology, such as lasers for surgery or other devices, we refine the alien designs, adopt them for human use, and license them out immediately.

"One big advancement we are currently working on is in computer design. As you know, if you have ever seen the insides of a computer, data links flow along straight lines with 90-degree turns. We are working to revolutionize that design by allowing data to flow in a circular manner. If we are successful in sending and retrieving data from the liquid inside the implants we talked about, just think what it would mean. There would not be a need for a hard disc, computer speeds would dramatically increase, and the storage capacity would be far beyond what most computer designers can only dream about today." Chester let that last bit of information sink in for a second and then turned toward Scotty and added, "Scotty, when I return from Puerto Rico, after seeing Captain Montgomery, I'll come out and give you a full rundown on our little capitalist endeavor."

"Thank you, Admiral. I look forward to it," Scotty replied and was a little startled when the telephone in the center of the table rang.

Morrison reached across the table and picked up the receiver and handed it to Scotty as he said, "It's for you, Admiral. You're in command now."

Scotty took the receiver from Morrison with a friendly frown on his face and spoke into the receiver. "Yes." His new secretary, Chief Petty Officer Marcy Franks, informed Scotty that Dr. Hewitt was in the outer office with a preliminary report for him about the girl. Scotty instructed Marcy to have the doctor leave his report.

"How long are you going to keep him on a string?" Morrison asked.

"Until I am satisfied that he is treating the girl with dignity and respect. I didn't like what I saw in sick bay. I got the impression that he was sustaining the poor girl's condition instead of trying his best to help her recover. When he shows me positive efforts toward her recovery, I'll cut him loose," Scotty replied.

"Okay, Scotty. It's your decision. But please keep in mind that we have always found his assistance most helpful. We also place a lot of trust in his talents," Morrison stated in a voice of conviction.

"I will, Admiral. There's just something about his mannerisms that I don't like," Scotty replied as he first looked at the admiral and then at a smiling Doreen. She knew that Scotty had more than championed her cause to cure the young girl.

In order to relieve whatever tension there was in the room between Scotty and Morrison, Vinson tried to change the subject. "Admiral, earlier today you made reference to the fact that we are dealing with two kinds of aliens. Any idea who they are?"

"That's a tough question, Commander. Other than say that they are from two different worlds, I really don't have an answer for you. I can, however, tell you what we have speculated about them," Morrison answered, forgetting about the doctor.

"Please do!" Vinson quickly answered.

"As I said earlier, the small ones, the Grays, seem subservient to the seemingly more intelligent and dominant aliens, like the alien you encountered on your way to Zambia. How that came about, we don't have any idea. The Grays may be a conquered race that are now fully dependent on the taller race or they may, in fact, serve in exchange for something.

"Personally, I do not believe that the Grays are a conquered race. They seem to act in concert with the humanlike aliens. Therefore, I firmly believe that we are under attack from two alien races acting as allies in pursuit of their end-game. Whatever that may be.

"If, as Scotty suspects, they are here to harvest organs, then one can only speculate as to which race reaps the most benefit. From the autopsies that we have conducted, our physiology is somewhat similar in form and function. For example, our hearts are almost identical to the humanlike aliens', while they would be too big for the Grays. Our lungs do not process enough oxygen for the tall aliens but are a match for the Grays. Our blood and livers seem compatible for both races, as well as our kidneys, gallbladder, and intestinal system.

"Taking all that into consideration, I fear that Scotty is correct. What I wonder about is why. Why would they be doing this? And if they have been doing this for a long period, then something is wrong in their individual civilizations.

"Let me explain what I mean. Let's go on the presumption that Scotty is right, the aliens have been coming to Earth for a long time to ply their deadly trade. It would follow, then, that their need is great, if you take into account the number of reported sightings throughout the world. Just in the last five years alone, reported sightings have continued to increase at an alarming rate. I think, throughout the world, the number reached well over five thousand last year alone.

"This would indicate two things: First, the aliens are risking detection on an increasing scale. Secondly, something must be drastically wrong on their home worlds for them to act so desperately.

"Brazil was a warning, that much is crystal clear. But it also would indicate that they fear confrontation. Otherwise, why drive a lesson home so dramatically if you don't fear your adversary? I believe that they are more than aware of our military capability and know that we can give them one hell of a fight." Morrison concluded with conviction in his voice.

"Sir, we mentioned why the aliens don't destroy our satellite grid, but do they allow our space program?" Cunningham asked.

"I think that it is more toleration than anything else. Remember that our space capability must look feeble to them, given their obvious superiority in space technology. As you may recall, some of our astronauts have reported sightings of alien craft shadowing the earlier Gemini, and now our shuttle program. In fact, the incidents became so numerous that in the mid to late 1980s, NASA decided that all transmissions from the shuttles to Earth were to be encrypted. Our astronauts and shuttle crews were constantly reporting sightings of alien craft. NASA, of course, did its best at damage control. They would claim that the sightings that leaked out to the public were space ice or flakes of paint separating from the shuttles.

"One of the more dramatic sightings was filmed by a shuttle crew and eventually showed up on national television. I'm referring to the one when a shuttle crew was filming the Earth for a weather study. Suddenly, a saucer, or Z-1, came from behind the shuttle and began entering Earth's atmosphere. This base didn't know that the shuttle was filming at that time, and after following the Z-1, we decided to test the plasma cannon. We only fired one shot from the cannon, intending to miss the Z-1 by one thousand feet. Once the shot reached the upper atmosphere, the Z-1 took off back into space like a bat out of hell. You can imagine when we saw, on national television, the saucer fleeing back into space with the plasma shot chasing them, just how surprised we were. NASA explained away the incident as space ice. On the positive side, though, it showed that the Z-1 was afraid of the cannon shot.

"But getting back to your question. If they were to knock down a shuttle or some other space vehicle, all of a sudden the great lie that aliens don't exist would suddenly become true. Throughout the world people would come out of their houses armed and ready to take them on. They wouldn't have one nation against them, but rather, an entire world united against them. I think that is what they fear the most, a unified world ready to fight them," Morrison concluded, knowing that he was right.

There was a slight pause in the conversation, until Vinson once again spoke up. "Admiral, if I may, I'd like to go back to the alien physiology for a moment. If our organs are somewhat similar to the aliens', why is it that they appear so different?"

"There's an old aviator's saying: 'Gravity sucks!'" Morrison immediately replied, but when he did not get any laughs, he continued, "A few years ago, NASA funded a study to determine what the long-range effects would be on man if he were to live in a settlement on another planet for an extended period. The basis of the study assumed a gravitational force roughly 45 percent of that on Earth. Another assumption was exposure to that gravity regularly due to exploration and work outside of the settlement. The settlement itself would maintain artificial gravity somewhat equal to Earth's, but slightly less. An effort would also be made not to oxygen-enrich the atmosphere inside of the settlement, but rather to keep the same mixture as on Earth. The last factor in the experiment were the people themselves. They would live in the settlement for at least fifty years.

"The results were a little scary. They pointed out that if we are to remain as we appear, our exposure to space has to be somewhat limited. Let me explain. If man were to live long-term in space, his physiology would be determined largely by gravity and environment. Taking the example NASA set forth, in a little over one hundred years, the descendants of the original settlers would appear entirely different, provided two generations remained in space.

"Due to gravitational factors, the descendants would be about one foot taller than their ancestors. Their cranial bone would thin and flatten outward, changing the entire appearance of their face and head. Also, the texture of their skin would have changed, as well as the possibility of the growth of additional appendages, such as a sixth finger or toe. Oh, and the entire bone structure would also thin. In essence, an entirely new species of man would have been created in a relatively short period.

"Pretty interesting how simply gravity could bring about all those changes, isn't it?" Morrison asked as he glanced around the room and saw the puzzled look on most of the faces.

Vinson turned toward Scotty and requested, "You have to promise me, Scotty—er, Admiral—that there will be no space for this Earth creature. I don't want to come back looking like some weirdo!"

Laughing, Scotty replied, "I promise you, Vinson, there will be no prolonged space trips for you."

"How come you didn't say no space trips?" Vinson quickly asked.

While still laughing, Scotty answered, "I thought that once I learned to fly the X-aircraft, we would take it out for a ride. Say, to the moon and back."

"I don't want to go into space," Vinson pleaded. "I'll come back with a flat head and won't even be able to wear a hat to hide my new, hideous face. That probably won't matter, though, since I'll more than likely have elephant-size ears and a superlong nose to go along with them!"

"Don't worry, I'll buy you a nice cardboard box to put on your head. That is, provided that they make one big enough," Scotty answered, trying to keep the joke going.

"Oh, man!" was all Vinson could say as he looked down at the floor in resignation while shaking his head back and forth as if to say no.

"Why, Vinson, I'm sure that the women will still find you very attractive and you will still break many a heart," Doreen added to the joke.

Still looking down at the floor, Vinson muttered, "Yeah, great. Flat head, wide face, thin skin, a giant nose, and superlarge ears. Oh, and don't forget the six fingers and toes. Life is going to be just great. Thanks a lot, guys."

Scotty turned from looking at his friend, as Vinson was obviously contemplating his new life as an alien species, and looked at Admiral Morrison. He had seen the new missiles earlier in the morning. Instinctively, Scotty knew that there was more than what he had seen.

Knowing that the admiral would have talked to him later about the missiles, Scotty was anxious to get the discussion over with. Actually, Scotty feared that he was to be the guardian of man's insanity, nuclear weapons. With the smile disappearing from his face, Scotty broached the subject. "Admiral, how many of the new missiles are available right now?"

"Your current stock is one thousand five hundred and twenty-six. Your total stock should shortly reach operational level of three thousand shortly," Morrison replied in a monotone voice, knowing what was coming next.

"Is there a dark side to the missiles?" Scotty asked as he looked at Morrison and then around the table. Scotty noted that Vinson had a puzzled look on his face, while Doreen and Chester had slightly bowed their heads and were staring at the table. Cunningham looked at Scotty with a look of bewilderment on his face. Morrison, Scotty noted, was looking directly at him with a look of concern.

"Yes, there is," Morrison replied, paused for a second, and then continued. "The missiles were designed as a penetration weapon very effective against the Z-1s. What we don't know is their effectiveness against the Z-2 spacecraft.

"To counter this threat, a nuclear variant of the design was also put into production. Currently, there are eight on the base, with another seventeen due to arrive in the next few weeks. My operational order is that these missiles are only to be used in space and as a weapon of last resort.

"There are, however, two more variants of the basic combat missile available before the jump to nuclear weapons should be considered. The second variant is an adoption of a cluster bomb. When this missile penetrates a Z-1, the nose cone explodes, launching one hundred and fifty tiny, smaller bombs. One second later, these smaller bombs explode, spreading shrapnel throughout the spacecraft." Admiral Morrison paused again before he continued. He knew that there was not an easy way to say what he had to. "The second alternative is a binary warhead adapted to contain either a chemical or biological weapon. The binary design was used for safety reasons in storing and transporting the weapons. Alone in each container of a two-container system, the chemical or bioagent would be harmless until the contents of the containers mix after penetration.

"While we have the weapons on hand, right now we haven't decided on a chemical or which biological agent to use. It is my sincerest prayer that neither of these weapons ever be used. I just don't want to go there."

Scotty looked at the admiral with compassion and felt the pain that he must be feeling.

But the admiral's nightmare just became his own. Speaking softly, Scotty replied, "Admiral, I feel the same way you do. I swear that I will never use the binary-design missiles or the nuclear warheads unless all hope is lost and the survival of our country is in doubt. I disdain these weapons, but they are a reality and must be dealt with. I just hope our adversaries feel the same way."

"So do I. And thank you, Scotty," Morrison replied.

"Admiral, how many of the cluster missiles do we have?" Scotty then asked, leaving the dark side of warfare.

"There are about fifteen hundred currently on hand. My goal is to maintain their stock on a level the same as the standard missile," Morrison answered.

Morrison paused for a second after answering Scotty's question. Then Vinson spoke up. "There's something I'm a little curious about. If we have the X-aircraft and it's adopted from a NASA design, then why aren't they flying a similar aircraft into space?"

Chester adjusted his sitting position and spoke up for Morrison. "NASA is in the heavy-lift business. They have to lift satellites, parts of space stations, and other materials that they have to place in orbit. Additionally, they have to constantly bring supplies and equipment up to the space stations. Right now they have a dependable system that is very cost-effective.

"When they decide to utilize the new designs and finally build the new generation of shuttles, their main problem is selling the idea to the public. Currently, they are testing a design that takes off and lands like an airplane, but its cost is about three times as much as that of the current shuttle. Their savings is in the lifting capacity, about four times as much as the current shuttles, but it's a hard sell to the taxpayers.

"Just as a sidenote, NASA has designed a few interesting modules to fit into the new shuttles. There is one that is like the cabin of a commercial airliner, thereby opening travel in space to many more people. There is a pharmaceutical module for the production of new cancer-fighting drugs that can only be produced in zero gravity. Other modules they envision are ones for manufacturing delicate electronic components and exotic metal fabrication.

"Personally, I believe that NASA has a very bright future in space, provided that we can ensure their safety. Our X-aircraft is, and someone should really give this plane a name, is a scaled-down version of their design, but enhanced strictly for speed and combat."

"You're right, Admiral. And I can think of no one better than the program manager to name the aircraft." Scotty picked up on the admiral's suggestion and looked at Doreen.

Doreen looked back at Scotty and lightly punched him in the arm as she replied, "Just for that, I think I will call it the Michael Mobile."

Scotty blushed a little at being bested but recovered nicely by saying, "Seriously, I think that the honor should fall to Doreen. Her work and dedication are more than borne out by the aircraft and the weapons. She obviously has given us the tools by which we may—and I don't mean to sound odd—save mankind from a horrible fate."

Scotty flinched a little as he saw Doreen move her arm; however, she gently patted his leg and smiled an adoring smile at her champion. Almost at the same time, everyone in the room either said that they liked the idea or that it was a great one. Morrison summed it up best by telling the group that such an honor was never more deserved.

Chester waited patiently for the others in the room to settle down and then anxiously asked, "Scotty, you know that we have mostly dispersed the X-aircraft squadrons around the country and Canada. Do you agree with that reasoning?"

"Of course. In the next few days, I want to review their disposition. What I would like to do is put up an aerial umbrella. By that I mean that each base be close enough to the next so that in combat there is always backup available," Scotty replied, knowing that Morrison had already done that.

"That's the way Captain Stark and I set it up," Morrison added.

"I'd like to ask one more thing. We know the aliens are visiting the oceans of the world, but no one knows why. Are you able to track their activity underwater or at least see where they are going?" Scotty inquired.

Chester began to reply, "After the Shag Harbor incident, an effort was—"

But he was interrupted.

"What was the Shag Harbor incident? Uh... I'm sorry, sir. I shouldn't have interrupted." Cunningham spoke up and nervously added an apology.

"That's okay, Mr. Cunningham. It's always best to speak up when you don't understand something rather than try to fake it," Chester answered.

"Thank you, Admiral. Please continue," Cunningham replied.

"Okay, Shag Harbor," Chester began as he repositioned himself in his chair. "Shag Harbor was an incident that took place off the coast of Canada. Civilian witnesses observed a UFO enter the ocean and promptly notified the authorities. The Canadian Navy immediately investigated and committed what one would call a small battle group to the immediate area.

"The UFO was located on the floor of the ocean. It was just resting there and not moving. The Navy set up underwater surveillance of the craft and, at one point, connected hydrophones to the shell of the saucer. All that they heard was a constant humming noise coming from the UFO.

"Suddenly, after one week, the saucer began to move away from the battle group at an accelerated rate of speed, while still underwater. The saucer then breached the surface and began to accelerate even faster. Land-based radar tracked it as it left Earth's atmosphere and re-entered space.

"At the time of the incident, the United States had established a rather-basic hydrophone antisubmarine net down the coastline of Canada and the United States. When a submarine crossed over the net, the sound of its engine and the noise caused by the sound of its propellers were transmitted to the War Department. A comparison was then made against a library of what are called a ship's signature. When a match was found, the ship could then be identified.

"During the Sag Harbor incident, we were able to record the passage of the UFO, but we didn't respond. It was a Canadian issue, and since they didn't ask for assistance, the United States just observed from afar. The only sound the net picked up was again a low humming noise. The War Department concluded, from the recordings, that the sound the UFO made was from a propulsion system not manufactured on Earth."

Chester was interrupted by laughter from around the table, and even he had to laugh.

"Hey, remember, that was a long time ago," Chester pleaded.

As the laughter died away, Chester added, "Today the underwater net is a very highly sophisticated system capable of incredible results. We can not only detect a submarine's engines but can also listen in on what people are talking about on board. Also, you will be pleased to know that today we have a little over 75 percent of the world's oceans under the watchful eye of our submarine net—"

Chester was again interrupted.

"How about UFOs? Do we track them today?" Cunningham asked.

"Yes. During the past twelve months, we have tracked no fewer than one hundred underwater contacts of alien spacecraft. Slightly over seventy of these contacts were identified as being the Z-1 saucers. Twenty-one have been identified as being Z-2 craft, or what we describe as the cigar-shaped spacecraft. The remaining contacts, we have not yet been able to identify.

"What is interesting is the fact that out of all the Z-1 contacts, we have identified thirty-eight of the saucers making repeated visits to the ocean depths. Their visits to the ocean world are not always to the same exact locations, but rather, the aliens visit new areas in a somewhat-sequential order. By this I mean one saucer may enter a twelve-square-mile area of the ocean and leave. A few weeks later, another ship will explore the adjoining section. And so forth.

"I should add that our submarines have been successful in chasing away a few of the UFOs close to our eastern shoreline. These were just off the coast of New York City, the Norfolk Naval Base, our submarine base in New London and Cape Canaveral. What they are up to is anybody's guess."

"Sounds like they are mapping the ocean floor." Vinson spoke up.

"That's the same conclusion we reached, Commander, but I also think that they are looking for a way to hide in the thermal layers of the ocean as well as the currents," Morrison answered.

"Sir, if they are mapping the thermal layers, do you think they are looking for a way to hide in a layer and travel the Earth undetected?" Cunningham asked.

"Chester!" Morrison handed off the question.

"It could be. As you know, at different depths of the ocean, the temperature continues to drop. We think that the aliens are trying to find a certain thermal layer where an underwater river is present. If they find such a river deep enough where the water is more dense, they would be able to cut their propulsion system and glide in the current. The denser the water, the harder it is for sonar to detect them. And if their engines are off, sound detection would be very difficult, unless we knew just where to look," Chester answered.

"You mean there are actual rivers in the ocean?" Vinson asked. "It doesn't sound possible."

Chester paused for a few seconds, trying to think of an example. "Yes, beyond the surface currents of its waters, there are underwater rivers throughout the oceans of the world. Perhaps the best example is one right out of the Devil's Triangle.

"A couple in their midforties left Miami along with four of their friends and headed for a shopping trip in the Bahamas aboard their cabin cruiser, *Starglo*. Port records in the Bahamas indicated that they arrived at 2:15 p.m. and departed at 7:30 p.m. for the return trip. The owner of the boat reported in to the harbormaster's office every half hour, giving his current location, speed, and estimated time of arrival. When they were one hour away from Miami, they made their last transmission. Once they didn't report in that they had arrived, the harbormaster's office tried to raise them by radio, but to no avail. When it was confirmed that the *Starglo* didn't arrive and was over three hours late, a search was begun. For the next three days, the Coast Guard and the Miami Harbor Patrol searched for the *Starglo*, but their efforts went unrewarded. It was assumed then that the *Starglo* had fallen prey to modern-day pirates or drug runners and the people had been killed and the boat stolen.

"Approximately five years later, the story dramatically changed. Deep-sea divers off the western coast of Ireland were conducting an underwater survey for the location of an offshore drilling platform when…what do you think they found? The *Starglo* resting quietly on the bottom of the ocean at a depth of three hundred and sixty feet.

"Needless to say, the discovery set off a detailed study to determine how the ship got there. A British research team found an underwater river flowing from off the coast of Miami to the coast of Ireland at a depth of three hundred feet and a width of one and a half miles.

"Somehow, the *Starglo* was caught in this river on her way to the bottom and managed to travel across the Atlantic."

"Sir, did they ever figure out what happened to the people or how the boat sank?" Cunningham asked.

"Well, the people, or any trace of them, were never found. As to the boat, now that is the really odd part—it was sunk on purpose, which tends to rule out pirates or drug runners. When the divers examined the boat, they found that the seacocks, two valves that would allow ocean water to flood the ship, were opened. It had to be done on purpose. The valves had to be opened manually.

"The case is simply one of the great mysteries of the Triangle, as well as hundreds of others," Chester replied.

"Are we to be concerned with the Devil's Triangle?" Cunningham asked as a follow-up question.

"Not really. We simply haven't had the time or the personnel to really take a good look at it. Scotty could probably tell you more, though. Scotty?" Chester replied and managed to shift the discussion away from himself.

"Yes, sir. But let me get a bottle of water first. I'm a little thirsty. I must be adjusting to the prospect of living underground. For some reason, it really makes me thirsty," Scotty replied as he left his chair and went to grab a bottle of water from the lunch table.

"Sounds good to me. It's time for a little snack, anyway," Morrison declared as he also left his chair and eyed the food.

"Yeah, Scotty, the change in air takes some getting used to. But you know, the air down here is almost pure, free from any contaminants. You are right, though, when I first came to the base, I drank a lot of water also," Chester offered as he, too, went for a bottle of water and nibbled on some lunch meat.

Doreen and Vinson likewise sought out the lunch table. Doreen chose coffee, while Vinson grabbed a soft drink. Cunningham chose to remain in his seat but was grateful when Chester placed a bottle of water in front of him. Morrison returned to the table with another large sandwich. Doreen couldn't help herself and, as she looked at the sandwich in front of Morrison, said, "Admiral, that's your third. Not that I'm counting or anything. Remember your triglycerides. We need you around."

In a voice of utter frustration, Morrison countered, "Thanks for reminding me, Captain. However, I'm hungry, and dinner is a few hours away—oops! Forgot a pickle." After getting a pickle, actually three, Morrison sat back down, and as he was about to take a bite out of his sandwich, he said, "Scotty, please continue."

After taking a large sip of his water, Scotty screwed the top back on the bottle. He placed his water bottle on the table and then began, "To answer your question, I guess I should begin at the beginning. First of all, the term *Devil's Triangle* didn't come into use until sometime in the 1960s. An article about the area appeared in a magazine and renamed what used to be known as the Bermuda Triangle. Whatever name you use, the area is well-known for what most call mysterious disappearances of ships, boats, and airplanes.

"Oh, I almost forgot. The area runs from Miami to Bermuda and then southwest to Puerto Rico and then back to Miami. Many researchers differ on the points of the triangle. Therefore, the size of the area may vary from a low of five hundred square miles to as much as six million square miles. In either case, the area that the Triangle occupies is pretty significant.

"The earliest recorded occurrence of something strange going on in the Triangle may be found in the journal entries of Christopher Columbus." Scotty looked around the room and saw the expressions of surprise on everyone and then continued, "While Columbus was sailing through the Triangle, he made special note of two strange things. First, his magnetic compass, for a short period, spun wildly and was of no use. This is very similar to what happens today to ships and airplanes. Their magnetic compasses sometimes will spin around and around and are useless. Secondly, Columbus observed a green light or aura over the water. Witnesses today also report the same thing. So what Columbus first experienced is still happening today.

"The Triangle is also subject to electromagnetic variances that occur at almost any given time. This will interfere with radio transmissions and electronic instruments on ships and planes, as well as magnetic compasses. This brings to mind the disappearance of the infamous Navy Flight 19.

"As you may recall, five Navy torpedo bombers were on a navigational exercise within the Devil's Triangle. During the exercise, a radio message was received from the flight leader that all the aircraft compasses were acting strangely and were unreliable. From that point onward, the situation worsened. In the end, contact was lost with the flight and they never returned. A subsequent search didn't turn up a trace of the missing aircraft or their crew.

"Most people want to believe that Flight 19 disappeared under very mysterious circumstances. In a way, it did. To be sure, there was a navigational problem with the flight compasses. When a pilot is out over the ocean, with no land in sight, he depends upon the compass as a necessary point of reference. Without the use of a flight compass over water, even the best of pilots can become disoriented, and disorientation can very quickly lead to panic.

"In the case of Flight 19, I don't believe that they panicked. You have to remember that these were trained naval aviators who constantly flew over the ocean. I think that once they didn't have the benefit of a compass, the flight leader would have logically headed in the direction he thought would bring them back home. Unfortunately, they might have run out of fuel before they crossed back overland. More than likely, they ditched their aircraft into the ocean. Even if some of the men survived the ocean landing and managed to get into their life rafts, the area is rife with sharks and barracuda. Their chances of survival were therefore minimal at best. Whatever their fate, the legend that was created by their disappearance will live on until some remnant of the aircraft is found.

"Boats and ships that disappear in the Triangle are another story. The speculation of many people who are seeking a mysterious answer to any event in the Triangle blames disappearances on everything from giant squid or the devil himself to UFOs and even to government experiments. I, however, think that there is a more rational explanation to many of these disappearances.

"Within the Triangle is the deepest part of the Atlantic Ocean. It is known as the Puerto Rico Trench and is approximately thirty thousand feet deep. Beyond this, the whole area is a meteorological nightmare. Never mind the hurricanes that frequent this area. There are also what are known as meso-meteorological storms that can't be predicted with any degree of accuracy. These storms form suddenly without much warning and may take the form of waterspouts that can reach thousands of feet into the sky, thunderstorms containing lighting and ball lighting, and what may be called miniature tropical cyclones. In addition, waves have been known to form a vertical wall of water over forty feet high. If a boat cannot survive a full emersion of water from one of these waves, the result is obvious. As suddenly as these storms form, they will dissipate just as quickly.

"I would like to believe that the vast majority of occurrences are a result of a natural phenomenon, and they are probably so. But the reports of green lights or a green mist in the sky followed by some catastrophe require further study. I just hope that it is not the aliens. In the future, I guess, we will have to pay more attention to the area if the disappearances in the Triangle increase or we have some reason to suspect alien activity." Scotty concluded by looking down at the table, obviously lost in thought. Then looking over at Cunningham, he asked, "I hope that answers your question?"

"More than enough, sir," Cunningham answered quickly.

Clearing his throat, Morrison asked the group, "Before we adjourn, is there anything else we should talk about?"

"Yes, Admiral, there are two things." Scotty spoke up.

"Okay, Scotty, what are they?" Morrison asked.

"Admiral, it's just what we talked about before. I would like to have Jonsey here ASAP, and I want Art Giovanni here as soon as possible. Hell, kidnap both of them if you have to. I need them right away," Scotty requested.

With laughter in his voice, Morrison answered Scotty's plea, "I promise, Scotty. I'll give the order for Jones as soon as we break up.

Giovanni may be another matter, but I'll also issue the necessary orders to have him cleared right away. But if he can't pass a quick background investigation, then no, he will not be allowed on the base. Okay?"

"Fair enough, Admiral," Scotty replied, knowing that Arty, as long as it didn't involve women, could pass any background investigation.

"Scotty, I know that you need both of these men to hunt down the spy that you suspect is on the base, but are you really convinced that there is a spy here?" Morrison asked with a trace of hesitation in his voice.

Not wanting to offend Morrison, Scotty chose his words carefully. "Yes, sir, I am. There is just too much of a coincidence in the two air attacks. Coincidences just don't repeatedly occur."

"Then go find that spy, Scotty. I may have just missed something," Morrison ordered and with hesitation asked, "Was there anything else, Scotty?"

"Just one more thing. I know that you have placed a lot of importance on the meeting on international terrorism next month, but I think that the meeting of the association you told me about should be canceled." Scotty almost demanded by his tone of voice.

"Scotty, the conference presents one of the rare opportunities for us to get together and exchange notes on alien activity. It is at these meeting that we also agree on a strategy to deal with the aliens. Also, it is an opportunity for you and Vinson to meet all the associates and help formulate the direction of the group for the future," Morrison pleaded.

"I know, sir, but I think that this meeting may be a trap of some kind. I just want to know one thing. Was the satellite net used to communicate with the other principals about the conference?" Scotty asked, sure of the answer.

"Yes, that's right," Morrison answered, not quite sure where Scotty was going.

"If the satellite net has been compromised by the aliens, and I am sure that it has been, then they also know about the meeting and who is going to attend. Brazil was a warning, like we talked about, but it could also be a trap. In other words, the aliens would think that because of Brazil, the meeting of the association would definitely take place. Since all the organized resistance to the aliens will be in one place at the same time, the target is just too sweet for the aliens to pass up. In one quick instant, all organized resistance fades away." He paused. "I'm sorry, Admiral, but the meeting has to be canceled." Scotty stated his case not sure what Morrison would do.

Without a trace of an expression on his face, Morrison stared at Scotty and then glanced over at Chester. Slightly nodding to Morrison, Chester saw the logic of Scotty's argument and agreed with him. Looking back at Scotty, Morrison replied, "Chester and I agree with you. The meeting will be canceled." After pausing for a second, Morrison then asked, "How do you want to play it, Scotty?"

"I would like you to contact each member in the next few days in the same code that you are communicating with them now. Use the net as you normally do and confirm in your message the meeting time of 9:00 p.m. and the exact location. I assume that the location is away from the conference?" Scotty asked.

"Yes. It's in a hotel on the other side of town," Morrison answered.

"Good. Include in your message that a personal representative of yours will visit them personally to discuss the agenda. Vinson here will be that representative. He will bring with him a copy of the film Mr. Cunningham is going to prepare tonight. Vinson will show each of them the film and instruct them that the meeting is canceled for the reasons we have just discussed. He will also instruct them that any communication in the future will be by encryption and burst transmissions.

"At the time of the conference, I would like all the principals to attend the opening ceremony. They can then slip away that night since none of them have an active role at the conference. I want them scattered around the globe by 9:00 p.m., away from France and the meeting.

"We will continue to act as if the meeting were going to take place. I will have some of our security personnel stake out the meeting site to hopefully stop whatever it is the aliens have planned for us."

Scotty planned his actions as he spoke.

Laughing slightly, Morrison replied, "Scotty, you have been watching too many spy movies!" Then turning serious, he continued, "It's a good plan. Chester and I will work out the messages and send them out in the morning." Turning toward Vinson, Morrison added, "Commander, you have a lot of dossiers to commit to memory. Are you ready for all this traveling?"

"Hey, it doesn't require space travel and I won't be in any jungles, and I'm sure that none of your counterparts keep snakes around their offices. I'm a lucky man. No problem, Admiral!" Vinson quickly replied, thinking about all the traveling he had to do. *Join the Navy and see the world. Just great!* Vinson concluded to himself, almost speaking his thought out loud.

"Sounds like we have a plan, then." Morrison summed up the meeting and then asked, "Anything else, Scotty?"

"Nothing, sir," Scotty replied.

"Okay, good. Scotty, I'll stay for the next three days and help you settle in. Captain Stark, I need you to return to Washington and hold down the office until I return. Then you are to return here and help Scotty out. I guess I have to start interviewing for a new assistant." Morrison issued his order with resignation in his voice and then perked up and continued issuing orders. "Chester, I know that you have to leave in two days to meet Captain Montgomery, but I'd like you to stay and help Scotty until it's time to go."

Chester spoke first. "Of course."

"I'll leave first thing in the morning, sir," Doreen replied with a big hint of disappointment in her voice.

"Well, I guess that's it. I would suggest that you all return to your quarters and put on those new uniforms of yours for the ceremony. You only have two hours," Morrison ordered and then, almost forgetting, added, "You will be escorted to the ceremony by Marine security personnel, so wait for them in your quarters. That's it, people."

As the meeting broke up, Morrison retreated to the food once again. As he was reaching for some bread to make another sandwich, Doreen cried out in a loud voice, "Admiral!"

With his back to Doreen, Morrison answered the challenge, "Captain, you don't outrank me yet. Let an old seahorse have his pleasure." He then piled the bread high with corned beef and Swiss cheese and then added a few pickles to his plate.

Once everyone had left, Morrison sat down at the conference table, enjoying his sandwich. He was confident that Scotty was the hope of the future. He smiled at the prospect of Scotty and Doreen becoming man and wife one day. But that thought quickly disappeared as he licked his lips and reached for the other half of his "snack."

CHANGE OF COMMAND

As Vinson, Doreen, and Scotty began their trek back to their quarters, the mood was somewhat mixed. Vinson and Doreen were laughing and joking, reflective of the excitement they felt over their new jobs and the challenges before them. Scotty was uncharacteristically quiet, as for the first time in his life, he was feeling the full weight of responsibility. Scotty was thinking about the future, and he knew full well that people's lives would depend upon his decisions.

When he was a naval aviator, life was simple. Scotty would receive his orders and he would follow them to the best of his abilities. But now he would be giving the orders. For a moment Scotty thought about the commander of the air group on the *Eisenhower* who couldn't or wouldn't give the order to launch fighter aircraft to come to his aid when he attacked the UFO. Scotty wondered if it was because he and Ice were probably dead men, anyway, attacking an aircraft with little chance of success, and the CAG didn't want to risk any more lives. Or did the pressure of possibly ordering people to their probable death become too much to bear? Scotty resolved at that moment that he would give orders based upon need, and if it meant ordering people into life-and-death situations, well, that was the way it was. He knew that the loss of one life would affect him, but Scotty also knew that he had a job to do and that people would die along the way. What mattered most was the end result, protection of the United States from these bastards that some people lovingly called aliens.

As the threesome approached their quarters, Scotty was surprised to see six Marines standing by his door at attention, in full dress uniform. Major Whitney was also there, pacing back and forth, carrying a briefcase while repeatedly glancing at his watch. When Scotty was approximately ten feet from the door to his quarters, Major Whitney snapped to attention and saluted. Returning the salute, Scotty ordered the Marines to stand at ease. Scotty invited Major Whitney into his quarters and instructed him to cut his men loose and have them return in one hour. After the major released his men, Scotty also asked Doreen and Vinson to join them.

Once everyone was seated, Scotty began, "Major, this morning you told me that your command consists of roughly two-hundred-plus combat-ready Marines."

"Yes, Admiral. It's two hundred and sixty-three to be exact," Major Whitney answered.

"Major, do me a favor and call me Scotty. This Admiral stuff is all new. Besides, everyone calls me Scotty," he ordered more than asked.

"Yes, sir. But you have to call me JW. My parents hung that on me when I was a kid. People have been calling me JW as long as I can remember," Major Whitney pleaded.

"Done. JW, how many of your men have had SEAL training and bodyguard training?" Scotty asked.

"Well, sir, only twenty-five of the troops are graduates of the Navy SEAL program. God knows I've requested more SEAL-trained troops, but—and forgive me, sir—Admiral Morrison has ignored those requests. As far as bodyguard protection, none of the men have been trained in that area," JW replied.

"Okay," Scotty answered and turned toward Doreen, who was quietly sitting on a couch across from Scotty. "Doreen, after you get back to Washington, I want you to make arrangements to have the entire Marine contingent trained in bodyguard procedures. Only send a few through the program at a time so as not to tip our hand. I'll see if we can't also"—Scotty then turned back toward JW—"get our hands on more SEALs for you, JW. I would like to see a larger corps presence on the base, not only for security reasons, but also because once we have all our ducks in place, things are going to change. It's my full intention to carry the fight to the aliens. Tomorrow you and everyone else on the base will see a film documenting what happened in Brazil. The time that the aliens freely roam Earth and kill or kidnap its occupants is quickly coming to a close. I'm going to depend greatly on your Marines, and I know that they will meet the challenge." Scotty paused for dramatic effect.

"They are the best the corps has to offer! They are ready, sir!" JW declared.

"Now, one more thing. From what I've seen so far, your security protocols are way above average and are to be commended. However, I believe that there is a spy, or perhaps more than one spy, in the complex who is getting intelligence out through the satellite net.

"I base this conclusion on two separate incidents when the aliens intercepted aircraft in flight. The first one was against Rear Admiral Braddock, and the second incident was against Admiral Morrison and the rest of us as we were returning from Brazil. It's gonna be hard to catch this spy, or spies, and I need your security force at the top of their game." Scotty paused, waiting for a reaction.

"How can I and my Marines be of help, sir?" JW replied in a voice of concern.

Scotty was glad to see that JW didn't offer excuses for any lapse in security that might have allowed a spy to operate but instead offered to help in any way he could. Yes, Scotty liked this man, and with that his trust of him was growing. Gathering his thoughts, Scotty replied, "For now just keep your present measures in place with a thought to enhance them any way you can. Also, I want you to personally review the log of admissions into satellite control every day. Look for anything unusual. When you have the time, review the surveillance videotapes of Space Command sporadically. Just keep it quiet and looking that everything is normal. Who knows, we might just get lucky."

"Scotty, you know about Carolyn Gibbs. Do you suspect her in any way?" JW asked.

"No. While she obviously has the knowledge and skill to carry something like this off, I sincerely doubt she has ties to the aliens. I think the base has been penetrated with an alien presence somehow. Vinson will give you the full rundown later. There are a couple of other things I want to talk to you about first.

"Tomorrow morning, Doreen will be returning to Washington for a few days. I want two of your Marines assigned to her as bodyguards. Also, Vinson will shortly be leaving for a trip, and I want security around him as well. From now on, whenever a member of central command travels away from the base, they, including yourself, are to have protection assigned to them. Is there any problem with that order that I should be aware of?" Scotty asked.

"No, sir. It's a damn good idea. Long overdue, I might add," JW replied.

"Good. Now, is there a way that the central command can be in instant contact with one another rather than having to use the intercom system or take the time to go to a telephone?" Scotty asked.

"Yes, that's one of the reasons I came down here," JW replied as he reached for and opened his briefcase. Scotty watched closely as the major withdrew from the briefcase what appeared to be three watches, two men's and one ladies'. After he placed them on the coffee table in front of him, JW continued, "I have a radio for each of you that can only communicate with others on the same frequency. Each member of the central command wears one of these twenty-four hours a day. In particular, executive officer Beverly Hocker; Commander Mark Bowman of Space Command; air commander—CAG, if you will—Captain Theodore Kendall; weapons officer Captain Raymond Bone; flight surgeon Captain Shena Gordon and her assistant, Commander Jerome Hewitt; my assistant, Captain Linda Clark; and of course myself." JW paused as he adjusted one of the radios.

"Does the watch work as well, or is it just a radio?" Vinson asked as he remembered reading about such a device in a science magazine.

"Remarkably, yes, it does," JW replied as he handed each of them a watch.

"How long does the battery last?" Scotty asked.

"They last about a year, but a member of my security team will visit you at three-month intervals and change the battery. It's better to be safe than sorry," JW replied and added as an afterthought, "Also, sir, your secretary will be able to contact you through the device. I don't know if Admiral Morrison has told you yet, but your office is manned around-the-clock. During regular business hours, Chief Petty Officer Marcy Franks is on duty, and in the off hours, I have two Marines from the guard division man the office and direct calls to either yourself or the exec and, in the future, Commander James."

"Very efficient, JW. Sounds like you covered all the bases," Scotty replied and sat back in his chair.

"Sir, about the protection service, how do you want the Marines dressed? And what weapons would you suggest they carry?" JW inquired, wanting to please the new base commander. "Also, I'm thinking that we should have at least four Marines assigned to each individual, which would allow them to work in shifts."

"What you are going to have to do is set up a weapons protocol for the protection division. See, JW, you just got another division you didn't know you had a few minutes ago." Scotty paused while laughing.

"Thank you, sir," JW replied, also slightly laughing, but Scotty could see the seriousness in his face.

"As I was saying, a weapons protocol has to be established. I would like them to go out armed to the teeth, but that's not practical. Do you have any of the new ceramic handguns that are supposed to be undetectable by airport metal detectors?" Scotty asked.

"Yes, sir. We have a science officer here who is second to none. You give her a problem and she will overcome any obstacle. She is Commander Lattice Wyman.

"When ceramic handguns first came out, as you know, they were detectable by airport metal detectors and x-ray examination. I asked Lattice if she could perfect the design and make it a break-apart weapon so that the pieces could be disguised as something else.

"You wouldn't believe what she came up with. Airport metal detectors cannot detect the handgun even if it is assembled. An x-ray, because of some special coating she applied to the weapons, comes out foggy and distorted. Broken down, the barrel of the weapon becomes the handle to a razor, and the stock fits into a can of shaving cream. And yes, shaving cream comes out of the can.

"The remarkable thing about her work is the fact that she also redesigned the ammunition. The weapon takes a 9mm bullet, either standard issue or the new ones she designed. Somehow, Lattice manufactured a ceramic bullet casing. She also came up with a new mixture of gunpowder, twice as powerful, and very quiet. Then she designed a ceramic projectile that shatters upon impact. This new bullet causes a hole in a person about the size of a quarter and then expands further as it travels through the body. This gives my men a great advantage over anyone they have to fight with. Also, the bullets go through standard Kevlar bulletproof vests.

"Not only did she design and manufacture handguns, but she also made an M16 model and a shotgun, both short and long barrel," JW replied.

"Thank God that she is on our side. I'm sure you thought of the implications if one of these weapons were to get out?" Scotty inquired more than made a statement. "Imagine a hijacker armed with such an undetectable weapon."

"Sir, all weapons and the designs are locked away in my office. It takes a week to make one weapon, and the manufacturing process is broken down into parts, with different people handling each part so that no one knows, with the exception of a very few, just what it is that they are making. I am present during the final assembly of the weapon and immediately take it to my office and lock it up. As a sidenote, the manufacturing materials are closely watched and are kept under lock and key. During manufacture, the raw material is measured out before it is given to the person who will mold it, so that no duplicates can be made," JW concluded.

"Most impressive, Major. I'd like to fire one of these weapons one day," Scotty declared.

"At your convenience, Scotty. Just name the day. You know, we have a firing range in one of the subbasements of the energy plant. Just let me know when you are available." JW paused and then asked, "Sir, about the protection escort, what are your requirements?"

"I agree with your suggestion. Each person should be assigned at least four guards. I would like them to come from your SEAL-trained ranks, though. They should also be dressed in civilian clothing while traveling and be able to blend in. In other words, I want them to pass as civilians.

"As far as weapons go, while traveling in the United States, each member should carry a standard-issue sidearm and the carbon-type knives. The team should be looked at as a combat unit. By that I mean there should be heavy weapons as well. Two members should carry machine guns, while the other two carry a break-down rifle, and the other a sawed-off shotgun. There will be no trouble with carrying handguns on airliners, as each member of the team will be issued National Security Agency identification and will be permitted, in the civilian world, to transport such weapons.

"When they travel internationally, they should be issued the ceramic handguns. I can't stress enough that those ceramic weapons cannot fall into the wrong hands. Also, they should carry the carbon knives.

"One other thing, no one who leaves this base on business, except in an emergency, will fly out of here. Tomorrow morning, when Doreen leaves, I want her group driven into Denver, where they can board a commercial airliner. Also, no communication is allowed over the satellite net to the group. Restrict all communication to landlines and encrypted cell phones. I know it sounds crazy, but those are my orders for now.

"While Doreen is away, I want your team on her like glue. If she enters a public bathroom, I want someone in there with her. Even in the Pentagon. Is that clear?"

"Michael!" came a protest from Doreen, but Scotty ignored the plea.

"Yes, sir. I will send a female Marine along as part of the team. She is not SEAL trained, but she doubles as our hand-to-hand combat instructor. Will that be sufficient, sir?" JW answered, thinking himself lucky that he had Staff Sergeant Dawn Symick on his staff.

"That will be great. JW, I know that we are shooting from the hip right now with this protection business, but believe me, once you see the film from Brazil tomorrow, you will understand my reason for caution. I don't expect you personally to do this job. I want you to appoint a member of your staff to a new position in charge of protection services. You will, of course, oversee the operation. Whoever you appoint to this new position should coordinate with Doreen so that we can start the training as soon as possible.

"Just one more thing and then we have to break. Can't be late for the change of command, you know. Do you have a rapid-response force in place?" Scotty asked.

"I have one ready team of eight Marines standing by twenty-four hours a day.

"They are set up to handle emergencies within the complex. In addition to that, our defensive weapons are likewise manned around-the-clock, as well as patrols within the grounds. We also run patrols just outside of our property," JW proudly answered.

"I hate to dump this on you as well, but I want your rapid-response force enhanced. It should consist of at least sixteen Marines around-the-clock. Their duty station will be on the hangar deck. I don't know where yet, but I'll set that up.

"I know the CAG keeps four F-18s ready at a moment's notice. I am going to increase that force to include two Black Hawk helicopters and at least one Apache helicopter, should the requisition go through," Scotty ordered.

"It may stretch my men a bit, sir, but it will be done immediately," JW replied, wondering what kind of trouble his new boss was expecting.

"I'll also work on getting you some more Marines. Now, you are gonna have to excuse me so that I can get changed," Scotty replied.

After showing the major and Vinson out, Scotty walked over to where Doreen was sitting. He reached down and pulled her out of her seat by both hands and gave her a soft and long, passionate kiss as they each pressed their bodies together, groping for the passion building within them. Their embrace was broken by the sound of a ringing telephone on Scotty's desk. With great hesitation, Scotty walked over to the desk and picked up the receiver. Scotty immediately recognized the voice of the admiral, who reminded him that he was due on the flight deck in fifteen minutes. Scotty replied that he was in the process of getting dressed as he looked up for Doreen but only caught a glimpse of her as she quietly left his quarters and closed the door. After he put down the telephone, Scotty ran to his bathroom and took a quick shower.

After his shower, Scotty crossed the room to the closet. As he reached for his new uniform, he quickly withdrew his arm and just stood there staring at the uniform. Momentarily, he remembered what brought him to this point, and he silently prayed that he was capable of what was expected of him. With reverence, he then reached for the uniform and put it on. Anyone who knew Scotty could tell you that he was not a vain man, but after he was dressed in his finest dress whites, he couldn't resist the temptation to look at himself in the full-length mirror attached to the inside of the closet door. Scotty stood there with a broad smile on his face and marveled at himself. He then reached up with both hands and placed his hat upon his head. Making minute adjustments to the placement of the hat, as he wanted it to look just right, Scotty took a step back, turned serious for a moment, and saluted himself. Quickly Scotty turned from the mirror, closed the closet door, and walked away, whistling an ole sea chant about a drunken sailor.

When Scotty opened the door to his quarters, he immediately stopped whistling as the Marine escort had returned and snapped to attention. Scotty saluted them and ordered them to stand at ease. He then closed the door to his quarters and walked across the hallway and knocked on Vinson's door. Vinson slowly opened his door and was greeted by Scotty issuing orders. "Snap to, Commander!"

"Yes, sir!" Vinson replied as he exited his quarters.

Scotty then noticed Doreen leaving her quarters, and he quickly ran over to her. His first inclination was to hug her and give her a kiss, but manners and social pressure held him back. Instead, he uttered, somewhat stunned, as Scotty always was by her presence, "God, you look great."

"Thank you, Michael," Doreen replied as she looked down at herself and then looked up at Scotty, giving him a quick kiss on the cheek and saying, "You look very handsome in your new uniform."

Scotty was about to reach out for her when he heard Vinson fake a cough. Scotty turned and looked at Vinson, who was holding a hand in front of his chest, shaking a finger back and forth, and then pointed his finger at a security camera. Scotty then turned back toward Doreen and saw JW walking down the hallway toward them. "Seems like we are all dressed up tonight. I hope it's a damn good party," Scotty called out, much to the amazement and delight of the Marine escort.

As JW approached the group, he called out, "Marines, attention!" and walked up to the superior enlisted man, Staff Sergeant Michaels. "Do you find the words of Admiral Scott humorous, Sergeant?" JW bellowed.

Sergeant Michaels looked his major squarely in the eye and replied, "Yes, sir!"

JW was a bit taken aback by the honest reply and stated, "Good, Sergeant. I was worried for a minute that you might not have a sense of humor or, worse still, that you were dead." Turning toward Scotty, JW continued, "Admiral, it is my pleasure and that of my men to escort you and Captain Stark and Commander James to your new office and command."

"Thank you, Major. I am honored by your presence and that of your men," Scotty replied while looking around at the Marines and receiving slight smiles or winks in recognition of his remark.

"Sir, if you will be so kind as to follow me, we will escort you to Admiral Morrison," JW offered.

"Lead on, Major. We are in your care," Scotty replied as he glanced around at everyone.

To the casual eye, it must have looked like Doreen, Vinson, and Scotty were under arrest and being escorted away. JW led them off, walking down the center of the hallway, followed by Scotty behind him, Doreen behind Scotty, and Vinson behind Doreen.

Alongside each of them were two Marines walking in perfect step with their motions. As they approached the elevator, which would carry them up to the hangar deck, the Marines stood aside and let the soon-to-be-promoted threesome enter. The Marines then entered the elevator, and when JW was satisfied that everyone was present, he pushed the button to the hangar deck level.

When the elevator doors opened on the hangar deck, everyone resumed their positions and the party walked a short distance in the dark, except for a few glowing red lights, to a stairway that led to an office that overlooked the length of the flight deck.

Scotty thought it odd that the flight deck was dark and quiet except for the humming of machinery and air circulation pumps. He swore to himself that there were people there also, but he couldn't see them. JW stepped aside once they reached the stairway and allowed Scotty to climb the stairs and enter the office. Doreen, Vinson, and JW followed him.

When Scotty entered the room, he quickly looked around and noted that it was to be his flight control center. There were computer and video monitors everywhere arranged neatly in rows. Below these were radar and satellite monitors. *Where at least ten technicians must work,* he thought. On one side there was a wall of windows allowing a view of the hangar deck. In the center of the room were plot boards, where any reference point could be displayed relative to the flight of an aircraft. Off to the side, Scotty saw two high-back chairs mounted a few feet off the ground, which would allow the occupant to view not only the actions within the room but also what was happening on the hangar deck below. One of the chairs was stenciled with the words *Air Boss*, while the other was marked *Admiral*. Scotty's review of the room was interrupted when JW called out, "Attention on deck!"

At once, Scotty froze and came to attention and noticed for the first time that there were other people in the room off to the side. Admiral Morrison ordered the others present to form a line behind him, while Scotty, Doreen, and Vinson were ordered to stand in front of the assemblage. Once everyone was in place, Admiral Morrison read the orders promoting Scotty to rear admiral, lower half; Doreen to captain; and Vinson to full commander. Morrison then stepped forward, congratulated Scotty, and placed the symbol of his rank, a five-pointed silver star, in his hand and added, "Very soon I expect to give you another star." One that would promote Scotty to the upper half of the rear admiral rank. He next congratulated Doreen and placed a silver eagle in her hand, signifying the rank of captain. Vinson next received congratulations, and Morrison presented him with a silver oak leaf in his hand, the insignia of a commander. Congratulations were then exchanged around, and Scotty was introduced to the upper command of the base. Present were Captain Kendall, the air boss, who was lovingly called CAG by the aviators under his command; Commander Bowman of Space Command; Captain Bone, the weapons officer; and Captain Shena Gordon, the flight surgeon in charge. Of course, JW was present and offered his warmest congratulations to the threesome. Chester pulled Scotty aside and offered him a few words of wisdom, "to think with his head and not his heart," and pledged him his full support and help.

As the group was relaxed, Morrison called them to attention again and asked Rear Admiral Chester Braddock to present himself before the officers present. Chester was surprised by this request but stood at attention before his friend. Morrison read aloud the order of promotion advancing Chester to the rank of vice admiral. Morrison was almost in tears of joy when he shook Chester's hand and told him that the promotion was long overdue. Chester embraced his friend and thanked him. Morrison then asked Scotty if he was ready to receive command of the base.

"Yes, sir," Scotty replied in a somewhat-nervous voice.

"Good. Ladies and gentlemen, please follow me," Morrison ordered.

Morrison led the way to the door and held it open as the command staff exited.

When Scotty neared the door and looked out, he was amazed by what he saw. The hangar deck that had been dark when he entered a short time ago was now bathed in light. It looked like the staff of the entire base was there in their dress white uniforms. American flags decorated the walls, as well as the base flag, an admiral's flag, and the flags of the different aircraft squadrons. Stretched across the middle of the deck was a large banner that read, "Welcome Aboard, Admiral." Along one side of the deck, there were tables and tables of food that must have stretched for at least a hundred and fifty feet. On the opposite wall, a band was getting ready to play. The airplanes that normally occupied this area were parked together at the far end of the deck, roped off from those in attendance. As Scotty descended the stairs, followed by Morrison, he became a little nervous. He had thought that the exchange of command would take place when he received his promotion.

When Scotty reached the bottom of the stairs, Morrison directed him to ascend three steps to an elevated platform that had been set up. Morrison and Scotty stood atop the platform, looking out at the crowd, when JW came from behind, walked to the microphone, and called the throng to attention. Within a few seconds, the entire area was silent, and those present were assembled in neat, orderly rows, standing at attention.

Admiral Morrison approached the microphone with Scotty at his side and read the simple order of change of command. In less than a minute, Scotty was given command of the base and its many responsibilities. When Morrison finished reading the order, he turned to Scotty and said, "The base is now under your command. I congratulate you, sir." With a slight grin on his face, Morrison continued, "Admiral Scott, would you care to say a few words?"

Scotty gawked back at the admiral with a look of surprise on his face, and momentary confusion, as he was not prepared to give a speech. Nervously he approached the microphone and issued his first official order. He called out, "At ease!"

In almost-perfect unison, those assembled assumed the at-ease position. As Scotty glanced out at the large sea of white uniforms, he noticed more than a few Air Force, Army, and Coast Guard uniforms sprinkled in among the Navy and Marine ones. Scotty's mind was in high gear trying to figure out what to say. He knew that this would be the defining moment of his command, and if he failed at this simple speech, it would take a long time to recover his stature.

Carefully he began, "Good evening, ladies and gentlemen."

Scotty was interrupted when everyone replied in perfect unison, "Good evening, Admiral."

Scotty thought to himself this might be somewhat easy since everyone seemed to be in a good mood, and he continued, "As I look out among you, I see the finest that this country has to offer. Each of you has been very carefully selected, because of your abilities and dedication, to engage in a struggle that will be the defining point of the human race. You and you alone will determine what course that struggle will take. The path that we walk together will be twisted and fraught with danger. Together as brothers and sisters, for those who walk together and face many perils and hardships together are truly brothers and sisters, we will overcome any adversity that is thrown in our path."

Lowering his voice in a serious tone, Scotty continued, "Tomorrow each of you will see what some of us recently saw in Brazil. It provides the answer to the previously unexplained disappearance of people throughout the world. I ask you this: Whenever you are feeling down about your work or a solution seems beyond your reach, remember the people on the aircraft that was snatched from the skies over Brazil. Let that memory be your guidepost and a rededication of your purpose. Let the people of Brazil and the countless others throughout the world whose life was ended or interrupted by these heartless, murdering aliens, and most importantly, the people of the United States, be our war cry!"

Raising his voice for dramatic effect and looking stern, Scotty continued, "We have the tools, we have the people, and we have the ability to carry the fight forward. As a sidenote, based upon what I've seen, I'd be damn scared to come up against this group—"

Scotty was surprised as he was again interrupted, this time by cheers and clapping. In a few moments, it again quieted down and he continued, "I propose to name this group the Raptors. It was suggested that you be named the Grim Reapers, but I don't agree. I don't see anything grim about this group at all. Together we will sweep and clean this universe of the invaders—"

Scotty was again interrupted, this time by chants of "Raptors, Raptors, Raptors!" Putting his hands up to quiet the assemblage, Scotty continued, "Together as brothers and sisters, we will move forward united by our dedication of purpose. Shortly we will unsheathe our swords and carry the battle forward. Let the word go out to the galaxies of this universe that the planet Earth is protected by a band of brothers and sisters known as the Raptors and no one but no one is to mess with them!"

Scotty was once again interrupted by cheering and chants of "Raptors!"

Quieting the crowd down once more, Scotty was able to continue, "It is my privilege—nay, it is my *honor*—to be associated with you. Together we will accomplish what others may view as unobtainable. Together we will press on, and victory will be ours!"

Once again the room erupted in cheers. Having regained order again, Scotty called out, "Attention!" and everyone in unison snapped to attention. "Raptors, my order of the day is this: enjoy the evening. The food, I know, is good, and the band looks anxious to start. Dismissed!"

When the dismissal order was given, the room erupted once again in applause and cheers. Scotty motioned for the band to start playing, and everything settled down.

Turning away from the microphone, Scotty faced Morrison, who said, "Jesus, Scotty, I thought you were just gonna say hello and how proud you were to be here. After that speech, I feel like I am abandoning ship."

"You're more than welcome to stay, sir," Scotty quickly replied.

"Duty calls, Scotty. And besides, who is gonna watch your back in Washington?" Morrison pointed out.

Doreen then approached the two admirals. Grabbing Scotty's hand and pulling him away, Doreen loudly declared to Morrison, "Excuse me, Admiral, but this admiral owes me a dance." Doreen then led Scotty to the dance floor. The band was playing a slow song, which her mood demanded at that moment. Pulling him in close to her, she whispered, "Congratulations, Admiral. Now, just when and where are we going to be alone, away from all this?"

Scotty smelled her sweet perfume, was lost in its fragrance, and softly kissed her neck as she spoke. He was about to answer "Right now" as he wanted to whisk her away to his quarters when the song ended and Scotty felt someone tap his shoulder. Releasing Doreen, he turned around and saw Chester standing there with three champagne glasses filled with their bubbly content. Doreen reached out and took one, and Chester handed the other one to Scotty. Chester raised his glass, and all of a sudden, a crowd formed around them, also with champagne glasses raised. Chester, in a very loud voice, said, "Let me be the first to offer my congratulations to the Navy's newest and finest rear admiral and captain!" He then sipped from his glass, as did Scotty and Doreen, to the cheers of "Hear, hear!" Scotty then toasted the newest and best vice admiral in the United States Navy.

After the toast was completed, an informal reception line seemed to form around Scotty. For the next three and a half hours, Scotty stood there and received the congratulations of all those present. At first, Doreen stood aside as she watched Scotty get engulfed by the crowd. She realized that for the moment, her passion, which was growing stronger with each passing minute, had to be suppressed. Resigned to the fact that the moment was forever lost, Doreen went over to the buffet tables and ate some dinner.

For his part, Scotty realized that his passion as well had to be put on hold for the moment as he greeted each member of the crew individually. He didn't rush through the introductions but rather took an interest in each individual, asking them their job, where they were from, about their family, and what their outside interests were. Scotty would add favorable comments to each individual's background and told each person that he was proud to be associated with him or her. Each person came away from meeting Scotty with a sense of importance. They felt, correctly, that Scotty truly valued them, not just as a person under his command, but, more importantly, as an individual. Scotty was hungry and longed for something to eat but felt it more important to meet his crew. He was relieved when Doreen slipped him a small plate of miniature quiche to nibble on as he talked.

Doreen then turned her attention toward Admiral Morrison and his eating habits. Morrison had taken up a strategic position near the cold cuts platter. This time he wasn't bothering with bread but was piling pastrami, brisket, and corn beef on his plate, accompanied by a small quantity of sour pickles. Standing in horror as her mentor picked up a couple slices of meat with his fork and unceremoniously placed forkful after forkful in his mouth, she took his plate and threw it in the garbage can. Taking him by the arm, Doreen led the admiral to a table full of fruit salads and the ever-present carrot salad.

She then prepared a plate of cottage cheese, fruit salad, and carrot salad and handed it to the admiral with one word: "Eat!" Morrison did his best to protest her actions, claiming that all this healthy food would surely poison him, but he knew that it was a losing battle. Standing close to the admiral, Doreen ensured that he ate every last morsel. Once he was finished, Doreen then took him by the arm and led him over to the frozen yogurt dispenser. Doreen took a small bowl and obtained a medium helping of chocolate yogurt for the admiral. Again, she spoke one word: "Eat!" Morrison did as he was ordered and, when finished, said, "That wasn't half-bad, although I prefer chocolate ice cream with butterscotch sauce and strawberries topped with—and you will like this—wheat germ."

"The wheat germ is the best part. Look it, Admiral, either you change your ways or you aren't going to be around. Michael and I wouldn't like that. So please, if not for yourself, then for us, watch what you eat so you will be around for a while."

"I'll try, Captain. I promise. But please, there is a decadent chocolate cake over there with my name on a piece of it. Just this last time," Morrison pleaded as he looked longingly at the dessert table.

"Whatever," Doreen answered, throwing her arms in the air, and walked away shaking her head back and forth in resignation.

Meanwhile, Scotty remained where he was greeting each member of the base. He was surprised when Dr. Hewitt presented himself. Scotty greeted him warmly and inquired as to the condition of their visitor. The doctor replied that she was still resting comfortably, and expressed thankfulness for the suggestions of Captain Stark. Scotty inquired to his own health as the good doctor seemed to be wheezing somewhat. Dr. Hewitt replied that it was just his asthma acting up again and explained that he had never gotten quite used to living underground. Before they parted, Scotty instructed Dr. Hewitt to forward his reports to his secretary, Marcy Franks, once every day. Scotty decided that he would try to establish a new relationship with the doctor even though he inwardly knew that he just didn't like him.

A short while later, Captain Kendall appeared in the line. Scotty warmly greeted him as well and asked how his relationship with Dr. Hewitt was, since it was the doctor who determined which pilots were fit for flying. Kendall explained that he tried very hard to maintain a good relationship but that the doctor was really a sweet pain in the ass. Scotty laughed at his comment and appreciated his honesty. Scotty then told Kendall that he wanted to see him in the morning and asked if the F-18 invisibility demonstration was set up. Kendall replied that it was scheduled for 1000 hours, if that was okay. Scotty replied that it was and stated that he looked forward to seeing him in the morning.

After Kendall left Scotty, he sought out Dr. Hewitt, having decided to make a greater effort to get on the man's good side. He found him by one of the food tables, eating an apple. "Hi, Doc," Kendall began, then added, "What do you think of our new commander?"

"Seems like a reasonable guy, but a real sweet pain in my ass," Dr. Hewitt replied, wanting to add more but then beginning to cough and wheeze.

"You okay, Doc?" Kendall inquired.

"Yeah, it's just my asthma acting up again. It's this damn closed-air system," Hewitt replied.

"Better take your pill, Doc. It wouldn't look too good if our doctor were sick. I'm sure your boss, Dr. Gordon, wouldn't want to see you sick," Kendall replied good-naturedly.

"Yeah, you're right. Excuse me, Kendall. I'll see you later," Hewitt replied and walked away having thrown the apple core into the wastebasket.

"Good night, Doc!" Kendall called out as he watched Hewitt walk away and take out a pill bottle, which Kendall knew the doctor always carried with him. Kendall continued to watch the doctor as he took a pill out of the bottle and, putting his head back, swallowed the pill. After the doctor put the pill bottle back in his pocket, Kendall continued to watch him until he disappeared among the throng of the partygoers.

Kendall's last thought about the doctor that night was, *My god, is that guy an ass or what?* Kendall next turned toward the buffet table and picked up an apple, which he looked at for a moment, unaware of what the "Or what" could possibly be.

When the impromptu reception line died out, Doreen went to Scotty's side and took his arm in hers and whispered to him, "I think the time has come for us to engage in some military intelligence in my quarters."

Scotty looked at Doreen with passion in his eyes and replied, "I concur. I think the situation has become too much to bear, and what it needs is some deep, probing intelligence work."

Doreen blushed slightly but then took ahold of his arm even tighter and led Scotty toward the elevator. As they left the area, those whom they passed again congratulated Scotty on his promotion and wished him well. Doreen was disappointed when others gathered at the elevator and, when it came, boarded with them. Once they were in the hallway leading to their quarters, Doreen and Scotty didn't speak as they walked with determination and a common purpose in mind. When they were about twenty feet from Doreen's door, Scotty noticed an armed Marine standing in front of the door to his own quarters. Scotty approached the Marine and asked him why he was there. The reply he received, Scotty didn't particularly care for but appreciated its purpose. It seemed that Major Whitney had taken their earlier talk very seriously and was tightening up security. Scotty was now to be assigned a round-the-clock guard at the door to his quarters. Scotty thanked the Marine and instructed him to carry on. He realized that there would be talk around the base. But hey, he was human too, he thought as he walked back to Doreen, who was standing in front of the door to her quarters. Scotty took the key out of her hand and opened the door. Doreen walked in first as she reached out and took Scotty's hand and was in the process of pulling him in when his new wristwatch/radio came alive with the words "Admiral Scott, please report to Space Command. Condition red!"

Doreen let out a loud breath of resignation and said, "Just go, Michael. We'll get this together someday."

Scotty turned to walk away, and Doreen pulled him the rest of the way into her quarters, out of sight of the Marine. She pressed herself closely to him and kissed him again. *It seems like this is all we will ever get to do,* Doreen thought to herself.

Scotty broke the embrace and whispered, "I'm sorry, but I better go."

"I know, Michael. Someday things will work out. See you in the morning," Doreen replied, watching as Scotty walked out of the door and away from her for the moment. Doreen then gently closed the door to her quarters and walked slowly to her bedroom, dreaming about what almost was.

When Scotty arrived at Space Command, everyone was leaning toward their computer screens, typing commands into their keyboards. Commander Bowman greeted Scotty and directed him to what he called the war desk. Scotty sat down in a high-back leather chair in front of a crescent-shaped desk at least thirty feet long. On each side of him were two other chairs. Directly in front of Scotty were computer monitors mounted below the height of the desk and angled so that Scotty could see their screens. Mounted below the desk was a pullout keyboard, which would allow Scotty to change the view on any given screen. Similar stations were mounted in front of the other four chairs around the desk. When Scotty looked up, he was able to see the larger monitors in Space Command and had an unobstructed view of the whole area.

"I assume this is my station, Commander?" Scotty asked.

"Yes, sir," Commander Bowman replied.

"What's up, Commander?" Scotty asked.

"Sir, as you can see from the monitors, we have picked up three flights, each consisting of eight aircraft, about to enter our atmosphere. On their present course, one flight will enter over the Gulf of Mexico, and one over Central Europe, and the third over Central China. This is the first time we have ever detected such a large incursion," Bowman replied.

"Think that they are pissed because they weren't invited to the party?" Scotty asked, trying to take some of the tension away from Commander Bowman.

"Could be, sir. That was one hell of a party, at least when I was there," Bowman replied.

"Okay, Commander, what's your assessment?" Scotty asked, turning more serious now.

"It's anybody's guess right now. They have never come in with this many ships at one time. Due to the dispersion of the unknowns, it's not a concentrated attack. If I had to guess, it's a water run. They should separate once in the atmosphere. They are entering the atmosphere now, sir," Bowman replied, knowing he had stretched his neck out as far as possible.

Scotty spoke into his wrist radio. "JW, you ready?"

"Cannons and missiles ready and tracking, sir," came a quick reply.

"CAG?" Scotty next asked into his wrist radio.

"Ready flight going up now, sir. Fires are lit.[55] Prepping four more aircraft," Captain Kendall hurriedly replied.

"Okay, gentlemen, let's be cool until we see what develops," Scotty instructed.

Once the group of saucers, or Z-1s, as they have been designated, emerged over the Gulf of Mexico, they dispersed over the United States, Mexico, and Canada and sped off to sources of fresh water. Once over freshwater lakes, rivers, and reservoirs the Z-1 craft lingered for a few minutes. Scotty watched the screens as the blips representing the saucers slowly then began to head back to the Gulf of Mexico. *Another vulnerability,* Scotty thought to himself. *The bastards need our water!* Turning toward Commander Bowman, Scotty asked, "Is it the same story over Europe and Asia?"

"Yes, sir," the commander replied without taking his eyes off the monitors, then continued, "Look, sir, they are all in the process of moving now."

Scotty watched as the blips re-entered space and took off to who knew where. "How often would you say they go for water, Commander?" Scotty asked.

"About once a week, sir. But never in this large a group. This is the first time we have seen a group this large," Commander Bowman replied while repeating his statement.

"Okay, Commander, call me if anything else develops, and order the base to stand down," Scotty replied as he got up and walked toward the exit.

"Sir!" Commander Bowman cried. "One of them has turned back and headed for the Gulf of Mexico again."

Scotty reversed his direction and went back over to his desk and sat down. "Any ideas this time, Commander?" Scotty asked.

"No, sir. This is unusual for them. Let's see where he goes when he re-enters the atmosphere, which should be in nine…eight…seven… six…five…four…three…two…there he is, in and on his way at ten thousand feet, at 850 miles per hour." Bowman swallowed hard and said, "Sir, he is bleeding off altitude at a rate of five hundred feet per second, and his present course will lead him right to our front door. ETA eighty seconds."

"JW!" Scotty called.

"Got him, sir. Missiles and cannon," JW replied.

"Fire at 5-0 miles out. Cannon only. Do you confirm?" Scotty ordered and asked for confirmation.

"Confirm, fire at 5-0 miles out. Cannon only," JW answered and passed along the order to shoot at fifty miles out.

"CAG! Launch ready craft. Direct them southwest on a hook course to bring them back in behind the unknown. Weapons hot. Permission to fire," Scotty directed. "Confirm, CAG!"

Scotty listened intently as CAG confirmed his order while he was staring at the computer monitors. "Commander, call the distance at intervals."

"Yes, sir. Unknown is 8-5-0 miles out and closing," Commander Bowman replied.

"Just the mileage, Commander," Scotty ordered.

Scotty listened intently for the commander's voice as he continued to watch the computer blip come ever closer to his base. "At 7-5-0…6-5-0…5-5-0…4-5-0…3-5-0…," the commander's voice droned on and on. Scotty sat on the edge of his seat, half-wishing that he were the pilot of one of the launched F-18s getting ready to do battle with these bastards. "At 2-5-0…1-5-0…1-0-0…9-0…8-0…7-0…sir! The bastard is turning and gaining altitude. Shit, he's going vertical right back into space!" Commander Bowman cried out.

A few minutes later, Scotty watched with relief as the unknown went beyond their sensor range deep into space. "CAG, keep your boys up for another half hour in the area, then land them. JW, stay on alert until the aircraft are recovered. Well done, gentlemen. Please pass it on," Scotty ordered, thankful that the first incident was now apparently over, and correctly guessed that it was only the opening act of a long struggle to come.

"Thank you, sir," came immediate replies from JW and Captain Kendall. "Commander, I'm going to remain here for a while. If I fall asleep, and I am dog-tired, just give me a poke," Scotty pleaded, then added, "You and your command did good, Commander."

"Thank you, sir. Like you said, we have only the best working here," Commander Bowman replied as he watched Scotty begin to fall asleep.

Later, Scotty felt someone shaking his shoulder and opened his eyes only to see Commander Bowman looking at him. "Yes, Commander?" Scotty said.

"Sir, it's 0300 hours and nothing further has happened. Why don't you go to your quarters and get some good sleep? That's only a suggestion, sir," Bowman pleaded with his admiral, whom he had come to respect during the event earlier in the evening. Scotty had shown calmness and a willingness to fight if it was necessary. Yes, Bowman decided, this was a good man, and a damn good commander.

"And a good suggestion that is, Commander. What about yourself? When do you get to sleep?" Scotty asked.

"My relief is due shortly, sir. Thank you," Bowman replied, somewhat surprised, as a superior officer never expressed interest in him before. *Yes*, he thought again, *this is a good commander.*

Scotty pulled himself up from his chair, which was comfortable enough for him to sleep in, and walked toward the exit, saying, "Good night, Commander."

"Good night, sir!" Bowman proudly responded.

As Scotty approached his quarters, he thought about stopping at Doreen's door and knocking, but he realized that the Marine guard, a new one at that, was standing not thirty feet away. As he passed Doreen's quarters, he looked longingly at her door and could only imagine what lay beyond it. When he reached his quarters, the Marine on duty opened the door for him. Scotty thanked him and asked that he be awakened at 0600 hours. Once inside his quarters, Scotty dragged himself into the bedroom and fell into bed fully clothed with a smile on his face. His last thought of the day was of Doreen as he fell fast asleep.

---

[55] Engines started.

ANOTHER DAY

SCOTTY WAS AWAKENED FROM A deep REM sleep by the ringing of the telephone next to his bed. Feeling a little uncomfortable, he opened his eyes and looked down at himself. It was then he realized that he was still in his full dress uniform. He uttered, "Damn," to himself and then reached for the telephone. Before he could even greet the caller, a loud voice called out, "Good morning, Admiral! It's 0600. Is there anything the admiral requires?"

"Yes, the admiral requires more sleep!" Scotty replied to the cherry voice, wondering why some people are so damn happy in the morning.

"Admiral?" came a hesitant reply.

"That's okay, I was only kidding. Thank you for the call," Scotty replied and hung up the telephone before the caller could reply. Scotty then thought to himself, *My god, I am becoming like the admiral. I better stop this!* Getting out of bed like a bolt of lightning, Scotty quickly undressed and left his clothes in a pile on the floor, swearing to himself that he would pick them up later. He then entered the bathroom, shaved, and showered in near record time and quickly dressed into a fresh flight suit. For a moment, he thought about getting dressed into a more formal uniform in order to set the right example but then remembered just how comfortable he felt in a flight suit. Scotty walked out of his bedroom, left his quarters, said hello to the Marine guard, and knocked on Doreen's door.

Doreen hurried to the door, knowing that it was Scotty. When she opened the door, Scotty smiled slightly and looked her over from head to toe. Scotty thought to himself that she looked absolutely stunning in her dress white uniform, military enough to pass inspection but custom-tailored enough to reveal the gentle curves of the body hiding underneath. Doreen was taken aback a bit by his inspection of her, looked down at herself and then at Scotty, and asked, "What?"

Smiling with a slight hint of a smirk on his face, Scotty answered, "Oh, nothing. I was kind of hoping for your definition of *casual*, like in Zambia." He was rewarded for his observation by a punch in the stomach and being pulled, by both arms, into Doreen's quarters. For a second they stood apart looking at each other, then embraced. Scotty kicked the door closed with his foot and moved even closer to her. For almost a minute, their bodies were locked in passion while their minds could think only of each other and the joy and fulfillment each could give to the other. Doreen broke their kiss and looked at Scotty, saying, "I am so going to miss you—oh my god, I only have fifteen minutes!" She then separated from Scotty and crossed the room to get her gym bag, which doubled as her suitcase.

Scotty then realized what was wrong and reminded her that his order was travel away from the base was to be in civilian clothes only. Doreen then realized her mistake and entered her bedroom. Not to be outdone by Scotty, she stripped her uniform and undergarments off and put on a thin camisole and a pink thong. Scotty was sitting on a couch in the living room, paging through a magazine, about twenty feet from her bedroom door. Doreen walked two steps beyond the doorway and, in a soft, sexy, and drawn-out voice, cooed, "Oh, Admiraaaal." When she saw him look, Doreen drew her legs together, slightly bent to the right, thrust her left shoulder forward, and placed her hands on her upper thighs, tilted her head slightly, and pursed her lips in a kiss. As Scotty let out an excited "Wow!" Doreen quickly turned around, bent half-over, looked behind her at Scotty, and thrust her tush slightly upward. Doreen watched as Scotty quickly threw the magazine down, lifted himself from the couch in one fast movement, and came toward her. Doreen very quickly took the two steps back into her bedroom, closed the door, and locked it securely. Scotty reached her bedroom door just as Doreen turned the lock on it. To keep the game alive, Scotty cried out, "Ah, come on, Doreen, open the door…please." The only response he received was laughter from the bedroom. Scotty smiled to himself and went back to the couch and picked up the magazine.

A few minutes later, Doreen emerged dressed in black pants, a white silk peasant blouse, and a waist-length thin black leather coat. Looking at Scotty, Doreen asked as she spun around in a circle so that he could see her from all sides, "Is this civilian enough?"

"I wouldn't guess for a minute that you were a captain in the Navy," Scotty replied.

As Doreen busied herself with last-minute preparations, she asked, "Michael, could you do me a favor and watch what the admiral eats for the next few days? He can't keep eating like he is eating. I'm afraid something might happen to him, Michael."

"I'll do better than that," Scotty replied as he picked up the telephone and spoke to the head chef and then the mess hall.

Doreen listened to Scotty as he gave orders regarding the admiral's menu and silently cheered what she heard. When Scotty hung up, Doreen observed, "He sure isn't going to like it."

"Yeah, but it may keep him alive a little longer. Besides, over the next few days, he may like it and come to realize that he has to eat healthy," Scotty replied, also worried about his friend.

In order to lighten the moment, Doreen asked Scotty if he thought it was possible that they might be able to get away from the base when she returned. Scotty had been thinking the same thing for a few days now and replied, "I was thinking that maybe next week or so we could go to New York City. I have to break the news to my mother and Marlene. Besides, we have to rescue those agents the admiral left at the house.

"Knowing my mother and Marlene, they are probably driving them nuts. Never mind that they more than likely have gained at least ten pounds each from all the food that Mother and Marlene are probably serving up."

"What are you going to do with your house?" Doreen asked. "It's such a nice, warm house."

"I'm going to keep it. I love that old firehouse. Besides, from what I've gathered from our talks with the admiral and Chester, this job is regrettably going to involve some politicking, and some of it may be in the city. I suppose it can also serve as a safe house for us. I mean, let's say we need a secure location to meet someone from another country or something. It provides an ideal location. No one would ever believe that we are running a military operation against aliens from an old firehouse in the middle of New York City. I'll talk to JW about it and see what he has to say," Scotty replied, really unsure of just what he was going to do.

"I love your old firehouse too. You should keep it, Michael," Doreen replied.

Doreen quickly finished her last-minute packing, and Scotty stood up and walked over to her. Doreen looked into his eyes and whispered, "Well, I guess this is goodbye for a while."

Scotty was looking in her eyes and knew that the next few days would be intolerable without her. She had become his strength and wisdom. He wanted to say, "No, I won't let you go," but that was impossible. Scotty didn't respond but instead kissed her ever so softly, like the touch of a butterfly. Neither Scotty nor Doreen wanted the moment to end, but a Marine knocking on the door ended their moment. Scotty opened the door, exchanged greetings with the soldier, and invited him in. Marine Private David James picked up Doreen's bag and invited them to follow him. As they left Doreen's quarters and walked down the hallway, Doreen looked at Scotty and asked, "What was that you were saying about Zambia?" Scotty laughed slightly and remained silent until they reached the hangar deck and the waiting vehicles.

Scotty understood the standard government-issued sport utility vehicle, devoid of any markings and private license plates, but he couldn't fathom the beat-up old station wagon parked there. As Scotty pondered whether or not JW was going in the junk business, JW introduced Doreen to her security team, which consisted of three tough-looking male Marines and a woman who looked like she should be on the cover of a fashion magazine. While the men looked like Marines in their civilian clothes, Doreen and her new companion looked like two college girls on vacation. As the others exchanged small talk, JW walked over to Scotty, who was still examining the station wagon. When JW approached, Scotty asked, "JW, mind telling me what this heap is doing here? If this is your car, I'm gonna have to get you a raise."

JW laughed slightly and replied, "What you are looking at, Admiral, is a fifty-thousand-dollar car."

"You got gypped!" Scotty interrupted.

"Believe it or not, we bought this car new and then redesigned it. The boys in the paint shop weathered it and made it look real old. The blue door looks like it was purchased from a junkyard and clashes real well with the overall color of silver. Next, a special engine and transmission were put in. The car was armor plated under the body panels, and bulletproof glass was added. Special radio equipment was also installed. This car will be manned by three of my men, heavily armed, following the captain and her escort about two hundred yards back. Both vehicles will, of course, be in constant contact. I also have two men at the airport waiting for them, and two more already in Washington, awaiting their arrival."

"Seems like you thought of everything, JW. Most impressive," Scotty commented as he then walked over to Doreen and met her security team.

JW called his team together and issued last-minute orders as Doreen and Scotty said their goodbyes. Doreen said she would call, and Scotty cautioned her to remember to use a landline only. JW then ordered everyone into the vehicles, and Doreen kissed Scotty on the cheek and ran to the sport utility vehicle. Scotty waved at first, put his hand down at his side, and winked at Doreen as he watched the cars drive toward the rear of the hangar deck and disappear up a circular ramp to the surface. "She will be fine," JW reassured Scotty as they walked toward the elevator. As the two men waited for the elevator, Scotty said, "Thanks, JW." JW didn't answer because he understood what didn't have to be said.

JW went back to his office to sweat out the rest of the day as Doreen's party made their way to Washington, DC. He wouldn't leave his office until he received a telephone call from his team later that day confirming that they had arrived safely and all was well. Of course, the caller would be leaving a message on an answering machine and speak the words, "Hi, Dad, just calling to let you know that I made it back to college. Love ya! Talk to you later. Oh, hey, Dad, think you could send me some extra money sometime? I need another book for one of my classes. Bye!"

Scotty went to the admiral's quarters and knocked on the door. "Come in, Scotty," came a booming response. Scotty was surprised to find the admiral dressed in his uniform and working at a desk. "Captain Stark get off okay?" he inquired. Scotty reassured him that they left on time and should be back in Washington in a few hours. The admiral finished writing in his ledger, put his pen down, looked up at Scotty, and ordered, "Let's eat. I'm famished!" Scotty readily agreed to the admiral's suggestion and told him that he wanted to eat in the mess hall. The admiral protested but reluctantly agreed.

Together, the old commander and the new walked down the hallway, discussing their views on who would win the Super Bowl that year. Scotty then brought up the incident last night with the unknown and filled the admiral in on every detail. When Scotty was finished recounting the story, Morrison asked if he would have shot the craft down. "I gave the order, sir. But he turned away before he crossed the threshold I established," Scotty replied.

"I thought you were going to wait until you set up your bases before you were going to act," the admiral observed.

"That's true, sir, but the safety of the base was at risk. It's a different situation!" Scotty shot back.

"You're right. Actually, you showed great restraint and coolness. Personally, I would have shot the bastard down, anyway. You did good, Scotty. You showed the base that you are not afraid to act, and I am sure that has impressed the hell out of a lot of people," Morrison replied, and they both then continued on in silence.

As they entered the mess hall, Scotty asked the cook if the admiral's breakfast was ready yet. Cookie, as most cooks in the military are called, suggested that they sit down as their breakfast was still being prepared. Morrison wondered what the fuss was all about as he eyed the mountains of French toast and piles of bacon and sausage. Scotty directed the admiral to an empty table, as he knew that Morrison would not take kindly to his breakfast. Settling into a comfortable chair, the admiral started thumping his fingers on the table in anticipation of his meal. When he saw a cook coming their way with a platter, the admiral unfolded a napkin and placed it on his lap and looked down at the table as his breakfast was placed before him. He looked up and said, "Son, there must be some mistake." But all the admiral saw was the back of the cook as he scurried away. Morrison then looked at Scotty and demanded, "What's this, an appetizer?"

Cautiously, knowing full well that an argument was coming, Scotty replied, "No, sir. It's your breakfast."

"Breakfast? Hell, I wouldn't feed this to a dog! Where the hell are the bacon and biscuits. And I want some of those miniature cinnamon buns. What did you do, hire a cook from hell?" Morrison asked.

"No, Admiral. Same cook, better diet," Scotty replied, tongue in cheek.

"Diet! Hell, a bird wouldn't survive on this. By the way, just what the hell is this supposed to be, anyway?" Morrison asked, somewhat resigned to his fate.

"Four whole-wheat pancakes with fresh blueberries, topped with diet syrup. You have eight ounces of freshly squeezed orange juice, one cup of decaffeinated coffee with skim milk, which also, by the way, is in your bowl of oat flake cereal. Be sure to eat the bowl of fruit. It was freshly cut this morning," Scotty replied, expecting another argument, also trying to think what he would do if the admiral simply got up and walked to the mess line.

"You know that I can have you arrested for this. The charge would be attempted murder. You wouldn't like that, would you?" Morrison stated, deciding whether or not to go with Scotty's menu or go and get some real food.

"Look it, Admiral, yesterday you gave me command of this base. Part of my responsibility is to ensure the health and welfare of every woman and man in this base, and right now that includes you. I have always thought of you as a surrogate father, and I don't want to see you eat your way to a heart attack. Doreen and I want you to be around. So please eat your breakfast and try to reverse your eating habits," Scotty pleaded.

What Scotty said hit the admiral like sharp daggers. He lowered his head, tried to lighten the moment, and replied, "Then a son, since I have always looked upon you as the son I never had, should listen to the father and order him a real breakfast fit for a workingman."

"Sometimes in life the son has to help the father to make sure that he will be around for the son and grandchildren," Scotty replied, desperately trying to sway the admiral.

Morrison, still looking down at his meager breakfast, replied, "Touché!" picked up a spoon, and began eating his cereal.

Scotty let out a deep breath and, likewise, began eating his breakfast, the same food and portions that the admiral had. Morrison broke the silence as they ate and talked about the base as he began to educate Scotty as to its workings and the people who made it work.

As Scotty and Morrison were leaving the mess hall, a chef came up to them and handed each a small brown paper bag. "What's this?" Morrison asked as he began to open the bag.

"Midmorning snack. You have an apple, orange, and pear. Just for insurance, I asked them to include a health bar," Scotty replied.

"Great! I can't hardly wait for lunch," Morrison replied and then added, "Scotty, we have to stop at the hangar deck. The morning supply plane is due in, and I have a surprise for you."

As Scotty and the admiral stood side by side on the hangar deck by the aircraft elevator, the giant platform ground to life. Scotty watched in amazement as the huge elevator lowered into the hangar deck, carrying a C-141 four-jet-engine cargo plane. Being a naval aviator, Scotty was used to aircraft elevators carrying planes from the hangar deck to the flight deck of a carrier and then back down again in an endless dance of aircraft movement, but he was amazed at the size and capability of the two giant elevators in the base.

When the elevator came to a rest, an aircraft tow truck pulled up to the front of the airplane. Two crewmen hooked a tow bar onto the front wheels of the aircraft, and the tow truck pulled the cargo plane off the elevator and parked it in an open space nearby. A ramp door at the back of the aircraft slowly opened, and when it reached the deck level, a few flatbed trucks that seemed inches off the ground backed up to the aircraft, and pallet after pallet of food and equipment were loaded onto the trucks. When one truck was finished and pulled away, another would immediately take its place. In less than fifteen minutes, the cavernous interior of the aircraft was empty of cargo. While the cargo was being unloaded, a small team of aircraft technicians and maintenance people went to work on the aircraft. The pilots and crew of the cargo plane didn't leave their plane, as they were busy preparing the aircraft for their flight back to their base, only to have to make the same trip again tomorrow.

Once the cargo had been removed, Scotty stood and watched as a figure walked down the center of the cargo bay of the aircraft toward the exit ramp. Scotty couldn't believe his eyes when Jonesy emerged from the aircraft. Jonesy stopped at the end of the ramp and dropped his bags. Removing the sunglasses from his eyes, Jonesy cautiously looked around and spotted Scotty walking toward him. "Scotty, you old Pirate. I heard you were back!" Extending his arms away from his side slightly with the palms of his hands open, he continued, "You believe this?" Making reference to his uniform with the insignia of a lieutenant. "Some fool went and promoted me. Now, who in the hell would be that stupid?"

"That would be me, Lieutenant!" came the booming voice of Admiral Morrison.

Jonesy snapped to attention and held a salute as the admiral walked up to him and came to a rest one foot away from him. "What's the matter, Sailor, aren't you proud of that uniform?" Morrison asked, trying to keep the laughter in and a smile from his face.

"Y-y-yes, sir!" Jonesy was barely able to reply.

"Good," Morrison first replied and then returned the salute. He then turned away and told Scotty that he was going to join Chester in Space Command. Morrison walked away shaking his head, wondering why he had done what he did. Scotty's reputation for, shall we say, acquiring certain things was legendary in the Navy, and when he teamed up with Jonesy, well, that was when he earned the call sign Pirate. Morrison knew that the infamous list of their "acquisitions" went way beyond beer. As he walked, Morrison recounted a part of the list: one refrigerated shipping container of steaks, a couple of jet engines from the Marine side of a naval air station that were needed by Scotty's group, one truckload of computers that apparently wound up in a needy school district (but no one could prove anything), one shipping container of furniture belonging to an Army general that Morrison knew went to a newlywed sailor when he received a thank-you note from the grateful couple, one transit bus from the city of Norfolk that might have wound up at a retirement home newly painted and the vehicle identification numbers removed, and perhaps the best caper of all, a building. That one couldn't possibly be surpassed. Morrison laughed to himself as he recounted the story. It seemed that the Navy, at great expense, had constructed a building for officers to use while in transit. It was furnished with all new furniture and appliances and was truly a hallmark of comfort and convenience. One day, before the building was opened for use, a large flatbed truck and a crane were allowed on the Navy base. After presenting the proper paperwork, the construction crew went about putting the building on the truck. After a hard day's work, the truck left with the building in tow. The base commander made an inquiry two days later as to why, after the Navy had put so much into the project, it decided to remove the building. When he realized that he had been duped, the base commander set out to find his building. After a week of searching, he found an orphanage on the other side of town that had just opened, the exterior of which looked suspiciously identical to the missing building. Realizing that he was beat, the base commander returned to his command with his tail between his legs and an awful lot of explaining to do. When Morrison heard of the theft, he checked on Scotty, and sure enough, the *Eisenhower* was in port that day and, you guessed it, Scotty and Jonesy, as well as a large part of the crew, were on liberty the day of the building's disappearance, but somehow none of them were reported to have left the confines of the base. *My god,* Morrison thought as he walked to Space Command, *I've turned over command of this base to a master thief and his apprentice!* The admiral did find some comfort, though, when he concluded that it was best not to worry about some things. He did chuckle when he wondered what havoc those two would cause throughout the world when they had the time to go "shopping."

When Morrison turned and walked away, Scotty and Jonesy walked toward each other, shook each other's hand, and it was as if the years had melted into the past. "Red called the ship and told us about what happened on your way back from South America. Is that what this is all about? And you, an admiral? Congratulations!" Jonesy spoke up and saluted. He was proud to receive a salute back from his longtime friend.

"Yeah, I'll explain it all later. Let's get you settled in and get you started on your day first," Scotty replied as he and Jonesy started walking down the hangar deck.

"Why did you send for me, Scotty?" Jonesy inquired.

"I have need of your special talents," Scotty answered as he looked at his friend.

"Why? What are we stealing? It looks like you have all the toys you could possibly need right here, especially those sexy planes over there," Jonesy remarked as he looked around the hangar deck and paid special attention to the X-aircraft.

"Nothing yet, although I could use some regular automobiles around here, and we will always need computer equipment, but not till later. We have something more important to do first," Scotty replied.

As the two men walked, they discussed the *Eisenhower* and her crew. Jonesy brought Scotty up-to-date on the crew and the happenings aboard ship. Scotty was saddened to learn that Seaman Arthur Forrester, the man whose party they had stolen the beer for, was back in the Navy. It wasn't because a beached sailor longed for the sea but rather because his wife had lied to him. The child she bore was not his, and after the divorce, he went back to doing what he knew best.

Scotty went to Vinson's office and introduced Jonesy to him and left him in his care for the rest of the day. Those two, as well as Lieutenant Cunningham, had to get to know each other since they all would be working on the same project together, Scotty thought. He wanted to ask the admiral the status of Art Givone again, but he thought better of it and simply wished he would arrive soon.

Scotty walked to the movie theater and was surprised to find every seat filled a full twenty minutes before the film was to be shown. Finding Lieutenant Cunningham pacing back and forth behind the curtain, reading from some index cards as if he were trying to memorize something, Scotty went over to him and asked if he was okay.

Lieutenant Cunningham told Scotty that he edited the film last night and, as he had ordered, the film was vivid in its detail. Scotty thanked him and told him to take it easy and ordered him to try to relax. It now being time for the first showing, Scotty and Cunningham emerged from behind the curtain and walked to a waiting podium.

Upon seeing Scotty, the entire theater stood at attention and saluted. Scotty returned the salute and asked everyone to please sit down. Scotty gave a few introductory remarks and then turned the affair over to Lieutenant Cunningham. Cunningham was a bit nervous at first, but when the film began, he settled down as he gave commentary and remembered the sight and smells of the scene being shown before him. Scotty, in the meantime, had gone to the back of the theater and took up a strategic position out of sight of the exit, but from his position he would be able to see the people as they left.

When the film was over, Cunningham asked those gathered if there were any questions. Mostly people seemed to sit in silence, but a few brave souls spoke up and asked questions about the human remains. One individual asked if there was any hard evidence that tied the incident directly to the aliens. Scotty could see the look of surprise on Cunningham's face, but he very patiently repeated the facts leading up to the incident again and wove his statements into a concise report, leaving no doubt as to who the perpetrators were. Scotty stretched his neck trying to see who asked the question but couldn't. He recognized the voice but just couldn't tie it to a face.

When Lieutenant Cunningham finished and all the questions were answered, those in attendance seemed to just sit there transfixed and spoke with one another in hushed tones. Cunningham asked if anyone had another question, and when no one answered, he told them that the presentation was completed and invited them back for the other showings, should they desire to attend. Still, no one moved. When Cunningham left the stage and the lights came back on to their full brightness, people began to drift out of the theater. From his vantage point, Scotty wanted to observe their faces as they left. He saw the look of shock and horror on some, but what he mostly saw was a committed look of determination. After the theater had emptied, Scotty sought out Lieutenant Cunningham to congratulate him on his fine presentation. He found him hunched over a desk, busily sorting through some notes. "You did fine, Lieutenant," Scotty called out as he approached.

Cunningham stood up erect, saluted, and replied, "Thank you, sir. Do you think the message was received?"

"Thanks to you, yeah. I'd say it was not only received but also committed to memory and provided a new sense of purpose for the crew. You did real well. So why the long face?" Scotty was gaining respect for the young lieutenant and wondered why he looked so down in the dumps.

"It's nothing, sir." Cunningham looked at the floor and then back at Scotty, then continued, "When I was giving the commentary to the film, all the horror came back along with the smells of the tent and the area, coming alive in my mind as if I were back there in that tent. And the children…why the children? Hell, I have a sister no older than one of those victims. It could have been her, sir."

"I know, Lieutenant, I know. It was a nightmare, and to think that those bastards actually got away with it. But it's because of that film and your commentary that the crew of this base will be more committed than ever to accomplish what has to be done. You may not realize it, Lieutenant, but you have done more for the mission of this base in a few short minutes than years of planning and prodding could have done. I promise you this: one day we will be able to hunt these monsters down, and when we do, there will be no quarter. No one but no one will ever get away with what they have done. And you, Lieutenant, will have played a major role in allowing us to do that," Scotty replied, trying to change Cunningham's mood.

"Yes, sir. Thank you, sir!" came a quick reply and a flash of conviction over the lieutenant's face.

"We have a couple of hours until the next presentation so why don't you come with me and watch a plane disappear?" Scotty ordered.

ON THE RUNWAY

As Scotty and Cunningham made their way to the demonstration, they stopped in Space Command to say hello to Chester. Scotty also wanted to remind Morrison that he would be back to eat lunch with him and Chester. That reminder was met with pleas and accusations of cruelty and physical torture. Scotty simply laughed it off and said goodbye as he and Cunningham next made their way to the operations office, where Jonesy was still being processed. Once his medical record was examined to make sure that all his immunity shots were up-to-date, Jonesy was allowed to leave. Talking into his wrist radio, Scotty asked Vinson to join them and asked him to bring along Executive Officer Beverly Hocker. Scotty knew that he had to start developing a working relationship with her, and besides, he wanted her to meet Jonesy as soon as possible. Scotty knew that Jonesy tended to become a pain in the ass when he got down to work and totally disregarded rank and protocol.

As the small group gathered on the hangar deck, Scotty made the introductions, and to his surprise, Jonesy and Beverly Hocker seemed to be hitting it off. Captain Kendall came over and announced that the test aircraft was on the runway and ready for the demonstration. He then invited them to get into a vehicle for the drive to the surface, and once they were on the surface, Scotty found himself squinting as the sun was burning bright and he had not been on the surface for almost two full days now. Donning sunglasses, as the rest of the group did, Scotty suggested that they step out from under the green lights of the hologram. Of course the group followed the direction (order) of their new commander and stood approximately fifty yards away from the hologram projection.

Once everyone was ready and binoculars were handed out, Scotty gave the order to Captain Kendall for the aircraft to take off. The group followed the sound as the plane screeched down the runway and then emerged from the green light of the hologram. Captain Kendall informed the group that the pilot would fly over the base from left to right at a speed of slightly under four hundred miles per hour at a height of one thousand feet. As the aircraft gained altitude and disappeared off to the left, Captain Kendall told the group that the pilot would make four passes. The first one visible, and the next two hopefully invisible, and the last pass visible.

As the F-18 approached from the left, all heads were turned skyward, following the progress of the aircraft streaking overhead and then turning to make another pass. Seconds later, the group heard the sound of the engines as it approached but could not see the aircraft. Confused faces looked at one another, trying to get help in locating the aircraft as the noise grew louder. When the plane sounded as if it was almost upon them, Scotty could detect a very slight distortion in the sky, but all that he saw was clear sky and some clouds. Scotty likened the experience to driving down the road on a hot summer day when, occasionally, when you approach an inclination in the road, you are able to see the heat waves emanating from the hot surface.

When the aircraft passed overhead and was going around for another pass, the small assemblage busily asked one another if they had seen anything. Of course the replies were negative. As the aircraft came in on another pass, all eyes were determined to find it in the sky. Vinson was the only other person who detected the slight distortion as it passed overhead. On its last pass, Captain Kendall radioed the pilot and told him to turn off the masking device as he passed overhead.

As the group followed the sound of the engines and guessed that the airplane was really close, suddenly the aircraft became visible, to the cheers of those on the ground. "That's one hell of an aircraft!" Scotty commented to Kendall. As the group began moving back to the vehicle for the ride belowground, Scotty pulled Kendall aside and told him that he wanted to meet with him and Captain Bone after dinner.

Once back on the hangar deck, Vinson, Jonesy, Hocker, and Cunningham went on their way to lunch. Scotty lingered and went with Kendall over to the X-aircraft. Kendall asked Scotty when he wanted to start learning to fly the aircraft. Scotty replied that he wasn't sure when he would be available. Scotty and Kendall then discussed the readiness of the aircraft and the status of the pilots who were to carry the fight forward. Kendall expressed confidence in his men and women but regretted that he might shortly be ordering some of them to their death. Scotty understood how he felt, but what had to be done simply had to be done. Scotty left Kendall and went to Space Command to meet the admiral and Chester for lunch.

LUNCH: ACT 2 OF THE DIET

S COTTY, CHESTER, AND MORRISON WALKED the mile or so through twisted corridors to the mess hall. Of course, the admiral was grumbling all the way about what he wasn't going to be able to eat. As they neared the mess hall, Morrison began to think out loud. "I can smell hamburgers, french fries, and also fried onion rings. Wait, I can also detect a faint wisp of corned beef!" With the aroma of corned beef in the air, he cast a stone-cold look at Scotty. "And rye bread and mustards. God, I can even smell the pickles! It also smells like pizza, some vegetables—probably overcooked—and cake, yes, chocolate cake." Turning toward Scotty again, as they were now entering the mess hall and were being directed to a table by a mess steward, Morrison asked, "What's for lunch? Probably peanuts and water, followed by a snack cracker, if we are lucky."

As the threesome sat down, Scotty asked back, "Look, if you would like, I'll have some peanut butter put on that snack cracker. Will that keep you happy?"

Morrison was a little surprised when a cook set three identical meals down on the table consisting of a cup of French onion soup, a mixed green salad, a small filet mignon steak, fresh string beans garnished with sliced almonds, a glass of water, and a small piece of chocolate cake. Of course, a pot of decaffeinated coffee was added to the table, as well as a pitcher of skim milk. Glancing over at Chester, Morrison winked at him and then turned toward Scotty and continued his complaining. "You know, when I was a kid, we had a family dog and we fed him more than this!"

Scotty didn't play into the little melodrama and let the remark pass. Instead, he turned his attention toward Chester and inquired about his trip to meet with Captain Montgomery. Chester expressed his regrets that he had to leave in the morning in order to arrive just as Captain Montgomery should be docking at the Navy base in Puerto Rico.

For the remainder of the lunch, they talked about the possibility of what they might find off the coast of Hawaii. As they were leaving the mess hall, Scotty again received snack bags, but this time the admiral accepted the bag without comment. Scotty was a little disappointed that the admiral didn't even look in the bag, as he had ordered a small bag of chocolate candy to be put in the bags along with fresh fruit and a health bar.

Once on the elevator, Morrison told Scotty that an important piece of equipment was on the afternoon supply run and asked him to meet the aircraft and ensure its safety.

Scotty readily agreed and followed the admiral's order.

DON'T ICE CREAM TRUCKS RING THE BELL ANYMORE?

B Y THE TIME SCOTTY REACHED the hangar deck, the afternoon supply aircraft had already arrived and the unloading had commenced. Scotty again watched in awe as the trucks used to unload the aircraft danced their dance of efficiency, and in no time the plane was unloaded. Once the trucks were gone, Scotty walked up to the loading ramp in time to see the shadow of a man walking toward the back of the plane, flanked on each side by two larger men. It appeared from the position of the man in the middle that his hands were bound. As they emerged into the light, Scotty and Art Givone eyed each other at the same time. Art tried to walk faster toward Scotty but was restrained by the two men. Scotty let the drama unfold before him, trying desperately not to laugh. As they approached, Scotty noticed that Art's mouth had been covered over by surgical tape to prevent him from talking. Once they were close to each other, the larger of the two guards spoke up. "Admiral Scott, I am Agent Brewer. I was instructed to deliver this package to you and use any means available to expedite the matter."

"Well done, Agent. But were the handcuffs and mouth tape necessary?" Scotty asked.

"Sir, we handcuffed him in order to protect him. We were afraid that when he woke up from the drug we gave him, he might go a little crazy, considering the circumstances. When he did wake up, he started hollering at everyone about his rights as a taxpayer and all. It was pretty distracting for the flight crew, so purely in the interest of safety, we covered up his mouth," the agent replied in a humble voice and then paused and continued, "Sir, would you like the restraints removed now?"

Scotty put his head down and stared at the floor, trying to hide his smile, knowing how Arty, because of his skills, could drive the most humble of men to drink. "Yes, Agent, remove them now. And thank you. You are both dismissed."

One agent removed the surgical tape from Arty's mouth while Agent Brewer inserted a handcuff key into the lock and removed the bracelets. Both agents then quickly walked away and reboarded the supply aircraft. As they walked away, the agents heard Arty shout, "You sons of bitches! Who do you think you are? I got both your names, and I'm gonna report you both. How do you like that, you bastards?"

Scotty reached up, placed his hand on Arty's shoulder, and in a strong voice, told his friend, "Arty, calm down. There is no one to report them to. Officially, they don't exist."

"What do you mean they don't exist? They are right there!" It was then that Arty grabbed ahold of his senses and sized up the situation and noticed Scotty's uniform. "Where the hell am I? And since when are you an admiral? The law business boring or something? This is the United States, isn't it?"

"Arty, I'll answer all your questions in time, but yes, this is the United States, and yes, I am an admiral. But no, the law business wasn't all that boring, but this..." Scotty paused as he raised his hand and pointed to the aircraft and people around him. "This is far more important than you can now realize."

Arty followed Scotty's lead and looked around and noticed the variety of aircraft parked around him, but he wouldn't let go. "You know what those bastards did? I was driving to work this morning when they hit me from behind. Before I could get out of the car, one of them was by my window. When I lowered the window, he stuck his hand in the car and sprayed me in the face with something. I couldn't move, but I was awake. In seconds, a tow truck and an ambulance arrived. They removed me from the car, tied me down to the gurney, and put me in an ambulance. Then a nurse—maybe she wasn't a nurse—gave me a shot of something, and bingo, the next thing I remember is waking up in an airplane. And by the way, what was all that green light when we landed? Where the hell is this place? Come to think of it, I have to call work. Where's a phone?"

"Art, I'm sorry for the way you were treated. I'm afraid it was my fault. It seems that the admiral took me in a literal sense and had you kidnapped." Scotty paused and looked at his disheveled friend, then continued, "I desperately need your help, my friend. Give me one day, and if you don't want to be here, you can leave and return home. You'll just have to sign the National Secrets Act and promise not to reveal what you will see and hear today. By the way, it's damn good to see you."

Cracking a smile for the first time since his arrival, Arty extended his hand and shook Scotty's extended hand, saying, "It's damn good to see you too, Scotty. Or should I say Admiral Scott?"

"Scotty will always do, Art. Before you start asking a lot of questions, I want to show you a few things first, okay?" Scotty replied as he and Arty began to walk toward the big doors at the back of the hangar deck.

"So why did you quit the law?" Arty asked as they continued to walk. "I thought it was going great?"

"You heard me talk about Admiral Morrison. Well, he asked me to do a job for him, and I did. When the job was over, he made me an offer that I just couldn't refuse. It wasn't the money or anything like that. I'll be making less now than what I made in a month in civilian life. It may sound corny coming from me, but it was a moral obligation that made me sign up," Scotty replied.

"And probably a pretty face too," Arty shot back, knowing that he was wrong, as Scotty was always a man guided by principle rather than by rewards.

"Yeah, that, too, but she didn't have anything to do with my decision," Scotty answered in a low voice as they approached the doors.

"Does she have a friend by chance?" Arty asked, always interested in the fairer sex.

"Perhaps," Scotty off-handedly replied as they stopped in front of the doors and returned the salute of a Marine dressed in combat gear with a loaded M16 in his other hand.

"Open them up please!" Scotty ordered.

Scotty and Artie took a few steps backward as the giant doors opened. Arty's mouth hung open as he visually examined the flying saucers within the room. At first, his only reaction was "Holy shit!" but after a few seconds, he commented, "So you guys are the aliens. I knew it! It's a government conspiracy. You guys have been flying these things around and telling people that there are aliens visiting Earth."

"No, Arty, these are for real, and the aliens are for real," Scotty replied.

"As in little-green-men-from-Mars real?" Arty excitedly asked.

"No, as in thieving, murdering bastards for real!" Scotty replied with conviction, then continued, "The one off to the side over there is the infamous Roswell craft, but it didn't crash in Roswell. The other three saucers were found close to here. That triangle-shaped one over there, it was built and designed by the crew of this base. It's sort of a test bed. Come on, let's get you a closer look."

Scotty led Arty into the room and let him roam around, examining the exterior of the craft. When Arty returned, Scotty led him into one of the craft and let a technician give him a brief explanation of the workings of the craft. When they were finished, Scotty and Arty left the room and began walking toward the elevator. As they walked, Scotty explained the events leading up to the present, from the encounter when Ice was killed to the events in Brazil. Arty listened to his friend talk and didn't interrupt even though he knew about Ice's death. To most, the story would seem fantastic, but Arty had seen the evidence and knew his friend well. Of course, it was hard to believe, but so were the events of his day so far, and yet here he was, walking in an underground military base, surrounded by aircraft and, of all things, flying saucers.

Once on the elevator, Scotty explained that they were going to a movie theater, where Art would see a film detailing the events in Brazil. Arty wanted to ask a thousand questions, but he remained silent as Scotty talked. Each sentence that his friend spoke was like a new revelation, some horrible and others filled with hope and promise.

As they exited the elevator and walked toward the theater Arty began to adjust his clothing since his shirt was half out of his pants, his suit coat torn, and his pants looked like they spent the night crumbled up under a pile of books. Scotty took notice of what Arty was doing and promised that after the film, he would get him some fresh clothes to wear.

When they entered the theater, almost every seat was taken up. Scotty directed Arty to two empty seats in the back, and they both sat down. Scotty glanced at his watch and noted that he was fifteen minutes late. Lieutenant Cunningham walked across the stage to the podium and began his introductory remarks. Scotty was supposed to have opened the meeting, but the lieutenant properly carried on after waiting a respectable period. Shortly the lights dimmed and the movie began. A faint light was left on at the podium for the benefit of Cunningham as he carried on with his narration.

During the film, Scotty could hear as Arty let out his feelings and passed comments such as, "Oh my god!" "Jesus, no!" "Those bastards!" "Jesus, how can this happen?" and what Scotty was waiting for, "You son of a bitch, I'm gonna kill ya!" When the movie concluded and the houselights came back on, Scotty could see that Arty was visibly shaken. His hands were actually trembling, and the color from his face had drained away. When questions were being taken, Arty paid close attention to every word asked and every word in the answer.

Moving ever closer to the edge of his seat, Arty couldn't contain himself any longer and stood up. Lieutenant Cunningham pointed at him and said, "Yes."

Arty spoke up. "Are we able to stop this from happening again?"

Lieutenant Cunningham noted that Arty was not dressed in a uniform and asked, "Are you a member of this base, sir?"

"No...no, I'm not. I just arrived," Arty humbly replied.

Lieutenant Cunningham spoke bluntly. "Sir, I can tell you this: The men and women that you see gathered here today are working toward that very end. Together we can and will stop this. Admiral Scott wanted all gathered here to see this film to show all of you what we are fighting for. The people on that plane could have been our brothers or our sisters or our mothers or fathers. They could have been our wives, our husbands, and even our children. No entity in the universe should be able to get away with what they have done. Our struggle will be long, but we will stop this. Sir, you are in the home of a proud band of people. We are called the Raptors, and as our name implies, we will hunt down these creatures and ensure that they will never again look upon the Earth as their murdering ground."

When Lieutenant Cunningham finished his remarks, the assemblage broke out in cheers and chants of "Raptors! Raptors!" Quieting the crew down, Lieutenant Cunningham looked directly at Arty, who was still standing, and asked, "Does that answer your question, sir?"

"Yes…yes, it does. Thank you," Arty replied and sat back down. He then glanced over at Scotty and felt as if he, too, should be part of this.

After Arty's question was answered, the meeting broke up. Scotty stood by the back of the theater and greeted the people as they left. He was happy to see the same looks of determination on their faces as he had seen earlier. Occasionally, he would glance over at Arty, who remained in his seat with his elbows propped up on the armrests and his fingers placed together with his index fingers against his lips. It was easy to see that Arty was deep in thought, probably considering what he saw. After the last person had left, Scotty walked over to his friend and asked him to accompany him. Arty rose from his seat, faced Scotty, and said, "Okay, where do I sign up?"

Scotty was a bit surprised by his fast decision and asked, "Are you sure you want to do this? It means giving up an awful lot."

"Hell yeah, I'm sure! How could anyone turn their back on what happened to those poor people? I'm not sure what I can contribute, not being a pilot or a scientist or anything, but I could at least polish the airplanes or something," Arty replied, now sure of his decision.

Scotty laughed at his comment about polishing the aircraft and said, "I have something a little more adventurous in mind than that. But that can wait until tonight. Here comes Lieutenant Cunningham. I want you to meet him since you will be working together."

When Lieutenant Cunningham reached them, he saluted Scotty and stood rigidly until the salute was returned. Scotty spoke first. "Very well done again, Lieutenant."

"Thank you, sir. Sir, I'm sorry that I began without you. I waited fifteen minutes and the crew seemed to be getting a little antsy, so I started!" Cunningham exclaimed, hoping not to get reprimanded.

"Nonsense! You did the right thing. I like officers who can think on their own, up to certain limits, that is," Scotty replied, noting that the last part of his statement sunk in as the expression on Cunningham's face registered the comment. Scotty then turned toward Arty and continued, "Lieutenant, I'd like to introduce Mr. Art Givone, soon-to-be Commander Givone. He's decided to join our growing family, thanks in no small part to your talk."

Arty looked at Scotty somewhat stunned by what he just heard and then reached out and shook Cunningham's hand. Scotty then continued, "Lieutenant, I'm going to leave him in your charge for the rest of the day. Please get him something to wear, not a uniform, since he hasn't taken the oath yet. In fact, just give him a flight suit. Also, before your next talk, kindly drop him off at base operations so he can complete the paperwork, and direct them to send him to medical when he is finished there. If you could, pick him up from medical and get him settled in. Then, please see if you can get him situated close to my quarters.

"One other thing, bring him up-to-date on our activities. Oh, I want to meet with you both in my office in Space Command at 2000 hours. Any questions?"

"No, sir, it will be my pleasure," Lieutenant Cunningham replied and then turned toward Arty, shook his hand, and said, "Welcome aboard, sir! I think you will find this place very interesting and challenging."

"Okay, then, I'll see you gentlemen later this evening. Art, thanks," Scotty said and turned and walked away but then turned back around and added, "Oh, Lieutenant, take Mr. Givone to dinner also. Okay?"

"Will do, sir. My pleasure," came the lieutenant's quick reply. Scotty then turned back around and headed off to Space Command happy with himself. His investigative team was now complete.

As Scotty turned a bend in the corridor, his wrist radio called out, "Admiral Scott." Scotty recognized JW's voice and promptly answered, "Go ahead, JW."

"Sir, I want to let you know that Captain Stark and her team arrived safe," JW replied, knowing that his news would be one less thing on Scotty's mind.

"Thanks, JW. See you later tonight," Scotty replied as a broader grin now crossed his face.

SPACE COMMAND

"HI, MARCY!" SCOTTY CALLED OUT as he entered his office area. "Good afternoon, Admiral," his secretary answered.

"Marcy, please call me Scotty."

"Yes, sir. Admiral, the admirals are in your office, waiting for you. Oh, and I have a few reports from Dr. Hewitt regarding our visitor," Marcy replied as she handed Scotty the reports.

Scotty stood by her desk and casually read the reports. Basically, they were the same: "Resting comfortably and prognosis hopeful." He concluded that the reports were as they appeared, sterile pieces of paper. Looking up, Scotty asked, "Marcy, could you do me a favor? A couple of times a day, go down to medical and look in on our guest. Most of all, make yourself visible to our good doctor. Let me know what your observations are and what, if any, progress is being made."

"It will be my pleasure, Admiral," she replied.

"Marcy!" Scotty said as he looked into her eyes.

"I mean Scotty," Marcy replied, a little uncomfortable at calling the commander of the base by his nickname.

"Good, that's—"

Scotty allowed himself to be interrupted as he heard shouts of "You're cheating!" coming from his office. Looking toward the door to his office, he noticed that the door was slightly cracked. Turning back toward his secretary, Scotty asked, "What's going on in there?"

"You have to see it to believe it, Admiral. Oh, I ordered up some popcorn for the admirals at their request. Unbuttered, of course. I hope that was all right," Marcy replied.

Scotty turned back toward the door to his office, handed Marcy the doctor's reports back, and replied, "Yeah, fine." He then slowly made his way to his office door. Trying not to make any noise, Scotty pushed the door gently open and walked in, closing the door behind him. Not believing what he saw, Scotty crept up to the conference table behind the admirals, who were sitting with their backs to him. Unable to contain his disbelief any longer, Scotty called out, "Video games!"

"Oh, shit! The ole man is here, Chester!" Morrison exclaimed.

"Sit down, Scotty. We have a controller for you. Here, we'll restart the game," Chester ordered.

Scotty sat down, picked up the controller, and played with the buttons as Chester gave Scotty a brief explanation of the functions of the different buttons. Indicating that he understood the buttons, Chester reached over and reset the game. Morrison cried out, "I'm number 1!"

Chester told Scotty that he could be the number 3 car and explained that video games sharpen dexterity skills. Scotty agreed with that statement in a positive but seemingly unbelievable tone. Once the game began, Scotty became involved in an imaginary world as he raced his car around the track and tried unsuccessfully to pass his two adversaries. It became clearly apparent to Scotty that Morrison and Chester had spent many hours developing their "dexterity skills."

After an hour, the game was put away in a cabinet along with the three controllers.

Morrison proudly announced that he was giving Scotty the game and expected better competition the next time, especially from a fighter pilot, who should be used to thinking fast and moving his hands as an integral connection to his brain. Scotty defended himself by saying that fighter pilots usually play pool in order to study the angles of attack and flight. Morrison replied in disbelief and promised to bring a video pool game back with him the next time. Scotty reminded Morrison that there were ample pool tables in the recreation area and perhaps they could play a game sometime. Morrison declined the offer, giving the excuse it would not be proper for two admirals to be seen matched against each other in a game in front of the crew. Scotty suggested that such a sight might in fact be fun for the crew to watch, but Morrison simply replied that one day Scotty would understand and it would be best, for the time being, to stick to the video games behind closed doors.

Once they were seated around the table, Scotty brought up the upcoming conference on international terrorism. Together the threesome devised a plan where all would appear normal, at least in the communications traffic. Morrison agreed to compose a series of messages to be sent out at regular intervals to the principals involved. The messages would contain the location and time of the conference dealing with the alien problem. Additional messages would detail the agenda and who was going to make presentations at the meeting. Scotty insisted that one item on the agenda be titled "Organizational Structure of Alien Resistance." Morrison and Chester agreed with Scotty's proposal but added one of their own, entitled "Conclusions of Investigating Board Regarding the Brazilian Incident." It was felt that the aliens would find this subject too good to pass up and would show their hand by trying to send a spy into the meeting. It was hoped that the security forces would be able to capture the spy and then interrogate him. Scotty felt that it was a good plan but doubted the aliens would try to penetrate the meeting with a spy but instead would electronically try to eavesdrop on the meeting.

Morrison pointed out that if they went that route, any electronic surveillance would be detected and they would be able to backtrack the device and might just as easily capture an alien. In either case, it could be a win-win situation for the good guys, Morrison concluded.

Scotty didn't feel totally at ease with the plan as presented, even though it was basically his plan. Something was nagging at him from the back of his mind, and he had a feeling that they missed something. Then he recalled an image from the video game they had been playing. When Scotty was trying to maneuver his car around the track, his car crossed into another car, and for a brief second, the images merged as if they were one car. Then it hit him: if he were an alien trying to spy on a meeting, he wouldn't just rely on electronic eavesdropping and try to figure out from the voices how many people were there. He would also want an infrared image taken to see how many people there were and use the beam as a backup for voice transmission.

Scotty carefully explained his idea. When Chester asked how they could overcome this shortcoming, Scotty's face took on an expression of frustration. Readjusting himself in his chair, Scotty suggested that they start at the beginning and talk the problem through. Morrison told Scotty to go ahead and that he and Chester would point out any possible shortcomings. Scotty got up from his chair and walked over to the small refrigerator hidden behind a wooden panel and took out a bottle of chilled water. Both Morrison and Chester declined his offer of water and instead called out for coffee. Scotty hoped that it would take a while for the coffee to arrive, to give him time to think, but in less than three minutes, the coffee arrived with a tray of water crackers. Morrison, upon seeing the crackers, asked Chester if he remembered when pastries used to be served with coffee in the afternoon. Chester mumbled a reply, not wanting to offend Scotty or his friend, about budget cuts and the quality of the food. Once Morrison and Chester were settled into their chairs with their coffee close at hand and the tray of crackers placed close to the admiral, Morrison told Scotty to begin.

Still pacing the room, Scotty took a sip of water and laid out his plan. "Let's start with what we know. The site of the meeting is in a small hotel on the outskirts of town. The structure is five stories high and is almost equal in height to the buildings surrounding it.

"Two weeks prior to the date of the scheduled meeting, I suggest that we send in four teams of security people to settle in close to the hotel and act as tourists. One of the teams should, however, settle in at the subject hotel, with their goal to monitor and get to know the other guests. Three days prior to the meeting, other teams should move into the area and set up surveillance around the hotel. One day prior to the meeting, since you have rented the entire floor, anyway, a security team should take possession and sweep the area for explosives and listening devices. Their presence should be obvious, but not too obvious to the casual observer. For example, while they will be secluded on the floor, they should eat in the restaurant of the hotel and also order up food later in the night.

"Also, they should work with the hotel staff to make sure that everything was set for the meeting. Their main goal, while providing security for a meeting that will not occur, is to ferret out any possible spy.

"In the meantime, the members of your committee should be making preparations to attend the conference and should be sending confirmations over the satellite net regarding the meeting on aliens and other relevant information, such as suggestions for the agenda and topics they would like to cover. Things must appear normal.

"On the day of the conference, the members of the committee should attend the opening ceremonies and the reception that follows at 1500 hours. After the reception is over, everyone should return to where they have been scheduled to stay.

"Shortly thereafter, everyone should slip away and return to their commands. Our security people can make a show of people arriving at the hotel just prior to the scheduled start of the secret meeting. The decoys will enter the hotel and slip out a back way or change their clothing so no one can recognize them and walk out the front door.

"Five minutes before the scheduled start of the meeting, I want our people to leave the hotel. The security set up around the hotel can monitor the entrances at that point. I don't believe that an alien will try to penetrate the hotel. If there is one around, he will likely be on the outside. But we have to also prepare in case they send a team of assassins to kill the members of the committee.

"There is, however, one last glitch that has to be overcome. Like I said before, the alien will probably also use, assuming that he is outside the hotel, an infrared beam as part of his listening device and to confirm that people are in the room. Somehow we have to put dummies in the room and have them emit a heat signature that matches the human body—"

Morrison interrupted Scotty. "There's no worry on that count, Scotty. We have such devices and have used them in the past as decoys. They're made out of a neoprene material and circulate heated glycol throughout the body to match the heat zones of a human. Hell, we can even have faces painted on them and dress them in the uniforms of the committee. Actually, forget the uniforms. We'll put them in civilian clothes," Morrison stated, helping Scotty along.

"Somehow the dummies will have to be sneaked into the hotel," Scotty added, fishing for an answer.

"No problem there either. When not in use, the entire package for one decoy fits into a small suitcase. When opened, Voila, you have one passable human decoy," Morrison replied, overcoming another problem.

"Wow, that's great! Anything else up your sleeve?" Scotty jokingly asked.

"Not for the moment, since you obviously had someone remove my personal stock of snacks from the refrigerator over there," Morrison pointed out.

"Must have been an alien invasion. I hear they like chocolate cake with whipped cream in the center. Oh, and don't forget the hard chocolate topping. Can't imagine how they got in here, though," Scotty shot back in a friendly manner.

"Scotty's right. I think I saw them leave. At least I think it was them. They had chocolate cake and whipped cream all over their mouths. Kind of hard to tell, actually. Could have been elves, though," Chester added with a laugh.

"Okay, okay, you guys have me beat. Please continue, Scotty," Morrison surrendered.

"There are two other things to consider. First is weapons. I have given orders that when the security teams travel outside of the country, they be issued the new ceramic handguns and a carbon knife. I don't want the ceramic M16 and shotguns to leave just yet. When the security teams arrive at the hotel, their weapons inventory will have to be augmented.

"The second problem is communications. I would like to have real-time communications without any delays. Since the meeting will be held in France, it might be possible to set up a ground link into Spain and then back to us. If we have to use a satellite, we should hide the signal in a carrier stream. For example, we could attach it to a broadcast we normally receive and then recode it upon its arrival. Also if possible, Chester, could we have a satellite over the hotel, say, ten minutes before the scheduled meeting time until the proposed ending time?" Scotty asked.

"No problem in either department. I'll have a satellite reprogrammed for that track immediately. As far as the signal goes, there are a variety of broadcasts we can piggyback it onto," Chester replied, glad to help.

"Then I think that's about it," Scotty concluded.

"It's a well-thought-out plan, Scotty," Morrison remarked and then added, "Tomorrow morning I'll meet with Major Whitney and Commander James and work out the details for you. One thing, I want you here monitoring the situation and giving any last-minute orders. Also have Major Whitney with you at the time. Chester, I also want you to be in your office when this happens and provide whatever support you can to Scotty. Also think about moving a backup satellite into the area. We can't lose our eyes should something go wrong.

"We only have three weeks to prepare, so we have to get on with it. Scotty, when do you think Commander James will be ready to leave?"

"He's been going over the files all day. I want to send him out the day after tomorrow at the latest," Scotty replied.

"Okay, we'll set the appointments tomorrow. Scotty, I sure hope that you are wrong about this, but we'll play it out just as you outlined."

"I hope that I am wrong too, sir," Scotty replied just as his intercom came alive with the voice of his secretary, Marcy.

"Yes, Marcy," Scotty answered.

"Sir, I have Captain Stark on the telephone for you," Marcy answered.

"Put her through, please," Scotty pleaded as his desk telephone rang. Scotty turned around away from his visitors and talked in hushed tones. After a few minutes, he hung up the telephone and caught the admiral sitting up erect, as he had obviously been straining himself to hear the conversation.

"Chester, what was that? It sounded like someone made a noise as if he was blowing a kiss or maybe kissing the telephone," Morrison joked.

"Sounded like a kiss to me!" Chester added, looking at Scotty and noticing that he was beginning to turn a little red in the face.

"Scotty, you didn't kiss the telephone, did you?" Morrison asked.

"Ah…no, sir," Scotty answered.

"Thank God! I was worried that you were going weird on us. Well, what do you say we go eat? It's past the dinner hour. Besides, I can't wait to see what treasures lie before us!" Morrison ordered.

"Let me just call the mess hall and let them know that we are on our way," Scotty said as the two admirals stood up and began to walk out of the office.

"Oh, great. Looks like more bird food tonight, Chester," Morrison commented just loud enough for Scotty to hear.

FOOD, I WANT FOOD

ALONG THE WAY TO THE mess hall, Morrison lectured about the restaurants he was going to visit when he returned to Washington. From memory he recited what each establishment had on its menu. He talked about the succulent leg of lamb at one restaurant, the fried onion rings and thick steaks at another, and about his favorite hot dog stand by Museum Row. Scotty took it all in stride, hoping that the admiral was just ribbing him and really wasn't going to go wild with food when he was alone in Washington.

When the three eager diners were approximately fifty feet from the entrance to the mess hall, Morrison suddenly leaned against the wall in the hallway and grabbed at his chest. Scotty ran over to him and asked what was wrong. Chester also ran to his side and said, "Arthur, what is it? Scotty, call for help!"

Scotty was about to speak into his wrist radio when the admiral spoke up. "Chester, do you smell it? It smells like fried chicken, onion rings, and I'm guessing now, but I detect coleslaw and, yes, it must be, sweet corn bread. Do you think we will have some?" Morrison and Chester then began laughing, and the admiral stood up and put his arm around Scotty's shoulder. Seeing that Scotty at first looked scared and now anger was creeping onto his face, he offered, "Scotty, lighten up. I was only kidding."

"It wasn't all that funny, sir," Scotty snapped back and walked a little ahead of the two clowns.

Morrison turned to Chester as they strove to catch up and said, again, just loud enough for Scotty to hear, "Boy, since Captain Stark left this morning, he has really been crabby."

Once they were seated, their food was immediately served. They each were given a cup of vegetable soup, a small salad, a large portion of a swordfish steak with carrots and string beans, along with a generous piece of chocolate cake with a marshmallow topping. The standard pot of coffee was placed in the center of the table along with a small plate. Morrison surveyed his meal and had a slight smile on his face. He then reached over to the small plate and picked up a small round item. The admiral then placed his elbow on the table and held the small delight about six inches from his eyes.

Pretending to examine it closely, Morrison asked, "Chester, do you have any idea what this is?"

"It kind of looks like a miniature flying saucer, but it has an irregular shape. I don't know, but it does look familiar," Chester answered.

"You know what? I think this is called a biscuit. I seem to remember these. People used to eat them with meals," Morrison added.

"Oh, yeah. I remember them. If I recall correctly, you are supposed to cut it in half and then put butter on it, or some people might put jelly on it," Chester jokingly responded.

Scotty let out a breath of frustration, and his arms across his chest as he asked, "Are you two comedians finished? There's something we have to talk about."

"Time to get serious again, Chester. Okay, Scotty, what is it?" Morrison responded.

Scotty uncrossed his arms, leaned into the table, looked at each of them, and in a hushed tone stated, "The next time we play the race game, I want to be car number 7."

Morrison and Chester then laughed, and the rest of the meal was punctuated by friendly, light conversation. When they had finished eating, Morrison and Chester went to the atrium to enjoy an evening cigar while Scotty went back to his office for a night of meetings and planning.

A TIME TO PREPARE

WHEN SCOTTY REACHED HIS OFFICE, Captains Kendall and Bone, along with Major Whitney and Executive Officer Beverly Hocker, were waiting for him in his outer office. Scotty invited them all inside and directed them to take a seat around the conference table. Once everyone was settled in, Scotty began to outline his goals for the deployment of the unit. He explained that, while the force, for now, could not take an offensive posture, Scotty envisioned that once their presence and capability became known, the aliens might, in fact, become more desperate in their actions. Beverly Hocker pointed out that the aliens were obviously in need of something desperately and agreed with Scotty that it appeared that they were desperate to obtain human organs. Hocker then concluded that their need would cause the aliens to become reckless and more aggressive in their actions. Captain Kendall stated that after he saw the film this afternoon, it was his impression that a war of survival was coming with the aliens. Captain Bone expressed his hope that the aliens would not step up their activity or engage in similar behavior, which would force them to react before they were adequately prepared.

Scotty followed up on Captain Bone's thoughts and began to explain that the only effective way to counter the alien threat was to spread the force across the United States and, in the future, expand into Canada and Mexico. At the present, Scotty explained that he envisioned the unit to be headquartered in the base they were in and at least eight to ten other units be located in such a way to be able to support an adjoining unit should it become necessary. Scotty realized that with the X-aircraft, such a setup would really not be necessary due to their speed capabilities. He based his plan on the combat range capabilities of the enhanced F-18. Support for his plan was received from around the table, but Scotty was the one who expressed reservations about the plan until a full complement of aircraft was secured.

Scotty's plan called for each unit to be comprised of eight X-aircraft and eight F18s along with all the support material and men necessary. Along with this, an adequate supply of the new missiles, both the penetrators and cluster type, was needed. In order to maintain those unit levels, Scotty also felt that a 10 percent surplus should be maintained within each unit, as some losses were inevitable. Therefore, if the operational strength was to be ten units with sixteen planes, eight of the X-aircraft and eight F-18s, each for a total of eighty aircraft, then eight additional aircraft must be in reserve combat-ready. When asked, Captain Kendall enthusiastically explained that while seventy-two of the X-craft were on hand, the remaining aircraft in production would be arriving in groups of ten shortly. Therefore, within a month they would be able to deploy the X-aircraft in strength. The inventories of F-18s were more than enough at the moment, but replacement aircraft would be needed to maintain reserve levels.

Scotty also added that he desired each unit to be backed up by a force of Marines with an appropriate number of vehicles and helicopters should ground action ever become necessary. Kendall admitted that this added requirement would complicate matters but resolved to work on it with Captain Stark when she returned. With conviction in his voice, Scotty told Kendall that he expected results and it would be wise not to wait for Captain Stark's return to begin solving the problem. Tongue in cheek, Kendall agreed with Scotty.

Scotty next turned his attention to Captain Bone, the weapons officer. Captain Bone explained that his present store of rockets was below what he considered to be the operational need of at least five thousand of each type. Bone went on to explain that current supply levels were increasing with weekly shipments of one hundred of each type.

Bone then added that he had been in contact with the manufacturer and production would initially be doubled and increased thereafter. Explaining that he would prefer operations to wait until his requested level of supply was reached, he promised that no matter what the level of supply, he would be ready at any time, provided that an all-out war with the aliens didn't start right away. When asked about the Gatling guns on the aircraft, Bone replied that current stocks consisted of ten million rounds, with one hundred thousand rounds arriving every week, more than enough to begin operations.

Scotty next expressed concern over the defensive posture of the base. Captain Bone replied that the defensive missile batteries and the two plasma cannons were manned around-the-clock. Scotty wondered about the plasma cannons and what their firing capabilities were. Captain Bone related that one cannon could fire two times per minute and the second cannon, which was an enhanced version, could recycle and fire every fifteen seconds. He went on to explain that the first cannon was scheduled to undergo enhancements next week to improve its rate of fire. Scotty expressed that he would like each of the future bases where the air units were to be stationed to have identical defensive capabilities, but he knew that the technology of the plasma cannons would only be limited to the Colorado facility. Captain Kendall reminded the group that future X-aircraft would have a smaller version of the plasma cannon as part of its weapons system, and perhaps the aircraft could also be dedicated to base protection. Scotty agreed with the assessment but realized that such a mission would require additional aircraft that they just didn't have at the present moment.

Scotty next inquired about pilot and technician training. Captain Kendall covered his operational plan now in place and his future needs. At present, there were ten trainers of the X-aircraft being flown out of the venerated Area 51. Kendall went on to explain that at present there were fifty men and women training in the X-aircraft and that their training consisted of three hundred simulator hours, one hundred and fifty hours of flying and maneuvers in Earth's atmosphere, and an additional one hundred and fifty hours of training in space. The difficulty of the training was that, for security reasons, all training took place at night. He went on to explain that the UFO watchers that surrounded Area 51 each night had probably taken photographs of the X-aircraft, but as yet no definitive, clear photos had shown up in UFO publications. This was due in part to the departure procedures that forced the pilots to maintain a high climbing angle, which would only give an outside observer a quick glimpse of the underbelly of the aircraft. Additionally, while the X-aircraft were somewhat similar to the stealth aircraft, a decision was made to have the same running light configuration as the stealth. Scotty liked that idea and knew that one day one of the UFO chasers would snap a photograph of the X-aircraft and the proverbial cat would be out of the bag.

Scotty was satisfied with the training schedule and only expressed concern that they would be able to find enough qualified pilots for the program. He then asked for a review of the technical training. Kendall explained that they used a feeder program from both the Navy and the Marine Corps. All aircraft technicians that were selected came to the program with at least two years' experience in their respective fields, whether it was hydraulics, electronics, or other areas of maintenance. It was expected that the current training program would more than keep up with deployment plans, Kendall pointed out. Bone added that his technician programs were equally on track, and once deployment was begun, all positions would be fully manned.

Scotty was satisfied and impressed with the preparations that had been made and were in progress. He just wanted to cover one more thing before they broke for the night.

While Area 51 had long been known as a testing facility for new aircraft, Scotty was concerned that his group had enough room to carry on their program. Kendall assured Scotty that their workspace was more than adequate. Their group was given two adjoining hangars with underground facilities capable of handling twice the number of people they had there. Scotty asked if the hangar space could handle their aircraft along with the new arrivals. Explaining that the facility was large enough to accommodate one hundred and twenty aircraft along with slightly over one thousand personnel, Kendall was confident that the facility was not only large enough for present needs but also allowed for adequate growth.

"Okay, you are both to be commended. Gentlemen, I know I may be pushing you somewhat, but after Brazil I am afraid of what may come next. I want this base and our other bases to not only answer the threat but also crush it. I won't be satisfied until the alien threat is all but eliminated. Now, when do I begin flight training?" Scotty pushed them on and was anxious to feel the X-aircraft under his control.

"Sir, whenever you want to. We have a simulator here, and I can schedule you whenever you want," Kendall replied, anxious to please.

"How's tomorrow morning at 0800? But only for an hour," Scotty replied, anxious to start.

"That's fine, sir," came a quick reply from Kendall knowing he had to adjust the simulator schedule to accommodate his boss.

"Okay, gentlemen, you'll have to excuse Ms. Hocker and me as we have another meeting in a few minutes."

After Kendall and Bone left the room, Scotty asked his executive officer what she thought of Kendall and Bone. Hocker replied that they both knew their jobs well enough but she felt as if the CAG didn't quite believe in what they were doing. It was as if it was like a big joke to him. Sure, he rode his men to the point of perfection and would accommodate whatever Scotty wanted, but he seemed to be holding something back; it was as if he believed that they would never enter battle with the aliens. Scotty asked if she thought Kendall should be replaced. Hocker stated that she didn't personally like the man but, at the present, felt him capable and decided that he needed watching. Scotty agreed with her observation and asked her to watch the man and report anything that appeared out of the realm of normalcy to him immediately. Hocker readily agreed to do so as a knock on the door rang out. Hocker left her seat and opened the door and admitted Vinson, Lieutenant Cunningham, Arty, and JW, again, to Scotty's office.

As everyone sat down around the table, Scotty went behind his desk and retrieved his briefcase. He then walked to the front of the table and opened it so that those sitting around the table could not see its contents. Scotty remained standing and called Arty to his side. He turned toward his friend and asked him to raise his right hand. Arty did so, and Scotty swore him into the United States Navy with the rank of commander. Scotty then asked a surprised Lieutenant Cunningham to present himself before the flag. Standing as rigid as a picket fence, he was promoted by Scotty to the rank of commander. Next to be called before the flag was Executive Officer Beverly Hocker, who Scotty promoted to the rank of captain. Next, Scotty informed JW that he was likewise being promoted but that the Marine Corps Board had not yet returned the paperwork. Scotty assured him that Admiral Morrison, upon his return to Washington, was going to "nudge" the board along. Scotty then asked JW to prepare a list of promotions for his contingent. JW thanked Scotty and realized that Scotty was a man who thought of everyone and, most importantly, paid attention to the details that always save lives.

Once congratulations were exchanged, Scotty called the group to order. Scotty asked Vinson to explain to the group the results of his inquiries into the implantation cases. Vinson began, for the sake of Arty, a review of alien abductions and the subsequent implantation of the BBs and the improved devices being found in people. Arty asked quite a few questions about the devices and their possible function, but most importantly, he took the revelations extremely seriously. Vinson then moved on and related that there are 244 recorded cases of implantations.

Thirteen of those individuals had passed away since the removal of the devices, leaving a total of 231 people still living. At this point, Scotty took over.

"Commander Givone and Commander Cunningham,[56] I have a job for both of you. You heard Vinson say that the implantees have basically nothing in common beyond statistical probabilities. Well, I don't believe that. These people were chosen for a reason, and it is your job to find out why. I want you both to split up the files any way you want, but make the division geographically reasonable, and I want to know everything about these people. I want to know what they eat, when they eat, when they go to the bathroom, what kind of clothes they wear, what time they go to bed—in essence, gentlemen, I want to know them better than they know themselves. It means that you will have to interview them and their doctors, get new and updated copies of their medical records, and hell, even talk to their relatives. What you are looking for is some point of commonality. It could be a behavioral pattern or something physical. Whatever it is, find it. It is going to take a long time to complete the mission, but I don't expect either of you will take any shortcuts. Vinson will give you both the files tonight. For the next two days, I want you to review the files and decide who is doing what. On the third day, you will depart and begin your investigations. Also, before you leave, make arrangements for you both to meet somewhere and compare notes, say, in two weeks from now. If you find something in common among the people that you have investigated up to that point that is hard evidentiary fact, then we will know where to center our inquiries.

"As for security, using the net for communications is a big no-no. In fact, I do not want any communications with this base unless it is an absolute emergency, and then only over a landline. You will be traveling on commercial airliners and using standard rental cars. I want your trip to appear as a business trip, and you both are midmanagement career employees of, let's say, a computer firm." Scotty was on a roll now and turned his attention to JW.

"JW, I know I am straining your troops more, but we need two more security teams. Also, I want IDs issued to them and the team. One set will be National Security Agency identification. Another set from the International Institute on Health Affairs.

"Along with that, also print up business cards for a computer firm and have a telephone line installed dedicated to the telephone number on the cards. If someone should call, your office will answer the phone under the heading and provide confirmation of employment. You never know, someone could get nosy, and the nosy one's fears are quickly dispensed with once they have a phone number to call. Thirdly, each team member should have IDs for the computer company they will be traveling under. All reservations should be made under the computer company's name. Also, your office will once again make all the arrangements." Turning back to Arty and Cunningham, Scotty continued, "I want you all to get together with Captain Hocker tomorrow night and keep her informed as to your progress. I know I'm giving you each a lot to accomplish, but I just can't believe that this is a total random act on the part of the aliens. We are missing something, and it's up to you, gentlemen, and your Marine escort to find out what it is," Scotty concluded.

Scotty asked for questions and patiently answered each one, driving home that security was of utmost importance. When everyone seemed satisfied, Scotty wished them well and told the travelers that he would see them before they left. Scotty also reminded Vinson that he also had to leave in another day. Vinson had come to realize that his life had now completely changed around. As they left the room, Scotty shook their hands and reminded them that their and their team's safety came first.

Scotty saw Jonesy in his outer office, waiting for his meeting. After he invited him into the office, Jonesy sat down in one of the chairs around the conference table. Immediately, Scotty reviewed with him the purpose of hijacking him off the *Eisenhower*. Jonesy listened patiently as Scotty once again explained his theory that intelligence data was being sent out of the base as a carrier signal on transmissions to the satellite net. Agreeing that such a process was not only probable but was also entirely possible and was being utilized by some sections of the military, Jonesy only asked when he could begin his work. Scotty explained that Captain Hocker would set him up in an office in Space Command, from where he could conduct his inquiry. Jonesy asked that he be placed in the big room of Space Command as he would then be able to get a feel for the people who worked there. Scotty agreed and directed Captain Hocker to get Jonesy a workstation in a corner, out of the way of most people. Scotty then directed him to start with the tapes on the day Chester's plane was attacked and move forward from there, paying close attention to the day they were attacked on the way back from Brazil. Jonesy wanted to get started right away, but Scotty ordered him to get a full night's sleep and start in the morning.

When they had finished talking business, Jonesy asked Scotty when the real fun would begin, the redirection of needed supplies away from those who ordered them to the base that needed them. Scotty assured

Jonesy that after his present assignment was finished, then the world was theirs.

As Jonesy left his friend, he found discomfort in the fact that if Scotty was right and the net was being used to convey intelligence to the aliens, then there were one or more spies in the complex. As he walked to his quarters, Jonesy vowed to himself to find the signal Scotty was looking for. He knew from experience that Scotty's instincts were rarely wrong about anything.

After Jonesy left, Scotty and Captain Hocker sat around the table and reviewed the meetings and their expectations. When they were finished, Captain Hocker asked, "Sir, what did Lieutenant Jones mean by the redirection of needed goods?"

"Nothing, really. Jonesy and I would secure items we saw being misused and redirect them to those who needed them," Scotty replied hesitantly.

"Like a shipment of beer for a party, or a bus, and some aircraft engines, and maybe a building?" Beverly asked.

"Could be," Scotty replied.

"So you are the mysterious Captain Aldridge the admiral is always telling stories about," Captain Hocker declared.

"Someone called me that one time," Scotty answered with a devilish grin on his face.

Captain Hocker was gathering up her material and was in the process of leaving when she said, "Admiral, life is going to get very interesting with you here. Good night, sir."

"Good night, Captain. See you in the morning," Scotty replied as he put his papers away and turned the light out in the office as he left for the night.

Scotty first went to sick bay and checked on their visitor. He was delighted to find a nurse in the softly lit room as the girl slept. The nurse brought him up-to-date on her progress, which had physically stabilized. She expressed concerns over her mental state but pointed out that the overall prognosis was positive.

Leaving sick bay, Scotty proceeded to Admiral Morrison's quarters. Scotty was surprised when Morrison answered the door eating an apple.

He decided not to comment on this miracle but instead informed the admiral of the night's proceedings. Morrison agreed with everything Scotty said and offered his help in any possible way. As Scotty was leaving, Morrison asked, "Are we going to have the same breakfast tomorrow?"

"If you want, Admiral," Scotty answered as he yawned.

"Yeah, you know, this health stuff isn't so bad," Morrison answered and saw a smile cross Scotty's face.

"Good night, Admiral," Scotty replied as he opened the door.

"Oh! Hey, Scotty, it's good to know that…ah…ah…somebody cares, especially you, Doreen, and Chester," Morrison declared.

Scotty looked at Morrison for a second and then repeated himself, "Good night, Admiral."

"Good night, Admiral," Morrison replied as he winked at Scotty.

Scotty closed the door to the admiral's quarters and then entered his own. He quickly made his way to the bedroom, undressed this time, and fell into bed thinking of Doreen. He silently told her that he missed her and wondered what she was doing at that moment as he fell asleep.

✦✦✦✦✦

[56] He sat erect with a broad smile on his face at being addressed as his new rank for the first time.

DON'T TELL ME THE DOG
ATE YOUR HOMEWORK?

S INCE SCOTTY HAD GIVEN HIM the assignment, Vinson had buried
himself in dossiers.

He was amazed at the apparent completeness of the documents,
which detailed almost every aspect of the lives of the military leaders
whom he would be visiting. Not only did Vinson know their professional
backgrounds, but he also became acutely aware of their private lives.
Vinson could recite from memory their educational and military
experience, what foods they liked and didn't like, their sexual preferences
and habits, and all other information about the men, which could prove
useful as a bargaining chip, should that ever become necessary.

Vinson placed the men in two general categories. In the first group
were the privileged ones. These individuals came from families steeped
rich in generational military service. Through skill, talent, and a very
large helping of political influence, they quickly rose to power. The
second group were men devoid of a family history of military service.
These men clawed their way to the pinnacle of rank, helped along
by their own skill, determination, and perseverance. For these men,

privilege didn't exist, and that void was filled by ambition and desire. Qualities Vinson liked and trusted. Both groups of men, Vinson correctly perceived, were, however, united in a common fear of alien incursion into their own individual countries.

Realizing that the real danger of his mission would not come from the aliens, Vinson knew that he would be walking a very fine line of diplomacy. The association that Morrison had put together was fragile at best. True, a united fear bound them in a common goal, but one misplaced or misinterpreted word or gesture on his part could damage the delicate alliance. With this in mind, Vinson realized that he had to stick solely to the purpose of his mission.

Vinson decided that, in dealing with these men, he would appear firm in his resolve but strike a delicate balance in friendliness. Inwardly he knew that he would probably be visiting these men again and again. There was a reason Scotty had trusted him with this mission, and knowing the way Scotty did things, his trip was not for a single purpose.

While he would like to have some social time to spend in Russia, Vinson knew that he simply didn't have the time. It would be a great coup if he could find out if the Russians knew about the large object Commander Cunningham had detected on the satellite search. If in fact the Russians knew about the object, Vinson would like to find out just what, if anything, they learned. If only he could find out something, it just might save Captain Montgomery a lot of trouble.

On the positive side, Vinson was secretly glad to be leaving the complex. If he had been fully truthful with Scotty, Vinson would have told him that he was not particularly wild about living underground. Every time he would go to the bathroom, Vinson would carefully check the toilet bowl to make sure that an errant rat or snake hadn't emerged in his toilet. Vinson knew that his paranoia was a silly fear, but he had heard of such things in the urban legends of New York City. Somehow, Vinson had reached the conclusion that such things were more probable underground. *After all,* Vinson thought, *it's always easier to go down rather than climb upward through the plumbing.* So far no one had seen the heavy weight Vinson placed on his closed toilet seat. It wasn't much protection, but it gave Vinson some sense of security.

On the morning of his departure, Vinson arose early, somewhat from the excitement of his trip, but more out of need to secure his bathroom. He doubled the size of the weight on the toilet seat and left a note for the cleaning crew not to remove the massive bulk from the plastic lid, lest they suffer the pangs of a slow, torturous death. Satisfied that his quarters (toilet seat) were secure, Vinson dressed in civilian clothes and joined his security team for breakfast.

JW presided over the breakfast and used the opportunity to instruct them on security matters. Once satisfied that everyone knew their duty, JW escorted them to the hangar deck. Scotty was waiting for them and greeted each member of the team individually. Pulling Vinson aside, Scotty gave him a short pep talk about the importance of the mission. Vinson tried to listen intently, but he was worried if he had put enough weight on the toilet seat cover.

Scotty watched as Vinson's team entered their vehicles and drove up the ramp toward the surface. It had always been hard for Scotty to say goodbye never knowing if he would ever see that person again. But it was even harder for him to say goodbye knowing that he was sending someone into danger. It was part of the job, if they were to survive, and Scotty knew that.

CAN I GO HOME AND GET SOME SLEEP NOW?

W ITH ONLY TWENTY DAYS UNTIL the passage of DG122 near the Earth, Dustin would linger at the observatory long into the morning hours after his shift ended. During this time, he would quietly sit at his desk reviewing the raw data from the night's observations, radio frequency readings, and soundings. His morning review would always reach the same conclusion as the day before and the day before that. The asteroid was on course and proceeding just as Dustin had predicted. DG122 would pass through the meteor shower two days before its final passage by Earth.

Before Dustin would leave for some much-needed sleep, Victoria would always manage to recruit him for the daily press briefings. In truth, Dustin would do anything for Victoria if it meant that he could be with her. Dustin didn't particularly like the press and their endless questions, but he recognized the need for the relationship.

What troubled Dustin the most were not the questions the reporters asked but, rather, the way some of the news people twisted his answers to fit their own spin on the story. Dustin had thought that by giving careful, straightforward answers, he would help calm the fears of some of the public. But instead, Dustin watched as some of the reporters seemed to sensationalize and alter the facts. Dustin only knew one thing: the facts were the facts.

I'LL HAVE ONE OF THOSE DRINKS WITH THE SMALL UMBRELLA

CHESTER WAS A LITTLE EXCITED about his trip to see Captain Montgomery. For the first time in his life, he was being sent out on a "secret mission." Since he had to travel on a commercial airliner to Puerto Rico, Chester put a lot of thought into what kind of disguise he should wear. His first choice was a blue button-down shirt with a pair of black slacks, but Chester decided that it looked too much like relaxed business attire. He ruled out a collared pullover shirt for the same reason. No, Chester had to appear as a tourist, and for that look he had to come up with something special. So shopping he went. He went from store to store at the Potomac Mall just outside of Washington, DC, in Virginia. He would buy one piece of his disguise in one store and then would go to another. He didn't want to buy everything at once, in case one of those evil aliens was watching him.

At the end of his shopping trip, Chester was proud of himself. He thought the items that he purchased would make him fit in with the rest of the tourists. That night, Chester laid his disguise out across his bed, stepped back, and was proud of himself. No one but no one would ever guess that he was a man on a secret mission.

The next morning, Chester took a taxi to Ronald Reagan Airport and proudly walked into the terminal and up to the ticket counter. Amid the business suits, casual business dresses, and families leaving for vacation dressed in casual wear stood a man separate from the wandering crowds who couldn't possibly draw attention to himself.

Chester wore a wide-brimmed tan straw hat with beads dangling off the back of the hat. This was complemented by a pair of dark wraparound sunglasses. For a shirt, Chester chose a loud red flower-print pattern. To be really casual, he left the first four buttons open, exposing his gray-haired chest. But not to fear, attention was drawn away from his chest by a few strands of seashell beads around his neck. For pants, Chester wore a pair of baggy surfer shorts that ended right below the knee. For footwear, Chester was simply going to wear a pair of slip-ons but decided instead to wear a pair of buckled sandals complemented by a pair of white socks. Lastly, Chester carried a well-worn black leather travel bag that he slung over his shoulder. A tourist he was; an undercover agent, he wasn't.

After arriving in San Juan, Chester made his way to the Navy base and the *Salisbury*. He found her at the end of a dock with a small army of people loading supplies onto the ship. Chester walked up to the gangway and stood there for a moment, looking at the ship. A sailor approached him, thinking that some weird-looking tourist was lost.

"Can I help you, sir?" the sailor asked.

Chester turned toward him and replied, "Beautiful ship, son. You should be proud of her."

"I am, sir. Best damn ship in the Navy," the sailor answered, not sure where this was going. At this point some of the men loading supplies stopped where they were and stared at Chester.

"Son, please tell Captain Montgomery that Admiral Braddock is her to see him," Chester ordered in a low tone of voice.

The sailor didn't know what to do; he just stared at Chester for a moment and then uttered, "Sir, do you have some kind of identification?"

Digging into his pants pocket, Chester withdrew his ID card and handed it over to the sailor and asked, "I guess my disguise really works, huh?"

The sailor looked at the card and back at Chester and then at the card again and replied, "Yes, sir. It's a really good...disguise. Please wait here." The sailor left Chester at the gangplank and went to the bridge of the ship and announced to Captain Montgomery, "Sir, there's some overage hippie at the gangplank saying that he is Admiral Braddock. Here is his ID."

Captain Montgomery took the ID from the sailor, looked at it, then crossed the bridge of the ship and looked toward the gangplank. As he was smiling to himself, George turned back around, handed the card to the sailor, and ordered, "Show the admiral up." When the sailor left, George couldn't help himself and laughed.

Once greetings were exchanged, the two men retreated to George's cabin to enjoy some lunch. As they ate, Chester explained why George had been ordered to Puerto Rico. Chester was glad to hear that the civilian scientists had left and were on their way home. George gave him a status report that the *Salisbury* should be refitted for sea later that day and that they would be ready to sail in the early evening.

After the dishes had been cleared, Chester very slowly and in a carefully prepared fashion explained the alien problem. Chester didn't leave a thing out, with the exception of the Colorado base and anything to do with it. George had a skeptical look on his face as Chester talked, but when he showed him the DVD of Brazil, that changed everything.

Once that was over, Chester explained his mission to him. The *Salisbury* was to proceed immediately, at flank speed, to Pearl Harbor. Once there, his ship would be resupplied. The *Salisbury* would then set sail again and join a combat fleet with support ships over the unknown object. Their job was to locate and determine what the object on the floor of the ocean was. Any decision as to possibly salvage would be made later by Admiral Morrison and Admiral Scott. Almost as an afterthought, Chester told George to expect Vinson once he docked in Pearl Harbor.

To say the least, George was floored by Chester's revelations. It was too outlandish to believe it, and at the same time, it was too outlandish not to believe it. But George saw the look of conviction on Chester's face, and that, more than anything, convinced him that it was the truth. Once he crossed that threshold, George asked a million questions and received more than adequate answers. Convinced that the fleet he was going to be sailing with had enough firepower to take on the world, George began issuing orders to make his ship ready for immediate departure. With a little luck and the best crew in the Navy, George expected to be in Pearl within five days. For the moment, he would treat it as just another scientific expedition, but with an alien twist.

When it came time for Chester to leave, George somehow managed to convince him that he should really change into some not-so-obvious tourist disguise. Accepting the suggestion, Chester donned some clothing left behind by the scientists. He left in someone's pair of jeans and a casual golf shirt, minus the straw hat and beads.

When Chester returned to the airport and boarded his flight for home, he said a silent prayer for George and his crew, because an inner voice told him that this wasn't going to be any walk in the park.

SO YOU WANT TO PLAY DETECTIVE?

Commanders Art Giovine and Richard Cunningham were busy themselves, while Vinson and Chester had prepared for their missions and had already departed. They had buried themselves in the files of the people who had had implants removed. The problem that they had faced were remarkably the same as before they began their review. First, the people that had implants removed were scattered throughout the United States, and therefore, geographic location was not a common factor. Secondly, women who were implanted with the BBs or the newer devices outnumbered men by almost three to one. Some had given birth to children, while almost an equal number had not. Thirdly, all implantees appeared to have nothing medically in common beyond what statistical probabilities of disease would dictate. Lastly, on a social scale, the group was spread out across the spectrum. There were people who were poor, while others might be considered middle income, then there were some that were considered rich, while a rare few could be called the superrich. There were homemakers, truck drivers, computer operators, teachers, secretaries, doctors, mechanics, nurses, and representatives from just about any occupation someone could think of.

In order to accomplish an investigation of such magnitude, Arty and Richard thought it best to do as Scotty had suggested and divide the country in half. Arty would tackle the eastern half of the nation, while Richard would concern himself with the western half. Objectively, they had estimated that their assignment would take at least three months to complete. To speed things along, Arty suggested that they enlist the members of their security team to help. Richard, however, would not hear of it and insisted that he perform all the work himself. Regrettably, Richard felt that their security teams were just that, people to provide security so he and Arty could do their work. Arty tried to point out that they would be able to cover more ground more quickly if the security teams helped, but Richard pointed out that Scotty had placed the responsibility on them and them alone. Arty wanted to discuss the matter with Scotty but was overruled by Richard's seniority in rank.

Once that conflict had been resolved, the two amateur sleuths decided that they would meet every two to three weeks to discuss their progress and see if any points of commonality in the investigation could be determined. Arty suggested that after they investigated the first group of people, they might just find what they were looking for. Richard, however, countered with the assumption that they would not know anything until each person had been fully investigated and all the facts had been reviewed. This time Arty didn't bother to argue and just replied that Richard was probably right.

So that they wouldn't have to carry around bulky files, Scotty had arranged for Carolyn Gibbs to copy all the implantees' files onto notebook computers. She didn't just load all the files onto the computers; Carolyn also added security features that Fort Knox would be jealous of. If one of the computers should fall into the wrong hands and be turned on by someone else, that person would have two chances of entering a password, which was twenty-seven characters long, within ten seconds. If the user failed the first time, a worm program would be activated to begin gobbling up data in a random order. The user then had ten seconds to re-enter the password. If the wrong password was again entered, a vial of acid would break open and wash over the hard disk, destroying the information.

Late in the afternoon on the day prior to their departure, Arty and Richard went together to see Carolyn. When they entered her research lab, it was hard to believe that they were still on the base. The neat and orderly military style didn't apply here. There was clutter everywhere. Computer parts were all over the place; there were glass prisms on one table, while on another there were some weird-looking bandages or some kind of a patch.

To say the least, Richard was not impressed, but it didn't bother Arty as he had been here before.

Caroline had her back to them when they entered the laboratory and was so lost in thought that she didn't even hear them come in. She was busy at work writing mathematical calculations on a row of shiny white boards, like a classroom chalkboard that stretched at least twenty feet long. Arty didn't have a clue what she was working on, mathematics not being one of his strong points, but was impressed when he noticed that whatever she wrote on the boards was replicated on a large computer screen.

Carefully, Arty and Richard weaved their way through the room, being careful not to step on anything. Richard had called out when they entered, but Carolyn was lost to her work and did not answer. They stopped about six feet behind her and waited patiently for her to finish. When Carolyn backed away from the board and stood reviewing her work, while tapping a magic marker on her chin, Arty coughed loudly to get her attention. The magic marker flew into the air as Carolyn let out a scream and turned around, only to see two men staring at her with their mouths open.

"Commanders! Don't ever do that again!" Carolyn burst out.

Richard replied in a conciliatory tone as Arty laughed, "We did call out, but I guess you didn't hear us. I'm sorry."

"That's okay," Carolyn replied, smiling sweetly at Arty, and then began to laugh.

Carolyn directed them over to a workbench that was only partially covered in computer parts or what looked like computer parts. Once they were gathered around the table, Carolyn pulled out two ultrathin notebook computers and instructed them on their use. After an hour of instruction, they entered their passwords and closed their computers. When they both thanked her for her work, Arty shook her hand and winked at Carolyn. She smiled and bowed her head ever so slightly in recognition, trying to hide her body language. Richard didn't catch onto their ploy and said goodbye.

As they walked back toward Scotty's office, Richard couldn't help himself and praised Carolyn's brilliance again and again. Arty, on the other hand, made more favorable comments about her sweet personality, attractive body, and the killer dimple in her smile. Richard ignored those observations and turned red when Arty commented about the more-than-ample size of her breasts. Richard quickly changed the topic of conversation and walked a little faster, but Arty was not paying attention. He just walked fast enough to keep up with a smile on his face and his imagination working overtime.

Once back at Scotty's office, they sat around the conference table and listened as JW once again lectured them on security measures and what not to do. Scotty would have preferred that they and their security teams not be away from the base during the conference on terrorism, but there just wasn't time. He simply didn't like leaving them out there on their own, away from the safety of the base.

Once JW was finished with his mini lecture, Scotty suggested that they all go to dinner. Arty excused himself, explaining that he had a few things to do first but would catch up with them later. As JW, Richard, and Scotty walked toward the mess hall, Arty raced back to see Carolyn.

JUST ONE MORE BYTE

"AH, COMMANDER. BACK ALREADY?" CAROLYN asked with a softness in her voice and desire in her heart. An inner voice told her that her infatuation was wrong, but ever since she had been exposed as a spy, her husband had ignored her. She was simply an embarrassment to him. Sure, at first he was the supportive husband and lover, but that had waned. Even the birth of their baby hadn't changed him. He paid them little to no attention. Carolyn wanted to desperately take her baby and run away, but for her there was no escape. Due to the inattentiveness of her husband, her sexual desire had withered—that is, up until the time she met Commander Arthur Giovine.

"Hi, Carolyn. I got away as soon as I could. Is the other computer ready?" Arty asked. He knew that he was violating orders, but he had decided to use his security team in the investigation no matter what the proper Richard Cunningham thought.

"Oh…yes, the computer," Carolyn replied with disappointment in her voice as she walked over to the same table that they were at earlier. From underneath a pile of rags she extracted another notebook computer.

While Carolyn was doing this, Arty couldn't help but notice the smooth, shapely curves of her body and how her long brown hair gently swung back and forth as she moved. *And the sweet scent of her perfume—a man could get lost in her scent!* Arty dreamily thought.

As Carolyn handed him the computer, she related, "It is configured the way you requested. I set it up for internet use with encryption-breaking software to get past any walls you may come up against."

Taking the computer, Arty began, hesitating a bit, "Carolyn…" If he would go any further, he would be breaking all his own rules. *Hell! She is married,* he silently told himself. *And besides, Scotty would kill me.*

"Yes," Carolyn quickly replied as she looked deeply into his eyes.

"Carolyn… I… I…," Arty stammered as he drew closer to her and became lost in the beauty before him.

"Arty," Carolyn replied as she as well moved closer. She felt moisture and arousal where there hadn't been any for a long time.

"I…," Arty began and then very quickly put his arm around her and kissed her.

Carolyn welcomed the advance and embraced him as well as she pushed herself into him. Arty's last logical thought was, *Oh well, explanation later.*

As they kissed, Arty began unbuttoning her blouse. In response, Carolyn started to take his pants off. She reached for him at almost the same second that Arty had pushed her blouse open, unhooked her bra, and softly suckled her nipples. Arty pushed her against the table as Carolyn arched herself backward. She felt Arty's hand slip under her skirt and move upward along her inner thigh. As Carolyn felt his hand between her legs and slip into her underwear, her excitement increased. As his finger penetrated her, Carolyn let out a soft, pleasurable groan. Quickly Carolyn looked over her shoulder and, with her arm, swept the computer parts off the table and onto the floor. Arty supported her as she lay back on the table. Reaching over, while still standing, Arty kissed her breasts as Carolyn put her arms around him, locked her legs around his hips, drawing him inside of her. She applied more pressure on her legs and drew him in deeper. She wanted to scream out his name, but speech was impossible as passion and desire had overcome her. What had been dormant for so long awoke like a tiger hungry for food and wanting to consume everything. Since Arty first saw Carolyn, he had dreamed of this moment, and now it was reality.

Just as their passion had climaxed, they heard running footsteps out in the hallway.

Quickly they helped each other dress. As they turned toward the noise and the doorway, a Marine, with his weapon drawn, pushed the door open and entered.

"Is everything okay?" the Marine shouted.

"Everything is just great, sir!" Arty replied, half out of breath.

"The video surveillance camera is out. We thought that something might be wrong, sir," the Marine replied with a very slight devilish grin in the corner of his lips. After holstering his weapon, the Marine walked over to the surveillance camera in the corner of the room.

It was at that moment that Arty saw Carolyn's thong on the floor where he had thrown it earlier. Once the Marine walked toward the camera, Arty quickly bent down and picked it up. Carolyn, with a smile on her face and while giggling slightly, snatched her thong out of his hand and put it in the pocket of her skirt. "Holy shit! I forgot about the damn camera," Arty whispered to Carolyn.

Carolyn leaned toward Arty and whispered, "After you were here earlier, I wrote a program to scramble the video system in this room. I was hoping…well…that we would do just what we did. When you came back for the other computer, I executed the program."

Arty didn't reply but stared at her with a coy grin on his face as he thought to himself, *My god, where have you been hiding?*

Arty began, "Carolyn, what are we going to—"

But he was interrupted by his new love. "Shhhh! He's coming back," Carolyn whispered.

"I'm going to have to call a diagnostic team to check out the connection in this room. I hope you don't mind, but I'll have to wait here until the repairs are made," the Marine stated with an air of authority.

"Not at all. Please make yourself comfortable. There should be a chair around here somewhere," Carolyn replied as she looked around her laboratory and then turned toward Arty and asked, "Commander, do you have any other questions about the computer?"

"Er…no, Ms. Gibbs. I understand everything," Arty answered, not knowing what else to say.

"Good. Then let me walk you out," Carolyn replied as Arty picked up the computer and walked toward the door. Once out of sight of the Marine, they kissed and pledged their love to each other. Arty then left, but not before lightly slapping Carolyn on the butt.

Arty then raced back to his quarters, dropped off the computer, and then ran to the mess hall. He joined Scotty and the others just as they were finishing desert. Scotty asked if he was feeling okay because Arty looked red in the face. Arty replied that he was fine and, in fact, never felt better. He did, however, wonder what he would say the next time he confessed his sins to his God. For the present, though, Arty was more worried about what Scotty would do if he found out about his indiscretion.

While Arty ate, Richard led a discussion on the alien problem. While everyone contributed to the discussion, Richard had become a little fanatic on the subject. At that point, Scotty began to wonder if he had chosen the right person for the job. But it was a little too late for that.

Once dinner was completed, Scotty had Arty and Richard escorted back to their quarters with orders to sleep in preparation for tomorrow. Arty tried to leave his quarters and go look for Carolyn, but Scotty had placed a guard outside of his door. He was going to call her and say that he had a problem with his computer but decided against that since the telephones were tapped and another security guard would probably show up with her. In utter frustration, Arty went to bed and spent a restless night thinking about Carolyn.

The next morning, Scotty went to the hangar deck to see Arty, Richard, and their security teams off. JW, as Scotty expected, was also there, giving last-minute instructions to whom he lovingly referred as *his* Marines. Scotty stood off to the side and watched the organized disorder as JW did a final weapons check and once again reviewed security procedures with Arty and Richard.

As Scotty stood by waiting, he was surprised to see Carolyn on the hangar deck, walking toward him. "Good morning, Ms. Gibbs. Is there something wrong?" Scotty asked.

"Good morning, Admiral. I came up to wish them well and to see if they had any last-minute questions about the computers. With your permission, of course, Admiral," Carolyn replied, not sure whether Scotty would believe such a lame excuse.

"Sounds good. Go right ahead, Ms. Gibbs," Scotty answered, wondering what she was really up to.

When JW finished his briefing, he walked over to Scotty. Neither JW nor Scotty noticed that Carolyn and Arty, in the meantime, had disappeared behind a parked aircraft.

"Say, JW, anything up on Carolyn Gibbs?" Scotty inquired.

"No, we are continuing to watch her, and so far nothing is out of the ordinary. As per the original order, she does not have access to the outside world.

"There was only one thing that was unusual, and that was yesterday, when Commander Giovine was in her office. For some reason, the video surveillance camera went out. We lost the picture, but we had a separate audio track on," JW replied, not really wanting to reveal what he had heard.

Scotty laughed slightly, looked at JW, and said, "Let me guess, Arty and Carolyn are, shall we say, engaged in a rather-close working relationship, and her interest this morning is more than just computers."

"Yes, Admiral. I would say, based upon what I heard, that they have a very close working relationship, and an eager one at that," JW replied with a grin on his face.

"I knew that when Arty arrived we should have issued chastity belts," Scotty joked. Then he asked, "What about her husband?"

"It seems that the good Mr. Gibbs is more concerned about his career than his wife and child. He had remarked once that being married to a spy was a real career stopper. A few weeks ago, he went to a family counselor and inquired about a divorce," JW replied and then added as an afterthought, "Admiral, that was before Arty arrived on the base."

"I know, JW. Let's get them moving," Scotty ordered and swore that he would get Arty when he returned.

Scotty watched as both teams departed in separate vehicles. More importantly, he watched Carolyn as she stood by and waved to Arty as he left. When she turned around to walk toward the elevator, Scotty would swear that he saw tears in her eyes. The anger, or maybe it was more disappointment, was slowly building in Scotty. The last thing he needed now was a messy divorce on the base. Shaking his head, Scotty also walked toward the elevator but was stopped by Captain Kendall. He reminded Scotty that he had simulator time booked for the X-aircraft. A wide grin came across Scotty's face as he raced to put on a flight suit. All thoughts of Arty and Carolyn quickly disappeared from his mind.

SQUEAK, SQUEAK

THE FOLLOWING DAY, SCOTTY WAS on the hangar deck again, but this time it was to welcome Vinson and his team home. When they lined up in front of him and saluted, Scotty was amazed at just how tired they all looked. It appeared as though they hadn't slept in days. In truth, they probably hadn't, as they crisscrossed the world. Realizing just how much he had pushed these men, Scotty proudly returned their salute and thanked them individually for their efforts.

As the Marines departed the hangar deck, Scotty picked up one of Vinson's travel bags and walked him back to his quarters. Scotty listened intently as Vinson recounted each visit and gave his impressions of the people he had seen. Deciding that his friend was too tired to be debriefed, Scotty did not burden him with too many questions, as that could wait until Vinson slept for a while.

Once they reached Vinson's quarters, Scotty ordered him to sleep and walked away. Vinson reached into his pocket and withdrew his security card for the electronic lock.

Once the door was opened, Vinson entered his bedroom and collapsed onto the bed.

After a few minutes, he decided to get up, change into something more comfortable, and go to the bathroom. Undressing, Vinson entered the bathroom in his regulation boxer shorts and T-shirt. He was relieved to see things as he had left them.

After checking the shower stall, Vinson walked over to the toilet bowl and stood in front of it. Satisfied that nothing had been moved, he bent over and removed the heavy weight from the toilet bowl cover and placed it on the floor. With great anticipation, he slowly lifted up the toilet seat and peered inside. What he saw caused his heart to miss a few beats. He slammed down the toilet seat and raced into his living room and over to his desk. Vinson pulled open a drawer and retrieved a .357 Magnum handgun. Running back over to the doorway of the bathroom, Vinson began firing his weapon at the toilet bowl.

Almost instantly, alarms went off throughout the base. Within a few seconds, two Marines, in full battle dress, entered Vinson's room armed with a shotgun and a mini machine gun. Scotty, of course, was close behind them.

"Drop the weapon, sir!" the Marine with the shotgun ordered as Vinson turned around toward them.

Vinson, half in a daze from lack of sleep and shock, found himself looking down the wrong end of two very nasty weapons. He dropped his gun and just stood there speechless. One of the Marines asked Vinson what had happened, but all he could do was point toward the bathroom.

Scotty and one of the Marines approached the bathroom, the Marine with his shotgun at the ready. Very slowly Scotty peered into the bathroom and then chuckled to himself at the sight. The toilet bowl was in at least a hundred pieces, water was everywhere, and even more water was shooting into the air from the water valve that fed the now recently deceased toilet bowl. The Marine walked into the bathroom, amid the debris, and, when he was in front of the sink, bent down and picked something up. He held a dead rat up by the tail as he turned around and faced Vinson, who was now standing alongside Scotty in the doorway.

With a grin on his face, Scotty asked, "What is it, Sergeant?"

The sergeant looked at the rat, which he was now holding in the air close to his face, and replied, "It's another one of those damn rubber rats. Nasty little creatures, if you ask me!" He then tossed the rat into the air, caught it in his hand, and squeezed it hard enough so that the rubber rat produced the squeaking sound of a toy.

Scotty couldn't contain himself any longer and erupted into laugher, especially since he put it there to begin with. Vinson didn't seem to see the humor in it and just stood there with his mouth open. Scotty slapped him on the shoulder and told him to get some rest. He then ordered the Marines to call maintenance to clean up the mess and install a new toilet bowl. Scotty then left in good humor but, at the same time, was a little ashamed of what he had done. Scotty thought to himself, *But who would have guessed that he would shoot the damn thing!*

JUST KEEP THE JUNK FOOD COMING

W HEN JONSEY BEGAN WORKING ON a problem, it was as if the rest of the world didn't exist. Scotty had given him a mission, find out how the aliens were using the satellite net to send out their information. Jonsey loved a challenge, and he would work on it until he solved it. For him, time was irrelevant. There was no daytime or nighttime; there was only a problem that had to be solved. Everything else was only a nuisance. To keep himself fortified, as he sat at his workstation in Space Command, Jonsey ordered up a steady supply of coffee and chocolate snack cakes. Any kind of snack just had to be chocolate; nothing else would do.

Hoping to find an easy solution, Jonsey first reviewed all the radio traffic out of the base for the day that Chester left Bermuda and the day that Scotty returned from Brazil. Knowing deep down that it wouldn't be that easy, Jonsey wasn't surprised when he didn't find anything. Inwardly, as he had expressed to Scotty earlier, he felt that the only way to get a signal secretly out of the base was to hide it. What he wanted to examine was the telemetry that had gone up to the satellites on those days. But in order to do this, he would have to first write a computer program to detect any hidden activity in the satellite feed.

Somehow the minutes turned into hours as Jonsey worked. He finished a couple of programs within the first two days, but for some reason, the programs had bugs in them. It took endless hours to check and recheck his programing code, but it was to no avail.

As he worked, the clutter around his desk grew. The trash can under his desk was filled to the brim and beyond. Wads and wads of paper were crumpled up and thrown all over his work area. The packaging that once contained his snack cakes were wadded up and tossed into a growing pile on the floor. In one small corner of his desk, empty coffee cups were stacked four and five high. Thousands of pieces of sticky notes, with computer programming notes written on them, were everywhere.

Jonsey was on a mission. He knew that Scotty would be leaving shortly for a quick visit home, and Jonsey had wanted to surprise him before he left with proof that there were indeed spies on the base. But as the hours and days ticked by, Jonsey knew that he wasn't quite there yet. Like Scotty, Jonsey believed that there was a spy on the base, but catching him would be another matter.

AH, THE PLEASURE
OF BEING HOME!

ADMIRAL MORRISON ARRIVED EARLY ON the appointed day, just as he had promised. Scotty gave him a short briefing to update him as to the current status of the base and its many activities. Morrison listened intently, promising himself to babysit the complex and not change a thing in Scotty's absence. Actually, Scotty had, by far, exceeded Morrison's expectations. He seemed to have accomplished in a very short period what the admiral thought would have taken months. The admiral then ordered Scotty to go home for a few days. He then added, with a slight grin, that Captain Stark was already there, waiting for him. Morrison had ordered Doreen to assist Scotty in closing down his law practice. Scotty, with a very wide grin on his face, saluted Morrison and proceeded to leave. After taking a few steps, Scotty turned back toward the admiral and declared, "Looks like you lost some weight, sir."

"Oh, so you noticed! It's due to this new diet some pain in the ass put me on," Morrison replied, proud of his new physique; even if it was only five pounds lighter, it was progress.

"Well, it looks good, sir. Just who is the pain in the ass? I'll have him arrested," Scotty replied, not to be outdone.

"Get out of here, Mr. Scott. Otherwise, I'll cancel your liberty!" Morrison answered.

With that, Scotty saluted his friend and mentor once more, turned on his heels, and quickly departed the base with his security team in tow. Scotty wanted to fly right home to see Doreen, but he was trapped by his own orders. First, there would be the drive to Denver, where he and his team would board a commercial plane to Chicago. Then they would change planes to Charlotte, where they would transfer to another flight to Baltimore, where finally they would board their last flight to New York City.

For all the unnecessary travel, Scotty's twisted route home went agonizingly slow for him but actually quite quickly by the clock. In six short hours, he and his team arrived at Newark International Airport. An additional security team met them at the airport and drove them to Scotty's home. After crawling through late-afternoon traffic in New York City, they reached their destination in just under two hours.

Very quietly, Scotty inserted his key into the lock of the front door and noiselessly opened it. After stepping into his old outer office in absolute silence, Scotty turned toward the security team and put his index finger to his lips to indicate silence and ushered them in. When they were all inside, Scotty motioned for them to stay where they were. Scotty then stepped quietly forward and turned a corner in the outer office to look toward the other offices and the kitchen area. He stopped momentarily as Scotty saw the three most important people in his life sitting around the kitchen table, enjoying a cup of tea and laughing together. Momentarily he stood frozen in time, just taking the whole scene in. He then stepped into their full view and cleared his throat.

Scotty's mother and Marlene let out a startled scream when they looked up and saw him. Doreen, upon seeing Scotty, jumped out of her seat and ran to him, jumping into his open arms, and wrapped her legs tightly around his torso. Neither Doreen nor Scotty thought of the others present as they kissed a long, firm kiss of physical desire and relief that they were now together. Gone from their minds were the thoughts and fears of Zambia, Brazil, and aliens. Nothing would invade this moment except, of course, a protective mother.

"Michael!" Catherine shouted, disrupting Scotty's dreamlike state.

Scotty opened one eye and looked around. What greeted him were his mother, Marlene, and his security team staring at him and Doreen with their mouths slightly agape. Remembering where he now was, Scotty patted Doreen on her rump and broke the embrace. Scotty held her tightly as Doreen released her legs from around him and stood up on her own. For her own part, Doreen stared at the assembled group not embarrassed in the slightest for her show of affection. Instead, she reached up on her toes and kissed Scotty on the cheek and slapped his behind loud enough for all to hear. *Score a big plus 1 for Doreen,* Scotty thought.

Catherine and Marlene then ran up to Scotty and embraced him in turn. After the required number of kisses had been exchanged, they all sat down at the kitchen table and caught one another up on their individual lives. Scotty hated to lie to his mother and Marlene, but he stuck to the cover story that Doreen had told them. As best as he could, Scotty patiently answered their questions about oceanographic research and did pretty good, considering that he didn't know the slightest thing about it. In any case, they seemed satisfied with his answers. The good thing about the cover story was that it would explain his prolonged absence from home in the future. Where better to be than on a ship in the middle of the ocean, doing who knows what?

Catherine couldn't help herself and expressed her relief that Scotty was now doing this "research thing" and would no longer be flying those god-awful jets around the skies. Of course, she just had to add, "If man were—"

Scotty cut her off and repeated her battle cry, "If man were meant to fly, God would have given him wings. I know, Mother."

"That's right. A son should listen to his mother," Catherine quipped back.

"I do, Mother. Every day of my life. I carry the lessons you and Dad taught me, and I practice them every day," Scotty replied and was a little upset when he saw a tear in the corner of his mother's eye.

Marlene then spoke up in order to relieve, not the tension, but the awkwardness of spoken love between a mother and son. She explained that since Scotty had left, she had two of his friends seeing to the business and brought him up-to-date on pending matters. Explaining that Scotty's two friends seemed more than capable to take over the business, Marlene suggested that they do so. Scotty readily agreed to her suggestion and decided to act upon it immediately.

Scotty excused himself from the table and went to his office. When he opened the door, what was his office had been transformed into a bedroom. Turning around, he found Marlene on his heels. She explained that she had to make a few changes in order to accommodate the security teams. Each of the three offices were now bedrooms, and his treasured conference room had likewise been transformed into a lounge for the people. Marlene directed Scotty to a "cozy" back room, where he could make some calls. Scotty was frustrated by her definition of *cozy*, which meant a transformed four-by-four-foot storage closet. With any luck, Scotty thought, he would be out of the law business shortly, and it didn't matter where he made the calls from.

Scotty first called his two friends and successfully convinced them to take over his business. It meant that his two friends would have to now form a partnership, but they seemed eager enough to do it. After all, it's not every day that someone gives you a business, and a successful one at that. For the next few hours, Scotty then called each of his active and nonactive clients and explained that he had been called up to active duty in the United States Navy and that two of his associates would be servicing their needs. His clients did not take the news well and pleaded with him to somehow retain their files and service their needs. Scotty knew that their requests were impossible to fulfill and told them so, as gently and as firmly as he could. In the end, all of Scotty's clients accepted his explanation and wished him well.

After the last call was made, Scotty closed his leather-bound address book and sat back with his feet on the desk and his hands folded behind his head and smiled. A major change had just taken place in his life. He was now officially out of the law business and relieved to be so. It was time for a change, and he had made it. This stolen moment of relaxation quickly passed as he thought of Marlene. What would she do now? Scotty wondered. Sure, she was a millionaire a couple of times over, but she needed a purpose in life, and Scotty knew that he had to find her one. Scotty then sat up, looked one last time at the file folders of his clients piled high in the corner of the tiny room, and smiled to himself the smile of contentment. After leaving the "cozy" office, Scotty went downstairs to talk to the ladies, and especially Marlene.

Finding his mother and Marlene still sitting around the small kitchen table, Scotty sat down and asked where Doreen was. Catherine told her son that Doreen was upstairs, getting ready for dinner. She went on to explain that they were all going out to dinner at Antonio's tonight. Sheepishly, Scotty looked at his mother, then at Marlene, and asked what they thought about Doreen. As if on cue, Catherine and Marlene looked at each other with frowns on their faces, and then at Scotty. Very quickly, as Scotty's heart raced at their obvious disapproval, the frowns were replaced by laughter. Scotty sat back as Catherine and Marlene heaped accolade after accolade in Doreen's praise. "She's the one. She's beautiful, and what a sense of humor! If you let her go, you are a fool…" And on and on it went. When they were finished, Scotty looked at his mother and asked, "What do you really think?"

Catherine reached across the table and placed her hand on top of her son's and answered, "Michael, since Doreen arrived earlier today, she has not shut up once. It has been Michael this, Michael that, and did you know that Michael can do this? We have heard nothing but Michael, Michael, Michael all day long to say nothing of the way she greeted you. I say, enough already! She forgets that I am your mother and that Marlene probably knows you better than anyone." Catherine changed her tone of voice from lighthearted to serious and continued, "In all seriousness, son, it is easy to see that Doreen is deeply in love with you, and I dare say, you with her. Marlene and I think that she is an absolute treasure. Marry this girl, Michael! She is what every mother who has a son could hope for!" Catherine squeezed Scotty's hand and released it, changed her tone of voice back to lightheartedness, and added, "Oh, and have some grandchildren. It will give Marlene and me something to do."

Scotty, who was now slightly flushed in the face, reached over and kissed his mother, and then Marlene, on the cheek and thanked them. After sitting back down, Scotty began, "Now, about having something to do—"

Marlene quickly interrupted Scotty. "Now, don't you worry about us. Your mother and I are leaving for a much-deserved cruise around the world next month. When we get back, we are going to start a foundation to donate books and computers to deserving schools throughout the country. We already have some corporate sponsors, and the company you did all that work for, Spectrum, has been most generous. They have promised us two million dollars a year for the next ten years, as well as computer equipment," Marlene replied with pride in her voice.

"I see. And just how did Spectrum happen to get involved?" Scotty asked in admiration of these two connivers.

"Your mother and I met with their CEO yesterday and reminded him of your work and how, without you, they would be a few billion dollars poorer each year on their bottom line," Marlene again proudly answered.

Scotty couldn't help it and began laughing as he replied, "And they call me Pirate! Hell, give you two a telephone, a fax machine, a computer, and a healthy dose of moxie and you'll steal the world." Scotty then stood up and kissed them both on the cheek while slightly laughing in admiration for these tough ole ladies. He was about to ask what time their dinner reservations were when Scotty heard footsteps on the stairs, the kind of sound a small high heel makes on bare wood. Scotty turned around and saw Doreen descending the stairs. It was her appearance that held him transfixed. Doreen was wearing a white linen dress drawn tightly around her waist to accent the hourglass shape hiding beneath. The top three buttons of her dress were opened casually in appearance but teasingly allowed a bare hint of breast to be visible. The bottom three buttons of her dress were likewise unbuttoned, accenting her long shapely legs. Doreen smiled at Scotty, walked past him, and took her place at the small kitchen table. Marlene then chased Scotty upstairs, with orders to get ready for dinner.

Dinner was spent in endless good cheer and the constant sound of laughter. It seemed to Scotty that the three women had talked endlessly about what he figured was absolutely nothing. Scotty knew that it was only with family and very close friends that someone could spend an evening with, talk about meaningless dribble, and have an absolutely fabulous time. Here, together, Scotty felt safety, comfort, and trust. It was a feeling he didn't want to see end.

During dinner, Doreen would hold Scotty's hand under the table from time to time. Scotty would do his best to brush up against her at almost every opportunity and quickly became intoxicated by the sweet and fruity aroma of her perfume. When the last laugh had been laughed, the last cup of coffee and cognac consumed, and the last promise of future dinners sworn to, it was time to leave.

Together they drove back to Scotty's in Catherine's limousine. Arriving home, Scotty quickly opened the car door and stepped out. He then reached in and took Doreen by the hand and helped her out of the cavernous interior of the car. Scotty waited for his mother and Marlene to exit, but when they didn't, he stuck his head into the back of the car and asked if they were coming.

"Heavens, no! The night is too young for us older people. You two go and get your rest," Catherine replied.

Scotty blew them each a kiss and wished them a good night. He then closed the back door of the car and watched as the car drove off and made a left-hand turn onto Fifth Avenue. Smiling to himself, Scotty wondered just what his mother meant by the night being too young. Turning back toward Doreen, Scotty said with a devilish grin, "Well, I guess that it is just you and me tonight." And as an afterthought, he added, "And our ever-present security detail."

"Let's forget about them and go upstairs," Doreen replied and slipped her arm around Scotty's.

Arm in arm, Scotty and Doreen entered the old firehouse, checked to see that the security team was settled in and comfortable, and then went up to the private part of the house. Doreen crossed the living room and sat down on the couch after lowering the lights to a soft, dull glow. Scotty walked over to the stereo and popped a soft jazz CD into the player. He then went into the kitchen and returned with a bottle of red wine and two short-stemmed glasses.

As Scotty approached Doreen, who was now standing by the bookcase, admiring a keepsake memento from his Navy days, she turned and smiled warmly at him. When Scotty was close, Doreen reached out and took the glasses from him. Scotty placed the wine bottle down on the coffee table and carefully inserted the corkscrew. With one quick motion, he uncorked the bottle. Scotty smiled to himself at his little triumph of not spilling any wine in the process as he recalled that this was the first time that the whole process went off without a hitch.

As Doreen held out the glasses, Scotty poured each glass half-full and set the bottle back down on the coffee table. Doreen then handed Scotty one of the glasses. Scotty stood there holding his glass of wine and searched for something either terrible, witty, or romantic to say. But the words did not come. Instead, Scotty just stood in front of Doreen, looking into her eyes. Doreen reached out and took the glass out of Scotty's hand and placed both glasses down on the coffee table next to the bottle. She then took two steps closer to Scotty, put her arms around him, and pushed herself into his warm embrace. She smiled slightly and, at first, kissed Scotty on the cheek. She then pressed her lips against his, softly at first, and then with an increased intensity of desire and want. Her tongue slipped between his lips in search of her soon-to-be lover. Scotty received her expression of desire and held Doreen even tighter to confirm that this was not a dream and that nothing would take her or this moment away.

As they held their kiss, Doreen slowly withdrew her arms from and around Scotty and began to unbutton his shirt. Scotty was thankful that Doreen began to undress him. His desire for Doreen had been driving him crazy, but in the back of his mind, he was fearful of trying to fulfill his dream, somewhat unsure of the response he would receive. Her simple action expressed her desire and removed whatever hesitation Scotty felt. Doreen finished unbuttoning Scotty's shirt and slid it off his body, letting it fall to the floor. She then began to undo his pants, which equally fell prey to her quick and nimble movements.

Scotty, in response to Doreen's direct approach, had likewise withdrawn his arms from around her and began to unbutton her dress. When the first button was opened, Scotty broke their long kiss and softly kissed her chest. As he worked his way down Doreen's dress, where a button had been buttoned, Scotty would softly and passionately kiss her body and move on to the next button. Doreen, in response to his attention, was moaning ever so softly and was pushing her willing body toward Scotty. When Scotty unbuttoned the last button, he stood up and watched in anticipation as he pushed Doreen's dress off her shoulders and beheld the treasure beneath.

Doreen reached out, put her arms around Scotty, and kissed him again. Scotty, likewise, put his arms around Doreen and, with one quick motion, unhooked her bra.

Scotty broke the kiss and lifted the bra from around her chest. He then, with his right hand, reached up and gently squeezed her soft and firm left breast. Bending slightly over, Scotty at first kissed her hard nipple and then softly sucked as passion continued to increase with each passing second. Doreen threw her head back with her eyes closed while moaning, then reached out for his rising testament of desire. Scotty let go of her left breast, only to be rewarded with the temptation of her right breast.

Softly he sucked and drew Doreen in closer. Doreen, holding Scotty now, aware of the heat and pulsation of what lay ahead, gently and slowly stroked her soon-to-be lover.

Scotty, pleasurably aware of her touch, now also let out a slight moan as he continued to suck her breast. After a few more seconds, Scotty closed his lips and then kissed her nipple in farewell as he fell to his knees. With his arms around her torso, he kissed her body in pursuit of his real prize, her private of privates. He, at first, kissed her softly through her underwear and then pulled the thong down and away. With his eyes closed, Scotty's tongue searched her out again. As Doreen's body pulsated, Scotty found her prize and kissed her again. Doreen, with fire growing within her, slightly bent over and drew in Scotty as close as he could be to her.

Doreen wanted Scotty now, but his preparation was not yet complete. Scotty then turned to her left leg and kissed where her stocking ended in its rise on her long thin leg. Doreen fell backward into a chair as Scotty knelt before her. She pulled him closer with her arms. Slowly, Scotty rolled the stocking down her leg, kissing her where the stocking had been as it descended. Doreen lifted her leg slightly as Scotty reached her ankle and took the stocking off and threw it aside. Scotty then turned his attention to her other leg and again set Doreen afire. Doreen, as Scotty took off the other stocking, melted into the cushion of the chair. She was wet with anticipation and desire as she sat there and felt Scotty's touch. Doreen reached out with her hands and squeezed her breasts as she felt Scotty remove the second stocking. Scotty kissed her body as he ascended and, reaching out with his arms, pulled her out of the chair as he stood up. They embraced again, Doreen feeling his passion and Scotty feeling her desire as their bodies willingly drew closer and closer until they were one.

Doreen broke their kiss, softly kissed Scotty's neck, and then buried her head in his chest. She felt his passion and wanted him. She locked her arms around him, holding him closer. Slowly she kissed his chest and worked her way downward.

Dropping to her knees, she at first held his expression of love and then wrapped her lips gently around him. She passionately sucked as her tongue stroked him. But she wanted more. Her emotions were but one, desire. Swiftly she drew all of Scotty inside of her as her tongue worked its own magic. Scotty wanted to scream out in pleasure but could only softly moan. He then reached down and pulled her upward by her arms until they were standing again. They kissed a kiss of true love and desire. Doreen loved this man, as he had become her life. Scotty loved this woman, but he didn't just want to make love to her; he wanted to consume her.

In one swift movement, Scotty placed one arm around Doreen's shoulder, broke their kiss, reached down and put his other arm under her knees, and picked his lover up in his arms. Doreen melted inside and softly kissed Scotty's neck as he walked slowly to the stairway. Scotty could feel one of her breasts against his chest, and his desire continued to grow as they slowly ascended the stairs.

Once in his bedroom, Scotty gently placed Doreen down on the bed, their bodies dancing in the soft shadows from the light of candles she had lit earlier. As Scotty removed his arm from her back, Doreen pulled him down on top of her, just as one candle extinguished its glow. Scotty and Doreen madly kissed as their bodies slithered in the serpentine dance of love. He reached down and sucked on Doreen's breast as she spread her legs even wider. Doreen guided him upward until their lips met in a soft, passionate kiss. Doreen slightly wrapped her legs around Scotty's and accepted her lover. The rest of the night belonged to the lovers as each candle burned out, but a fire was alive in the bedroom that lasted throughout the night.

AH, COME ON, MOM!

DOREEN GENTLY NUDGED SCOTTY ON the shoulder, waking him up from a restful sleep. When he opened his eyes, Scotty looked into the eyes of the woman of his dreams. He could only smile a warm and loving smile. Scotty then reached out and put his arm under Doreen's shoulder and pulled her close to him. He wanted to kiss her, but all he received was a slap across his chest. Doreen whispered that it sounded like someone was lightly knocking on the bedroom door. Scotty lifted his head up, stared at the door, and listened. Sure enough, there was someone outside of the door. But he thought that someone was kicking the door rather than knocking. "Who is it?" Scotty called out as Doreen lifted the sheet around her neck.

"It's Mother and Marlene," came a muffled reply from the hallway.

Without thinking, Scotty shouted out, "Come in!"

Doreen instantaneously screamed and hid under the covers.

Scotty could hear his mother struggling to turn the doorknob, as if she was holding something in her hand and trying to open the door. Scotty was about to get out of bed and open the door when he realized that he was naked. After a few seconds, the door swung open. In walked Catherine and Marlene, each carrying a white wicker bed tray with breakfast. Marlene walked over to Scotty's side of the bed and placed a tray over his legs as he sat up and rested his back against the headboard. He then reached over and placed Doreen's pillow on its edge against the headboard. Doreen, however, remained curled up in the fetal position, with the covers over her head. "You idiot, why didn't you tell them to wait a minute?" Doreen whispered to Scotty in frustration.

Catherine was standing on Doreen's side of the bed as she waited for her to sit up. After a few seconds, Catherine pleaded, "Doreen, I know that you are in there. Believe it or not, I was young once. You don't think I was born this old, do you? Please sit up. This tray is getting heavy."

Doreen knew that she couldn't pretend that she wasn't there any longer.

She straightened her legs out and slowly pulled the bedsheet down across her face until it was just below her eyes. When Doreen looked up, she saw Catherine looming over her. Again Catherine pleaded with her, "Come on, dear! Please sit up. There's nothing to be embarrassed about."

Doreen was resigned to her fate and carefully lifted herself up while holding the bedsheet just above her breasts. Once she was sitting up, Doreen tucked the sheet under her arms and smiled at Catherine. Catherine then placed her food tray down over her legs as she returned the smile. Walking over to the window, Catherine parted the curtains and lifted the room-darkening shade halfway up as she pointed out that it was a beautiful day that should not be wasted in bed. Catherine's smile turned to sadness as she looked out of the window at the tree in the backyard. She stared for a moment and remembered a time not so long ago.

"On second thought, just be happy and treasure these moments," Catherine declared as she relowered the shade, turned around, and smiled at her son and the woman he loved. Reaching up with her hand, Catherine wiped a solitary tear from her eye, looked at Marlene, and said, "Let's leave these two alone."

As Catherine and Marlene walked out of the room, Scotty called out, "Thanks, you two ole romantics!"

Scotty looked down at his tray, and his mouth watered at the sight he saw.

There were Belgian waffles smothered in fresh strawberries, with a generous helping of whipped cream. (Not the kind you buy in the store, but homemade, rich whipped cream.) This feast was accompanied by a small glass of orange juice and a steaming cup of black coffee. Scotty then looked over at Doreen's tray and noticed that she had something that he didn't. Looking up at Doreen, Scotty smiled and said, "Gee-whiz! I didn't get a flower in a small vase." He and Doreen laughed and then attacked their breakfast. As if by magic, when the last bite was eaten and the last drop of coffee drank, Catherine and Marlene knocked on the door again and entered the bedroom before Scotty could say anything.

"Good. I'm glad to see that you two enjoyed your breakfast. You sure must have been hungry after last night's activity," Marlene declared with a twinkle in her eye and a soft laugh in her voice. Before Catherine could pick up Doreen's tray, Marlene had already scooped up Scotty's tray, placed it over Doreen's, and lifted them both up at the same time. Catherine asked if she could help, but Marlene stated that she could handle them both and motioned for them to leave.

Catherine held the door open as they left, then closed the door.

Once the door was closed, Scotty reached over, took Doreen in his arms, and kissed her as he gently pulled the sheet away from her breasts. As they were kissing, Catherine, without knocking, opened the door and walked in. Doreen screamed out and retreated once again under the bedsheet. Catherine let out a sigh as she crossed the room and walked over to the bed. As she reached out and handed Scotty a piece of paper, Catherine said, "I forgot. Some guy named Jonsey has been calling all morning. He's been going on and on about discovering something or another. He wants you to call him as soon as possible. His number is on the paper."

"What? Why didn't you wake me? How come the phone in my room didn't ring?" Scotty exclaimed as he threw off the covers and stood up.

"Michael Scott! Get some clothes on you!" Catherine shouted as she turned around, looked down at the floor, and hastily began her retreat from the room.

Scotty looked down at himself and realized that he was dressed in his birthday suit. Reaching across the bed, Scotty picked up a pillow and held it in front of him and pleaded, "Sorry, Mom. But why doesn't the telephone work?"

"We didn't want you two to be disturbed, so Marlene and I turned the telephones off up here. I'll go down and turn them on," Catherine quickly answered as she left the room, without looking back, and closed the door.

"Thanks, Mom!" Scotty shouted out and then looked at Doreen, who was laughing.

"Very funny!" Scotty remarked as he threw the pillow at Doreen, missing her by inches as it whizzed past her face. He then crossed over to the dresser, withdrew a pair of boxer shorts, and put them on.

"'Sorry, Mom.' Is that the best you could come up with?" Doreen asked as she continued to laugh.

Scotty picked up the telephone receiver on the nightstand and was disappointed when the line was still dead. Turning back around, he leaned against the dresser, folded his arms across his chest, and softly whispered, "Damn." Doreen looked at Scotty and instantly knew that their minivacation was over.

Throwing off the covers, Doreen stood up, looked at Scotty, and in a tone of disappointment, declared, "I guess we will be going back to the base. I am going to take a shower." Scotty could only nod in agreement.

As Doreen walked to the entrance of the adjoining bathroom, she felt that Scotty was looking at her. Stopping just short of the door, Doreen stood still, turned her head and shoulders to look in Scotty's direction. Her feeling was confirmed when Doreen's eyes met Scotty's. Doreen blew him a kiss and then entered the shower.

Scotty continued to look at Doreen as she entered the bathroom and then the shower. He was still staring after her when the telephone rang. Picking up the receiver, Scotty softly answered, "Yes," since he was lost in his thoughts and dreams about Doreen.

"Michael" Catherine replied and then continued, "The telephones are on now. But that pest is on the phone again. Do you want me to tell him to call back later?"

"No, no. Please put him on," Scotty pleaded.

"Okay, but if you ask me, you ought to tell him to call back in a few days so that you and Doreen can get some rest," Catherine replied as she switched the call to Scotty's telephone.

Scotty heard a soft click on the telephone and then spoke up. "Jonsey?"

Jonsey anxiously replied, "Scotty? Hell, man, I've been trying to get in touch with you. Scotty! I found it! I—"

And he was interrupted by Scotty.

"Calm down. What do you mean?" Scotty asked, hopeful of the answer. "I know how they did it. It's the damndest thing...," Jonsey again anxiously answered.

"Jonsey, calm down. Don't say anything over the telephone. Who else knows?" Scotty directed.

"JW. He's the only one," Jonsey replied.

"Okay, now listen up. Doreen and I will be leaving shortly. Don't tell anyone what you found. Just keep it between you and JW for now," Scotty ordered. Then he added, "Jonsey, you did good work!"

"Thanks, Scotty. Hurry back. You were right all along! Goodbye," Jonsey replied and hung up.

Scotty placed the receiver on the telephone and half-ran into the bathroom. "Jonsey found the signal!" Scotty shouted out.

Doreen peeled back the shower curtain just enough so that her head stuck out. "That's just great!" Doreen answered in a depressed mood, then added, "Too bad he couldn't have found it later. Say, a few more days from now." Opening the shower curtain a little more, Doreen reached out and pulled Scotty into the warm water of the shower. She put her arms around him and whispered, "This is New York and not Colorado." Scotty bent down and kissed her as Doreen pushed his boxer shorts off. Scotty then reached down and lifted one of her legs around his hip. Doreen held her arms around his neck as she wrapped her other leg around his hip and whispered, "Do admirals do it better in the water?" As the water cascaded down over their bodies, they again were joined as one, and the reality of the world left them momentarily. Taking a shower took on a whole new meaning for Scotty, an experience he would never forget but would often long for.

CONCLUSION

S COTTY CALLED DOWN TO HIS security force and instructed them to have the car brought around as they would be leaving within the next half hour. He then called flight reservations and purchased two tickets on a direct flight to Denver. They would be flying direct to Space Command rather than taking multiple flights back to the base.

After dressing, Scotty and Doreen went down to the kitchen and joined Catherine and Marlene for a cup of coffee and couldn't help themselves as they indulged in a piece of French pastry. The conversation around the table was full of light banter and regrets that they had to leave so suddenly. When it was time to leave, the foursome exchanged hugs and kisses all around. Scotty noted that he saw tears in the eyes of his mother, Marlene, and even Doreen. As the front door opened, Catherine ran to Scotty and hugged him again as she whispered in his ear, "Don't let Doreen get away as she is the one for you." Scotty broke his mother's embrace and simply offered a sly smile back as he emerged from his home.

Once in the car, Scotty and Doreen held hands as they drove through the streets on their way to the airport. As Doreen stared out of the window, she became a little jealous of the people they passed by. Most of the people were smiling, laughing with a friend, or listening to music on earbuds. Doreen did not envy them of their life, but rather their peace of mind, of their not knowing of the alien threat that was lurking in the shadows.

Once they arrived at Newark Liberty Airport, they were met by two Marine security officers, who escorted them to their waiting aircraft. Once they were airborne, Scotty looked out of the window and wondered about the future. He knew that he was in love with Doreen and wanted to marry her, but he was more worried about Space Command and an epic battle that would have to be fought with the aliens. But that is a story yet to be told.

ABOUT THE AUTHOR

Michael Albright was born in Elizabeth, New Jersey and lived there during his formative years. He comes from a military and government service family. After 37 years of service, he retired from the State of New Jersey as Assistant Director of Criminal Investigations.

He has a BA degree in History and Education, an MA degree in Chinese Area Studies, and a Juris Doctorate in Law. He was admitted to the New Jersey Bar.